THE STORY OF A MAN

JOHN JOHNSON

Table of Contents

This is a work of fiction;
to say otherwise
would simply be misguided.

The glass was empty, but then it wasn't.
It all makes sense; now really, does it?
A fairy tale or every wonder,
Kneel ye down, torn asunder.
To those offended, to those so clear,
Cry "Yahushua, let me hear!"
JJ

BOOK ONE: PREPARATION

BOOK ONE: CHAPTER ONE

This is the story of a man. Of time, of how it changes. Of a time when the world's waters boiled. When some men were frogs and some men went BANG!

Second-in-command Sergeant Illeo's body draped over a fallen tree berm, face up, minus the eyeballs, as if his head were cut straight through with a buzz saw. Corporal Jack Finnigan could see two VC in the tall bamboo directly off his left flank. He quickly threw a white phosphorus grenade—a Willy Pete—followed by a frag. No more movement, just smoke and a pair of toasty dinks.

"CO dinks in the bamboo tops," yelled Corporal Finnigan, sure to make eye contact with his team and motioning with his hand.

"Sixties and grease guns in the tops, full grenades." First Lieutenant Dannie Blake was a real warrior out of Lon Hoi, and Hatchet Team Twenty Three unloaded their arsenal of sixty millimeter grenades and sub-machine guns into the bamboo.

Thud, thud.

Corporal Finnigan could hear Charlie hit the deck as he unloaded the third clip from his CAR fifteen, a shortened-down fully automatic version of the M Sixteen.

"Fuck the fog. What do you mean, no air support? Wait till I'm off this mountain, mutherfucker," Blake spoke into the radio. Then turned to the team. "No help tonight, boys." Lt. Blake threw three gas grenades about fifty meters in front of the perimeter.

That will send those slope heads into our sixties, Finnigan thought. *Hell of an arm on Blake.* Then he saw a Chicom grenade fly in over his head and turn PFC Adams into hamburger meat. The concussion knocked Corporal Finnigan unconscious. Two or three seconds later he awoke, mud in one eye and a Chicom in the other.

"FUUUUCCK," Finnigan yelled, curling into a ball. *Plunk.* Nothing, a dud. He hurled it past the perimeter.

"FINNIGAN!" Lt. Blake motioned for Corporal Finnigan to move back behind the next berm. SP four Simmons, the radio transit operator, had his guts spilled out as Finnigan turned the corner of the berm.

"Shrapnel through his ass, out the stomach. Let's go." Lt. Blake stated Simmons's condition calmly.

Finnigan and Blake carried the RTO to the next berm, as Lt. Blake pulled a poncho over the three of them to focus on the task at hand. Corporal Finnigan quickly hit Simmons with a syrette of morphine through the leg of his camo Strikers. This was the sort of pain Finnigan would not endure; he would ask someone to put a bullet through his brain.

"Pick up his guts. I'll wash them off, then put them back in."

Corporal Finnigan picked up the intestines and felt the cool water wash the warm blood from his hands. At least the blood was not as visible in the dark of the night. He held a penlight in his mouth under the poncho but felt it necessary to close his eyes for a moment or two. When his hands warmed, he looked down and returned Simmons's guts in the hole that started low in his gut and went over the top of his pants line, past his navel. No way he was making it through this.

"You'll be fine," Finnigan muttered, penlight still in his mouth.

Lt. Blake put five or six bandages on Simmons's hole and laid him face up in the mud.

★★★

BANG! Corporal Finnigan awoke cold, naked and sweaty. He could feel hair in his right hand. As he turned, his head and eyes came into focus, gazing at the jet-black hair beside him.

"Jack! Jack, it's Della, baby. Wake up. It's just a bad dream."

He looked over, short of breath, and saw Della Tomasini, naked and covered in sweat as well, beside him on the floor of their apartment.

"Fuck." Jack stood up and helped Della to her feet. "That Agent Orange did something to my head." Which was true and untrue.

True in that it was all over the hills surrounding Chu Chi, Parrot's Beak and Fish Hook, where Jack spent time. Also true that the white malaria pills made him feel a bit different—not hit with diarrhea, like many of the other guys—but his stomach seemed a bit more unappreciative of certain foods upon his return to the States.

Untrue in that last night was not about Agent Orange, but Nui Ba Den, The Black Virgin Mountain. While Jack was certain Agent Orange was not last night's culprit, it was at least relatable. Certainly a better cause than nightmares. At least he hadn't hurt her. Once before when he awoke, he found himself kneeling, grasping her windpipe. Della had clawed at his face to snap him out of it. He had seemed more fazed than she had at the time.

At least he didn't piss the rack tonight, which had happened twice after he had returned, but July Twelfth, Nineteen Sixty 9 was almost seven years ago now. Jack was born Nineteen Forty Seven, ten months to the day after his father, John, was demobbed from service in the Pacific War against the Japanese.

He was named John after his father but never called by his name out of respect for the old man. His father was a WWII Purple Heart recipient who served under General MacArthur. Strangled Japs with his bare hands and roasted them alive with napalm flamethrowers. While Jack was only a child at the time, he didn't recall his father having any war-related outbursts—and certainly not seven years after the old man returned home.

"You know, we didn't fuck last night."

Dropping his seed seemed to make Jack sleep more soundly, even though a full-size mattress was small for two people night after night. The mattress was starting to cut a nerve.

"You said you were tired, fell asleep, almost burned a hole in your shirt again," Della said, putting on her bathrobe and sitting on the edge of the bed.

Jack was developing a habit as of late, falling asleep while smoking an Embassy. "Cuming makes me more relaxed. You like me when I'm relaxed, don't you?" He grinned with his chilled blue eyes as he drew out the O in *don't*. He stood up, arching his back, still grinning.

"Of course. I love you. I'll make a better effort. Sorry," she said, as she looked straight at his cock.

"It's OK. It's OK." Jack stepped near her and stroked the back of her soft straight jet-black hair. He held her head against his belly.

Della reached out kindly and touched Jack's hands; she brought them to her breasts. "Lie down, relax." She lay him down upon their bed. "Close your eyes."

His body was different than hers but the same together.

He was Irish, white, while her skin was Sardinian olive. His body hard, worn; hers soft. His hair was long, more brown than red, pulled back in a ponytail most days. His beard, trimmed short, was more red than brown, topped off with piercing blue eyes that sometimes hurt. Five foot ten, lean with muscles that were taut from use. Della was tall for a woman: five foot eight, toned with curves. Silky long black hair that was ironed straight, with even silkier skin. Skin that was naturally bronzed by the olive oil of her ancestors and perfected by the sun.

She slid on top of him, sitting upright. "There."

"Aahhhh," He felt her moist sex, warm and familiar. He always enjoyed it when she just let him lie there and appreciate her work.

As he closed his eyes, his mind always seemed to wander to his father's handwritten note that he had always carried in the breast pocket of his Strikers:

Son, best said by our man Patton to the Third Army, more important now after Truman's give to the Red Chinese. Stay safe.

-Your Father

"When you, here, every one of you, were kids, you all admired the champion marble player, the fastest runner, the toughest boxer, the big-league ball players, and the all-American football players. Americans love a winner. Americans will not tolerate a loser. Americans despise cowards. Americans play to win all of the time. I wouldn't give a hoot in hell for a man who lost and laughed. That's why Americans have never lost, nor will never lose, a war—for the very idea of losing is hateful to an American."

-Patton

There was more to it than that, inspiring words for an inspiring time, to an inspired people, written but now forgotten. Something about making the other man die for his country. Corporal Finnigan moved quietly, swiftly, though the jungle, sweat dripping the camo paint into his eyes. In his left gloved hand, a double-edged hatchet. He was walking point now for two teams, Hatchet Teams Twenty Three and Twenty Five, clearing the brush in triple canopy. Having come from the whore mountain, Nui Ba Den, he was salivating for any dink to shred. The rotors whirred as the UHID flew them over the canopy tops, above the river, past Fish Hook, just inside Cambodia. Time for some real payback.

Recon gave us intel on a trail heavily used for enemy troops and cargo between one and three am. As the two teams crossed through a rice paddy to stop for a moment, Lt. Blake noticed a village dink out using a radio. "You have got to be kidding me," Blake murmured. The dink had clearly seen us but kept using the radio. "Stay quiet," Blake whispered into Jack's ear. Jack passed it down the line quietly, as Blake slipped through the rice paddy and slit Charlie's throat, sliding his black steel knife into the side of Charlie's throat and out the other. Pushing forward hard, dark-red spray gushed. Dannie cut half the dink's head off. Done from behind, not a drop of splatter on Dannie. Smart. Radio smashed and body hidden under a haystack. Even smarter.

Off to the ambush zone. Another three klicks, single canopy.

"Ants, ants." Jack ran backward toward the teams and was out of his clothes in 11 seconds flat.

"Water, water, water." Jack grabbed a canteen and dumped it over his head, nuts and ass, whisking the water-covered ants away with his flat hand. "Fucking fire ants covered me head to toe in two seconds."

The teams roared and howled as loud as they could without getting their heads blown off.

"Laugh it up, girls. A real riot. Ha, ha." Jack smirked, with about a hundred bites to boot. "Could somebody grab my gear, please, and carefully."

"Go, careful please." Blake motioned to two of the PFCs. "Thanks for providing some comic relief and a damn fine guide as always." Dannie rubbed Jack's shoulder. "Suit up. Time to go."

They quickly found the trail and a wide path, maybe thirty meters long, marked by broken vegetation, clear-cut ruts, regularly used by carts.

"Set up," Blake said drily. "Time to hit these Commie bastards in the gut." Hit their supplies and take out senior officers. Decimate them the American way: completely. Bring back any papers that were left. Time for payback, you dink cocksuckers.

"Harder, Della, harder," Jack groaned.

Claymores every ten meters for the thirty-meter length of the path, interlocking M sixties on either side at the top of the berm. Two men at the left pinning the start of the trail along with the M sixty. PFC Anke and two other men on the right with Lt. Blake on the trip-wired grenade. The kill zone is set.

Bang. The grenade is off. The CAR fifteen zips.

Clack. Corporal Finnigan squeezed the firing device to his claymore. *Woooooosh.* The feeling of a jet airplane, flying five feet overhead.

"Swiss cheese, Jackie special." Jack gave a grin, then tossed a Willy Pete white phosphorus, followed by a frag grenade. "Fry, you sons-a-bitches." Let their friends watch them blaze up the night, then be turned into mincemeat by the frag. Not some cheap Chicom either. Corporal Finnigan thought more to himself than aloud as he squeezed five clips into the trail and moved around down the berm to the front of the convoy.

"Keep it together, Anke," Finnigan yelled at the puking PFC, mostly to keep from vomiting himself. Dinks fucking vaporized against the back trail wall. Pink goop, the smell of burning hair and flesh—the caustic chemical smoke was thick. Bicycles, carts, an ox bleating with its guts spread halfway across the path. The bleating was ghoulish, like something out of hell itself.

Harris unloaded half of a CAR fifteen to make the bleating stop. Then Harris pulls out his knife and stabs it through the chest of a slumped-over NVA. He cuts off the bastard's ear.

Gunfire off in the distance. NO! Corporal Finnigan's mind raced. They couldn't get pinned down here, not on the other side of the river. A LAW rocket careens toward the noise.

"Time to go," Lt. Blake yells.

Not pinned down yet, but no time to lose. Another smart move by Blake. Finnigan reached down to fold back the dink's jacket, from what was left of the officer's upper torso. Really just the left half of the head, nose, half a mouth, chest and left arm. Papers grabbed from the torso, along with the officer's ear. Jack slid the ear into the back pocket of his Strikers, for a good laugh with the boys back at camp.

Finnigan's heart beat near maximum as he ran through the jungle, leading the charge back to the clearing for rendezvous with the slicks—the choppers. The ten-minute run was exhilarating. Finnigan feels satiated. PFC Anke, hit by shrapnel in the ankle, was able to keep up with Lt. Blake's help. The jungle was black, darker than hell itself. Tears of exhilaration well up in Finnigan's eyes as the slicks appear above the clearing.

"I'm cuming. I'm cuming. Don't stop," Jack moans.

So beautiful, the jungle at night; without the war—if only for a moment—serene, stunning. The first slick picked up the wounded and four of the men. Dannie and Jack look out over the lush canopy tops.

"Nice work out there tonight." Dannie rubbed Jack's shoulder, while the second slick appeared in the clearing. The wind was refreshing on their faces, as the gunship's miniguns blazed down near the kill zone.

"I needed that, seriously." Jack rolled Della over, kneeling above her. He kissed her gently on the lips. He touched her hair near the top of her head kindly. "You complete me." A popular catchphrase, though silly, was always well received.

"I love you too." Della smiled, knowing that he only said it that way to seem hip.

Jack grabbed the Jameson Irish Whiskey and poured five fingers into a crystal tumbler from his mother's china hutch. Two swallows, warm belly, warm balls, nice.

Hard to drink away that feeling of being betrayed by your own government, however. Your own fucking government. Allowed to be spit on in uniform on his first day home from the airport. At the fucking airport, in mutherfucking uniform. If that had happened to Dad, the country would have executed the traitor. Back then the country knew what it meant to be patriotic, to sacrifice. Nothing done to the perpetrator. A new day had dawned.

Missed his own welcome home party for what, for backhanding a traitor in the face? Thankfully Chief Warrant Officer V. John Finnigan was there to save the day as usual. Whisked Jack off to the VA for no reason other than saving face.

Jack was sick of saving face, sick and tired of it. Sick and fucking tired of it.

"Suit up. Time to go."

Della put on a pair of tight jeans and a tie-dyed undershirt tank top, a *guinea T* as they were called, referring to the white undershirt as part of the official Italian wardrobe. Their railroad apartment consisted of three rooms all in a row: kitchen, den and bedroom. The front door entered into the kitchen, and the doors ran along the left side near the wall. It was sparsely furnished but cozy. A comfortable couch that Della found at the Goodwill store; she had made some cool dark-purple tie-dye covers for it. Found some fun knickknacks over in Chinatown, a big brass hookah with four tubes, and some little Buddha statues and bamboo plants. She thought they might let Jack look back and find something worthwhile from that shit hole they had sent him to. The couch was great for when they wanted to stay in and watch the boob tube, as he liked to call it. He liked *All in the Family* and *Welcome Back, Kotter*; she liked *Happy Days*, so they watched that also.

Della knew that they were going to see John and Patricia today, his parents, but knowing it did not make the trip any more relaxing. She found Jack's mom to be cold, and his father, John, asked a lot of questions that no one besides himself knew the answers to. Still they were always polite and never said anything nasty to her face, so she considered them pleasant on the whole.

"We'll take the Plymouth, so we can smoke a joint on the way." He always carried a folding buck knife in a leather pouch on his belt and a black double-edged Special Forces knife in his boot.

Jack walked into the kitchen, and Rufus, Della's twenty-five-pound gray tabby with a stump instead of a tail, rubbed against Jack's boot. Jack had had quite a catalog of childhood pets, but they had never included cats; his mother had thought they were filthy. And while he found the litter box foul and three cats FAR too many, he had grown accustomed to the gray-and-white tabby. Especially after the beast had clawed and chased away four mangy strays that were hanging around the house as of late.

It was nice to have a little smoke before having to deal with his folks. Lately Jack's side business was proving almost as lucrative as his tree trimming. Plenty of Jamaican Red for his personal use was an added benefit as well. A little smoke calmed his nerves and helped him to be a little less intense. His friends appreciated it; he suspected Della did too. *Episodes*, as Jack referred to them, exclusively within the innermost recesses of his mind, were decreasing in occurrence, but steadily increasing in concern. When they took hold, he had no memory afterward, a complete blackout.

The *nightmares*—which was the uttered name for the violent-natured scenes contained within his mind—were manifesting in his physical body. The Veterans Health Administration proved to be uninterested and unhelpful. His father's example of some evening whiskey had not provided the relief it should have. Whiskey in the evening was eventually wrapped in a cloud of pot smoke, followed by whiskey in the mornings, if the nightmares had manifested, as they had last night. Still they persisted.

"Come on, hon." They walked out hand in hand past Jack's new Nineteen Seventy Five Harley Shovelhead to his olive-colored Nineteen Seventy Two Plymouth. While the Harley was the go-to ride, it was not the go-to ride for smoking a joint, and Jack could do without the looks from his old man as well. Pops thought the hog was for troublemakers who needed to get a job. Case in point, Jack thought.

Jack opened the passenger side door of his Plymouth, and Della slid in.

"Spark one up," Jack said lightly, as he turned the key in the ignition.

Jack drove off from their little apartment in Brooklyn and headed for the Long Island Expressway to Levittown. This present-day hamlet of four large suburban developments had been nothing but old potato fields until after WWII, when Arthur Levitt and his sons had bought up the fields during a potato blight and had turned them into affordable housing for the returning GIs. John, Jack's father, had received one of the first houses in Nineteen Forty Seven, the year Jack was born.

Jack was tense, as usual, on the drive to his childhood home.

Della opened the dash and took one of the joints from the pile of three. She reached into the front right pocket of Jack's jeans to grab his Zippo lighter, which was always in the same place. She opened the shiny metal lighter with the initials JF on the outside; she held the tip of the joint to its open flame. Jack always said that was how you kept the joint, from running down one side and smoking unevenly. Della held the joint to her lips with the tip still in the flame and breathed in slowly.

"It's lit perfectly," she said, passing it over to Jack and popping in the new Bob Dylan album *Blood on the Tracks*.

Jack already looked more relaxed as he took in his first lungful of smoke. "Jamaica Red, nice burn, good light. I guess practice makes perfect." He chuckled. Always good to have a bit of a laugh.

As if his father was not glorified enough already, now Jack owed his freedom to his dad as well it seemed. While it was never discussed, it became the filter through which all events now passed through first.

"Did I ever tell you about how I got out of Nam early?"

Della shook her head to say no, although Jack had, indeed, related the story twice before while drunk. She would always say no when asked if a story had already been told, if only because she liked to hear him talk. Through his stories, she was able to share in some of his most private dialogues, his personal demons.

"So you know Dannie Blake, my first lieutenant. Was with him for six months. The guy with balls of steel."

"Blake, of course I remember him. He was with you on that mountain you told me about."

"That's right. That's right," he said, not wanting to discuss Nui Ba Den but glad she remembered. "Well, Dannie gets reassigned, and we get this shiny new first lieutenant—First Lieutenant Brown." Jack stroked the underside of his beard with the back of his four fingers, then grabbed the wheel as he placed his right hand on the inside of Della's thigh.

"You know this piece of garbage almost gets us killed on two different occasions? Third time around, he wants me to teach him how to walk point. I fucking protested of course, so did half the team, the half that had spent hard time in the field—Mike, Benny. Well, Brown's up there with me, and I stop him three inches from pulling a line on a VC booby trap and turning us both into hamburger.

"So look here, Brown," Jack said, looking deeply into Della's eyes, keeping the car straight in its lane. "I've got four months left. Four fucking months. I'm not going to let some green piece of garbage send me home in a black bag. After all I've been through and four months before I'm States-bound, no fucking way."

"Of course not. How could you?" Della spoke softly, stroked his arm and shoulder, then his hair and the side of his short-trimmed red-bearded face.

Jack appreciated her soft touch; he wasn't agitated, just passionate. He tried to contain his tone and took two large lungfuls that made him cough heartily.

"So we get back to the base, after this dirtbag Brown almost blows us to hell. He gets drunk and passes out dead in his hooch. Well, you know, that just sealed it for me, just fucking sealed it. Look, everyone wants to pass out sometimes, right? But you have a system. One guy always looking out. Sometimes it's you. That keeps everyone sharp, safe. Well, this asshole has been there for two weeks and nothing. So me and a couple of the guys think it's time to send him a wake-up call. We take some wire, wrap it around his tent with some ammo cans, along with a note scrolled on one at the front of his tent that says, BANG!"

"Ha, ha! Clever!" Della laughed out loud, in part because it was funny, and in part because she had heard the story before and realized this was a laugh break.

"I know. I know!" Jack roared with laughter. "You should have seen his face, hungover, caught in the wires, ammo cans clanging, stumbling out of his tent for morning chow." Jack slapped the steering wheel.

"Well, this prick doesn't think it's so funny. Has the MPs come to our tents, harass the team, talking about court-martial unless the culprit cops to it, in which case said culprit will be reassigned. Well, I copped of course. No reason for everyone to go down. Clearly this Brown had the whole thing set up so I would get reassigned. Clever bastard." Jack shook his finger.

"Was probably for the best." Della grabbed his arm and put it back down on her thigh.

"Probably for the best. Reassigned as a door gunner, shooting an M sixty on a helo. Got to hang out the door on a bungee cord. Soar down three thousand feet, unload some serious lead into Charlie's ass, rockets blaring all the way." Jack smiled.

"That must have been some sight."

"Some sight, some sight. You should've seen it at night. Looked like Armageddon, beautiful. On this end of it at least." Jack's hearty laugh was cut short, as he took two more deep pulls off the almost finished joint.

"So one day we're pulling into base, and I see that son of a bitch Brown at the edge of our camp. Perfect position for me to unload a belt into the canopy over his head. You know, scare the shit out of him, but still be able to say I saw some movement in the canopy.

"Well, he was scared shitless. Probably pissed himself, the pussy, but again turns it into this big fucking deal. MPs don't care about my side of the story. Brown's saying I was trying to kill him. Total bullshit."

"Bullshit," Della repeated back.

"I know. I know. Well, more talk of court-martial and dishonorable discharge, but this time they were fucking serious. Sent me back on a plane Stateside that same night. Same fucking night. You think Simmons with his guts hanging out got a flight back that night? Fuck no. Fuck no, he didn't."

"Bastards." Della rubbed his hand hard.

"Hate to say it, hate to fucking say it." Jack tapped the top of his steering wheel twice and grinned with a laugh. "Pops lives up to his name again. Wouldn't tell me how later, but, when I got off the plane, there were no MPs waiting to escort me. Instead I walked down the ramp with the rest of the boys returning home."

Jack hadn't expected to be home free, but he had heard there was jeering at some of the airports. He didn't expect it to be like that though, not at John F. Kennedy.

"So JFK, end of the tarmac, this girl is screaming same as the rest, 'Baby killer, murderer.' I turn and, as I make eye contact with her, she spits right in my face. Well, needless to say I was stunned, for about a tenth of a second, then I smacked the bitch right in the mouth." Jack made a backhanded smack with his left hand in the air.

"Not hard, but hard enough to make her bleed unfortunately. Next thing I know, there's this policeman holding me around the bicep. I look at him, and he looks at Pops, who has jumped over from the sidewalk and is now holding the cop by the bicep. The old man stares the cop in his eyes and says, 'Jimmie, he just back today from walking point on hunter-killer teams. Today, Jimmie, we're going to the VA straightaway.' Pops looks at me and says, 'Let's go.' To which the copper replies, 'Take him straightaway.' That's why Jackie had no welcome-home party, folks!"

"Who wants a big party after all that anyway, right? At least not with your parents." Della slides her body up against Jack's straightened arm.

"You're right. You're right." And she certainly was; he didn't want to hang out with the folks, especially with his dad's endless questions. "So I don't know who Pops spoke to, but I ended up with a General Discharge under Honorable Conditions. No brig time at all."

John had asked his son one question when they got in the car, before driving to the VA. It was this: "Look me in the eyes, boy. Did you come home because you were a coward?"

"No, Dad. I swear. I wasn't scared. I did my duty, but that son-of-a-bitch lieutenant was going to get us killed." Jack looked back without fear because that was mostly the truth.

"I knew it was the truth, son. Just had to hear it from your lips while I looked you in the eyes. You fought honorably. Everything is going to be fine. That broad deserved a belt in the kisser. Just don't do it again," and John thought about putting his hand on his son's shoulder.

The VA prescribed nothing except rest.

Jack took another lungful, then he reached his right hand over and touched Della's denim-covered thigh. They passed what was left of the joint between them and leaned back into the drive, as she stroked the hand that lay familiarly in its place. They both had paths to walk, but walking together seemed comforting, familiar, safe. Della provided nurture, stability. She took care of him and was a vixen in the sack to boot. Jack made Della feel safe. While there were a few incidents, they were never intentional. She had been intentionally hurt before and found that sort of hurt to be of an extremely different nature.

They worked together and were happy, save an increasing government cataract that blurred the vision and filled the void where innocence once lived. This country, this America vaulted to greatness, was forced by nature itself to look evil directly in the eye during the Great War. We did not blink. In fact we kept our eyes open and had our eyelids seared in Vietnam. Our values questioned by Jonestown and Kent State. Our innermost faith punctured by the bullets destined for Kennedy and King. The great men were killed, and the people began to find their voice. With the two hundredth anniversary of the country coming next year, change was in the air, and the air was becoming hot.

BOOK ONE: CHAPTER TWO

The tires of the Plymouth rolled closely to the curb, but not so close to touch. Jack opened his door as Della waited for him to come round and open hers. It was, after all, proper manners. A chain link fence ringed Jack's childhood home; green plastic strips were woven through the holes. John, Jack's father, liked the added privacy it provided. He had installed it himself many years ago, when it was clear that Jack's dog, Salty, would be a permanent addition to the family. Salty was a black-and-white Boston terrier, nearly the size of the home's current sheltie, SNAFU—military speak for "situation normal, all fucked up." Both dogs were akin to their names.

The house was large, seventeen square feet, expanded from its original 9 hundred square-foot frame. John had added a second story. The converted attic was now two full bedrooms and a full bathroom. He also added a new TV room downstairs. John did all the work himself, including the plumbing and electrical. A detached garage kept the family car warm during the snowy winters.

The front door was painted fire-truck red, and a wagon wheel of the same color leaned against the family home's white siding just to the left of the front door. It had been painted the same red since Jack was a child. It made the house unmistakable as you drove down Barbara Lane. Jack remembered helping his father retouch the dark blue trim of the home's windowpanes and shutters.

"If she starts in, just nod and say, yes ma'am." Jack's mother could be a real ballbuster. His suggestion came from years of experience and was given freely, as he rang the bell.

Jack no longer had a key to the house. It had been taken, and his bags had been packed almost three years ago. Coming home sloshed one night, after consecutive nights of near blackout benders, he had been rearing for a fight. His father had given him a curfew of midnight as a condition for continued residence after weeks of nonstop reverie. Leaving the bathroom covered in puke for his mother to clean had put him at the top of his parents' shit list. As a combat Vet, Jack found the curfew as ludicrous as it was insulting. An insult to his very manhood. It was also unenforceable, since his father was old and his mother always caved when push came to shove.

After a night at the pub, Jack had stumbled in around three a.m. He was looking to send a message.

His father threw a packed duffel bag at Jack's feet as soon as he had entered through the front door.

"Leave your key on the mantel. You are done here," John said from his easy chair in the corner. He had spent the evening waiting for the front door to open.

Time to send a message, Jack had thought, as he stepped toward his father, with an outstretched finger. He would remind the old man just how old Pops really was and that it would be best if he just kept quiet.

He was surprised when his father repeated his words. "Leave your key on the mantel. You are done here."

This time Jack was looking down the barrel of his father's Colt forty five.

An equalizer, touché. Jack placed his key under the watchful eye of the black iron eagle that hung above the brick mantelpiece. He grabbed his bag on the way out.

Today when the bell rang, Patricia opened the door quickly, wearing a plain white dress as if ready for church. Her hair and makeup were impeccable, both coiffed with white powder. She was hardly five foot two and seemed frail in body. With her china-white skin and white hair, she would have seemed a specter if not for the dark red lipstick.

"Come in. I thought you were coming earlier. Your father is watching TV." Patricia was surprised to see her son had not yet moved on from his latest flusie as she escorted them into the kitchen. It was clad with stained brown wood paneling like the rest of the house, along with wrought iron fixtures.

SNAFU, the family's dog, ran between their feet, as Jack reached for a piece of pizza from the box that sat upon the counter.

"That is your brother's pizza," his mother quickly quipped.

Jack put his hand to his mouth and shouted upstairs, "Bobby, I'm eating some of your pizza." A cheese pie from Mama's, a family favorite.

John bellowed from the TV room, "Son."

Jack walked into his father's enclave, leaving Della alone to deal with his mother. The TV room was furnished with a dark brown leather couch and a brown leather La-Z-Boy, his father's throne.

An American flag from the Great War hung in a triangle-shaped box upon the wall above a map of the United States.

"If you can drink like a man, you are free to join me." John lifted his crystal tumbler, a match to the one upon Jack's nightstand. "There is ice in the bucket."

"Thanks." Jack filled a glass with ice and poured himself two fingers, the respectable amount for a man, according to his father.

John was not as much disappointed in his son as he was disappointed by his choices. His son had always been unbridled; he remained so to this day. John thought that it was a trait passed down from Patty's father, a redhead with a fiery streak, to say the least. But Jack was almost thirty now, and John was convinced that Jack's tree-trimming business was a worthless endeavor. Certainly it had not provided a steady paycheck nor steady hours. John suspected the real allure was not having a boss, not having to be accountable, and not having to work a forty-hour week. But the war had been hard on his son, hard on a country that had not fully realized the foul fruits of its labor.

"Sit down, son."

Jack sat upon the couch beside his father's chair.

"It is said," John continued, "the Tree of Liberty must be refreshed from time to time with the blood of patriots and tyrants." John gazed into his son's light blue eyes. "We both know it. We have seen it. I am sorry this country forgot, son. It is not right." He reached over and gently touched his son upon the shoulder.

The thirst of wickedness must certainly be quenched for it had drunk deeply from the bowels of patriots.

It was rare for his father to be physically affectionate, being Irish Catholic and a combat Vet to boot. His father's touch was welcome but also strangely uncomfortable. Jack swallowed the last mouthful of whiskey to keep down the well of emotions in his throat. He fought back the tear in his eye from becoming an endless stream. The war had been painful, but his country's disdain, even hatred, had been almost unbearable. Jack got up and poured himself three fingers. He looked out the window into the backyard, past the green grass into the rain basin that used to house potato fields. "Thanks, Pops." Jack sat again on the couch.

"You know, son. We have a big problem here in this God-given America. Do you know what it is?" John took a sip from his watered-down Jameson.

"Not beating those Commie bastards?" Jack felt change was in the air as of late. He suspected a diatribe was coming as well. Something about buckling to the Chinese in Korea, laziness, drug use by the youth—all the popular buzz words.

"Son, this country has lost its way. We fought the most evil, vile men and nations the world has ever seen. One of their wicked philosophers said this, 'Whoever fights monsters should see to it that, in the process, he does not become a monster.' Now, son, I love this country, America.

We have both fought for that flag hanging there on the wall behind us and what it stands for—freedom, truth, justice." John turned and glanced to the flag on the wall, gesturing with his cup. "Now I am not saying that we are monsters, son, not yet, but I fear we have picked the wrong fork in the road. The fork that leads us away from our founders, away from true liberty, away from God."

"Yeah, Pops, I know. Our music is of the devil. People are lazy." Jack hoped to get his father off the subject quickly and onto something else. He added, "You remember when you ran the station wagon over my hamsters, when I left their cage in the driveway?"

John smirked. "I remember. What a mess! Lucky for you, you are not the one who had to clean it up!" John laughed as he sat on the edge of his chair and shook his finger.

Jack had, indeed, left the hamster cage on the driveway, so that his hamsters could get some air. He had forgotten about them, while lying on his bed, thumbing through his baseball card collection, until he heard a crash down below his window. His heart sunk into his stomach as he ran down the stairs. His father, quickly aware of the massacre, whisked Jack inside the house to save him from the horror of seeing smashed hamster guts. After the cage was cleaned up, they had a little ceremony over a hole in the backyard that contained the hamster remains.

"Did you really bury my hamsters in that hole?" Jack asked his father.

"What was left of them." John's big smile showed off all of his white teeth. His brown hair was still cropped short, and he was fit, even with the twenty pounds put on his six-foot frame since retirement. "Son, who do you consider some of the great men of history?"

Jack thought to himself, then said, "Christ, Washington, MacArthur, Kennedy." Finally a softball. Kennedy was a zinger right down the third-base line, him being a Catholic and all.

"What do those men all have in common, son?"

"Umm, they're all dead?" Jack responded, puzzled.

"Indeed they are. Kennedy shot down in his prime for the whole country to watch. Finally a man ready to stand up to the Communists and"—John smiled sadly and touched his heart—"a Catholic."

Jack's mind raced as he tried to find an easier line of conversation. His buzz was already dwindling. Should he talk now about his parakeet frozen solid, hanging upside down on its perch the morning after the power went out, or his bunny's heart attack from a lightning storm? Nope, the hamsters were the best pet story of the bunch. This was going to require something stronger. Jack reached further back into his memories. "Do you remember when we used to live with Grandma on Forty-Seventh between Eighth and 9th?"

"Do I! That was just after the war. I guess they call that Hell's Kitchen now. We lived there till just after you were two." John sat back and crossed his legs.

A little cold-water flat on the second story with a communal bathroom in the hall. They had moved in with his mother and two sisters after Patty was pregnant with child. The only privacy to be had were draperies hung from the ceiling, used for partition walls. Coal and ice were delivered by truck back then.

"Saturday night was bath night for you and your cousins. Oh, I guess there were about six of you. My sister Quennie would heat the bathwater in a big kettle on the stove, mix it in the tub with equal parts cold." John turned his hands, as if he were dumping out a big vat of water. "It was a big tub. Took about an hour just to get it ready. We had a big aluminum cover so we could use it as a sideboard during the day."

Playing in the tub with his cousins was one of two memories Jack had from the flat. The other was looking out through the window, watching the coal truck drive to the curb below.

John went on, "Well, we were living high on the hog back then. That is for sure. Unlike a lot of other folks in the area. You kids all had clean water on Saturdays. Most families had to share one tub of water." John crunched up his nose in disdain. "You can bet your sweet ass it was the babes that went last. The water looked like motor oil by that time." He laughed and slapped his knee.

John paused, leaning back into his chair and looking into his color Emerson TV. "Bend steel with his bare hands." He looked over at his son beside him and, with his two fists knuckles up, bent them down together as if bending a piece of rebar into an upside-down U.

"This is my favorite part." John coughed slightly before getting himself into character, for his favorite line. "Fights a never-ending battle for truth, justice and the American way," John repeated; his voice was deep and bold.

Jack laughed aloud as the theme song from an old George Reeves's rendition of *Adventures of Superman* rolled on the boob tube. Laughing as it were because his father's routine was pure to form all these years later.

John leaned forward and looked his boy in the eyes in order to drive home the importance of what was said next. "Son, with the defeat of the evil that attacked us during World War II, America was given a great responsibility. Bretton Woods, as it is called, made the United States the world's reserve currency. Our dollar would be the yardstick against which all the other currencies of the world would be measured—the light of the world, as it were."

Jack recalled hearing something about Bretton Woods in high school, but, by his sophomore year, beer and girls were his chief concern; his grades were hardly passing. He could tell that his father was set on a train of thought. Perhaps it was better to let him run for a bit and hope he ran out of steam. Jack was certain Della was not having an easier time with his mother in the kitchen.

"Do you know how much money we spent in Vietnam?" John asked inquisitively.

"Too goddamned much or maybe not enough," Jack replied with a hint of anger.

"Mouth," his father replied; taking the Lord's name in vain was not something he tolerated.

"Nineteen Fifty, after the Great War, we owed two hundred fifty billion. That is billion with a B. You know, you could stack hundred-dollar bills on top of each other and a billion dollars would reach almost thirty-five stories."

"Bullshit," Jack retorted.

"True. I know you fought hard, son, like a warrior, but we tied your hands." John raised his two hands together, as if they were bound. "We lost that war because the great men were dead or retired. We lost that war because the country lost its resolve. We forgot just how brutal war was. We forgot the nature of the actions necessary to vanquish a determined enemy. Now we owe damn near a trillion dollars. A goddamned trillion dollars is over six hundred seventy eight miles high. Pardon me, Lord." John looked up briefly to the heavens. "You understand, son. America now walks the path to destruction, destroyed as it were from within, after all that we fought for, all that those who came before us sacrificed." A sad and defeated look came over the old man's face.

"Son, Jefferson warned us." John prepared to riddle off from memory more words from a great man of yesteryear.

"'If the American people ever allow private banks to control the issue of their currency, first by inflation, then by deflation, the banks and corporations that will grow up around will deprive the people of all property until their children wake up homeless on the continent their fathers conquered.'"

John paused and stated the last line slowly. "'The issuing power should be taken from the banks and restored to the people, to whom it properly belongs.' Until this happens, we are ruined, son. Maybe not today, maybe not tomorrow, but ruined sure enough. You see, we fought and lost that godforsaken war with borrowed money. That liar

Nixon spent us into oblivion because he did not have the balls to let his generals fight." John paused.

"You see our dollar, it was backed by gold then. You could take your dollars in and redeem them for actual gold, if you wanted." John extended his hands as if he were making a deposit across a bank teller window. "Of course FDR's chicanery took a larger piece of that gold for the government, but at least that son of a bitch knew how to fight a war. That gold standard is what kept these filthy politicians from spending us into the poorhouse. More spending is always their heart's desire.

"That liar Nixon blew up the whole damn system, because we spent our asses off, spent money we simply did not have. The French and Swiss suspected as much. When they wanted gold for their dollars, we told them to screw off. America would no longer use the gold standard. The French and the Swiss were right. We were printing money. We blew up the system. Blew the whole damn thing right up. What a disgrace."

Jack was bored and was having a hard time even feigning interest. He swirled the melting ice around in his glass.

"You see, son, once we start down the road of unchecked spending, these crooks grow accustomed to it, even feel entitled. They won't stop. They never do. Sure, we might slow it down for a time, but you will see. We will not stop. Eventually, when we cannot get our hands on another red cent, we will just print more and more, like the crumbled empires piled upon the ash heap of history." John clapped his hands and stood from his seat. "Then BANG!"

Jack jumped.

"Sorry, sorry," his father said, his palms headed toward the floor, making a quiet-down motion. "I just hope I will not be here to see it."

"What is going on in there?" Patricia yelled from the kitchen.

"Nothing. Nothing, sis. Just boys being boys. *Shhh.*" John put his finger to his mouth and looked at his son with a big smile. "Freshen up?" Jack nodded as his father grabbed their glasses and poured them each two fingers of Jameson.

One last curveball deep to the inside. "Do you remember when you wouldn't let me do karate?" Jack thought on the moment with faint sadness.

John remembered back to Nineteen Fifty Seven, when his son was only a boy of ten. John's defenses had been worn down after weeks of a prolonged frontal assault on the matter by his son. Upon entering the class, John sat with his son on a wooden bench near the door, and watched the teacher and students prepare. They were mostly Asians, and the teacher was a Jap. His disgraced flag hung on the wall behind him. The students sat down with the instructor at the front of the class; they began to breathe slowly in what John assumed was some sort of meditation bullshit.

Jack replayed the scene over and over again in his mind: being yanked out the door by his wrist after the instructor had the students repeat something in Japanese and bow their foreheads to the ground.

"No son of mine is going to bow to some Nip flag."

His father's blaring words were still etched in his mind.

"Well, I lost my temper, and, for that, I have apologized." John's blood was boiled in an instant as he saw Americans bow before the cowardly flag that flew for the nation which had attacked them on Pearl Harbor. No son of his would bow before it.

"I did get you into that junior boxing league. Not too many punks messing with you after that, right, Champ?" A large toothful smile arose upon his father's face.

"Right, Pops." And right he was. Jack was quite good; he was the Long Island Junior Boxing Champion runner-up when he was only fourteen. That legend ran strong, until he was forced to join the service or do jail time after he was caught stealing jewelry from the local department store at eighteen.

★★★

Della sat uncomfortably on a stool in the kitchen across from Jack's mother. She thought to herself, if there was ever a home that was Spic 'n Span clean, it was the Finnigans' house. The wall adjoining the living room had its center cut out, like a window, so that you could see in. There was a little counter in between.

Patricia sat at the round oak kitchen table smoking a Virginia Slims, very chic for professional women of the time.

"Did Jackie ever tell you that he was an altar boy?" Patricia asked, as she took a drag off of her cigarette and placed it in the small green glass ashtray on the table.

"Yes, and that he went to Catholic school as well," Della replied. She also knew that the nuns beat him with rulers because, as Jack said, "They were sexually repressed and sadistic." Plus she knew that he had received ten severe lashes on his back as a boy of twelve with a belt, while attending a Catholic boys' camp. He and some of the other boys were caught skinny-dipping in the lake one night. He had never told his father about the beating. Jack had been truly heartbroken when his father hadn't let him do martial arts that year. He had found a Bruce Lee book in a neighbor's trash can and thought it would be a surefire defense against sadists, but the book alone wasn't enough. He needed training. Thankfully his father got him into boxing.

"So you are *Eye*-talian," Patricia said, pronouncing the long I, like in *ice cream*. "Your family goes to church then?" she asked, waving her cigarette in a circle, then taking another drag.

"No, ma'am. We do believe in God though," Della answered.

"Going to church and believing in God are synonymous, my dear. One cannot be extricated from the other." Patricia took the last drag from her Virginia Slim and lit another with a little brass lighter.

"Yes, ma'am," Della answered, as she bit her tongue. "My sister goes to church."

"What diocese?" Patricia asked curtly.

"They use the high school gym over in Lindenhurst."

"That is certainly not church." Patricia leaned into her high-back wooden kitchen chair and pointed to the ceiling with her cigarette. "You know, I was studying to be a Carmelite nun, before the War, before I met John."

"I heard you work for Western Electric now. That's pretty cool," Della threw her hat into the mix.

"Who told you that? Jackie?" She looked sternly. "Really?" she said drily. Patricia made a mental note to reprimand her son and took a long slow drag off of her cigarette. She worked on the DEW project, an early warning radar system to keep the country safe from Soviet missiles and certain annihilation. Patricia had top secret clearance. She was not surprised to hear her son did not keep his mouth shut. He always was a little braggart.

"Being a wife is a real responsibility, dear. Taking care of the family, the home, still making time for the higher things. You know, Mass prepares you for the challenges of the day. That is why I attend Monday through Friday, five thirty a.m. sharp. I never miss. On Sundays John and I go together. College, dear?"

"No, ma'am. I work in a diner. The tips are really great." Della was proud. She liked having her own money; she was saving some. Soon she would have enough for a Camaro, her dream car.

Patricia leaned forward; her bony fingers brought a cigarette to her lips. "As school trains the mind"—Patricia tapped her temple with her hand holding a lit cigarette and coming dangerously close to her coiffed hair—"so the church trains the soul. Do you understand, dear?" Patricia tapped her chest over her heart.

"Yes, ma'am." Della's attempts to steer the conversation were not going well; perhaps a change of topic was due.

"That really is a lovely plant you have here on the counter. My girlfriend has one just like it, but yours is even more beautiful, very lush." Della smiled and ran her fingers over a leaf.

Patricia rose to her feet, walked across the kitchen and touched one of the leaves. "Well, thank you for saying as much. John's sister got it for me a few months ago. It does have lovely foliage. Very unique. I have never seen anything quite like it."

"Oh, yes," Della replied, finally being on the winning end of a question. "It's called a Wandering Jew."

"Excuse me?"

"It's called a Wandering Jew. I'm not really sure why. I know because my uncle has a flower shop."

Patricia was instantly blind with rage. She lifted the plant in its ceramic pot above her head and with outstretched arms shaking, flung it to the floor violently with more force than her thin arms suggested was possible. The pot shattered, and dirt washed over the spit-shined linoleum floor.

It certainly was not the first time Della had seen something smashed in anger, but the way Patricia's blood boiled beet red within her white skin was unsettling.

"Defile my house, how dare she!" Patricia stormed into the TV room.

John was sitting forward in his seat, waiting for what was to come, as Jack sat back and looked out the window at nothing in particular.

"She will answer to Christ Himself for this one, John. Believe me, she will. She knew very well! A plant named for the killers of our Lord and Savior! Quennie, that little witch, she will be sorry when her eternal soul fries. But it will be too late then, too late, John. Just like the rich man in Luke Sixteen."

"Yes, dear. Della, why don't you come join us?"

Bobby, Jack's brother, younger by almost fifteen years, came bounding down the stairs. He must have been about fifteen. He wore a flannel shirt; his long brown hair rested upon his collar. He was blind in one eye, which was noticeable; he was not handsome like his brother.

Patricia had stopped drinking liquor altogether while she was pregnant with him. She had also cut her smoking in half to be on the safe side. He was sickly right from the start though; it forced Patricia to take a few years off work. While she was home, she did not breast-feed as there was something about it that had seemed heathenly to her.

Jack noticed that his mother was kinder to his brother; she would even hug him. He resented it.

"Buzz off, meathead." That was Jack's name for his brother, since finding it hilarious on *All in the Family*, especially since it cut a real nerve with Bobby.

"Be nice to your brother. Bobby, go sit down." John had seen this act too many times before.

They sat in the TV room, while Patricia cleaned up the mess she made, dust pan and broom in hand, skirting around the floor on her knees.

"Hey, Della," Bobby said, as he sat next to her on the couch.

Jack had had plenty of pretty girlfriends, but there was something about Della that was particularly attractive, something more than just her looks.

"Hi, Bobby." Della liked Bobby; he was dorky. She didn't like that Jack was mean to him, so she made a point to be particularly friendly to his brother.

"Dad, tell Della the story about the equalizer," Bobby said excitedly.

"Shut up, meathead." Jack groaned.

John laughed heartily. "The equalizer. Great story," John said with a grin. "Well, Jack was about eight at the time. Our next-door-neighbor's boy was 11, a real punk of a kid. Well, one afternoon some of the neighborhood kids are out front and, Joey was his name, pushed Jack to the ground. Right in front of the other kids." John pushed his arms forward.

Jack sunk into the couch, as Della leaned forward. "What happened then?" she asked.

"Well, Jack came home and got a ball-peen hammer from my toolbox in the garage. He walks next door, rings the doorbell, and, when Joey answers, he clunks the boy right on the forehead." John made a hammering motion. "*Boink*, knocks the boy clean out. Well, Jack walks back home, puts away the hammer and goes up to his bedroom. Two hours go by, and Joey's mom is over here, furious, screaming at Patty. You should have seen Ma's face. She was mortified." John laughed with a slap of his knee. "Well, she tells me to give him a good whopping. I grabbed the belt and took him out to the garage. Sat him on my lap, looked him in the eyes and asked him what he had learned today. Well, he fires right back and says, 'An equalizer works just like you said, Dad.'

"Well, I just about burst my gut again, trying to hold down a laugh. Lesson learned."

John slapped his knee another time and laughed a laugh deep from within his belly, which had in fact been burst once before in the Great War, from his breastbone to his navel. Damn Japs.

"Well, I told him that I was going to have to make a fuss to appease his mother. So I hit the work bench with the belt a few times, hooted and hollered about never again, and how Joey could have been really hurt. Learned the lesson of the equalizer at eight years old." John laughed again, and Jack laughed along with him.

"That kept the older kids off your heels for a few years, son, hey?"

"It sure did, Dad." However, Jack was getting antsy and was ready to be off the corner of Reminiscing Street and Education Lane. He leaned over closer to Della beside him on the couch and said softly, "Will you call your sister, and see if she and Paul are hanging out?"

"Sure." Della loved seeing her sister Roxie.

"Have your sister ask Paul if they're up tonight."

"OK." Della stood and walked through the double door into the kitchen. "May I use the phone to call my sister, ma'am?"

"Is it local?"

"Yes, ma'am."

"Then of course," Patty replied, as she put her apron into their front-loading Bendix washing machine in the family's mudroom. The floor was spotless, and any evidence of the lifeless plant was removed. Patty poured herself a cup of tea. Lipton's, two tea bags, one sugar and milk.

Della lifted the handset, placed her finger in one of the circular holes within the base and turned each of the seven numbers around the round dial. "Hey, Roxie, are you and Paulie hanging out? . . . Yeah, Jack wants to know if Paulie's going to be up tonight? . . . OK, great. We'll see you guys in a bit." She turned around. "Thank you, ma'am." Della walked back to the TV room, past Patricia.

Patty remained in the kitchen, drinking a mug of tea and sparking up another Virginia Slim.

Della sat back down on the couch next to Bobby and leaned over to Jack. "Paul said they'll be up."

Finally, Jack thought. "All right, Pops. We're getting out of here. Good seeing you guys, meathead." Jack stood and gave his brother a light tap on the back of the head. He extended his hand to his father.

John stood to his feet and grabbed his son around the shoulders, pulling him tight. "You take care of yourself, son."

"I will, Pops. I will." Jack patted the old man on his rib cage. He grabbed Della by the hand and walked into the kitchen. "Mom, I hope you didn't harass Della too much. Nice seeing you," he said snidely.

"She was a dear," his mother replied, "for an *Eye*-talian that is. Get to church. You should come with the family on Sunday."

"Yeah, yeah, Mom. You know I gotta work on Sundays. See you soon, Ma." And he was out the door quickly with Della behind him.

"Nice to see you, ma'am," she said over her shoulder.

And with that they were off to her sister's apartment a few towns over in Lindenhurst.

"How did it go with my ma?"

"Not bad, though she's very concerned for our immortal souls." Della giggled.

"Glad you find it funny." Jack gently pinched her ribs. He liked that Della was so lighthearted, even when it came to his mother. Impressive.

"Six of one, I had a workout session with the old man. At least he always has booze." Jack laughed. He would have had Della spark up another joint, if the ride to her sister's wasn't so short.

Roxie lived in a basement apartment with an entrance around the back of the house. It belonged to some retired couple with no kids. The separate entrance was nice and made the place feel more like a home.

Della walked down the little concrete steps, rang the doorbell and opened the door. Jack walked in behind her and locked the dead bolt.

"Roxie, hey, baby," Della said in a funky voice as she ran over to the kitchen and threw her arms around her baby sister. She gave her a big kiss on both cheeks.

"So glad you guys came over," Roxie shouted, wiggling her hips.

Della was six years older than her eighteen-year-old sister Roxie, who recently had moved out of their parents' house and in with her boyfriend, Paul. She was wearing a red string-bikini top and a pair of cutoff jeans, with the bottom quarter of her ass hanging out. Other than that, there was no doubt they were sisters. They both had jet-black hair, hazel eyes, smooth bronzed skin, with very sleek lines and some curve to their hips. Roxie at five foot ten was two inches taller than her sister. Tonight, as usual, Roxie was wearing heavy red lipstick, baby-blue eye shadow and red rouge. Another girl might have been laughed at, but not Roxie. She looked hot, damn hot.

"Hey, Paulie. What's happening, my man?" Jack strolled over and reached an outstretched arm to hug Roxie's boyfriend. Paul was wearing skintight red jeans with cowboy boots and no shirt. He was devilishly handsome and had hair like Ted DiBiase, the professional wrestler, only more wild. Paul was Italian mostly, tan, lean, with a smooth stomach and a real baby face.

"Hey, Roxie." Jack gave Roxie a hug; he enjoyed feeling her smooth skin.

There were lines of coke all ready to go on the kitchen table. On the other side of the half-partition wall, separating the sink and fridge from the eating area, was Rock Murphy. Jack and Rock had lived four houses apart growing up. Jack was a year and a half older. They were neighbors more than friends but had shared an unstated bond after the war. Rock was a stupid ass; he had willfully joined the marines, after Jack was sent to the army.

Jack walked around the partition to the sink, where Rock had a little blonde girl's ass bent over the kitchen sink; his cock was still inside.

"Aw, you fucking animal. You marines are such fucking animals." Jack laughed, bending his knees. "Hi, cutie. What's your name?" Jack tilted his head down so as to be level with her eyes.

Rock leaned his hips forward into the blonde, whose pert ass was in the air, bent over the counter, her head half in the sink.

The pretty-faced girl looked over and replied, "Debbie."

"Her name's Debbie." Rock laughed, looking over his shoulder at Jack, as Rock smacked her ass. Rock was stark naked. He put his hands on his hips and arched his back. "Watch this. Stay," he said, as if talking to a dog. He pushed the little blonde's head back into the sink. Rock grabbed a mirror off the counter. He poured a little bit of white powder onto Debbie's ass and carefully cut it into a line with a razor blade. He held one of his nostrils closed and snorted up the fat line quickly.

"Oorah, Marine Corps!" Rock straightened up and pounded his chest with one hand.

"Get the fuck outta here, you jarhead. You're a maniac." Jack grabbed a dish towel, spun it around tightly and snapped Rock on the ass. "Animals," he roared and ran around to the other side of the partition. "All right, line me up, Paulie. Della?" Jack motioned inquisitively to Della.

"Tiny." Della held up her thumb and forefinger an inch apart. Coke was not really her thing, but doing a small one would keep the harassing comments at bay.

Paulie quickly chopped up a line and a small one beside it.

"Half that size," Della replied, stepping toward the table.

"I'll take her half and one like Jack's." Roxie smiled, clutching her hands to her chest and jumping like a bunny to the other side of the wooden table she had picked up from the local Goodwill store.

Della grabbed Roxie by the wrist. "That's too much."

"*Puh-lease*, it just looks that way because you're doing a baby line," Roxie jested, drawling out the words slowly. She leaned over from the hips, freeing herself from Della's grasp. The lines were quickly up her nose, and Paulie grabbed a handful of ass, as she leaned over the table.

"Mmm, nice, baby. Watch this!" Paul yelled, as he picked up a straw. He inhaled his two large lines quickly, one up each nostril.

Jack and Della followed suit.

"Thanks, man. Nice." Jack walked over and patted Paulie on his bare back. Jack was vibrating, a nice numb to it, but a little too fast for his taste.

Jack moved his mouth close to Paul's ear.

"Dope? Yeah, yeah, of course I do. You want some?" Paulie said, "Happy to be of service."

38

"Just a hit." Jack needed to be a little mellower. The great thing about Paulie was that he was always ready to party. He always brought the party with him and could do enough of whatever to kill three people.

"All right, hold on. Let me get it ready in the bathroom." Paul walked through their small living room and into the bathroom at the other end.

"So you like driving that bus?" Della asked Roxie, as they both leaned against the high-back wooden chairs. After high school, Roxie got her license to drive a school bus. She drove for the junior high in the next town over.

"Groovy, baby." Roxie pointed her left arm straight up in the air and then straight out in front of her toward her sister, shaking her finger back and forth. "Ha, ha, ha! All the little junior high kiddies think I'm Farrah Fawcett with black hair or something. I'm so hot." Roxie snickered, as she bent her knees and put her hand to her head, pointing her elbow up in the air.

Della thought the job was a bit embarrassing, especially since her sister could make more than twice as much working at a decent diner.

Paul walked out of the bathroom. "It's in the top drawer. All yours," he said with a smile.

"Thanks." Jack strolled into the bathroom and locked the door behind him. It was a gloomy bathroom, no windows, brown tub with shower, a brown ceramic sink, a dark stained wood medicine cabinet and toilet seat cover. Jack looked in the mirror. His face seemed a little more gaunt lately. He raised his hands and stroked down the few straggling hairs around his ears and smoothed his beard against his face. He looked down and opened the little drawer on the left. A six-inch piece of tinfoil, folded in a little V, plus half of a plastic straw with a lighter.

Jack put the straw in his mouth and saw a little piece of black tar heroin about a quarter the size of his pinkie nail in the middle of the aluminum V. He picked it all up and pulled his lighter from his pocket. He held the flame beneath the tinfoil. Smoke rose off the black tar in a little stream, and Jack sucked it up from the straw until his lungs were full.

Exhaling, he could feel his heart begin to slow. He took one more large hit and crumpled up the tinfoil, placing it, along with the straw, back in the drawer. As he exhaled again into the vent fan, he felt euphoric, at peace. His whole body warm, relaxed. As he opened the door, he was tranquil, as if everything was going to be just fine.

"You have any pot?" Paul asked, as he strolled into the kitchen, looking relaxed.

"Of course, no sweat, out in my car. How much ya need?"

"Just a dime." They walked out the front door. Paul walked next to Jack with his arm draped over Jack's shoulders. "Nice, huh?"

"Wow, great. Been a while," Jack responded, feeling relaxed and fluid.

"I know. I love that shit. You have to be careful with it though." Paul had had a friend of a friend who had overdosed. "You still trimming those fucking trees?"

"Not really. A couple times a week for some extra cash. Making more money selling pot, a few pounds at a time now." Margins were thin, but Jack was able to pay some bills.

"With your network, you could be making five times as much moving dope and have a little extra to party when you want." Paul winked.

"Not for me. This is working pretty well." Jack handed him a plastic baggie from out of the trunk of his olive-colored Plymouth. "Now we're even. Thanks for inside. Totally chill. Just what I needed after hanging out with the old man all afternoon."

"Seriously." Paul started down the cement steps to the door.

"I'm toast. Send Della out. Tell Rox and Rock that I said good-bye."

Della came up the steps to see Jack leaning against the metal railing.

"Will you drive home?" he asked.

"I thought you were going to drive." Della did not want to drive after doing a bump, even if it was only a small one.

"I know. I know. Super tired all of a sudden, even after that line. Not sure why. I'll watch the road for you."

"Fine." Della was irritated, as Jack always seemed to pull stunts like this. Unlocking the passenger door, she opened it, and Jack oozed onto the seat. Heading over to the other side of the car, Della hopped in, moved the seat forward and adjusted the mirrors. Forty minutes later they were lying side by side, naked in their little full-size bed. Jack's arms lay on the bed above his head, and Della cradled beside him, her head on his chest, floating quickly to sleep.

Jack's mind was slowed but fluid, like his body. Going to see his father was always a bit much. At least Della fended off his mother like a pro. Everything seemed a bit *much* lately, his parents, people, life. He wanted to go someplace slower, more real, connected. Upstate maybe. A little place in the woods, a few acres that could be cleared. Get some goats and chickens, live with his hands, away from the world that seemed to becoming an ever-growing irritation.

It would be great for Della too; she certainly wouldn't realize it at first, but, if he could save enough money and buy some land, she would come. Sure, she would hate it for a while, but, without all the oppressive noise from the city, she would learn what it felt like to be free.

He remembered his father saying that the house was worth about thirty thousand dollars; how he had only paid seven thousand seven hundred dollars for it in Nineteen Forty Seven. He had put down a hundred bucks and, with his GI Bill, still had ten dollars left to take Mom out for an Italian dinner at Caruso's. Jack's GI Bill didn't have quite the same perks, and things had gotten a whole hell of a lot more expensive. If he could save up, it just might work.

A nice place upstate, no neighbors and a few acres must cost about forty grand, he figured. He was relaxed, and the pressure of Della's head against his chest was comforting, as he breathed in and out.

Maybe he could sell a little dope. Just for a while, to save enough so he and Della could disappear, make their own way, live on their own terms for a change. Work the land together, be free.

If anyone knew whether it was feasible to make money on dope, it was his cousin Stan who still lived in Hell's Kitchen. Jack made a mental note to give Stan a ring as Jack lay back into the soft green grass of the riverbank in his mind. He wriggled his feet in the smooth pebbles of the cool creek that ran beside his little cabin, deep within the forests of upstate New York.

BOOK ONE: CHAPTER THREE

It was three o'clock in the afternoon, and Della was already tired. She took the bus crosstown, as she normally did, and walked the last two blocks to her apartment, now shared with Jack. The lunch rush was always exhausting. Her feet were more tired than usual and swollen, but, from behind, you couldn't even tell she was already six months pregnant.

As Della opened the door, she had hoped to find Jack ready to leave for dinner at her parents' house but instead was irritated to find him lounging on the couch with his cousin Stan Sesla and his low-life friend Ritchie Nazzle. The trio clearly cut short their conversation and were hurriedly rearranging the magazines on the coffee table.

"Hey, babe. How was work? Stan and Ritchie just stopped by to say hi. They wanted to make sure the baby was cooking all right." It was clearly a lie, but it sounded nice and would go unquestioned, Jack thought.

Jack had been hanging out with his cousin Stan more often the last few months, since Della got pregnant. Jack needed to find a way to make a few more bucks, and Stan had a connection for dope back in the neighborhood. It was certainly paying off, as Jack was able to dump the tree-trimming business entirely and still have a few more bucks in his pocket than before. He had bumped into Ritchie at Stan's; Jack and Ritchie used to run in some of the same circles in high school. Jack forgot what a riot Ritchie could be, and, at six foot three, he was good to have along for the ride.

Della was beginning to think that Jack was not taking having a baby seriously, as if he stopped listening when she spoke. And while she couldn't smell it, she was sure they were smoking pot before she came in. With the rustling of the magazines, they were probably hiding a joint. Which was stupid because she had told Jack, several times, that she didn't care if he smoked pot in the house, as long as she wasn't home when he did—because of the baby and all.

Della was sure he would settle down now that there was a baby in the picture. He asked her to marry him right away when she had announced she was pregnant. A much better reaction than she had hoped for. He suggested they go to the county clerk since his parents would make things difficult. She didn't get a fancy ring or anything, but she really didn't care.

Instead of focusing on his business, Jack started selling more pot and hanging around friends who Della considered creepy. Ritchie being king of the creeps. At six foot three, he was almost as tall as her father, but greasy. Not greasy like one of the guidos from the neighborhood either, but like used grease from the deep fryer at the diner. He had long thin, stringy brown hair down to the nape of his neck and was just on the shy side of being called a fat ass. Big and hulky enough that he scared people, especially when he grinned. His teeth were yellow, and several of them had rotting brown decay around the edges. It was disgusting. Della felt like she would puke whenever he smiled, especially now that she was pregnant. He had a dark, disturbing sense of humor that matched his teeth nicely.

Stan, on the other hand, was shorter than she was, only five foot six, stalky and strong like a gorilla. When he shook your hand, you felt as if it had been placed in a vise. He was Black Irish, dark hair, black eyes that looked dead unless you looked long enough to feel scared.

"Why are they here? Didn't you remember we're supposed to go to my parents for dinner?" Della showed her frustration with Jack's persistent lounging around. It seemed to be an increasing occurrence, shared with a decreasing quality of characters.

"Yeah, I remembered." Again untrue.

"Are you going to change?"

"No need," Jack answered. He was in his standard attire: black army boots, blue jeans, white guinea T, topped with an unbuttoned long-sleeved flannel shirt. His black leather jacket with the Tweety Bird patch lay beside him. It was his favorite; underneath Tweety, the patch read Everyone Enjoys a Little Pussy. He found it very clever.

"I'm going to change, then we need to go."

"Putting on a few pounds there, eh, Dell?" Ritchie shot out jokingly.

Thing was, Ritchie's jokes weren't funny; they were just mean and sometimes downright cruel.

"Fuck you, Ritchie. You're just a fat piece of shit not even a mother could love," Della answered, which was true. She shut the door to their bedroom.

"Hormones, damn," Ritchie replied, as Jack snickered at him.

"She works hard that girl. Ain't had it so easy neither," Jack replied, looking Ritchie dead in the eye.

"OK, easy. I was just messing around." Ritchie held up his hand in front of him, sitting in an armchair across from Jack and his cousin.

"So, like I was saying, we got a grand, just from the tellers. No need to go to the bank vault or nothing. In and out, me and Vinnie." Vinnie was his younger, but far taller and handsomer, brother.

43

"Good for you, Stan. I've had my fill of guns," Jack replied. He carried knives now; he could easily cut down ten men, even an untrained man with a gun. If it took more than that, he wanted no part of it; no more guns, never. While money was appealing, with a little more effort, his new endeavor should yield him that house in woods.

"You guys are gonna have to get outta here when she's done. Forgot we have dinner at her mother's. She cooks the hell outta spaghetti and meatballs, straight from the Old Country, made from scratch, and chicken parmesan!" Jack made a kissing motion as he put his hand to his mouth.

"Great, count me in." Ritchie laughed.

"Yeah, you wish. There isn't enough food on the island to fill your piehole. I'm hitting the head, then you guys need to split." Jack walked into the half bathroom attached to the living room and locked the door.

It all seemed a bit surprising to Jack, if he had bothered to think about it, so he tried not to. Della was real great; he pictured her on the farm with him, but a baby was not in the original plan. Sure, he could see himself with kids eventually, once he and Della settled in and figured things out. A baby wasn't rugged, and being a bit rugged was going to be necessary for his plan to work, at least on the front end.

He took out a hygiene bag from under the sink. It had a razor and a sock inside, just in case someone happened to open it. Jack took his kit from the sock and smoked a large hit. He crumbled up the tinfoil into a ball and put it back inside the bag. Once every week or so, when he had the place to himself, he would tear apart fifteen pieces of tinfoil and put them in the bottom of the bag. That way, on a day like today, he could be in and out in under a minute. Nice. Jack held the air long enough so that there was very little smoke released when he exhaled. It always gave him a bit of a head rush. Other than that, he felt perhaps a little calmer, but the euphoric feeling had long since passed.

Jack opened the door and saw Ritchie asleep with his feet on the coffee table, his head against the back of the chair. Stan was sitting with his legs crossed, quietly dangerous as usual, wearing black jeans, a tight black leather jacket over a black ribbed T-shirt.

Jack kicked Ritchie in his jean-covered calves, sending his size 11 Converse shoes to the floor.

"What the fuck," Ritchie snarled, awakened from his dozing.

"Time to go." Jack kicked at Ritchie's heels.

"Let's go. Nice to see you, Della," Stan yelled, as he stood and gave his cousin a hug. He turned and pushed Ritchie Nazzle up into the kitchen and out the front door.

"I hate those guys." Della stepped out of the bedroom upon hearing the front door close.

"Hey, that's my cousin." Jack rose to his feet, figuring Della was ready to leave for her parents.

"Ritchie's not. He's just a low-life scumbag, totally gross. I know Stan's your cousin, but I also know he robs banks. He's *scary*!" Della said.

"He's always nice to you. He's *polite*," Jack said. Which was true, but it had a chilling effect. As if he were overcompensating for something hidden from view. "I know Ritchie's a dumb ass, but he's a good guy at heart. He's someone who'd watch your back. I trust him."

"Can we go to my mother's already?"

"Let's go already." Jack walked to the door, holding it open.

As they exited the Long Island Expressway, Jack decided to get off in Amityville, on the way to Dell's parents' house in Lindenhurst. He found it intriguing to cruise by the DeFeo house. Late last year the whole family was murdered—four kids and the two parents. They pinned it on the older brother Butch. Jack figured it had to do with drugs or the mob maybe, since the family were guineas.

He hopped back onto Old Sunrise Highway and saw three black men in their early twenties leaning against the lamppost, drinking beer on the corner. Jack slowed the tires near the curb five or six feet from the corner. "Be right back." And with that he was out of the car.

They were all over six foot and muscular, wearing black jackets, trying to pull off a Black Panther look. Amityville was one of the few towns on Long Island where some blacks got a toehold.

The largest of the three dropped a cigarette in the gutter and passed his beer to a buddy. "Is there a problem?" he asked, standing up straight to show his size.

"I'd say so. You just littered. There's no drinking beer on the corner here either. Not on Long Island and certainly not by a bunch of stupid niggers." Jack cared for niggers no less nor more than for spics, kikes, guineas, drunk mick bastards or ninety 9 percent of the rest of society. But it was an easy way to get a rise.

"That's a pretty dumb thing to say when you're outnumbered, white boy." The largest of the three gestured to his friends and took a step forward.

With his right fist, knuckles pointing out, Jack threw a fast punch, landing it square on the boy's chin. It knocked him out instantly. On his way down, Jack lifted his left knee into the falling face and then added to the momentum by thrusting his hands on the back of the falling boy's head. He landed facedown in the gutter, unconscious.

In an instant Jack grabbed the beer from the man who had been leaning against the pole. Holding the back of the man's head, Jack beat the guy's face, using the bottom of the beer can. Blood began to spray, and his knees crumbled. Jack stepped to the third man, who, like the others, was still a boy. He stood paralyzed by the seven-second fury. Jack looked him squarely in the eyes, until he was able to see through the shock.

"Stop, help," the boy gasped, as if the air were sucked from his lungs.

Jack grabbed him around the bottom of his chin, his hand in the shape of a U; he squeezed it tightly like a vise.

"No littering, no drinking outside. Tell your friends, all of them." Jack threw him by his face, so he fell into a heap of black trash bags. With that Jack slid back into his olive-green Plymouth and said to Della, "Don't talk to me like that in front of my friends again." Jack pulled back onto the highway.

"What are you talking about? What are you doing?" Della turned toward him in her seat with a look of disgust and amazement on her face.

"*Why are they here?*" Jack said mockingly, mimicking Della's voice, referencing her comment from when she had arrived home from work. "What's with that bullshit snotty attitude?" Jack said with arrogance.

"Are you serious?" What nerve, Della thought.

"Of course I am."

"Just drive to my mother's." He was so unbelievable sometimes, Della thought. She wished he would just grow up.

Jack parked in front of Della's small family home. It was only eight hundred square feet, crowded growing up with the three girls and their brother. It was tiny, but quaint from the outside, brick red with white trim, a nice front lawn. Her father, Ray's, white work van was parked in the driveway.

Jack and Della walked up the little concrete walkway hand in hand to the front door. Della walked them into her parents' living room.

Her sister Pricilla ran quickly to put her hands on Della's soccer-ball-size belly. "Ooohh," she squealed."

Della, Roxie and Pricilla—Prissy as she was called—were all variations of the same mold. Long dark hair, smooth bronzed skin, lean, toned, one's face more beautiful than the next.

"Hi, baby. It's your favorite aunt, Aunt Prissy. Your aunt Prissy loves you. So does Jesus," Prissy said in baby talk, with her mouth next to Della's belly.

"Prissy, it's so great. You can feel him kick now. Feel." Della held Prissy's hand to the side of her protruding belly.

"Ooooh, I felt him." Prissy giggled with excitement.

"He's so strong. Some nights he kicks me all night long," Della said with a weary smile.

"You said *him*." Roxie inserted herself into the conversation.

★★★

Jack walked around the girls to find Ray in the kitchen. Lilian, Della's mother, was at the stove, stirring a giant cast iron pot. It was more of a cauldron filled near to the brim with a sweet, pungent sauce. Meatballs bounced up and down in the bubbling red sauce, like a witch's brew.

Jack inhaled deeply. "Smells delicious as always." He hugged her, a plump woman with short gray hair and thick glasses. She wore an apron and a dress that seemed more like a smock or a nightgown. Lily was a sweet lady, but, if you spoke with her for long, it became clear that she only had a sixth-grade education. She could hardly write and could only read certain words, but she was ever stirring, stirring, stirring. Jack teased Della that her mother's parents were first cousins, which was funny, because it was true.

"Have a taste." Lily lifted a large wooden spoonful of the red sauce with a broken piece of meatball to Jack's bearded lips, blowing on it first to cool it down.

"Awww, heaven," Jack said with a half-open mouthful of sauce, as it was too hot to swallow. "Ray, nice to see you. Carl." Jack nodded to each. Ray was standing up near the kitchen table. Carl, Della's brother, was sitting in his seat at the far side of the table near the wall.

"Boy, the neighborhood sure has changed some, huh, Ray." Jack extended his hand to Ray for a shake.

Ray grabbed Jack's hand, making it seem small in his own. Ray was six foot four and strong as an ox. Probably from waxing floors night after night, lugging those heavy machines in and out of his truck. He worked in the dead of night, alone, because the owners of these schools, gyms and buildings that needed their floors waxed did not want to have its occupants' eyes bothered with the waxers. Ray was a recovered alcoholic; it took Alcoholics Anonymous to have him quit drinking in the end. He was sober three or four years now. It had been a long, long journey.

"Niggers everywhere," Ray blared out. "All started when that old mick bastard MacNamara sold his house to that nigger family." Ray was visibly irritated and shook his finger. "Did it just to spite me, that son of a bitch. Couldn't sell to niggers before that. It was the goddamned law. But that set some sort of precedence." Ray threw up his hands in the air. "Now look. What do you see? Niggers everywhere, that's what."

"Yeah, well, I just taught a few of them some manners off Old Country Road."

"You mean those sons-a-bitch niggers with the black jackets?" Ray asked with wide eyes. If Ray was a younger man, he would have kicked the shit out of those thugs himself.

"That's them," Jack said, smiling.

"Tell me it's so." Raymond stepped toward Jack and looked him dead in the eye.

"It's so. It's so, I swear." Jack held up three fingers giving the Boy Scout salute. "The moolies were drinking and smoking out on the corner. So I told them, it just wasn't allowed," Jack said coyly. "Rearranged the two big niggers' faces and told the scrawny kid to let his friends know." Jack gave two swift uppercuts to the air.

"Hot damn." Ray jumped up and slapped his knee. "Hot damn, hot damn, hot damn." Ray danced around his plump wife, Lily, whisking her off her feet, spinning round and round, singing a little tune he just concocted over and over again.

"Bash the nigger's face. Bash the nigger's face. Don't kick the niggers out of town. We're better off with 'em dead." He put down his wife, and, as an Irishman, he started a little Irish jig. He would have asked his son to join him, but, being half Italian, he never quite got the hang of it.

"Dinner!" Lily put a pot of spaghetti noodles on the table, along with a smaller cauldron of homemade sauce filled with steaming plump meatballs.

Ray sat at the head of the table, his son, Carl, to his left, his wife on his right. The girls sat round the table next to their mother, usually from oldest to youngest: Pricilla, Della and Roxanne. Since Della was carrying Jack's baby, she exchanged her customary seat with Roxie. So Jack sat down next to his wife.

Lily began spooning out the pasta and sauce, fitting the stereotype of an Italian mother well. With an inherent desire to fill guests to bursting, she always made more food than could possibly be eaten. She served Ray first, then Jack, Carl and the girls. Everyone drank water, and Della was glad of the fact. There was a time when her father drank vodka at the dinner table straight out of the bottle.

"When Della was in high school, there were only two niggers in the whole school. One was that nigger family that bought old MacNamara's house. After that, the goddamned school recruited that nigger football player, right, Dell?"

"Dad, enough with the Lord's name in vain, please," Prissy chimed in. She was a born-again Christian now. She attended Pentecostal revival meetings in a tent, similar to the circuit riders of yore. She had given her life to Christ a year earlier, after she had seen the miraculous change that took place in her brother. That could only have been God at work.

Carl had gotten progressively crueler as a big brother over the years, especially as his addiction to methamphetamine grew. It had caused him to drop out of college and had created several miserable years for the family. He progressed from smoking and snorting to shooting up. Eventually it appeared as though he had lost his mind after being *up* for nearly a week. Drove his car all the way to Texas, convinced he was getting secret messages from the radio. It sounded amusing in hindsight, but it wasn't amusing, not amusing in the least. Carl was brought to a point of mental insanity. The point where one truly does not know what is real and what is not. A feeling that would become more common. For Carl and for a world changed by time, truth was no longer absolute.

By the time Carl got to Texas, his car broke down, and he was coming down as well. He spent a night and a day sleeping in his car. When he went to wander around, he ran into a Pentecostal revival in process. He came home a changed man, truly. Not a great man, but no more meth. With a new crowd of friends, he spent time helping out at the meetings. That was eighteen months ago. The family noticed, Prissy in particular.

"His name was Steve, Dad, and we made it to the semifinals," Della chimed back at her father. Steve was a nice guy. Things were different when Della went to high school, even though it was only a little more than six years ago. Girls had to wear skirts with stockings. Boys had to wear slacks, no jeans; collared shirts, no tank tops; no sneakers; no long hair. It seemed strange to her now. That's why she hardly ever wore anything besides jeans and tank tops now.

"At least we've got a good Irish lad in the family now. Right, Jack?" Ray twirled a big bite of spaghetti into a cylindrical shape with his fork. He was able to twirl it with just his fork now, like the guineas, no spoon needed. It took Ray some time to drop the need for the spoon though.

Raymond took a large gulp from his clear glass, having only recently become a vessel for water. He still filled it to the same height, except not with cheap Russian vodka. The tattoo of a naked girl in a martini glass on his forearm was evidence of his proclivities. A design that was popular when he was in the navy.

Raymond Tomasini loved to drink, even when he didn't. It got progressively worse as the children got older, if that was even possible. He would often drag an assortment of kids down to the bar, making them sit underneath the bar stool, until he stumbled home at three or four in the morning, often without them. Lilian would search methodically, bar by bar, as Ray never remembered where he had been. She was no longer frantic about it, as the scene was repeated, repeatedly. She seemed unable or unaware of how to make it otherwise.

By the time Della was eight, her father would regularly come home after work drunk, his temper violent. He liked to scream and break things. Della and her sisters would flee through the front door to where it was safe across the street, to their aunt Carmella's house.

Ray came home one day when the family was listening to some music on the radio. It was the family's only entertainment and escape. He was in a murderous rage. His eyes said he would gladly rip off the arm of his own children and bash their brains out with it. Della remembered how he yelled something about the radio and showing them what poor looked like. He proceeded to break all the furniture in the house—all of it, every single piece. Every mirror, every cabinet, every window in the entire house. He threw the radio against the wall. They should feel lucky to have a roof. It took a month and a half before her uncle forced their father to help him fix the windows.

The family had no furniture again until Della was a junior in high school. The family slept with blankets on the floor. The girls handed down one set of clothes between the three of them. Della finally got the courage in high school to start buying some furniture from the Goodwill store. It started with a mattress on the floor, eventually a couch. Her father broke the couch until it was just a pile of wood. Della moved out with her friend Cheryl as soon as Della turned eighteen. She hardly spent any time at home her senior year after her father broke the couch. She had been scared to the very core of her soul.

The summer after graduation Della sniffed half a line of methamphetamine with her brother at a party as a graduation present. When Carl dropped her off at home, she went in and saw her father crouched over, hands to his mouth, staring out the glass door in the kitchen into the backyard. He was shaking his head side to side. Della pulled back into the shadow of the living room and watched paralyzed by the sight. Her heart beat so loudly in her chest that she hoped it did not draw attention.

"No, no," her father shouted in a whisper, as if terrified and insane all at once. He pressed his face close to the glass and gazed intently as if he saw something impossible off in the shadows. He began to hiss like a cornered alley cat and then began to shout, "No. No, I can't. I can't. Don't ask me to. No!" Then he sobbed uncontrollably.

Della thought she would throw up; her father never cried.

He sat down in a kitchen chair and pulled a blanket over his shoulders and head; he gazed out the window. He would move his head side to side, his body slowly bouncing up and down like a rocking chair, as if to gain a better view. Periodically he would clutch his heart, then his mouth; he was hyperventilating.

Della was certain he would go to the garage, grab an ax and cut up the family in their sleep. She grabbed her sisters from the blankets on the floor in the living room and crept quietly over to Aunt Carmella's.

"This spaghetti's really amazing, Lily. Seriously, best meatballs I've ever had, ever, even in a restaurant." Jack was flattering her, but it was all true. Lily made the best Italian food Jack had ever tasted.

Lily filled up his plate again.

"He's doing somersaults in my belly. Must like pasta, just like his daddy."

"There you go with the *he* again," Roxie noted, slurping up a strand of pasta.

"It's a boy. I know it is," Della continued to rub her belly.

"Delicious, Lily! Well, Ray, happy to keep the neighborhood clean, glad to be part of the family." Jack rose and gave Ray a firm handshake; they looked each other in the eye like men. Jack bent over and gave Lily a hug; she kissed him on both cheeks. "You behave and eat. Make sure she eats, for the baby. You're too skinny, both of you." Lily pinched Jack's waist.

"Hey, you keep making that spaghetti and meatballs, and you'll have nothing to worry about."

Prissy and Roxie took turns kissing and rubbing their sister's belly until she was out the door.

As they rode back, Jack was tense. Still he enjoyed Della's family. Her dad was a racist riot; it was fun and easy to jerk his chain. Boy, could Lily cook, and she always did. There was no booze there, and no weed-smoking in his own car with Della pregnant and all. They were home before long thankfully, in their room, their bed. Della had found a nice queen-size mattress from Goodwill. Jack would have never bought something from Goodwill, but Della was right. The bed was a steal and slept like a dream. Plenty of room to stretch out at night. And stretch Jack did, feeling warm after a five-finger slug of Jameson Irish Whiskey. Jack and Della lay together, naked as always, her belly pressed up against his ribs.

"I felt that." Jack felt a kick in his ribs, which was cool and strange at the same time.

"He's moving all around. He says, 'Hi, Daddy.' He moves around a lot right before I go to sleep, like he's saying, 'Good night,'" Della said quietly.

A bit corny but still cute. The moonlight filtered in through the curtains covering the bedroom window, lighting the room as if by dim candlelight. Jack drifted and heard the sound of a car driving by, slightly slower than the rest. BANG, BANG, BANG!

Della screamed.

By her scream, Jack knew he wasn't dreaming. "Don't make a sound." He pushed her face toward the bed, crouching, with her slender wrist in his hand and his body protecting hers. He grabbed a machete beside the bed, dragging them inside their bedroom closet in less than two seconds. It was a good thing too, as more shots rang through the living room and into the bedroom.

"Get on the ground," Jack whispered.

Della sat on the ground behind him, uncomfortably, naked, in the corner of their closet. Jack stood in front of her, machete raised at his side. He breathed evenly through his stomach to slow down his breathing; he slipped into combat mode. If anyone opened the closet, he would make them hamburger before they could fire a shot. His wife was pregnant, and this civilian had been trained to be a Ranger.

They heard the crashing sounds, like someone kicking in the front door. Three more shots rang out with what sounded like a lamp getting blown apart. Jack heard two sets of footsteps; one of them opened the door to the bedroom and walked in. He pushed Della close to the floor with his left hand and squeezed himself in tight to the left side of the closet. Footsteps walked over to the bed. Jack could hear the comforter being thrown to the floor. The footsteps walked back out of the room; Jack's pulse began to slow.

He could hear someone say, "Nobody here."

Jack's pulse began to steady. Ten seconds later Jack heard the car in front speed off, spinning its tires. He waited in the closet for another five minutes just to be cautious. He counted Mississippis in his head.

Della was still cowering in the closet as he slid open the sliding closet door.

"It's all right." Jack lifted Della to her feet and brought her over to the bed.

"Holy shit," Jack said, sitting beside his wife and running his hands through his hair.

"Oh, my God, what the fuck was that?" Della was shell-shocked, and the baby was still.

"I don't know," Jack said, holding his head in his hands.

"What do you mean, you don't know?" Della's fright was turning to anger. How could he place their baby in such danger? Getting married and having a baby was supposed to slow down him down, but things only seemed to be getting more chaotic.

"I don't know, really." And he didn't, specifically. Jack assumed it had something to do with the dope he was moving lately. He was able to cut out some of the competition with a better product and cheaper price. Thinner margins weren't a problem for him, as there was previously no margin at all.

Della wasn't going to press the issue for now. She couldn't tell if Jack really knew what was going on or not. She suspected he did, and she suspected it had something to do with his cousin Stan and that scumbag Ritchie. A real nefarious trio.

"Well, turn on the light. Go see what's left. Should we call the police?" Della was tired and resigned.

"Nothing the police can do now." Jack went to survey the apartment, which was thoroughly shot up and upended.

"Couch looks OK," Jack shouted from the other room.

Della closed her eyes, laid back upon her pillow and let the tears stream quietly down the sides of her face. The baby remained silent.

BOOK ONE: CHAPTER FOUR

It was past six, the evening before Christmas Nineteen Seventy 9, and Guy—as he was named by Jack, his father—was just more than three and a half years old. His father had thought it best in the world, as it was, to be just another guy. Guy was born April thirteenth, the year America celebrated its two hundredth anniversary. Today he sat upon a dark red leather bar stool with a high back, his blond head jutting just above the stool's backrest.

His mother was serving food to a packed crowd of patrons with Christmas money in their pockets at a pub called Potters off Hempstead Turnpike. Potters had a long bar that could seat near thirty people, with more seating available at tables along the side and in the back. The bar was dimly lit, well suiting the epic drinking of their clientele. The food was not like Lily's, but, for a pub, it was top-notch. The manager, Timmy Flynn, was a traditional Irishman of the wild-drinking variety. If there was any other kind of Irishman, they certainly weren't to be found on Long Island. He wore most of the hats in the pub: helping to create dishes in the kitchen and putting on the best bartender show on the island—some would say even within the city. He twirled bottles above his head with ease and blew six-foot-tall flames in the air with Everclear.

Potters was across the corner and down the street from the diner where Della used to work. Timmy would stop in periodically to get a roast beef sandwich; he thought Della had real charisma. He told her that she could make a lot more money working at the pub. By the next week it was a done deal. The drunk patrons tipped the pretty young lass handsomely.

Guy was at the bar, sitting next to Ted, a construction worker who stopped in most nights to grab a beer before he went home. Ted looked over at Guy sitting in the seat next to him drinking what was left of a Coca-Cola in a tall skinny glass with a skinny red straw. Guy was watching the hockey game on one of the two TVs mounted above the bar.

"Hey, kid. Who do you like, the Rangers or the Islanders?" Ted asked boisterously over his frothy mug of cold brew.

This was the first time Guy had ever seen hockey. He was only watching it because it was on. Guy liked lots of shows like *The Electric Company*, *Mr. Rogers* and *Sesame Street*. He watched reruns of *Get Smart* with his grandma; it had fun music. Guy knew that his grandma and grandpa lived on the island.

"The Islanders," Guy said loudly, so he could be heard.

"Ha, ha. The Islanders! You hear that? This kid likes the Islanders! Kid gets another Coke on me," Ted said loudly, lifting his mug of brew above his shaggy brown head.

"I'm allowed to get my own sodas for free." Guy slid down and put his foot on the rung at the bottom of the bar stool. He was wearing his little black-and-white saddle shoes, dungarees and a long-sleeved red shirt. His short sandy-blond hair framed his his chubby cheeks and fair skin.

Guy walked around Ted, and, as Ted looked over his shoulder, Guy pushed open the little wooden swing door, letting himself in behind the bar. Getting soda was fun, because the soda maker looked like a gun. Guy put his glass in the sink and picked up a new one off the ledge that came to his chest when he stepped onto the little plastic step. Guy grabbed the ice scooper, shoveling himself a glass half full of ice. His favorite part of course was the soda gun. Guy grabbed the black gun with buttons on the back; he pushed the C for Coca-Cola, which was his favorite! He picked out a new bright-red straw.

"I'm allowed to have a new straw and a cherry," Guy shouted to Ted, who was looking at the boy with amazement.

"Who is this little kid?" Ted asked Timmy, who was busy pouring drinks up and down the other end of the bar.

"Della's boy." Timmy pointed to Della, who was carrying five plates of food to a bunch of Wall Street guys in ties.

Guy was back at his seat and, with firm resolve, said, "I'm not little." Guy unbuttoned his dungarees to show Ted his Superman Underoos. "See? I'm a big boy," Guy said with a smile upon his face as he rebuttoned his dungarees.

"Woo hoo, does your mom do tricks like that?" Ted asked with a hearty laugh.

"Only in our house." Which was true, Guy thought, since his mom did walk around the house in her girl underwear.

"I know my ABCs." Guy proceeded to recite the alphabet. "I can count to a hundred."

"Wow! Hey, Timmy! You seen this kid?"

"Yeah, he's a real riot, smart little booger." Timmy wasn't the tallest of his brothers, nor was he the shortest, standing at six foot four. He had long shaggy blond hair and broad shoulders. Timmy was slim like a swimmer, with a burly mustache. He was the youngest brother by age. He had an older brother by two years, Mack, and George by two years again. George was six foot six, and, though a monster of a man, he was a bit gangly for his size and not handsome like his brothers. A gentle giant, as long as you were on his good side.

Mack was six two, the shortest of the brothers, with brown hair and a thick mustache. The next year people would say he bore an uncanny resemblance to Tom Selleck in *Magnum, P.I.* Mack was sitting with the Wall Street crowd—bankers actually.

"All right, kid, you know how to add? What's three plus one?" Ted asked with a grin, hoping to get Guy to shut up. He supposed all that soda was not helping his cause.

Guy began counting, holding up his pointer, middle and ring fingers on his left hand. "One, two, three."

"One." Guy held up his pinkie finger as well. "One, two, three, four. Four."

"No shit." Ted was stunned.

"That's not a nice word."

"Not for kids, it's not. All right, wiseass, what about subtraction?"

Guy was not sure what *subtraction* was, but he was pretty sure donkeys were not wise. "I can do take away." He held up two fingers. "Two take away one is one." Guy proudly held up his pointer finger.

"Holy shit! This kid's a little fucking whiz." Ted turned around to face the tables behind him. "Della, your husband a doctor or something?"

"Yeah, right. You think I'd be working here?" Della placed five large mugs of beer down on the table and gave him a wink.

"Your kid's like a little fucking Einstein. Where the hell did he learn to do addition and subtraction?"

"*Sesame Street*. Kid loves *Sesame Street*. He's a sponge, picks up all sorts of crazy stuff."

"Bullshit," Ted said sarcastically. "No little kid learns that from watching *Sesame Street*."

"I don't know what to tell you. He says stuff every day that makes me shake my head!" Della replied.

"No shit. Well, I'd offer to buy you another Coke, kid, but looks like you got that one covered. Timmy"—Ted parked a five-dollar bill at the end of the bar—"see you tomorrow."

Timmy slid down the bar, picking up his tip from the edge.

"Wow! You're rich. Five bucks!" Guy said with wide eyes.

"If five bucks made me a rich man, I'd be in good shape, kid." Timmy laughed and rustled Guy's fair hair.

"Trade that Coke in for a Shirley Temple?" Timmy reached across for Guy's glass.

"Hurray!" Guy loved Shirley Temples, but he couldn't make them by himself. You needed the red syrup, which was kept out of his reach.

"Mack, get a load of this kid. He's smart as a whip."

Mack walked over from the suits' table. He was a banker, in the commercial real estate division for Chase Manhattan, of the increasingly rare variety who did calculations in their heads.

Mack sat on the stool next to Guy, still wearing his navy blue suit, a starched white shirt with the top button undone and a loosened maroon tie.

"Thinks I can retire off of five bucks." Timmy laughed, pointing his thumb at Guy and cleaning glasses in the stainless steel sink. "My brother's a banker. Mack here knows all about money, kid."

"I know about money too," Guy stated confidently, in a way that made the adults forget they were having a conversation with a three-year-old.

"Really?" Mack pulled out the change he had in his pocket and put it on the bar: a quarter, two dimes, a nickel, two pennies and a subway token.

Guy automatically counted it. "Twenty-five, thirty-five, forty-five, fifty, fifty-one, fifty-two. What's this?" Guy asked, moving his tiny fingers to the subway token.

"That's a subway token. You use it to pay for a ride on the subway. It's like a train. Impressive counting! Go ahead you can keep them." Mack looked over at Timmy. "You're right. This kid is smart as a whip!"

"Della's kid. She's our best waitress. The guys love her."

Mack knew who Della was; he could understand why the guys loved her. She was a knockout and fun, always laughing. She never got offended, even with the drunk knuckleheads. She made a point to ensure no one's glass ever ran dry, even if it was not her table.

"Hey, Della! Your kid's a real riot," Mack yelled over.

Della stepped over, rubbed the top of Guy's head and gave him a kiss. "So I keep hearing. He's something special. Started walking just before he turned 9 months. He was using four- and five-word sentences by the time he was a year old. At a year and a half, he decided diapers were for babies." Della chuckled; she liked Mack. He was the classiest guy who came in—and funny, like his brother. When the two of them got together, it was a real hoot.

"Look, money." Guy chimed in. "You can have it, Mommy." Guy extended his closed hand with a quarter and dime peeking out from between his tiny fingers.

"Where did you get that from?" Della stood with her hands pressed into the green-and-white dress above her hips, the uniform of Potters Pub's for Irish lasses.

"From him," said Guy, pointing to Mack beside him.

"You know we don't take money from strangers," said Della, shaking her finger.

"No, no, it's fine. I gave it to him. We were counting, and, hey, it's Christmas Eve."

"Please, Mommy?" Guy looked up pleadingly.

"OK, OK. Let me finish up, so we can get home and get you into bed."

Mack was fascinated by Guy. He was like a little man, but sweet.

"So what's Santa going to bring you for Christmas tomorrow?"

"Christmas is Jesus's birthday. He was poor. He was born in a stable with animals."

Mack was caught off guard by the little man's response; his mind fumbled for something appropriate to say. "Ah, yeah, that's true." Whoa, I barely dodged that one, Mack thought. "So what do you want to be when you grow up?" he redirected.

"I want to be a policeman."

"Ah, that's a great job!" Mack lifted his hand for a high-five, and Guy smacked him hard with his little hand. Mack thought very highly of policemen, had a few uncles and some close friends who were cops. One of them, Clarke, was his roommate all throughout college. He was a lieutenant for Suffolk County now. They were men of honor who put duty above self. Men of real character who stood up for what was right.

"So why do you want to be a policeman?"

"So that way I can put the bad guys in jail," Guy replied with excitement, now kneeling at the edge of the bar stool.

"Easy there, you don't want to fall."

Guy sat back down and leaned forward to eat the maraschino cherry from his Shirley Temple. "Mmm." Guy loved cherries, and he loved Shirley Temples even more than Coca-Cola, if that were possible. "What's your job?" Guy asked inquisitively.

"I'm a banker," Mack said, proudly sitting up in his bar stool and straightening his tie.

"What do you do?" Guy liked to know what people actually did, not just what they were called.

"We work with money."

"Fun. Maybe I could be a policeman and a banker!" Guy was kneeling on the bar stool again, this time with his little hands resting upon Mack's knee.

"If you study really hard in school—careful there, sit back." Mack nudged Guy gently back into his chair and laughed heartily.

Guy laughed too, as he squinted and scrunched up his little button nose.

"All right, time to go." Della, with apron removed, ran up to her son and scooped him into her arms, twirling themselves together. She was making three hundred sixty eight dollars gross a month now and could take home almost that much in tips, especially if she got extra hours. Rent was three hundred fifty, which she could cover now, since Jack's "cash flow" was sporadic at best.

"Mack's funny." Guy touched his mother's nose.

"I'm sure he is, but we have to go. We don't want to miss the bus," his mother answered.

"What are you talking about, take the bus?" Mack stood to his feet, "I'll drive you guys."

"Thanks, but it's OK. We don't live on the island. It's quite a drive. Completely unnecessary. We do this five or six nights a week."

"You're kidding me, right? It's Christmas Eve. I don't mind, seriously."

"I don't want to put you out." Della walked toward the door, holding her son.

Mack ran beside them. "I won't take no for an answer, not on Christmas Eve. My car's right outside." Mack smiled and held open the door.

Della walked out with Guy in her arms, following behind Mack in the crisp air of the night. Mack came to the pub regularly to visit his brother Tim. Sometimes on the weekend he would come in wearing short lifeguard shorts. Timmy and all of his brothers had been lifeguards during the summers. She thought Mack looked as if he was carved from oak.

"Wow, that's yours?" Della followed Mack to the rear of a brand-new Nineteen Seventy 9 Datsun two eighty Z, dark green.

Mack popped open the rear hatchback door. "Look, you have your own little compartment," Mack said to Guy.

He peered into the back, which was flat, covered in carpet and had lots of room for a boy. "Yahoo." Guy leaped out of his mother's arms into the back of the green Datsun.

"Keep your head down while I close this." Mack shut the top gently and went around to open the door for Della. He closed it as she sat down.

"Cool car," Della said as Mack started up the engine.

"Like Flash Gordon," Guy yelled from his capsule.

"I like it. Just got it last month. The last one on the lot as they were bringing in the Nineteen Eighty models. Negotiated a great deal. Plus it's my favorite color. Where to?"

"Brooklyn. I told you it's a drive."

"Oh, it's no problem. Comfortable back there, Guy?"

"This is *sooooo* cool, Mom. It's like a rocket ship." Guy was flat on his back, his knees bent, looking out the bubble window toward the infinite night sky above.

In what seemed like no time, Mack pulled the Z in front of Della's first-floor railroad apartment in Brooklyn. Guy was just beginning to fall asleep, which never happened on the bus. Mack and Della opened their doors together, and Mack opened up the glass top of his dark green Z.

"Come on, sweetheart." Della reached down and scooped up her son. "Thanks for the ride. That was really nice of you."

"No problem. No problem at all. Anytime." Mack waved as Della carried Guy hurriedly through the front door.

"Daddy." Guy perked up hearing the TV and seeing his father home.

"It's bedtime. Santa doesn't come for boys who aren't in bed asleep," Jack said, sitting upon the tie-dyed couch. He waved Della to their bedroom.

Della could see that he was in one of his moods, which seemed to be happening more and more often lately. She hated to think it, but she was glad he was spending less and less time at the house. Jack seemed to be envious of the time she spent taking care of Guy. As if a child were a burden, some sort of wedge between them, instead of the ultimate expression of love. She took Guy and settled him down on the small mattress in the corner of the bedroom. He had a Superman blanket and a little stuffed Ernie that had been replaced twice. There were black marker circles where his eyes had once been.

"Sweet dreams, Guy." Della kissed his little lips and pulled the covers snug up to his chin.

"Don't forget prayers, Mommy." Guy sat up and folded his little hands.

"OK, quick." Della folded her hands.

"Jesus, thank You for being in our hearts. Happy birthday for Christmas. Thank You for being born." Guy laid back on his pillow. He felt sorry for a moment that he didn't have a present for Jesus's birthday. But then he remembered he had fifty-two cents in his right front pocket.

He stopped his mom before she got to the door. "Mom, I need the money in my pants for Jesus's birthday," Guy said quietly.

"OK, OK." Della picked up his dungarees from the floor and felt into the pockets for the change. She pulled the coins out of the little pocket.

"Here." Della handed Guy the coins.

"There's one more penny, Mom. Fifty-two."

"OK, let me see." Della rummaged again through the little pockets. "OK, here it is." She passed Guy the worn penny.

"Thanks, Mom. Mom, can I give them to Jesus tomorrow?"

This was Prissy's area, Della thought. "Give them to me. I'll tell Santa to give them to Jesus."

"Mom, Santa's not real." Guy handed his mother the change.

Della kissed her son on the forehead and closed the door behind her. She walked over to her purse to deposit the change.

"What the fuck was that?" Jack rose to his feet.

"What are you talking about?" Della closed her purse and turned around to face her husband. Jack had begun to look disheveled; he had a look in his eye that seemed different, vacant, at times mean, then apologetic.

"You know exactly what the fuck I'm talking about. The fucking suit."

"Oh, you gotta be kidding me. Are you fucking serious? It's Christmas Eve, for Christ's sake. That's the manager, Timmy's, brother. He felt bad for us. He didn't want us to have to ride the bus on Christmas Eve, so he took us home." Della spoke Italian with her hands; she had had enough of his same ole shit lately. "You're really going to start, huh? What happened to the goddamned bedroom furniture? What about the money I gave you for Christmas presents?"

"There wasn't enough money. We're going to have a big Christmas now, OK? What do you think of that?" Jack said snidely. Which was true now for sure, because he was going to be forced into using more of the money than he wanted to for presents. Untrue in that he really needed the money to re-up his drug stash.

"So you what? You sold our furniture?"

"Yeah, my grandparents' bedroom furniture," Jack said slowly. "I got two hundred bucks for it."

"For your grandparents' heirloom furniture? You have got to be kidding me." Della threw up her hands in disgust. "Two hundred bucks. What are we going to do for a bed?"

"We'll get a new bed, relax." Jack was certain of that and irritated by Della's insinuation that it would somehow be otherwise. He would have the money for a new bed soon. He seemed to have done more of this last batch of dope than he should have, and now he had to make up the difference. Especially if he wanted to have enough to start over again. Plus he didn't really give a shit about his dead grandparents, or his mother either to be honest. He used some of the money that Della had given him for a fix this morning, while trying to come up with a plan, and a plan had finally come to mind: selling the furniture.

"So where are the Christmas presents? It's 9 o'clock," Della asked still wearing her pub uniform.

"That's where I was just going when you came home." Which was again true and untrue, as he was planning to cop a quick fix before hitting the store. He would have done it here, but Della was such a downer lately and suspicious. Jack didn't want to give her concrete proof that he was not simply consuming Jameson heavily. He would get up and pour some down the sink once or twice a week, to make it seem excessive. This caused his liquor expense to go up as well, which was unfortunate.

"I'm taking a shower and going to bed. Don't be too late. The presents still need to be wrapped."

"OK, OK, I love you." He gave Della a hug and walked toward the front door.

"I love you too. Wake me up when you get home. Don't be too late," Della repeated, as she walked back into the bedroom.

A hot shower and then to bed, back on the floor. At least her comforter and pillows were still here. Della grabbed them and made a space near her son.

Jack's quick stop turned into a king of the party, which was no surprise since he had had a pocketful of cash. Jack awoke to the sound of a blaring horn—his horn—his head resting upon the steering wheel. His mind was blank, and, as he lifted his head and opened his eyes, the blaring of the horn halted. With his vision still hazy, Jack could see that he had inconveniently parked his Plymouth with two tires on the front lawn of the three-story apartment building where they lived. The front end was resting on a pile of metal garbage cans. Fuck, he thought, but at least he was closer to the door. He laughed internally, until his heart sank, as he realized it was Christmas morning.

"Was that Santa Claus?" Guy sat up in his little bed on the floor. His mother was curled up beside him. A campout, Guy thought. Fun!

"I don't think so. *Shhh*, stay here, quiet." Della rose to her feet. Crouching slowly, she took her bathrobe off the wall hanger and then walked quickly to the front door, just as Jack came walking through it. She could see the car parked on the front lawn on top of the trash cans.

"No, no, *nooo*." Della cupped her hands to her mouth. "Where are the presents?" Della screamed quietly. Rushing toward the door, her stomach sank to her bowels as her blood rose. Jack, while wobbly, grabbed Della around the arms above her elbows.

"Calm the fuck down. I was robbed, OK? I was out all night looking for the presents."

"You're a fucking liar. You're wasted. You ruined Christmas. There, you happy? Did you get your son a present, even one?"

"I told you, they were stolen when I came out from the last place, which didn't have anything worth buying anyway. The trunk was jimmied opened. Everything was gone, everything, a whole trunk full of presents."

"I can't believe this, you piece of shit!" Della stormed out of the house and down to the car parked on the lawn. She went right over to peer down at the lock on the trunk. "Nope, no marks," she said loudly.

Jack followed her out the front door and down the steps.

"You liar," Della hissed. "You ruined Christmas. Happy now? Hey, everyone, my husband, Jack, ruined Christmas," Della began to shout. "My husband came home loaded and parked on the lawn. Hope you don't mind. Merry Christmas! And not one present for his only son!" she shouted with her hands to her mouth and rushed back in the house past Jack who was standing in a haze. He followed her in, then closed and locked the door behind him.

"Who the fuck do you think you are?" he said with condescension and a look that made Della freeze, paralyzed where she stood. Literally paralyzed with fear, like when you were a little kid and tried to scream but the sound just wouldn't come out.

"In front of the neighbors, the whole fucking neighborhood. You've got some nerve woman." He walked toward her slowly, his eyes fixed with intent that would make a strong man shudder.

Della peered back like a deer staring into headlights before it's crushed by hurtling steel.

As he stood before her, Della was able to reach her hands to her mouth, as if in slow motion. Perhaps she could muster a scream.

Crrack was the sound of Jack's backhanded fist against the bone under Della's eye socket. He struck her swiftly with his right hand, fist closed, only a fraction of a second spent. Della's eye was the size of half a grapefruit instantly, and so purple that it looked as if the top right quarter of her face would explode, an eyeball leading the charge. As Della fell to her knees, she saw Jack walk out the front door, down the steps. She heard the motor turn and the wheels screech, as her head hit the floor hard.

Jack hadn't meant to hit her so hard, but he was furious inside. How could she push him like that, that far on Christmas? Of course he had planned on getting presents, but it's not like they couldn't go and get a couple things now, like she didn't have some cash stashed away someplace, right? A disrespectful mouth and she had been using it more and more. It just needed a little pop. He hit her too hard; that was true.

He shouldn't have used a closed fist, but she had her part also. He was sorry he took his end too far, but she needed to recognize her part. Maybe she would learn something from this.

He thought it best to cool off for a couple days; he certainly couldn't stay with Ritchie, who was living back home like a loser. Staying with his cousin would get word back to his folks. So Louie it was. Jack had been hanging out with Louie the past few months, turning their relationship into one of his more profitable business ventures. Louie was a Hells Angel; he had a beautiful hog. Jack had to sell his Shovelhead before the baby came, a total drag. Louie let Jack ride the hog whenever Jack wanted. He rolled the Plymouth to the closest pay phone, and, although it was five in the morning, he figured there was a good chance Louie and his lady, Barb, might be still be up.

Jack picked up the receiver and listened for a dial tone. As he did, he saw a police cruiser with two strapping bucks pull up and park behind his car. That fucking bitch called the cops, unbelievable. Jack composed his thoughts.

"Yeah, Uncle, sure. Where do you want to meet for breakfast? Hang on a sec, Uncle. A couple nice officers are walking up."

"Is everything OK?" the first officer asked.

"Yeah, sure. Talking to my uncle about breakfast. He's a captain on the job, in the city." Jack placed the receiver back against his ear. "Yeah, sure, you can talk with them, Uncle." Jack turned toward the officer and took the receiver away from his ear. "My uncle wants to talk to you." Jack extended the handset to the officer.

The officer looked slightly perplexed as he reached his hand for the phone. As he did, he was coldcocked with a right cross and knocked unconscious, lights outs. Before the second officer could process half of the scene, Jack was stepping over the first officer, striking the second squarely on the chin, right on the button, with Jack's left rendering the second cop out, like the first.

Jack passed by them both in five seconds flat, got into his car and back onto the street, hightailing it over to Louie's.

The officers had, in fact, just been checking to see if Jack was OK, since his car was pulled over and it was early in the morning. Della had not called the cops but instead had called her parents crying. She had asked for her sister Pricilla.

She relayed the story over tears and gasps of breath, telling her sister that she would be lying down in the bedroom with Guy, that the front door would be unlocked.

Della felt woozy, so she laid down directly. Had she gone and looked at herself in the mirror first, which was not possible yet, she likely would have puked, making matters worse. She sobbed silently.

Guy reached over and touched his mother's face, which made her cry less silently. He touched her eye softly. "Boo-boo, Mommy. Ouch." He started to cry.

She held him tight. "It's OK. It's OK. Prissy's coming. We're going to Grandma and Grandpa's."

Guy touched his mother's hands with his tiny fingers. "Jesus, please heal Mommy's boo-boo on Your birthday. Amen."

Della fell asleep with Guy in her arms, until her sister's gasp woke her. Prissy helped them to the car, carrying Guy in one arm, the other over her mouth, trying to fight back the sobs, as tears streamed down her face. She drove them home, walked them both into her parents' house and Della directly to her bed, which was covered by curtains in a corner of the living room. Della laid down, and Prissy whispered to Guy, "Go tell Grandma 'Merry Christmas.'"

Guy ran into his grandma's kitchen. "Merry Christmas, Grandma." He leaped into his grandmother's cozy arms. She was wearing a white apron and felt like a marshmallow pillow.

"Merry Christmas," his grandmother said, beginning to develop a bit of a lisp.

"Merry Christmas, Grandpa."

His grandpa picked him up so high that he was almost to the ceiling. "Merry Christmas." Ray whirled his grandson like a helicopter above his head

Lily pushed a little package toward the edge of the table.

"Yeah," Guy squealed, pulling out a kitchen chair and standing upon it. "Can I open it?"

"Open it. Open it." His grandfather touched his fair little head.

Guy was still in his one-piece Superman pajamas with the feet. He tore into the paper to reveal six glass containers, each half the size of a roll of film, along with two paintbrushes. Guy thrust the paintbrushes above his head, one in each hand. "Paint!" he shouted. Guy spent a lot of time at his grandparents' house. One of his favorite activities was painting rocks from the garden with nail polish that Aunt Prissy gave him.

"Santa brought it for you." His Grandma smiled.

"No, he didn't. You did! Thanks, Grandma. Thanks, Grandpa. I love you." Guy put down his paintbrushes and arranged his paint all in a line.

"Here, come help Grandma. We're having chicken parmesan tonight."

And by *tonight* Lilian meant from noon onward.

"Can I eat the eggs?" Guy loved the eggs, and he was getting hungry.

"After we finish. Come help." She pulled his chair over to the counter.

Lily had two paper grocery bags, flattened out on the countertop. She pulled out a big glass bowl and the Italian bread crumbs from the cupboard. She spread some on one of the flattened bags. She added some seasoning atop.

"Raymond, get me the chicken breasts and the eggs out of the fridge." Lily's voice always seemed slightly shrill when she was ordering Ray around.

Ray passed her the chicken breasts he had picked up from the butcher and a carton of eggs. Lilly cracked the eggs into the glass bowl. She would use all of them for the chicken. Lilly took the first breast and dunked it in the egg, then into the bread crumbs with seasonings on the first brown paper bag. After the flip, she turned the chicken over to Guy, who would smoosh it around in the bread crumbs some more and then place the finished cutlet onto the second brown bag. If he was moving too slowly, holding up production, his grandmother would help him along. She had years of experience, dunking, breading, flipping, moving. Soon the chicken cutlets were in a large breaded pile.

"OK," his grandma said, as she moved his chair back to the table. She poured what was left of the eggs onto the bag with the leftover bread crumbs and handed Guy the fork.

Guy eagerly mixed the bread crumbs with the egg into what most closely resembled a sandy turd. Then he ate it. "Mmm." Guy scrapped every last bite off his brown bag "plate." His grandmother was already working a pot of seasoned meat into balls on a tray to put in the oven. She broke off a piece of the raw chopped meat and fed Guy like a little bird, putting the uncooked meatball into his mouth.

"Yummy, more please." His grandmother passed him another piece as she slid the first tray of meatballs in the oven.

★★★

"No, I'm telling you, I'm done. This was it." Della rolled onto her other side, facing the wall, away from her sister.

"You need to go to the hospital." Prissy rubbed her sister's back.

"Not now, I'm tired. Call Roxie. Tell her what happened. See if she'll come over."

"OK, but then you have to go."

★★★

Roxie was planning on going to her parents' place for Christmas to enjoy a hearty meal. She had two kids of her own now. Paulie was two, twenty months younger than his cousin Guy. Paulie looked like a miniature version of his father—a sweet face with an impish smile and tan skin. Roxie had named his brother, the baby, after her grandfather Durante because he was nice. Durante was an Italian name, and she remembered it meant enduring, steadfast.

The children were enjoying their toys near the poinsettias in their living room. Paulie had liked Guy's Ernie so much that Roxie had bought Paulie a stuffed Cookie Monster. Jerry, as Durante was called, was playing with a new set of wood blocks. There was a similar larger set at her parents' house that Jerry was crazy for.

Big Paul walked out of their bedroom, wearing a pair of blue jeans, his hair wild. He held his white T-shirt in both of his hands.

"Where's my shit?" He stormed up and over to Roxie.

"What shit?" Roxie played dumb. She had had a feeling he was using heroin, but Paul had always denied it. She had found his stash last night.

"You know what I'm talking about, bitch. Where's my shit?" He stepped to within an inch of her, peering down, with venom reeking from his pores.

"How could you, with the kids? They could have found that shit. I flushed it down the toilet," Roxie said defiantly, her arms crossed.

Paul was blind with rage, and, with his right hand, he grabbed Roxie's right wrist with all his might and twisted it, throwing her to the couch. *Crack*. Roxie heard her wrist break; white heat soared up her arm. With a scream she began to sob tears of anguish and pain.

"Paul!" She hardly got the word out, but he was already on top of her, straddling her on the couch holding both of her arms above her head. She felt that, if he didn't let go of her shattered arm soon, she would never be able to use it again.

"You threw my shit away, you stupid cunt. You stupid cunt, you don't ever touch my shit." He let go of her arm to slap her in the face and followed through with a backhand.

Roxie screamed blood-curdling murder.

Little Paulie, holding his Cookie Monster, walked from the corner, where he had been playing, to the couch.

"Daddy, stop. Please don't hurt Mommy," he begged, with tears running down his cheeks.

His father turned. "Get!" He flailed his arm toward the boy, "I said get!" Paul screamed at his son with murderous eyes and shooed him back toward his brother and the poinsettias in the other corner of the living room.

"I will fucking kill you, cunt. Don't you ever fucking touch my shit again, never."

Roxie gasped; his weight on her chest was making it hard for her to breathe. Her arm felt like dead pain.

The phone rang suddenly, and little Paul walked to the end table near where he was playing and picked up the phone.

"What the fuck is going on over there?" It was Rock yelling into the phone. He was the kids' babysitter since he lived in the next building over.

Rock could hear Paulie crying on the other end of the receiver.

With the last of what Roxie could muster, she yelled, "HELP!"

And so did little Paulie, over and over again. It wasn't more than ten seconds later that Rock—who found the front door of Roxie's apartment locked—promptly kicked the door in. He was wearing tighty whities. His body was still chiseled; his brown hair still cut short. He was carrying a samurai sword and quickly absorbed the scene.

Paul was on top of Roxie who looked near dead. He was smacking her back and forth across the face, over and over.

With Paulie and Jerry huddled in the corner, Rock flew across the room, as if a gust of air, and in an instant held Paul's long hair in Rock's left hand. Paul's hair was greasier and stringier than in days past. Rock stepped up on the couch with his right leg, and, as he pulled Paul's head back, he lifted his samurai sword and, with a swift blow of the hilt, knocked Paul's two front teeth down his throat.

Blood poured from Paul's mouth as he choked on teeth mingled with blood. Still holding Paul by the hair on the back of his head, Rock put his face to within an inch of Paul's and stared deeply into his eyes.

Then Rock promptly bit off the tip of Paul's nose, about a half inch or so. Paul rolled over onto the floor in pain, and the children sat quietly in the corner.

Rock spit the severed nose back into Paul's face. "Don't ever fucking touch her again, or you're dead, got it? Not so pretty now, huh, mutherfucker?"

Rock kicked Paul so hard in the stomach that Paul thought his guts would gurgle up from his mouth, if only he had the air to let them out.

"Come on. I'll take you to your mother's. Come on, fellas. You are brave little soldiers. Your daddy is never going to hurt Mommy again. Neat Cookie Monster."

"I got it for Christmas," Paulie said and held it tightly to his cheek, and Rock held the boys to his bare chest. He placed the boys with their covered-feet pajamas into the back of his Buick. "Stay right here. I gotta get your mom." Rock ran back inside, picked up Roxie, still in her cotton pajamas.

"To Grandma's, yeah," Rock said and drove the trio to Ray and Lily's. Rock was still clad only in his underwear.

A trip to the hospital was on the docket for both sisters at the request of Prissy, the nurse in training.

The three boys helped Grandma taste dinner until it was ready. Guy intervened when Paulie broke his baby brother Jerry's block pyramid and pushed him to the floor. Guy told his cousin that God wanted us to be kind to babies.

The girls made it home from the hospital in time for chicken parmesan. Roxie's arm was in a cast past her elbow; it would stay that way for three months. Della had a giant white gauze bandage over the top right side of her face, eye included. It was much more pleasant for all to look at that way, Della included. As they sat down to chicken parmesan, Ray, Lily, Carl, Prissy, Della, Roxie, Guy, Paulie and Jerry held hands.

Guy looked up. "Can I pray?"

"Sure," Ray answered. It was better than Prissy's prayers. Guy was cuter and would keep it short, a much better alternative when there was Lily's chicken parmesan on the table.

"Jesus, happy birthday for Christmas. Please come into our hearts and help us to be kind. Amen." Guy knew about having Jesus in your heart from his aunt Prissy. He got to go to church and sing and dance with her sometimes. He asked Jesus in his heart when she told him that he could. He even asked Jesus if He needed air in there, in Guy's heart, then Guy would go through the motions to open a little door atop it.

He hoped he could paint rocks after dinner.

Jack and Paul spent their Christmas with the dregs of society, whether with someone else or alone. Jack made it out to old Louie's house. Paul lay on the floor of his apartment, a giant wad of blood-soaked toilet paper covered his nose. He spent most of Christmas upon the linoleum floor of their bathroom. As he lay on the cool floor, he coughed periodically. The blood from his busted-up mouth slowed to a trickle and dripped down the back of his throat, which seemed oddly comforting. As a cockroach ran over his hand, Paul was alone, with no shit, feeling sick.

BOOK ONE: CHAPTER FIVE

It was Thanksgiving Nineteen Eighty; Guy was four and a half years old. His fair hair was beginning to turn brown, and his chubby legs had lengthened and slimmed. He was enjoying the extra time he got to spend with his new housemates, Grandma, Grandpa and aunt Prissy, along with his mother of course. Though his mom and dad were still fighting, at least it was not in the same house. Guy was able to hold his head up a little higher.

While time had moved on since Della had had her eye split and since she and Guy had moved out, she had not really moved on. Not for lack of trying. The mistake was in not cutting things off immediately. She had seen Jack off and on for a year, sometimes with Guy, all the while hoping he would move on or get arrested for something. He didn't, and so she filed for divorce. The choice was a difficult one for Della, because she was certain Jack would get unsupervised time alone with Guy once the divorce was finalized.

Of course he was smooth in court, charismatic. Jack knew the right buzz words and was able to paint Della in this light or that. But Della knew the truth: his friends and lifestyle were dangerous, and Jack certainly did not know how to take care of a little boy, even if it was his son.

Della was able to drag out the date for Guy's first unsupervised visit with his father until October. She was nervous, but when Jack showed up to see Guy that Friday night, the boys were so happy to see each other. She actually felt happy on top of all the sadness. She thought perhaps they could finally move on. Jack dropped Guy off Monday at eight in the morning, though he was due home by dinner on Sunday. Della gave Jack the benefit of the doubt in an effort to start things out with a clean slate. Guy was white as a sheet, which was generally the case, but he looked clammy and seemed hot and cold all at once. Della took Guy straight to the emergency room, where he was admitted for three days with viral pneumonia. It sounded as if his tiny lungs could only take a teaspoon of air at a time.

After Guy recovered, his mother asked him what he did while spending time with his father. Guy related that he had spent Friday night at his grandparents' house—on Jack's side. On Saturday they had watched TV. Later his dad had let him play up on the roof. No, Guy was not wearing a jacket, and, yes, it was wet up on the roof, but, no, Guy wasn't cold.

Della took Guy to what seemed to him to be a doctor's office, but it had a large play area, bigger than his grandma's living room. There was a tricycle and blocks, a table with crayons and books. There was a nice lady with black hair who came in and colored for a while. She asked the same silly questions his mom did about spending time with his dad.

Jack pleaded ignorance in that it was a cold October, and he would never be so foolish again. It seemed credible to the court, and all was forgiven. Jack was however getting sick and tired of explaining the relationship with his son to the government. It's not like he had done anything intentionally wrong, and, in all reality, the whole thing was really an outgrowth from Della's unwillingness to reconcile.

When Thanksgiving rolled around, Jack was sick and tired of being told where and when he could see his son. Guy was his son for Christ's sake. It was Thanksgiving, a time for a father and son to share a meal. He didn't give a shit if Thursday was his day or not.

Jack pulled the green Plymouth onto the Tomasinis' black asphalt driveway. His blood was boiling before his car door even closed. Being relegated to babysitting duties every other weekend was bullshit, and he had had enough of it. Jack loved his son more than anything in the world, in his mind. Not that things were easy as it was, what with his business and all. Guy sure was a little riot, but he was also Miss Manners. All of which made doing business difficult. But today was Thanksgiving— Thanksgiving was spent with family, and his son was the only family left that he gave a rat's ass about.

Lily, Ray, Carl, Prissy, Della, Guy, Roxie, Paulie and Jerry all sat around the table in the kitchen. Two large trays of lasagna—with chicken parmesan of course—and bowls of plump meatballs and pasta were in the middle of the table.

"Happy Thanksgiving," Ray said sweetly to the children, leaning over, so his face was low to the table like theirs. "Prissy, will you get us started?"

Prissy closed her eyes, bowed her head, and took her brother's hand in her right and Della's in her left. Della took Guy's hand; Guy took Paulie's, and the family joined hands in prayer and thanksgiving around the dinner table.

"Lord Jesus, our God, we have so much to be thankful for this Thanksgiving Day. Thank You for allowing us to sit around this table, spread with bountiful food, as a family. For these little babes that You have brought into the world. Thank You for providing a country where we can worship You in freedom. May You comfort those who are persecuted for Your name. Please help us to seek Your wisdom and guidance. Offer us protection under the hem of Your cloak. Amen."

And everyone around the table said Amen. As the N rolled off their lips, so a car rolled into the driveway, followed by a door closed loudly.

"I want to see my son" was heard by all round the table.

The front door leading to the kitchen was open, save for the screen door. The adults sat upright, startled, putting their hands upon the table in unison.

Lily rose in a flash, scooping Guy up in her arms, walking him through the living room and into the bedroom behind. She placed him on her bed and bent her chubby knees to look into his eyes. "OK, sweetheart. You have to be quiet as a little mouse now, OK?"

"OK, Grandma." Guy nodded, his hands held by his grandma's chubby fingers.

"Time to be a big boy. Under the bed now." Lilly lifted the comforter that hung over the side of the bed touching the floor.

Guy hopped off his grandmother's bed. He was wearing brown corduroys, a long-sleeved tan T-shirt with a brown kitty cat, along with a pair of saddle shoes. His light brown hair looked even darker in the shadows.

"OK, all the way under." Lilly motioned, and Guy crouched down low on his belly to crawl under his grandmother's bed.

Lilly crouched down and looked under the bed. She whispered, "All the way down to the middle and quiet like a little mouse. Don't come out no matter what. Only when your grandma calls."

"OK, Grandma." Guy shuffled to the middle of the floor underneath the bed upon his belly.

"Don't come out for anyone, not Grandpa, not even Mommy. Only Grandma, OK, sweetheart?" Lily might not have gone to high school, but she was no dummy. She knew that men were cunning, and a man like Jack might try to force Della to call for her son to come out.

"Yes, Grandma." Guy curled up into a little ball and closed his eyes. He didn't like when his mom and dad fought. His grandma said it would be over soon, because his mommy was in court. His mommy spent lots of time in court. Guy didn't understand how spending time at Court's Carpets off the highway was going to make things any better, but he trusted that his mommy and his grandma knew what they were talking about. He just wanted all the fighting to be over.

Lilian walked out past Della back into the kitchen. Della was sitting on the living room sofa, shaking like a leaf, her arms crossed over her chest, staring into her lap, rocking slowly back and forth.

Jack peered into the kitchen through the screen door. "Guy! Guy, it's Daddy. Happy Thanksgiving. Come say hello to Daddy." Jack put his hand above his eyes, as if to get a better view as he leaned into the screen door.

"Guy!" Jack shouted loud and with heat. Jack turned his gaze over to Ray. "It's Thanksgiving, Ray. I want to see my fucking son now!"

Ray stood to his feet. "It's not your day, Jack, goddammit." And, as if Italian, Ray flung his hands from his chest outward above his head.

"I came to see my fucking son, Ray. It's Thanksgiving, and you're feeding him fucking lasagna. Where's the goddamned turkey and stuffing?"

"Relax, Jack. You get him tomorrow." Ray held his hands out at his sides with the palms up. "You can feed him a whole damn turkey. Enough is enough, come on, Jack."

"I came to see my son. Bring him out, Ray." Jack's stare focused, cooled. He spoke slowly, clearly.

"It's not your goddamned day, Jack. Leave the boy alone for Christ's sake. It's dinner. He's hungry." Ray stomped his foot and became angry. He had had about enough of this horseshit. Whatever was going on between Jack and Della was their problem but leave the fucking boy out of it, Ray thought to himself.

Perhaps it was the hopelessness of Jack's current situation, the loneliness mingled with drugs. Perhaps the war, divorce, money. Perhaps all, perhaps none. It was, however, the proverbial straw. At that moment something deep inside Jack snapped. Where or what precisely it was would be hard to say—somewhere deep within the inner recesses, someplace unknown even to himself. It would never be made straight again, never. He turned around and walked back to his car.

Ray walked to the screen door. It looked like that had done the trick. Ray walked onto the concrete stoop to make sure that Jack continued on his way. Ray's son, Carl, followed.

Jack walked to his trunk, placed the key in the lock and opened it. Jack looked into the black-carpeted trunk to the multicolored piece of carpet rolled up into a cylinder. He unrolled it and grabbed his sawed-off twelve-gauge pump shotgun. The same one that he had bungee-corded to his utility belt over in the shit. Old man had sent it over to Jack. Once, when walking point through elephant grass, he had stumbled on three dinks, sitting on their helmets, smoking reefer. He blew off all three of their heads with this gun before they even startled. Got a nice big bag of reefer too.

Ray's heart fell into his stomach as he ran down the two stairs onto the lawn, cutting Jack off from the house. Carl followed behind his father.

Ray jumped up and down in the air, waving his hands wildly. "What are you, an animal now?" Ray shouted and pointed, as if he had at once become insane.

"I want to see my son. I'm not leaving without him," Jack said calmly, with cold, vicious eyes. He pumped the shotgun.

"What are you, an animal now, a fucking nigger? Look at you, a fucking gun, a fucking gun? Oh, my God! Oh, my God!" Ray howled like a cornered animal, flailing his long arms and kicking his legs in the air wildly.

"Bring him out now," Jack said coolly, extending the shotgun toward Carl's nose, who stood next to his father.

"You're not getting that boy! Do you hear me?" Ray was a man possessed, he took a step toward Jack. "You'll have to kill all of us! Do you hear me?" Ray screamed as tears began to steam down his face, red with anger and fear.

Khkhoooo. The shotgun blast tore a few inches off Carl's right ear. He fell to his knees screaming, clutching his ear in agony. Jack walked to his left around Carl. Ray crouched over him, gazing down at the blood that flowed from his son's ear. Jack barreled up the stoop, where he could see Roxie standing at the screen, her arms tucked behind her.

Roxie gazed through the screen into Jack's icy-blue eyes. She had seen that dead look before, but this was colder. Eyes that had moved past violence for fun or hatred to violence as a tool, as a solution. Roxie tried to keep from fainting or throwing up. "What? Are you going to kill us all, you maniac? Leave us the fuck alone," she said with as much force as she could muster through her bandaged nose—her latest injury, courtesy of her own maniac husband—and twisted insides.

"What are you hiding behind your back? I'm taking my son, Roxie." Jack certainly was going to take his son. He was not intent on hurting anyone, though everyone had choices to make. He didn't understand why they wouldn't just bring his son out to begin with. They had escalated what was an easily resolvable situation.

Roxie brought her arms partway forward revealing her two sons behind her.

"And . . ." Jack screamed.

Roxie turned to show that no one else was hiding behind her back.

His facial expression contorted. "Where's my fucking son!" Jack screamed violently now. Having completely lost whatever composure remained, he grabbed for the knob of the screen door. He never liked

75

seeing little children hurt. However, his hand had been forced. He just came over to say "Happy Thanksgiving." Now he had to take the boy with him to prove a point. To assert his rights as a father.

When Della heard the gunshot, she had called the police. They knew very well who Jack Finnigan was, and, yes, ma'am, they would be there momentarily.

The police had found it necessary to broaden their tactics, increase firepower and bone up on conditioning. They had been caught with their pants down on a number of occasions when dealing with combat veterans home from Vietnam, especially with the increased drug trade involving those Vets. A badge and a six-shooter did not scare these guys. In fact they had begun to adapt military-style tactics in their crimes. The police knew they were increasingly outmaneuvered.

Nothing that couldn't be rectified with the proper federal funding and alliances.

Yes, the police were well aware of who Jack Finnigan was, and they parked their patrol cars four houses down on each side. House by house, bush by bush, they crept down low. 11 officers slowly snuck around to the Tomasinis' yard.

Just as Jack reached for the knob of the door, a burly officer brought down the butt of his rifle upon the back of Jack's head, and Jack's world went black. The patrol cars and an ambulance were brought in quickly after that. Jack was strapped to a gurney and wheeled away. Carl was taken away in an ambulance of his own, and the remaining police officers took Ray's statement on the front lawn.

Guy was quiet as a mouse, partly because he had fallen asleep. He was having a terrible dream—standing on a grassy field, staring at a king on a galloping white steed off in the distance. The king violently struck the horse with the reins, then the king became a blur as the white horse frothed at the mouth. Guy was paralyzed as the horse's face grew clearer and closer. Guy could hardly mutter the word "Jesus" as a loud BANG woke him from his fretful slumber. Still he was quiet as a mouse.

"Sweetheart, it's Grandma. Come on out. Time to eat."

Guy recognized his grandma's voice and wiggled on his belly out from under the bed.

"I was quiet as a mouse," Guy whispered, which was true. Guy kept quiet even when he awoke to the loud bang with a startle.

"You sure did, my big boy." Lily scooped him up in her arms and carried him out into the kitchen. There was a big piece of lasagna, half of a chicken cutlet and a whole meatball waiting on Guy's plate, with his very own can of Coca-Cola.

"Where's Grandpa?" Guy asked. He didn't ask about his dad, because no one liked talking about his dad. It always made people uncomfortable.

"He's helping the neighbors. He'll be back in a minute." Lily hated to lie, but Ray was, in a way, helping the neighbors, by getting that damn maniac out of here. This had gone on long enough. Ray was getting old, and he was going to get hurt. Tonight her son had been hurt.

Della sat on the couch, wiping the tears from her eyes with her father's handkerchief. Life had become a blur, as if she were on a long, dark stretch of highway with no off-ramps and a fuel gauge on empty. Her mother walked in with fire steaming from her ears.

"Your father could have been killed tonight, and your brother might be deaf. I love that boy, my God I do, but what choice do I have? You have to leave tomorrow."

"Mom, no, please."

And her mother walked out the door.

"Mom, no, you can't!"

"Parmesan cheese, please." Guy loved lots of parmesan cheese on Italian food.

"Here you go, sweetheart." Lily passed the shaker to Guy.

Jack was locked up until the end of January. Della thought it was nice not having him around for Christmas; it made things easier. While the Thanksgiving Day situation was difficult, it did result in no more unsupervised visits for Guy with Jack. Now they would take place in a medical facility, where nurses and a therapist would be able to watch from behind a mirror. Not that it was permanent, but at least until Jack could prove he was capable of unsupervised visits again. Della hoped that would be never.

Twice in the past two weeks she had taken Guy to the Social Services' building in Westbury, Long Island, so that he could get used to the surroundings before seeing his father. There was a large play area with books, crayons, a tricycle. The meeting room was clean, white, sanitized. It had a large one-way mirror, which Guy thought was cool. His mother was clear. There would always be someone watching him.

"Happy you're getting to see your father today?" Della held Guy's hand as they walked through the large glass doors of the lobby.

"Mmm-hmm," Guy said. He was looking forward to seeing his dad. He loved his dad. His dad made other people scared, but Guy wasn't scared. Guy would be five next month and starting kindergarten after summer. Guy was never scared of his father, because he knew his father loved him and would never hurt him. He was glad that they were going to play at the doctors though, because going to his dad's house was not always fun.

77

Guy rushed to the elevator and pushed the Up button, a small delight. As the elevator doors opened, he pushed the three button and took his mother's hand. Guy knew the doctor's playground was on the third floor. Della walked down the long corridor, holding Guy's tiny hand, going through the first door on the right. There was a high counter with a pretty receptionist and a small waiting room with a swinging door leading to the supervision rooms.

Della waved to Daisy and pushed open the swinging door.

"Guy," Daisy cried out, her arms open, her body crouched low to the floor to greet him. Daisy was a blonde, about thirty-five, absolutely beautiful, dressed all in white.

Guy ran and gave Daisy a hug. She was always happy to see him. She even colored with him once. And she always gave Guy a lollipop on his way out.

"I'm going to color." Guy opened the door and ran into the play area. He was easily seen from the glass panel in the top half of the door, as well as through the see-through mirror.

"Hi, Daisy." Della gave Daisy a big hug.

"Hi, Della. How are you doing, dear? A bit nervous?"

"A little," Della admitted.

"Don't be." Daisy shook her head. "He's fine. We'll be right here, watching the whole time," Daisy said assuredly.

"I know, but I told you what *he*'s like, Daisy." Della's heart quickened, and she grasped Daisy's forearm with both hands.

"It's OK, dear. I know. It's OK." Daisy patted the top of Della's hand. "But like I told you, this is what we are trained to do. We deal with this same situation every day. The police station is right down the block. We have security right here in the building. It's going to be just fine. It'll be better without you. Trust me. You'll see." Daisy winked and gave Della a big hug.

Daisy was extremely comforting and confident. "All right." Della opened the door to the playroom. "Give your mom a kiss." Della knelt down and extended her arms.

Guy took a coloring break to give his mom a big hug. "I'm fine, Mom. I'll see you when we're done."

"OK, have fun with your dad."

"I will." Guy smiled.

Della squeezed him tight, then left the room. "Watch him carefully, please, Daisy."

"I will. Don't worry." Daisy patted Della's shoulder.

Della walked back to her car in the parking lot quickly. She made sure to leave sufficient time between her departure and Jack's arrival.

As Jack drove to see his son, he was confused and angry. Surprised more than confused by his current state of affairs. Sure, he had pushed the envelope too far on Thanksgiving. He knew better than to point a gun at someone if you weren't planning on pulling the trigger. He had, indeed, pulled the trigger, but only for effect. A little more than sixty days in the pokey only seemed to fuel his anger, as if somehow this was all his fault. Like he was a bad guy, some sort of criminal. He was no fool though—told them that he had daily nightmares from Vietnam and was self-medicating with booze and heroin to keep them at bay.

It had worked, and he had been immediately transferred to the medical wing. From there he was able to work the system and was out in sixty days. He agreed to take twenty milligrams of Mellaril as well as Haldol while he stayed. He liked neither, but the Haldol made coming off the junk a lot easier. He agreed to keep taking the Mellaril in order to be released. He did and grew a bit accustomed to it. It took him down a few notches. It also made him feel peculiar, however, sometimes as if he were an actor in a movie, somehow disconnected from the reality of the moment.

Jack's blood was on a slow simmer since being released. The effects of the Mellaril seemed to be diminishing with time and the existence of the real world. Perhaps dampened by drinking and using as well. Shotgun aside, it was simply shocking that some government bureaucrat could tell him, a man who had served his country, when and where he could see his son. Sure, he could see that, with the divorce, it would have to be split say fifty-fiftyish, but he had been relegated down to an every-other-weekend dad. Not that it was a problem in practice, with his business and all, but that was not the goddamned point.

Now the government was going to tell him that, in order to see his son, he would have to agree to be supervised in one of their facilities. It was the fucking government that needed to be supervised. Like the fucking government knows a goddamned thing. They certainly weren't capable of winning a war, even with the best damned troops and machinery. And it was clear by their public statements that they were nothing more than liars. Crooks and fucking liars thought they were going to tell Jack that he couldn't see his own son. Yeah, right. Bullshit.

As Jack walked into the third floor office, he had already decided that he was taking Guy with him for the day, perhaps for the whole fucking weekend. Jack surveyed the little lobby.

"Can I help you?" the pretty receptionist asked.

Jack surmised that the little swinging door was the entry point. He walked swiftly toward it, extending his left arm.

"Sir, you can't go back there before you're called," the receptionist said to his back.

As Jack walked through the swinging door, he immediately saw Guy coloring at a desk in the room on his left. He stepped forward, gazing through the glass window of the door.

Daisy was standing at the other end of the hall, flanked with rooms on both sides of the corridor. She saw a man looking through the glass of the room closest to the exit door and assumed it must be Jack Finnigan. Clearly off on the wrong foot already, seeing as she had not yet been rung that he was waiting. He was dressed in black biker boots and faded blue jeans. His denim jacket was of a similar color and worn over a white T-shirt. His hair was pulled back straight, tight in a ponytail that went down past the nape of his neck. It was thick and had several rubber bands down the ponytail, every three inches or so. His beard was trimmed but bushy, at least an inch or two long. He looked something like a mountain-man biker, if that were possible. Daisy decided she would not make a big deal of being notified; she would be extrafriendly, unintimidated.

"Hi. Is it Jack?" Daisy smiled, extending her hand, putting out a cute-and-friendly vibe.

"Yes, I'm here to get my son," Jack said slowly, looking at her coldly and leaving her hand unshook.

"Here, he is," Daisy said cheerily. "He loves to color, that boy. Keeps inside the lines already. Come on in. It will be fun. You'll see." Daisy reached to push open the door.

Jack was not in the mood for redirection today, nor for pretending not to be heard. He sidestepped toward the door. "Listen. I'm here to get my son. Go get him now," Jack reiterated slowly and precisely. With his dead blue eyes, he looked deeply into Daisy's gaze.

For the first time Daisy had truly been scared. At times she had called security in the past, but this fear came on suddenly, and she was instantly numb. "Ahh, umm, that's not the way it works, sir," was all Daisy could stammer out.

Jack stepped to her close, so close that Daisy could feel his body heat. He snatched Daisy's face quickly with his left hand. He took her jaw between his thumb and four fingers; he squeezed tightly like a vise. So tightly that Daisy would have screamed had she been able. Just then another nurse dressed in white entered with a security guard. Jack turned, still holding Daisy by the jaw.

Jack moved his coat to the side, to expose his large buck knife still in the sheaf on his hip. "Hands above your heads, over there next to the fucking wall, now!" Jack shouted, not loudly but violently. The nurse and security guard were chilled and did as they were told. A security guard without a gun—what a joke, Jack thought.

Jack moved his nose to within an inch of nurse Daisy's and continued to squeeze her face as hard as he could. This time she let out a yelp like a wounded puppy. "Get my fucking son," Jack said calmly, murderously, and then screamed, "Now!"

It had the desired effect, and urine flowed vigorously down nurse Daisy's leg onto the linoleum floor in a big puddle.

Jack let go of her face and pushed open the door.

Daisy stepped into the room, bright with florescent lighting, dazed, as if just standing to her feet in the fiftieth round of a heavyweight bout and waking up from a nightmare all at once.

"Guy, time to go. Your father's here."

Guy looked up from coloring, holding a green crayon. "Mommy said we're not allowed to leave."

"It's time to go, Guy." Daisy extended her hand and bit her lip hard to keep from crying. For, if she had, she would have fallen down to the floor weeping, becoming part of its very fiber, never to be moved again.

Guy grabbed her hand and walked out though the door with her. He saw his father standing next to a big yellow puddle. Guy lifted his feet slowly so not to get all wet. He looked at Daisy and saw that she was wet, her stockings and shoes too. She must have peed her pants like a baby. Guy thought that was embarrassing, so he reached his free hand over and patted Daisy's hand as he held it. "It's OK. Everybody has accidents," Guy said warmly.

Daisy looked down at him, with tears welling in her eyes. A nod and a glance was all she could muster; she began to weep.

"Time to go, Guy." Jack grabbed his son's little hand and whispered in Daisy's ear, "No one is coming between me and my son. No one." Jack swept his lips close to Daisy's face, lingering long enough to look her brutally in the eyes. "Black Chevy out back, yeah, and I know where you live, cunt. Stay the fuck out of this," he whispered directly into her heart. Then Jack walked out with Guy, pulling him alongside. Before they were through the door, Jack swept back the hem of his jacket to reveal his cased buck knife once more. He looked over his shoulder and made eye contact with the security guard and the other nurse, who were both still frozen against the wall.

"I'll come back to say hello if I need too." He put his right hand to his mouth with the pointer finger up. "*Shhhh,*" he whispered, and they were out the door.

Guy complained that he didn't get to push the button for the elevator, but his father explained that they were in a hurry.

Daisy, Nancy—the other nurse—and Fred, the security guard, stood as if on an Oklahoma street that had once been a neighborhood, now swiped away by a twister. Nancy quietly put her arm around Daisy, who was crying inconsolably now and repeating, "The boy, the boy." Daisy cried through hyperventilated sobs, her hands pressed to her face, her head shaking back and forth. Nancy took her into one of the side rooms to get her cleaned up, and showed Fred where the bucket and mop were.

The trio were in shock from the lighting strike that had rained down upon their heads. Their confusion was further mingled with the guilt of being unable to prevent the ponytailed man from taking Guy, which left them in a state of paralyzed inaction, as if they themselves were waiting to be rescued.

"Mommy said we're not allowed to leave," repeated Guy, sitting in the passenger seat of his father's Plymouth, moving on down the road. This time he pulled up the emergency break that was between their two seats.

The tires screeched, and Jack released the emergency brake quickly. "Your mother doesn't know everything." Jack looked over at his son, fiercely, but only for a moment.

"Where are we going?" Guy asked quietly.

"To your uncle Louie's house," his father replied, with one hand on the steering wheel and the other on the emergency brake.

"I don't have an uncle Louie," Guy replied, sitting Indian style in the front seat.

"Yeah, ya do. Relax. Take a nap, will ya?"

Guy wished they were going to his grandparents' house—his dad's parents' house, that is. His grandmother always made him the most delicious tea with milk and sugar. She was wrinkly. Guy was allowed to put in his own tea bag and then fish it out with a spoon. His grandma let him have two spoonfuls of sugar.

Guy liked to sit on his grandpa's lap and watch *Superman*. His grandpa was funny; he would sing along with the song. Grandpa had strong muscles like Superman. He had a magnifying glass and showed Guy how to look at things to make them bigger. Grandpa would hold it in front of his face to make himself look silly. He always told Guy how handsome he was, and that he was going to be big and strong when he grew up. That it was important to get As in school and to work hard at your job, whatever it was.

Bobby was his uncle; Bobby was nice, but he liked to tease if Grandpa wasn't around, and Bobby liked scary movies. Once when Guy had a sleepover, Bobby woke Guy up in the middle of the night, after everyone was asleep, to watch *Invasion of the Body Snatchers* in the TV room. Guy thought it would be fun to sneak downstairs and watch a movie with his uncle, even though he was tired. He was wrong though, because the movie was very, very scary. Guy tried to hide under the blankets, but his uncle kept pulling them off. He tried to keep his eyes closed, but it still sounded scary.

★★★

Della could sense that something was wrong when she walked through the third-floor waiting room door. The pretty receptionist was pale; she pointed to the swinging door and looked down when she saw Della enter the waiting room.

Della's stomach sunk—like in one of those dreams where you fall off a building. She darted through the swinging door and felt as if she would pass out when she saw the empty, sanitized room. Perhaps she would throw up instead. Della put her hand to her mouth, as if throwing up would stop the sick feeling in her stomach.

She saw Daisy standing there with a blanket wrapped around her. Nancy was beside her; both of them were shaking in concert, as if they had just been pulled out of a frigid lake. Fred looked at his shoes.

"No, no. I warned you!" Della grabbed Daisy by the shoulders and shook.

"He took him." Daisy began to weep.

"Where are the police?"

"They said there was nothing they could do for twenty-four hours," Nancy said, trying to stand upright. Since no one had been hurt and since no weapon had been used and since he is the boy's father. Call back if he hasn't returned the boy in twenty-four hours."

"The 'boy' has a name. It's *Guy*." Della clutched her mouth and began to cry; the tears ran down her pretty face.

Daisy's arms were folded across her chest, hands clutched in tight balls at her shoulders. Her face no longer seemed pretty. Aside from the messy running mascara, she seemed somehow hollow, sunken. "Disappear. Get your boy back. Disappear the both of you. Don't tell a soul where you are going. Disappear, run, run for your life!" Daisy gasped, wide-eyed, as if with some religious conviction.

The three employees walked into one of the rooms on the side of the corridor.

Della's mind was frozen. She walked as if in a stupor down to her Nineteen Eighty cream-colored Chevy Camaro. Two doors, four seats, sticker price.

As if she were on some strange acid trip, she stumbled into Potters Pub, her face covered in tears, trying to discern just what was going on. She ran to the counter, and crying, she screamed, "He took him."

Timmy, donning a green apron, dashed out the little bar door and grabbed Della by the top of her arms. He knew full well what she meant. So did the rest of the regulars round the bar. The patrons stood to their collective feet, and, for a moment, drinking beer faded into obscurity. Mack Flynn, Timmy's older brother, leaped to his feet as well.

"Holy fuck. Calm down. It'll be all right. What happened?" Timmy said, as he gave Della a hug while mouthing *holy fuck* to his brother.

Della stood up and tried to compose herself. "Jack took Guy from the court-ordered Social Services' visit. The police won't do anything for twenty-four hours."

"Bullshit, they won't." Mack pounded the bar fiercely. "Where are they? I'll get him right now," Mack said with a slow, steely rage.

Timmy turned around and put his hand to his brother's chest, easing him back toward the little swing door behind the bar. He looked his brother in the face. "Not this one, Mack. This guy's the real deal, OK? Airborne Ranger, in the shit. I met him. This one's a killer, no joke." Timmy stepped back behind the bar.

Mack paused. Timmy had always been more reckless, and he could tell that Timmy wasn't kidding. But that boy—Mack had met Guy, what a kid. If anything happened to that kid, Mack would make sure that scumbag paid for it. He would use his last nickel if he had too. He felt as if he would explode.

"OK, let's not get out of control. This has happened before, right? Jack took Guy for a few days," Timmy asked, coming to the edge of the bar.

"Yes, that's true." Della wiped the tears and snot away from her face with the back of her hand as she sniffled.

"OK then. This is going to be no different. Give it twenty-four hours." Timmy took his hands off the edge of the bar and stood up straight.

Della looked as if she had been hit by a truck that was driven by a ghost. "I'm staying in a basement down the block from my mom and dad." Della did not particularly want to go back to her new place, which was composed of a pullout couch and a black-and-white TV in a dank half-finished basement belonging to a friend of her aunt's.

"By yourself? No way." Mack stepped closer to Della. "You can stay at my place tonight. I have a little house in Wantaugh, with an extra bedroom. I'm serious. No monkey business. Come on." Mack placed his arm around Della.

"Sure." Della nodded.

"It's going to be OK. Timmy, call her sister. Give her my number, and her parents, so that, if there's word, they can reach her."

"OK. No sweat. Don't worry." Yet Timmy began to think that they were playing with fire.

★★★

Guy sat with his father at Louie's kitchen table.

Louie was forty-five, but much of his hair and beard had already gone gray. His wild gray hair was pulled back behind both ears to the back of his head with a rubber band, then allowed to flow down to his shoulders. His face was red from too much liquor and bloated with a bulbous nose. He had a beard of a similar color and texture as his hair—straight, neither coarse nor soft. His beard hung down to his chest, and his large belly protruded though a white Harley-Davidson T-shirt.

Louie's Hells Angels' vest hung with pride on a peg in the corner of the wall. His woman, Barb, was at the stove, making eggs for everyone. She was fat, not as fat as Guy's grandma, and, though she was younger than Louie, she appeared older.

"Let's go with those eggs. The boy's hungry," Louie bellowed across the kitchen.

"All right already. They're done, but they're hot." Barb carried the pan with an oven mitt and scooped out four healthy portions.

Jack looked at Louie. "I'm going to take care of business. Eat your eggs, son. I'll be back in two minutes." He would be back in two minutes, as that was all it took him now to cook a fix.

Louie had become one of Jack's best customers, plus Louie had lots of friends. He was a good guy; they had become close friends. Plus Louie had the best setup. New needles, cotton, lighters, spoons, rubber tubing, even Band-Aids. No shit. Jack locked the door of the bathroom off Louie's living room and rolled up his sleeve.

Guy bent his head and folded his hands. "Jesus, thank You for this food and please help to keep us safe. Amen."

Louie and Barb looked at each other awkwardly, then back down at Guy.

Guy took a bite of his eggs, which were runny.

"Good eggs, huh, boy?" Louie pointed at Guy with his fork.

Louie and Barb hadn't been mean to Guy, but there was something about them that just didn't seem right.

Louie reached for the Heinz bottle and coated his eggs liberally with ketchup.

Guy's chest got tight; he felt as if he couldn't breath. His eyes widened. Ketchup on eggs? Guy knew there was something very, very wrong about ketchup on eggs. He became afraid in general, but specifically of Louie.

"By the Blood of Jesus," Guy said quietly yet clearly. His aunt Prissy had taught him that the devil himself was frightened to flight by the very mention of the Blood of Jesus. Guy's favorite story in the Bible was about Noah, then also the tale of David and Goliath.

Louie was so caught off guard by the whisper that he choked on his eggs and spit up ketchup all over his beard. For a moment his eyes looked as if they would pop out of his head.

Barb passed him a glass of water, and he was able to compose himself, more or less.

Louie and Barb were disoriented, until Jack came out of the bathroom and sat down at his seat. He seemed tired.

Guy leaped out of his seat and grabbed his father around the waist. "I love you, Dad." Guy put his face against his father's side.

"I love you too. Go finish your eggs. It's almost time for bed."

"I'm not hungry," Guy whispered. He had lost his appetite completely.

"OK, sit and wait till I'm done." His father touched his back as Guy clung fiercely to his side.

"Can I sit on your lap, please? I'll be quiet as a mouse," Guy whispered. Otherwise his seat was closer to Louie.

"Go sit down. I'm a quick eater."

Guy did, and Jack was.

Jack made a space for them in the extra bedroom on the floor with a couple pillows and blankets. It was dusty, and Guy did not like Louie's house one bit.

"Dad, what if somebody tries to get me?" Guy whispered, curled up in a ball on the floor under his blanket next to his father.

"No one can get past your old man. I used to sleep in the jungle. I sleep with one eye open." Jack closed one of his eyes.

Guy wasn't sure why his dad slept in the jungle, but he didn't believe his dad could really sleep with one eye open. That was impossible. Guy closed his eyes despite this thought and eventually slept.

Jack knew how the cops worked here. As long as he dropped off his son within twenty-four hours, the worst that would happen would be a slap on the wrist. Return his own fucking son.

Mack's telephone rang before noon the following day. He was making pancakes and coffee. It was Prissy calling to say that Guy was with her at their mother's, and, yes, he seemed fine.

86

Mack raced Della to Lindenhurst from Wantaugh in his two eighty Z before the receiver clicked. They were both on the stoop in an instant. Standing on the other side of the screen door was Guy in his little Superman shirt from the day before. Della opened the door, knelt down and squeezed him tightly while she cried. "It's OK. It's OK." Della wept.

"I know. Mommy, you don't have to cry." Guy patted her back softly. "Nothing's wrong, see?" Guy made Della smile. He was a darling; he made everyone smile. Mack rubbed his little head.

BOOK ONE: CHAPTER SIX

April Thirteenth, Nineteen Eighty One, had finally arrived. For Guy there was something special about turning five, something transitional. He had been looking forward to it since the day after he had turned three.

Della and Guy enjoyed the security and happiness Mack's abode provided them. Guy hadn't seen his father since they had left the playground that day.

That day had left Della in a state of perpetual alert or, more accurately, a state of low-level shock. She had been in some scary situations in the past with her own family, as well as with Jack no doubt. But something had changed on that previous Thanksgiving. True, there was always an underlying danger to Jack's character. Della wasn't sure if the war had magnified an existing sore or if it had, in fact, created the canker. But as the wound deepened, Jack seemed detached from the moment at hand, irrational.

Nurse Daisy had been shaken to the core, out on disability, never to be the same. Her joy had leaked, not like an old oil pan but ruptured like a fatal aneurysm.

Della could not shake Daisy's warning from her head. She seriously considered disappearing, but she had no means. Her car could only take her so far without gas, and she only had enough cash to last a couple weeks.

Della had jumped at the opportunity when Mack had offered to let them stay with him after the ordeal with Social Services. Mack was kind, a real gentleman. He didn't even try to get into Della's pants until she was ready. He was supersmart, ten times smarter than anyone she had ever known, even college professors she had met. Della thought it was cool, that it was great when they were hanging out with friends. He took a shine to Guy and got a real kick out of teaching him new things, especially math.

Mack's house in Wantaugh on the south side of Long Island was lovely, right across from the water. He had purchased it wisely of course, which was a surprise to no one. The house was yellow with a screened-in porch filled with exotic plants in clay pots. Dracaena, snake plants, barrel cactus. Guy loved to hide behind the tall dracaena which towered above his head. Mack and Guy would play hide-and-seek all around the house. When Della was working, Mack would order Guy pizza and chase down the ice cream man when they heard the bells ringing up the street.

The cherry on top was the return of the two cats from their exile to the hard streets and back to the cozy comforts of indoor living. Once Della and Guy had left his grandparents' house for the dingy basement apartment, the cats had to live outside. Guy had cried about how unfair it was, especially since the basement didn't even have all of its walls. Even though they were living in a house owned by friends of Aunt Carmella, the landlords were firm on their no-cats policy. Della had no other good alternatives on such short notice. Roxie was certainly not an alternative, what with Paul still being around and all.

Della and Guy had had two cats: Rufus, a twenty-five-pound gray tomcat, and Tasha, his orange, black and white queen. They were comfortable both outdoors and in, but preferred the choice to come and go as they pleased. Then Rufus went missing for nearly a month. Della and Guy had searched the whole neighborhood for weeks, checking with neighbors, vets, stores, street after street. Three weeks later Della was walking six blocks up, calling for Rufus, when she heard moaning coming from inside a broken-down car. Della recognizing the moan of her beloved Rufus, and, as she peered into the engine from underneath the car, she saw him.

His bulky frame was gone, withered away, oily and matted. His tail was wrapped around a piece of metal keeping him trapped. His tail looked like a shredded banana peel. Della dislodged his tail and wrapped him in her sweatshirt. He didn't fight at all; he knew his guardian angel had arrived.

Rufus's tail was amputated; the veterinarian took pity on Della's pocketbook. Rufus's tail healed quickly into a little stump. The weight, and then some, came back even more quickly.

On his fifth birthday, Guy was happy as he awoke to the smell of pancakes; he dashed down the hall into the kitchen.

"Happy birthday to you, happy birthday to you, happy birthday, dear Guy, happy birthday to you!" Della and Mack sang in unison upon Guy's entrance.

Mack delivered a stack of freshly made pancakes, slathered in butter and syrup, the way Guy loved them. Mack liked his plain.

Guy could tell this was going to be the best birthday ever; he was five now. He was big.

"This is from your mom and me." Mack handed Guy a card and placed a present—wrapped in red and green, about the size and shape of a mason jar—on the table.

Guy was so excited; he could hardly open his card. On the outside was a picture of a fat gray cat wearing a birthday hat. Guy read the inside. *"To the best kid in the world, happy fifth birthday. Love Mom and Mack.* Thanks, Mom. Thanks, Mack." Guy beamed.

"What's this?" Guy held up three pieces of paper that were cut and colored to look like movie tickets. *The Empire Strikes Back* was written down the middle. Guy knew they weren't real movie tickets, and *The Empire Strikes Back* wasn't even showing until next month.

"They're vouchers for three tickets to *The Empire Strikes Back,* opening day." Mack thought the move was inappropriate for a five-year-old, but Della had insisted it was fine, and Guy spoke of it as a matter of fact. Mack came around to the idea, mostly because Guy didn't act like most five-year-olds. He knew more about the plot and characters than Mack did. Guy saw *Superman* on opening day in December of Nineteen Seventy Eight, when he was almost three. He had waited in a line which had wrapped around three blocks for the entire day with Della. He sat through *Star Wars* when he was one; Della held him while he watched the whole movie quietly.

"Yes!" Guy raised both hands, holding the vouchers above his head. He ripped into the wrapped present on the table.

"Money!" Guy roared, as the torn paper revealed a mason jar filled with coins of all types, predominately silver in color. Sticking out of the top of the jar were coin wrappers.

"Wow! Thanks, Mack. Thanks, Mom. I love you!" Guy dove off his chair and gave Mack a mighty hug.

"You're welcome. Glad you like it." Mack smiled, still wearing his calf-length blue bathrobe.

Guy turned and gave his mother a hug and a big smile.

★★★

Jack was still asleep after a raging night out with his cousin Stan. He was shacking up with his old lady, a rather unremarkable girl named Denise. Jack's growing disillusionment with the current state of the world was only moderately constrained by dissociating mixtures of just about anything. He seemed to find himself on the end of every losing transaction: his marriage, his son, his business.

Aside from losing his temper once with Della, he had never truly hurt anyone that he could think of. Hurting people was always a possibility, and at times an attractive one, that was only staved off by strength of mind and fortitude of will. Thinking about it some, he guessed maybe he had hurt a few people but never that badly. In reality they usually deserved it; he would never hurt family. Except for that time he had beat the living shit out of his brother after Jack had been home from Vietnam for a year. He had warned Bobby repeatedly not to leave his damn bike in the fucking driveway. But the wiseass little shit had a hearing problem. It had been a bad beating too, though broken up quickly by their father and his Colt forty five.

The fact that the government could keep Jack away from seeing his son, who he had never hurt, was maddening. He loved that boy deeply, though it was a love expressed only within his mind.

Jack had not seen Guy since the government's attempt to begin monitoring their relationship, their every whisper. His own boy.

Jack felt as if he couldn't lose to win. Heroin, his big moneymaker, had turned out to be a dangerous bedfellow. Heroin eased at times the seething betrayal Jack felt, along with the help of booze, pot, Mellaril. Fortunately he didn't have to pay rent at his old lady's.

Either way he was a veteran of a foreign war, and he would see his son on his own terms. Today, being Guy's birthday, was the perfect day. Jack wasn't even going to make a big fucking display over the situation either. Or over the fact that his whore of an ex-wife was shacked up with some suit playing Daddy to his son. Jack knew where they were too. He hadn't even caused any trouble, and, with the way Della was throwing it in his face, they should have expected some.

He would swing by to say a quick hello, and this time he would leave the shotgun at home. He had heard about the giant birthday party planned at Mack's. Jack's friend Marty had garnered an invite, since he was a friend of Paul and Roxie. Jack figured he would be able to slip in and out, Ranger style, since the party was sure to be festive. He even set aside ten dollars on the dresser before he went out last night, so he would have money left to buy his son a present.

Jack and Stan made a hundred bucks the previous night, selling fifty hits of acid to Louie. They bought it from a guy on the island who went to the same high school as Jack, a few grades behind. Stan and Jack came up with the two hundred fifty bucks to buy the acid and sold it to Louie for three fifty, an easy score. Jack and Stan tried a hit two weeks prior, which had melted them into the floor. Good product makes for an easy sale. It was a good thing Jack had left the ten dollars at home last night. It was certainly one of those nights that left a man's pockets empty.

The strong daylight illuminated the bedroom even through the shade on the window, and the incessant ringing of the fucking phone finally rose Jack from his coma.

"What?" he answered angrily and half awake.

"What? Are you fucking kidding me? Where the fuck have you been?" came the voice through the end of the telephone.

"Louie, I just woke up. Late night with Stan," Jack said, rubbing his eyes, still coming too.

"No shit, Sherlock. I've been calling you all damn night. You sold the boys bunk acid. Are you fucking serious?" Louie growled.

"What? What are you talking about?" Jack stood up straight as a line.

"That acid was bullshit."

"What do you mean, *bullshit?* I did the same shit two weeks ago with Stan. It knocked us on our fucking asses. How much did you take?"

"All of it, the whole fucking lot, one or two hits apiece. Not a damned thing."

"Bullshit," Jack said, with a hint of rising alarm.

"Are you hearing what I'm telling you? That acid was bunk. We had the whole damn night planned too. It was supposed to be a bonding experience for the crew, you know? Something a little spiritual."

"Louie, don't fuck around with me. Are you fucking serious or what?" The tone of Jack's voice was agitatedly concerned.

"For the last time I'm fucking serious. The boys were about to come unglued, but I said, no way Jack tried to fuck us." Louie's voice was firm.

"*Oooh*, that mutherfucker. You have got to be kidding me. Who does that mutherfucker think he's fucking with?"

"Jack, the boys are cool for now, but we want our money back."

"Of course, Louie. It's my problem, not the club's. You have got to be kidding me. Un-fucking-believable. That little piece of shit." Jack's blood boiled, like viscous oil coursing down the side of an iron cauldron, hissing and popping as it gushes onto the flames below.

"Settle down. Not the end of the world. I told 'em it wasn't your fault. But, you know, they wanted to hear it firsthand," Louie said evenly.

"Louie, you know I love you. I'd never disrespect you like that. This kid, this piece of shit, spit right in my face. I'm sorry. I, I can't believe this." Jack was astonished that someone would rip him off so blatantly, so out in the open, so disrespectfully. Who did the kid think he was messing with? Almost everyone on Long Island knew Jack was a combat Vet, one who had seen the shit war. Everyone knew he had a short fuse and that he liked to back it up. Some thought he was a few cards short. He didn't mind; it played to the image.

"It's all right. Cool it."

"This kid is gonna get cooled, Louie. I can't believe this shit!" Jack was fuming.

"Easy, just get the three fifty," Louie said lightly. He had no doubt that Jack would get his money back. Plus everyone was really only out ten bucks a head.

"I'll call you." Jack replaced the phone in the cradle, grabbed a baseball bat and smashed a hole in his old lady's wall.

"What the fuck!" Stan jumped off the couch in the living room and rounded the corner, still wearing his clothes from the night before. His cropped black hair was tousled, and sleep still clouded his eyes.

"He robbed us!" Jack had the Louisville Slugger draped over his right shoulder; his eyes felt as if they would bleed.

"What?" Stan cocked his head to the side, still in a haze and not sure what the hell Jack was talking about.

"That mutherfucker Mick sold us bunk acid."

"Bullshit." Stan stood up straighter, brushing the bangs off his forehead.

"Does it sound like I'm bullshitting?"

Stan looked deep into his cousin's icy eyes. "Fuck."

"Dead. Who does that cocksucker think he's fucking with?" Jack could not believe the nerve. Disrespecting him, in front of his friends, his family. Certainly this piece of shit knew of Jack's reputation. There were only so many pubs in Long Island, and Jack was known at most of them.

"You said it then." Stan sat stiffly back upon the couch.

"They want their money back." Jack walked to the living room, holding the fat end of the bat in his hands.

"Of course they want their money back. That's not the point clearly." Stan shook his raised index finger in the air.

"No shit, so?" Jack asked his cousin, as a plan formulated in his mind.

"All right, get a bag." Stan had become quite the accomplished bank robber, pulling off more than a half-dozen heists. One had required shooting a guard, though not critically. After that Stan went to Ireland to lay low, visit family for a while. In the Old Country he had established connections already moving heroin right out of New York City. His was the sort of family who despised heroin but used the proceeds so that their collective voice could be heard clearly. Collectively against oppression, occupation—and, for the love of Christ, through his church. An Ireland independent from the Colonial Brits who claimed to be a brother but acted instead as a master.

Jack smashed the already smashed drywall in the kitchen again. Lately his short fuse seemed even shorter. The only solution that came to mind was to make the wick wetter. That worked until the wick ran out.

★★★

Guy's party started at noon, which seemed to him like forever from now. His aunt Roxie and uncle Paul showed up first around 11 thirty a.m.

94

with his cousins Paulie and Jerry. Roxie and Della were both wearing skintight blue jeans. Della was wearing a gray fitted T-shirt with the sleeves cut off. Roxie was in a low-cut beaded tank top, her hair feathered with a crimper. Just in case her five-foot-ten frame didn't catch everyone's attention, its balance upon five-inch red heels ensured a glance.

"Wow, would ya look at this place? This is really amazing, Mack, incredible." Roxie shook her head in amazement; she had never been in a house as nice as Mack's, especially one so close to the water.

"We did it together." Mack was referring to the red, blue and yellow streamers that hung all throughout the house and the backyard. The party was Superman themed, of course per Guy's request. Hence the colors, plates and cups. Superman logos were hung all about.

"Come on." Guy grabbed his cousins' arms and ran through the open double doors into the backyard. "Ta-da." Guy opened up a giant cooler, overflowing with ice and sodas of various delights.

"*Oooh.*" Jerry's feet danced as he dipped his little arm into the ice. He was promptly punched by his brother, who pulled out a can for himself.

Guy grabbed his cousin Paul by the arm. "That's not nice. No hitting. Say sorry," Guy demanded, as if it had been a personal affront.

"Sorry, Jerry." Paulie lowered his head and took a sip of his root beer.

"You pick, Jerry." Guy put his arm around his cousin's slender shoulders. Jerry was thin, pale, with blond hair, unlike his brother, father and mother.

Jerry picked his favorite, Sunkist orange soda. He popped the top. "Mmm, delicious!"

"Mack said we could have as many sodas as we want and pizza!" Guy's eyes beamed with delight.

"Pizza!" Paulie and Jerry squealed and joined hands. They never had money for pizza. Nor for white socks. They wore the same green-and-blue athletic shorts with black socks. Black socks didn't need to be washed very often.

"And"—Guy paused—"Superman ice-cream cake for dessert!" Guy held his arm above his head with his fist closed, his left arm at his hip, with an intense look on his face. Flying, after all, took immense concentration.

"Ice cream!" Paulie and Jerry were now interlocked, chest to chest, twirling around in a circle. At times Jerry's feet flew off the ground.

By twelve thirty, a case of beer had already been dispatched, and nearly fifty people had arrived: folks from the pub, Mack's brothers and his younger sister, Joan.

Della's Italian heritage was apparent in the ordering of the pizza pies. More food than could possibly be eaten at once was needed, especially since their friends would be here late, drinking and dancing to the music. Mack moved the speakers into the backyard so everyone could hear. His backyard was decorated with beautiful clay pots just like the patio, including some elephant foot trees that he had planted in the ground with trunks almost half a car tire in diameter.

"Can you believe these bullshit interest rates, Mack?" Paul tilted his umpteenth beer to Mack as they stood around the ice coolers and pizza. He was donning blue jeans with dingy red cowboy boots. His shirt was already off.

Mack was wearing a blue tank top and short green athletic shorts, which were popular among his group of friends. Many of Mack's friends were former lifeguards from Jones Beach, where he had worked during the summers through high school and college. Mack taught Guy to swim in two and a half weeks at the YMCA's indoor pool.

Mack responded kindly, "No, but completely necessary. We have a serious inflation problem. The only way to squeeze it out of the system is by raising interest rates. Guess we'll see if Reagan and Volcker are up to the job." Mack thought they very likely were. Prime was down to seventeen and a half in December.

Della snuggled up to Mack's arm, hugging it tight.

"Who gives a shit about inflation?" Paul yammered, rather than asking what *inflation* was.

"Ask the Germans after the first World War. It took a whole wheelbarrow full of money to buy a loaf of bread, if there was even one to be found."

"Bullshit." Paul waved his hand and pulled out another beer.

Della knew it wasn't bullshit, because Mack said it, and he was always the smartest one in the room. She was irritated that her sister Roxie hadn't thrown out that bum Paul on his ass. It's not like he paid the bills. Hell, he wasn't even handsome anymore, what with part of his nose missing and all. Plus he looked strung-out and grimy. Della worried that the kids weren't getting enough to eat, but Roxie did always keep the house stocked with Wonder bread and Jiffy peanut butter.

"Nope, true as all hell. They printed their way right into hyperinflation. By the time hitler arrived, they were begging for him to save them."

"OK. OK, whatever. Now, on a serious note, thanks for your generosity. Beer for everyone!" Paul raised his bottle. "I heard there were a few bottles of Jack Daniel's?" Paul gave Mack a joking elbow to the ribs.

"Cabinet in the front room. Three bottles. Help yourself." Mack knew how to throw a party. His brother was a bartender after all.

Mack would give one last attempt for those in the group who might have been paying attention to the economy talk. "You see, there's just too much debt out there. People had been borrowing at crazy terms. All the money in the system drives prices up to unrealistic levels." Mack took the last slug of his Budweiser and grabbed another.

★★★

Jack and Stan drove up to the Green, a park in Levittown, to find Mick Knall. Jack was in a focused fury and had not thought once about his son's birthday since the phone had rung earlier. He pulled his green Plymouth slowly to the Green, which was a popular hangout spot for disenfranchised youths of the age. The cool air coupled with a nice buzz seemed to calm the teens' nerves, or at least cool their ambitions. Jack scanned the park as he drove slowly along the curb.

"I don't see him, but those kids are friends of his. Piece of shit loser hangs out with nineteen-year-olds." Jack took off his jean jacket, revealing his taut build underneath a guinea T. He slammed the door behind him. He held a folded yellow piece of paper in his left hand, hiding an open six-inch buck knife.

Stan closed the passenger door. He looked a bit like a gorilla with hairy, wide forearms bulging from beneath a tight black T-shirt—his standard attire with jeans and black motorcycle boots. Stan was carrying a tire iron shaped like an L, wrapped in a dingy white towel.

Jack walked swiftly to the trio of Mick's friends. They were typical nineteen-year-old knuckleheads of the goofy variety. Jack handed the yellow paper to the kid on the right, a dweeby kid with long shaggy black hair.

"You're friends of Mick's, right?" Jack said coolly, tapping the open knife blade on the palm of his left hand. "Think carefully before you answer."

The boys looked at Jack, then at Stan, and quickly realized their best and only choice was to play it cool. They had heard from Mick about the fake acid, and, while he had been convinced of the merits of the scheme, they were certain it was a bad idea. Especially when they had heard that Jack Finnigan was involved. He was one of those crazy Nam Vets—and not one of those guys trying to milk it. He was dangerous. These teens didn't know Jack personally, but they knew very well that he was not the guy to pull a fast one on.

"Ah, yeah," the boy on the end, Chris, said, now holding the unopened note.

"Open it. Go ahead, read it." Jack stared into the back of Chris's brain.

Chris opened the yellow paper and read the words written in thick black marker:

One Thousand Dollars

COD

Brothers Pub

Seven Seven Three - Six Eight Four 9

Chris looked up at Jack with confusion. Stan moved to Chris's left, so that he was directly in line with the left side of Chris's head rather than in front of him and his buddies. Seeing Stan stand just outside his periphery with what was clearly a tire iron wrapped in a towel made Chris feel as if he couldn't breath. He thought he might puke.

"Let them see the note. What? Do you boys think you're in the army?" Jack said, touching the tip of his knife to Chris's camouflaged field jacket purchased from the army navy surplus store. "Hey, Stan, these kids want to play army."

"No, we don't. Sorry." Chris adroitly took off his jacket and rolled it into a ball, holding it next to the pit in his stomach. Squeezing the balled-up jacket, like a child's blanket, made him feel a bit more comfortable as he stared at the ground. The note was passed back to Chris, the group's unelected whipping boy.

"Nobody robs from us. Got it?" Jack held the buck knife straight up in the air, the tip at chin level. "Eyes up, you little cocksuckers." Jack made sure the trio got a good look at him and the knife. "Where is he?"

"We haven't seen him today. Maybe at his mom's or Susie's," Chris said, hoping truthfulness would bring the current situation to an end quickly.

Jack looked to the other two. "Haven't seen him?"

"No," they responded in unison with pleading eyes.

Jack turned his attention back to Chris. "You're gonna give that note to Mick. Got it?"

"Sure, I swear, as soon as I see him." Chris was ready to get the hell out of the Green and wasn't planning on coming back anytime soon.

"Not good enough. Your new job is finding him. Got it?"

"OK." Chris was looking back down at his shoes.

"OK? Do you see Mick in the fucking park?"

"No," Chris replied sheepishly.

"Then you'd better go find him." Jack pressed the tip of his knife lightly into Chris's T-shirt-clad chest, and, with that, he ran at a full sprint all the way to Mick's house.

Chris's friends followed Chris out of the park, but, until he got to Mick's stoop, Chris realized they hadn't followed him all the way. He was covered in sweat. His heart was about to explode out of his chest, and he was heaving so hard he knew he was about to puke.

Bluuuaaach. Chris hunched over the black wrought iron railing and puked his guts into the Knalls' flower bed to the left of their stoop. He walked up the four steps to the door and rang the doorbell.

Mick opened the door, and Chris tore through the opening, running into the kitchen and peering out through the blinds.

"Oh fuck, oh fuck, oh fuck."

"Hey, relax. What's the deal?" Mick was neither handsome nor ugly, but was larger than most of his friends at six foot and two hundred pounds. He liked hanging out with Chris and his buddies because they were fun. They had no responsibilities, so they were always available. They had money from their parents, so they were always ready to party. More rightly put, they were rarely sober.

Chris handed Mick the note. "It's from that guy you sold that fake acid to."

Mick opened the note. "Is this what you are all wound up about? Are you kidding me? Relax."

"No, you don't understand, Mick. This guy's serious. He pulled a knife on me. Had some other scary guy with a fucking tire iron."

Mick was surprised to hear that. "Seriously don't worry about it. Jack and I went to the same high school. We're old buddies. He's just messing with you."

"Mick, he wasn't messing around. He's fucking crazy."

It takes one to know one. Mick laughed. He had studied up at Pilgrim State and Mid-Hudson Psychiatric Center. His mom thought he had needed the help. Jack was a few years older than Mick and might have been in Nam, but Mick had thirty pounds on him. Mick had met some returning Vets who weren't all that tough—mostly booze and hot air. He grabbed his mom's purse and pulled out a hundred and fifty dollars. That was more than half of the purchase price. He would get the rest, if it came down to that.

"See, no big deal." Mick held up the money he had just taken from his mother's purse. He had already blown the two fifty Jack had paid. Half last night at a few pubs in the city coupled with a big steak dinner. The other half he spent on Susie and their two kids, Cammie, five, and Nick, two. They took the train down to the Freeport mall to buy clothes. Susie loved buying clothes. Mick was certain his generous gesture would go a long way toward mending fences with his ex-fiancé. Mick had never wanted a family, nor a job for that matter. At least with disability pay he was able to spend his money the way he wanted, without having to answer to anyone. And without having to pay rent at his parents' house, he was free to spend it on getting loaded and hanging out with his friends.

Mick swept Chris back out the door he had come in through. God help him if his mother heard all the commotion. He'd never hear the end of it. She nearly had a conniption when she saw Mick making his wares, a concoction of grape juice, coffee and cut up pieces of white construction paper. He had used an eye dropper. Clever. He told his mother it was art therapy, ordered by his doctor, but she wasn't buying it. When she pressed, he admitted he was going to sell it as acid and make a cool two hundred and fifty dollars. She hemmed and hawed as usual, but what did his mother know about making a million bucks anyway?

Mick locked the door and put the folded note in his pocket. "Mom," Mick yelled up the stairs, "if anyone asks, I'm not home. I think I'm getting sick. I'm taking a nap. Remember, if anyone asks, I'm not home."

"OK, OK. I heard you," his mother yelled down.

Mick went into his bedroom, locked the dead bolt, dove onto his bed and put the pillow over his head.

★★★

Guy was enjoying his umpteenth Coke and his best birthday ever. His belly was full of pizza, as were his cousins' along with some other children who were tagging along with their parents. It was six o'clock, and the light was leaving the sky, turning it to sapphire, where some would say the gold meets the blue.

"Watch this." Paulie jumped toward the big plastic bucket, holding the aluminum keg with mountains of ice, used to keep its malty delight crisp and cold. Stacked red plastic cups looked like a giant pyramid on the table next to the ice-mountain keg. Paulie bent over, pulled his pants down and waggled his bare butt at Jerry and Guy.

"*Eww*, stop it." Guy turned and looked over his shoulder.

Mission accomplished. Paulie had, in a flash, grabbed a red cup and poured himself an inch or two of beer. He dropped the little spigot into the ice and took a big gulp holding the cup with both hands.

"Mmm." Paulie smiled widely, adorning a thick new foam mustache.

"Hey." Guy walked to Paulie with little Jerry behind. "What are you drinking?"

"Beer." Paulie giggled mischievously and took another sip. Then he held the empty cup still in both hands above his head, triumphantly. As he turned it upside down, what little foam remained drizzled upon his head.

"Beer's only for grown-ups." Guy put his hands on his hips and bent his front knee.

"Mmm-hmm, I'm allowed. Ha, ha, ha, ha." Paulie pointed at Guy and his brother, and lifted one foot at a time, up and down, in a little dance.

Thankfully big Paul was walking by, and Guy grabbed a hold of his pant leg. "Uncle Paul."

Paul turned and finished a large guzzle from the upended Jack Daniel's bottle in his right hand.

"Paulie's drinking beer." Guy looked up at his uncle. He didn't like going over to his cousins' house. His uncle wasn't very nice, and he frightened Guy.

"Oh, do we have a little tattletale here on his birthday?" Paul reached over and grabbed the red cup out of Paulie's hands.

"A baby sip for a baby." Paul looked down at what was left of the foam in the bottom of the cup and flicked it onto the dirt. Big Paul primed the keg and grabbed the spigot. He tilted the cup filling it with three fingers' worth of beer and passed it back to his son.

"Party time!" Paul said, raising both hands above his head. He took another big slug of JD.

"See." Paulie shook his heinie and extended his arms, holding the red cup to mock his two playmates. Paulie took two big sips of the cold beer, poured correctly without all the foam.

"I want some." Jerry looked up at his father sweetly.

"Next year," Paul said coarsely.

"Ha, ha. You're just a baby!" Paulie took another sip of his beer.

"That's enough teasing." Paul slapped Paulie on the back of the head. "Give your brother a sip."

Jerry eagerly took a big gulp of his brother's beer while they held the cup in unison. Guy knew that Uncle Paul was wrong; beer wasn't for kids.

"Cake time!" Della swooped up Guy in her arms. "Ah, what are you doing, Paul? You're letting them drink beer? Come on. You didn't drink any beer, did you, Guy?"

"No, mom." Guy knew they weren't allowed to drink beer.

"You trying to turn these kids into a big mess like you, Paul? For Christ's sake, come on. It's time for cake." Della dumped Paulie's beer into the bushes and then scooted Jerry and Paulie along.

Mack was finishing up a conversation with his brother and a group of friends on the importance of savings. Mack was taking advantage of the newly enacted Four O One (k) plan. Sure, it was no pension, but it's not like you could leave money on the table either. The Dow Jones was gaining momentum, looked like it might even break through the thousand-point ceiling. Yes, it had been over a thousand a few times in the seventies, but it had never really broken through, created a floor. Mack thought there would be some creeping asset inflation over time, now that the gold standard was eliminated.

Mack had a long wooden picnic table with long benches and chairs at both ends. Guy was at the head of the table with his Superman logo ice-cream cake with six candles—one for good luck. All the partygoers rounded the table, beers in hand, to sing "Happy Birthday" to Guy. Guy wished, as he blew out his candles, that he and his mom could live with Mack forever, and the day danced away its last breath.

★★★

Jack and Stan were steamed, having wasted the whole afternoon searching half the pubs and hangouts in Long Island for Mick and coming up dry. Bad luck. They decided Mick must be hiding out, at a friend's maybe, or with his ex, perhaps even at his parents' house. Time to smoke him out.

Jack had exchanged his green Plymouth for his father's light-blue Chevy—his father having passed rather suddenly with a problem related to his gut. Jack tapped the Chevy's wheels against the curb, and, in a moment, he was out of the car solo, ringing the Knalls' front doorbell.

Mick's plump black-haired mother answered the door with a pleasant "Hello."

"It's Jack Finnigan, ma'am. Is Mick home?"

"No, I'm sorry. He's not home right now." Mrs. Knall began to close the door which was open about a foot.

"Excuse me. Ma'am, it's important. Can I leave a message?" Jack yelled through the cracked door as he stopped it from closing with his foot.

"OK." Mrs. Knall opened the door once again.

"Thanks. You see, Mick owes me some money, and he was going to trade me some parts for my car. I really need them. Can you please have him call me?"

"OK, let me get a pen." Mrs. Knall's heart quickened because, while she knew it was likely her son owed someone money, it was impossible he would have said he would give them car parts. He didn't even know how to drive.

"That would be great, please."

Mrs. Knall came back to the door, pen and paper in hand.

"OK, have him call seven seven three, six eight four 9. Ask for Jack."

Mrs. Knall read the number back as her stomach churned. "That was seven seven three, six eight four 9, ask for Jack."

"Thanks, ma'am." Jack walked back down to his father's light-blue Chevy.

Mrs. Knall locked the dead bolt and watched the blue Chevy pull away as she peeked out from behind the curtains. She waddled down the hall, both hands over her mouth, until she pounded furiously on her son's door with the palms of her hands. "Mick! Mick, open up!"

"I'm sleeping, Mom. I said leave me alone."

"Mick, open up. Jack Finnigan was here, and he said to call him at this number immediately." Mrs. Knall pushed the paper under her son's locked door. "He said you owed him money, Mick. Honey, this guy was really scary."

"Mom, it's no big deal. Stay out of it," Mick yelled through his locked bedroom door but began to wonder if this, in fact, was a bigger problem than he had realized.

"Mick, I'm serious, sweetheart. I don't want you to get hurt."

"Shut up, Mom." Mick decided he would call Missy and Sara; they were both friends and loved free drinks. He would take them to the bar with him to cool down the situation. Offer up the rest of the cash as a peace offering too, no hard feelings. If it really came down to it, he could always grab a bottle as a weapon. He had been in fights at a few pubs, and everyone said he punched hard as a mule.

When he sat down at Brothers Pub, he put Missy and Sara on each side.

"What? Are you fucking crazy or stupid, Mick?" Shep, the barkeep, crouched down and got in Mick's face. Shep had no love lost for Mick— he always ran his bar tabs too high for too long. Bringing Missy and Sara was a plus. They were fun on any other occasion, except one involving a hot Jack Finnigan.

"Three beers, please, Shep." Mick laid down a twenty and flashed the rest of the bills. "See, not a problem."

"Mick, I don't know if you're stupid or what, but Jack Finnigan is not the sort of guy you rip off. If I were you, I'd get the hell outta here. You hear me?"

"Don't worry about it, Shep. I got it covered. Me and Jackie are old high school buds. Not a big deal, just a misunderstanding."

"I'm just saying." Shep threw a bar rag into the sink.

Mick knocked back his beer and another quickly. He began to feel a bit more at ease, and, as he did, a storm blew in through the back door.

Jack was instantaneously hostile when he saw Mick there at the bar drinking Jack's money away with a couple hookers. Mick hardly had time to stand before Jack was upon him, like a lion enveloping an antelope.

Jack took the empty plastic vial from out of his pocket; it was cylindrical, coming to a cone at the bottom, with a little plastic flip top. As Jack stepped into Mick's personal space, Jack tapped the pointed cone end into Mick's chest, hard, repeatedly. "Who the fuck do you think you are?"

Mick was caught off guard by Jack's ferocity. Mick's mind seemed scrambled, and he found himself struggling for the words, any words. He was able to make out something like "Huh?" with a shrug.

"You think you can sell me fake acid, huh, mutherfucker?" Jack said loudly, further enraged over the fact that this piece of shit was actually sitting here drinking a beer, rather than cowering in some corner. He would find out what it was like to cower.

"No" was all Mick could get out; his fright was mixed with embarrassment, and he began to make his way toward the back, so that they could talk privately.

Before he could say a word, he was thrown hard out the rear door, face-first on the black asphalt parking lot. He was wearing jeans, but his hands and shoulder were scraped bloody. The side of his head hit the ground hard. "Hey, hold on. I've got money right here. Look." Mick peered up and pulled out the wad from his right front pocket, using his left hand. His right arm ached.

Thank God, Jack thought, and he reached down, snatching the money from Mick's hand. "Not even a hundred and fifty fucking bucks." Jack tried to stay cool. "Where's the rest?"

"That's all I have, seriously." Mick pulled out his pockets and stood to his feet.

Jack looked into Mick's gaze deeply and, with a cool cadence, he said, "Then go ask your mom or your ex or find a cock to suck, because you're getting us our money tonight. Got it?" Jack tapped Mick in the chest. Jack needed to pay Louie and the boys back quickly to save face, especially since Louie had put his neck on the line for Jack. Louie was Jack's biggest customer now.

"All right, fine. My girl, Susie, always keeps an emergency fund. Chill out, Jack, jeez."

"Get in the car. I'm having a drink." Jack opened the backseat of his Plymouth and yelled for Stan, still inside.

"Any deep water close by?" Stan asked Shep, leaning in over the end of the bar. Shep did shit with Ritchie, and Shep knew who Stan was.

"Yeah, five miles north and south. You got a boat?" Shep knew a guy who rented boats.

"Thanks." Stan turned to meet Jack at the back door.

"He's in the car. We're going to TJ's to get some money from his old lady. He had about one fifty on him."

"That's a start." Stan got in the passenger side door.

Jack pounded the bar next to his friend and former business partner, Ritchie Nazzle. Shep knew that was the signal and put a four-finger glass of Jameson Irish Whiskey down in front of Jack. Everyone in the vicinity was hoping it would cool his jets.

"Can you believe the nerve of that piece of garbage?" Jack said loudly, his face uncomfortably close to Ritchie's.

"I got it. Cool it down, baby." Ritchie was a regular at Brothers. He liked the crowd; it was always relaxed.

"Cool it down? Seriously?" Jack could not take being made to look like a chump, a sucker in front of the whole island. "Are you fucking kidding me, Ritchie?" Jack was incensed. He put his mouth to where Ritchie's ear would be, if it wasn't covered by a stringy drape of greasy brown hair. "He made me look like a punk, Ritchie."

As Jack stood up, Ritchie looked into Jack's eyes. They seemed vacant. Not high or wasted, but perhaps as if operating in neutral.

"I'm fucking serious." Jack threw back what was left of his Jameson, leaning in, with his palm placed against the edge of the bar. He was past irritated that Ritchie didn't understand what the fuck was going on. That people could actually think they could pull a fast one on him. Jack pushed off the bar and flew out the back door.

Jack drove. Mick's ex was likely at TJ's, he had said, a few blocks over, a biker bar. That must mean Mick's ex was a little slut. Hopefully for him, she had their money, because payment in kind was not going to suffice tonight.

Jack put the car in park, looked over to Stan. "You're up." Stan got out of the car and opened the back door.

"Let's go." His voice was gravelly, though he was a man of few words. Some would say a man of few thoughts, but just fewer areas of thought.

"Hey, you can't park there," a burly bouncer in a black leather vest yelled.

Jack rolled down his window. "His old lady owes us some money. Need a quick check to see if she's inside."

Stan pushed past the bouncer quickly with Mick in tow. Unfortunately for Mick, they were back out almost as quickly. No sign of Susie.

Stan threw Mick forcefully into the backseat.

"Jack, I don't know what to tell you. I'll get your money, I promise." Mick was still not as frightened as he ought to have been.

"What about your parents?" Jack said, coldly staring straight ahead.

"I already hit my mom's purse. Susie's gotta be home. It's almost midnight."

"She better be." Jack pulled onto the highway.

"Let's be clear, Mick," Jack spat out, with a heavy emphasis on the CK, the last letters of his name. "Because apparently I haven't been clear, have I Stan?" Jack spoke more slowly toward the end of the sentence, all the while looking straight forward.

Stan turned around in his seat and swiftly brought the towel-covered end of the tire iron down upon Mick's left forearm. It broke clean through.

The fire in Mick's arm felt as if he were being electrocuted. He began to scream out a horrific, blood-curdled scream. It was, however, muffled back down his throat, as Stan shoved the curve—where the two pieces of the tire iron met, still wrapped with the towel—into Mick's mouth, like a bit.

"Like I said," Jack continued, "we want our money tonight. *Now*. It's nonnegotiable. Tonight is already tomorrow. Got it?" Jack turned around and stared at Mick, bit still in mouth. Now he looked scared, like an animal that suddenly realized it was about to be devoured, unaware of the lurking danger until it was far too late. Jack came unglued. "Last chance, mutherfucker! You fucking hear me? This is it!" Jack screamed with the fierceness of a warrior from antiquity—a guttural scream from a time long before guns and bullets.

Mick began to sob uncontrollably, like a man who has been struck suddenly by tragedy. His bit was removed. He was broken, as they pulled up to Susie's apartment. He was hopeful still, because of her steadfastness. Mick was certain she would have her emergency fund.

Jack looked over his shoulder. "Play it cool. Got it?" With that, he went around and opened the back door. Jack pulled Mick out by his collar and pushed him up the stoop toward the front door.

Mick rung the doorbell. "Susie, it's me. Open up," Mick called through the door, cupping his right hand to his mouth.

He rang the door repeatedly. Susie was out of her bedroom and crouched halfway to the floor toward the door in the dark. With Mick and the lateness of the hour, she was immediately concerned, nervous. She walked softly and put her ear toward the door, her mouth squeezed tight, so as not to scream.

"I don't know, Jack. She's not answering. Susie! Susie, it's Mick. It's an emergency. Open up."

Once Susiew heard that Mick was not alone, she knew for certain she would not be opening the door, and she crept quietly back toward the kitchen and the phone.

Jack grabbed Mick by his shirt and threw him in the backseat of the Chevy. Mick was thrown so hard, he was pretty sure his limp arm would have to be amputated. It felt like spaghetti.

"That's it." Jack looked over at Stan. He turned around quickly and came down hard on the corner of Mick's jaw with the towel-covered tire iron. Stan had broken a few jaws in his day, and this one was hit just right. Not even a spurt of blood. After the initial shock and panic, Mick was out like a light.

★★★

Guy was out like a light as well, almost. He had burned up the fumes of exhaustion with a day of celebration, filled with his every delight. This was the best birthday ever, just like Guy had dreamed of. He had hardly even noticed that his father wasn't present. Except for a moment, when Guy had opened the present from his dad's friend Marty. It was a gun! Guy was head over heels; he could finally shoot rattlesnakes in the backyard, like a real cowboy. Not that there were any rattlesnake sightings yet, but Mack's ample backyard seemed to provide more than enough hiding places.

The gun was more precisely a twenty two caliber rifle. Guy read it on the side of the box, as his mother screamed at Marty. Guy tried to help Marty plead his case. Guy only held the rifle for a mere moment, and his mother swore it would be the only time, as five-year-olds were not allowed to have rifles. Guy insisted that, if the five-year-old were a real cowboy in the Old West, they could.

Guy's Superman ice-cream cake was the best cake he had ever tasted! Made by Carvel of course. Vanilla ice cream with a cookie crumble in the middle. Guy gave his last bite to Rufus, the beggar cat. Tasha didn't like cake.

This was the first time ever that Guy got to stay up for his entire birthday, past midnight. His cousins had long since fallen asleep, but his party kept going until Mack sent everyone home shortly after midnight, which had been a point of discussion with Guy before the party.

Guy had a whole arrangement of stuffed animals now, stacked in around him. That made him feel safe and happy. Guy lay comfortable, safe in his bed, and hoped his birthday wish would come true.

★★★

Jack closed the back door to his green Plymouth. Mick was in the backseat, half conscious.

"You can turn around," Jack instructed his younger brother Bobby. "Take Dad's car straight home. You got it? No stops."

"I got it. No stops," Bobby repeated, trying to pull off a look similar to his brother's. He was, however, a smeared carbon copy, born blind in one eye.

Jack stood in front of the back window to block his brother's view. "I'm serious, meathead. No stops. Get outta here. Now." Jack motioned with his head for Bobby to pull out of the parking lot behind Brothers. It was late, and no one was watching carefully.

As Bobby pulled the light-blue Chevy out of the parking lot, Jack grabbed the black bag from the trunk of the Plymouth and passed Stan the keys. Jack got into the backseat and straddled Mick, who began to moan like a dying, bleating ox.

Stan silently drove the car.

"You like making noise, huh?" Jack grabbed a gym sock and stuffed it into Mick's mouth. He grabbed the duct tape and wound it around Mick's mouth and head tightly. Mick began to breathe in a panic through his nose, and, with what little strength he had left, futilely attempted to buck Jack off with his hips and arms.

He was however handled like a roped calf—and soon found his arms bound to his sides with duct tape, and his legs as well.

"You want to fuck me, mutherfucker? Nobody fucks me!" Jack screamed primitively. "You want to fuck me, steal from me? Time you learn some mutherfucking RESPECT!" Jack roared fiercely as he said *respect*, as if a man possessed, perhaps out of his mind. Terrifying. Jack pulled out a spool of wire and some wire cutters. He unwound the spool, pulling off several feet of wire. Jack snipped and repeated the process.

He took a length of wire and wrapped it around Mick's arms above the elbows, around the chest, twisting the ends together with pliers. Jack twisted the ends tightly until they tore through the duct tape and Mick's skin underneath. He quickly repeated the operation at Mick's elbows, wrists, knees and ankles. Mick could hardly flinch as each new tourniquet was applied, and he was in anguish, knowing that they would not be enough to end his suffering. All the pain became one, except for the rag down his throat. That stood out. The seething, the never-ending fiery choking, the endless suffocation. Please let it end, Mick could cry out only in his mind.

"Oh, you like that, huh, mutherfucker? See I'm just getting started with you tonight, bitch." Jack hit him and hit him and hit him in the face until he just didn't feel like hitting anymore, or because his hands were too sore; he wasn't quite sure.

Blood flowed from Mick's face. It was bloated, bruised, bloodied, beyond recognition. His jaw, which was covered in duct tape, was swollen to telltale proportions and caused him to look other than human, like some deformed experiment.

Jack put his mouth next to Mick's ear, so Mick could feel Jack's breath. He whispered, "You see, I still don't think you've learned your lesson yet. I'm sending you to burn in hell tonight." The black tip of Jack's knife cut through the cartilage at the top of Mick's ear, removing it quickly, cleanly. Jack straddled Mick's stomach; Mick's eyes were opened widely now, the final look of terror on a wild animal half consumed.

Jack held the ear he had cut off close to his mouth. "Do I have your attention now?" Jack threw Mick's ear upon his open eyes. "No fucking stealing! Thieves will be punished. This is a little game I learned in the field called pin cushion. It works especially well with pricks." Jack smiled; he was particularly witty tonight. Mick hardly had life left in him to move an eyelash, let alone his lungs, still suffocating slowly, choking.

"Oh, you like air, do you, bitch?" Jack pulled out a thick cargo belt with a metal fastener and looped it around Mick's stomach. It squeezed out all but the very last of Mick's life.

"Ten minutes," Stan said from the driver's seat, looking in the rearview mirror.

That was hardly enough time, but it would have to do, Jack thought. Mick heard *minutes* through a distant fog and hoped his journey was about to come to an end.

Jack took his long black blade in hand, the one that he carried in his boot. The one that never got pulled, that no one ever saw. He pushed the tip slowly into Mick's cheek bone below the eye, about two inches deep. Jack repeated the process never going more than four inches deep and making sure to miss any vital organs or arteries, but being thorough, very thorough.

Jack finally felt as if a powerful wrong had been righted, as if someone had finally gotten what they deserved. Deep down he knew it would come to this—not this exactly, but . . . "You see, it was your choice, this whole thing." A clear message needed to be sent after all.

"We're almost there," Stan said more quietly.

Jack pulled a twenty-five-pound plate from under the front seat. He placed it on Mick's chest and taped it firmly to him, round and round with duct tape.

"Nighty night, mutherfucker." Jack pulled a little blanket over the sausage that was the dying Mick and leaped into the front seat.

Stan pulled over to the side. The Verrazano bridge was quiet this time of night. Jack and Stan were out of the car quickly. The night air was cool. Jack felt calm like the night. He grabbed Mick and pulled him out by the hair; Stan caught his feet.

"You're garbage," Jack whispered in Mick's ear, and, with a heave, Jack and Stan watched him hit the water below. It was so far down, they couldn't even hear the splash.

BOOK ONE: CHAPTER SEVEN

Detective George Donovan had seen this scene repeatedly, more often in his last five years on the force than the previous seventeen. It was hard to believe he was closing in on twenty-five years. During that time, there was certainly a steady increase in all crime: vandalism, drunk and disorderly. In his estimation, it was drugs and Vietnam that brought a noticeable escalation. The violence level had swelled, and the novelty that a murder call once brought now turned his stomach sour.

Detective Donovan, or Georgie as his wife called him, was a throwback. That man, like a wasp covered in amber, remained unchanged. Yet the perception of its nature had changed dramatically by the passage of time. Yes, time does change things, but it seemed as if time was beginning to change everything more rapidly. George was one of those good-natured guys with a consistently happy disposition. It served him well, because everyone knew he was uncompromising—some would say a stick in the mud. A straight arrow who refused to cut corners for principles' sake. His wife was certain it kept him from advancing up the chain faster, that and the fact that his buzz cut went out of style shortly after he had joined the force.

Detective Donovan's boots shone like glass when he stepped down onto the craggy shore off the Belt Parkway in line with Seventy-Seventh Street in Brooklyn.

"Detective Donovan, I secured the scene. A very nasty one this morning."

"Good morning, Officer Grabowski. Thank you." Detective Donovan was the only man on the force who referred to the stout black-haired man as Officer Grabowski. His name in high school was Henry. It had been wisely changed early on in life by his parents. However, at the academy, it was discovered that his proper Christian name was Hienek, the Polish version of Henry. It was promptly shortened to Hiene by all on the force for the perpetuity of time.

The body that washed up on the rocky shore was a white male, late twenties, early thirties. George had run this drill a few too many times lately, and Hiene was right. This was a nasty one. The victim was gagged and had been bound repeatedly; his hands were still tied behind his back. George knew it was the body of a man, not by the face, which seemed hardly human, but by the open trousers. These days the sex of a victim could not be determined by the length of their hair. An ear was clearly severed. George checked the pockets and could see that the man was tortured. Dozens of stab wounds covered his body. If George were a betting man, he would put his money on drugs or a Vet, perhaps a twofer.

"Have them get this boy out of here."

"Right away. Good to see you, Detective Donovan. Hope the family is well." Heine waved as Officer Donovan strode back up the shore.

George stopped and turned back, absorbing the iconic view: a stout Pollock, draped by the quiet gray-blue expanse and flanked by a deformed corpse. Detective Donovan could imagine Welcome to Brooklyn billboards framing the scene off in the distance. "And to your family as well, Officer Grabowski."

Mick Knall was identified by his fingerprints, which were readily available on file at multiple locations. His mangled face could have made him an extra for *Night of the Living Dead*, that is if the movie had been filmed in color and was actually disturbing. The victim had been tortured. The coroner counted forty-four stab wounds, all from two- to four-inches deep, and all missing vital organs.

Mrs. Knall broke down in tears, when George broke the news. She wasn't surprised, however, and related a story of unresolved mental health issues and poor decision-making skills. The latest included Mick selling fake LSD. She told Detective Donovan how the neighborhood boys, Mick's friends, had come over in a panic yesterday. They were worried something bad had happened to Mick and had begged her to call the police, but it wasn't unusual for him to disappear for a week or more. They were young and anxious, she thought. She had been riding the roller coaster for years.

The leveling off of her tears was cut short by a new pod of wails when the portly woman remembered that a man named Jack came to the door the last day she had seen her son. He was looking for Mick, said he was picking up some parts in place of the money Mick owed him. She knew at the time that it couldn't be true. Mick couldn't even change an oil filter. Her demeanor devolved into a sludge of sobs and repetitive lamentations of "It was him. I should have stopped him. It's all my fault." He was a man still under the care of his mother; she too was lost now.

It didn't take long for Detective Donovan to track down the details of the story. The neighborhood kids were lazy potheads and scared to the bone of this character Jack Finnigan. They needed little coaxing to relay the story of Mick's fake LSD scam on Jack. Finnigan had forced them to pass a note to Mick, while yielding a large buck knife. He was accompanied by some other gorilla, carrying a crowbar.

At Brothers Pub the bartender attempted to play dumb as a rock. Clearly not far off the mark for the dolt. However, with the promise of a squad car checking in on the place multiple times a night till forever, he became slightly less dimwitted. Finnigan's gorilla was an accomplice, a fella named Stan Sesla. They were seen with Knall by multiple patrons, including a neighborhood lowlife named Richard Nazzle. Finnigan was wildly agitated, and Sesla might have gone unnoticed, if it had not been for the crowbar. While it didn't stick out in the dolt's head at the time, perhaps the question concerning "deep water" seemed not so strange in light of new developments.

The mother of Knall's children related a story where Mick came to her door late that night with another man. She heard Mick call the other man *Jack*. She knew then in her bones that something was dead wrong. Her gut told her not to open the door; she had been petrified. George told her to always trust her gut. It was what had kept him alive on the job this long. The fact that Knall was dead seemed to bring her a somber relief.

★★★

Ritchie Nazzle was living back in the quiet neighborhood of Levittown with his folks. His various business ventures had failed to yield significant fruit, through no fault of his own and to none's surprise than his own. He nestled back in his downstairs bedroom, which looked much as it did in high school. When Jack came falling in through the kitchen door, on the side of the house, Ritchie was unamused.

"Body floated up," Jack mumbled, as he reached for the kitchen counter, steadying himself upon a stool. It must have been 11 thirty a.m., and Ritchie was hardly up, still in his drawers and undershirt beneath his robe. Ritchie blocked Jack's path to the living room. Jack looked like shit, as greasy and grimy as any gopher gut you had run across. Ritchie was particularly nervous, not because of the generally wasted, yet crazy Jack Finnigan but by Detective George Donovan, a real-life Joe Friday.

"I know. I know. What the fuck are you doing here? You can't even sit up. How much shit did you do?" Ritchie grabbed Jack around the bicep.

His head bobbed, as his eyes moved down to his lap. "Too much, not enough, I don't know."

"You gotta get out here, lay low, disappear for a while." Ritchie tried to steady Jack to his feet and back out the door.

"Whatever." Jack's resolve to stay steady on the stool increased.

"Look, I'm fucking serious. This detective was here two days ago looking for you and asking questions about that night at the bar."

Jack sat up like a lightning bolt. He moved his long hair away from his face. "What? What did you tell him?" Jack stood to his feet.

"I didn't tell him shit, but he already seemed to know a whole hell of a lot." Which was true. Ritchie didn't tell the detective anything that he didn't already know. And Ritchie was more unsure and ambiguous than anything. Hey, he was loaded that night.

Jack lowered his head and rubbed his forehead. "Like what?"

"Like that you, Stan and Mick were all there. That you were agitated. That we had a drink and talked."

"All right, all right. What else?"

"Nothing really, just trying to confirm details. What time you came in. What time you left. How many drinks did you have. I told him that I really didn't remember. That I was loaded. He asked if it was around midnight, and I said I wasn't sure. Maybe. He said four drinks. I said I think just one." Which was pretty much the case from Ritchie's perspective.

"OK, not too much damage done. Just keep your damn mouth shut." Jack leaned back against the counter.

"You better disappear right now. This detective is a little goose-stepper. I'm telling you, he's got a nose for you." Ritchie tried to steer Jack back toward the door.

"You're right. You're right." Jack was surprised that they were on to him at all, let alone so quickly, but he had already forged a story to explain why he and Mick were together. Time to lay low. They would eventually pull off resources, and the case would go cold. In the long run, nobody cares about a low-life dirtbag, especially the cops. *Good luck finding the knife, boys. Can we see the murder weapon, please?* "Call Louie when you have more on the heat."

"I will, of course. Now get lost. Seriously." With that, Ritchie was finally able to whisk Jack back out through the kitchen door.

★★★

Della had stepped into the kiln of her own accord. It wasn't so much a choice, as the walls of her life were already set ablaze. Once the firing in a kiln is completed, either a thing of beauty has been created or a broken vessel is revealed.

The lunch crowd had subsided, and Potters had its midafternoon lull buoyed by those who drink when others do not. Filling half-empty Heinz ketchup bottles was not enough of a mental distraction to keep the knots in Della's stomach from being uncomfortably noticeable. She suspected that even the alcoholic contents within the bar's full cabinets were not likely to do the trick either.

It had been three months since Guy's fifth-birthday blowout in April. Della had never seen Guy happier; what a party! Mack had gone all-out; he had included all of Guy's favorites. Della had never met anyone like Mack—nobody in her circle of friends or family. He was one of those old-time gentlemen and not just wearing it like a jacket, then taking it off. A man with real principles, like something out of a hokey movie; plus he looked great in his suit! This one day, in the alley behind the bar, a guy sitting in his car dumps an ashtray full of cigarette butts on the parking lot. Well, Mack tore across the lot, and, within seconds, the guy was on all fours picking up the butts and putting them back in his ashtray, apologizing all the while. Littering was wrong, Mack had said.

But the birthday balloons were quickly deflated once morning came after Guy's birthday. While his father's absence had not gone unnoticed by Guy, it was diminished by the euphoric festivities. Della did not let it show to Guy, but she was downright pissed at Jack. Was he so damn selfish and insecure that he couldn't even wish his own son a happy birthday? And then to send Marty with a damned rifle? What bullshit! She had planned on giving Jack a real earful. Mack's house was still a mess, and they were only a few sips into their coffee that morning when Roxie and Paul came screeching into the driveway, bursting in through the screened front porch.

Della knew something was wrong immediately. Roxie should have just been getting to bed by this time of the morning. She was too worked up to talk, and Paul explained that Jack had murdered some guy named Mick from the neighborhood.

Della had momentary vertigo as she was vanquished by dueling emotions, elation and terror, freedom and the feeling of being seized all at once. It was an early rumor, but it was the same one being repeated in various circles all over the island. It was certainly true that Jack and Stan were with Mick at Brothers Pub that night.

The gnawing terror festered as the days rolled to weeks and the weeks to months. Rumors of Jack's arrest seemed to be all the buzz, but the passage of time smothered the din. Della became certain that another escalation was imminent. Her rotted innards told her that, if Jack was not arrested, he was going to take Guy away, right after bashing her brains in. Mack was big and strong and wonderful, but Jack was a trained maniac; he thought about things differently.

Detective Donovan stopped by Mack's house to see whether Della would be willing to get into the kiln. You see, the rumors were correct; the police were onto Jack Finnigan, and they were ready to make an arrest. Except the police were having a hard time locating him; Jack was keeping an extraordinarily low profile. Could Della help by setting up a meeting? No need, since Jack had a supervised visit with his son scheduled.

It seemed too much to ask, to let Guy be used as bait, to catch his murderer of a father. Detective Donovan swore it was the only way to get Jack off the streets. They would get Jack, before he went inside, so that Guy never even noticed. Mack was reluctant at first, but, as always, he asked all the right questions. In the end he agreed with Detective Donovan, and the plan was set in motion.

Everyone agreed that having Della present would only increase the tension. Mack promised that not even a pack of fierce lions would be able to tear Guy away.

Well, today was that day, and the gurgling of the ketchup bottles was drowned out by the gurgling in Della's stomach. The lunchtime crowd here was quiet, as usual. She had asked Prissy to pray for her; maybe, for once, God might actually be on her side. He certainly couldn't be siding with Jack.

Not long ago, on the night before Detective Donovan had come to Mack's looking for a big juicy night crawler, Mack had been presented with an opportunity. He had been taking his usual subway ride home with four senior officers from Chase Manhattan. They were excited about starting a new office in Los Angeles, to expand the bank's lucrative commercial real estate lending into the largely untapped Western market. Untapped by the large Eastern megabanks, that is.

A wife of one of the officers had refused to go; she made it the end of the story. Mack jumped right in and offered to take his place. The four senior officers agreed on the spot to send Mack. Mack asked Della if she and Guy would move with him to LA. If they liked it, they could stay; he would take Della as his wife and adopt Guy as his very own son. They had decided to look at L.A. houses once Jack was arrested. They were going to leave tonight. The bank was giving Mack a two hundred thousand dollar loan to buy a house; they were going to buy a mansion. Della had always wanted to go to L.A., although this was not quite how she had envisioned it. She wondered if there would be movie stars at the hotel where they were staying for this trip.

"Hey, Dell."

A gravelly whisper near the front door was all it took to snap Della back to reality. The snap was less like that of a teen girl's bra and more like that of a chicken's neck. The mere sight of Vinnie made Della nauseated; perhaps she would just pass out. Della tried to keep her composure. "Hey, Vinnie."

"Come on outside. I need to talk to you for a sec."

Vinnie Sullivan was a full head taller than his brother, Stan Sesla. Other than sharing the same crazy Irish mother, the boys shared little else in common physically. Vinnie was considerably taller and larger framed than his brother. Vinnie had fair brown hair and was considered handsome, especially when next to his brother. They were both violently crazy and shared a love of sticking up banks. Both viciously cruel. Where Vinnie was loud, boisterous, always at the middle of a scene, Stan was cold, quiet; he gave you the creeps.

Della's knees buckled. "I'm working, Vin. Come in, sit down. It's been too long. I'll get you a big steak, on the house."

Vinnie stood up straight and took off his sunglasses; he was wearing a long black wool trench coat. "I'll have a beer."

"Great. Come on in. Take a seat. I'll get you a cold beer."

Vinnie sat himself at one of the dark tables in the corner.

Della tried not to panic and decided to take a quick shot at the bar to calm her nerves, while she fetched Vinnie's beer. She ducked quickly behind the bar, swallowing two fingers of Jack Daniel's, and grabbing Vinnie an ice-cold Budweiser.

"Here you go, hon. Whatcha been up to? You shouldn't be such a stranger." The small two-person table separated Della from Vinnie as she leaned against a chair.

Vinnie took a nice long swig of his beer. "Ah." He tilted his beer slightly, as if in a toast. "Did you think I came all the way over here for a steak and a beer, cunt? What did you say to the cops?" Vinnie leaned back against the booth.

Della could feel her cheeks begin to flush. She stuttered out, "What are you talking about?"

"Don't play stupid with me, bitch. You know what I'm talking about." Vinnie leaned his chest forward over the table.

Della stood up straight. "Oh, no, Vin. *That.* Of course not. What are you even talking about? Seriously I don't even know anything. I didn't hear anything. I didn't see anything. I don't know anything. Come on, Vin." Della could feel the blood rush to her face.

"Look, we know you talked to the cops. Last chance, sweetheart." Vinnie moved his trench coat to the side, revealing a holstered Colt nineteen 11—which wasn't really necessary since Della had spent more than enough time with Vin to know the gun never left his side, unless it was in his hand.

Della thought about running. Could he really know that she had spoken with Detective Donovan? What if Vin, Stan and Jack knew about the whole thing? Maybe Vinnie was here to take care of her, while Jack and Stan went for Guy. Della swallowed hard. "I didn't say anything,

Vin. All I know is, they've been asking all over town about Jack, but nobody's seen him. Certainly not me."

Vinnie smashed down his beer on the table, exploding the bottle and sending the table careening to the floor. "If you're fucking lying to me, bitch . . ." Vinnie leaped to his feet.

"I'm not lying, Vinnie, I swear." Della's hands were instinctively clutched to her chest.

"Hey, buddy. Leave it alone already." Mel was one of the regulars, a chubby, bald mail carrier who always enjoyed a pint after lunchtime.

With the speed of a predator, Vinnie was upon the mailman.

Dell realized that Vinnie was about to change Mel's calendar for the next couple months, so she draped her body over the mail carrier like a suit of chain mail. "Vin, he's an idiot. Just leave him alone. It's not worth it, Vin." Della pushed against Vin's chest.

"You're lucky, asshole." Vinnie turned and strolled to the door. "Nice seein' ya, Dell. Stay smart. See ya again *reeaal* soon." He was coy and walked out the door without turning around.

Della decided another two fingers were needed, and Mel decided he would not be showering tonight.

★★★

Jack was caught off guard by the current turn of events. Sitting in front of Judge Goldstein's Supreme Court of the State of New York County of Kings on July Seventh, Nineteen Eighty One, was not Jack's idea of a long Independence Day weekend in Brooklyn. The severity of the current situation was missed by Jack. Being arrested had come as a surprise; being incarcerated had caused some nervousness that perhaps things were going the wrong way. But Jack had kept his cool; he was no dummy. There was simply no case. No murder weapon, no eye witnesses, no hard evidence, no case.

Ritchie was right about one thing. The lead pig sure was Mr. Joe Friday, all right. Had a real hard-on for Jack, coming down with all his pig buddies to arrest Jack in front of his son. What a little pussy piece of shit. Jack would teach that guy a thing or two about manners when he got out of this case. There would be too big of a spotlight at first, but you know what they say about revenge.

Sure Jack would play the part. He came to court, clean shaven, wearing a suit and tie. He would not be shy about his service to the country.

This was Jack's second time appearing before Judge Goldstein, black robed, bald and bifocaled.

"Mr. Finnigan, I felt it necessary for us to meet again today for the purposes of restating, or better yet, to reclarify two points. Two points specifically. The first concerns your representation and the second the charges against you. Do you understand?"

"Yes, Your Honor." Jack did not understand specifically, but he was sure the kind judge was about to enlighten him.

"As discussed at our initial meeting, Mr. Finnigan, your counsel, Mr. Louse, was also counsel for the prosecution's witness, Mr. Richard Nazzle, when he came in to talk to the police about the homicide in which you, as the defendant, are now charged. In doing so, Mr. Louse may have learned confidential information from Mr. Nazzle. Do you understand, Mr. Finnigan?"

"Yes, Your Honor." Of course Jack understood. His attorney had a knack for beating murder raps alleged against his clients. He had been used regularly by Stan's family. Stan's side of the family habitually broke the law and had learned to navigate the system well. Mr. Louse was sent right over for both Jack and Ritchie, free of charge. Stan had a nose for these things. He had hopped a boat to Dublin three days later. Way before the fuzz were even sniffing—smart.

"Do you understand that Mr. Louse's representation could hinder proper cross-examination of the witness against you, especially if there was communication between Mr. Louse and Mr. Nazzle?" Judge Goldstein leaned forward grimly.

"Yes. I understand that. I still request Mr. Louse to be my attorney, because I know personally there was no communication, Your Honor." At least no communication that the court needed to be privy of.

"Well, the court cannot understand, Mr. Finnigan, and will not ask you questions in that regard, about how you can know there was no communication." The judge folded his hands and looked more gravely at Mr. Louse.

Jack had dodged the first bullet. Concerned about Louse and Nazzle? That was a crucial angle. Jack would use Louse to feed Nazzle info for the witness stand and turn the prosecution's case right on its ass. Having a family lawyer you could trust was golden, especially one who was familiar with the finer nuances.

"On the second matter, and I say this to you directly, Counselor. On the subject of murder in the second degree versus the charge of manslaughter in the second degree, did you have a detailed discussion in furtherance of our previous discussion, with your client, as requested by the court? To include the differences in the preponderance of evidence and the severity of penalty upon conviction?"

"I have conferred with the defendant, Your Honor, and we talked about it, as Your Honor has said, and we prefer not to have the lesser included." Mr. Louse was disheveled in appearance. His suit was brown and was covered with a uniformly applied coating of faded oil stains, and, while his suit was large, it seemed not quite large enough. His just evidenced and much-boasted-of oratory skills were hardly overshadowed by his well-kept comb-over.

"With your permission, Counselor, may I address your client directly?" Judge Goldstein motioned with his hand, standing on formality now that the issue of representation was finalized.

"Yes," Mr. Louse motioned back with a slight bow.

"Do you understand what your attorney has said?" Judge Goldstein removed his glasses and rubbed the bridge of his nose.

"Yes." Keep it short and sweet. Did this guy think Jack was a moron? He was not going to jail for a case where the cops had no evidence. Did the judge really think a Long Island jury would send a military hero to jail for the murder of some drug addict in a case with no evidence? Jack would make the jury decide. Including the manslaughter charge gave them an easy out; he was going home after this. Then maybe that cabin in the woods after all.

"Should the jury find you are not guilty of murder because you lacked the intent, they could still find you guilty of lesser crimes, including manslaughter in the second degree, which will call for a much lesser sentence." Judge Goldstein was adamant on the point.

"Just the one charge, no lesser included. We don't make the request." Proud Mr. Louse poked his round belly forward, his hands in his front pockets of his pants.

"In effect then, not only do you not make a request but you are waiving the request for a charge of manslaughter in the second degree?" The judge's emphatic tone conveyed his disapproval.

"Yes, Your Honor." Mr. Louse was very pleased.

★★★

"Dad! Dad, watch this!" Guy ran from the back of the diving board, leaped into the air, spinning like a corkscrew, and plunged into the deep end of the pool. Guy's feet did not touch the ten-foot bottom. He thought only parks had pools that were inside the ground.

"Woo hoo. Great jump, just like a corkscrew. Careful though—when we jump in the pool, we jump from the end, no running, especially on the diving board. When you run around a pool, you could slip and fall, because it's wet. That's very dangerous."

"OK, Dad." The warm pool provided insulation from the crisp, cool air. Guy swam into Mack's strong arms and grabbed hold around his neck. Mack had been a lifeguard at the ocean; he knew all about swimming. He could do a swim called the butterfly. His whole body came out of the pool; he could make the biggest splashes you ever saw. Guy learned all about water safety when they came out to California the first time to find their new house.

They had decided to stay at the Westwood Marquis Hotel. As it just so happened, the hotel was booked solid with young ladies in town for a beauty pageant. Seeing as it was Los Angeles, frolicking by the pool was the only item on the agenda for the afternoon. Mack and Della were busy enjoying piña coladas in a pair of lounge chairs when a stunning blonde in a bright turquoise bikini, no more than nineteen years old, came running toward them. She was soaking wet and held Guy clutched to her tanned bosom. She related a dramatic tale of Guy falling in the pool near her; he was drowning, flailing his arms. She had always been a quick thinker and had plucked him to safety. She was going to give him mouth-to-mouth first aid, but one of her friends said that, if he was talking, he was breathing. That made sense.

Guy smiled, and Mack and Della laughed out their last sip of piña colada. Della informed the young lass that Guy could swim like a fish. "Probably better than you, my dear." Guy said thank-you in his sweet tone, and, with a kiss on her cheek, they all had a riotous laugh, even the blonde with the pretty, but now red, face.

No pretending you are drowning and no running by the pool, Guy had learned.

Mack found the perfect house on their first trip. It was a mansion, by all standards except Los Angeles's. Mack and Della had designs of living by the ocean, Malibu or Santa Monica. Not on two hundred thousand dollars, so instead it was Porter Ranch, a little suburb twenty-five miles north of downtown Los Angeles, on the north side of the San Fernando Valley. Mack and his business partner, Don, looked at different neighborhoods; they both settled on Porter Ranch. It was the best value considering commute time. L.A. traffic, you know; no more subways. Plus it would be nice to have their two families together, Don and Karen had two girls, the eldest would be in the same grade as Guy. It was a blast; the ladies loved the idea of a life of matching pool parties, cocktails and carpooling, not necessarily in that order.

The day they saw the house, the broker didn't have a key; so Guy had to go in through the doggie door and unlock the front door for everyone. So cool!

The house was part of a tract, nestled among the holes of the Porter Valley Country Club in a safe, quiet neighborhood with no crime and great schools. Theirs was twenty two hundred fifty square feet with a two-car garage, just two houses off the sixth green. The steep driveway was wide enough to fit two cars tandem or side by side. The house was about thirty yards from the street and about ten feet higher in elevation. Looking at the house from the sidewalk, the driveway on the right of the dwelling was cut out of the hill, and the residence was flanked on the left by rectangular-shaped shrubs which butted against a white stucco capstone wall with black wrought iron decorating the top that made a ring around the property. The main path to the front of the house, left of the driveway was flanked on both sides by lush green grass and seven cedar trees.

The top of the path gazed into the living room through a fifteen by five foot window, and the front door was the biggest one you had ever seen, with glass all around reaching up two stories!

The house—which looked to be two stories from the front—was white stucco, with wood shingles and a big square column topped by an overhang from the roof and anchored where the paths from the driveway and front walkway met. The house was in actuality a trilevel, with a bedroom, bathroom and living room on the bottom floor. There was a real wood bar with a sink. Sold! The wall behind the bar was cut through, so you could see up into the kitchen, which was wrapped around by a large L-shaped dining/living room. Upstairs included a master with its own en suite bathroom. Who had ever heard of two sinks? It had its own balcony overlooking the backyard. In addition to the master, there were two more bedrooms with another bathroom upstairs as well. Mack said Guy could pick one of the upstairs bedrooms. Guy picked the boy's room that had been filled with Star Wars toys. Guy's room was as big as his grandma's whole house; he didn't think it could possibly be true.

Two weeks before Christmas Nineteen Eighty One, Mack heated the pool to ninety-two degrees, so they could go swimming every night and on the weekends. The steam floating off the pool made it seem as if they were in an ethereal mist. The backyard was serene. The neighbors were not too close, like some of the other houses Mack had seen.

Growing up, Mack remembered none of the houses on his block had even had fences. The layout of this yard was great. There was a patio off the bottom floor with a built-in gas barbecue. With weather like this, Mack could grill every night of the year. The bottom patio had a small grass patch with a Jacuzzi and steps that led up to the pool, which was across from the formal dining room. But maybe the best was the big hill at the back of the yard—no neighbors behind him. Some oleanders covered the hill now, but that was a space Mack could really work with.

Mack had called his friends and family the night of the Long Island blizzard. He told them that he had just finished a swim in his backyard and that they were never coming home.

Guy thought swimming at night was the coolest thing ever. "I love you, Dad." Guy hung off Mack's neck and kissed him on the check. He had started to part his hair on the left, just like Mack, except when they were in the pool. There they would tilt their heads back, blowing bubbles out their noses, so that, when they came up, their hair was slicked back out of their eyes.

"I love you too, *Roooaha*." With little effort Mack heaved Guy high up in the air so that he came down with a splash.

"Do it again!" Guy had hardly taken a breath.

"What about me?" Della called from her usual spot on the foam raft that let her sit half in and half out of the water, so she could work on her tan all day. It was still comfortable in December in California.

"You want to be thrown? Get over here." Mack pulled Della toward him by her ankle, planting a big kiss on her lips as she squealed.

Della Tomasini, floating in her very own heated pool at night, in Los Angeles—who would have ever guessed? She looked through the sliding glass door to the lit Christmas tree in the sparsely furnished living room. Mack had such a good heart, and she could really get used to this. After Jack was arrested, the court had been so accommodating in letting her move out to Los Angeles with Mack and Guy, circumstances being what they were and all.

Back in the beginning of October, just after Guy had started his new school, the verdict came in. Guilty. Della felt as if she had won the jackpot. The pun made her laugh; she was queen of the world.

★★★

The only swimming that Jack was doing was within the recesses of his own mind. It was impossible, simply incomprehensible to him, that the jury had found him guilty. They simply had no cause to convict. The entire case had been circumstantial. No one had even seen Mick Knall killed. Yet somehow Jack had managed to torture him while leaving no evidence of a crime scene. No murder weapon was ever found; Jack had been insistent on this point at trial. The buck knife that he always carried on his hip was presented into evidence, just as Jack knew it would be. That was the knife Jack made sure everyone knew about; he used it for intimidation. The lab reports were clear, there was no blood or human tissue found on the knife. The lab report also stated that it could not be conclusively said to be the same knife that had caused the wounds to Mr. Knall. Jack knew specifically that a buck knife could not have caused those wounds. His boot knife was of a completely different make. It had a different blade: longer, thinner, with a serrated portion. Jack made sure to always keep it hidden from sight, and that certainly hadn't changed. How could they just make believe like it was the same damn knife?

There were also numerous inconsistencies in the witnesses' testimony against him. What color was the paper of the note? How about the ink? Since Mr. Finnigan is a military veteran and always keeps his knife sheaved on his hip, and you say he had it out, how come you can't recall exactly what it looked like? Jack's defense was strong in his own mind.

Jack was beginning to wonder if perhaps he had not been seeing things clearly. And to so wonder was to sew wonder. Even at the outset, Judge Goldstein had attempted a verbal gaveling for the dissolute decision concerning the manslaughter charge. The nature of the prosecution's circumstantial evidence had seemed to the jury rather specific and enveloping. A reed picked, and then another and another, all woven together, then tightly forming an impermeable vessel.

The prosecution was clear. Mick Knall had sold Jack Finnigan fake LSD, and Jack Finnigan was not a man who took to being made the fool. The neighborhood boys were trotted out and respectfully told the same story. Jack had forced them at knifepoint to pass a note to Mick, demanding a thousand dollars, assisted by an unknown gorilla with a tire iron. With tearful testimony, Mick's mother accepted responsibility for her son's death. Yes, it was true. She had found out Mick was making fake acid to sell. She would have called the police, but her son just wasn't cut out for prison. She knew something was wrong when Jack Finnigan showed up that afternoon, saying Mick had promised to give Jack car parts in exchange for the money he was owed. After that, she was inconsolable and had to be helped out of the witness box. The jury's collective heart sank with hers.

Then there was Susie, plain but prettier than the circumstances of the case would have led one to imagine. Her voice cracked as she remembered Mick calling out to a man named Jack. She was wearing the new pajamas Mick had bought her in town that morning—the kids too. He must have spent at least a hundred dollars. It was the nicest thing he had ever done for them.

There were plenty of witnesses at both bars who placed Jack, Stan and Mick together, both coming and going. From all accounts, it was clear that it was not a friendly gathering. The bouncer from the second bar related that they were trying to get money from Mick's old lady as well. Oh, and on the matter of the cargo belt that was used to bind Mick's torso, it just happened to be from a company called Aeroquip. Jack was shacking up with Denise Hagerty at the time, whose father worked in cargo handling for Aeroquip. Very circumstantial, indeed.

But none of that seemed to resonate with Jack at the time. It was Ritchie Nazzle who pushed the blade in deep between Jack's shoulders. Two weeks before the trial, Mr. Louse, who was supposed to be feeding Ritchie testimony points, told Jack that Louse was so sorry, but Mr. Nazzle would be truthfully testifying for the prosecution. That they have him on a warrant for cocaine possession in Florida. And, by the way, things have gotten more expensive than expected. Mr. Louse would be needing some additional funds from Jack for the trial. The money from Stan's uncle had simply run out.

Ritchie testified that Jack had confessed to Ritchie about getting money from Knall and dumping him over the side of the Verrazano. Pointing out the prosecution's deal and the other inconsistencies to the jury had held no sway over them whatsoever in the end. Jack's three alibi witnesses—including his brother, Bobby, who had no police record by the way—meant nothing. His military service, the lack of hard evidence—none of it mattered. When the judge read the verdict, it was as if Jack was shocked back to reality by a heart defibrillator. His first instinct was to run, but it would have made no difference. Except, had he been shot, but he wasn't that lucky, was he.

He managed to get himself transferred to the psych wing, but Jack could tell that it wouldn't be long till he was sent to general population. How could this be happening? Jack was sure he would lose his mind, and perhaps that was the angle. He would certainly appeal. Losing his lawyer, Mr. Louse, two weeks before trial seemed like a valid point also. How could Jack trust the fool when Louse had let the heat get to Ritchie and then had the gall to ask for more money right before trial? His new attorney, Mr. Shewlik, did an admirable job for the price and time, but Ritchie had placed the dagger in just the right spot.

Now Jack had time to think. As he looked back over the chain of events, Jack realized there were some things he could just not remember. Maybe there was something more to the nightmares; plus he certainly had been self-medicating. Maybe this was all related to his military service? Post-traumatic stress disorder was the new buzz around the wing. The convicts said appeals were always rejected, but Jack knew his case was unique.

Everybody simply must understand: they had to let him out. He simply could not spend the rest of his life in prison. Twenty-two years to life, for the murder of some low-life scumbag? You have got to be kidding me. What cruelty. When his mind rested upon the time of his sentence, his stomach sank, and he would nearly vomit. Yet this was not a place to show weakness. He would have to let people know he was not to be fucked with when he got out in the yard. He would get his case appealed, and, if not, he would show them. He would show them just what a government machine would do locked in a cage with animals for the rest of its godforsaken life. He was a man locked in a cage and thrown into the deep, dark bowels of the sea.

★★★

California had long been the destination for those seeking new beginnings; it would be here that the newly forged Flynn family would pan for gold under the warm western skies. Skies that held promise, not the dark clouds of times past. Guy missed his grandparents, his aunt Prissy especially, but his parents promised they would visit. Guy's new bedroom cushioned the blow, and by August the room next door would be occupied by his new baby sister. Now Mack would never leave. Guy would be the best big brother ever; he would never let anyone be mean to his sister. He looked forward to teaching her all the new things he was learning at school.

First and foremost being how to tie a shoe. How could his teacher expect him to know how to tie a shoe if no one had ever shown him before? He didn't even wear laces; his shoes had Velcro fasteners. But still the teacher made him try. Guy was incensed upon returning home the first day. The little man's red face made Mack feel embarrassed, as if he had himself set up Guy for intentional failure. But this was all new to Mack, and, as was his style, he made sure that, from that day forward, Guy was at least two grades ahead in his studies, especially with anything pertaining to numbers.

The clear California skies made it apparent to Della that they were a little too rough around the edges for their new country-club lifestyle. With Mack's help, she worked hard to tone down her Long Island accent. She was able to move the knob from obnoxious to disagreeable. Guy certainly needed exposure to the arts, and what could be more edifying than ballet? Karen was in full agreement, and Lacy and Guy were promptly enrolled.

Guy was initially sold; they were going to perform *Star Wars*, and he was going to be Luke Skywalker. But, by the second class, Guy was informed that his shorts would have to be traded in for tights and his tennis shoes for ballet slippers. His lightsaber was just a stupid foam stick, and there was no fighting or bad guys at all, just silly prancing and marching with a bunch of girls.

Thank goodness that pool parties at Don's house included the Chang family from next door. Their son Lawrence, or Larry as he was called, was two years older than Guy. He was chubby and wore glasses but had studied martial arts with his older brother, Henry, at their father's Chinese school. Henry was sixteen years older than Larry and had trained with Dan Inosanto, Bruce Lee's protégé. Guy's pleading to dump ballet for martial arts was soon echoed by his new friend Larry, and the mantle of Eastern wisdom was hoisted high by Larry's father, Winston. He would extol the benefits of the ancient Chinese art of martial arts. Winston was not, however, aware which martial art this was in particular. Jeet Kune Do, Larry would chime in. But as always, in true Winston fashion, with a beer in each hand, his performance was more than enough to persuade even the soberest observer, which was to be found only in the children.

The world was changing rapidly, and their new position in life had allowed the Flynns, as they were soon to be legally known, to be on the cutting edge of those changes. Mack bought them a VCR. Now Guy could watch *Superman* and *The Empire Strikes Back* any time he wanted to. Mack even filmed Guy during his martial arts class, so Guy could watch himself on TV. He felt like a real-life movie star. Especially on their new twenty-four-inch JVC. The coup de grace though came on Christmas. For the first time in history, technology had caught up with the magic of Santa. Santa was caught red-handed delivering presents underneath the tree. He had brought Guy a new bicycle, Superman sheets, a football, an Atari, Matchbox cars, and there was a puppy! Santa bore a striking resemblance to Don.

They decided to call the puppy Tramp, because he looked a little bit like the dog from *Lady and the Tramp* mixed with a giant schnauzer. He actually came two days before Christmas, since they had rescued him from the pound. He liked the cats, who were finding the sprawling hills of California a true delight—filled with unknowing field mice and gophers that were no match for the urban hunters, Tasha and Rufus. They left carcasses of skulls, guts and the occasional tail in a show of their undying appreciation. Tramp proved to be quite the guard dog as well, but only if you were black or delivering a pizza. Long Island would have suited him well.

As the California sun penetrated Guy's soul, it was rebuffed by the craggy hills holding the memory of his first father. Guy understood what *jail* was now, but not what had caused his father to be locked away. He knew the situation was difficult for his mother; it was a topic that was never to be discussed or mentioned. To fade away like a dream half remembered. But Guy would not forget, and one day he would see his father again. As Guy lay in his bed, tucked safely beneath his Superman sheets, he snuggled his little brown bear, Beary, in the crook of his arm, and thanked God for all that He had done for him and his mother. Tomorrow he would ask his parents if they would let him go to church and if Larry could come over and play.

BOOK TWO: TRANSFORMATION

BOOK TWO: CHAPTER ONE

Guy's frame extended the full length of his twin-size mattress—his Superman blanket long ago exchanged for a simple plaid navy comforter, his Superman Underoos for a plaid pair of Joe Boxer. As the family grew into the upstairs bedrooms, Guy withdrew into the only bedroom on the ground floor, where he spent most of his time, alone, with his 11th grade precalculus text and a twenty-inch JVC, ingested by the white-walled room. Aside from the bed, there was no comfort to be found. Something had changed; perhaps it hadn't. He would have wondered what it was, if it had mattered, if he had cared.

The skies were always sunny in California despite the climate; lately they were a damn scorcher. The sort of days that made young girls shed their clothes, and young boys shed their manners. The Moorish blood that ran through Della's veins from her Sardinian ancestors was warmed, turning her skin to an alluring Puerto Rican brown. She gave Mack a couple kids of his own, a little girl named Pearl and a son they called Herman Mack. They were angelic in appearance: blond hair, blue eyes, tan skin, as if the California sun had bathed their bodies in the womb, or perhaps it was just the Sardinian blood. For Guy the sun was poison; the blistered shoulders of summers past had created an enduring friendship with Coppertone. If one were to look, it would seem that all the Sardinian blood had accumulated in his eyes—his fierce, fierce eyes.

California, with Los Angeles as its hub, was a monument to American exceptionalism. The conquering of Communism's tyranny by the freedom of capitalism had arrived. The days of Jimmy Carter's groveling, with America on bended knee, were replaced by Reagan's trickle-down economics and an army of men ready to subdue the world. This particular army made their base on Wall Street. Fatigues were replaced with gabardine, bullets with dollars. America told the world how it would be, and the world rightly listened. The world made sense this way; the world was better off when it did what America said. Mr. Gorbachev, tear down this wall. Yes, sir, was the correct answer.

The world had not become smaller; America had simply become bigger. We showed the Soviets that our freedom would not prevent us from doing those things necessary. The velvet glove was alluring, but the rise of CNN made it more difficult to keep things like Iran-Contra out of the public's sight. The fall of the Commies clearly justified the ends over the means. The Chinese were innocuous; they knew the only people they would be permitted to run over in tanks were their own. Their endless supply of cheap knickknacks was certainly not . . . overlooked.

The frigidity of years spent in Manhattan preserved Mack's brain and kept him head and shoulders above his sun-basked competitors. He ended up doing quite well—for the bank, that is. His salary of a hundred and fifty thousand dollars a year provided a nice upper-middle-class lifestyle for his expanding family. Though, in L.A., it certainly wasn't going to get you rich. Chase Manhattan supplied him with the East Coast's best financial weapons to fillet the silly Western regional banks. Never heard of lending on LIBOR? Really? There was such a spread between the West's use of the prime rate and the East's use of the LIBOR that Mack had to raise his pricing by two hundred basis points just so people didn't think him a con man. No derivatives? Back up the swap truck, boys. He was funding more than two billion dollars a year in outstanding debt now.

The early eighties were off to a rocky start, but that was certainly due to the Carter malaise and the Volcker squeeze. Reagan and the Wizard of Wall Street, Alan Greenspan, had turned economics into a science. Calculable, with an ever-growing trajectory. Voodoo economics stuck after Black Monday when the Dow dropped over five hundred points, twenty two percent of its value from its high of over twenty two hundred. But it was simply a test. Did we really have the courage of our new convictions? We learned from Milton Friedman that individuals pursuing their separate interests made America great. Greed was great, and we were great, indeed!

The last decade had grown our revenue from five point eight trillion to over eight trillion, while our debt only expanded from seven hundred 11 billion to two point four trillion. It was hard to argue with a thirty three percent debt-to-GDP ratio. A chicken in every pot had literally become a house in every hand. The American dream was in full force, and those who disagreed with it would see where our hard-earned capital was spent: TVs and bullets, bitch.

We moved past actors in office. Our new commander in chief was the former head of the CIA, and he wasn't going to take any shit, especially when it came to our economy's life blood, oil. He let the world know, in no uncertain terms, that the time had come for a New World Order, and, in case no one noticed, America was the last man standing.

Della was feeling her strength as well. Two more kids did not slow her down at all, though they certainly tried to cramp her style. She bounced back to bikini shape with the help of Bally's and doubles tennis at the club. The babysitting co-op, along with the pool, kept the younger kids entertained. Late nights of babysitting became Guy's first job before he was a teen. He was six years older than his sister, eight older than his brother, and very responsible. With Mack now an executive, those fancy dinners out with Della were all part of doing business.

Something was wrong with the world, but Guy couldn't seem to put his finger on it. He always did what he was supposed to do, follow the rules. He was voted most likely to succeed in sixth grade, which was certainly more valuable than most popular. He studied hard and learned the value of perfection. After coming home with a ninety 9 percent on a math exam, Mack had asked him what happened to the other point. Guy learned the valuable lesson that perfection precluded criticism. Until it didn't, that is.

Martial arts provided a spirit of discipline that was carried into his studies, into tennis. His skills in the martial arts studio were unparalleled for his age. Guy started martial arts at six, but by twelve he was training in earnest. Saturdays at Winston's Chinese school was not enough. Guy was already a full head taller than Henry and Larry, and nearly as strong. Dan Inosanto, Bruce Lee's protégé, had a protégé of his own, Cassimore Magda, or Sifu Cass as he liked to be called. While Dan's school was all the way down in Marina Del Rey, Cass decided to open a school in the San Fernando Valley, on Reseda. The rent was cheap. He called it the Magda Institute. There were no silly belts, not even uniforms at first, just a concrete floor in a garage. A grand master, teaching the art of compound fractures, mingled with stick and knife fighting. No tournaments here, just street fighting of the kind that sent people to the hospital.

Henry pushed to have the boys included at the new school. Cass thought it was a joke at first; he wasn't teaching kids-level classes. That was until Henry had the kids demonstrate a free flow sumbrada stick fight, complete with disarms, and a finishing neck choke. Yes, they knew all the footwork and the proper boxing technique also. It's not like Henry hadn't spent all day every Saturday, some Sundays too, for the last seven years teaching them everything he had acquired from Dan.

No, they did not get in fights at school. That is, except once, in first grade, with a bully who liked to bite. He bit Guy hard on the playground one day. Guy looked over his shoulder to his friend Larry, a third-grader, for moral support, who gave him a nod. One bloodied nose assured that Jaws no longer roamed the playground looking for snacks.

Since there was no kids class at the Magda Institute, the boys trained alongside the men, and the kids' technique was better than most. Guy became Sifu Cass's instruction dummy. The extreme flexibility of Guy's young joints allowed Sifu to demonstrate how to really crank down an arm bar. When Guy hit the ground, the thud wasn't quite so loud either.

They started contact boxing when Guy was fourteen. After coming home with a black eye, Della said it was time to stop. Guy carefully explained how he had purposely dropped his guard. Sifu had said it was important to know how it feels to really get punched. If Guy was going to take a punch, it was going to be from Matt, who was twenty-five, with arms like a gorilla, a real iron man. So Guy made some adjustments after that. It was clear that his fifty percent power and Matt's fifty percent were calibrated differently. Guy hit harder; his classmates no longer dropped their guard when they boxed with him.

His mother certainly didn't mind Guy's ferocity when they were out on the tennis court. In fact she liked it, especially when playing doubles at the club. Guy's forearm was wicked; it kept the people playing the net honest or, from a different perspective, nervous. Della liked the attention winning brought; they had fun together when they were on the court. Sometimes they would play at the park, if all the courts were filled at the club. While finishing up a set, Della, in her customary way, had words with a loudmouthed foursome who were waiting for the court. Della had no problem letting the men, who were in their forties, know they could, in no uncertain terms, go fuck themselves. The court was theirs after the set was over, not before.

Set complete, and racquets packed, one of the gents made sure to let Guy know that his mother had a mouth like a horse and a face to go with it. The complainer was a little more than surprised when he came nose to nose with a teenage Guy who posed a question of his own.

"What the fuck did you say about my mother, bitch?" The man was surprised to speechlessness. Especially as he unexpectedly found himself on his heels, backed up against the green fabric-covered chain link fence. "Say it again, mutherfucker, huh? Thought so. What about the rest of you pussies? Real tough now." Guy peered into the eyes of each man individually. "Talk trash to another woman down here again, and you'll see how little I enjoy talking to scum."

Guy's request of his parents to allow him to attend church was a successful one. Since Della was Italian and Mack Irish, it was only natural that they go to the local Catholic church, St. Euphrasia. It was a good time to be a Catholic; the prejudicial looks and sneers had passed. Priests were more than happy on Sunday to forgive their parishioner's sins in exchange for a few Hail Marys and a few more delicious children. And by *children* they meant boys: tasty, delicious boys. A time when men of the cloth could indulge in the darkness they preferred, away from prying eyes that peered after things they shouldn't be concerned with.

Guy enjoyed Sundays at church. He convinced his parents on the merits of catechism classes as well. Guy loved reading stories from the Bible; he only wished they would do it more. His catechism class focused mostly on Catholic rituals and holidays. They hardly ever even read the Bible. Guy did not want to be out of anyone's good graces, let alone God's, so he performed the rituals with vigor. He received all of the available Sacraments. When it was time, he would be Confirmed. Unfortunately for the priests, he had no interest in being an altar boy. Father Sapilis was not only mean but also a bore. Della had no desire to add a third or fourth day of carpooling either.

In sixth grade, Chaminade College Preparatory came around to catechism classes looking for recruits from families with deep pockets. A school where you learned about God with real religion classes. You got to study the Bible in school. Guy was sold. If he could only convince Mack, which seemed doubtful, as Guy was sure the school was expensive. When he worked up the courage to give Mack the brochure, his heart beat with anticipation. Mack related how he had attended Chaminade in New York; he thought it was a great idea.

There Guy had deepened his love for books, great books, classics that stood the test of time. His mother had already fostered in him a desire for the written word. In elementary school, she had taken him to the book mobile and had picked out books for Guy above his age group but not above his intellect. Guy loved being transported to another place, to another time, to see how others lived, to see how we got to where we were. Reading was now compulsory; he had to read ten novels every summer alone. By the time Nineteen Ninety Two rolled around, he was in the 11th grade and had already read many of the great works. Certainly more than anyone who he had met, except for some of his literature teachers.

Guy was a dichotomy in his own right. His martial arts gave him great physical confidence. When he got to Chaminade, a friend of his, the only other kid in school who studied martial arts, beat the shit out of an eighth-grade bully in front of the whole cafeteria. He let the school know that the bully was just lucky he tangled with him instead of Guy. All of the students took notice. It was tested once, on the playground, when one of the kids had kicked Guy in the thigh as hard as he could, after a dispute on the basketball court. Guy only used three-quarters' power, but a Thai roundhouse to the leg fractured the boy's femur, and he had to use a wheelchair for the rest of the year.

Despite this, Guy was a nerd though and through. Being near the top of his class in all of his studies, along with a severe acne problem, had kept all but the smartest girl in school at bay. It wasn't till he began thinking about girls and showering after gym class that he realized how uncomfortable being uncircumcised made him. It was a mental challenge to be an outlier, to be in the minority on something so private, so intimate. He would eventually date the school's brain, Wendelyn, but Guy's chivalry, mixed with acne and shame, meant he was not interested in anything more than heavy petting until he got married. The hot girls liked the jocks anyway. Jocks were assholes, not a one in upper-division classes. Guy would never forget sophomore year. In religion class, they were instructed to tape a piece of paper to their backs and walk around the room writing something nice about the person on their piece of paper. When Guy took his off, someone had written *tomato face*. Guy's face burned brighter than a beefsteak. He had walked around the whole class; everyone had read it. No one had said a word. Guy made sure the offender was ratted out—some stupid jock. Knocking the wind out of him in front of the class did not made Guy feel any better, nor less embarrassed. He didn't even punch him hard.

Guy made a few good friends. It was enough, until the hole growing in his stomach, maybe someplace deeper, said it wasn't.

Guy spent most of his time at home in the downstairs bedroom now, which provided both a space for the gnawing hole in his stomach to grow and some relief from the dramas at home.

His beautiful sister occupied one of the two children's bedrooms upstairs. She found night unconducive to sleep. She was up three, four, five times an evening, crying. She said she saw ghosts.

Della had no patience for foolish nonsense, especially every fucking night, and the frustration became a continual eruption. "Shut your fucking, goddamned mouth, you little piece of shit. Did you hear me, you mutherfucker? Do you want me to give you away? Fine, I will. I'll give you the fuck away, you little piece of shit." All night, every night.

Guy finally moved into the downstairs bedroom when his little brother came. Guy could still hear the noise, but not the words; he guessed that was a bit better or a bit worse, depending on perspective.

His brother was quickly a mama's boy. When he was a toddler, they would regularly have babysitters on the weekend. Herman would make himself so hysterical that he would throw up, every time. Della made sure he got plenty of practice. When Guy was ten, his favorite babysitter was a girl named Cheryl. She was beautiful and kind, with long blond hair. She spoke to Guy like he was a grown-up. One day she told Guy how she smoked pot. Guy was horrified. He had been through D.A.R.E classes in school. He was no dummy, and drugs were for dummies.

She laughed. She guessed Guy was just too little to understand. She promised he would get it when he was older, that he would even smoke pot himself. Never, he promised. He found Cheryl disgusting after that. He told his parents that he and the kids, as he called his siblings, no longer needed babysitters.

Guy wasn't sure why his mother was always so angry with the family, though most of it was directed past him. He wouldn't stand for it like everyone else did. When his mother became particularly vicious with the children, he intervened. Like the time she had ripped his brother down both flights of stairs, his feet dangling above the floor, while she clenched his wrist and swung him. Guy thought his little shoulder would pop out. She screamed what a stupid little boy he was. "You like to cry, you little shit? I'll give you something to cry about."

Guy flew down in a rage. "He's not stupid. You're stupid. Let him go now, or I'll make you cry!" She did let him go. She hurled the same insults at Mack, who had learned to keep his head down and his mouth shut. To make sure he shut off the lights at the office personally. By the time Guy was twelve and had started seventh grade at Chaminade, he garnered only criticism from Mack. Finally no more criticism; then no more speaking, only silence. It was preferable to interaction.

Guy poured himself into his studies, until the mixture was homogeneous. By his junior year in Nineteen Ninety Two, Guy's perspective lacked hope; it lacked joy. He found some excitement with one of the guys from the drama club. Last year on a Friday night, they had told their parents they were sleeping over at a friend's house and drove down to Tijuana. They got into a real Mexican club using their high school IDs. Kenny spoke decent Spanish for a white kid from the Valley.

"Traer la bebida mas fuerte de mi amigo en el bar." Kamikazes, zombies, coco de nadas, and white Russians were all knocked back with ease. The blackout and alcohol poisoning that ensued was severe. But nothing that two white college-prep kids did not plan for well in advance. True, they hardly got back across the border, but Kenny, as the designated driver, was not drinking, and they made sure to pack plenty of trash bags. A night spent sitting on the toilet of a San Diego hotel, vomiting, without being able to raise his head, had left Guy a little closer to death than he had realized. The mere thought of alcohol made him sick. They played Nirvana's *Nevermind* over and over on the car ride back. Guy found it soothing.

Other than that, sneaking out after midnight to drive down to Jerry's Deli on Ventura Boulevard was his only other excitement. He and Kenny would gawk at hot girls in tight dresses coming back from the clubs, while munching on greasy french fries.

137

But it didn't quench the need to pursue the perfect score, the perfect paper. Guy found Vivarin; it helped him stay up all night and study. He bought the little yellow packages from the supermarket; he had a car now that he was sixteen. The more he pursued perfection, the more perfectly round the hole became. His family was an American family, living the American dream. A few kids, a nice house in the 'burbs, his dad had a fancy job. And his parents hated each other.

None of Guy's other family members kept in regular touch, except for instructional Buddhist letters from his father in jail and his less-than-regular phone calls. Jack loved him, as well as Guy could figure, but it was a David Carradine love, detached and didactic. On the Flynn family's last trip to New York, Aunt Roxie had finally told Guy why his father was in prison. She told him all about the brutal murder, the drugs, the times Jack grew up in, the Vietnam War he had served in, the nightmares thereafter. It made sense; at least some things did.

If this was what the fruits of hard labor brought, Guy decided it was not worth the toil. It wasn't an immediate decision, but a gradual sliding down the slope. When awakened to this perspective, it was surprising how you found yourself at the bottom of the mountain you once stood upon. Not quite certain how or why you got there, but certain of its permanence.

Della and Mack stopped going to church when Guy went to Catholic school. Dragging the kids around had become more of a chore than it was worth. Pearl and Herman took First Communion. That should be enough to appease God. Guy dropped martial arts in his junior year in favor of precalculus and AP History.

Guy stared at the popcorn ceiling above his bed, the heels of his six-foot, one hundred fifty five pound frame hung off the bed. He counted in his head: one, two, three, four, five, six, seven, eight, 9, ten, 11, twelve, thirteen, fourteen, fifteen, sixteen, seventeen, eighteen, nineteen, twenty, twenty-one, twenty-two, twenty-three, twenty-four, twenty-five, twenty-six, twenty-seven, twenty-eight, twenty-nine, thirty, thirty-one, thirty-two, thirty-three, thirty-four, thirty-five, thirty-six, thirty-seven, thirty-eight, thirty-nine, forty, forty-one, forty-two, forty-three, forty-four, forty-five, forty-six, forty-seven, forty-eight, forty-nine, fifty, fifty-one, fifty-two, fifty-three, fifty-four, fifty-five, fifty-six, fifty-seven, fifty-eight, fifty-nine, sixty, sixty-one, sixty-two, sixty-three, sixty-four, sixty-five, sixty-six, sixty-seven, sixty-eight, sixty-nine, seventy, seventy-one, seventy-two, seventy-three.

Guy removed the pressure of the razor blade from his left forearm. The four-inch-long gash was clean, deep. The blood, rich and thick, not black but dark. Guy felt a brief calm come over his body. He counted to seventy-three twice more, and then to thirty-seven another seven times. His soul became as deadwood; he wasn't sure when it happened, but he had developed some tools to reconnect with himself, to feel, to order his mind.

Once dead, pain can seem preferable to numbness, to nothingness. Guy would cut his way to the hole and hope it leaked out. It meant wearing a turtleneck under his Sue Mills uniform, but it was worth it, and turtlenecks were in. Confining it his to his left forearm felt controlled. Guy found that ripping off a hard scabbed-over wound allowed him to keep from expanding the real estate used, and provided a trail of blood in place of the tears he wished he could cry. When steel became imperceptible, fire found its mark. Guy let a wooden match burn till it went out. The wound it left was severely painful, not clean, puss-filled, dark and distorted. Guy was thankful for it. He found a Zippo lasted longer.

While it worked, Guy used numbers to keep his mind at bay, combinations of sevens and threes worked best. One of Guy's friends noticed his darkening mood, and, when he saw Guy's arm, he threatened to tell a counselor. Guy talked him out of it. However turning a test in blank, that the teacher knew Guy had the answers to, required a trip to the school counselor nonetheless.

Guy was no fool; he would keep his damn mouth shut. He was tired, and, while only sixteen, he already had his fill of what the world had to offer. After an hour of intense interrogation at the hands of the school counselor, he could keep up the ruse no longer. In a pool of tears, he admitted he was going to kill himself. He would sit in his car in the garage, when everyone was gone during the day. A hose from his tailpipe in through his driver's side window. He thought it was a bit cowardly, but he didn't have access to a gun. No specific date yet but sometime in the next couple weeks, he figured. He wasn't going to make a big deal and cry to everyone about it first, but he didn't like lying either, and the counselor's persistent questions broke down Guy's wall. Sympathy wasn't the point—just quiet, nothingness.

He hoped God would forgive him, but he suspected not. People who killed themselves burned in hell. What a state of despair, when eternity in hell mattered not. Guy tried not to think about that much. They told him to go home; they would call his parents. Guy was crying hysterically by the time they were done. He wasn't sure why, but it still didn't matter; it changed nothing.

The knock at his bedroom was followed by his mother's face looking in at him through the cracked door. About the last person Guy wanted to see.

"Heard you were having a hard time at school. Maybe you should see Dr. Katz." Dr. Katz was Guy's pediatrician.

"Really, Mom? Whatever." And by *whatever*, Guy meant *fuck off*. He picked up his Game Boy, as if he were interested.

"You've got some nerve. What the fuck is your problem, huh?" Della opened the door and walked into Guy's room, looking down on him as he lounged in his boxers on his twin-size mattress.

Guy hurled his Game Boy against the wall, smashing it into a million pieces. Della was startled and took a step back. Breaking something was completely out of character for Guy.

Guy looked at her with fierce, dead eyes. "Like you give a fuck. Get out!"

She did.

An hour later there was another knock at the door. This time there was no delay in its opening. There were three men, two of whom were so large that they crouched their heads to get beneath the door frame.

The men were white. The two in the back must have been nearly six foot seven and easily three hundred fifty pounds each. The one in the front was smaller, six foot four, two fifty. They all had shaved heads and were dressed totally in black. The smaller man was carrying a cylindrical black leather bag.

"We can do this the easy way or the hard way" was how the small man made his introduction.

Guy was caught off guard in a way he found more amusing than alarming. Not off guard like with the counselor, more intriguing. Could it be that something interesting was actually afoot? "What?" Guy sat up in his boxers, smirking.

The gentlemen stepped in closer, and the smaller brute clutched the black bag with both of his hands in front of his body. "You're coming with us. We can do this the hard way or the easy way."

Really? Now this was interesting. Guy summed up the situation quickly. Who were these guys? Where were they going to take Guy? They were certainly former military and definitely combat trained. Probably not with the sort of sophistication that Sifu Cass supplied. These guys were real fighters though, not just classroom students. Guys that liked to fight. Their weight alone, coupled with the small space, made the situation ugly and the outcome uncertain. It was likely Guy would end up going with them, but would there need to be a hospital stop along the way? A simple protest would surely leave him unconscious, until they arrived at their destination. What fun would that be? Especially after he was tied up and beaten with whatever was in that black bag.

"Interesting. I'll get dressed."

"Pants, socks, shirt. We'll grab your shoes. Now."

"Relax, tough guy, unless you feel like doing a round the hard way. Let's go. Wait. Hang on, I want my hat." Guy never wore his Yankees hat.

"Fuck your hat." And the small man grabbed Guy by the bicep.

"I'm taking my hat." With a quick turn of his arm, he was free of the man's grasp. He donned his Yankees hat, backward.

Guy followed between them up the short flight of stairs to reach ground level and to leave out the front door. His parents and siblings had fled the scene—pretty pansy, but still amusing.

There was a white utility van parked at the bottom of the walkway.

"Get in."

"No shit, where're we going?"

"You're going to a mental hospital, where you belong. Keep your mouth shut, and don't try anything stupid, or I'll make you sorry."

"A mental hospital? Are you fucking serious? Oh, this is rich." Guy laughed heartily. OK, was this some sort of joke or what? Why would they take Guy to a mental hospital? It's not like he was crazy. He didn't even think those things really existed outside of the movies or for homeless people. You have got to be kidding me, he thought.

"Keep your mouth shut."

Boy, these guys were edgy; they must have been fed some cock and bull about Guy being the next Bruce Lee. What an amusing and unexpected turn. A mental hospital, who would have thought? Guy recognized the streets as they drove. The same route as to martial arts, straight down Reseda Boulevard. They made a left at Roscoe and turned into Northridge Hospital.

They headed into the ambulance bay, with fifteen doctors and orderlies outside. Guy was obviously quite the big deal.

"When you get out, do as you're told, and that's it. No funny business."

"Relax already, commissar. I've been quiet the whole time, haven't I?"

"Get out."

Guy stepped down onto the parking lot, the three giants behind him, as the guards in white began an encircling movement. The one in the middle pushed a wheelchair forward.

"Sit down, son." He spoke with a thick Indian accent and wore a turban.

Guy turned around and sat down politely. "Nice meeting you, fellas. Look forward to seeing you again soon." Guy waved.

They were not amused. Another hand was before his face with a small white paper cup holding three pills. "Take these."

It did not have the ring of a request. Guy swallowed them down.

Another hand offered a paper cup of water.

"No thanks," Guy replied. He recalled being escorted up through some elevators and multiple locked doors, into a large lobby. He remembered some blurry-faced boys and girls, peering out from cracked doors around the perimeter, but it was more like he was dreaming it.

★★★

"You were off your ass last night, man. They probably gave you Haldol and Ativan. That's what they do when you don't behave. I'm C.J. We have to be up and ready for breakfast by seven o'clock. I already showered. I don't sleep a lot, learned how to cheek my meds. If I'm going to use them, I might as well take a bunch at once, catch a buzz."

"What the fuck?" Guy rubbed his eyes. As if it were possible, this bed was smaller than his own. One against each wall of the small room. Guy's head felt cloudy; he didn't remember falling asleep or even getting into bed. This was certainly the first time he remembered seeing C.J., a Mexican with a teardrop tattoo under his eye. "This is a mental hospital" was all Guy could drawl out.

"That's right, *esse*. You're fucking batshit crazy! Ha, ha, ha." C.J. laughed loudly and pounded his fists on his bed like a gorilla. "What's your deal, *holmes*. Blow? You like to smoke?"

"What? Hell no. I don't do drugs. Why, do you?"

"Hell yes! I've tried it all, homey. PCP, coke, speed. But it's that *yesca* and Marlboro Reds that get my daily attention."

Guy's brow furrowed.

"All right, all right, it's all good. Well, at least there's some fine-ass *heinas* in here."

"Cool." Guy gathered that *heina* was slang for *girl*, since it wasn't a word that came up in Spanish class. "What the hell is *yesca*?"

"Weed, homey. Ganja. Dang, C.J. is going to have to school your ass. Hey, you like to fuck, right? You ain't no virgin or nothing?"

Guy was sixteen, and, yes, he was a virgin, not that it was anybody's business. He got up and looked for his clothes. Time to take a shower.

"No way, man. Bullshit! You a virgin?"

"Yes, as if it matters. Fuck off," Guy said callously.

"Hey, this is Grape Street, *muthafucka*." C.J. held up his two hands in the shape of a G.

Guy's blood was boiling. He turned and stepped to C.J.'s nose, looking him dead in the eye. "My name is Guy. You better hope your friends show up real quick."

"Whoa, *esse*. I was just fucking around, man. No biggie. I didn't lose my virginity till I was thirteen. We're cool, man. You're my friend now. That means Grape Street has your back, *esse*. You're fucking crazy, man. I love you. I'm going to get your ass laid. I'm being serious now."

C.J.'s hug caught Guy off guard. This place was strange.

"Tonight I'll show you how you can order a milkshake for breakfast. I'll get you one of these foam egg crates for your bed. I have two. They're comfortable."

"OK, that's cool."

The day was spent being introduced to staff, and answering questions and questionnaires from all manner of nurses, psychologists and psychiatrists, intermixed with group therapy and mealtime. It was clear right off the bat that the whole wing was filled with fuckups, dropouts, druggies and sluts.

"So what brings you here?"

The first interesting question and it was posed by Dr. Milton Steiner. From the name, Guy guessed he was a Jew. The doctor was handsome, short, five foot eight or so. Gauging by his eyes, it was clear he was highly intelligent. "That's a good question. I was wondering the same thing myself." Guy looked at Dr. Steiner blankly.

"You don't know why you're here?" Dr. Steiner glanced down at his clipboard and back at Guy.

"I'm here because three big guys brought me here in the back of their van," Guy said coldly and flatly.

"Oh, really? That's it?" The doctor stared at Guy inquiringly.

"Look, I don't belong here, OK? I don't do drugs. I get straight As, and I'm a fucking virgin, OK?"

"What does being a virgin have to do with killing yourself? May I see your arm, please?"

"Here it is." Guy rolled up his right sleeve.

"The other one, please."

Guy rolled his eyes and turned his head to stare off into space as he revealed his other arm for inspection.

"Wow, that's one of the worst ones I've seen. So you don't think you belong here, huh? Are there more?"

"That's the only spot," Guy replied, which was true.

"Does it make you feel better?" The doctor spoke softly.

"Sometimes."

"We're going to work on that. So I saw in your chart, you count numbers in your head?"

"Yeah seventy-three, thirty-seven."

"You like to wash your hands a lot?" Dr. Steiner asked.

It seemed a peculiar question. "Not especially."

"Ever heard of obsessive-compulsive disorder? You do anything else with numbers, touching things, repetition?"

"Well, I like the TV volume on twenty-one, and it needs to be turned off on Channel seven, but after it was on Channel three."

"You don't find that strange?" the doctor asked, a puzzled expression on his face.

"It just makes me comfortable. Why?" Who really cared what channel the TV was on? Big deal.

"Well, I guess they don't teach you about obsessive-compulsive disorder in upper-division math at Chaminade, huh? I hated math. Never got through calculus at Columbia."

"What? What are you some kind of wiseass?" Guy found the remark witty rather than offensive, but it still needed to be mentioned.

"Just trying to make you smile. You're wound a little tight, huh? Taking Vivarin and not sleeping doesn't help, sorry to let you know. I'm going to give you some Anafranil. It works great for OCD and will help you get a decent night's rest. It's going to be OK. I saw your picture from the art therapy class this morning. A big tree with a knothole in the middle. Very clever. You read that in a book, I gather?"

Guy smiled. "Yeah, I was at least trying to amuse myself." Somewhere along the line Guy had read that drawing trees with knotholes was a sign of sexual abuse.

"Very amusing. I'm sure Kim thought so. You'll hear she's been raped a few times."

"Wow, shit, hold on. I was just fucking around. OK. I got it. No problem."

"It's not a problem. We are all open about our problems here, all of them. No embarrassment. We support each other. We find new ways to cope. You do need to be here. Just give it a chance. You'll see. Things can be different."

"Fine, whatever."

"Fucked-up, insecure, neurotic and emotional. F-I-N-E. That's the way most of the kids feel here at first. It's OK. We have group therapy Tuesday and Thursday evenings, parents included. Your mom and dad will be here if a couple of weeks. I'll be here too. It will be OK. We will take things slow. And if you want to tell me to fuck off, just tell me to fuck off or whatever." Dr. Steiner gave a smirk and half a wink.

Guy found Milton Steiner as intriguing as Guy's new set of circumstances. Things were regimented and ordered; he liked that. He wasn't allowed to worry about homework; that was weird. He had no idea where this path was leading, but it was different, interesting, so Guy walked and inhaled. There was lots of talking too, which was weirder than no homework, so Guy mostly listened. The medicine he was taking seemed to give him some nervous energy; he burned it off by pacing, which had become a bit of a peculiar habit since he had started taking the Anafranil.

He enjoyed listening to the other kids. They were real, not like most of the kids at his school. They had real problems, fucked-up parents, most of them were poor. The same themes in different variations, all forms of abuse: physical, mental, sexual, neglect, just downright cruelty. They turned to drugs and gangs for solace, most of them had never read a real book. But they were real, and they felt. Guy began to feel an emotional connection with some of them which brought an unusual comfort.

For whatever reason, they all seemed to like him. They thought he was the crazy one.

He taught C.J. martial arts at night when everyone slept. C.J. made Guy laugh. C.J. taught Guy about drugs and girls, tagging and gangs. How things really worked out on the streets. Guy even let C.J. show him how he could make himself pass out. C.J. went first of course. Guy stood up with his head down near his waist and hyperventilated for two minutes. Then he took a giant breath of air and held it, standing up straight against the wall. C.J. pushed both of his hands against Guy's chest as hard as he could, until Guy fell to the floor like a sack of potatoes. Guy woke up with a strange spinning in his head. He didn't even remember falling. C.J. told Guy you could also do it by strangling the person, but pushing on the chest worked best. After that C.J. flooded the carpet with water and soap, and played like it was a Slip 'N Slide in his boxers. Guy wasn't much into property damage, but he still couldn't hide his smile.

Guy enjoyed visiting time, but tonight, when the bell tolled, it meant Guy would be seeing his parents for the first time, and a numbed nervousness set over his body. Yesterday Kenny, his friend from drama class, came to visit Guy with some McDonald's and a carton of Ben & Jerry's chocolate chip cookie dough ice cream, a new favorite. He let Guy know that Kenny's parents had said Guy and Kenny couldn't be friends anymore. He was genuinely sorry. Guy was a legend at school now, if he cared. Kids were saying how he threw a chair through the principal's window. Kenny got invited to a couple parties.

Guy could see that things were not going to be the same anymore; he just wasn't sure what they would be. At least C.J. and Kim had friends who came to visit every night.

"Bro, we are going to get you so fucking stoned when we get out of this place!" C.J. was laughing and smiling so big, it looked as if his face would split.

"No shit. I can't wait! I have the sweetest little pipe and chocolate Thai stashed in my closet, for when I get home." Kim was fourteen but could run social circles around most of the guys. Her long brown hair framed her impish face. She was cute and a real wiseass.

"Oh, just wait, Kim! My mom got the fattest new bong, that shit gets you *hiiiigh!*" John Brown was Kim's friend from school, when they bothered to go.

Freaky but damn cool. The sort of kid who did whatever the hell he wanted to. That certainly didn't include school. He was sort of a gothic gangster. He had cool-kid hair. Shaved all around the sides and back, long on the top, pulled back into a little three-inch ponytail. Black jeans, black Doc Martens boots and a wallet chain. He would come in wearing sunglasses, after riding his bike across the valley. It didn't have brakes, only Doc Martens. He was certainly getting laid. "I'm John Brown, bitch" was his favorite retort.

"Look at this." John pulled back his lip and showed Kim how he was filing his incisors to a point.

"Hot!" Kim smiled.

"Sara thought so! Ha, ha, made her neck bleed." John laughed as he opened his mouth and touched his tongue to the tip of his incisor. "She was so fucking hot. She gobbled my cock right up to the balls. I was like, holy shit! Busted a nut right down her throat. She swallowed most of it. Ha, ha. Said it was her first time swallowing. Yeah right. You just swallowed a python right out the gate. Sure, honey." John cracked himself up, and everyone else along with him.

"Oh, shit." C.J. reached across for the high-five. "Who's down with OPP."

"Yeah, you know me," John shot back, quick as a whip.

"You guys are so stupid." Kim laughed. "Fucking Sara. What a slut! Once Guy gets out of here, we are on a mission to get him stoned out of his face, and then he's getting his cherry popped." Kim punched Guy in the belly.

While he wasn't an athlete, all those years of martial arts had kept him lean and hard. Yet he turned red, just as she knew he would. She thought it was cute. She was one of the few who was still able to embarrass him.

146

"All right, anybody who's not here for group, time to clear out." Achmed was looking specifically at John Brown.

"*All right, anybody who's not here for group, time to clear out,*" John parroted back in his most obnoxious Indian accent, shaking his head back and forth, and doing his best to look like a moron. The group laughed loudly.

"Tell your mom I said hey." John looked at Guy and laughed. "Seriously, good luck. See you guys tomorrow." John went for the door.

"Thanks, John." Guy meant it. He was nervous; he was not looking forward to seeing his parents.

Though she wasn't allowed to, Kim took Guy by the hand and led him into the large room used for group. The chairs were already arranged near the walls in a circle. She sat Guy beside her.

"C.J., sit down next to Guy. It's going to be fine. We're gonna be right here. I think my mom's coming tonight. You'll see what a cunt she is."

"My dad would come, but he's drunk by now. At least I get free beer." C.J. laughed; his joke came across more sad than funny.

The rest of the kids and their parents poured in along with Dr. Steiner and his colleague, Dr. Karen Horney. She was blonde, beautiful. Smart and funny but without Dr. Steiner's wiseassery. Still, Dr. Steiner was smarter. One of the few men Guy found at times a step ahead of himself. Whenever it happened, he was thoroughly amused.

Kim and her mother certainly could go at it, and they did. They chewed through nearly half the time for the ninety-minute group. Guy was relieved.

"You think you can just do whatever the fuck you want, don't you? Well, you can't. You're fourteen, and, when you're home, there's going to be no more smoking pot, no drinking, no boys in the house, and you're going back to continuation school."

Kim's mom sure was a bitch; they had been going back and forth now, more or less heatedly, for forty minutes. Kim's mother, Kandy, short for Kandace, was wearing short jean shorts and a white T-shirt whose contours seemed to mesmerize the eyes. It was easy to let her drone on for a while. Poor Kim.

"I learned it from watching you, Mom, OK?" Kim and a couple of the other teens laughed; that was the line made famous from the regularly aired government commercial for the antidrug campaign at *http://www.youtube.com/watch?v=rfj3dPkeaqi*. "You're such a whore, Mom, God! Why don't you take your own advice? Why do you think Dad left you in the first place?"

"You little wretch. I will beat your ass, sweetheart. You hear me?" Kandy was up to her feet.

Guy unglued his gaze from her and shifted it over to Kim.

"Settle down. That's enough for tonight." Dr. Steiner motioned Kandy back to her seat.

"What a circus act, wow!" Della gasped. "Does anyone else get a turn?"

Mack sat beside her, looking defeated, quiet.

"Please, that's why we're here, Mrs. Flynn. We're here to support each other, to talk about our problems in a safe environment." Dr. Steiner motioned for her to continue.

"Well, it's hard to see how, after a show like that, but whatever, I guess."

As his mother looked over, Guy reluctantly made eye contact.

"So are you done with this shit or what?"

Guy looked over at Kim and then to Dr. Steiner. His mom really was clueless, wasn't she?

"Nothing to say?" Della shot back across the room sharply.

"What do you want me to say, Mom?" Guy said drily. You've got to be kidding me, he thought, this cannot be happening. He knew this was going to be a disaster.

"I want you to say you're ready to come home," Della said pointedly, sitting up straight in her folding chair.

Guy looked to Dr. Steiner and took a comforting glance into Karen's eyes. She was younger than Milton, and her demeanor was more sensitive and comforting, especially the tone and inflection of her voice. Her blond hair came down to her shoulders, and sometimes she ran group by herself. Guy found her to be one of the kindest people he had run across. She was witty too; she had to be sitting next to Milton.

Karen addressed his mother. "Mrs. Flynn, Guy's not ready to come home yet. We take things slow, especially the first time we have the family back together. Why don't you start with how it feels to have Guy away from home?" Dr. Horney looked at Della directly; her words were calm and succinct.

"Perfect. That sounds like a great place to start. Because you know what? I've had just about enough of everybody's bullshit, all right? Enough of his bullshit." Della pointed down at Mack in a most demeaning way. "Enough of your bullshit too." Della looked over at Guy. "I'm done, you hear me? I've had enough. I'm taking care of me now. We're getting divorced." Della's finger whipped back and forth between herself and Mack. "Mack moved out of the house." Della was finally able to get it off her chest.

"What?" Not what Guy was expecting. If Mack was the sort of man to cry, he would have.

"Yeah, that's right. I'm seeing Paul Blobel from up the street. You know his son Chris."

Chris and Guy were the same age; they went to the same elementary school. Chris was a snot-nosed dumb jock. Chris was ranked number one in men's and boy's juniors at the club. His father Paul was number two.

"The fucking pool man? Are you kidding me?" She was fucking their pool man.

"He's not just a pool man. He has his own pool company. He's getting divorced too. He moved in over the weekend."

"You have got to be fucking kidding me. Have you lost your mind?" So his mother was going to burn down all of their futures, so she could fuck the pool-cleaning stud at the club.

Kim grabbed Guy's hand and squeezed it tight. "It's OK," she whispered.

Guy made the mistake of looking back at Dr. Steiner and then to Karen; the tears welled up in his eyes.

"I'm done, thanks." Guy rose to his feet.

"Get back here. We're not done yet." Della stood to her feet, as Guy rushed out the door.

Kim was up to her feet as well. "Anyone ever tell you that you're a real cunt, lady? I'm sorry your wife is such a bitch, sir." Kim looked down at Mack, who seemed to crack half a smile. "What is it with L.A., huh? All the women here are whores." Kim held up her fingers in a peace sign but continued to glare at her mother and Della. "Might help to keep those legs crossed, sluts." Kim then crossed her fingers after she said *sluts*. With that, she stormed out, toward Guy's room.

Guy's hand was swollen and purple; his wall had taken a solid shot. With the thud, group ended early. All visitors were sent on their way.

Guy had snuck out a plastic knife from the cafeteria at his very first breakfast here. He sat on the floor against C.J.'s bed, so Guy could look toward the door. The little plastic knife would be difficult to cut with, but it was serrated. With some effort, Guy pressed it hard into his forearm, with his thumb over the blade, so the knife wouldn't snap. The white layers of skin peeled away, but no blood. He moved the blade quickly until the blade began to blur. Red warmth, deeper than he had thought. Not in some failed suicide attempt, but simply for the pain that cut through the numbness and for a moment to let the rot out.

"No, Guy, stop, please." Kim stood at the foot of Guy's bed. "You've been doing so good. Please stop. Guy, I hate to see you like this. For me, please."

Guy put the knife on the floor next to his hip.

"You should have seen the look on your mom's face when I called her a cunt." Kim smiled and put her hands on her jutted-out hips, with a look of accomplishment upon her face.

"You called my mom a cunt?" Guy looked up from his work to Kim's smiling face.

"Yeah, she almost shit herself!"

"Thanks."

"Code Red. Back to your room, Kim." Achmed pushed Kim out of Guy's room quickly.

"Relax, Achmed. He's fine now. His mom is just a stupid cunt, that's all."

"Code Red, Code Red" came over the loudspeakers, along with buzzing noises. The children were locked in their rooms; nighttime activities were off the agenda.

Really? Totally unnecessary, Guy thought, but if that's the way they wanted it, OK. "Achmed, I'm calmed down. Let it go. Don't make this into a bigger deal than it needs to be." Guy placed his palm over the top of the little knife. As Achmed stepped toward him, Guy put the knife back in his wound and extended one of his legs.

"Time to go get your friends, Achmed. Fuck off."

Seemed like a wise suggestion. The ensuing standoff lasted for nearly an hour, which gave Guy plenty of opportunity to expand the real estate on his forearm. All the king's men were scared of Guy and his little plastic knife. Guy found it pretty pathetic. In the end, as a personal request from Karen, Guy gently tossed the knife to the door.

He was then promptly bum-rushed by fifteen of Achmed's closest, largest friends. Guy had no intention of actually hurting anyone, but he wasn't going to make it easy for them. It took them another hour to pin him down enough to finally shoot him up. Guy hadn't even thrown a punch; he was just a good wiggler. Once they got the needle in, all the wiggling stopped.

★★★

When Guy woke up, he wasn't sure when it was, but it seemed to be morningish. He was in a room by himself, strapped to a bed with restraints. He was on his back; his hands were cuffed next to his ears, his ankles in leather leg cuffs. Leather belts were positioned at his knees, waist and chest.

"Really, Achmed? Are you fucking kidding me, you pussy? Good morning, everybody. Is it morning?" Guy yelled out, feeling a bit jovial.

"You made it, Guy. Good morning." Kim's voice rang out first, coming through the walls.

"Good morning. You guys have to see this. They have me strapped to a fucking bed."

"It's almost good 'afternoon,' *esse*." C.J. laughed. "I've seen that shit personally. Never again, homey. I do not fuck around with those restraints. Gives me claustrophobia and shit. C.J. does not go on red, homey."

Achmed poked his head through the door. "You feeling better?"

"Why don't you take these restraints off and find out? You know, you kinda deserve to have the shit smacked out of you, Achmed." Guy laughed.

"OK, then, see you later." Achmed closed the door.

"Seriously, Achmed, I didn't even touch you yesterday. You hit me like twenty times. I was just fucking around. Come on." The restraints were uncomfortable now that Guy was awake; he tried fruitlessly to regain his slumber.

"Settle down, Guy, or they are not going to let you out of there," Kim yelled through the door.

"OK, OK." Guy tried to let his mind drift.

BOOK TWO: CHAPTER TWO

The engine to Guy's Nineteen Eighty Two black Mustang GT was loud enough that the neighbors knew when it was started and when it drove by. Guy first car had been Mack's old Volvo, but an accident and four thousand dollars in insurance money purchased the 'stang over the summer. The Mustang was parked on the street in front of the house as Guy pulled up with Mack on the way back from the hospital.

Mack was quiet. He had said he was sorry; he looked defeated. Guy asked Mack why he didn't beat the shit out of Paul. Mack recited a poem about setting a bird free; if it doesn't come back, it was never really yours to begin with. Horseshit, Guy thought. A blue pickup truck was parked in the driveway, clearly Paul's. Mack made Guy promise to keep the peace for the sake of his younger brother and sister.

His mother's chicken cutlets were about the only thing that was delicious about dinner, but they were delicious, indeed. Paul, Herman, Pearl, Della and Guy all sitting around the table pretending to be normal as best they could. Everyone was happy to have him home, though *nervous* seemed a more apt description. In two months it seemed his life was turned upside down, permanently altered. How time changes things.

The changes were swift, different than Guy could have imagined. Guy lost control of his destiny. Shunned not only by his friends but his school as well. He thought the Catholic school had wanted to help, but the administrator said Guy was too far behind to be able to get caught up. He was locked away for just over two months; it didn't seem to matter that he was a year or two ahead of the average students in most subjects. The only way Guy ever spoke to hot girls was in his math class, when they needed his help with their homework. Julia Cernelia or Michele Dowthwaite, among others, were a sort of high school goddess, so beautiful that their every line, every curve, was seared into your permanent memory. Guy would let the hot female volleyball players a year older cheat off of him.

After that first group therapy, it took another month before Guy spoke to his mother again, and another month before he was released on the twenty second of December, Nineteen Ninety Two. He had spent Halloween and Thanksgiving in the effective and safe looney bin. *Merry Christmas! This year Guy gets to be the only kid in his class who doesn't get to go to college, hurrah!*

Not like Mack was going to pay for Guy's school after all this. He could imagine that conversation: *So I know Mom is fucking the pool man and you live in this shitty apartment on Reseda Boulevard, but can you pay for my college?*

Kenny had placed one last call to Guy while he was still in the hospital. Wendelyn was dating their friend Ryan. Kenny wanted to tell Guy before Guy got out, while he still had time to think about it, to take care of himself. Guy and Wendelyn hadn't dated in a while, but it sure was a dick move on Ryan's part.

Wendy was one of the few people Guy could ever really talk to. That's because she was smarter than he was. She was so, so smart. She probably wanted to lose her virginity, now that Guy looked back on it, but he would have never done that to her.

Guy figured this was why kids got stoned. He was about to find out— once he made a side trip.

Guy was feeling frisky; he was free, alive and you know what? Now nobody was going to tell him what to do. As he turned onto Ryan's block, he drove slowly to keep his engine from roaring. He turned off his headlights and parked two houses down. The night air was cool for L.A., low sixties. It was almost 9 o'clock, dark. Guy walked halfway up the driveway, knelt to the ground and pulled out a large black Sharpie marker. He wrote:

ANTICIPATION OF DEATH IS WORSE THAN DEATH
ITSELF.

He used capital letters, about twelve inches long. Not like he was going to kill Ryan or beat him up or ever even talk to him again. But there was nothing like a good Steven Seagal line to strike fear into the heart of a man, let alone a boy.

★★★

Guy turned on his JVC detachable-face CD player. The album was *Appetite for Destruction.* The song was "Mr. Brownstone." Guy cranked up the volume, seventy-three, no seventy-one. Guy was no one's prisoner now. He chuckled to himself. *Mr. Brownstone* meant *heroin.* How many times had he sung this song without even realizing? He thought back to the dances in high school. Never was the floor more packed than for Grandmaster Flash's "White Lines." Guy thought it was *white lies,* but really the song was so popular because, when they shouted *freeze,* everyone would stop dancing and freeze in place. When they shouted *rock,* everyone would start dancing crazy. The song was about freebasing cocaine. Guy laughed heartily. He knew none of his friends realized it either. A bunch of white kids dancing while the song played. There were some things Guy could laugh at.

Guy pulled onto Rinaldi and drove east toward Van Nuys Boulevard. Seeing Kim away from any confines—what a delight. He would normally take the One Eighteen over to Van Nuys, the shit part of the Valley, but tonight he was in no rush. The change in the Valley, it was part of the reason he had really wanted to go to Chaminade for junior high, even though all his friends were going to public school.

Guy was in fifth grade when they started busing kids in from the inner city. The kids were black and Mexican. They were nice kids; a couple of the guys were great at kick ball. But in school, they were far enough behind to be considered stupid. Guy knew it wasn't their fault. It wasn't like it was just one or two of them—it was all of them. They all wanted to be smart, and they were embarrassed when they became aware of the disparity.

Guy remembered Keisha, a pretty black girl, dark as anyone Guy had ever seen, even in a magazine. Oral book reports were assigned; the teacher was clear on the parameters. Keisha presented *Dumbo*, the picture book. She flipped through the pictured pages and fumbled through a weak recollection of the story. Reading the one or two sentences per page would have been better. Most of the kids laughed; Guy didn't. She had picked the book she thought she could do best.

Guy's report was on a biography for George Washington Carver. Carver did all sorts of amazing things with peanuts, and saying he was born into slavery puts his early family life mildly. Guy wrote a five-page report which was required as well. His oral presentation in front of the class was from memory. How could you be expected to know how to tie your shoes, if no one ever taught you?

So this was Van Nuys at night. People were out walking around. Guy pulled his Mustang one house past Kim's. She told him to honk, but that seemed rude. Guy turned the engine off and got out of his car. The one-story houses were small, ringed with chain link fences. Probably built in the fifties, a bit dilapidated.

Kim came bounding down from the side of her house like a little bunny; she was so cute and perky. Her long brown hair bounced. "Dude, I told you to honk." She punched him right in the chest. At the hospital, Kim was always on yellow; she didn't care.

"What? That's rude." Guy shrugged his shoulders.

"Oh! I have so much to teach you, Smallville."

Guy used to wear his hair like Clark Kent, parted on the left. But one night C.J. helped Guy slick back his hair, the same way C.J. wore it. The

155

same way Pat Riley did and like when Guy was in the pool with Mack. Guy wore it that way ever since.

Kim leaped into Guy's arms. When he caught her, she felt so good, safe.

"I love you. I'm so glad you're out." She squeezed Guy tightly with her arms and legs. "Like I said, I'm getting you high as a mutherfucker." She giggled; her nose ticked Guy's ear. "Is that your car? *Sooo* fucking sick!"

"It's quick." Guy smiled.

Kim jumped down and pulled him by the hand. He unlocked the passenger side door and let her in. It was a two-door, but the backseats were roomy; you could put three in the back if you wanted, two real comfortably. Kim slid into the front seat; she was wearing baggy blue jeans, a black sports bra with an open jean jacket. She had a Rastafarian bandanna tied around her head and big silver hoop earrings.

Guy wore blue jeans and a plaid shirt; he sat in the driver's seat and turned the power to Accessory. The volume on the radio was low. *Appetite for Destruction* was a hit with most crowds.

"I need you to listen to me for a minute, Guy, OK?"

"Of course, what's up?"

"Well, you and me, Guy, we both been through a lot, right?"

"Of course." In that sentence was hidden their deepest, darkest secrets. Those things they had shared with each other through circumstances and conversation, the matters at the core.

"I mean, we know everything about each other, right? Like everything. You know it's been hard, but we made it through, and we're gonna make it though."

"You know, I'm always there for you, no matter what."

See, the thing about Guy was, he was nerdy. Nerdy in that he knew all sorts of stuff about all sorts of stuff. And not just a little, but real things that happened, or things people wrote about or thought. Guy was logical, rational, well-spoken, except that . . .

Except that it became clear, to everyone, that, while it was rare, you didn't want to see Guy angry. Guy wasn't cruel, but when he saw people taking advantage of the weak, it boiled his blood. He would seem to become disconnected, fixated, without fear or concern.

"That's why I love you, but you are seriously crazy, you know that? You need to chill the fuck out. I'm being serious, Guy. Everyone knows you're wound way too tight."

"Only a little too tight." Guy laughed lightly and touched her hand gently.

"A little too tight?" Kim looked in his eyes and stroked his cheek softly. "It's OK. You know you're one of the few good guys out there, Smalls."

"You're always too kind to me." Guy looked up at the ceiling of his car and fought back a tear. Kim's words were always touching, and the feel of her hand against his cheek melted his heart.

"No being sad." Kim made her voice deeper, stern. She draped her body against Guy's shoulder; he looked her in the eyes. "Look, I know you're not out there beating the shit out of people every day, and, if you did, they'd damn deserve it. But you're going to be eighteen soon, Guy. You'll go to jail, just like your dad, OK? It doesn't matter who started it. You're dangerous and, when you get that look . . . You promise me right now that you are going to chill the fuck out. Milton and Karen already told you like a hundred times."

"I know. I know." Guy looked at her gently.

"No, you don't know! That's why you're lucky you have me, fucker. I'm gonna show you how to relax." She talked slow and touched his chest.

She pulled a ziplock bag from her baggy pants. The pipe was dark brown wood; it was about as long as Guy's middle finger, smooth. About an inch and a half thick, with a bowl cut into the middle. Kim pulled some marijuana from the bag. It was brownish green and looked a little like a juniper bush.

"You have a book or something? Of course you have a book. Pass me a book." She looked at him.

"Ah, sure." Guy grabbed something from the backseat. "I have a notebook."

"Perfect." Kim grabbed it excitedly. "So much potential, Guy. You have such a good heart. You always know the right thing to do. That's part of the problem though!" She wagged her finger. "You can't *not* relax when Mary Jane is involved!" Kim sang "Mary Jane."

When finished singing, she said, "Then I'm gonna make you cool." Kim puckered her lips and pointed.

"Get out of here." Guy pushed her and laughed. "Are you going to load that pipe or just poke fun?"

"Poke fun." Kim giggled and poked Guy in the ribs. "Lesson one. Break apart the weed." Kim broke up the weed on the little white notebook. "It'll smoke better."

"Why does it smoke better?" Guy wanted to know. He figured it better to ask Kim than to look foolish with someone else.

"Because you take out the seeds. They pop, and the stems don't taste good." She broke apart the small quarter-size nug.

"Do the seeds or the stems get you high?" That was a good question, Guy thought.

"Nope, throw 'em away." Kim opened her door and dumped a little handful of stems and seeds into the gutter. She loaded half the pot into her pipe.

"When I light it, breath in deep, all the way in. Don't be a fucking pussy. Now, you will probably cough like a pussy, which is fine. Everybody coughs." She put the pipe to his lips and lit the plastic Bic lighter.

Guy inhaled deeply. He could feel the smoke in his lungs. It felt a little uncomfortable, no pain though. Guy could hold his breath for almost two minutes when he was messing around in the pool. He let out a little cough so as not to be rude.

""That's right." Kim took two big lungfuls. She blew a smoke ring from the second. She lit the pipe for Guy again. "Take two hits this time. I want to see smoke!"

Guy did as requested and turned the bowl to ash in the process. "Sorry, I think I finished it." Guy laughed a bit.

"Yep, you cashed it, perfect! Pretty good hit. Feeling it?" Kim rubbed his arm.

"I don't think so." Guy didn't think he felt anything yet.

"Where is Angie when you need her? Her dad always has the bombest weed. She was supposed to hook. I have one more big bowl. Twice as big as the last one, and you're smoking the whole thing." She packed the rest of the marijuana into her pipe.

"Let's share it. It's totally cool." Guy wasn't going to be bummed if he only caught a little buzz, or no buzz at all for that matter.

"I said, I was getting you high your first time. I've been high like a million times. Like seriously fucking high, OK!" Kim laughed. "Just like I promised. Plus I have a whole pack of Reds. You know I was dying for my Reds." Kim pulled out a pack of Marlboro Reds and lit one up. "OK, your turn. Smoke the whole thing please, and then tell me you're not high yet." Kim took a long drag from the Marlboro Red she held from between her unpainted fingernails.

Guy took a nice big hit.

"So did you get that Cypress Hill album yet?" Kim looked at him inquisitively.

"Yep." Guy motioned to the glove box. Kim opened it and pulled it out, still in its wrapper.

"Already got it, nice. Listen to it." Kim read the back of the CD case. Guy had been introduced to Niggaz wit Attitudes by his friend Larry of all people. It was popular in public school.

"This is the shit. Just came out last week, Dr. Dre, *The Chronic.*" Kim pulled out the CD from her pants pocket.

"Dr. Dre, he's from NWA." Guy smiled, pleased with himself.

"Yes, but this new shit, is the bomb-diggity. Best shit ever! Just wait for your high to kick in." Kim exchanged *The Chronic* for Guy's *Appetite for Destruction.*

"You high yet?"

"Wow, holy sh . . . wow." Guy rubbed his forehead and laughed. His body was numb and soft. Just so . . . relaxed.

"Listen to this shit." She turned up the volume.

Guy was overcome. The beats, the words, pulsed through his body. Hard and smooth at the same time.

"Snoop Dog, huh? Wow, holy shit." This is what D.A.R.E. wanted to keep him away from? Friends, music, feeling?

"I know. He's the shit, right?" Kim laughed and squeezed Guy's hand. "I told you I was gonna get you high. Popped that cherry. One more and you'll be all growed up." They leaned in toward each other.

"You're the shit. I love you. This is amazing. I so love you." Guy couldn't believe how new and fresh, how OK, things felt.

"I love you too. I told you, I'm going to teach you how things work, so relax. No scores to settle. I know you would do anything for me, so don't do anything. Just be here."

The music rolled off the singers' tongues and into Guy's ear like warm whispers of truth.

Guy would have been happy to sit here all night.

"Shit. John's blowing up my pager." Kim looked at her see-through pink pager attached to her belt loop with a silver chain. "His code is 6669. You need a code—well, you need a pager too." She blew a big smoke ring, clear and dense.

Guy thought it must have taken a lot of practice. Cigarettes killed you and didn't make you feel like this.

"Your hair looks good but shave the sides. Nice jeans. Get a pair of Adidas Kicks. So many things to do, but, tonight, we relax. I'm so glad you're out, Guy." Kim reached across and gave Guy a giant hug.

The skin on her back was smooth and soft.

"We are going to do this all the time, just wait. John said you were going to pick him up. If you told John that you were going to pick him up, he's not going to stop blowing up my fucking pager until you pick him up."

"He said it was his birthday. I wanted to see you. I want to stay with you. He was so cool coming to visit all the time." Guy was high and happy, all smiles.

"It's his birthday, but, so you know, John's full of shit. He's awesome, and he will totally have your back, but he's full of shit just the same. And he always wants a ride."

"OK."

"So you have to go pick him up. He's cool, so listen to him. Deranged, yes, but cool. And get a pager, OK?"

"I will. Your hand is so soft." Guy stroked her hand.

"You think so? You should feel my tits!" She put Guy's hand to her breast and laughed.

Guy laughed nervously and pulled his hand back. "I thought we were just going to be friends." As friends they had become so emotionally close, it was something he wanted to keep.

"I was just fucking around, relax. That's why I love you, Guy. I could take off my panties, and you would offer me a blanket. Anyone else . . ."

She was something more than a sister to him.

"You're going to have to be a little less nice in order to lose that cherry." She smiled.

"Whatever you want, just touch my face again."

"Like that?"

"Yes."

And she did, and they listened to *The Chronic* album as it blazed, hypnotized, mesmerizing them in the moment.

Her beeper buzzed, and she read the latest one: Three Five Seven Six 9 *Bitch!* She said to Guy, "Can you remember those digits, John's address?"

Five numbers, yeah. Guy was pretty sure he could remember. Even while stoned, it turned out. Guy was glad John lived close by, right near the Four O Five and the One Eighteen.

John was sitting in the dark on a little brick wall outside his grandparents' house. The small house was a dwelling for his mother, her sister, plus his younger brother and sister as well. Guy might have missed John sitting on the wall, dressed in black, had it not been for the red cherry of his lit cigarette. Guy pulled the car to the curb and got out. John was wearing a black Megadeath shirt with skulls. Loud and angry. Guy wasn't a hard metal fan; he never liked skulls either. He thought they looked evil, not tough. They made him think of the devil.

"Shit, you have a five-o. It's the GT, damn." John went around the back to confirm, then over to the hood.

"Yeah, it's pretty quick. Got it the month before I went to the hospital. Had a Volvo before that."

"Open up the hood. Let's see." John was excited; his hands were already by the grill.

"Sure." Guy opened his door. He knew the hood release was somewhere by the lights. "Hang on a sec. OK, there you go."

As soon as the hood popped, John released the lock. He knew exactly where it was.

"Yo, this engine looks brand-new. A three o two small block. *Shiiit*, a four-barrel Holley carb. That's not factory standard." John leaned his head down under the hood.

"That's how it was when I bought it. It's a stick too."

"No shit, Sherlock. You're gonna drive a car like this in an automatic? *Heeell* no. I gotta drive. Let's go." John held out his hand for the keys.

"You even have a license?" Guy knew John was a year younger than he was, but Guy was pretty sure John did not have a license. He certainly did ride his bike everywhere, and, while that did not preclude a license, Guy could usually tell if a kid had a license or not.

John let out a smirky laugh. "No, but I'm a great driver. Come on. Let's go." John reached his hand forward.

Guy paused and rolled his eyes toward the sky. *Ugh*, he was not going to act like a tool, especially on John's birthday.

"I bet you don't even know how to change the oil on this car." John looked at the hood, and Guy handed him the keys.

"Hell *yeayah*." John strapped himself in, while Guy got in shotgun. Guy couldn't believe he was letting John drive his car, but he was still stoned and relaxed.

"Be careful," Guy said slowly. "Seriously." Guy made eye contact with John.

"Relax, bro. I'm a good-ass driver. My dad's a mechanic. Well, my stepdad. He's got a new family. My real dad lives in his piece-of-shit car. He comes by every once and a while and says he's going to buy me a car. Really, Dad? With what? Recycled cans? Why don't you just go live under a bridge and give me that piece-of-shit car?" John fishtailed the car as he pulled away from the curb. He did it twice, on purpose.

"*Ta-dow*. My name's John Brown bitch."

They laughed heartily.

"Where are we going? Kim got me stoned, damn." Guy leaned back; he had never been driven in his own car before. It was nice. He could devote attention to the radio now, cool. He unwrapped the new Cypress Hill CD. "Kim said this is awesome."

"Oh, you got a CD player in this mutherfucker too. Damn! I got a radio in my room. Doesn't even have a tape player. This car is fucking tight. Oh, cruise control too. Shit. Turn that up."

A police call center pumped through the speakers.

"Topanga Boulevard? Damn these guys are local too?" Guy slapped his knee and leaned back in his seat. The song *Pigs* played on.

Guy had wanted to be a police officer when he was four. He admired police officers; he considered them the good guys, honest. Yet Cypress Hill was lyrical poetry; something about the way the music sounded when you were stoned was consuming.

"Shit, I hate pigs." John had booked it from the pigs a few times while smoking weed in the park. They were always fatties. *Good luck hopping the fence, piggy.* John revved the engine at a stoplight. "You ever been to Captain Ed's?" he asked.

"Nope, where's that at?" Guy had no idea where or what Captain Ed's was.

"You've never been to Captain Ed's? *Ooohh*, best head shop around. Captain Ed's it is."

Guy looked at John inquisitively.

"Fuck, dude, I keep forgetting." John laughed with amusement. "A head shop. They sell bongs and shit, fucking crack pipes, all sorts of crazy shit."

"Where is it?"

"Reseda past Sherman Way, west side."

"No shit?" That was literally a block past Guy's martial arts studio. He never went farther south than that. The studio was east on a side street, so not like anyone was going to see him. Not this late anyway.

Reseda Boulevard was lined with palm trees, right out of a movie. In reality, used as scenery for many movies. This part of the Valley was seedy, mostly Mexican, which was not bad, just noticeably poorer and uniformly so.

John pulled in front of Captain Ed's. It was painted with graffiti, crazy colors and papers plastered up around the front door.

Guy grabbed a bunch of change from his ashtray. There was metered parking. He put in a few quarters.

"No need. No parking patrols this late." John walked to the door.

"It was only seventy-five cents." This place was like something out of the sixties. Psychedelic colors all over, glass displays for jewelry, filled with all sorts of pipes and bongs. "Those are bongs." Guy pointed.

"Yep, yep. You put water in the bottom, then you put the weed in the bowl and smoke." John pantomimed the ritual. "The smoke goes through the water so you can take a bigger hit."

"Sure, the water acts as a filter, cools the temperature." Guy nodded.

"Gets you high as fuck is what it does. Oh, I wish I had one of those." John leaned over the glass counter.

"Happy birthday then." Guy patted his back.

"I wish. Those are like a bill. Thanks for remembering." John smiled.

"Oh, for sure. Seriously, having you come by the hospital every night was a real treat. Not that close on a bike either. Look, I got no friends. Not because of that, but just because I want to, so pick a bong."

"Bullshit," John said with irritation. Why did people always end up being dicks? he thought.

"No, serious." Guy pulled out his brown folded wallet. "I got like five hundred bucks here."

"Bullshit." John reached to help open the wallet and looked inside.

"Serious. Got five hundred twenty six dollars."

"Bullshit, mutherfucker! How did you get five hundred twenty six mutherfucking dollars?" John's head bobbed back and forth between his shoulders. John's grandpa got a pension check every month, and he didn't have five hundred dollars. The bar down the street probably got five hundred dollars a month from his grandfather.

"The glory of savings." Guy looked at John and chuckled. "Babysitting, birthdays. I've got like two grand at home."

"Bull-mutherfucking-shit! Oh, we are going to to have some crazy fun. Let him see one of those wallets right there, one of these dope-ass denim ones. Can I see that bong right there?"

"Get whichever one you want. I got cash."

"All right, let me see that sweet-ass bong right there, bro." The kid behind the counter was about nineteen, half white, half black, dreads.

"My mom's going to flip. She always wanted this Graffix bong, bro."

"Your mom smokes pot?" Guy looked at John incredulously.

"Bro, my mom will smoke your ass under the table. Where do you think I get my weed from? She used to do angel dust. That shit will fuck you up."

"Damn." Guy wrinkled his forehead.

"She's totally cool now. When she smokes, she's like *whatever*."

Guy thought that *whatever* wasn't so bad after all.

Guy looked at one of the K-Rave flyers on the counter. Knott's Berry Farm was turning the whole park into a giant rave for New Year's Eve, from 9 p.m. until five a.m.

"This looks kinda cool." Guy passed the flyer to John.

The kid behind the counter became animated. "That ain't *kinda cool*. That's gonna be the hottest party ever attempted. I know some of the people behind it. The whole park's going to be one big crazy-ass rave. DJs all over—all sorts of crazy shit. Twenty thousand people rolling their asses off." We could see the excitement in the kid's eyes.

163

"We're in. We are so in, baby. You have tickets or what?" John was holding up his hands, as if he were stopping traffic.

"Hell yeah, I have tickets. Twenty-five here or thirty at the door, if they're still available."

"What do you think, homey?" John looked inquisitively and seriously at Guy.

"Hell yeah. Can we take Kim?" Guy asked.

"Hell yeah, we're taking Kim. Three tickets, this bong right here, get my boy that cool glass pipe right there and that little brown bag. Get us two Bic lighters, green, and hook us up with some pokers. My boy needs a new wallet. Throw in that dope denim one right there."

When they got back to the car, John looked over to Guy. "We're best friends from now on, not because you bought me that shit either." John rubbed the back of Guy's head.

What a weird thing to say, Guy thought, but nice. John was weird but he was cool and fun. He did what he wanted and said what he thought. Guy thought he was rude, but the girls loved him, especially the hot ones.

They went to the K-Rave. Kim flipped her lid when she heard they had bought her a ticket; she couldn't believe it. The look of appreciation on her face would have been worth it to Guy, even if they hadn't gone. It was decided. John would drive; Kim and Guy would trip. Kim and John were adamant that Guy would do acid his first time at the party; it was going to be epic. Guy worked on his look: two earrings in his right ear to match the three in his left plus one up high. A pair of baggy sand-colored jeans and shell-toe Adidas. A cool T-shirt with a cartoon gangster kid—a popular line at the time. His hair, Pat Riley slick, the sides and back shaved. His hair wasn't long enough for a ponytail.

John was certain they would be able to find acid at the rave.

Trust me, he had said. It didn't take John long, and, after a few interviews, he decided pink elephants were the way to fly. One each, five bucks a pop. It was just a piece of paper, not even as big as Guy's pinkie nail. That's it, Guy thought? He put it in his mouth and made sure to keep it there. He made a point not to talk. After a half hour went by, he didn't seem to feel anything. Guy and Kim began to think maybe they got ripped off.

"Relax," John said. "I'm telling you, we didn't get ripped off." After about forty-five minutes, Guy thought maybe he was seeing some purple spots. Holy shit, they didn't get ripped off. An hour in, an hour before the New Year, Guy's world changed. He was alive, happy. Everything was new, wonderful, beautiful. He danced his ass off. He got lost in a girl's ass, or more correctly the black-and-white checkered miniskirt she was wearing. The girl cracked up. When she heard it was Guy's first time tripping, she touched Guy's hand to her ass. It was as if twenty thousand people were best friends—more than that—feeling the same, thinking as one.

Guy danced with Kim and John; they fell into each other. Guy felt as if his face was going to open like a Pez container. When he laughed, he put his hand over his mouth, so his head wouldn't flip open. He could see his fingers stretch and melt; it was amazing. Everything was Eden, until they decided to ride the Kingdom of the Dinosaurs around three a.m., a popular ride at Knott's Berry Farm. Kim freaked out; she was seeing blood everywhere. John said it was time to go. By the time they got to the parking lot, it was as if Guy had left the Garden of Eden by choice, not by edict. Kim calmed down, but John insisted it was time to leave. Guy was so disappointed, he did the only thing that seemed natural at the time: he spit right in Kim's face. Kim and Guy were both stunned, but somehow it allowed them to put the party, cut short, behind them.

As they sat in the parking lot in the backseat of the car, Kim's and Guy's very beings melted together. They needed each other's touch, each other's breath; they made out passionately until sunrise, getting lost in one another. Just kissing and touching, it was special. In that moment they knew each other completely, still friends, not lovers. Friends expressing themselves, sharing something new and special in the safety of each other's arms.

In that moment Guy was not alone.

Without much to do, and plenty of time to hang out, Guy needed money. That meant a job. After the New Year, he enrolled in Granada Hills, the public high school. The classes were the equivalent of what the dumb kids at Chaminade did in the eighth grade. More than enough idle time for a job with not much homework on the agenda.

Guy procured a job at Kentucky Fried Chicken. Minimum wage, four dollars twenty five cents an hour. At least he was up in the front with the customers and not cooking in the back, with the Mexicans. Cooking sucked; most of the cooks didn't speak English. Guy's Spanish allowed them to have basic conversations; they thought it was cool as shit. Most of the cooks had tattoos on their faces and necks, with names like Napo, short for Napoleon.

Guy was sent to make coleslaw his first day with some big-ass white kid, who was there for his first day too. Boy, they really threw you into the fire. Blind leading the blind, guys. As Guy looked over from the coleslaw station, one of the cooks, Marcello, held a whole chicken by its wings from inside the freezer so only Guy could see. Marcello, pants still on, began to fuck the chicken vigorously. He made kissing noises and spoke romantically to the chicken in Spanish of course, since he couldn't speak a lick of English.

"Tu pollo es muy bonito."

Your chicken is beautiful. Guy laughed, Marcello laughed louder and danced in a little circle, like performing a Mexican hat dance.

"Hey, look at Marcello." Guy motioned over with his head.

"That guy's crazy. He pinched my ass earlier." The kid looked nervous.

"I'm Guy, Guy Flynn. You should probably tell the manager," Guy said firmly.

"You think so? Shit. I don't know. This is my first day." He was clearly nervous.

"Of course you shouldn't tell the manager, relax. Marcello was just screwing around. He's a total whack job. Your name's Bear, your real name? Where you from?" Guy read the kid's name tag; it was clear Bear was not a local.

"Yep, Bear. I'm from Flint, Michigan."

"Welcome to L.A. I'll cut the cabbages, onions and carrots. You put them through the shredder, good?"

"OK." Bear was one of those big dorky kids, especially noticeable as a California transplant. Big, like six-foot-four big, red hair and all.

"You got many friends yet?" Guy asked, wondering.

"Not yet. I got a brother, who's twelve. I'll be sixteen in June."

"Well, we're friends now. I'll be seventeen in April. You smoke?" If you wanted to be cool in L.A., you had to smoke.

"Cigarettes? No." Bear shook his head.

"I hate cigarettes." Guy said.

Bear scooped the shredded cabbage into the big white plastic bin.

"Everyone smokes weed in L.A., homey. Time to get high." In L.A., if you were cool or you wanted to fuck hot chicks, you smoked pot. Plus what could be more relaxing?

"Cool." Bear was happy to have been given the time of day.

"How're you getting home?" Guy chopped the cabbage in quarters, then chopped the stem off each quarter.

"I walk. It's only a few blocks. My mom works. We live with my aunt." Bear hated living there; her house was too small for everyone. But, even with no friends, Bear liked L.A. better than Flint. Bear's neighborhood was the poster child for white flight, but his mom had had no wings.

"I'll take you home. Let's take a look at our shifts. If we work together, I'll pick you up."

"Wow, that would be super cool." Bear smiled.

166

"Does your mom care if you chill out after work?"

"She's been hoping I'd make some friends." She was actually starting to worry; Bear looked down.

"*Sweeeet*. You can meet my friend John. He's crazy, bro, but the girls love him."

"Lucky." Bear blew out air dejectedly.

"No joke, I know. Just takes some practice. A little bit of herb doesn't hurt." Guy laughed.

"I'm in," Bear said, pushing the cabbage through the shredder forcefully.

"That's all of it, nice. I'll pour in the dressing. You get to mix." Guy put the big butcher's knife in the sink.

"Oh, this is nasty. Gross." Bear waded his gloved-covered arms into the coleslaw.

"Looks like cum. Make sure you mix it real good. All right, here's a good-ass story. So there's this girl, Lesanne, who I met at Granada. One day I bring these whippets over to her house. Whippets are laughing gas. They sell them at head shops. They look like CO_2 cartridges for a BB gun. You put the cartridge in this little thing that looks like a brass pipe. It's called a cracker. Twist it together and the gas comes out of a valve into a big balloon at one end. It's actually nitrous oxide. They use it to make whipped cream." Guy twisted his hands together for illustration, as Bear mixed the cumlike-slathered coleslaw.

"When you inhale the balloon, you get this amazing head rush. John showed me. It's awesome. Well, Lesanne begs me to bring a box over after school. She's a total hottie." Guy looked at Bear with eyebrows raised.

"No joke?" Bear's eyes widened, as he waded up to his elbows in creamy goodness.

"For sure. So she does one, and it gives her an orgasm. A fucking orgasm, no joke. She starts to finger-bang herself right there. She took off my pants and gave me a blow job, swallowed the whole load. First one I'd ever had. Seriously." Guy started to laugh and threw up his hands.

"That's the craziest thing I ever heard." Bear picked his jaw off the floor.

"Tell me about it. Wanted to lose my virginity while I was still sixteen, was starting to get nervous. A night in the Jacuzzi and done. We're so hanging out."

"Totally rad." Bear beamed.

They were done by ten thirty. The cleanup was definitely the worst part. Guy, Bear and a few of the Mexican cooks came out together.

"*A noche*." Guy nodded.

"*A noche piche cabrone.*" Napo laughed.

"You want a piece of this, bitch?" Guy laughed heartily.

Freddie and Gabe started in. "Hell yeah, he wants a piece. Go get a piece, Napo." Freddie and Gabe laughed as they bent over and slapped each other on the back.

"Hey, fuck you. You go get a piece." Napo was laughing and pointing back at them.

"Fuck no, *esse*. I ain't gonna get my arm broke and shit. Hey, white boy, show Gabe how you did that shit to my arm." Freddie was twisting his own arm. He had two black teardrops under his left eye.

They had grilled Guy on martial arts right off the bat. They even knew who Royce Gracie was. Guy had trained with Royce when he had come to pay respects and teach seminars at Magda. "You guys smoke or what?" Guy looked over to Napo.

"Do we smoke or what? Listen to this fucking cracker. Of course we smoke, esse. Why? You got fucking smoke?" Napo stepped across the parking lot, intrigued.

Guy unlocked his car and pulled out a baggy from the center compartment. "Take a look." He passed the ziplock baggie with an eighth of weed over to Napo. Guy had figured out how to make a few bucks, but really it was about free pot.

Napo opened up the bag and looked in. "Shit, white boy's got the kind bud, Freddie."

Freddie stuck his nose in the bag. "That ain't no Mexican dirt weed. That's the chronic, damn!"

"Lemon Thai. Gets you high as a mutherfucker. I got a pipe." Guy did indeed have a pipe.

"Light that shit up, *holmes*. You smoke me out on breaks, we're gonna be homeboys for life." The three cooks crouched over, clapping their hands in excitement.

Along the night air a black El Camino ebbed by slowly. As the window rolled down, a tattooed Mexican in a white T-shirt stuck his hand out the window and yelled, "Blythe Street, mutherfucker," as two shots rang out. The car sped away quickly. Napo, Freddie and Gabe crouched down low as the car pulled onto the street. Then Freddie ran toward the car and let a shot of his own fly from a little twenty two.

"Pacoima Brown Stone Locos." Hand signs flashed.

Guy didn't even flinch. He wasn't sure why; he just knew it wasn't necessary. Bear stood behind him, unflinching. Bear was *down*—cool Guy thought. Napo, Freddie and Gabe wanted to jump him into their gang. As the only white boy, it was a big deal. While flattered, Guy declined—a better ally than a master. While they smoked half the bag, Napo promised Brown Stone Locos would always have Guy's back.

BOOK TWO: CHAPTER THREE

The world was a better place in Nineteen Ninety Three because America was the world's only superpower. The European Union would attempt to gather and bind people together financially rather than at the edge of a sword, a truly negligible difference. The Russians were, as usual, angry at themselves, and, in another October Revolution, nearly two hundred lost their lives. Bill Clinton was everyone's friend. Especially the Middle East and gays in the military. Until one of our buildings was bombed, that is. Some of the world had not yet learned their lesson. America does not negotiate with terrorists, and we believe all people deserve freedom. That cost can be high. Bill showed he was willing to pay the price in our own domestic operation, when the flames of little children and women were made to shine brighter. Come simply to be known as Waco.

Guy learned about style from his mother. Style mixed with violence was timeless. Slicked back hair, shaved around the sides. The guinea Ts of New York were recoined as *wifebeaters* on the West Coast. They highlighted Guy's taut physique. Cartoon images of criminals with guns were popular on T-shirts. Baggy jeans or jean shorts below the boxers, shell-toed shoes by Adidas with fat laces. Guys who didn't give a shit had both their ears pierced.

Cruising round the streets of L.A., music and mad-dogging—intimidating stare downs—were obligatory. Peacocked confrontations, yelling "Where you from?" and giving hand signs. Those with ambition obtained a fake ID off of Alvarado Street. Living on Cypress Hill was a not-so-small amusement for Guy. John and Bear showed they would walk to the gates of hell with him. The three of them tattooed HB4L over their left shoulder blades. *Homeboys for Life*, in Old English green ink. It showed nicely in a wifebeater. Their moniker was two eight three Killers—two eight three was "bud" spelled numerically by phone. It worked for paging and throwing hand signs, with B-U-D-K spelled out with one or two hands. John liked to tag two eight three K in green spray paint. Guy thought it was destruction of property, but he also had bad penmanship so tagging wasn't an activity he engaged in. The only C he ever got was in handwriting.

Guy listened to no one, which was convenient since no one told him what to do. His mother and Paul went their own way, did their own thing. Guy finished up junior year in public school. The basic classes were not deserving of any remedial attention, but the lead in the school play made sure Guy attended theater class. Having attended theater class regularly, he was surprised by a ring at the door from a large sheriff. Did they really still have truant officers? Amusing. The officer wanted to know why Guy wasn't attending all his classes. Guy was pretty sure the slammed door in his face provided clarification.

The HB4L boys bought weed from some guys at Kennedy, John's high school. Guy wanted to go direct, around the middleman. An opportunity presented itself one night in front of a liquor store when Guy overheard a stoner in his twenties talking on the pay phone. Witty conversation and some bud Guy had in his own pocket had made a new friend and distributor. Better quality bud at larger quantities and vast discounts, plus acid.

It caused sore times on the rare occasion when John attended class. Particularly with the CHBs. Guy only knew that you called them *cheeseburgers* to make fun of them. They were taggers more than gangsters, from Guy's perspective, but that was true of most in the Valley, except the Mexicans up and down the east side. One particular day that caught John in attendance, he came close to getting his ass kicked in the corner of a bathroom.

Guy asked John to relay a message after that. Whoever their leader was, he's a pussy, and Guy would like the opportunity to let him know firsthand, one on one. The challenge was accepted, and John was to fight their lieutenant as well. John was nervous, but Guy and John spent the next three nights training. Get to the ground quick. That's where it will all happen. They practiced strikes, locks, chokes, defense, knees, elbows, boxing.

The fight went to the ground in three seconds. Mostly rolling around with a few shots. It was declared a draw after a few minutes. John perhaps got the slightly worse end of the stick. The main event attracted dozens of observers, most of whom Guy didn't know.

C.J. along with Guy's new friend Elvis were in attendance, plus many others representing both sides of the fights. Elvis was black, from the Jungle of L.A. He was cool, hence he cared not for his namesake one bit. Eli the giant, Elvis's friend, was six foot eight and not gangly. He even looked big next to Bear—not that he was tougher than Bear, just a giant.

The other kid, the one to fight Guy, was smaller than Guy. The kid had a bad case of the nerves when he stepped into the circle. He claimed he was getting over the flu, but severe taunting from the crowd shut him up. The kid really was a full two inches shorter than Guy. The kid was scared and clearly not a regular fighter.

Guy was so looking forward to a good fight. If he had the opportunity to look someone directly in the eye, in the moment, it rarely led to a fight. Verbal humiliation at least seemed necessary in this case. "How about one hand behind my back or no return blows from me for a full sixty seconds?" There was no fight, just crying from the kid. The *cheeseburgers* were tossed. John was dubbed the King of Kennedy.

Working at Coco's restaurant as a host paid Guy more than KFC; so with his job, he would take his GED instead of finishing high school. Most of the kids at his school failed, John said. Guy got a ninety-eight, even though he and John didn't sleep the night before. Why waste time repeating eighth and 9th grade material in 11th and twelfth grade? Granada Hills High School did supply the girl, and by proxy the Jacuzzi, for Guy to lose his virginity, however. He even went to prom with a senior, a friend of his. Guy found a few girls to hang out and have sex with.

John seemed to always be at the buffet table, while Bear looked on hungrily. Bear was shy with the girls, but so damn funny. He wouldn't make a move, no matter how much you prodded, no matter the clarity of the path. Bear was big, but he preferred not to fight. When he and Guy worked the focus pads, Guy assured Bear that his fists were like ham hocks. "You hit almost as hard as I do. Twist your hip, pivot like this. You'll knock a mutherfucker out cold. Trust me." And Bear did—trust Guy, that is.

Guy, John and Bear spent their time and their thoughts together. They stood against the world and cared when no one else seemed to. The streets provided an outlet for anger and a path with companions. Guy wasn't sure where the path would lead or whether he cared. Fun with the boys and chasing skirt was paramount, imminent—the future far off. Pot and beer, along with Boone's Strawberry Hill for the ladies, made the days and nights spin smoothly.

Guy, John and Bear found hotboxing the car while talking about life was one of their most cherished activities. They would park on some side street and take off their shirts so they could endure the hundred-plus-degree California summer. Eventually the car would be so filled with smoke, the lighters would stop working due to lack of oxygen. That became the ultimate goal. Roll down the windows so the lighters work, just not too long.

They carried a travel shaving kit with all their paraphernalia inside: a little bong, pipes, weed. It had to be replaced when Bear left it on top of the Mustang pulling out from Guy's house one afternoon. The next-door neighbor was watering his lawn. John asked the guy if he had seen a little black bag lying around. Thankfully he didn't see the bag, since Guy's neighbor was a sheriff. They didn't lose much weed either.

They lost the bag again one night, while smoking bowls in the park with Shanna, a stunning little blonde Guy was spending time with. Her mom had died from a cocaine overdose, and her dad was a dirtbag. Somehow Shanna retained her innocence. Guy spent less time with her because of it. One night at the park Napo and Freddie were being real wiseasses. They were messing around with a Maglite, pretending to be cops. Guy was sitting quietly with Shanna, when he saw the lights come up the path. He couldn't make out the figures, but he knew instantly that they were cops.

Guy grabbed Shanna by the hand. "Cops," he yelled and was off to the races. He pitched the pot bag into the thick hillside brush and slid down the hill, across the street to the creek, a favorite smoking spot. Only Bear and John followed; they knew the plan, if cops came. They waited at the creek for an hour. Bear's car was parked next to the park. He had bought a new Plymouth after his old truck had overheated, then went up in flames on the roadside. It even caught a tree on fire and nearly burned down a house. Anyway, after an hour Bear went to the car by himself; the cops were still waiting. He got a curfew ticket. He told his mom that Shanna and Guy had gotten in a fight, that she had opened the door and had run into the park. So Bear had waited on them to return.

Shanna was never allowed in Bear's house again. Guy found it a shame. Bear's mom, Bea, had bought a little mobile home in Sylmar, a prefab. She got the money from a work-related accident. It became a regular smoking spot since Guy and John started smoking Bea out. Bear was too embarrassed to smoke in front of his mother. No more Shanna though; it was best for her.

The parties at Bea's house were great. Shawn, a School Yard Crip, recently released from prison, was living in Bea's neighborhood. He had an SY tattoo, one letter on the back of each of his massive triceps. He was cool enough to hang out with, and super appreciative of being smoked out. Guy would take massive rips off the three-foot glass bong they kept at Bea's. Smoking often took on a competitive nature. One of Shawn's friends wanted to show his bong-smoking prowess; he took a big rip from the three-footer. He pounded his chest when he stood up, showing off his skills. He then promptly passed out, smashing his face upon the railing of the open sliding glass door, all while having a full-body seizure. He was fine when he came too, said it didn't even hurt. They gave him frozen peas for his bloodied face.

Guy regularly attended group therapy with Milton and Karen; he enjoyed it. They met once a week—eight kids, boys and girls. They ate dinner together, usually Italian but sometimes sandwiches or Chinese. There was no short supply of craziness. Guy shared himself intimately, becoming especially close with Carrie, a crazy but passionate blonde. They were really just close friends, outside of a few months of heavy sex. They were gasoline, and when Carrie lit the flame to ride the dragon, Guy was sure they would spontaneously combust. Guy had tried stimulants; he was not a fan. They led to a corner not worth exploring. So did Carrie.

One evening while Guy was strolling along outside his mom's house—or Mack's house or the pool man's house or whoever's house it was now—a car drove past slowly with its lights off and pulled to the curb. It was dusk. Four tatted-up Mexicans got out of the car. One of them yelled, "You know Guy Flynn?"

"Nope," Guy replied and continued his walk down the street. He could see one of the guys grab a shotgun from the trunk. Guy walked quickly until he was out of sight and hid underneath a parked car. The Mexicans drove slowly, up and down the street.

Carrie had said she was dating some guy affiliated with the Mexican Mafia, but she was known to blow things out of proportion, and Guy had discarded the comment out of hand. Guy learned that they were not quite Mexican Mafia. They were MS thirteen—not much better. The kind of guys who were not to be fucked with, not even looked at.

After that Guy acquired a gun from Elvis with an FBI emblem on the grip which had been sitting in Elvis's grandpa's closet for the last twenty years since retiring. Bear had slept with Carrie, even though Guy had warned him of her wiles. A small ripple between the two eight three Killers emerged. Bear, the perpetrator, was concerned it would tear apart the group. Guy figured as much would happen, but, if it meant Bear would finally lose his virginity, Guy thought it was worth it. Maybe now he would have some confidence with the ladies. Posse before pussy, he reminded Bear.

★★★

Life's party emanated a hazily drifting fog that ebbed and flowed. A night of wild partying with friends from group became a memory that seemed so distant there was no proof it ever existed. All that appeared now was noxious fog; it invaded Guy's mind and leaked out, trapped within a craggy rock ceiling. The misty walls of rock seemed to breathe, a ring of torches provided scant light. Guy could feel the dank warmness of the room against his naked skin, as he lay upon a giant black rock platform. It was smooth as glass, except for the intricate carvings all over. His hands were extended out from his sides, his body like the shape of a cross.

Guy tried to sit up, but it was as if a millstone were upon his chest; he attempted to scream, but he was paralyzed, unable to make the slightest noise, like a frightened child. Then suddenly standing at Guy's feet was the devil himself, lucifer.

"I am he who gives light."

There was fire above the creature's head. It turned from a burning flame to a glow—like white lava—as he spoke. It was mesmerizing. Guy shifted his gaze to the creature's eyes. His head was something of a bull and a goat with ragged brown hair. There was a pentagram, an upside-down five-pointed star upon his forehead. It too glowed like a jack-o'-lantern, emanating a mixture of green and red light. His two horns were more like an antelope's, long and slightly curved. He had two large beautifully formed, but hairy breasts along with his hairy shoulders and arms. His hands were of a man. He held up two fingers and a thumb on each hand, one hand pointed toward the floor and the other toward the heavens. His legs were of a large goat or bull, his penis of a donkey or a horse.

There was a giant medallion bolted into the beast's stomach. From behind it, a wriggling mixture of guts and snakes protruded. Guy's faculties eluded him. Was he dreaming? Was he dead? He was having a hard time putting a thought together.

"Show him the pain," the beast said calmly.

The torches ringing the ceiling lit up with intensity. Chains with hooks came into focus as they lowered from the foggy void above. Suddenly around him were old men in red robes with hoods. Their demonically wrinkled hands held the chains. In unison they were lowered; the hooks pierced Guy's flesh. A hook on the left and a hook on the right, from his chest down to his ankles. Guy could feel the hooks pull his skin. The pain was real; this was no dream.

satan floated above Guy's feet. His hooves were crossed in the lotus position. "I am lucifer, prince of light, he who rules the world. Its subjects do my bidding."

The beast stretched out black hairy wings behind him as he pointed below. Guy lay in the middle of a pentagram; its open spaces revealed a lake of liquid fire beneath. Some Hebrew-like characters were all aflame at each point on the pentagram. One of them looked like the mathematical symbol for pi.

A giant circle opened up around the room; Guy could see he was on an altar of rock that extended all the way down to the lake of fire. He gagged and thought he would throw up, but he couldn't. How could this be?

"Show me," the beast said.

The red-hooded men comprising the inner circle pulled their chains. Guy felt his flesh rip away from his body, revealing his innards. He saw his beating heart, his guts; he was hot, sweltering. He saw the bones sticking out from his shins.

"It is I who decides," said the beast. "The name Guy Finnigan shall not be written in the Lamb's Book of Life. Your soul belongs to me for a thousand eternities."

Guy wished he would pass out, but there was nothing to alleviate his circumstances. The fire licked at his sides, its glow and roar more violent than a tempest at sea.

"You are garbage, and you shall be treated as such. Your God does not love you. He has thrown you away like the worthless trash you are. The box—"

A black-hooded creature could be seen off in the background. A clawed hand extended, holding a shiny black cube.

lucifer grabbed the box and floated above Guy's head. lucifer stuck the black cube deep inside Guy's open guts.

It felt as if a hot coal were being thrust into his bowels; the cries were only in Guy's head.

The beast walked upon a small stone platform that appeared, extending from Guy's feet.

The chains grew slack, and Guy's skin reattached to his body, as if cauterized in place. His fear grew. Suddenly Guy was on his feet, naked, standing at one end of the altar.

The beast sat on a wriggling throne made of children at the other end of the room.

There was a slide, like a chute next to the throne. A small child tumbled down into the beast's waiting hands. On the other side of the throne, there was a giant jar with molten gold that bubbled over the sides. The beast held the crying, wriggling boy by his heel and dipped him into the bubbling melted gold. The cries quieted, and the beast promptly bit off the young child's leg, then his groin.

"Tasty." The beast looked Guy in his eyes as the beast devoured the rest of the boy. His disgusting smile revealed pieces of flesh stuck to decaying, pointy teeth.

"Now," the beast said, and a black-robed figure appeared at the other end of the large rectangular altar upon which Guy stood. Guy dared not peer into the hooded cape; he saw only a large gun pointed at his face. When the trigger was pulled, Guy could see the bullet travel out of the barrel toward him. He was frozen and felt the bullet enter between his eyes. He could feel his brain leak out a large hole in the back of his head. He crumbled, tumbling back into the lake of fire.

As Guy tumbled, he saw a giant frying pan come into focus above the lake of fire. There were rocky outcroppings with demons hovering all about. They hopped and hollered, screaming among putrid sulfurlike smoke. Guy fell upon his stomach, like a pat of butter into a sizzling pan. Guy pushed himself to his feet, but he could feel them begin to melt from underneath him. As they did, he thought about diving into the lake, but he knew that would not bring his suffering to an end.

Guy's legs were no more; his body began to seep together like a molten slug.

satan descended into the dark cylindrical cavern, hovering above Guy with beating wings. "You are less than worthless. You are nothing."

Guy became a bubbling liquid pool of himself, frying in a pan. It felt as if only a distorted face remained. With it, he looked upon the winged beast.

"He doesn't love you. He's cruel. He's always been this way." lucifer looked down at the bubbling mess that was Guy.

It wasn't true. Jesus is love; Guy knew that. satan was the wicked one. "God, why? Why, Jesus? Please help me!" Guy's tortured soul cried out for his mouth.

When Guy opened his eyes, he was in a hospital room. He was dazed, unclear, but this was reality, and he was not dead.

"He's awake," said a nurse, with short brown hair and a clean, crisp white uniform.

A moment later a gray-haired bespectacled doctor came in. "You made it. We weren't sure . . . What drugs did you take, son?" It came back to Guy in a flash. The party with group at Colleen's place at the Summit at Warner Center. They were all going to do acid; he remembered having a little baggie full of tabs. Guy feigned being tired and closed his eyes. "I don't know. I'm so tired."

He was in a hospital gown; his clothes sat on a chair behind the door. As they let him be, Guy moved to get up, only to be stopped in his tracks by a tube coming out of his penis. A catheter. He pulled the tube out quickly; it burned like fire and made him regret it. Guy was able to get his clothes on quickly. He was out the door, in his car and home. He checked for his gun; it was gone from underneath the seat.

Calls to John were unanswered until about ten a.m. He said Guy had gone crazy, had ripped a door right off its hinges, that he had ripped a bay window out of the frame. Colleen had called the cops. It took a dozen of them nearly an hour to get Guy hog-tied. It was all blurry to John. He wasn't quite sure if he actually remembered or if someone had told him. He was tripping balls.

The next day Guy received calls to the house from a detective asking about a gun that was found in his car. Guy told the detective that someone had given him acid for his first time, and he had a bad trip. He went to hell. He didn't know anything about a gun; he had no recollection whatsoever of the night, no idea why it was in his car or if it had his prints on it. "A horrible nightmare of a night, Detective."

John arranged a little get-together over at Guy's house to recoup. Guy's house was quickly becoming John's house; he spent enough time there to treat it as his own. He drove the Mustang while Guy was working. John would bring some girls over. Just chill out on the side of Guy's house as usual, to smoke, drink and laugh.

"Yo! Did you hear that?" Guy heard a car drive by unusually slow. He motioned to John with the glass pipe he held in his hand.

John heard it too; he opened the wrought iron gate that separated the two six-foot stucco-covered walls and walked into the front yard.

The house had been remodeled with FEMA money after the Nineteen Ninety Two quake. Della was off leading her new life; she was attending Trade Tech. She was going to become a fashion designer and help Paul grow his pool business. By *helping*, Guy was sure it meant spending Mack's money that Della got in the divorce.

Guy sat in a plastic lawn chair on the side of the house. It was paved with concrete now because Paul thought it would be a good place for a basketball court that never materialized. Nobody bothered Guy and his friends during their late-night revelries, but then again no authority figures wanted to be bothered with them.

John strolled up the mauve stone walkway through the grass and the seven trees, back through the gate. The warm summer evening left John clad in a wifebeater with black baggy jeans and a new pair of Doc Martens. John never wore shorts, even when it hit a hundred and fifteen degrees outside.

John made eye contact with Guy as he walked through the gate; John held a machete up in the air. It was properly called a garab sword, depending on where in Southeast Asia you were from. It had a curved blade and was slightly longer than John's forearm and hand. It looked almost rusted but not—just old, fifty years, maybe more, maybe less. Still had its original leather sheath, but the tip was torn off, so the blade stuck through. Guy had found it at a garage sale for ten bucks.

"All good. Marie, let me bum a smoke," John said.

"Sure." Marie got up from her chair and pulled out a pack of smokes from her purse. "They're Marlboro Lights though."

"Lightweight." John smoked Reds of course; he reached out for the cig.

Guy had tried cigarettes; they were gross. They killed you and didn't even make you feel good in the process. Mack's dad had died of lung cancer; it was a hell of a way to go. They called Mack's dad, Big Mack. He made sure to let everyone know he had used the name decades before McDonald's. He laughed that he should get royalties, but his name was different, spelled with a K after all.

John nodded his head as he took a drag. As if Guy needed a head nod to see Marie's ass, holy shit. Marie's jeans were a bit baggy, but the entire ass was cut out, up to the top of the back pockets. Her ass was milky white, firm, like two little midgets where walking around underneath, holding it up. Its perfect shape was framed by a burgundy thong. Guy's cock was hard.

John had his eye on Marie too. Marie had brought her friend Lisa. Lisa wasn't hot, but not ugly either, just a bit plain. She had blond hair with a bit of curl. She seemed nice enough, a bit one-of-the-boys-ish. For Guy, Marie stole the stage; he could hardly pull his gaze off her from the minute she had stepped into the yard, and that was before he saw her ass. She was five two or so, slim. B cups, Guy figured. As if her face was not hot enough, her ass had him hypnotized. Her hair was red, which was not normally Guy's thing. But it was not that red-red or that orange-red but more a raging fire that emanated her heat.

"Damn." Guy put his hands to his mouth. It was normally smart to play it cool with a girl like this. But with a girl like this, you also had to lay it all out there.

"I told you that ho was hot." John pointed at Bear, with two fingers and his thumb positioned like a gun.

"You did. You did!" Bear raised his palms to the ceiling, Arsenio Hall–style.

"*Ladies* not *hos.*" Guy put his palms out facing the floor, letting the boys know to cool it. He hated when girls were called *hos*, even when they were *hos*.

Marie looked at Guy, dead in his eyes. "I ain't no ho." She swung her hair as she turned her head to John. She was wearing a skintight black spaghetti-strapped camisole. "You wish." She smacked her own bare ass and pointed to his crotch. "Whip that shit out, and I will Lorena Bobbitt it, mutherfucker." She walked over and sat in the seat next to Guy, smiling at him all the while.

"You'll need a chainsaw, *beeeeaaach.*" John laughed. "Pass me the bong."

"So what do you guys think? He killed her or what?" Guy leaned back in his chair and opened his arms, addressing the question to all four.

"What?" John looked puzzled.

"O. J. Simpson, U.D." Bear cocked his head and coughed out some smoke. U.D. was short for *ugly dog*—a reference John had created one night while at a frat party in Santa Barbara. John had made some drunk guy wear a little cape after he had spilled booze all over himself. "Ugly dog," John had blurted out; it was eventually shortened to U.D.

"So sad. I hate to even hear about it." Marie took a long drag off of her smoke.

"Hell yeah. He cut both their heads damn near right off." John tapped the side of the garab against his neck.

"Guilty," Bear yelled out. "He'll only get life though, because California is full of pussies. Just about anywhere else he'd get the needle."

"A piece of garbage." Guy thought that was enough said. He agreed with Bear. O.J. would certainly get life but deserved a needle.

"What scumbags his lawyers are too. I mean, I get it. Everyone deserves a fair trial, but how are you that guy? The one who uses every trick in the book to get some piece of trash off that you know is guilty," Bear continued.

Guy shook his head.

"Disgusting," Marie threw in.

"My brother's attorney got him off for two grams of meth." Lisa took a hit of herb from the glass pipe.

Ugh, Guy thought. He hated tweekers. Guy had tried speed and coke but found he didn't like stimulants. His mind already moved too fast, thinking and analyzing things continuously. It gave him trouble sleeping. Guy didn't need any additional spark and the whole not-eating-and-sleeping thing, no thanks. You could take a single look at anyone who used for any length of time and see there was something off about them. Pot brought Guy down to normal speed; he slept well too.

"Nice." John took a hit off the pipe and passed it to Marie; their hands touched.

"So what up for tomorrow, nigga?" Guy looked over at John. *Nigga* was a term of endearment. Nothing like the *nigger* of times past used by his grandfather. The word had been adopted and used to mean *friend, homey*. Guy found, in certain circles, especially with his black friends, that you weren't cool if you didn't use the word. And if you weren't cool, you couldn't use the word. They called Guy *nigga* too; it was a mark of identification and belonging. It was used by people who just didn't give a fuck about what certain other people had to say. It wasn't simply about race; it was about a system of power, about glaring inconsistencies and abuse. Some people had just had enough.

"Watching the kids. Your mom's got school." John babysat for the kids when Della went to fashion school. Guy found the whole situation absurd. But John made breakfast, let the kids watch TV while they ate.

"Cool, I gotta work early, eight in the morning. Gotta leave like seven forty five." Marie's hand lingered as she passed the pipe back to Guy.

"No worries. I'll be asleep. The kids usually don't get up till about 9." John looked down at his pager. "Bear, you spending the night or what?"

"Uh, sure. I don't have to work till four." Bear usually slept on the couch; it was pretty comfortable.

"Cool, I'll take the ladies home. It's late." It was only twelve thirty, but Guy could see Marie's eyes saying the same thing. The party feels a bit big.

The girls followed him out quickly to the Mustang. Guy opened the passenger door. Granada Hills was only a few miles away. Lisa suggested she get dropped off second, but her house was on the way to Marie's. Guy insisted he'd drop her off first.

Guy looked over into Marie's eyes. "Are we finally alone? Oh, my God, girl. You are so fucking wow." Guy took Marie's hand in his. "Who are you?" Guy's eyes were puppy-dog wide; he put his other hand to her pursed lips, and took a loud breath in and out.

"Marie Trouble." She touched his nose.

She was spicy. "Middle name?" Guy raised his brows, above his quickened heart.

"Nope." She smiled. "You?"

"Hmm." No one had ever asked Guy for his middle name. Interesting.

"Kerry. From my dad. Well, my birth dad. Wait, you wanna chill someplace or get some food?"

"Sure. Can we make a quick stop to see my dad first, please?" Marie clapped her hands together.

"*Oooo*," Guy moaned. Even if her dad were chief of police, he'd meet him and say, "Hello, sir."

"He's totally cool. He'll give us some bud. He gets pot from the kids at his school. He's a teacher." Marie stroked Guy's hand.

"Girl, if you touch my hand like that again, I'll build your daddy a new shed in the backyard. Well, I'll pay John to do it." Guy laughed.

Marie laughed too and touched his face with the back of her hand. "What if I do this?"

"If you do that, I'm going to take your clothes off, but not before I let John know we're together."

She laughed and wondered how this was the guy she had heard so much about. Really? He was so nice. So handsome he took her breath away. Made her gasp when she had first seen him.

Guy smelled chronic as they walked, holding hands, toward the side gate of Marie's house. The house was small, one story, but this part of town had big flat yards. Marie opened the gate. Her father was sitting on the cement steps, smoking a little brass pipe. There was a six-pack of Mickey's big mouths by his side, three of them empty.

He looked a little like a troll, Guy thought, but a happy troll. He was gray haired, balding. Stout. The type of man you would expect were a baker if you saw him on the streets.

"Hey, Dad. I'm going to be out late. Can I have some weed, *pleeeeaasee*?" Marie begged and stomped her feet jokingly.

"Of course. Here, smoke this. It's the good shit." Her father smiled, passing her the pipe.

"Can I see?" Guy looked to the bag. He was wearing a Grateful Dead tie-dyed shirt.

"Oh, it's the good shit. I only smoke the good shit." Marie's father, Arnie, passed Guy the bag.

Guy opened the ziplock and took a smell, then a close look. "That's the chronic. That's some good shit right there." Guy smoked more chronic lately as it showed up on the scene. It was wicked good, hardly ever seeds, stinky, moist. It was different, kind.

"Try it out." Her father motioned, and Marie passed the pipe to Guy. He took a big lungful and passed it back to Arnie.

"Can we have the chamber weed, Dad? Please!" Marie giggled.

"OK, OK, only because I love you." Arnie cashed the bowl and unscrewed the middle chamber. He passed a large resin-covered nug to his daughter.

"Take two of these and call me in the morning." Arnie handed over two of the big mouth bottles of Mickey's to Guy.

"I'm good, thanks. We have plenty of weed too."

"Just take 'em," Arnie insisted.

"Just take them." Marie hooked onto Guy's arm, and Guy grabbed the beers. "Thanks, Dad. Love you. See you tomorrow." Marie walked Guy back toward the gate.

"Nice to meet you. Have a good night." Guy made eye contact over his shoulder. Guy would kill his daughter before he let her do this—you have got to be kidding me.

"There's a park up the street that's fun. It's quiet. Nobody will bother us the whole night."

"Are you sure?" Guy thought and asked from experience.

"I've seen the sun come up plenty there." Marie's smile was warmer than the rising sun.

"Cool."

They settled on Taco Bell and had a Mexican pizza, two soft tacos with sour cream, sodas, cinnamon twists. Plus Marie got a bean burrito with cheese.

The night cooled, but it was still warm. The moon's light shone off the hills of the grassy park like the rolling waves of the sea. Guy and Marie walked over to the merry-go-round, hand in hand. They rarely had the spinning disks at parks anymore, as Americans deemed them far too dangerous. Marie sat toward the center of the circle.

"Come here." She motioned to her lap.

Guy looked at her strangely.

"Lay your head down, silly."

Hmm, that caught Guy off guard. There was one thing he needed to address. "I don't date tweekers." Guy looked at her truthfully.

"Well, I'm not a tweeker, and I won't do speed at all, if you don't want me to."

This girl was so peculiar. Guy laid his head into her lap, and she began to stroke his hair. It might have been the nicest thing someone had ever done for him. He looked into her eyes, she into his. They saw each other so deeply it was as if they had become one. Her eyes were starrier than the night above, but Guy looked and tried not to be overcome.

Each time she stroked his hair, she said, "I'll always be there for you, no matter what. Everything is going to be OK." She was gentle and kind. "You're not so scary with those eyes and all, you know." She put her hand under his shirt and felt his tight stomach.

"Most people seem to think so." Guy smiled.

"I'm not most people." She looked at him like a fox, a vixen. "You think that I'm scared of you, just because the boys are?" Marie could see now why the boys were scared of Guy. John and the rest of them were usually dumb and full of shit. But there was something intense about Guy.

"You should be." Guy rolled over and bit the inside of her thigh. He rolled back and looked in her eyes. "Do you know what I would do to you?" he whispered.

"I'd like to find out," she whispered back and touched the top of his ear.

"*Ahh.*" Guy bit his thumb. "Just wait." He stared deep into Marie's eyes, until he could see her blush in the moonlight. Her skin was fair and radiant with youth. "So how old are you?" Guy looked at her, having turned eighteen before summer.

184

"Fifteen," Marie said unabashedly.

"*Uuhhh*." Guy put his hand over his eyes.

"Are you kidding me?" Marie asked with an irritated tone. She pried Guy's hand off his eyes. "Seriously I've probably slept with more people than you have. You want to bust out a list? Ask the thirty-six-year-old who raped me." Marie was still calm as she stroked his hair.

Whoa, this chick was something. Guy was consumed by her. Why were guys always scumbags with girls? "Are you kidding me? Like every nice girl I meet." Most of them hot and raped, Guy thought. He was so sick and tired of this shit. "You want me to beat the fuck out of him? It would be a pleasure."

"No, besides, there are too many assholes. My stepdad used to slam us up against the wall and lock us in a dark closet for hours."

"What? Are you kidding me? What sort of sick fuck does that?" Guy began to sit up.

She pressed his chest back down, "Exactly. There are plenty of them. Trust me." Marie liked him. He was sensitive; he was a gentleman with morals. Here today, but in a way from a time in the past.

"I know." It was a shame Guy didn't run into any of these fucks firsthand. He took her hand which was on his chest and held her index finger to his lips. When he looked in her eyes, it was the most intimate moment either of them had experienced. They felt safe, understood.

"I was going to kill myself, so I got locked in a mental hospital for a little over two months. Kicked out of private school, lost all my friends. I was the smart kid, but no college money for me, because my mom decided to fuck the pool man and get a divorce." Guy put his hands down by his side.

"It's OK." She stroked his hair, and he knew it was. "So you never finished telling me why your middle name is Kerry. I think it's sexy."

"My real dad, Jack Finnigan, was an Airborne Ranger in Vietnam. A friend of his was killed when his position was overrun by Vietcong. He fought them back so the rest of the men could escape. They later found his body with forty dead Vietcong around him. They said he had killed them all because he still had his rifle. If the VC killed you, they took your rifle. He was awarded a Congressional Medal of Honor. His name was Kerry. My real dad came back from the war all messed up, stabbed this guy forty-four times over the fake drugs he had sold." Guy had found out all this from his aunt Roxie on a trip to New York when he was fourteen. "Threw the guy off a bridge while he was still alive. The guy died."

"I'm sorry. That's hard." She touched Guy's face. She knew it would all be OK, and she knew why the other boys were scared. She felt safe with him. His body was strong, lean, snow-white like hers. He was handsome but didn't seem to realize it. He wasn't a pretty boy.

"You have brothers and sisters?" Guy looked back into her beautiful brown eyes, her long bangs swept over her right ear with two studs and two hoops.

"That's an interesting question. It depends on how you look at it. Full biological, there are five of us. My brother, Arnold, is the eldest. He does martial arts too. Older sister, Champagne, and two younger sisters, Jackie and Maybel." Marie was counting on her fingers; she paused to take a breath. "Then there's the youngest, my half sister, Sunshine, from my stepdad, along with two stepsisters and a stepbrother, who I grew up with from the time I was seven—when my parents got divorced—until I was fourteen, and I moved in with my dad. My dad's bitch wife has two daughters, who are strange to say the least. My stepmom's a total bitch, and, no matter which group you look at, I'm always the middle child. Does that mean I am forgotten? For some reason, in this case, yes." Marie raised her voice for the first time and leaned back against the pole of the merry-go-round.

Guy turned on his side so his mouth was facing Marie's stomach. He enveloped her small frame with his arms and pressed his face into her. "How could anybody ever forget you?" Guy held her tightly. "I know I'm not crazy, but what's going on between us?" Guy blinked a few times longingly.

"You're not crazy." She stroked his face. "I know we just met, but I feel like we were meant to be together. Does that sound crazy?"

"Only because I'm thinking the same thing." Guy was lying on his side now, with his face in Marie's lap, looking up at her. With his arms wrapped around her tiny frame, they both felt safe. Where he could feel her skin, it was soft and smooth, erotic. He knew he would find out all about Marie; he was already sure she was girl who he would do anything for, even lead a good life.

"So my whole family is Mormon—except my dad was, now he isn't. His new wife is, so he kind of is again, I guess, but he really doesn't do anything. My brother's not Mormon either. But my older sister, who's down here, she's Mormon. And all my sisters are and my mom is, and my grandmas and blah, blah, blah." Marie was surprised she was telling him all this, but being with him felt right.

"Do they believe in Jesus?" If you didn't believe the right things about Jesus, you were going to hell, as far as Guy could tell. His lifestyle didn't always portray it, but he knew Jesus was real. He wanted to get married in the Catholic church one day.

"Yeah, but it's not that simple. They believe in all this other stuff too. I learned some of the differences from Christians at my school. I got sick of it. I never really believed all of it anyway, glass-bottom boats and all. I used to sneak out the window before Sunday school." She smiled.

"Hmm, hmm, hmm." Guy snickered except with a *hmm* instead of a *ha*. Marie was a pistol; she could take it too. Guy wanted to give it to her, bad. He laughed again. Guy felt as if the weight of the world was beginning to lift. When Marie said everything was OK, it was. Guy's journey as a man was just starting, and he had plans. He knew Marie was going to be part of those plans.

"I was a Catholic. Haven't been to church much lately though. Believe in Jesus, the Bible, Noah, Moses, the whole thing." Not that Guy knew exactly what *the whole thing* was, but he had read the Pentateuch—the first five books of the Bible—as well as the four Gospels in Catholic school. He stopped and breathed into her hand on his chest. "So, let's hang out, yes? 'Morrow night, I'll pick you up. After work, ten thirty?"

"A haiku, how cleverly cute. You are so silly, Guy Flynn or Guy Finnigan. To me, just my guy. I don't know if I can wait till tomorrow night." Marie would have slept with him right here in the park, even without a condom. She was on the pill. But that wasn't the type of guy he was.

Guy's head was about to explode. His references often went unrecognized or came off peculiar because of it. Guy didn't mind; he was regularly funny, but at times he did things for his own mental amusement. If other people caught on to the allusion, it was a real hearty laugh, but pointing it out seemed arrogant. Saying it without anyone catching on seemed arrogant too, but the mental distraction was alluring. Did she really just send a haiku of her own back at him? Guy's heart melted.

Marie made Guy feel complete. When they spoke, when they touched, he knew he never wanted to be without her. The fact they both felt the same amplified their own feelings. Guy had never met a girl like her, confident. She had survived her own trials. She had some innate understanding of Guy, even more than Milton. Plus Milton didn't have an ass like this, nor such deep eyes.

"A haiku of your own, you blow my mind. Don't tell me you read books too, please?"

"*Jane Eyre* is one of my favorites. Blow your mind, huh?" Marie laughed under her breath.

"Nice." Nice and boring, not like Dostoyevsky or Tolstoy, Dickens even, but that was for another night. This one seemed over in a blink, as the dawn of a new day arose.

Guy cleaned his room, not that it was ever particularly messy. He let John know he and Marie had made a connection. They didn't make out yet, but they were an item. The blacklights around his room illuminated the otherworldly posters. His room was warm, so he and Marie lay on top of his blue comforter. The twin bed was small, so they lay close to each other, in each other's arms. Her skin was so white and smooth, it glowed slightly from the blacklights. Marie's skin was so soft, the only thing Guy could think of to compare it to was a baby's skin. Hers was better—tight, sexy. When their tongues touched, they wanted to dive within each other.

Her nipples were light pink, hardly darker than her skin. Her breasts were firm, and she quivered when he touched them or brought them to his mouth. She wore black panties; they felt like velvet except they were wet now as Guy stroked her thighs and caressed her body.

Guy thought he would erupt, he was so full of desire and devotion. "We're going to do it twice, because I'm going to explode when I get inside of you." Guy thought about taking her panties off. It was like a present he had been waiting his whole life for.

"At least"—Marie smiled and dragged her nails over his back—"I'm on the pill, so you don't have to wear a condom." Marie liked the feel of Guy's body; it was hard, lean. His chest was smooth. He was a great kisser; she felt she could burst with happiness and wake the neighbors.

By the time they were done, they had explored each other's body with vigor. Guy used the jackhammer technique. A version of the missionary, where he put his hands behind Marie's neck and pulled her whole body down in rhythm as he thrust up. She had an orgasm, then three and four; she lost count as Guy came deep inside her. It was her first orgasm; her body and his had consumed each other.

"You know we're going to get married someday, right?" He kissed her head and stroked the fire flowing from it.

"I know," she said and squeezed his chest to hers.

BOOK TWO: CHAPTER FOUR

Guy and Marie wanted to be married, but they were in no rush. It seemed people with a short-term perspective on marriage never experienced the long-term rewards. To find a long-termer who wasn't from his grandparents' generation was rarer and rarer these days. While there was no rush, Guy and Marie fell hard and fast. Aside from responsibilities, they were inseparable. They would look into each other's eyes for hours on end, saying all that needed to be said in silence. It made people sick, especially Bea, Bear's mom. Guy and Marie could talk all night long. Often there were no words to express the depths of their feelings, so they simply consumed each other. It was an understanding, an acceptance, that they had both been missing in their lives. If Marie were the only thing the world had to offer, it would be a world worth living for.

Marie spent most nights in Guy's tiny bed. He would drive her home at five in the morning before the house was awake. Today Guy had the day off. He was enjoying an afternoon of Street Fighter II on his Super Nintendo.

John was Ken in the game. He was free as usual, since getting a job never made it to the top of his agenda. Bear was at work; he was putting in a lot of hours lately. Guy, as Chun Li, was effectively kicking Ken's teeth in. Guy knew how to use most of the characters. He and John were pretty evenly matched except when Guy did acid. Then he would go on three- or four-hour streaks without losing a battle.

"We're going to need another pound soon." Guy sat up on his bed.

John was on the floor. Guy did a Chun Li flutter kick which John followed with ten fireballs in a row. "Oh, don't cheese."

"I'm not cheesing. I'll tell Birdie we need another one, five hundred." Pounds were cheap. They only needed to sell twenty percent to make their money back.

"Cool, I'll get you cash."

Bear would pitch in. "So I think you're spending too much time with Birdie. Those guys are bad news, bro. I'm telling you."

"He's cool, nigga. Don't worry about it. You should come kick it." John let out a flying spin kick.

Guy had no interest in hanging out with Langdon Street. Those guys were gangsters, like Pacoima, not just some tagging crew. John had met them at the Winnetka Drive-In. The whole gang worked there. They used the theater to sell crack.

John had seen six giant bags of it in the back of one of their cars—along with three hand grenades, real ones.

"I'm serious, bro. Those guys are a one-way ticket to jail or a bullet." Guy took the second round.

"Ah, fucker. It's all good. They get cheap-ass weed, don't they?" John elbowed Guy's leg.

"For sure, but that doesn't mean you need to be best buds." Guy looked away from the JVC TV on his dresser, across from his bed, and over to John.

"All right, whatever." John picked Ken again.

Guy picked Ryu. Guy was going to win in two straight rounds, just to be a dick. He didn't like being told to fuck off, or whatever, especially where John was concerned.

Light entered the room when Marie opened his bedroom door. She still looked hot despite Subway's desire to hide her away in a pair of poorly fitted black pants, a green collared shirt and a green hat.

"Hey." Marie seemed distraught.

Guy put down his controller. "What's up?" Guy stared at her with lowered brows.

"I was just about to kick your ass." John looked up.

Marie shook her head as she took off her hat. She usually took it off when her brother picked her up, but she had been so mad. Her hair was long and thick. It would still be damp after her shift if she washed it first.

"Work. It sucks sometimes, that's all." Marie studied the floor.

"Marie, what happened?" Guy could tell something was upsetting her, something out of the ordinary course of work's general irritations. He went over to her and took her hand.

"Some people are just assholes. I don't want to talk about it. You'll just get all crazy." She looked toward the ceiling and put her hand on his chest.

"Are you fucking kidding me? What happened?" Now she had to tell him. He would do his best to stay calm.

"John." Marie turned to John for support.

She had a look in her eyes that let John know this was serious, that Guy was going to be pissed.

"Shit." John faced Guy. "You promise not to do anything stupid, to let me take care of this?"

Guy looked at John, then back to Marie "Are you fucking serious?"

John's eyes were wide, and he nodded.

"All right whatever." Guy shook his head. "Well?" he asked Marie.

"This guy Ernesto from work has been bugging me. He sexually harassed me today. I told the manager." Marie sat down on the bed, which was in the corner of Guy's room.

"What do you mean, *sexually harassed*?" Guy said calmly.

She met John's gaze again.

"What do you mean, *sexually fucking harassed*?" John asked.

"He fucking came up and tried to kiss my neck, then he grabbed my tit and pressed himself up against me."

Guy jumped in the air and put his hand to his head. "You have got to be kidding me. What did the manager say?" Guy tried not to lose his cool.

"She asked me if I could still work with him. I said if he could keep his hands to himself and his mouth shut, then, yes." Marie laid her head down upon the pillow.

Guy looked over at John with fire in his eyes.

"Let's roll." John held out his hand for Guy's keys.

Marie put her hands to her mouth.

"We're not gonna hurt him," John said in a long-drawn-out tone. "I promise. We're just gonna talk to him. I'll make sure Guy behaves himself. Ernesto's not gonna bug you again. Trust me."

"I'm sorry. It's OK." Guy kissed Marie's tender lips and followed John out the door.

Subway was close to Marie's house, off Zelzah. John tore the blocks up like Mad Max.

"I'm doing the talking. I'll put this fool on blast. Keep your mouth shut."

Guy promised he would, and he didn't break promises.

"Tell this fool, if he ever so much as talks to Marie again, I'm going to kill him." Guy was boiling over, but he would stick to the script and let John run point.

They were into the yellow-and-green-walled store quickly and quietly. John looked over the glass partitions to where the sandwiches were being prepared. Guy stood at his shoulder.

"Hey, is Ernesto here?" John yelled out loudly enough that anyone in earshot could hear.

"I'm Ernesto," a uniformed Mexican in his early twenties replied. He was about as tall as Guy, but lanky with long black hair to his shoulders.

"You know Marie who works here?" John looked him dead in the eyes.

"Yeah, I know Marie. Why?" He put his hands on his hips defiantly.

"Well, that's Marie's boyfriend behind me." John pointed over his shoulder with his thumb. "If you ever touch her again, if you are ever so much as rude to her, next time, you're gonna have to talk with him. Trust me, no one ever likes talking with him. He's fucking crazy. Don't make us come back again, or you'll regret it. You understand me?" John was loud enough for everyone in the store to hear, which Guy thought was well and good.

Ernesto was stunned.

"Got it?" John asked again. This time he leaned over the counter.

"Got it," Ernesto answered back. Guy's stare burned a hole in Ernesto. Ernesto looked at him only once, briefly.

John looked over his shoulder to his friend. Guy nodded and walked for the door. When they were outside, John put his arm around Guy's shoulder and squeezed. "Did I do good?" John asked.

"Did I?" Guy laughed, looking straight forward toward his Mustang. "Yeah, you did good. That was perfect. He just better keep his damn mouth shut now."

The problem was Ernesto had only kept his mouth shut for about three shifts.

Guy was at Bea's when he had cajoled the truth out of an exasperated Marie. Ernesto had looked her up and down, and had mentioned that she "looked extremely hot today." It was the stare afterward that left her really uncomfortable.

A look was all Bear needed to follow Guy to the car. They arrived after 11p.m., after Subway was closed. It was dark, and the commercial center was reasonably quiet, except for people at the gas station. Ernesto was due out by 11thirty. They would have time to listen to half of *It Takes a Thief* by Coolie, track five "Ghetto Cartoon", always made Guy smile.

Track six blared as Ernesto walked out the front door.

Guy was across the parking lot in a moment. Bear sighed deeply following behind; this was going to get ugly, he thought.

"What were you told, asshole?" Guy yelled as he strode over to Ernesto.

Ernesto turned and stopped; he clenched his hands into fists at his side.

"You were told to leave her alone, but you just couldn't keep your fucking mouth shut, could you?" Guy stopped just out of Ernesto's reach.

"Fuck you, asshole," Ernesto shot back.

Great and surprising, Guy thought. He jutted his forehead forward quickly a few inches. As was hoped, Ernesto took a swing. He was actually going to stand his ground. The punch was sloppy, a bit of a haymaker. There was plenty of time for Guy to adjust; however, he decided to play things Hulk Hogan, Superman style. The punch landed on the side of Guy's face. He hardly flinched, staring all the while into Ernesto's eyes, before he threw a right cross with all his force directly at Ernesto's chin. He was out immediately, on his back unconscious. Guy straddled his chest and waited for him to wake up. Once he opened his eyes, Guy grabbed him around the windpipe with one hand and began to squeeze. Ernesto's eyes held the fear of a man about to die.

"Never, ever talk to Marie again. Never look at her. Never speak to her, ever," Guy screamed with fury. He never screamed. He hated yelling. He was usually able to get his point across without it.

Ernesto squirmed underneath him like a dying animal.

"Stop! Stop, you're going to kill him. We're calling the police." A woman with pixie-cut hair ran over from the gas station with three or four onlookers beside her.

Guy was not going to kill him. In fact Guy was not even going to strangle him long enough to make him lose consciousness again. "You never want to see me again." Guy looked into Ernesto's eyes and gritted his teeth. Guy stood up and passed the car keys to Bear. They smoked a bowl on the way back to Bea's, so Guy could cool down and Bear could get high, since he was still keeping up pretensions in front of his mother.

It was just one of those weeks. John was off-kilter too. He seemed unhappy lately; he was spending more time with the guys from Langdon Street.

Guy knew John was smoking P dogs, joints laced with crack. Guy had tried it; it made your lips numb, which was fun, but crack was dangerous as fuck. It was also a stimulant, so no thanks. Heroin was a downer. That's what his dad did. That shit could ruin people's lives, first try. They said the same thing about crack.

John had stolen some speed about the size of a baseball, or grapefruit, from some kid John met while cruising town with his new friend Birdie. John had sat in the passenger seat when he had asked the kid in the back to see his ball of meth. It had been such a beautiful specimen that John had decided to keep it. The kid had pleaded and cried, but stopped when John had opened his four-inch serrated Gerber knife. It was a gift from Guy and had HB4L engraved on it. They then kicked the kid out of the car.

When Guy had heard the story, he wondered what the hell John wanted with a big rock of speed anyway.

What the fuck was John going to do with it? It truly was a beautiful specimen, but it's not like they were going to use it or sell it or even keep it the fuck around. What the fuck was John's problem? Guy knew John well. He didn't have much of an education, but he was great with his hands; he could make a real life for himself. After some serious prodding, John became unraveled, and his woes flowed along with his tears. His uncle was calling around the house lately. John had two uncles, brothers; they had molested him. They did every despicable thing imaginable. John just repeated, "Everything, everything," as he shook his head and cried.

Less than a week later, Guy received a call while working at Coco's. John's uncle was at the house. It would take Guy five or six minutes to get there. He told his boss there was an emergency and tore across Reseda Boulevard from Coco's to John's house. John's mother, Ann, was not happy to see him as Guy walked through the front door and into the kitchen of their small house.

"Where is he?" Guy asked, looking about.

"He's taking a walk around the block." John was standing beside his mother in the cramped kitchen. Ann's hair was blonde, crimped. She was a heavy smoker.

"Look, Guy, I know you're tough and all, but John's uncle is a gorilla. He's a real bruiser, Guy. He was just telling us how he goes down to the bar and gets in fights with five or six guys at a time. His arms are as big as a bodybuilder." She grabbed her bicep. "I'm telling you, Guy, you need to leave before he gets back here. I don't want you to get hurt." She looked at him with dead seriousness.

Guy sighed and looked at her calmly. He touched her shoulder. "Ann, when I said I studied martial arts all those years, I wasn't kidding. Don't worry about me." He looked over to John. "Let's go." Guy walked out the front door with John following behind him.

"So when he comes up, speak your peace. Now's your chance to say whatever you want to this piece of shit, to get everything off your chest. When you're done, just look over at me, and I'll knock him the fuck out." Guy looked at John firmly. "It's OK. This is it." They waited in the driveway of John's grandfather's house. The grandfather's name was John also; Ann had named her son after her father.

John's uncle Merl was burly, a cross between a bodybuilder and a lumberjack. He strolled down the sidewalk, hemmed in on one side by the grass strip running along the curb and the modest homes on the other. His arms swung back and forth nonchalantly. John stood at the edge of driveway and the curb.

Merl and his taut T-shirt were greeted by John's now deeper voice.

"What you did to me really fucked me up. I have a hard time with relationships, with the way I treat girls. I hate you for what you did to me." John looked his uncle dead in the eyes. His uncle had fractured his very being. The things done too hard to even think of. So they weren't thought of, nor spoken of, never, ever. That still wasn't enough. It didn't go away. John's sex life was robust, but it didn't feel right. He just couldn't; he wasn't sure what.

"What are you talking about? Are you being serious?" Merl said snidely.

Tears welled up in John's eyes. "After all that!" He screamed, "You lying piece of shit!" He looked over his shoulder to Guy. "I'm done with this piece of trash." John took a step back.

"Time to deal with me, asshole." Guy stepped a right arm's distance from Merl and removed the veil from his eyes. He allowed Merl to see how his dirty deeds made Guy seethe. To know in advance what was coming. Merl did know, but this time groveling would not suffice, and so Merl was put on notice, so as not to be surprised.

"Time to get knocked out, mutherfucker." Guy put up his dukes and allowed his eyes to speak for one more moment. He threw a right cross, with all his body weight, like a flash, center chin. Guy stepped in quickly, expecting a heated brawl. But knocked out was the right phrase, indeed. Merl fell like a sack of potatoes, his knees to the left, his head back, then to the right. Guy was actually a bit surprised. He looked to John with raised eyebrows, whose expression was mirrored by John, except with his hands over his mouth.

"Damn!" John said through cupped hands.

As Merl lie upon the ground and he slowly opened his eyes, he appeared as shocked and frightened as a deer meeting a semi. But then in a flash, he was off to the races. Merl was fast, as fast as a deer. Guy had never been a fast runner. Merl's car was at the end of the next block, and he was at it fast. His car sped off before Guy and John got close.

Guy and John ran back toward the house and hopped in the 'stang. They chased Merl onto the Four O Five North at Rinaldi, just to give him an extra scare.

"You all right? Did you say what you needed to say?" Guy looked over to John as they drove back to his grandfather's.

"Hell yeah, I did! Did you see that fool? He got dropped like a little bitch! Thanks, bro. Nobody ever did nothing like that for me before. That mutherfucker really messed me up." John shook his head.

"My pleasure. Fuck that mutherfucker."

John took a big lungful and passed the glass pipe to Guy.

It wasn't enough though, not enough to free John's mind from its cellar. John was having more of a I-could-give-a-fuck attitude, papered over regularly with P dogs. Guy loved John, not in a sexual way, but in that he cared for him deeply. John extended a hand when no one else would. Not simply extended, he grabbed Guy's hand firmly. John wouldn't have been able to pass seventh grade at Chaminade, but he was loyal, he spoke his mind. John cared for Guy too; he showed it in his actions by spending time, in thoughtfulness. It got to be so they, along with Bear, knew each other's perspectives and reactions before they occurred. Consideration was made in advance.

John was in that place where Guy once was, wandering around the entrance to a dark tunnel. Guy wasn't sure what the problem was. Guy had hoped, by John expressing his feelings to his uncle, that John's direction would begin to change. The dangerous path, however, continued unabated. Guy tried ribbing, then kindness, but each time John would say he was fine, mirroring the tone in which he was asked. Guy knew John lying. It was time for a more serious conversation.

"So what's really going on?" Guy asked as John opened his bedroom door.

"What up!" John asked elatedly. He held out his hand for a palm slap to be followed by a fist bump.

Guy stood by his bed, obliged, then stepped to John's chest, looking him in the eyes. "What's going on?" Guy spoke slowly and deeply.

"What's up, fool?" John looked Guy in the eyes, then up at the ceiling.

"Yo, what's wrong? You know I can tell when you're lying." Guy held out his hands casually; he was half Italian after all. "You know I've been in that dark place. I thought you wanted to take care of your uncle. What the fuck's up?" Guy touched his temple.

"Nothing." John dove on the bed, onto his stomach, putting a pillow over his head.

Guy sat down next to him and put his hand between John's shoulder blades. "You've seen me at my worst, bro, how many times? Strapped to the gurney at the hospital, trying to kill you while freaked-the-fuck-out on acid, hello?" Guy's tone was joking and empathetic.

"Fuck, dude. Yes, my uncle, but"—John pulled the pillow down harder upon his head.

"It's OK. Let it go." Guy rubbed his back.

John began to sob. When he caught his breath, he said between the tears, "I can't stop thinking about his brother too."

Guy looked up at the white-popcorn ceiling of his room. "Older or younger brother?"

"Older. Fucking asshole." John loosed his grip on the pillow and rolled over onto his back, keeping the pillow pressed upon his face.

Guy rested his palm on his friend's chest. "I'm sorry. What do you want to do?"

"I want that mutherfucker to get what he deserves. It's all I can think about." John took the pillow off of his face and sat up against the wall.

He looked at Guy. "He's a crazy-ass drug dealer, OK? That's why I didn't say anything. That's why I was just trying to forget about it. Everyone thinks he's so great, Mr. Big Shot." The tears streamed down John's face.

Guy's heart ached; it seethed. There was nothing worse than the taking of a child's innocence; it could never be replaced.

"A big scary drug dealer." Guy put his hand to his mouth and pretended to bite his nails, like a wide-eyed cartoon character.

"You're so fucking stupid." John laughed. You're crazy, he said with his eyes.

"What does John want to do?" Guy asked wistfully. "Totally your call."

"I wanna get that fool," John said with disturbed quietness.

"Then we get him, but only if it's really going to make you feel better. Put an end to this slump. No more hanging out with fucking Birdie. No more P dogs." Guy put his hand on John's knee gently. John's left knee had a lump from a bike accident.

John raised his fists. "He needs a payback. That's all I can think about. You're right. No more Birdie. No more P dogs. I'm done. My uncle's name is William. We called him Billy."

They formulated a plan; they discussed scenarios, then particulars over and over again. They couldn't be recognized. They'd wear generic clothes: blue jeans, plaid long-sleeve button-ups, black gloves, and two green bandanas. One over the top of their heads tied behind, and one tied like Jesse James so that just a small slit remained for the eyes. Generic white tennis shoes. All thrown in a Dumpster behind a Ralphs grocery afterward.

They wanted to be in and out in seven minutes, no matter what. They didn't want to hang out long enough in case the cops were called. Arrest was always out of the question. Suicide by cop ended that scenario.

Guy parked two buildings down. It was a townhome complex. The units had a Nineteen Seventies look; they were two stories with dark wood trim. Billy's was an end unit.

It was late, after 11 p.m.; the complex was quiet. Guy and John crept up the stone path flanked by bushes shaved into spheres. Guy pointed the 9mm at the door and knocked. John had borrowed the gun from a friend, since Guy's had been confiscated. John had met some nerdy twenty-one-year-olds with legal firearms. For a reason unbeknownst to Guy, they let John borrow one of their guns. Actually because John smoked them out and always brought girls over. They wanted to be cool and allowed their guns to live vicariously through John.

John would not speak tonight, just to be cautious. Guy would do all the talking, and seven minutes would be more than long enough to send a permanent message.

Billy opened the door, wearing a dirty white T-shirt.

"Get on the ground, mutherfucker." Guy stepped in so that his foot was past the entrance to the door.

"Stop messing around." Billy waved his arm and laughed.

"I will blow your fucking head off. Get on the ground," Guy said slowly, deliberately. Billy keeled over on the floor like a fainting goat, except his face was more disturbed. His tongue stuck out, and his eyes rolled back in his head. Guy stepped over Billy into the entranceway. There was a stairway to the second floor on the right and through the entryway a living room where two men and a woman were seated. Guy pointed the gun toward the man on the right.

"Who's upstairs?"

"Nobody," the man answered quivering. All three sat with their hands in the air.

Guy checked. The man wasn't lying.

"On your bellies." He passed the gun to John. "We're not going to hurt anyone, except maybe that piece-of-shit Billy over there. Squirm over here on your belly, like the worm you are, Billy."

Billy obliged, as did the others.

Guy pulled out a roll of silver duct tape from his back pocket, so versatile. Guy quickly bound the men's ankles and hands behind their backs. He put duct tape over their mouths.

"Would you prefer to sit on the couch, dear?" Guy asked the girl with long brown hair and bell-bottom jeans, as he motioned to the olive sectional. "I could just do your hands, if you promise to behave."

"I'll behave." She sat back on the couch, and Guy put one loop of duct tape around her wrists.

Guy stepped back beside Billy, who was lying on the spotted cream-colored shag carpet. Guy held out his hand to John for the gun, then put his knee down hard on Billy's temple. Enough to make him moan. He grabbed Billy's hair with his left hand and turned him face up, looking at him through the slit of his bandana. Then Guy looked at the girl.

"Did you know this piece of shit likes to touch little children? Tell her, Billy."

"That's a lie!" Billy yelped out, hardly moving.

The girl held her hand over her mouth. "He would never." She looked as if she would cry.

"You lying piece of shit." Guy cocked the hammer to the gun and pressed it firmly to Billy's temple, as he lay upon the floor. Through the slit of his kerchiefs he would devour Billy.

"You like to have oral sex with little kids, huh? Sodomize them? You despicable piece of garbage!" Guy pressed his knee into Billy's side, and the barrel into his temple. "Bye-bye, trash. Last chance. Tell her or die!" Guy had no intention of killing Billy, still his blood was boiled. Stealing the innocence of little children who couldn't defend themselves. Innocence that could never be brought back. Guy hated when the strong preyed upon the weak; he hated bullies.

Billy cried, "It's true. It's all true."

"He's just saying that because he's scared." The brown-haired girl had both hands over her mouth now and looked as if she were about to cry.

"Tell her the names. I won't ask twice." Guy released the gun from Billy's temple and motioned as if he would put it back.

"Oh, God. Oh, God. Oh, God." Billy began to sob uncontrollably. He sniffled hard twice. "Matthew, Tommy, Darren, John, Stan, Davey, Joey and Bobby, Merl, Jeff, Paul, Thomas, Eric."

"Eric?" The brown-haired girl stood to her feet. She had known Billy since she was a kid. She was eight years older than her younger brother, Eric.

"Eric! Eric?" She walked and stood over Billy. "My fucking brother? Are you serious? You miserable piece of shit. How could you? No!"

He was in the fetal position on the floor.

She pounded his shoulder.

His hands were over his face. "Yes, yes, and more, more, oh, my God, no, no."

"You monster!" The small girl seized upon him with the rage of a mother grizzly and tore at his face. She flailed at his head. "No, how could you?" She sobbed over and over.

"I want all the drugs and all the money in the house right now." Guy looked down at Billy.

The brown-haired girl looked up; her face was red, and tears streamed down continuously from the wells of her eyes. "I'll get them." She stood defiantly.

"Go with her." Guy looked over to John. They returned quickly with a paper brick slightly wider but not quite as thick as a regular brick. John held up a thin wad of cash as well.

"Open it." Guy motioned to the brick.

"It's coke." The girl looked at the floor.

Guy removed the duct tape from the men's mouths.

200

"So that everyone's clear what this is about, it's about Billy being a serial child molester. Is everyone clear about that?"

"Yes" was whispered between the three.

"Are you going to report him to the police?" Guy looked to the girl with the brown hair.

"Fuck yes, I am," she said angrily.

"You promise?"

"That's my baby brother! First thing in the morning, that piece of shit is going to get what he deserves. Maybe you can get raped in prison, you piece of shit." She folded her arms angrily.

Guy looked over to John standing beside a glass table upon which the brick sat. "Flush it."

"No," Billy sobbed.

John cut open the package with his Gerber knife and dumped the contents into the bathroom hall toilet. Several flushes later, he rinsed off the package and his knife in the sink. Not a sniff left.

When John returned from the bathroom, Guy picked up Billy by the hair. He grabbed Billy's hand tight and pulled a straight razor from his pocket. Guy held the edge to Billy's finger.

"If I ever, ever hear about you so much as looking wrong at another kid, I will find you and cut off your fingers," Guy said slowly. "Understand me?"

"Yes," Billy said defeatedly, hardly able to stand under the weight of his own convictions. Guy pushed him back to the floor, like a falling glass.

"Call the cops in the morning."

"I will." She nodded.

Guy was pleased. Hardly more than six minutes, mission accomplished.

The time since he had met Marie was a blur, because she blurred his vision. Guy was not pleased with the new escalation taken to bring closure with Billy. Ann had heard from her sister two days later that the cops had arrested Billy the day before at his house.

The world changed when Marie softened Guy's heart. He wouldn't have agreed to join the Marine Corps if she been there at the time, but it could provide a good foundation for them. A foundation for the wife who she would be, for their not-yet-materialized family. Without the ability to pay for an education, Guy was extremely unlikely to crack the hundred-thousand-dollar salary mark. In California, Los Angeles no less, a hundred K was simply living reasonably, not richly. After his hospital stay, Guy had decided to enjoy the world's view without following a road map to see where he was going. He figured he was smart enough to make some money, if he set his mind to it.

He was eighteen now. Guy had reflected over the course of the last two years since he had gotten out of the hospital. He could clearly see the escalation in his dangerous activities. The Marine Corps was an emergency chute he had hoped he wouldn't have to pull. Bear's mother had signed his waiver, since he was only seventeen at the time.

John stuck to his end of the bargain and stayed close to Guy and Bear. He smoked nothing, aside from cigarettes and weed. He was drained, nothing cheered him up. He needed a trip to a facility himself. Ann coordinated with Oliveview, a county facility. It was nice and available. It worked.

After a week of pleading, John convinced Guy to sneak a whippet in during visiting hours. John did the nitrous oxide in the bathroom and gave the brass cracker and balloon back to Guy. He wanted John to focus on getting better, to not rush getting out.

When John did get out, the spring was back in his step. He got his first job at Captain Ed's and had politely said the Marine Corps was no place for him. It was too big a thing to ask, but Guy knew in his heart Marie would say yes. Yes to waiting for him until he got out of the marines. Eventually they could live off base, once he got stationed, hopefully down in San Diego at Camp Pendleton. At least that's what the recruiter said was most likely.

He and Bear were scheduled to leave in the spring of ninety five. The world was a quiet place. Guy had his list of reasons why; he would get some money for school—not enough to attend a good school, but enough to help out. Also some preferred lending for a house; it would break his family's cycle. When Marie said yes, Guy kissed her a thousand times, all over her body. She was young, only fifteen. If it were another young lady, any other young lady, the waiting would simply be words. Four years and many fond admirers would be too much of a youthful burden. With Marie there was not the slightest concern.

Guy and Bear began to train. Bear needed to shed some pounds, and Guy needed to bulk up. They lifted weights, ran, did push-ups and pull-ups. Bear was big, not nearly as lean as Guy, but he could run. Guy hated running. They both worked on getting solid three-mile qualification times. They would run around the block across from Guy's house; it was a mile around. They could almost do twenty pull-ups, and Guy could do sit-ups and push-ups all day, because they were a staple at martial arts.

Marie took over babysitting duties with Pearl and Herman. They loved her; she was much more thoughtful and kind than the boys were. Everyone loved Marie though; she was one of the rare few who put others before herself. She wrote thank-you cards; she was like the Energizer bunny. She kept going and going and going. She rarely thought of herself.

That was OK, because Guy could never stop thinking about her. If he was concerned, even for a moment, that Marie didn't think it was the right decision for him to go, he would stay. That was the thing. She did trust his judgment, his decisions. Just as important, she knew what he needed, without him saying it, often when he wasn't quite sure himself. He spoiled her for it, emotionally, materially, sexually. He adored her, protected her, and now he needed to provide for her. Make a life for her. He never wanted her to be sad or in want.

Guy put on ten pounds of muscle. He weighed one sixty five now and was running satisfactorily by the spring of ninety five. They were going to leave in April, but Guy and Bear would receive the big green weenie, before they even knew what it was. During one of the final medical screenings, Bear was told he had a hernia that required surgery. He would have to push out six weeks later, if he had the surgery immediately. For some hard-to-explain reason, it was now completely impossible to keep them both on the same track; there were simply too many recruits. They were both disheartened but agreed the plan was crucial whether they went together or not. After boot camp, or recruit training, they would have infantry school, then the fleet. It was almost certain they would both be stationed down in San Diego. They would be together for most of the duration anyway.

Guy scored a perfect score on his ASVAB; Bear scored in the nineties. Their recruiter, Staff Sergeant Lucky, wanted Guy to go aboard a nuclear submarine; it had prestige. Guy was adamant he wanted to go into the infantry, but Lucky said that was where they sent the ASVAB waivers. Guy won; he and Bear would both go to the infantry. Guy had joined the Marine Corps for a challenge and a good old-fashioned kick in the ass. He was going to be a real marine, an infantryman. He would get a degree in something he could make money with, not something involving submarines or his hands.

Guy and Marie spent every moment of their 9 month romance together. Nearly as much time compressed as Guy, John and Bear had spent together over the previous two years. Guy needed Marie in a way that was feverish and unquenchable, but positive and alive. She was a woman beyond his dreams. They both knew in their hearts they would spend the rest of their lives together, so they felt no need to rush. They would do things right. Marie got her GED as well and enrolled in community college for the summer. She would work at Subway's until she could find something better, plus spend time watching Pearl and

Herman. She and Guy would write and see each other as soon as possible. Guy was happy he had his whole life, for he suspected even it would be too short to share with her.

BOOK TWO: CHAPTER FIVE

Six hours into today's Marine Corps thrashing, and Guy was surprised and a bit regretful of his decision. His mouth was so dry, he would have licked the sweat from a dead horse. Still he would not have changed his decision. He had joined the Marine Corps because it was the toughest of the tough. Guy had always considered himself tough. Now he was going to find out just what sort of ass-kicking he could endure. He saw *Full Metal Jacket* and the rest. Hollywood was illusion, and its air of hollowness did not prepare Guy for what was coming.

He thought back to his first day. The bus full of hopeful recruits had stopped at Denny's before they pulled into the Marine Corps Recruit Depot near San Diego. There was not much talk, just some nervous chatter while everyone ate. Silence as the bus pulled through the gate. When it stopped on the other side, a drill instructor appeared, wearing the familiar garb of old: an olive circle-brimmed hat, khaki shirt, green trousers held up by a bright belt buckle sporting a gold eagle, globe and anchor. The drill instructor tore onto the bus in a whirlwind that would have made the Tasmanian devil dizzy. The screaming and insults were first-rate, as if a core conviction rather than a portrayal.

Screaming and insults were child's play for Guy; yet some of the recruits were really rattled. Their heads were shaved; they were issued all sorts of gear and uniforms, two different types of boots. The all-leather boots were called cadillacs, and the pair with nylon webbing were called jungle boots. Everything had a different name. A flashlight was a moonbeam; a hat was a cover, which was always worn outside but never inside. A pen was a writing stick; you always used black ink, never blue. It was clearly all some form of brainwashing, but Guy allowed the information to flow into his mind and made the transition easily.

The first real tests for Guy were physical in nature and of the kind Guy wasn't expecting. *Hurry up and wait*, the Marine Corps motto was put to good use the first few days. They sat in rows on the floor, Indian style, so close that Guy's feet touched the person in front on him. Guy was surprised to learn that a couple hours sitting cross-legged brought unbearable leg cramps. They were so painful that no amount of squirming could ease them. Your mind settled on the absolute necessity of straightening your legs, the one thing that was, under no circumstances, allowed. Eight hours of pain proved that eventually your legs would go numb. One recruit who had dared to straighten his legs was yanked to his feet by his collar, screamed at in the customary inch-from-your-face fashion and thrown back to the floor with force. An hour later when he did it again, he was dragged away by the nape of his neck, not to return.

Falling asleep was another test Guy would not have envisioned as a problem. When the new recruits had arrived, they stayed awake for two days straight. Running here and there, only to sit cross-legged on a concrete floor for hours. You could see heads nod as the recruits started to doze. A loud smack to the back of the head—or *grape*, as it was called—from a scowling machine cleared the daze from the eyes. Sleep's mist is a difficult enemy; it permeates and suffocates until there is no fight left. Guy endured.

Guy joined Platoon 1113 in Delta Company. Their graduation date was June Sixteenth, Nineteen Ninety Five. They started with sixty recruits but were down to fifty quickly. They had four drill instructors, including their Senior DI Staff Sergeant Burrow. He was a nice man, firm, fair. He was black and rarely seen, which left the sadists to toil. There was another staff sergeant, SSgt. Garvas. He was Hispanic. Sergeant Willum was black, short and strong. Sergeant Sutherland was white and particularly sadistic. The cruelty of the drill instructors was new to Guy in that they enjoyed it; they relished it. Guy had expected it; he had expected to be pushed to his limits.

But the honed cruelty in an environment of unfettered power was more than Guy had envisioned. The dirt was their friend every day last week; they were thrashed without end. Push-ups, down but not touching the floor, hold it, no butts in the air. Running in place with arms straight out in front and knees lifted to the waist. Leg lifts on your back, chin to chest, both feet up, down, but not to the floor; scissor kicks; jumping jacks. Guy thought he could do jumping jacks all day, until he tried doing them in sand and cadillacs.

They rotated through the exercises quickly. Up, down; back, chest. No drinking water unless you were given permission. Permission was ten seconds' worth every two or three hours. About four hours in, men literally started to cry for their mothers. At about five hours, someone finally dropped, and an ambulance was called. Sitting cross-legged never felt so good. They faced away from the ambulance, straight backed, hands on knees. They were told to drink a whole canteen. The breeze was tranquil; it was important to stay hydrated.

Today made Guy long for the sand pit. Since the moment they woke up, they were playing fuck-fuck games in the squad bay, where no one could see. The squad bay was simple concrete floors with a row of metal bunk beds, called racks, down each side. This left a large corridor down the center and two smaller corridors down each wall. The walls were lined with large windows. Square support beams went up to a drop ceiling. Each bunk mate had a footlocker at the bottom of the rack closest to the main inside corridor.

The new recruits had just finished the duck walk. There was not much Guy hated more than the duck walk. They marched in circles around the racks. You crouched so low that your butt was just above your heels as you walked with your fingers interlocked behind the back of your head. Guy's thighs and calves burned as if they were actually ablaze. Simply falling provided a powerful extinguisher, but it was letting the body burn that allowed it to stand. Plenty of recruits did fall over; the DIs punched and kicked them in the guts like lively contestants on a game show.

"Waterbowls, POA." Sgt. Sutherland barked commands like a rabid dog.

Just standing in position of attention mediated the fire from Guy's legs. Guy grabbed his canteen and stood with his heels and toes touching, his gaze straight ahead. His left hand in a fist at his side, his right the same but cupping his canteen.

"Are you fucking kidding me?" SSgt. Garvas tore across the floor and grabbed Recruit Makandog's canteen from his hands. Makandog had twisted off the top of his canteen, wrongly assuming he had been given permission to drink. Makandog looked Southeast Asian, perhaps Indonesian or Vietnamese. He certainly spoke English as a second language. He had trouble following instructions to the letter and was also weak at PT—physical training.

"Did I tell you to hydrate, recruit?"

"Yes, sir," Recruit Makandog answered in a less-than-blistering tone.

"What?" The Staff Sergeant's tone was incredulous.

"Yes, sir," Recruit Makandog answered with more force.

"Are you just plain stupid or what, recruit? Now, did I tell you to hydrate or did I tell you to get your fucking waterbowl, genius?"

"This recruit was told to get his waterbowl, sir," Makandog answered as loudly as his lungs allowed.

He was Guy's height, about six foot, and gangly with tanned dark skin. He spoke with a thick accent, and, though he didn't seem like a dolt, he had a difficult time processing orders instantaneously. Peculiar verbiage did not make things easier.

"So why did you hydrate, recruit?" SSgt. Garvas snarled.

Recruit Makandog proved he was no dummy and gave the only answer that was likely to get him off the hook. "This recruit is stupid, sir," Makandog said directly.

"Recruit Makandog is stupid. Do you hear that, platoon? Recruit Makandog is a dumb shit who doesn't like to follow instructions. Time for the electric chair. Say 'Thank you, Recruit Makandog.'"

"Thank you, Recruit Makandog," the platoon repeated, exhausted and defeated.

The one thing Guy hated more than the duck walk was the electric chair.

"Backs to the fucking wall. Three, two, one." Sgt. Sutherland spit his commands as he pointed to the walls with both arms straight out. "Did I say put down your waterbowl, Bugal? Get that waterbowl in your dick skinner, boy!" Sgt. Sutherland charged him like a bull elephant.

"We will play fuck-fuck all day and all night. Do you sons-a-bitches hear me? Waterbowls up." The platoon squatted against the wall, extended locked arms in front of them, holding the waterbowl. Guy was so parched he felt as if his throat would close.

"Assume the position." Sgt. Sutherland's voice was especially powerful.

The recruits spent the first two weeks of boot camp coughing away. Raw throats from sounding off mingled with bugs from anywhere west of the Mississippi. Guy had it bad for a week or two. The drill instructors told everyone to suck-it-the-fuck-up. Guy sucked it up; no way he was going to be a broke dick and go to sick bay. Peculiarly he noticed he hadn't had an erection since he had arrived, not one.

"Bugal, get that ass down, you cock guzzling faggot," Sgt. Willum said slowly and deeply through grated teeth. He pushed Bugal's shoulders down until his thighs were parallel with the floor.

Guy had hoped for push-ups, anything but more legs. His legs were not as strong as his arms when it came to endurance games, especially when compared to others. Guy's thighs shook violently in place; his burning legs approached collapse. His shoulders and forearms began to lower, imperceptibly for now. He hoped someone would break first. The drill instructor's need for blood was rarely satiated, and Guy tried to keep himself out of the DI's crosshairs.

Recruit Bugal hit the floor hard. He appeared more sixteen than eighteen, a pale waif of a man. His buzzed brown hair made him look more like a cancer patient than most of the others. He hit the floor with a thud, as his strength left him entirely.

"You worthless maggot, get up before I stomp your brains out." Sgt. Willum raised his combat boot over Bugal's head which had careened against the floor.

Bugal staggered to his feet, slumping his thin fame against the bulkhead.

"Recruit Digrigli requests permission for Platoon 1113 to hydrate, Staff Sergeant," the guide—the senior-most recruit—blared loudly, still in the electric chair position, his eyes locked forward. Digrigli was short and amazingly fit. He already ran a perfect PT, three miles in under eighteen minutes, and he could crank out twenty-plus chin-ups with ease.

"Shut your cock washer boy." Sergeant Sutherland strode to the end of the line pointing his finger directly at Recruit Digrigli with a steely stare of death in his eyes. A stare that men had seen in Guy's eyes, but Guy had rarely seen outside of a mirror.

"Get these recruits hydrated, Sergeant Sutherland." Staff Sergeant Garvas waved his hand as if shooing a fly from his chest while walking out the squad bay door.

"You heard, Staff Sergeant. Waterbowls up, time to hydrate." Sergeant Sutherland began to count backward from thirty, which was the time allotted for a recruit to finish his waterbowl of water. Not a lot of water for a prolonged time, but a lot of water to drink all at once. Guy was able to guzzle a lot of water fast, the same way he was able to inhale his food by taking large bites. This came in handy when the drill instructors informed everyone that they were done eating only five or ten seconds after Guy sat down. Certainly not a single occurrence nor an every-meal occasion.

Everyone finished their waterbowls in time, though a few recruits took the last mouthfuls down their shirts.

"Open your waterbowl. Thirty, twenty-nine, twenty-eight."

The recruits picked up their second waterbowl and began to guzzle. While it was tough, most people could drink a full waterbowl and most recruits could drink one quickly. Two waterbowls was a different story.

Guy was often a man of extremes, and yet he found a second waterbowl extremely challenging.

Two recruits, who had trouble with the first waterbowl, quickly began to gag.

Out of the corner of his eye, Guy could see one of them begin to puke. Guy breathed in through his nose slowly and swallowed hard, finishing the last ten ounces or so of the waterbowl's half-gallon capacity.

Five or six more recruits threw up before zero.

The third canteen was a near disaster for Guy. He got it down over a few gags, but nearly everyone puked. Guy's stomach wished he had. Wearing puke-covered clothes, while getting thrashed in the dirt, was standard training.

Thankfully the night was already late, and it was straight to the showers, after the pukers had cleaned up their mess with the clothes they were wearing.

The showers were all in one silver cylinder with spray nozzles all around, placed too close together around an open room. They were sure to receive instructions on how to wash their shit holes and under their ball sacks from Staff Sergeant Garvas.

Before the lights were switched off, the recruits faced their racks at the position of attention.

"Ready to fight. Ready to kill. Ready to die, but never will. *Oorah*, Marine Corps," Platoon 1113 blared with murderous eyes. With closed fists, chests were pounded twice like King Kong. "*Uhhh, uhhh, ahhh*." The recruits pounded their mattress at the end and leaped beneath the covers from the position of attention. The lights were off, and the night's firewatch would hopefully be the only break in precious slumber.

Guy had a bottom rack, not that it was his choice, but it was certainly his preference now. Certainly after Sergeant Sutherland had strangled Recruit Makandog with the laundry bag that hung from his bunk while Sergeant Willum whispered in his ear. They promptly flipped his mattress from the top bunk onto the concrete floor. He landed with a *crack*.

Guy would have chosen the beating over last week's humiliation in the shower. Aside from having to wash their cocks, ball sacks and shit holes long after they were already clean, it was also routine for Recruit Bugal to drop his soap.

As if the DIs were waiting for the cue, the platoon was marched out into the squad bay, soaking wet, as soon as the soap hit the floor. The recruits were forced to form two lines, then made to move closer until they were all back to chest. No way to keep your junk from touching your neighbor's behind and vice versa. They were forced to put their hands over their heads, and jump up and down repeatedly, until they were drip-dried. It would have made some sicko a great whack-off movie.

Abuse of power and humiliation were right up some folks' alley; they went hand in hand. Try as they might, they could not steal Guy's mind, and he used it whenever he wanted. When things were at their worst, he would prewrite letters to Marie. Once permission was given, he was able to get three letters written quickly once they were begun. The letters in the envelope were all written upon the same paper.

He placed all three letters to Marie in an envelope and mailed them off at the first opportunity. At night he would reopen envelopes he had received to bring his mind some comfort. The letters and unending thoughts of Marie passed the endless days and nights for the three phases of boot camp and his duration at the School of Infantry Training. During his time, the DIs would tear at Guy's chest, attempting to rip out his heart and emblazon it with the eagle, globe and anchor. Their efforts were in vain, for Guy had already given his heart to another.

Envelope One

From Guy Flynn, MARINE CORPS RECRUIT DEPOT, San Diego, CA

Addressed to Beautiful Trouble

Marie,

What's up, baby? Today is Wednesday. I have been here for a little over a week now, and it is definitely worse than I had imagined. And the worst thing about it is how bad I miss you. It makes me want to cry most of the time because I miss you so much, but I have to hold in the tears. Can't wait to be done with this crazy phase. You have to do everything in about half a second, and you always have several drill instructors screaming at you. Let me give you some of the highlights.

One of the first days they said we weren't drinking enough water so they made the whole platoon—which was about fifty-five guys then, but now is only fortysomething recruits—drink water till we puked. I puked pretty good. They also wouldn't let a couple guys use the bathroom, and so they pissed all over themselves and the floor. I'm sorry I haven't written till now, but I haven't had any free time. The training is hard. Yesterday we did some of the obstacle course: all sorts of high things you have to get over and also a rope climb. Quite a few of the recruits couldn't do it, but I did. We also had our run, pull-up and sit-up test.

Today was one of the harder PT—physical training—days. We have them every morning. First off we have to do a number of things to warm up: push-ups, sit-ups, knee bends, jumping jacks, etc. Then after that we had to circuit train, which was so hard. There were all these different stations. We had to do curls, military presses, rows, pull-ups, inclined push-ups, crunches, inclined sit-ups. Holding a bar, leg lifts, dips, and the list goes on.

After that we had to run one and a half miles. We will end up having to do a ten-mile hump at the end, which is with sixty-five pounds on your back. They say your hands and feet get all swollen. We also do a lot of drills (marching). It's actually pretty tough.

One thing that sucks when people mess up is the DIs send us to the dirt to be thrashed. You have to do push-ups, but they say *down*, and you can't touch the ground or come up till they say, which gets impossible. Also jumping jacks, which get hard quick with combat boots on, and running in place. Then leg lifts, where your feet can never touch the ground. You think you will die, and it lasts too long. I have big-ass blisters on my feet and a sunburn.

We took apart our M Sixteens today. Well, that's pretty much the lowdown. We get up at five thirty and also have to get up for one hour in the middle of the night to do a watch. I hope things are a little bit better back there. This is definitely the hardest thing I've ever done. One guy refused to follow orders, so the Military Police came and locked him up. I can't even wait till it's over.

You don't even realize how bad I need you. I really would think I couldn't do it, but I have to, and I will be happy later. I love you so much. How is everybody doing out there? Please write and send those addresses and a picture. :)

Please take care of yourself. I'm sure it's hard for you too now. What's up with Bear? Don't let him wimp out.

Love always,
Guy

★★★

Dear Marie,

Standing firewatch right now; it is about one in the morning. I'm not supposed to be writing letters now, but fuck it. They make us go to church here on Sundays. It's really weird; I enjoy going. It touches me. I don't know but maybe it's like a sanctuary for me here. It's cool. Well, happy Easter. I know this is probably your favorite holiday, since you will get piles and piles of chocolate. Tomorrow we go swimming in the morning and a three-mile hike after lunch.

So what all have you been up to? What have you been doing for fun? Smoking any bud? Have you been up to Bea's?

Nothing fun to report up this way. We've had to drink water till we puked about seven times now. The food here actually isn't bad. You don't get much time to eat, but that doesn't bother me since I eat like a maniac.

It gets hard for me here a lot of times. But I just try to think of the future and how it will be worth it. All I want in the world is to have you and to make a good life for us. I know this was a good thing to do. It is just hard and much too lonely without you. I love you and never want to be without you. I really miss making love to you. I had a dream about you. I'd tell you about it, but then I would not get back to sleep later.

Eternal love,

Guy

★★★

My love,

Sitting up in my rack in the middle of the night. Just finished my watch and ironing my cammies. I received that giant letter from you. It means a lot to me; it helped get me by, and I really liked that one—I'm sure you know which. It was hard to sit still and read it. We are definitely going to have some fun when I get out of here. Being without you is so hard, especially since my love for you is so deep. I don't know much, except that I want to be with you always, and that makes everything else OK.

I love you more than you can imagine. I fall in love with you more every day, even though I don't know how it is possible to want and love you more than I already do. I'm glad you have been doing good. And I trust you more than you know. I am a worrier sometimes. I'm glad you signed up for group. Just remember that, down the road, this will all be worth it. That's what I have to keep saying to myself; otherwise, I would never make it through.

My love is yours forever,

Guy

PS: Please send those addresses.

★★★

Honey,

I got your pictures today Thank you. I especially liked your cute butt. It just made me want to take a bite. You look more beautiful than ever. All of the recruits think the same. They said I better not bring you around. They also really liked that letter. Just kidding! Didn't tell anyone about it. I hope my siblings aren't treating you too badly.

We had to drink water twice more till everyone puked. The platoons here are broken into four squads. Now I am one of the squad leaders. I lead the line in drill and yell at everybody to make sure they are doing what they are supposed to.

I miss you more than you can imagine. I can't wait till graduation. In a couple weeks we go to Camp Pendleton to train out in the field for a month. Shooting, plus five-, seven-, ten-mile hikes, all with sixty-five-pound packs. You're the best thing that has ever happened to me, Marie. My heart is yours.

Your eternal lover

***

Envelope Two

From Marie Trouble

Hey, lover,

Well, after careful consideration, there's something I want to share with you. Last night I had a very vivid dream about you. We were at a beach house overlooking the ocean. After whispering my desires to make wild passionate love to you until your cries of pleasure filled the night's air, I restrained you to the bed. Looking deep into your eyes, I slowly began to bathe every part of your body with my lips (occasionally focusing on one area), :), stroking and caressing you until I could hear you moaning softly. I crawled on top of you and brushed my breast across your lips.

As you began to suckle, I felt pleasure sweeping through me. Straddling you, flesh against flesh, while nibbling on your ear, breathing hot and heavy, I asked you if you wanted me. As you began to reply, you were silenced by the beginning of lovemaking. Allowing only a little bit of you inside me, I teased you until you cried out. Then, slowly but firmly, I made love to you, building up my movements till they were quick and firm. Then I began to call out, overwhelmed by pleasure. Gripping your sides in fevered passion, I let out a moan so loud, God could hear it. Shortly thereafter you gave in to the intense pleasure, moaning as you came inside me.

That night may have been a dream, but I want to live it (HINT). I couldn't help myself. Sometimes I think of you, and it gets me so freaking hot and wet, it's fuckin' unbelievable. When we do make love, it'll be the bomb. Love you dearly, not queerly!

With all my love,

Marie

[Over one hundred XOXOs surrounded a red-lipsticked kiss at the bottom of the page.]

★★★

Envelope Three

From Marie Trouble

Dear Guy,

Well I got my braces off today. It feels fuckin' awkward as hell. Too bad you're not here to hear how I talk! I sound like a five-year-old with slurred speech. It's pretty funny.

I'm doing better. I've been happier the past three days. I'm babysitting for your parents and two of the triplets from across the street. And Farood has a death wish! He's sitting here right now and fuckin' annoying me really bad! I miss you so bad, honey. Come home please. I can't believe how much I miss you. I hate this. IT FUCKING SUCKS, GODDAMN IT!!

Dude, the fuckin' pig's dog from next door, Copper, almost snapped Cypress's neck today! Poor little kitty cat! Herman and I pretty much chucked the dog back into their yard. I fuckin' bitched-out the pig. I was so happy. I got to yell at a pig for something.

Well, I love you more all the time, though you're not here, but you already know that! Take care of yourself, lover.

Love always,

Marie

[Another flock of XOXOs here.]

PS: Write me back or you'll get a beating you'll never forget. I'll tie you down and do all sorts of naughty things to you. :)

PPS: I was thinking about writing you a letter so hot that your eyes would burn up! But I didn't want to get you in trouble!

★★★

Dear Guy,

What's up, honey? Guess what? Pops almost got in a fight at a market, but I got in front of him and started yelling at this dickhead, who was complaining about how my dad was in line and then I came up with another cart. This guy just went ballistic. My sister Jen was there, and she stared crying when my dad threw up his hands. It was funny as fuck.

Anyway I went to Casa de Coffee on Monday. They're going to try me out. I told Scott about how you're in the Marines, so I'll see what I can do about Saturdays.

Baby, today I couldn't get you out of my mind, not that I would want to or anything. It's just I was losing it. I would be doing something to keep myself occupied, and you would flash through my mind. I miss you so much. I miss cuddling with you and wrestling with you. Maybe now I'll give you a bit more of a challenge. I've been lifting weights. I remember how you get me excited just by looking at me with your enchanting eyes. I always want to rip off your clothes and make love to you. Or go down on you and taste you. No one ever loved me the way you do.

Also you treat me better than anyone has ever treated me. You're the best thing in my life, and, believe it or not, you're the sexiest man who I've ever laid eyes on. And I'll tell you why: One) If you didn't notice, when we met, how I put my hand on my chest and got shy when I shook your hand. Two) You're modest. Three) You're such a beautiful person inside, I couldn't ask for more. Four) You care for me. Five) A million other things. Six) Last but not least, you gave me my first orgasm. Now don't get cocky on me now, ya hear? Remember, you're a special person in my life and take care of you. I love you with all my mind, soul and body. My heart you hold in your hands.

Yours for forever and eternity,

Marie

PS: Sweet dreams, my love!

PPS: Please don't show anyone this (not even your best friends).

I thought you needed some affection. Verbally is the only way I can give it to you now. I was thinking of sending you pictures of me that only you would ever see (if you know what I mean), so If I can and you want me too, you know I will! :)

I love you.

★★★

Hey, sweetheart,

How's my marine stud holding out? Surprised you haven't gotten those addresses. I sent them a while ago. I'm sorry I haven't written you sooner. I've been really sick. The longest I've been outside is four hours, and I get to bed at 11 p.m. That's way early for me. I sleep for a good twelve to fourteen hours and have hardly any energy at all.

In about a week I'm getting my permit. Scary, huh? Darling, I miss you so much. At times it's unbearable. Baby, I love you more than anyone else alive. You mean the world to me, and that'll never change. I know that now. My heart belongs to you and you only. The time we've been apart, I realize you are the only one for me. There's **no one** that could take your place, ever. No one has touched my soul as deeply as you. None have loved me completely—only you have. Only you have made me feel good about who I am. You made life fun again. You're sharing a beautiful dream with me, and I'm really thankful.

I miss making love to you too, baby. I get so hot with memories of how you touched and caressed me. How your breath feels on my skin. The way you gaze at me with that look in your eyes that made me melt. I miss how you made me scream out in ecstasy. It's turning me on just thinking about it. Sometime in the future I want to try something different (sexually). I'm not going to tell you till you get out of boot camp. I want your imagination to run wild and free. :)

Guy, I want you to know that you're a really great person. I don't know what I'd do without you. You're everything I've wanted. (You probably don't want to hear it, but tough fuckin' shit). You're caring, generous, very intelligent, stubborn (it's very sexy). You make me laugh. You are honest. I can trust you. You're drop-dead, fuck-me-now fine, :) and the bomb in bed! There are so many good things about you, I could go on for days. That's one millionth of the list. I love you with all my heart, soul and mind.

All my love forever,
Marie
[A flock of XOXOs here.]
PS: See you in your dreams, lover! I'll have a "phattie" for you, honey.
[Red-lipsticked kiss imprints.]

★★★

Dear Guy,

Hey, baby! How's it goin'? Good I hope. I just wanted to say hi and see what's up with you! But Marie wouldn't let me write on her paper. Oh, well.

Be sure to be good! Take care, OK!
Love,
Champagne
PS: Men are scum!
PPS: I suppose you can be the exception. The **only** one though. :)
(Heart) me. Jackie says "hi".

★★★

Envelope Four

From Colleen

Dear Guy,

Wow! I finally got a letter from you. I have been checking the mail every day for over two weeks. I am so glad to hear things are going well for you. You're going to be mad because you left right when things got crazy in group. To start things off:

One) C.J. and I broke up on Easter due to the fact I told his parents **all** about his drug problem. :)

Two) C.J. went into Northridge Hospital for one week and is now thirty-days' sober in one week. :)

Three) C.J.'s parents found his bud plants growing in his room.

Four) C.J. and I got back together. :)

And most important:

Five) Are you sitting down for this one? I'M PREGNANT! Boy, I'm sure you saw that coming, before you even read the letter. I wrote it so damn big. Anyway C.J. and I have prom, but we would love to come to your graduation. So unless an emergency comes up, consider us there. Do you get to come home for a few days after you graduate? If you do, we **must** do something. I miss you so much. You know, after we said good-bye to you, C.J. and I went home and cried. We just couldn't believe you were leaving. Well, it makes me so happy to hear from you and that you're well. You are like a brother to me, so you best keep in touch.

Oh, yeah. You tell those son-of-a-bitches not to make you drink water till you puke, or else I'll have to bust their asses when I come down there. :) Yeah, right! **Hardly**.

(Heart) Always,
Colleen
PS: Remember you are supposed to write three times a month. Keep in touch. I will tell the others to write you.

★★★

Envelope Five

From Jack Finnigan

To Number One Son

Date May Twenty Fourth, Nineteen Ninety Five

Hi, Guy!

Hope you enjoyed your birthday as best as possible. Just received your letter of May twenty first. It got here May twenty fourth. Not bad, hey? It takes a bit longer for mine 'cause I send them out to somebody to mail. You understand.

I was wondering what you're doing for a wallet? Would you like me to get you one made for your birthday, a "Bikers" type or a regular? Let me know.

Glad to hear that you made squad leader. Good going, lad. I know it's hard, and some of that shit may seem senseless, but it will soon be over, then you'll be a real jarhead. :) Do you want some Taoist sexual secrets? Do you eat pussy? They say, if you eat pussy, you'll eat asshole. So what's up? :) With all the sexually transmitted diseases, you should keep your passion just for Marie. Stay away from those Marine Corps–town hookers. I caught the clap over in Nam. It's a drag.

Even in you don't have quality time to do meditation, try just layin' in your bed and doing it in the morning or at night. Spend just five minutes, bring that breath (inhale) through the nose and fill the lower lung (belly breathing), you remember? Put a boot over your navel. Inhale, push the boot up. Exhale, let the boot fall. Just put your mind into the belly breathing. After that, now see in your mind what time you want to get up or what you want to achieve the next day. See yourself doing it, accomplishing it. These are the basics you have to master: holding your mind on your belly breathing. Every time it wanders, realize it and return your attention to that belly breath.

Our Buddhist Event (Buddha's birthday) is this Sunday. Twenty-eight monks and lay practitioners come over from the monastery. We

219

have a service and then serve lunch. We have a Buddhist band that plays sometimes for our teacher. He likes the Blues.

OK, here's a Taoist Sexual Energy exercise for you and Marie. First, to experience the action of the muscles involved, you must, while taking a piss, stop the flow of urine in middle of the flow, before the bladder is empty. This is done by contracting the anus muscle (sphincter). This is a good exercise for keeping the male and female sex glands healthy. It is also good for the woman, as it keeps the pussy tight.

Sitting naked (yau) on a pillow (whatever is comfortable), legs out in front of you, some foreplay may be needed so that your cock is hard. She would mount you, facing you. (Sitting down onto your cock, taking you into her pussy.) Place each other's hands on each one's nipples and lightly stimulate. You visualize taking in a white light through the top of your head. White light continuing through your cock (seeing it going into her pussy). As you get to the point where all the air is exhaled, you then flex your asshole muscle (exercise from above).

Now she begins to inhale, bringing that white light into her belly breath. She sees it in her mind's eye. White light in her belly, she begins her exhale, sending the white light back into your cock. As she reaches the end of her exhale, she flexes her asshole muscles. Now you begin to take the white light into your belly breath, filling it up (inhale).

Now start the exhale and the whole process over again. You have to get your breathing down, you and her. And you should do this exercise for about twenty minutes. No fucking. This is strictly a sexual-energy transfer. It will take you a while to get it down. We'll talk more about it, after you've tried it. You can keep hands on nipples if you like or simply embrace.

Any questions? Let me know. :)

Remember, a woman needs lots of foreplay—slow, extended intercourse. Where she will experience multiple orgasms, you have to learn not to reach climax too soon. Control the desire. There is a nerve—allowing blood flow to your cock deep at the base into your nuts almost—if you squeeze there, it will keep you from ejaculating too soon. Experiment with it, let me know. Don't jerk off. Save that energy for the PT course! Do you know the location of your girl's clitoris? Ask her to show you. That's what you want to lick and suck on as you're eating pussy. Well, that's my sex lessons for today! :)

About the mind, it plays a big role in SEX. One more thing, you ever give Marie a warm oil massage? She'll love you for it. Women need to be nurtured, hugged, kissed, talked with on emotional things. Comb their hair, wash their bodies, take baths together. Candles and wine. You know, Guy, women are wonderful creatures. Learn to appreciate the way a woman's mind perceives the world. Being emotional beings, they're very intuitive, dig? Always listen to your woman when she speaks from that "I just have a feeling about this" type of thought.

See, that's where we try to go in Zen. Learning to think from intuitive-mind thought happens **before** left-brain/cognitive thought and NEVER lies to you or is deceptive. A way to use it is to ALWAYS look deep into a person's eyes when he's speaking with you. You'll know after a while of sitting Zen, called zazen, whether a person is telling the truth or not. Heavy, right? Remember to have me tell you the story of how my teacher showed me his intuitive mind some time.

Well, lad, for other trails to travel, get a book on tracking. Hope to get some flicks taken Sunday. Will send ya one.

Stay strong, keep trucking. When the going gets tough, the tough get going. Can you run sixty one hundred yards with a guy on your back, under fire, on a hot extraction to a chopper? Sure you can. Just see yourself doing it. Love ya. HAPPY BIRTHDAY, MAGGOT.

Taian (Pronounced TIEANN my formal Buddhist name given me by the Teacher)

XXXOOO

PS: Dig knees in when walking—use ass muscles, push off with toes. Use whole leg. When running, crouch a little. Indians run like this. Doing lower- and upper-lung breathing? When it gets hard, keep a small stone in your mouth to make saliva. Focus your mind on your breathing, as you evenly breathe, not on how far you have to go. Keep mind in control.

★★★

Envelope Six

From Della Flynn

Happy birthday! I mailed this a little early. It seems like it takes a while for you to get our letters. Sorry you're not home to celebrate. I'm going to attend as much of your grad ceremonies as possible. I'll be there for most of the weekend. Tonight is the Fashion Show and next Thurs. is my graduation from school. I may pass on that grad ceremony. It starts at three in the afternoon, and they only give us two tickets. I'd rather the kids miss school for your graduation than mine. They scheduled the day real poorly. They have something early in the morning, then a bunch of hours with nothing planned, then the three o'clock graduation. And you can't bring any guests to the morning event. So I may just go in the morning alone or skip the whole thing altogether. Anyway I'm so glad to be finished. Looking forward to seeing you. Time is going so fast. I'm sure you'll be really glad when boot camp is over. Sounds like you're in great shape. Have you lost or gained any weight? I feel good already, tighter. I've lost three or four pounds and want to drop another five. Tramp is happy. I am taking him walking again. No sign of Buster. We put up signs, but so far nothing on that cat!

I'm happy to hear you're making a savings plan. Have you found out about taking your car? Would you be able to use it much? Do you know we never found your pager? Have any thoughts on this? Everyone saw it in your room, and then it just disappeared.

Can I bring you something for your birthday? I don't know what to get. Some suggestions, please.

Thanks for all the letters. It's great to hear of your boot camp escapades. Looking forward to your graduation.

Happy birthday!

Did you get the card from my sister Prissy?

Take care of yourself,

Mom

★★★

From Pearl and Herman

[There was a cloud at the top of the page, containing a big red heart sticker and a little brown bunny sticker with this note: "I got the rabbit a new really big cage. She loves it!"]

Dear Guy,

Hey! Did you get my last letter? I hope you did. I haven't been doing much but watching TV. I'm on spring vacation. It is really boring. Dad is thinking about taking us to Magic Mountain. I hope he says OK. What have you been doing? After reading your letters, it sounds like you're doing a lot of tough stuff. I hope you didn't get too sick from drinking that water. When I read how you did that, I cried. And when I heard about the guys peeing on everything, I felt sorry. When I heard about your sunburn, I asked if we could send sunblock, but Mom said that we can't send packages. When I heard that your feet were blistered, I thought about how much pain you were in, so I wanted to send Band-Aids. Are we allowed to do that? I hope so. Please tell me in your next letter home.

I feel sorry for that guy who passed out. If he's your friend and you see him again, tell him I said I hope he feels better. Please take care of yourself and make sure that never happens to you. I know you can do it! Just hang in there! Could you also tell me the day of your graduation?

Because I am going to camp in Utah with Molly Engles. If the dates are too close, I'll skip camp because I miss you so much. I need to find out the date soon. I love and miss you tons and tons! Please take care of yourself.

Sincerely,
Pearl

★★★

Hey, Guy, having fun? The turtle got out of the tank twice since you have been gone. Pearl, Mom and I finished a five-hundred-piece puzzle that I got for Easter. The puzzle only took us five hours. Cypress is learning how to hunt. Pearl and I had McDonald's last night. I love you.

Love,
Herman

★★★

Envelope Seven

From Mack Flynn

Hi, Guy!

I wish you a happy birthday! I **wish** you have (or *had*, if this is late—which is likely) a great day, but I'm sure each day looks the same where you are. Happy birthday anyway!

I got your letter. It's always good to hear from you. We all miss you here. My pool game has leveled off. I still play OK. But since I'm lucky to play one night a week, I'm not really improving. But when I'm on, I still kick butt. There seems to be a babe drought in the San Fernando Valley. I should live down at Manhattan Beach.

You know I really enjoyed the trip to St. Thomas too. I had hoped you'd like it as much as you did. And you're right. Going out together was great. Hopefully it will always be like that. It can be tough being a parent, judging the best way to relate to and raise kids. We really had some rough spots, but if you focus on solving problems, the situation gets better. I think we've both realized that, at the core, we are there to support each other. I guess that's family working together. It means a lot to me, but sometimes I don't know what to say. That was true much of the time you were in the hospital. But I had hoped, by being there, you would see that how you felt was very important to me. I'm glad to hear how you felt about it. I miss playing Ping-Pong by the way.

When Timmy and I would ask Grampa to take us camping when we were kids, he never would. He said he had camped out for a few years in Europe with Gen. George Patton and the boys, and had had enough of that for a lifetime. I suspect you will have better food and weather than he had. You'll probably have fewer people shooting at you too. I hope you get a kick out of it or at least survive. Don't forget your compass.

So you're in the field now. Well, turn the compass one hundred eighty degrees, because, in your letter, you asked how many people are going to come "up" here. From L.A. we come "down" to San Diego. I'll bring Herman and Pearl on Sunday (the last day). I believe Mom is coming then too. I told Marie that she can come with us, if she would like. I tried to talk to Mom about who is going and when, but she's not done with school till the Thursday before and wants to go over it when she's done. I guess her head is still spinning a bit. She won third place for one of her designs. Not bad, huh! I'm glad she seems to be doing well.

So have you gone on any interesting nature walks lately? It sounds like fun hiking through the rolling hills of beautiful San Diego with a group of your closest friends. You get to camp out, sit around a roaring campfire, roasting marshmallows and telling each other scary stories. Let us know which of God's furry critters you've seen. Yeah, it must be nice strolling around bird-watching. Do you guys compete to see who can spot the most different species? And you get to do all this for free. I'm jealous! Wish I could be there—NOT!

By now I'm sure you know you can handle whatever they dish out. It may hurt, feel miserable, but somehow you find it within yourself. Hope there aren't many days that are real bad.

By the way Herman is campaigning for playing hooky one day when you're home so we can go to Raging Waters. How do you vote?

We're looking forward to seeing you!

Dad

★★★

From Pearl and Herman

[A new page was decorated like for a party, with squiggly lines, flowers around the border, balloons with smiley faces written in them. A banner across the top that read "We love you!!!" Little partying stick figures were all over.

There stood Guy and Pearl in profile. A bubble containing "**You**, muscleman, bald," with an arrow pointing to said muscleman. Pearl with her bubble saying, "I love you," and another bubble saying, "**Me**, short, wimp!" and an arrow pointing to said wimp.]

Dear Guy,

Happy birthday! I bet it doesn't feel so great at the moment, but you probably feel big and strong. After going through a gas chamber, I'd feel like I'm the toughest thing on Earth if I survived. I would be really proud of myself. I'm definitely proud of you. I miss and love you tons and tons!
    Sincerely,
    Pearl

★★★

Happy birthday. How are you doing? I miss you very much. I can't wait to see you at your graduation. I have to go now.
    Love,
    Herman

★★★

Envelope Eight

From Robert "Bulldog aka Bobby" Finnigan
11Three Barbara Lane
Levittown, NY 11Seven Five Six
To Recruit Flynn, Guy #Three Three Seven Eight Three Eight
Four Five Six
Third Battalion D, Camp Platoon 1113
Forty Thousand Midway Ave, Unit Three
San Diego, CA 9Two One Four Zero-Five Six Six One

Date: May Eighth, Nineteen Ninety Five, Twenty One:Thirty
Three VE Day, Fifty-Year Anniversary

Dear up-and-coming PFC Guy,

Thanks for the call today. Read your letter. You must improve your penmanship. Remember when in the field or in war games, bury your shit, toilet paper, butts, etc. So the enemy won't know your position. Wear no cologne, jewelry, deodorant, etc. It can be heard and smelled. Try not to leave bootprints. Use a branch to erase them. Pick up two books: *Knife Throwing: A Practical Guide* and *Knife and Tomahawk Throwing*. Both by Harry K. McEvoy. When you are issued your gear, let me know. I can get you an excellent combat and survival knife, plus a throwing tomahawk, if you're allowed.

Well, today is Sunday, product distribution day around here. So I've been listening to my radios and using my visual aids. And tomorrow I get to pay a seventeen hundred dollar plus tax bill, done four times a year for the privilege of living in Levittown, watching these dopers do their thing. But very soon the Enola Gay is going to drop the Little Boy on these lowlifes. So I've invested in more special equipment for home security.

Jack and I are not talking. I won't accept his calls or mail. I didn't like his uncaring response when I told him Sylvester, my cat, has diabetes and a fibrosarcoma tumor. These I just found out. But Jack never liked cats anyway. Isn't your birthday soon? *Happy Birthday*, if I missed it. Memory isn't up to par lately. Over, please.

Remember that this family has a long and honorable tradition of service to its country, going back to the Civil War, WWI, WWII, Vietnam. Be proud of this and make your own marks.

I'm not exactly sure, but I think you're the first Finnigan who's a jarhead. See if you can get me a USMC baseball cap with your unit insignia for the back window of my car. And also a USMC sun catcher for the front bay window of the house, remember? You would have to join a branch of the service I can't find online that sells shit.

Well, lights out for now. Be careful. Keep up **good conduct**. Remember school choice.

One) OCS = Officer Candidate School.

Two) OTS = Officer Training School.

Three) NCO = Noncommissioned Officers School (Sgts.)

Four) Get a copy of *Navy Times* at PX. Check available MOS— Military Operational Specialty. And starting dates of above schools and colleges.

Be careful. Be cool. Keep low.

Sincerely yours,

Bob

★★★

Envelope 9

From Marie

Dear Guy,

How are you? I'm not doing good. I'm really depressed. This morning I woke up, and it was like living through the day was going to be one of the more difficult things I've had to do. You want to know how I feel inside? I feel like there's a big fuckin' knife stuck in the center of my heart. Lisa moved to Woodland Hills. Every day I wake to find someone else gone. Sometimes I don't want to care, but I do. I cry every day about all sorts of shit. I've felt this way for a very long time. I chose not to tell anyone. When I'm at my house or anywhere else, I feel as though I don't belong. I've lost my will to help myself. I've been helping others so much, I forgot how to help myself. It's like part of me doesn't want to. Last night I totally fuckin' tripped. John wouldn't give me a cigarette, so I took off, and he had to chase me so I wouldn't buy any. Then we went to Burger King, and I just started crying. Dude, I don't know what it is. Maybe these pills from the psych doctor? Or am I going crazy?

Anyway, when I went out with my mom, we had a good time. Please don't worry too much about me. I'll live. I'm not gonna off myself or anything. Sometimes I feel sanity thinning. I don't know, maybe I'm having one of those days. I try to think of the future and what I need to do, and remember it'll be worth it. But it's hard. There's so much I want to get out. Well, I have to eat. I love you, more than life itself. Never doubt my love.

Marie

★★★

Envelope Ten

From Guy Flynn

My love,

I'm sorry things have been so rough for you lately. I wish I could take all of your pain. You don't know how bad I wish I could be with you through all this trash. I'm worried about you, baby. I really think that you should keep going to counseling. If you didn't like the person you were seeing, find someone else. Better yet, ask my mom for Karen's number from group. She's great, or she could recommend someone else who is.

Maybe you should stop getting loaded for a while. I know it seems like the worst time, but maybe it's the best. You need to clear your head and work all this shit out, otherwise it will keep bugging you. That's what I had to do before. It seems like bullshit, but, once you get that haze off, you can get to the root of shit and find ways to resolve it. When you're loaded so much, it just dulls everything and changes it. I'm sorry if I sound like an ass. It's just that I love you so much, and I'm worried about you.

Things have been really rough here. Since there are a couple individuals who don't put out, we can't work as a team. That is about the worst thing that can happen. We pay for it every day. It is really wearing me down. I try hard every day, and, because a couple people don't, it doesn't matter—we all get punished. I'm sure I have no voice from sounding off so loud all the time. It sucks. Today we had a killer run. It really kicked my ass. It was only one and a half miles, but it was in combat boots, and you had to hold your rifle out in front of you.

We ran in formation, and it was hard because you have to sound off real loud all the time, so you don't get enough air. You have to keep up the same pace the whole time too 'cause you are in formation. I didn't think I would make it. I was so tired, yet I made it though, and I didn't fall back at all. A couple guys fell out. We got in trouble for that. It really pisses me off, 'cause I am one of the weaker runners, and I made it. Some people just don't put out. I need you. I can't wait.

Love you now until forever,

Guy

PS: What's up with Lisa? Why doesn't she write back? Call her. I'm sure Bea has the number on her phone bills.

★★★

Love,

Hi, honey. What's going on? Got a letter from Bear. He seems like he is doing good, and he is actually talking to his mom.

Things have been busy and crazy up here. Today was qual day. Shitty conditions, real windy and drizzling. I was three points away from expert but, oh well. The other day the DIs made us dump out everything in our footlockers, kick it all over the squad bay and march on it. Then they pulled off all the mattresses and sheets. The place was a wreck, and no one had their own gear. So we had to get up on the middle of the night and change, which took forever. Also today, after we ate a real big dinner, they made us drink enough water so we all puked three or four times. It was nasty. The whole place was a puke puddle. I am now halfway done cleaning it up again.

In the morning (Saturday), we have a four-mile beach run, which I am sure will kick my ass, but, oh well. We go into the field on Monday. Sleep in tents, that type of shit. It is going to be real tough, tough. Lots of humping. We will also get to shoot grenade launchers, M Sixteens, machine guns, plus shoot at night. I hope this last half goes fast, because I am going through major Marie withdrawals, and I don't know how much longer I can hang on. I love you more than words can say. I can't wait to be back. It will probably be one of the best feelings in my life. I am going to eat like a fucking horse too. I miss food, real food, a ton! Take care, babe, and I'll do my best to do the same.

Eternally yours,
XOXO Guy

★★★

Baby,

Well, I only have one week of second phase left, then I am in third and on the home stretch. The first week of being in the field was OK. We stayed nice and dirty. You hygiene using the water in your canteen. We are back to the barracks for the weekend, so I got some nice warm food and a good shower. Glad to hear high school is going good. Today we had to go through the gas chamber—CS gas. It makes it so you can't breathe. Your eyes burn, plus your mouth and nose. Snot goes everywhere, and it makes your skin burn. Some people really freak out. It sucked, but it wasn't unbearable, after you got out at least.

I hope I see Bear at church. I miss you a lot. Make sure you talk to my mom, or dad, and get a ride up here for grad, visitors' day, etc. Will you send me Bea's address? I want to say "What's up?" Say hello to Bea for me.

You want to know something really weird? I don't know if it is because everyone is so stressed out or what the deal is, but no guys in boot camp can get a hard-on. I had one when I had a dream about you when I got here, but I swear no one ever does. Strange. When I see you, stand back, cause I will probably poke your eye out.

Next week we shoot all sorts of cool weapons. Tomorrow we are either having a seven- or eight-mile hump. It should be pretty killer. There are still a couple of stupid asses in our platoon who need to get their asses kicked on a regular basis. Gosh, I have so many cravings—it is sick. Well, take care of yourself. I love you with all my being.

Forever yours,
Guy

★★★

Dear Marie,

Sorry I haven't written much lately. I haven't gotten any time off at all. Especially because I am a squad leader. We started Mess Week today. We work seventeen hours straight. Come right back and hit the rack. We have to get up at three thirty, so I probably won't get time to write this week. I'm really sorry. It's not that I don't want to, you know I do. Mess ends one week from today. The good thing is, we get to eat a lot!

I know I sounded weird on the phone. It was 'cause I was trying to make sure nobody heard me, because we were at the travel agency, and they asked who needs to call their parents to see if they need to buy an airline ticket. Well, I said yes, even though I didn't, just so I could at least hear your voice.

We will be able to see each other soon! Argh! I love you, baby. You mean the world to me. I'll write whenever I can. When we aren't on Mess Week, we have to get up in the middle of the night and have about two hours' worth of stuff to do, so it's hard for me to write during the middle of the night like I usually do, 'cause we hardly get any sleep in the first place. Well, I long for you in every way you can think of, if you know what I mean. :)

Your love slave,
Guy XOXO

Envelope 11

From Marie

Dear Guy,

Have you gotten any hands-on training with explosives, etc., yet? I know you're lovin' it! I went to Bea's yesterday for a little while. Remember her dog, Brandie? Well, she's pregnant! Bea also rearranged her house. It looks better. It's all clean 'n' shit. Of course I'm religiously getting **fucked up**! John just recently accomplishment a mission I gave to him, to get so blitzed that he didn't know where or who he was! Cool, huh?

Honey, I don't know how much longer I'm staying with my dad. I'm going to end up killing his dumb fuckin' cunt of a wife. I was so close to kicking the living shit out of her. She was runnin' her fuckin' mouth, trying to be my mom and shit.

Have I ever told you how much I love you, and you're everything I ever wanted? I often think of being held by you. Feeling the warmth of your body next to mine. Hear you telling me that you love me and able to look deep in your beautiful eyes. To taste your sweet lips. Last night I had a dream about you. I'll just leave it at that. I love you more than you know.

Only yours,

Marie XOXOXOXO

PS: Keep your head up. I'm positive you'll be fine! Heaven knows you're as fine as they come! Seriously!!!

PPS: If you didn't already know, somehow John got chlamydia and cheated on Jamie with Robin. Well, she (Robin) got it and guess what? Bear's brother Diamond fucked her!

★★★

Boot camp had opened Guy's eyes in many ways. The physical and mental endurance necessary had surpassed any of Guy's expectations and would surpass any sensible man's rules of decency. In Phase Three, Platoon 11Fifteen had all of their DIs summarily relieved. Guy knew that platoon's DIs were sadists as well.

Guy also knew that, during war, all sorts of horrible things happened. His biological father was living proof. Yelling was something most men could eventually put up with; some had plenty of experience from their own mothers and fathers. It was the punching, choking and sleep deprivation that got everyone's attention. It was the withholding of drinking water, toilet privileges and food that brought anxiety. It was forced vomiting through hydration, with regular and sadistic pleasure, that caused most men's minds to panic.

The physical training was grueling, but it was thrashing and playing fuck-fuck for eight to twelve hours that made recruits cry for their mothers and drop unconscious. Deck toweling was always a favorite. In two lines, the recruits would deck towel the squad bay. The squad leaders were forced to fill large gray trash cans with scalding water and dump them on the squad bay floor. With their hands on the floor holding a deck towel, the recruits would pump their legs, wheelbarrowing round and round the squad bay. At the end of a lap, they would stand and squeeze their towel into a trash can. Four hours straight was their record. Guy had cried quietly to himself after two and a half.

Marie sent Guy a bag of chocolates for his birthday. He was able to eat them inside the drill instructors' hut. Sergeant Willum helped Guy along with one hand round his windpipe, and the other shoveling the bag of chocolates down Guy's throat, wrappers and all. Guy glared angrily into Sergeant Willum's eyes, and, for a moment, they had an understanding that it was Sgt. Willum who was fortunate he held a position of authority. Guy was made squad leader.

He was surprised not so much by the torture of it all, but by the spirit of the torturers. Clearly some men were just doing their job, but some men were truly sadistic. These men were of a cruelty uncommonly witnessed—rare men, indeed. It was strange these days that such human relationships were allowed to exist. It was an opportunity for these men to practice cruelty unrestrained. Guy got the feeling some of them had done much worse than he had experienced at MCRD or later at Camp Pendleton.

The Marine Corps was designed to test a man's mettle. One of those tests was the gas chamber. They learned about chlorobenzalmalononitrile firsthand; it was more commonly called CS gas. Each platoon was led into a windowless concrete room with benches ringing the walls. They were told to don gas masks, and two large canisters of CS gas were opened. Of course the seals on the gas masks didn't work, but it didn't matter as they were soon taken off. The thick yellow smoke removed all oxygen from the lungs immediately and set everything it touched ablaze. Fire down the throat, the eyes, skin. As you choked for air, it felt as if your nasal passages and your eyes would drip upon the floor. Don't rub; rubbing only made it worse.

The toughest guide in the company, aside from Digrigli, was a black kid who was strong as a bull. He tried to run out while his platoon was inside. They made him go three more times in a row with the other platoons. They held him down. He seemed to lose some of his fighting spirit after that.

But Guy made it through. Marie was shocked by the physical transformation. He had weighed a hundred sixty five pounds when he left for the corps. He had put on an additional ten pounds ten in boot camp, so he was now one seventy five. When Mack, Della, the kids and

Marie came up on visitors' day, Guy ate twenty pieces of chicken parmesan, along with a dozen sandwich rolls. The pizza a couple hours later was outstanding.

The ten-day leave was ephemeral. Guy and Marie drank of each other heavily, as wisps of others floated on by.

Dearest Guy,

I don't remember if I let you see these pieces I wrote, but now's a better time than ever. It's a little reminder of how I feel for you, since I can't tell you every day.

December Eighth, Nineteen Ninety Four

The agonizing pain that seemed endless is finally coming to rest. The love I feel in my soul would be enough to keep the sun burning for eternity. . . . A taste would spark a flame in a dead fire. . . . Even though I was down to the last bit of emotion, someone gave that back to me. . . . Everyone notices the glow about me now. Sometimes my heart burns so bright that those who do look inside see my heart.

December Twenty Fifth, Nineteen Ninety Four

Never before have I felt as strongly as the love I feel deep within my being. . . . Often I've wondered what it's like to have someone have the same feeling burn within them. . . . Now that I know, I don't ever want it taken away.

December Twenty Fifth, Nineteen Ninety Four

In the back of my mind the words he softly spoke are said again and again. . . . One might question our love, whether it is true or infatuation. . . . How do we know? Because I feel whole—all the emptiness I felt is filling quickly with a sense of belonging.

I would willingly die if I could look into his eyes one last time to see his heart and feel peace before it closed my eyes forever.

The whole point was to let you know I love you and think of you twenty four seven and to hang in there. I'll be here with open arms, baby.

Heart)

Marie

Envelope Twelve

From Guy Flynn

My love,

How have things been? Smoking any good weed? School of Infantry training is tough, it's only been one week since I saw you last, but I already miss you so much. Hopefully I will be able to come home next weekend. I will, if I don't have watch. I hope to see Bear soon. I've talked to some of the other guys ahead of us, and things are going to be really tough. The humping is hard. I went to the E Club last night and got drunk out of my head. I was so sloshed, I puked at the end of the night, but not very much. :) I can't wait to see you again. I'm so in love with you. We have been doing land navigation, where we use a compass to locate all these boxes that are spread all throughout the mountains.

My uncle Bobby might get sent to jail for four years. That would suck.

So what have you been doing? Have you been looking for a job? Yuck!

My dad is so lucky. He went to the Virgin Islands this weekend. We will have to go someplace cool like that sometime, baby. Gosh, I can't wait till I am out of the corps, and we can be together. I still have to go to college, but that won't be nearly as bad. What would be awesome is if I got sent to Australia, when I have to go overseas. I've always wanted to go over there. If I ever got sent to Amsterdam, I think I would die. I wouldn't be able to "hang" with you. My boots make my feet hurt so bad. I've made a couple cool buddies in here.

Also sorry I was a bit distant on the phone yesterday, baby. I was just wasted and way fucked-up from that hump, baby. I think that was the hardest thing I've ever done. I couldn't hardly walk yesterday. I got to see Bear for about an hour and a half today, which was cool. We are going to come down as soon as we don't have watch. I miss you, baby. All this stuff is damn hard. It really takes a toll on me. I can't wait till I am done with it forever. I've been having very erotic dreams about tying you up and playing games and teasing you all night long, so you get so excited you don't even know where you are.

So Jamie is going to introduce you to one of her friends? I tried to convince Diamond last week to break up with Robin. I wonder if he did. I love you, baby, and thanks for writing so much! I try, but we don't get much time, besides weekends. Take care and be prepared to be tortured. I'll have a sweet dream about you tonight to keep me going. See you soon, honey.

Your servant in love,
Guy
XOXO

★★★

My beauty,

Well, at least we got to talk this weekend. You don't know how bad I wanted to come down this weekend. It bummed me out really bad when I couldn't. I miss you a lot. I've had to try hard not to start crying today. I love you so much. We have to wake up at three thirty in the morning so we can go out to the field. We will be sleeping in two-man hootches. We stay out till Thursday. We will be shooting all sorts of cool weapons though. Big-ass machine guns and automatic grenade launchers. I will definitely come down next weekend unless I have firewatch. Then I will just die.

I'm listening to Pink Floyd. It always reminds me of you and makes me think about us. You were the first person who ever got me to listen to them—and Nails—and now I love them both. You remember some of the early times we spent together? Being in Diamond's room, smoking bowls. Then turning out the lights, listening to music all stoned out and kissing so passionately. I would just hold you in my arms all night, and that's the best feeling I've ever known.

You are so special to me. You make me feel like no one ever has. You've done so much for me, baby. Your love gives me strength and helps me in everything I do. I can't wait till I can be done with all this, so I can start my real life with you. Busy schedule for a few more years, but I know it will all be worth it. If I work hard now, and when I get out and go to college, then I will have a good life to share with you later. Well, at least if I cry myself to sleep, I'll get to see you in my dreams.

All of my love,
Guy

★★★

Love melted Guy's heart; it emanated from Marie. He knew she would become his wife and bear his children, the one person he would grow old with and reflect back upon life's experiences. What a gift, to be able to look back over a shared life together. The renewed knowledge of all the beauty life had to offer, this was a feeling he had not experienced since childhood. A life worth making required hard work but was worth it to share alongside a wife, a family. The dichotomy was Guy's work required a hardening of the heart. That was more difficult now.

For Guy, infantry training was less mentally exhausting though certainly more physically strenuous than boot camp. Guy had anticipated a de-escalation in the daily oppression but was surprised that the physical demands increased substantially. In SOI, School of Infantry, Guy decided to become a machine gunner. They said it was the hardest MOS you could pick. Guy joined the corps to do something hard. He felt he needed a proper ass-kicking, and he had received a proper one. Bear picked machine guns also; he thought it might increase their chances of connecting again. Guy and Bear both put in San Diego as first choice and Hawaii as second choice for duty stations.

Guy was able to keep up on the physical side, the runs, twenty-five-mile humps; the packs, helmets and rifles were heavy. Their longest hump during SOI started with Recon Ridge, a mountain that felt like it went straight up and wound endlessly behind Camp Horno. Guy thought his legs would give out from under him. Ten miles of flat terrain were at the top; Guy couldn't wait. Boy, was he wrong.

The sergeants called it the microwave. The ten miles were blacktopped, and it was called the microwave, because, during the California summers, after about three miles, your feet felt as if they were in a microwave oven. After ten miles, many men cried as they walked. Guy learned to dissociate from the experience. He performed different actions in his head for a distraction.

He found visualizing eating worked best. Imagining Thanksgiving dinner or a favorite steak. Going through each motion in great detail. The utensils, cutting each bite, chewing, the flavor, swallowing. Guy would eat all of his favorite meals. He would have conversations with Marie; thinking about sex was too much while humping. Singing a song was not enough for the brutal portions either—things like the microwave or a particularly long, steep stretch or double-time jogging. Guy's feet had blood blisters on both heels the size of large silver dollars.

SOI included tests for your specialty weapon. The machine gunners used three different machine guns. The first was a Two Forty Golf, a new version of the M Sixty machine gun used in Vietnam. It was belt fed, and shot in a two-man team. One person shot the gun which was usually mounted on a small tripod. The second man would lie halfway on top of the first man, spot the target, load the belts and change barrels when they got hot. They could theoretically shoot a thousand rounds a minute, somewhere between eighteen and thirty-five football fields away. They also shot the fifty caliber and the Mark Nineteen automatic grenade launcher. Both were shot as part of a weapons company and usually mounted on Humvees. The fifty caliber could go through ten people, back to chest, wearing bulletproof vests at one thousand yards and catch them all on fire, if you used incendiary rounds with tungsten slugs. The Mark Nineteen shot belt-fed Forty mm grenades. Each grenade killed everything within five meters and had a casualty radius of fifteen meters. It could rain down about three hundred fifty grenades a minute. Guy was able to take the guns apart and put them back together faster than anyone else. He could even take them apart and put them together with his eyes closed. He scored the only perfect score on the written final and graduated Battalion Honor Graduate. Guy found it somewhat amusing.

Guy made friends with a big Tongan fella. Guy taught him how to play knuckles. Like slapping hands, except you touch your fists together and try to strike the top of your opponent's hand with your middle knuckles. Guy was good at turning hands black-and-blue swiftly. The game took more time with the Tongan, who was swift despite his ham-hock hands. A high-speed version of the game evolved which involved punching your opponent in the ribs wherever and whenever possible.

Eventually the game achieved a superlative level that included the whole platoon. The rules were simple. Everyone played. All the time. You simply had a choice of whether or not you would hit back. With most of the guys, it was just a little tap to show you weren't paying attention, nothing too dramatic. When Guy and the Tongan stuck each other, however, an unguarded punch took the breath away.

While out in the field for lunch, they had the rare privilege of hot chow trucked in, instead of the thirty-year-shelf-life of rations called Meals, Ready-to-Eat. Heaven help you if you got the omelet with ham MRE.

The Tongan, Mahafatan, sat cross-legged, with his metal tray in front of him. He was just about to stuff a big bite in his mouth, when Guy noticed his elbow was at a right angle with his body, leaving his ribs wide open. As he placed the bite in his mouth, Guy crouched quickly and dealt Mahafatan a serious blow, which caused him to spit his chow everywhere. A few phenomenal shots he had landed on Guy earlier in the week had put Mahafatan in Guy's crosshairs.

A sergeant, who observed the entire incident roared over, screaming. As he arrived on scene, Mahafatan choked down his composure and stated simply, "It's a game." He explained the rules to the sergeant, who was flabbergasted, then intrigued and finally very supportive.

It happened to be the same sergeant who thought it would be fun to wake the company up with smoke grenades. He tossed several into camp one morning, around five fifteen. They filled the single-man hootches which lined the brown field with thick, noxious green smoke. One of the grenades rolled underneath Guy's tent. In less than a second the tent was filled completely with thick green smoke. Guy's tent and his cammie blouse caught fire; he was out of the hootch in an instant. *Stop, drop and roll* had been drilled into his head enough that it came naturally.

Two sergeants stomped out Guy's tent and looked at him with panic, the panic of men who thought they were going to be court-martialed. Guy didn't care about the tent since it wasn't his, but they were sure going to buy Guy a new pair of cammies—and woodlands at that. They were a little bit thicker, nicer. The sergeants agreed with exasperated relief.

San Diego would be Guy's duty station; Bear would eventually be sent off to Hawaii. Most weekends it meant Guy was able to see Marie. He brought his Mustang to base. His new company, India, was a boat company. Located at Camp Horno with Recon Ridge for a backyard, India Company liked to train hard. Many of the marines saw time in Iraq. The new drops were all roomed with older lance corporals. Guy's roommate was Lance Corporal Rebel.

He was one of the few cool guys, despite the fact that he had a large rebel flag tattoo and one hanging above his rack. He said there were no blacks in this company, because there were swim qualifications and blacks weren't good swimmers. Coming from L.A., Guy found it all rather backward. He was surprised there were kids his age who glorified the confederacy. Guy found it hard to rationalize and very peculiar. He spent all the time he could away from base.

Guy became friends with a weaker marine named Violet. They went out around town, tried different restaurants, listened to music. Guy was one of the only people in the company with a car. Violet got Guy to spend some time at a Hare Krishna temple. Guy found it more like an anthropological study than an enlightening experience, but it was amusing and relaxing. They ate some great vegetarian food with their hands. Violet was from Cleveland, and, when Guy took Violet back to L.A., he thought it was paradise. They smoked a joint one weekend right after a piss test. Violet was so hammered he was lucky to make it to formation Monday morning.

A year has passed since Guy had joined the corps. They were getting ready to train to deploy overseas on a ship for six months. It seemed someone had to protect the seamen. Guy wasn't looking forward to being away from Marie, but getting to see her on the weekends was ecstasy. He would not have been able to bear being stuck in Hawaii.

Now that he was done with training, Guy was surprised by the general atmosphere of the fleet. He was told they would be treated like real marines once training was done. He could see quickly that the lance corporals and corporals with seniority ruled by force and intimidation. Those with weaker minds and weaker bodies were feasted upon. Guy would not stand for it. He tried to tune it all out; he listened to music by The Beatles, The Band, Cat Stevens, Creedence Clearwater Revival, Pink Floyd. He found the music soothed his soul.

His soul needed all the soothing it could get. It surprised and then angered Guy that the men in positions of authority within his battalion were almost exclusively cruel men. Cruel and extremely fit. Unfortunately the nonsense was perpetual and not what Guy was expecting after enduring nearly six months of hazing that would make a frat boy blush.

Guy was privileged enough to clean up the first sergeant's office. The first sergeant was what you would expect from an old marine bird. The other PFC in the room took offense when he was told by the first sergeant that he "was more worthless than a nigger." The PFC lodged a formal complaint. Guy was lobbied heavily by both sides. When he was forced to give a statement, Guy confirmed the incident. He was not going to lie about it. He found degrading anyone inappropriate. The incident was swept under the rug, and the PFC was transferred to another company.

The company commander, a lieutenant colonel, addressed the company regarding the additional preparation for deployment. He said, "We have been training hard. We will train harder. When we go overseas, hopefully we will be able to utilize our training, travel to exotic locations, meet new people and kill them." The lieutenant colonel was a broad man with gray hair, tall. His statements were not made in jest, but by a man who takes his work seriously. It was met with devil-dog howls of approval. *Oorahs* rung out through the cacophony. A nice send-off for their seven-mile boots-and-UTES run.

Guy hated sounding off while running; he was usually winded enough. The cadences were racy, and Guy sounded off to tales of warriors' joys and fears. That is, until a catchy little tune about killing babies and raping women came along. Guy was stunned silent while everyone else sang along in tune.

One of the weaker marines in Guy's platoon was having health problems. Not much was hated more than a broke dick who got out of training. The marine had received a spinal tap that afternoon and was declared a malingerer by a group of senior marines by evening. His face was well broken, not figuratively of course. It was the last time he was seen.

Guy joined the marines in order to get some money for college, to challenge himself and to get his life on the right path. He would not have done it, however, if he weren't a patriot. He believed America was the land of the free, that America was a force for good in the world. He was willing to protect that freedom with his life if needed. What he did not appreciate was an attitude that looked forward to the opportunity of killing. Guy would, of course, pull the trigger if necessary, but not without much forethought. To have some innate desire to kill just for the experience of killing was twisted. Guy knew raping women and killing babies happened in war historically, but he did not find that glorifying it through song could in any way be morally justified.

While not in L.A., Guy spent all of his free time with Violet. Under the circumstances, they became good friends. Violet's soft demeanor brought increasing harassment his way, and Guy was concerned Violet would have his face broken as well. In his gut Guy thought it would be something worse.

Violet was on guard duty for the motor pool Friday night from midnight till eight in the morning. A shift he stood regularly. That particular Friday a group of marines, led by Sergeant Ravenclaw, snuck into the motor pool and made Violet get on his knees and plead for his life with weapons locked and loaded at his head. Cammies along with ski masks left no doubt that the perpetrators were marines. Violet was hog-tied with zip ties and left gagged in a parking lot until someone found him the next morning.

There was no secret made that it was Ravenclaw's operation. Violet rightly or wrongly said he would write his congressman. Then the wolves began to circle. When possible Guy and Violet would spend any extra time after chow relaxing and chatting in Violet's room. All the rooms were the same: not much bigger than the two racks, each with a metal wardrobe and end table. A desk with chair along with a bathroom. Violet sat on his rack which was closest to the door while Guy sat in the chair at the opposite end, his boots upon the metal table. Their chat was interrupted by the screaming voice of Sergeant Money.

Sergeant Money was an ox of a man, six foot four, two hundred forty pounds, with swastika tattoos and short, clipped blond hair.

"I'm getting really sick of all this shit, Violet." Sergeant Money held the doorjamb with one hand and the knob with the other as he peered at Violet through the crack in the door.

"I'm warning you. Let it go." Sergeant Money scowled.

"Or what? You and your buddy Ravenclaw will tie him up and leave him in a parking lot again, tough guy?" Guy leaned back in his chair, and the door flew open as Money tore inside.

"What'd you say, Flynn? Shut your fucking mouth." Money's eyes bugged out of his head.

"Or what? You and your buddies will break my face? Good luck," Guy said calmly but seriously, still leaning back in his chair with his feet upon the table, as he stared into the bugged-out eyes of Sergeant Money.

"Why don't we step outside, wiseass." Sergeant Money took a step back opening Violet's door wide. A smug smile exuded from his authoritarian self-righteousness.

In a moment Guy was upon him, standing at the close edge of his personal space. "Why don't you take off that blouse and chevrons, so I can cave in your fucking head, tough guy!"

While he had not been touched, Sgt. Money stumbled backward a few steps and knocked his head against the doorjamb.

As Guy stepped toward him again, Sgt. Money was stunned, the bugged-out look in his eyes turned to fright. Guy stared into his eyes intently. "If anyone touches him, something bad is going to happen to you. I promise." You had to state things clearly for some people in the corps to hear you.

"Jesus Christ, Flynn!" Money was out on his heels.

★★★

Guy shot as well as anyone; one or two guys shot particularly well. After they finished at the range, they rounded up by squad. Guy's squad was headed up by Lance Corporal Poltroon, a particularly nasty wanker. He was big enough, a hell of a PTer and acted tough. He was mean, but his sadistic side came off as a performance, rather than an expression of innate desire. Guy never got off well with bullies. He had the opportunity to meet some fine specimens in the corps, men who were festooned with power and authority. Guy noticed the infantry's complete lack of women led to a more openly devious atmosphere.

They rounded up after housekeeping brass, the empty shell casings. LCpl. Poltroon grabbed the top of Guy's magazine case and shook it. "How about snapping it shut, asshole," Lance Corporal Poltroon said loudly, looking around at the rest of the squad.

"Thanks, Poltroon. I mentioned it to Sergeant Money." Guy clicked closed the magazine case on his utility belt, then pulled up on the top to show that it opened readily as the latch was mostly worthless.

"You already mentioned it to Sergeant Money, huh?" Poltroon placed his face to within an inch of Guy's. "Shut your mouth when I'm talking, bitch." Now Poltroon was pointing with his thumb and finger near the side of Guy's face, "I am going to fuck you up when we get back to the barracks, smart guy."

Guy looked evenly into Poltroon's eyes. "I'm going to hold you to it," Guy said calmly.

Guy's blood boiled over as they ran back to the barracks in formation. Guy was sick and tired of men who ruled with fear and intimidation. It was a real picnic when they had an easy target. Guy would push the bully's line back and stand upon it. If the bully crossed Guy's line, Guy would not back down.

241

Such was the case with LCpl. Poltroon and some of his compadres after the range.

Guy came through Poltroon's door, not forcefully but with steam like rage, and Lance Corporal Poltroon's courage vaporized as Private First Class Flynn stood before him.

"I'm ready to get fucked up, bitch. Stand up," Guy said in a stern, wrathful tone.

Poltroon sat at the edge of his bed with the posture of a lady attending etiquette classes. He opened his mouth widely, but nothing came out. He started to shake.

"You want to fuck me up, bitch? Go ahead and try. I'm not leaving till you do," Guy said slowly. "Stand the fuck UP!" Guy roared.

One of Poltroon's lackeys slunk out the door and was back in an instant with the entire company. The day was late; the sky was dark.

Poltroon sat straight up, as if at attention, a fisted hand upon each knee. He looked forward blankly as he shook violently back and forth.

"Not so tough now, huh? Nothing to say, bitch?" Guy crouched down low and looked Poltroon in his blank eyes. "Everyone is real tough when it comes to marines like Violet or Manning, huh?" Guy addressed the gathered crowd.

Lance Corporal Rebel pushed his way to the front of the crowd. "Yo, Flynn. Come on, bro. That's enough." Rebel waved his hand, calling Guy back to their room.

"Oh, now it's enough, is it? After this piece of shit threatens to kick my ass? Well, let's go, pussy." Guy knew there was no opportunity for a fight, but he wanted all to revel in Poltroon's cowardice for as long as possible.

"Guy, the watch commander is going to call the MPs. Let the rat go."

"Let them call. They can hear all about how this piece of shit threatened me." Time to wrap it up. He'd make Rebel work for it. Rebel wrapped his arm around Guy's shoulders and escorted him back to their room.

Guy was promptly required to see a Navy Chaplain. Guy thought it seemed strange, considering the range of occurrences he had personally witnessed. Guy had not once laid a hand on anyone, not even in a thrashing. He informed the chaplain truthfully. He was surprised how the Marine Corps promoted fear and intimidation rather than honor, courage and commitment. Guy told how, while he found the former to be completely unnecessary, he possessed a strong skill set.

The chaplain promptly related how he thought the corps was no longer the place for Flynn, that he should consider going home. Guy was adamant. He had signed a contract and would not leave without an honorable discharge along with his benefits. If that were possible, was Guy interested in going home, the chaplain asked? Only a crazy man would refuse that offer, Guy replied.

It was made so. Guy was promptly promoted to lance corporal and wooed to forgo discharge by the gunnery sergeant and his staff. The wooing was consistent, including one morning when Guy passed out, standing in formation. No, his legs were not locked. They had just finished a seven-mile boots-and-UTES run, followed by "calisthenics" and pull-ups. Guy passed out when he was done, only for a second, but standing in the front of formation, the trickle of blood on his forehead gave him away. The Gunny was thrilled upon hearing the story from Guy's own lips. He told the company, "Passing out was the appropriate response for today's physical training, unless you are at your peak condition. Most of you are not."

Only a crazy man . . .

BOOK TWO: CHAPTER SIX

Guy wasn't crazy, and, as with most things *in the suck*, the time droned on slowly until he arrived back in the arms of his love, Marie. Before Guy was honorably discharged, he got a few months of downtime doing menial tasks. Mostly janitorial and yard work, which was fine by him. It was settled; he was going home. He polished off a few books he was looking to get around to. He had time to reflect. He wasn't disappointed he had joined the marines. He was thankful he didn't experience combat. What he did experience was beyond his expectations, but not beyond his mental endurance. His body was hardened, but it was the few rare men who dominated the physical endurance landscape. Some went down to Mexico to pick up steroids. Guy had tried a shot of Deca Durabolin once in his thigh. His leg ached so bad the next day he hardly made it through a hump. No thanks.

Guy realized the only limits you have are the limits you set upon yourself. That you can go harder, faster, farther, than seems physically and mentally possible. Even when you gave it your all and had nothing left, you could keep on going.

Guy arrived home in the fall of Ninety Six, and, though his bedroom remained the same, any semblance of a family was gone forever. His mother and Paul were still playing house while the kids played house swap. Guy spent two weeks inhaling Marie. A simple touch from her fair hand, the smell of her hair, a kiss on her neck, they were enough for a thousand tomorrows.

Guy was lobbied heavily to go back to New York and lend a helping hand to his agoraphobic uncle Bobby. Roxy and her second husband Ted helped Bobby refinance the house and get an equity line. He was using the line to pay bills. Roxy said Guy's grandfather would drop dead on the spot—if he weren't already dead—should he see the condition the house was in. Going back to New York would provide an opportunity to have a conjugal visit with his biological father, Jack. Guy held hope that someday Jack would get out of prison, that they could have a real father-son relationship. Guy needed to get a job and a place to live, and it seemed this was likely his only window of downtime. It was hard to leave Marie again, but he promised he would get them a place as soon as he returned, and that they would never have to spend another night apart again.

The external condition of John and Patricia's house was unnerving as Guy's cousin Paul drove Guy up to it. Paul thought it looked too dangerous to stay in, but Bobby was expecting Guy, so Paul dropped him off and drove away in his clean Nineteen Eighty 9 Lincoln Town Car. Guy's grandparents' home had been destroyed—everything his grandfather had worked a lifetime for. There was a rusty chain link fence running the perimeter, and the grass looked natural, as if it had never been mowed. The house seemed abandoned. The red wagon wheel still lay against the front of the white house with its faded shutters, door and cast iron fixtures.

Per his uncle's instructions, Guy went around to the side door that led into the kitchen. As he stepped up the concrete stoop under the faded red awning, the kitchen door opened quickly.

"I saw Paulie dropping you off in the Lincoln. Come inside." Guy's uncle extended the arm of his lanky frame. He was an inch or two shorter than Guy and weathered. His hair came down to the middle of his back and was braided into a ponytail. He wore a red plaid shirt beneath a camouflage field jacket. Jeans with a wallet chain, finished off by black motorcycle boots and a US Army hat. A cigarette hung from his lips, revealing his more-brown-than-yellow decayed teeth. They made Guy queasy, as he followed his uncle into the exact same kitchen Guy had been in as a young boy, plates and all.

Without taking a tour, it was clear the house was filthy, or better put, never cleaned, not once for years.

"Put your bag in here." Bobby led him down the small hall toward the only downstairs bedroom. The bathroom door in the hall was closed. Guy squeezed past his uncle and set his seabag down on the floor of the small bedroom in front of the twin-size bed. The room was modestly decorated from the Nineteen Fifties and remained just as Guy had remembered it, except for the thick layer of dust.

"Gimme your jacket." Bobby reached out his arm.

Guy took off his leather jacket; it was brown and extremely warm to wear in California. He began to lay it down upon the bed.

"Uh, uh, uh. Jackets belong in the closet. Gimme that jacket." Bobby stepped forward.

Guy dutifully handed Bobby his jacket. Some things were not worth making an issue over.

Bobby hung Guy's jacket in the closet outside the kitchen next to his own. Guy chuckled to himself that his uncle must not have received the memo about wearing covers inside. A kettle began to whistle, and Bobby, with the aid of a rooster-shaped oven mitt, moved the kettle to a cool burner. Two white ceramic mugs sat upon the original Formica countertops. The Formica was weathered; it was hard to tell if the countertops were off-white or green-gray, perhaps a light brown.

"Tea?" Bobby asked holding up the kettle.

When Guy was little, his grandmother always made him tea. He had never drank it outside of his childhood. "Sure," Guy said, seeing the two cups on the counter.

"Milk, sugar?" Bobby placed the Lipton's tea bags in the cups and poured the steaming water.

"Sounds great." Guy thought about the greasy walls as Uncle Bobby pulled the milk out of the refrigerator, an appliance which seemed new for the space, perhaps ten years old. "The milk's good?" Guy asked plainly, seeing no way to tiptoe around it.

Bobby held the quarter-gallon plastic jug up to his face. "Is it good? It's the yellow." Bobby tapped the yellow plastic cap. "Two percent." He looked over at Guy's raised eyebrows and bobbed his head. "Oh, is it expired?" he drawled. "I just bought it at the market yesterday, meathead. Grabbed a jug four back with a later date."

Guy chuckled; he did the same thing. He rarely took the first item on a shelf. "Just asking. I mean it's not like the maid came before I got here."

"The maid's off on Tuesdays. One or two sugars?"

"Two."

"I take four. You shouldn't. It's not good for you." Bobby tilted his head to the side and squinted. He sat down at the little circular wooden table, which was cluttered with magazines and newspapers.

Guy took a sip of his tea. It was hot, sweet and creamy; the tea bag and spoon were still in his cup. "So what's going on here, besides not having enough money to pay the bills?"

"Oh, I have enough money to pay the bills. I'm short about four hundred bucks a month. But I get it from the hundred and twenty thousand dollar line of credit on the house. And what's going on here is that I'm under attack. This neighborhood has been taken over by off-duty police officers dealing drugs, Long Island's finest. Come here. I'll show you. Bring your tea." Guy followed his uncle into the living room which was adjacent to the kitchen out the hall. Though it was daytime, the room was dim and dank. Heavy floor-to-ceiling curtains covered all the windows. Guy turned on a floor lamp in the corner which provided good light and another table lamp on an end table at the other end of the couch. The room had a dull gray tint from the thick layer of dust that coated everything in the room. Everything in its decades-old place.

"They deal drugs right out in the open. What do they think? I don't notice?" Bobby tapped a videotape recorder mounted on a tripod, set up to look out the window. "Oh, I see all right. I got months' worth of tapes. Did you know Grandpa built the entire second story of this house? He built the patio and TV room too. He wired the whole damn thing himself. Do you think he'd let this neighborhood get taken over by dopers?"

"Bobby, what's going on in here?" Guy walked toward the smell coming from the dining room. It was so pungent, it actually made him gag. The dining room table and chairs were covered with hair and, without closer inspection, what appeared to be feces.

"That's Grandma's cat, Clarabelle. I call her Clara, after one of our high school cheerleaders. Ooo la la." Bobby began to laugh, as he put his hand to his head. "She always has plenty of food and water, but I don't clean up cat shit. I tell her to go outside, but she's a dumb cat and prefers to make her bedroom a shit box." Bobby walked past the dining room into the TV room and began to pull some of the videotapes from the shelf, like he was checking the labels of fine vintage wine.

"Remember when we watched *Creature from the Black Lagoon?*" Bobby asked with a chuckle. "Now that's a classic flick."

"I found *Invasion of the Body Snatchers* to be more memorable." Disturbingly memorable. The vividly disturbing memory of body-snatching aliens had been seared in Guy's brain since his uncle had woken up Guy in the middle of the night all those years ago.

"Oh, yeah. I remember that. You kept trying to hide your head under the blanket." Bobby chucked loudly.

Guy sat in one of the matching armchairs. They were wooden, with sloped backs, big armrests and cushions. Comfortable, except for something poking Guy in the back. Guy dug his hand between the cushions and fished out a bayonet. Guy held it point up in front of his face.

"You never know where a battle's going to start, jarhead. There are weapons strategically placed all over the house: Special Forces knives, blackjacks, brass knuckles, baseball bats, no guns unfortunately. The man took them when I got arrested while you were in the corps. Wannabe soldiers. I hate civil servants. So the postman sees a hand grenade wired to the kitchen door, and, the next thing I know, I have the whole damn ATF busting down my door. Whatever happened to the right to privacy? It's my damn house! Don't want to get blown up? Don't come in the house without permission!

"Not like it was even a real grenade or anything. Well, it was real, but it wasn't live—no explosive or firing pin. I put it on the kitchen door latch, right where you can see it, so those damn doper cops would think twice before trying to sneak in here. The ATF confiscated Grandpa's guns from World War II. Can you believe that shit? That's part of history. Do you think they even bothered to compensate me? Nope, as usual, the man does as he pleases. Thieves. Took my Remington Eight Seventy shotgun too. Same one you jarheads use at embassy duty." Bobby sat down in the second armchair. It was separated by the first with a dark wood cabinet used as an end table.

"Watch some boob tube? If you're hungry later, I have a whole stock of Hungry-Man TV dinners. Turkey, steak, fried chicken, chicken fried steak. Fried chicken's my fav. I sneak out after hours once or twice a month to restock. Picked up orange juice, some bread, strawberry jam."

"Sounds tasty. I'll watch whatever. Go ahead and pick something. I gotta take a leak." Guy got up and made his way to the kitchen. He opened the refrigerator which had the aforementioned items and nothing else. The overhead freezer was crammed with about thirty Hungry-Man dinners.

Guy opened two cabinets. On one side were half-used spice containers, the other held formerly white plates. The dishes had been put away clean. They had sat so long, they were actually black with dust. The cabinets were dry and dusty; the Formica countertops virtually nonexistent as they were covered by all manner of clutter.

Guy opened the small bathroom in the hall. As he stepped in, the white porcelain sink was visibly black in a plate-shaped diameter near the drain. Not just dust, but some combination of grime, mold and hair. The same cocktail graced the toilet underneath the lid, and the tub shower near the fixtures and cracks. Guy peed carefully and was thoroughly disgusted.

As he stepped out of the bathroom, Guy crossed over into the unused living room and looked at his grandfather's brick fireplace. His grandfather's photo stood upon its mantel, along with pictures from times past, all forgotten and covered with dust.

Guy only had a few memories of his grandfather, but thought of the man he was and must have been. When his grandparents were alive, you could literally eat off the floor. They would lose their gourds to see it now. John had received this house as a reward from the Great War and then built most of what exists now with his own hands.

Guy thought of Marie, his beauty. Not just that she was his sexy firecracker, but for the mother he knew she would be. For the best friend, confidant, guide and lover that she already was. Their kids would live a different life where they were not scared, where their innocence was guarded. Where they were protected and loved. Cared for, educated, not poor.

Guy took a few big breaths in the kitchen before walking past the cat room and exhaling in the TV room. He sat down and finished his last few sips of his tea. "Good tea, thanks!" Guy lifted his mug in the air.

"I'll make you another." Bobby started to rise from his chair.

"No, no, thanks, maybe later. Bobby, I'm cleaning this house for you, and you're going to help."

"I told you the maid's off today. Plus none of this stuff is garbage. I'm not going to just throw it in the trash!" Bobby stood from his seat.

"Did I say anything about throwing stuff away? Sit down." Guy was sitting in the chair closest to the door, and, with his left hand, he nudged Bobby back toward his seat.

"Cleaning's a different story, Bob. Grandpa would kick your ass now, and you damn well know it. We're going to get this place cleaned up and take a look at the bills."

"Bills, bills, no need to look at the bills. Like I said, I'm four hundred dollars short a month—four thousand eight hundred short a year, every year, year after year. It's simple. I just gotta die before I run outta the hundred twenty thousand dollar line of credit money." Bobby put his index and middle fingers of each hand on his temples.

"Stop being so dramatic. For one thing, you could get a damn job. You could probably panhandle four hundred damn dollars a month. Outside of that, let's take a look and see what we can figure out."

"Fine." Bobby sat back in his chair.

"Good to go with cleaning?" Guy leaned forward.

"Fine. I said fine." Bobby waved his hand.

"The whole house."

"Fine, yes, fine." Bobby waved his hand again, this time with his eyes closed.

"You want to smoke some pot? Paulie gave me a care package when he picked me up from the airport."

"You have pot?" Bobby sat up straight in the chair, his attention piqued.

"Yep, and it's pretty killer."

"*Chronic?*" Bobby's neck craned forward; his hands were now upon his knees.

"For sure."

"I've always wanted to try that chronic. I haven't smoked Mary Jane in, wow, fifteen years, maybe more. I've got this great little bong upstairs. Get the pot."

Bobby was quickly out the room and up the stairs.

Three weeks of cleaning a house that required hazmat gear had left Guy with a case of serious bronchitis. The house looked as if a real person lived in it now, both inside and out. Lots of elbow grease, along with a neighborhood company to fix the roof and paint the house for 9 hundred dollars. Bobby spent more time out of the house with Guy than he had in the last fifteen years combined. They got a renter to help with the bills, some ex-con named Whitey. He had jailed with Guy's father and had been out on parole for two years. He would also pay four hundred fifty dollars a month.

Guy knew it was Paulie's Lincoln when he heard the horn. As he walked down the pathway, the front passenger door swung open. Guy could see Paulie behind the wheel.

The roomy Lincoln allowed the cousins a proper Italian hugging.

"Yo, yo. What up, cuz?" Guy buckled his seat belt.

"Ah, I've been waiting to take you out. We're gonna get blasted, baby! That's Mess and Charlie. Charlie's crazy, yo! Not like Guy crazy, but straight break-somebody's-arm-with-a-baseball-bat crazy. That kid didn't even do shit to you, Charlie."

"Yo, that kid was annoying as fuck. I told him to shut the hell up like three times." Charlie's words drowned in a thick New York accent.

Guy turned over his shoulder. "Nice to meet you, Charlie. What's your real name, Mess?" Guy looked over to the scraggly blond kid; his NY Mets hat was slightly tilted to the side.

"Mike."

"His name's not Mike. Hasn't been Mike since he pissed his pants in first grade." Paul laughed as he looked back at Mess through the rearview mirror. Paul's hair showed his Italian side, a bit greasy. He was tanning-booth burnt copper with a gym-hardened body that clearly had help from steroids. His ripped abs were clad in a tight-fitting Calvin Klein T-shirt finished with jeans and Timberland boots.

"Well, they actually called me Messy Mike at first, until second grade. Then they dropped the *Mike*. It was just Mess after that," Mess said forlornly, so many years later.

"Nice to meet you, Mike. I'm Guy." Guy extended his hand for a shake.

"OK, so tell these malooks about your crazy-ass uncle, and then I want to hear all about your visit with Pops. Was it crazy or what?" Paulie looked over to his cousin. "Wait. Quick pit stop first. Mess, you pump. Charlie, cuz, beer time."

Guy followed his cousin, who walked briskly into the little convenience store. "Hey, you guys know that I'm not twenty-one yet," he whispered in Paulie's ear, as they made a beeline to the back of the small convenience store. Paulie and Charlie pulled out eight frosty forty-ounce bottles of St. Ides.

"Saint Ides, it's all about the crooked I, bitch. Two forties each, you're gonna need it, trust me!" Paul placed four down on the small counter, which took up most of the space. "I got eight. Give me two packs of those Swisher Sweets, two lighters and a pack of Newports. Put the rest on 11." Paul paid the bill in cash; he wasn't even questioned for ID.

"What the fuck was that?" Guy looked puzzled as they walked back to the town car.

"What? That's not how you roll in L.A.?" Paulie and Charlie bumped hips since their arms were full of St. Ides.

Charlie placed his beer in the trunk, and they were off swiftly.

"Grab an Ides." Paulie passed three forties back, and Charlie immediately passed one back with the top off.

"What? Are you fucking crazy?" Guy assaulted Paul's ear as he guzzled down the neck of his forty ounce while cruising down the expressway. Paulie placed the large bottle between his legs. Before he knew it, Guy was the only one who hadn't cracked his frosty St. Ides.

"Drink the neck. You're gonna need it!" Paulie laughed heartily and slapped the steering wheel. "Load me up!" Paulie gazed into the rearview mirror.

Mess chopped up the cocaine with a razor blade on a little square mirror. He laid out two fat lines, leaned forward, and held the mirror just below and in front of Paulie's face. Mess held a little straw to Paulie's nose.

"Go," Mess spoke with a feverishly quick tone.

Paulie inhaled the first line and Mess moved the straw to his other nostril. Clearly a routine often practiced.

"Go," Mess repeated.

Paulie inhaled vigorously.

"Yeah, baby. That is the shit right there." He inhaled three more times deeply and wiped his nose with the back of his hand.

"I told you, drink up that neck, cuz. You need the balance. You're up next."

"Are you serious? You're crazy," Guy replied.

"That's how we roll, baby! One line, then you'll be ready for story time!"

The line Mess held was smaller than Paulie's, but large enough. Guy did it just so he wouldn't have to hear about it all night. It was strong. Cocaine sped him up, which was never necessary. It was good he had two forty ounces and some bud.

"So like I already told you, it was crazy." Guy turned from looking at Paul toward the backseat. "Like banned-from–Jerry Springer crazy."

"No joke, yo!" Paulie bobbed in his seat to Mobb Deep and looked in the rearview mirror.

"So, toilets and sink coated black with grimy hair and mold. Not like kinda black, straight black, yo." Guy looked to his cousin. "I had to use a screwdriver to scrape that shit off. So fucking nasty. It was like fused on there, it was there so long. I had to grind it off one layer at a time. Hella gross." Guy looked at Mess. "Learned all about spit-spot cleaning in the corps. That house is not quite spit spot, but as close as it's ever going to get again."

Guy stretched out his legs. The Lincoln was not his style, but it sure was roomy; it rode smooth. Guy wore a pair of Harley-Davidson motorcycle boots. Again not his style, but his uncle had had a matching pair and had been insistent. The toe was squared, and the front of the boot was embroidered with an eagle which remained hidden underneath his pair of jeans. There was a little silver ring near the heel with a strip of leather, kind of like a stirrup. Guy thought it looked cool. He wore a gray shirt with a half zipper made out of some sort of nice sweatsuit material. It was his guido cousin's of course. He was fortunate enough to be asked to wear it.

"And what did you get for all your help? Bronchitis, exactly. Wound up in the emergency room." Paul pounded the steering wheel and looked over to Guy. "What are you, a retart? You don't wear a fuckin' mask with a respirator or nothing?"

"I figured Bobby lives there, hey. And I left windows open while I was cleaning," Guy retorted.

"Left the windows open." Paul looked behind him to Charlie, "The cat uses the fucking dining room as a shit box, and he left the windows open. What? Are you kiddin' me? Retarted." Paul gave Guy a good shove in the arm. He was meaty, but Guy was solid.

"OK, so here's the crazy part," Guy continued.

"Here's the crazy part. You're fucking mint, cuz. I love you. Load me up." Paul grabbed the steering wheel with both arms.

"You said one round."

"One round for you, lightweight." Paul held up his index finger.

"You did two your first round," Guy pointed out.

"Yeah, but that's still one round. Listen to this kid. Yo, Charlie and I will do like three eightballs to ourselves and pound three forties a piece. Now listen, if I'm gonna drive, do cocaine and drink a forty, I need to concentrate. I can't have you here breaking my balls." Paulie chuckled. "Load me up."

"You're a psycho." Guy took three long swigs off his forty. It was already dark, and no one seemed to be watching. In California, Guy would never let anyone crack a beer in the car, let alone drink while driving.

"That's what Mom says. I tell her, talk to my dad about it. She says I would, but your dad's dead in the gutter from getting high. You're gonna end up joining him. Blah, blah, blah, blah." Paulie moved his right hand open and shut like it was a little mouth.

"*Sooooo*, all sorts of crazy stuff in that house. My grandpa's war medals, my grandma's jewelry. Found a little leather diary. Opened it up and all the pages were blank except for about a third of the way in. There was one page with a detailed entry."

"Oh, shit. Here it comes." Paulie slapped at Guy in disbelief.

Mess crouched into the front seat. "What it say?"

"So it was a detailed time line with the date at the top of when my grandma drowned in the bathtub. It had times in the margin, like what time she woke up that morning, what time she took a bath, what time Bobby found her in the bathroom, what time he did CPR. I got this feeling like, shit, my uncle murdered my grandma."

"Hell yeah, he did," Paulie blurted out.

"She cut me off when I was about ten. Wouldn't pick up the phone anymore, stopped sending mail and birthday cards. Looking back on it, my mom thinks Bobby might have been controlling Grandma or something. She was real old by then. He was always strange."

"Uh, that's an understatement. Mr. I-have-a-fake-real-hand-grenade-tied-to-the-door." Paulie laughed and shook his head.

"Well, it was only to protect against the drug-dealing Long Island Police Department." Guy smiled.

"Hey, that part's probably true, they sure were happy to take his guns" Paulie said emphatically.

"Probably true," Charlie chimed from the backseat.

"Where do you think we got this shit from?" Mess laughed. He had a voice somewhere between a mouse and a rat.

"So to be honest, seeing Pops was overwhelming." Guy touched his palm to his short-sleeved sweatsuited chest.

"For sure, for sure. I can only imagine," Paulie said compassionately.

"I was able to bring in two brown paper grocery bags full of food. They give you a list of stuff you can't bring. So I brought all this fresh fruit, vegetables and nuts. That's what my dad wanted. I also brought an apple pie, cherry cheesecake, steaks, chicken, ground beef, pasta. I fit a ton in those two bags. But, I tell you what, I didn't hardly eat the whole weekend. I had no appetite whatsoever. When you first get there, you go through all these gates and fences, metal detectors. They pat you down. They let us stay in this trailer for like a day and a half. There were three trailers in this chained-off yard inside the prison. They have a bedroom, bathroom, kitchen, living room. The outside was all concrete. We played handball, where you each have a concrete square, and you hit this racquetball in the other persons square with your hand." Guy mimicked the swing with his hand.

"Who won?" Paul chimed in quickly.

"Well, I had never played before, but I won," Guy said coyly yet valiantly.

"Of course you won, you competitive prick. This guy used to get straight As in school." Paul pointed with his thumb.

"So it was good, but it went quick. It was surreal. He likes to talk about all this Asian philosophical stuff. He's a Zen Buddhist. He was telling me this story of how he was working in the library one day, and he needed to use a typewriter but didn't have the code to the locker. Well, this Buddhist monk, who happens to be visiting the prison, comes along and tells him the answers to everything you ever wanted to know are out there, if you just know which questions to ask. Then he gives my dad the code to the locker. Well, my dad was like, I don't know what just happened, but he became a Buddhist after that."

"Like the monk didn't know the code, duh. Fucking Jack, maniac." Paulie shook his head back and forth.

"Well, fifteen years in the pen." Guy couldn't imagine being locked in a cage for fifteen years.

"No joke, horrible." Paulie opened his eyes wide.

"He told me how, when he first caught the case, he was an instigator on the yard. The guards locked him in solitary confinement for six months. They used to put him in this cell that had Plexiglas between the bars. Jack said it would get up to like a hundred and thirty degrees inside. He would flood the cell so he could lie in the water on the floor."

"That's some crazy shit, fucking pigs!" Paul pounded the steering wheel.

"So, Whitey, that former con my dad got to rent a room from Bobby told me some crazy-ass stories. He used to be a heroin addict. Told me that he started having problems with this black guy when he was mopping the decks. One day the guy asks Whitey if he can borrow the mop to mop out his cell real quick. Well, Whitey reluctantly agrees, and, when the guy's done, he leaves the mop in his cell. When Whitey mentions something, the guy says, sorry, go head and grab it.

"Well, Whitey could see it was a setup to get him in the cell and turns to walk off, but quickly gets surrounded by sixty black guys who start forming a ring around him. So all of a sudden my dad shows up and asks if there's a problem. Well, the problems disappeared. Whitey said Jack was the only white guy on Rikers Island who was allowed to use the black's phone. I guess that's what being an Airborne Ranger in Vietnam gets you."

"Damn!" Mess was up on the edge of his seat.

"He told me how he used to be friends with Eddie Money, whose real name is Eddie Mahoney. How Jack let my mother down, that she did what she had to do. How he didn't realize that he had post-traumatic stress disorder after the war, not that it was an excuse. He told me that he had murdered Knall, that he accepted responsibility for it. He told me how he had kept his mouth shut about his cousin all these years, and how he wished Ritchie had done the same. He told me that he never confessed to Ritchie about the guy he murdered. Other than that, it was like talking to Kwai Chang Caine." Guy could tell nobody caught the reference, but nobody asked. "So where we going?"

"We're going to Joey's. His parents are out of town. They're old-school Italian. They make the best homemade wine in five-gallon water jugs down in their garage. I always take some for my mother. It's the best. And I'm fucking mom's married friend Angie. Gonna give her the Paulie special. Put my feet against the footboard and wham, wham, wham." Paulie thrust up his pelvis.

"I put my hands together like this." Guy grasped his hands together the way you clap. "Put them behind her head and pull down at the same time you go up, bam!" Guy pulled his arms down. "I call it the jackhammer."

"I'm gonna leave the door open, so you faggots can hear that pig squeal. Seriously watch. It's gonna be epic." Paul looked back at Charlie.

"I'll be smoking a fat blunt," Guy threw in. His cousin was such a whack job. Guy had decked him hard in the stomach once when Paul came to California on vacation. Guy must have been about 9. Their parents had gone out, and Paulie had pulled Guy's shorts down in front of the babysitter, underwear and all. He punched Paulie hard. Paulie never messed with Guy again after that. He also left California with a fresh pack of white socks. Della told Roxie to use bleach so they would stay white.

Guy enjoyed spending time with Roxie, Ted, Paul, and Jerry. They had taken care of Lily and Ray, who Guy had loved deeply. His aunt and her family were crazy, so they were fun to visit. He would get to hear more about his father and the old days from aunt Roxie, since his mom and dad never spoke of such things.

Guy's night with Paulie went quickly as did his time in New York. He was sorry it ended on such a bitter note with his uncle, but, as he lay naked in bed next to Marie, he tried not to think about it and thought instead of their new life together.

When he had returned from New York, Guy and Marie found a little house in Reseda. It was great: three bedrooms, two big living rooms, a decent kitchen. The yard was large, and the grass-covered backyard had plenty of room for Marie and Guy to start a vegetable garden.

With John as a roommate, the thousand dollars in rent was reasonable. Guy and Marie took the master, which had its own bathroom. John took a bedroom for three hundred. Guy snuggled up to Marie's soft naked body, as if they were one; she was warm like a little hot tamale. Marie was a sound sleeper. Guy said someone could steal the bed right out from under her. Guy had seen that happen to a marine in SOI. When they were ready for bed, he always held Marie tight until she fell asleep. If he could sleep with her in his arms all night he would, but Guy was only comfortable sleeping on his stomach. Beginning and ending every day alongside his love, his very heart, provided Guy such joy and comfort that all the world threw at him no longer mattered.

Not surprisingly it only took John three months to miss a rent payment. He lost his job at the head shop. They said he was lazy, and John was already driving Marie crazy, leaving dirty dishes all over the house.

Surprisingly John found a replacement roommate, a white kid named Montel. He was pretty cool and always had great weed. He had the craziest pit bull Guy ever saw. It was a purebred, bought at a dog show for sixteen hundred dollars. Coco was brownish red in color with a red nose, not short in stature like most pit bulls. Coco could look you in the eyes when he stood on his back legs. He had a strange look in his eyes, something feral. When he latched onto something, you couldn't get it out of his mouth until he was done with it, no matter what.

Still Coco was a better addition than John's monitor lizard, which ate live mice. Guy found it cruel and disgusting. Sure, it happened in nature but was not quite the same when the mouse was put in a bag and banged against the table to stun it first. You wouldn't want the lizard to get nipped after all. John and Marie both held it. The lizard swam in the bathtub like an alligator. Guy didn't in fact consider it a pet at all. He didn't think squirrels were meant to be pets either, but John's pet squirrel, Squirrel Nutkin, turned out to be quite friendly. John's mother had rescued him from a fallen tree in her backyard. She nursed him back to health, and John got him a big hutch inside the house, until they set him free.

Marie asked if they could get a cat. Guy said no, and the next day, after he got home from work, Marie asked him to guess what she got.

His reply, "Not a cat," produced a black fluffy kitten. Guy named her Stinky due to her particularly odiferous fart-to-size ratio. She practiced guerrilla warfare, running out from under small things around the room and attacking Guy and Marie's feet as they got up to use the bathroom. Squirrel Nutkin taught Stinky how to make noises like a squirrel. Now that was cute.

Guy sat up on the edge of their queen-size bed. It was Marie's from her room. She got it from Ikea. It was a four-poster bed, light wood, and a hell of a bitch to put together. They had a little black dresser with three drawers about waist high, more square than rectangular. Guy made sure they always had a big plastic cup filled with water by the bed, next to his eighteen-inch glass bong with a bubble. He loaded himself a large snapper from the top drawer.

Guy had been quickly certified as a security guard; he was able to make decent money with a lot of shifts and still go to school. He worked the graveyard shift which allowed him time to study. Most of the places he guarded were technology companies. They were dead quiet at night. He found out about the company from Marie's brother, Arnold. Guy enjoyed feeding the feral cats outside the business and even made love to Marie on top of one of the polished wooden boardroom tables. Guy figured the table must have cost twenty thousand dollars, more than his yearly salary before taxes.

He lay back down and snuggled his chest to Marie's back, his pelvis to her butt. Simply lying here in their own room, in their own place together, was a fantasy. All that he needed and more than enough. Regular meals of pasta did not seem a sacrifice, nor was living in Reseda. While it wasn't the best part of the Valley, it wasn't the worst part of Reseda, and it certainly wasn't Van Nuys. They were committed to being together, no matter what, no matter where.

Guy breathed in the back of Marie's neck, and his final day with his uncle Bobby replayed itself again. He wished it had turned out differently, but it all had happened so quickly.

Paulie had dropped Guy off at the house, and, as he entered the kitchen door, he saw Whitey pinned up against the wall. Bobby was strangling him. With both hands wrapped around his neck, Bobby screamed, "I'm gonna kill you," over and over again. Guy shouted as he tore across the room to no avail. His uncle had a death grip that Guy was only able to pry away after putting his uncle's neck in the crease of his elbow and using his other hand to wrench back his uncle's fingers.

Bobby was like a mad dog that had lost its bite. He lunged back toward Whitey, and Guy pulled Bobby to the ground on top of him. Bobby hit his eye on a chair behind them as they went down; it was instantly a gruesome purple shiner. Guy couldn't see it at the time, not until the police arrived. Guy held his uncle until they did. Bobby screamed, "Mutherfucker, who said you could paint my walls!" until the cops arrived.

Whitey had taken it upon himself to paint the kitchen walls the night prior. He said the nicotine had leeched right through the first coat. He switched to exterior paint; it took two full coats to cover up the nicotine. Guy's uncle smoked four packs a day. What a show, Guy thought.

As Guy lay next to Marie, the bloody purple shiner filled his mind; it was more like he was watching the scene than reliving it. Whitey called the police, who arrived nearly instantaneously. Bob was checked into a county psychiatric facility. When Guy was finally allowed to visit, his uncle was despondent and heavily medicated. Guy apologized to his uncle for his eye and tried to bury the hatchet, but his uncle was removed, disaffected. Bobby told Guy he decided to undergo electric shock therapy. Guy's pleas for patience, research, and concern for the severity and permanence of the procedure were received as lukewarm bathwater upon the skin. The doctors were very enthusiastic.

After Bobby's therapy Guy received a call that he and Whitey were to be out of the house. Bobby was coming home, and, if they were at the house, the police would be called. Guy was glad he had decided to take his grandmother's pearl necklace for Marie and his grandfather's cuff links. They would be the only mementos from his side of the family. He didn't even have a picture of his grandfather.

Guy's subsequent phone calls weren't answered, and four trips to the house did not yield so much as a cracked door. Since then Guy received back two letters he wrote, both unopened and marked Return to Sender. In black marker, Guy's name was crossed out, and Benedict Arnold was written instead.

Perhaps Jack was right when he told Guy to seek conservatorship. Before Guy even went out to New York, his father had suggested getting Bobby declared incompetent by the court. Guy wanted no part in it. He wasn't sure it would have ended better anyway.

Guy was a light sleeper, and, as he seemed to doze, his eyelids brightened slightly, and the bushes rustled. Guy heard muffled voices in the back of his mind that brought him to his feet. Peeling back the curtains from the window by his head, as well as the sleep from his eyes, he saw twenty militarized police, clothed all in black, black military helmets, black assault rifles—all pointed at the house.

Guy pushed firmly against Marie's naked back. "The cops are here. Put on your bathrobe, don't say a word and do whatever they ask. Put your hands up. They have their guns out." Guy grabbed his bong from the nightstand and, like a gazelle, placed it on a shelf in his closet. He moved the small bag of weed in the top drawer under his socks. Guy pulled on a pair of Joe Boxer briefs from the floor beside his bed. He opened his bedroom door which was adjacent to the front door.

"Come out with your hands up!" Guy heard an officer yell.

Guy yelled loudly, "Coming!" and a little less loudly, "Montel, Tina, cops with guns all around the house, hands up. We're going outside now."

Guy put his left hand behind him as he would when walking through a store, because he knew Marie would grab it. She did, and Guy opened the front door, to a blur of black troops shouting commands for them to get facedown on the driveway. Guy and Marie did as instructed quickly. Her bathrobe was really just a negligee. They were lying on the slightly downward sloping driveway. Seven or eight cops were upon them instantly, and they were roughly cuffed. Guy turned his head to the side to see that Montel and Tina were just about to experience the same treatment. Montel, like Guy, was wearing boxers, and Tina's negligee allowed for a visual cavity search. Tina was a top-notch stunner who was in no way compensated for by Montel's Mustang, his decent job or reasonable personality.

Guy couldn't hear much except "Stay on the fucking ground!" He could tell that the ten cops pointing rifles at his head did not appreciate being looked at.

But Guy looked, and someone with rank stormed over from the direction of the house. His face mask was lifted. Guy could hear Coco going crazy and scratching at the front door, preventing the officers from entering the house.

"Whose dog is that?" the white officer with lifted face mask asked.

"It's his." Guy motioned with his head. "Coco, he's only ten months old." The concrete was cool, and the sun was just starting to break. There must have been thirty policemen: police in Guy's yard, police in Guy's neighbors' yards, police cars up and down the street.

"Don't you lie to me, boy." The man who looked more soldier than servant spat at Guy from under his sandy-blond mustache.

Guy thought what a sight this must be for the neighbors. The pervs were certainly enjoying the scenery. The mustached man walked behind them and picked Marie up by her hips and arm, placing her on her feet. He did the same with Tina. Guy lost them from view as they entered the house. A little more than an hour after walking away with the girls, the mustached man returned, sans helmet.

"Where's your brother Jeter?" The mustached man asked with irritation.

"I haven't seen him for like a week. Did you check my mom's?" Montel replied.

The mustached man walked them both into the house, and placed Guy on the living room floor, against the wall opposite the girls, who were also still handcuffed. Guy could hear Coco barking occasionally from behind the bathroom door. The police made the girls go in ahead and lock Coco in the bathroom. Guy watched as a uniformed police woman opened his bedroom door and was caught by a guerrilla ambush. In a black flash, Stinky used the officer as a climbing post, scaling to her neck and promptly diving back under the bed. Guy tried not to laugh; the other two officers who saw did not fare as well and nearly keeled over with glee.

The mustached man walked out of Montel's room holding a pistol; he pulled Montel up to his feet by his bicep. "Whose gun is this?" He looked threateningly at Montel.

"It's my brother's. He stays with me sometimes," Montel answered sheepishly.

"You ever seen this gun before?" The officer pointed the gun at Guy.

"No, officer," Guy answered courteously.

It took Guy four and a half hours to find out that the police were there looking for Jeter on a warrant for terrorist threats. It was an old warrant for making harassing phone calls to Tina. The same Tina who was friends with Jeter, and yet she sat mostly naked and still handcuffed on the living room floor with Montel. Jeter, who was about as dangerous as wet dishrag.

BOOK TWO: CHAPTER SEVEN

It took Montel five minutes to realize the cops had not only taken his brother's gun but had also helped themselves to an ounce of pot and an eightball of speed. Guy's eighth of pot along with his bong remained undisturbed. Montel was growing a pot plant in the spare bedroom. Guy wasn't using the room, and Montel offered to pay an extra hundred and twenty five bucks for it. Guy told him to keep it to one plant and was surprised to find that the police not only left it rooted but left the small halogen light on as well.

Montel's younger brother, Jeter, did crash at the pad periodically. He was a tool, totally harmless. The tool even made out with the Asian transsexual hooker from next door. The hooker got her hooks into the pocketbook of their next door neighbor, an elderly man. He was unaware that having nice boobs did not preclude you from packing a penis these days. Jeter seemed unaware as well; the transsexual told Jeter she was on the rag.

Guy was able to get his lease canceled the day after the raid. It was a good thing, because later that evening he received a call from Manuel, pronounced Manwell, one of the Valley's meth cooks. Guy had tried speed before; he hated it pretty much the same as coke, crack, or any other stimulant. As always Guy's mind moved fast enough, and the people associated with those drugs were always trouble. Manuel, or Manwell's, reputation preceded him.

Guy had never met him, but knew Manuel cooked high-quality glass. Manuel made a statement of fact that the gun was his, not Jeter's, and he knew Guy stole it. He wanted it back now. Along with four eyewitnesses, Guy told him to call the station and ask for it himself. Of course Manuel claimed a personal friend in the police department told him there was no gun booked into evidence. Guy hung up the phone. He didn't think the cops would take a gun, but they did steal the meth and pot, so he couldn't rule it out completely. The next day Guy purchased an HK Benelli semiautomatic shotgun.

They spent the week with Della at Mack's house in Guy's old room, just to be careful. Part of the allure of having some roommates was pooling money for a house and a yard. Guy and Marie had each other, and, though they were poor, they didn't feel poor. Reseda it was again. Reseda and Victory. Not as bad as Reseda and Roscoe at least. It was certainly seedy, with strippers and potheads, but not generally dangerous. Guy and Marie were excited to find a little one bedroom for six hundred fifty dollars a month. The summers were hot; it only had a window air conditioner in the bedroom. Stinky was very effective at keeping the roaches at bay.

The location was convenient, across the street from a grocery store, and right off Reseda Boulevard, which was nice if you didn't have kids. There was communal laundry and a sauna in the back of an unused rec room. The complex was two stories of units in a square, with an unheated pool in the middle. Between the parking lot and the street, there was always plenty of parking for guests. There was a gate where people entered a number to call your home phone. When you pressed the # key, it buzzed open the front gate.

There was nothing like not having roommates. Guy and Marie saved on laundry as they hardly wore clothes. Guy made love to her body with his eyes continuously. He loved to stroke her soft skin and could never seem to keep his hands from her ass. He couldn't help from giving it a little smack whenever she walked by; it was perfectly shaped and so alluring. She would giggle and wiggle it at him. They spent the weekends naked in bed, losing the time in each other's arms and watching episodes of *The Simpsons* that they taped every week. There was a place right up the street that rented porn for cheap fun on the weekends.

They took classes at community college, and, when possible, they took classes together. Marie was a diligent studier and consistently scored top marks. She was, however, generally irritated that, regardless of the class, there were very few total points that Guy missed out on. He paid close attention in class, always sat in the second row and took copious notes. He read all the chapters once and reviewed his notes. He was embarrassed by his grades, considering the amount of time he spent studying. He tried to make a joke of it. He begged her not to take it personally; she was getting straight As after all.

Guy realized how soft his heart had become one morning when Stinky went missing. Guy and Marie were awakened early by Mufasa, their orange tabby. Stinky did need a friend after all. Marie had found him at a pet shop. The screen door behind their bed exited onto Reseda Boulevard; it was open. Guy threw on a pair of shorts and was out the door, searching the neighborhood, calling, then screaming. As the search continued, tears streamed down Guy's face as he saw cars streak down the busy boulevard. He sobbed woefully, calling all the while, until he saw Marie, cat in hand. Stinky had gotten inside the courtyard of their sister building next door. Guy told her what a bad cat she was, then how much he loved her.

Guy spent five hundred fifty four dollars, which was his entire savings, on a simple white gold band with one small embedded diamond for Marie. On Christmas he got down on one knee and asked Marie to marry him. She said yes and wore her small ring proudly. They would be prudent and wait a couple years until they were making more money and had some more schooling done. Their love was eternal. They were together; there was no need to rush.

Bear got out of the corps, and Guy and Marie were able to roll their lease into one of the larger, nicer two-bedroom models. Roommates sucked, but it was Bear after all. It was great to have Bear back in town. Guy was twenty-three; it was Nineteen Ninety 9, almost a new millennium. Guy was working security at Citibank in Woodland Hills now, the day shift. No more graveyard shifts, no more study time, no more once-in-a-blue-moon auditions to see if he could pick up some acting money.

When Marie called in on the bank's branch line, it was shockingly out of character. Through tears, she quickly explained that the guard company would not relay her message, that her brother, Arnold, was dead. He had shot himself in the head. He lived in a little detached room in their father's yard, where his girlfriend had found him that morning. The coroner just took away the body. Marie was going to go help her father clean up the mess.

Guy was flabbergasted, shocked. Marie was devastated, broken. Arnold was the only boy, the eldest. No note, no reason. He wasn't high; he had a beautiful girlfriend and a decent job. His girlfriend, Paula, couldn't believe it; she thought he must have been murdered. The police did a thorough investigation; it was suicide. Paula joined the US Air Force.

At the funeral, much to his surprise, it was Guy who was inconsolable. He knew Arnold pretty well, but it wasn't like they had really hung out. He didn't expect to be so devastated. Guy wept through the entire service. It was Marie, however, afterward that slipped into a bitter depression. She could hardly function. Guy convinced her to start seeing Karen Horney. With regular visits, the passage of time and medication, Marie was considerably better. The pain was more like a dull ache that dissipated but never disappeared.

April of Two Thousand was already scheduled for Guy and Marie's wedding. They were sad that Arnold wouldn't be there. Marie's sister Jackie beat her to the punch by a month, getting married in March. She was pregnant enough to pop on the altar. Karen told Marie that siblings often get pregnant after the suicide of a loved one. It was a subconscious attempt to replace the love that was lost.

Guy left his job as a security guard at the bank when the security company had refused to let him go home that day Marie had called him about her brother's death. That made it that much easier to say yes when Citibank offered him a job as a teller. He would make nineteen thousand dollars, an extra two thousand a year. Plus it was more in line with what he was going to school for—Business Economics. Guy would transfer to UCLA. He wasn't exactly sure what he would do, but it would involve making money, and the financial world seemed like a decent place to do it.

The timing was good; it enabled Guy and Marie to save up a little more for their wedding. Guy did well at the bank; he was never out of balance, not even a penny. He won a bunch of national referral competitions.

The Finnigans, as they were called, were married for under ten grand, the whole kit and kaboodle. Guy decided they would use his birth father's last name. There was Guy's half brother, Herman Flynn, plus Guy's stepdad, Mack Flynn, who also had brothers; so plenty of men to carry on the Flynn name. If not for Guy, the Finnigan name would come to an end.

Guy always believed in his heart that the stories about Jesus and others from the Bible were true. He wanted to get married in the church, especially since he was confirmed while in the US Marine Corps. It ended up being a big process to get married in the church, but, as marriage was a once-in-a-lifetime experience, Guy thought it was worth it. They met regularly with a priest and completed questionnaires with hundreds and hundreds of questions that were fed into a computer.

The results showed similarities and differences in their responses which were discussed with a priest. Questions on everything: kids, money, faith. There was a mandatory weekend-long engaged encounter retreat in the hills of Malibu. It was beautiful, lots of questions, writing and facilitated talking. Guy thought it would be hokey, but it was neat. Guy and Marie had been together six years now. They felt like they knew just about everything there was to know about each other, but they got a lot more out of the experience than they had expected. They found a great priest from Our Lady of Grace on Ventura Boulevard to marry them.

It was April, and they weren't able to use the church because of Lent. They decided on the old San Fernando Mission founded in Seventeen Ninety Two. It was beautiful with an Old World feel. To get married in the church, Marie was forced to sign a contract, promising to raise the children Catholic, since she was once a Mormon.

The wedding was lovely. Guy wanted a full Mass, which was longer than he had expected, but Marie didn't mind. She was nervous and had dropped down to one hundred five pounds, but she was stunning. She wore an old-fashioned white lace gown and veil that they had found for five hundred dollars. She was a vision of beauty that, in all of Guy's fantasies, he could never have even imagined. Her sisters were bridesmaids and Bear, John and Herman stood alongside Guy. There were one hundred thirty guests, and, as Guy found out, a guest list was certainly not about who was getting invited; it was about who was not getting invited to keep the numbers manageable. The reception dinner was served at the Odyssey in the hills above the Valley. Only two people abused the open bar, which was impressive and amusing.

They had the time of their lives honeymooning in Della's time-share which they used for ten days in Aruba. Marie even went topless on a secluded portion of the beach, until she was worried that a plane overhead might catch a glimpse of her inviting, firm bosom. Their allure certainly caused Guy's brain to crash.

The Finnigans met Kevin and Shelly, a fun couple from Minnesota, also on their honeymoon, while taking a Jeep ride around the island. Guy and Marie expected a tour guide to pick them up; instead they drove along, following the tour guide in a caravan of Suzuki Samurai Jeeps, stopping for six-packs along the way. Guy screamed like a girl after he was convinced to stand upright in the ceiling flute of a cave. A shine from the tour guide's flashlight sent thousands of bats streaming down the flute over Guy like rushing water. He had screamed like a girl, all right, but made sure to note some people were too scared to even go into the cave.

They drove past the police on the beach, beers in hand. The white-lettered *Policia* on the side of their blue mail trucks was not particularly disarming. The police waved them right by. They went out for cocktails and dancing at Carlos and Charlie's with Kevin and Shelly. Shelly, a pretty blonde, started a conga line after she poured a beer down the front of her shirt. They were well drunk when they walked back to the Finnigans' hotel. The moon glistened on the ocean as Shelly yelled, "Skinny-dip!" and ran for the pool. Guy's shirt was nearly half off before Marie said good-night and dragged them both back to the room.

They decided they would move in with Guy's mom before the end of the year. They put all their newly acquired kitchenware and trinkets in storage. In a *Days of Our Lives* turn of events, Della retained ownership in the pool man's house, and Mack was back in his. The pool man's house was a block up the street and a mirror image of Guy's house, the exact opposite floor plan. Guy and Marie stayed in the mirror of his old downstairs bedroom that Marie used to sneak out of.

Della was having a hard time paying the mortgage and told Guy, if he paid half the payment, she would give him his money back when she sold the place next year. Fifteen hundred dollars was more than Guy wanted to spend, but it was like forced savings with free rent. Though being newly married and living with Mom was not a big plus, it would be worth it, if they could use the money as a down payment on a place. Guy limited the arrangement to no more than a year.

10-10-00, was a date to be shortly recorded in the books. The days were long and uneventful lately. A full day at work, then straight to class until ten. Guy usually didn't eat dinner until he got home. He was continually getting more responsibility at work; he was learning to open new accounts now. The people who opened up new accounts were officers; they definitely made more money. They had dual-control access and keys to the branch. Together Guy and Marie made about forty seven thousand a year; Marie was making more than Guy doing office work. Guy had just finished his economics class, which was significantly more interesting than Calc II. He was glad to have finished up his math units; he would have the necessary classes to transfer to UCLA before much longer.

That October night, Guy peered across the parking lot to his midnight blue Acura Integra. It was a great ride; he liked to play his music loud. Tonight he wished he had a map of the world, ranking the nations from highest to lowest in Gross Domestic Product per capita. Green for the top rankings and graded colors down to red for the nations with the lowest GDP per capita. Guy suspected it would show the countries with the most freedom had the most wealth per person. He thought there must be enough money in the world for people to be paid a living wage for a full day's work. A wage that a husband could support a family on. There were all sorts of reasons for poverty, unfortunately a chief one among them was laziness.

Guy turned east out of the Pierce College parking lot onto Victory. The night was cool, but not crisp, as steely drums began to bump through the speakers, playing "Churchez LaGhost," by Ghostface Killah. The sweet smooth voice of Madam Majestic began:

Tommy Mattola lives on the road.
He lost his lady, two months ago.
Maybe he'll find her, maybe he won't.
Oh, wonder, that love.

In a moment Guy was overcome. Overcome and aware. Aware of the Spirit of God. That God was in a manner speaking to him directly. Speaking not with audible words but with omnipotent power. The Spirit's mere presence revealed Guy's debasement next to God's pure holiness. Guy felt small, ashamed. He considered himself a good man in his heart. The Spirit illuminated the things Guy harbored in the inner recesses of his heart and mind. Guy was horrified. It was as if God had allowed Guy for a moment to see things from His perspective.

How God wept for His children who choose to turn their backs. He called for them throughout time itself, and His voice never grew weary. His love for us, so unfathomably complete. Guy's sins were so egregious, so disgusting before God's face, and yet God gave His only Son, so that Guy might be saved from his own filth. That His Son paid the penalty for all sin, all of Guy's, all of everyone's. All of Guy's future sins, all paid for, his burden carried. All Guy had to do was choose, to turn.

Scottfree and Chauncey, very upset.
They're sick and tired of living in debt.
Tired of roaches and tired of rats.
I know they are over.

A vision formed in Guy's mind of a mother and her little child asleep on a dirty floor. Their bellies full with only hunger as rats and roaches scampered over their bare, dirty feet. Their gaunt limbs framed the debasement of Guy's mind. *Poor people were poor because they were lazy after all. Because they didn't want to work to better themselves.* The shivering mother and her babe melted the cold indignity from Guy's heart. He was ashamed, and his heart was changed in an instant.

Regardless of the circumstances that brought them there, would an Almighty God not feel compassion for the suffering of the destitute? For a child whose belly is empty, whose heart is full of fear? Why allow it, God? Guy was utterly devastated; he sobbed violently.

God spoke into Guy's heart. He wanted us to live in splendor, happy and free from the wages of sin. Guy's sins, which he had always felt were so insignificant in the big scheme of things, affected people in ways he would never know. The effect was compounded; the desire for sin rather than God had turned the world into a dark and brutal existence. This was our desire, not God's. Our actions had consequences.

The Lord provided the world with more than enough resources for all men. But men had chosen to be poor stewards, to be unappreciative and greedy, filling their black hearts with treasure, as they stepped on the necks of the meek. The kings filled their rubbish heaps with rotted food, while babies slept with roaches and cried for milk. Now Guy saw a rich man in purple robes and a handful of gold looking up from a lake of fire, wailing in agony, his curly brown hair partly aflame. His fat arm grasped upward. The rich man could see directly into the heavens, where a thin Lazarus, still in rags, was held by Abraham, cloaked in a long white robe.

Guy was remorseful for the world and what it had become. Guy's feeling of sorrow was replaced with an ominous dread. The scale had been tipped; the path chosen. Enough was finally enough. The time had come to choose sides; a war was looming. The plea for repentance was personal, yet God's wrath burned against the nations. Burned against the rulers of the world who took counsel together against the Almighty. The call was personal; the love God felt for each and all of us was inexpressible, beyond comprehension. The dread Guy felt, however, was imminent, as if the world's cup was nearly full. God always gave a chance for repentance, but the nations of the world were about to collectively refuse. There would be no repentance; the world would choose rebellion, judgment. The Lord God Almighty had spoken; the stage was set. The time of the Great Tribulation was nearly at hand.

No, no, it wasn't possible, Guy thought, as he sobbed hysterically and covered the groans coming from his mouth. There was no mistaking the message. The die was cast, but the imprint had not yet been struck. In a blur Guy was home. He walked into their bedroom, inconsolable, unable to speak, as the tears streamed down his checks. Marie asked questions at first, but then just held him and stroked his hair. He cried in her lap for an hour until he was able to speak.

When his sobs subsided, Guy spoke. "I know this is going to sound crazy. If someone said it to me, I wouldn't believe them, but God spoke to me tonight." Guy sat on the edge of the bed next to Marie.

"I believe you. What did He say?" she said kindly and held Guy's hands in her lap.

"He said we have to change our ways. We have to figure out what God wants us to do with our lives. I'm serious. God is pissed off." He looked in her eyes.

"He's got plenty of reason to be." Marie's hand looked small as it stroked the back of his.

"Look, this whole thing is crazy, but God warned me the end of the world is coming. We choose our path as a people. We're not sorry anymore. We're not going to repent. I know it's crazy."

"I believe you. Why wouldn't He?" She brought Guy's head to her chest.

Destroy the world, Guy finished her sentence in his head.

Guy related his experience fervently to everyone he was close with. To his surprise it seemed most believed him. Guy could tell he was not simply being placated, but he was just as surprised that people weren't in the least bit concerned. Guy shouldn't be either, they felt. It was an opportunity for him to seek God and to learn more about Him. Guy was determined to learn all he could about God and what the end of the world really entailed.

On Sundays Guy and Marie began to attend Our Lady of Grace, a local Catholic church. Guy listened to the readings and the homilies intently. He received communion, but there were steps Marie needed to fulfill before she was eligible to receive the transubstantiated body and blood of Christ. Guy began to pray the rosary at night, and Guy and Marie began to read the book of Matthew from a Catholic Bible. Guy prayed to God with an earnest and open heart. "God, thank You for calling out to me. Please teach me about You. Please bring me to people who know You and Your ways."

In the spring of Two Thousand One, the Finnigans felt God smile brightly. The hunt for a place was real, something that would be theirs, something they could take pride in. With their rent rebate from Della, Guy and Marie had finally cobbled together enough money for a condo, in Reseda. They worked with a sharp real estate agent named Allan. Guy had met him at the bank. Allan worked hard to find them something great for their first house, something they would want to come home to. He convinced the Finnigans to stretch from a hundred and ten thousand dollar price range to a hundred and thirty thousand. This got them a two-car garage, two stories and a patio, instead of a condo, which was really just an owned apartment. A real house, a town house. The two-car detached garage opened into a patio, then to a sliding glass door into the kitchen. Two bedrooms upstairs, two baths. There was a nice large grassy area outside the front door and some talk of remodeling due to the Ninety Four earthquake. Guy and Marie were nervously excited. Marie was concerned it was too much, but Guy knew they could afford it now and that they would grow into it. He saw value.

Unsurprisingly to Guy, YTwoK went off without a hitch. The bank actually made him work on New Year's, just in case there were any problems. If the world's computers crashed, it would all be OK. Guy was on the job at a Citibank branch in Woodland Hills. The town house brought the American dream to the Finnigans; they were married, employed home owners. There was plenty of room for Buddy, a black-and-white cat saved from a rescue shelter. It was hard to choose from all the cats that needed a home. Buddy, a finalist, was selected under the "You broke it. You bought it" rule trotted out by Marie when the black-and-white kitten leaped from Guy's arms into the wall of his Plexiglas cage. There was an extra bedroom for a first baby. The one thousand three hundred sixty dollars a month covered their mortgage and HOA fees. Guy thought being part of the Home Owners Association would be great, until he went to a meeting and realized all of the people involved were crazy.

God smiled again that summer, when Guy received an opportunity to be an officer. The mortgage officer at Citigroup had a friend Bill Wilson who ran a First City office in Woodland Hills. First City, a service-oriented California bank, was on the high end of retail banking. Bill Wilson heard the tale of a sharp young kid who was going places. Bill was told by his friend that he would be stupid not to hire this kid. Bill offered Guy thirty four thousand dollars a year. The job was a bit beyond Guy's experience level; he had never worked with business accounts. There would be serious goals, imputing credit applications, lots of cross-selling. Guy was nervous, but confident; he knew he could learn anything that he was shown. An extra twelve thousand dollars was hard to fathom and impossible to pass up. The officers wore suits. Guy was thankful for the excess cash; he would need some money to purchase some suits for himself.

He would learn quickly that Bill could be a real ballbuster, but Bill was serious about business and serious about stack rankings of employees. He was gruff, but Guy learned all about cold-calling and door-knocking, trying to find new clients. The bank even paid for a multiday John Gehegan cold-calling seminar, flip chart included. The funny thing was, it worked as long as you had volume, lots and lots of volume. Volume of course came with voluminous rejections, but it was a numbers game after all, and Guy didn't take the rejections to heart. Guy was good at making connections and analyzing a situation to determine how he could help clients make more money. By listening to clients, Guy found he was able to add value by offering products and services that were appropriate to their situation.

He found that people wanted good service, someone to pick up the phone when they called, someone to provide a solution to a problem, someone to engage in good conversation, someone who was a creative thinker. If you could actually provide something of value, it was remembered, especially if it was saving time or making money. Bill had an officers' meeting in his office every morning before the bank opened. They would review overdrafts. Guy was able to overdraw clients' accounts up to ten thousand dollars. For the right clients, it was OK, and the office made amazing revenue on the fees. For some of the repeat offenders, the office made a hundred thousand dollars or more a year. Managing overdraft fees more than paid for the office's salaries. One of the worst offenders was a trashy family who would later become the nation's reality television darlings. Everyone called the husband the white Michael Jackson.

Having goals was stressful, but the money was certainly worth it. Guy excelled and found himself competing with some of the name-brand officers. He enjoyed wearing a suit every day. Guy was rarely up and running at six in the morning, as he only needed to leave fifteen minutes before his eight thirty start, but this particular morning something had prodded him from his slumber. Guy turned on the television—which he almost never did before work. Smoke and fire bellowed out of the World Trade Center for a brief moment before Guy watched a plane fly into the second tower. Guy was stunned to his feet in disbelief. What was happening? How could anyone do this to America? He was glad the country had a Republican in the White House; this called for retribution. He was also glad interest rates were high enough that the government had some flexibility to insulate the economy.

Guy's new job started him on the path, but 9/11 propelled Guy to become a voracious consumer of news content—anything political, economic or financial. Fox News and CNN on cable television, plus the Web along with Bloomberg. Guy found Sean Hannity, Michael Savage and a host of others on talk radio. They were engaging and informative. Guy found newspapers to be less relevant. The news they were reporting was a day late, and by then Guy was already well versed.

He was glad he had voted for George Bush. Bush took the fight to the enemy, hitting the Taliban in Afghanistan when they refused to turn over osama bin laden, 9/11's mastermind. The Republicans had the White House and most of Congress, which made the retribution swift.

Guy believed the president. osama was so dangerous that he needed to be personally stopped, eradicated. As Guy read osama's writings, an overarching goal became clear. Other than hating the West and Israel, the great and the little satans, for various perceived wrongs, osama was planning to use the West to topple the corrupt dictatorships of the Middle East. He would form a Crescent of Nations and reestablish the Muslim Caliphate. The caliph would be the political and religious leader for the world's billion Muslims. Now that sounded dangerous.

Al Qaeda must be stopped for the good of Western civilization and the world, which were pretty much one and the same. In conversations, Guy would discuss what people already knew; anyone could get across the United States' southern border anytime with anything they wanted. It was hard to argue with the tons and tons of drugs that flooded across it. How hard would it be for terrorists to smuggle suitcase nukes across the border into six or seven iconic American cities? Lowering interest rates would not save the economy from that hit. The Muslims had unlimited funding from oil, and everyone knew the advanced nuclear state of Russia was plagued by corruption.

Guy knew little about fasting except that it seemed like an appropriate way to honor God and remember how God had called out to him on that tenth night of October in Two Thousand. Guy decided he would fast every year in remembrance; he would drink only water for twenty-four hours. On 10-10-01, Guy kept his commitment to God and fasted. It was a Wednesday, and Guy thought of Matthew, chapter six, from the Gospels. When you fast it should not be to get attention. It should be a personal act between you and God.

After work, Guy spent some time reflecting in the extra bedroom upstairs; he prayed for the victims of 9/11. In his spirit, Guy began to feel that God was more angry than sad. Guy recounted his sins; he felt weak and ashamed. He was not boastful but thought as to his regular attendance at Catholic Mass.

An interview of a Catholic bishop replayed in his mind. At the time Guy was disgusted by the fact that the bishop would not accept any responsibility for the heinous, recurring, long-standing cover-up of child rapes within the worldwide Catholic church. The Bishop didn't even apologize; he wouldn't even say he was sorry for children being molested. Were these the men to lead Guy closer to God? Guy began to weep quietly. As he prayed, he felt led to leave the Catholic church, though no alternative solution was provided.

Guy felt convicted, as if God were asking him what Guy had done with the knowledge that was shared. Guy did tell all of his close friends and family. The seriousness of 9/11 began to weigh on Guy's soul. For the first time, he realized 9/11 was a warning, a trumpet, that the battle for the end of the world was rising over the horizon. Guy felt the call to repentance; it was strong, but it seemed the country didn't have ears to hear. Guy was compelled to write a letter of warning; it needed to be of record. The people needed to be formally warned. Guy wept quietly; he grabbed a pen and paper, and began to write:

My name is Guy Finnigan. On 10-10-00, I was driving home from school around Ten p.m., after just taking an economics test which I knew I had scored well on. A song played on the radio that I had listened to before. A woman sang, "We're tired of living with roaches and living with rats." Instantly I was overcome by what I knew to be the Spirit of God. I now know it to be the Holy Spirit. I was immediately thrown into the fits of inconsolable sobbing for nearly an hour. God told me, "There is only suffering because man takes advantage of one another." I felt in my spirit a collective and individual call to repentance.

Compassion and wrath all at once, but burning wrath, as if God knew that we would reject His call. The cup was nearly full. The Tribulation is about to begin. Beware! The Battle of Armageddon lies before us. All true believers in Christ, the Savior, must prepare like Noah many millennia ago. Our times call not for ships but for equipment necessary to survive when civilization as we know it comes to an end. We know not when the exact time will be, but remember that, when the flood came, men and women danced the night away until their deaths. Prepare with food, water and NBC—nuclear, biological, chemical—gear. Fear not, for those who love God, and Jesus Christ, His Son, heeding His Word, will be spared to see humanity's new dawn.

Guy photocopied the letter and handed it out to an expanded circle of people that included Milton Steiner. Guy also told John he thought President Bush needed to be made aware. Guy planned to send a copy of The Message to the president, but John cautioned that, if Guy did, he was certain to be put on a list. Not a good list, but some list you didn't want to be on. Guy thought it was a valid point, and so he nixed the idea.

The Patriot Act was passed with necessary rapidity two weeks later, and it ensured various agencies could access whatever information they deemed necessary to protect America from future such terrorist acts. Guy believed the president and Congress when they said the Patriot Act was necessary to stop terrorism. Good guys like Sean Hannity believed the same. We all knew we were living in a New World after 9/11, fighting an enemy with no country. Things had to change.

The Finnigans were moving out of their new home by the summer of Two Thousand Two. They were surprised, not disappointed, as they were going to receive a brand-new house. The entire complex would be brand-new in fact. The units would be torn down to the studs, with brand-new kitchens, floors, bathrooms. The fact that it came to fruition so quickly was a real shocker. The Home Owners Association had offered six thousand dollars to cover expenses for the summer move. The Finnigans were able to put the money toward Pergo floors and a wood banister since Mack, who was now back in his house, had offered, for free, Guy's old room to the newlyweds while the rebuilding took place. Marie would not even have to sneak out the garage door in the morning.

Guy could feel something big was coming, something outside the perhaps inconvenient but amazing remodel. Guy prayed for God to lead him to people who knew about Him, who would teach him God's ways. He began to read the Gospels over again.

Guy and Marie enjoyed spending time with Mack, though it caused their lifestyle to become more demure. Pearl and Herman bounced back and forth between Mack and Della. Herman was as tall as Mack now, six foot two, maybe an inch taller. He was blond and good-looking, a little chubby. In addition to being extremely smart, Herman knew oodles of obscure facts. Guy thought Herman should be on *Jeopardy*. He was socially awkward, which Guy attributed to him being a seventeen-year-old virgin.

Moreover he had a black-cloud countenance which was particularly disturbing. He could be downright cruel, especially to Mack and Pearl. Herman would yell and tell Pearl and Mack how they were stupid, that Herman hated them, that he wished they were dead. He told Pearl that he would chop her up with a chainsaw. Mack stayed even-keeled and made no attempt to resolve the situation or behavior due to his guilt over the divorce. As the escalations increased, Mack got frustrated and raised his voice to no avail. Guy found it necessary to let his brother know, if Herman ever threatened Pearl again, Herman and Guy were going to have a problem.

Mack was working with Bank National now. After over twenty years and billions of dollars' worth of business, Chase Manhattan had decided to pull out of the California real estate market. Mack would be promoted if he moved back to New York. He declined. He wouldn't leave his kids now, after everything that had happened. Though the divorce had been nearly a decade ago, the wounds to the family had never healed; they simply festered.

Pearl was dating Darnell; he seemed reasonably nice. Of course Guy placed a high mental bar for his sister's suitor, so the jury was still out.

Did Darnell have a career plan; what were his goals for the future? Guy noticed quickly that Pearl and Darnell bickered incessantly, at times heatedly. The only time Guy had ever raised his voice to Marie—and then only for a moment—was when he had found out she was smoking behind his back before they were married. A raised voice was almost always uncalled for; Guy knew the atmosphere of a room changed quickly if he got heated. He learned to keep his cool despite the temperature of the situation.

What Guy did find very interesting about Darnell was that he was a Christian. Darnell and Pearl were going to a church that was filled with the Holy Spirit out in Santa Clarita. Guy was intrigued, but even more so by the fact that Darnell knew about the Bible and wanted to discuss it. Darnell invited Guy and Marie to come to the Burning Bush Church with them.

When Guy found out that it was located in a retail strip center, he only said yes to be nice to his sister. A church in a retail center seemed a little embarrassing. When they arrived, they were greeted by friendly congregants who passed out programs and offered help in finding a seat. Everyone knew Darnell and Pearl well; they seemed excited to see Guy and Marie there as well. The retail center location felt like a church when Guy and Marie walked in. There were padded chairs instead of pews, and the room was bathed in a general purple hue. The hundred-chair church was near capacity, and you could feel excitement in the air. They worshipped, singing songs at the beginning of service, which Guy thought was odd. It was also like a rock band, except they were playing songs for Jesus. Everyone sang with their hands held up to God. It was strange but passionate and real.

It was predominantly a black church, less reserved, more outwardly passionate; Guy enjoyed it. Guy observed a sea of black faces, along with brown and white as well. From what Guy had heard, the church was not a good representation of Santa Clarita's fairly homogeneously white demography.

The preacher, Max, was a black man, a former football player in great shape. His wife, Sue, was white. Max was passionate and preached that he served a big God, the God of Abraham, Isaac and Jacob. He would pray in the name of Jesus, for the Word of God said there was power in that name. Guy noticed how everyone brought their own Bibles. If you didn't have one, the ushers would bring you one, a King James version. Guy was, for the first time at church, truly moved by the Word of God.

There was an altar call at the end of service. People who wanted to turn their lives over to the Lord Jesus Christ were called to front of the church to accept Him into their lives. Guy felt moved and went forward.

Guy and Marie became core members of the Burning Bush. Guy was quickly baptized. Marie followed soon after with an altar call of her own and was baptized as well. The feeling in Guy's spirit was right; that summer at Mack's house had bloomed into something more beautiful than a new town house.

It didn't take more than a month of Wednesdays and Sundays for Marie to clean the entire house of all pornography. She said she thought it wasn't honoring God. Guy's spirit agreed, but his flesh had a harder time letting go. Guy had masturbated since he was a teenager. He had a high sex drive, but it was more about bringing relief to tension. Even as the incidences got further apart, they brought Guy great shame. It was a constant source of prayer and quiet personal embarrassment. It made Guy feel weak and dirty, shameful.

Guy learned a lot about prayer. God should be praised, you should pray for others, pray for yourself. When it came to praying for himself, Guy would ask Jesus to squeeze the blackness from his heart, to help turn his back on lustfulness. That Guy would have ears to hear and eyes to see. That he would be a man who loved and recognized truth, a hater of lies. A man who loved the things that God loved, and hated the things that God hated.

Guy and Marie would leave their house at four fifteen on Friday mornings for prayer meetings with Max and ten other early risers. They would pray aloud for the needs of people specifically, for the needs of the church, for the country, for the world. Anyone who wanted to could pray; it was encouraged. So was speaking in tongues.

It seemed crazy to Guy, but he was told how it was like the tongues of fire from the book of Acts. That it was a way for your soul to communicate directly with God. It took a while before Guy was comfortable with it.

Guy had the power of fasting confirmed for him. The pastor often spoke of the need to fast for something important. Max fasted once a week. Guy learned that reading the Bible every day was a good way to cleanse your mind. That it should be studied like an instruction manual for life. Guy and Marie soon purchased their own King James Study Bibles.

Guy considered himself to be generous, certainly more generous than most. At the Burning Bush, or the Bush as the congregants called it, Guy learned the biblical principle of tithing, giving ten percent of everything you made to God. It seemed a real stretch. Max showed how the Word said you would receive a sevenfold increase. Guy wanted to be obedient to what God desired. Since Guy and Marie felt led to the church, they decided to give tithing a try. Another couple, Ronnie and Leda, had given the church nearly eighty thousand dollars that year. Ronnie was a shoe distributor who hoped one day to be able to live on ten percent of his income.

Guy learned the importance of service; he became an usher, and Marie worked in the children's church. Guy and Marie became more cognizant of how they lived their lives, what came out of their mouths, what was absorbed by their minds. They felt more fulfilled, more alive, more aware, and, if possible, more in love. The realness of spending eternity with each other, with a family, was overwhelmingly satisfying. They enjoyed being involved in the lives of others. People at work and church began to call Guy *Mr. Fabulous*, because he was always fabulous; he was always smiling and in a good mood. Guy played worship music in his car; he truly enjoyed it. He still found rap music auditorily appealing; but he stopped listening to it, because he could see it had a negative effect on the mind, the spirit. It was a shame, he thought. Eminem's *Marshall Mathers* album would go down as one of the best in history. Guy felt as if it gave his dark recesses a voice.

Guy formed strong relationships, especially since he was an usher and said hello to everyone who came in through the door. He organized everyone to donate gently used clothes and a variety of food for the poorer Hispanic-speaking community, Newhall, in the south. It took them nearly six hours to pass everything out. They did it on a Saturday evening when everyone was home. There were a few members who spoke Spanish; Guy spoke only a little. The neighborhood was shocked and appreciative. Women brought their neighbors, children and husbands to pick out items. Max printed up flyers with the name of the church and an offer to pick up anyone for service on Sunday. That was not Guy's intention with the giveaway; most of the community didn't even speak English. He knew there were people in the community who lived poorly, and others who had beautiful things they never even used.

The Finnigans made Jesus Christ the cornerstone of their lives and marriage. No longer would God be relegated to an occasional thought or prayer. God became the reason for each day. They spent time with people who felt the same. They became close friends with the Ebrahimis—Daroush, who went by George, and Anahita, by An. George was deputy director for the local congressman, which Guy was neither concerned with nor infatuated by. George and An were extremely hospitable; they had a lovely home, about two thousand five hundred square feet. Not as big or new as Max's three thousand one hundred square-foot home or Ronnie's three thousand eight hundred square feet.

The Ebrahimis had a son, Tyler, in 11th grade and a daughter, Becky, in 9th. They were amazing kids. They loved God, knew the Bible, and were smart and modest. An, who was very persuasive, convinced the Finnigans that they needed to take advantage of the market and trade up to a house in Santa Clarita. She even knew the right zip code for the best school district—theirs. There were a couple of neighborhoods she was certain Guy and Marie could afford.

The search for a home, a family home, began in the winter of Two Thousand Three. The Finnigans joined in prayer alongside others from the Bush to pray specifically for a house in an exact zip code that could be purchased within their price range. Max taught them it was important to pray specifically, to speak it, to claim it as a birthright of a child of the Most High God. Many people didn't receive simply because they didn't ask clearly.

Shortly after Guy's birthday, April Thirteenth, Two Thousand Four, Marie called him along with An one evening while he was in class. Guy had a cell phone now; one of his first big clients had told him to go out and buy one so that he could get hold of Guy whenever it was necessary. Guy was purposely part of a minority of people who didn't have a cell phone. He didn't like the idea of a constant leash and added expense, but he acquiesced. Marie called to say she and An had found the perfect house. It was everything the Finnigans were looking for: price, location and size. Guy told Marie to call the agent and to make an offer. They did, but the couple who owned the house would not accept until they met Guy in person.

They were the original owners of the house, which was built in Nineteen Sixty Four, when Santa Clarita was only onion fields. The owner, George, showed them slides, actual slides of the house being built. The four-bedroom track homes were two thousand twenty five square feet; this home had an extra window in the back bedroom that overlooked the mountains. George saw the builders getting ready to board up that wall and had asked them to cut an extra window. It cost him lunch for the crew.

Today Delores, his wife, made tea, and their adult daughter, Jordel, sat on the couch, petting her dog. They had raised their family in this home; it was a good home. They wanted to make sure it was going to be with someone who wanted the same. The family was retiring to Arizona and for five hundred and five thousand dollars a deal was made.

The Finnigans' town house quickly entered escrow and fell out just as rapidly when it was discovered that there was pending litigation with the Home Owners Association that prevented prospective buyers from obtaining financing from the banks. Guy and Marie were crushed. They had found their dream home—redbrick, a nice big yard, private, four bedrooms, two-car attached garage—across the street from the big

Central Park. The purchase of George and Delores's home was contingent on the sale of the Finnigans' town house. Guy and Marie asked to have through the weekend before their escrow was canceled.

The Finnigans were part of the Ebrahimis' home group. A weekly meeting of four or five families that provided for each other on a deep spiritual level. The home group asked for God to move; they knew what seemed impossible for man was possible for God.

Their agent held an open house the next day, Saturday, at the town house. An elderly couple offered a full-price, all-cash offer. Everyone marveled at God's awesomeness. The Finnigans' loan broker tried to talk them into a five-year, interest-only loan; it would be damn cheap. Guy insisted on a thirty-year fully amortized loan; he was no fool.

When everything was said and done, the Finnigans had the house of their dreams and forty thousand dollars in their pocket. After they ran all the numbers, they felt convicted about the hard work everyone at the church was doing to raise the thirty thousand dollars necessary to get camera equipment. Max said it would help them spread the Word of God to more people. They could win more souls, bring in more donations, so the church could do more, get a staff, a building eventually. Guy and Marie knew how fortunate they were; they were thankful God had reached out to them in such kindness. They decided to donate the thirty thousand dollars; Max was truly stunned. He told the Finnigans that they were going to be blessed beyond their expectations. That made Guy uncomfortable, as it was not his motive.

The Finnigans opened their house for a home group of their own; it was literally two minutes down the street from the Burning Bush. The Finnigans' house was two stories; there was a brick patio and planter box outside the front door. From the sidewalk you could see the inclined driveway on the right leading to a two-car garage which opened into the laundry room and kitchen. The front lawn to the left of the garage was chest level from the street, surrounded by a brick retaining wall. The glass-topped double front doors opened to an entryway with twenty-foot ceilings. To the right of the entryway was a stairway with a white wrought iron railing. The stairs went up to a double platform and doubled back up the same direction. They rose to two bedrooms, the master on the left. A hallway straight off the master led to the other two bedrooms, with a full bath halfway down. The rear bedrooms looked over the backyard with an even larger hill than Mack's. The bedrooms were roomy; the master bath was small, but it was all worth it. There were white oak floors throughout the house except for at the entry and in the kitchen/dining room.

To the left of the entryway was a large living room, with a checkered wood floor and high vaulted ceilings. At the end of the entryway was a double door frame leading into the dining room with a patio door to the left and open kitchen to the right. The backyard had a large grassy area. There were two sheds on one side of the house with the trash cans; the other side of the house had a grassy patch as large as the front yard. The Finnigans had a pine tree removed from the front planter box. It blocked the view of house, and Guy had always wanted to grow roses. He planted twenty-two rose bushes. A straight row lining the planter at the edge of the lawn and then in a square around where the pine tree had once resided. Guy got every color in the rainbow; some were so fragrant, they would fill up the whole house with their wonderful smell. Certainly not like anything you could buy from a florist. Sandy, an elderly teller at First City, grew the most amazing roses Guy had ever seen. He went to the same nursery she used, and bought all of his favorite varieties. She even let him in on all of her secret techniques. Roses, nice roses, that is, were hard work. The Finnigans left the black iron eagle over the garage door of their new tan-colored home.

The Finnigans' lives had changed greatly in the two years since attending the Bush. Guy had switched majors and had decided to study theology at King's College. He was doing well in his career, and, other than his wife, there was nothing more important to him than God. Guy didn't like that there were men who knew so much more about God and the Bible than he did. He wanted to learn for himself; he didn't want to take anyone's word for something so important. As usual, Guy began reading extensively. This time, volumes of Christian material on all matters and subjects. He found class discussions enlightening.

Pearl and Darnell were on the rocks, as usual, and were rarely ever seen at the Bush. Della turned her life over to the Lord after coming to the Bush as a guest on Mother's Day. When Max did an altar call, Della raised her hand and asked if this was going to require a lot of work. When she was told salvation was a free gift, she came forward, well pleased. The change was not instantaneous nor overwhelming, but it was noticeable. Della began to refer to God in her conversations.

The Finnigans had plenty of room for a dog now; getting one, however, was unplanned. They were watching Skinny Boots, Della's cat for her while she was out of town. While impossible, it appeared Skinny had escaped. The house was searched, so was the neighborhood. The pound was tried. Guy came upon Chance, a golden-colored Lab-boxer mix. His muzzle was brown, as were his sad eyes. Guy read his bio, which stated after having him for six years, the owners had found a dog too much work with the birth of their second child. Chance was set to be euthanized on Monday. A few sobs later, Guy and Marie were back the next day, Sunday, to retrieve Chance, who they renamed Lucky. He was sweet and loyal, a one-of-a-kind dog. Guy heard a dog was the last holdout before children. Skinny was hereafter found hiding in the cabinet above the refrigerator.

They acquired a forth cat, a black year-old kitten, Larry. Marie was at a prayer group with a new woman, who spoke of a sick cat with no money to take it to the vet. Marie's heartstrings were pulled, and she was back at the woman's house after the group.

The cat was not simply sick, but rather dying in the corner. The kitten's stomach was distended to the size of a cantaloupe, and he was covered in feces. Apparently the daughter, who was eighteen, had slammed the door in anger, and the kitten got stuck in the middle. He wasn't able to move since; that was nearly a week ago. Marie called Guy from the vet. The kitten's enlarged stomach was actually his bladder; it was nearly ready to burst. The vet expressed the urine manually. Larry was cleaned up and given an IV of fluids and medication. The tests and X-rays showed Larry's back was broken. The vet recommended he be put to sleep. He took a scissor and snipped poor Larry's little paw to show there was no feeling in his legs. The vet would give the Finnigans some time to hold Larry and discuss the situation.

Guy and Marie prayed together for an answer; Guy was certain little Larry needed to be put out of his misery. But, as they prayed, little Larry began to twitch his back legs. That was enough of a sign; they would keep Larry.

They converted the room next to the master into a cat room. Marie, of course, was industrious enough to add a plywood and linoleum top floor. Larry was incontinent, so they learned how to express his bladder, which needed to be done twice a day. They did it as a team on the front lawn. Larry was happy as a clam and got along great with the other three cats. They even got him acupuncture. Eventually, though wobbly, he was able to stand up. He could climb the stairs and even to the top of the cat tree. He would flop down a level at a time, happy as could be.

Guy found his heart was for the poor and downtrodden, especially the homeless. Guy and Marie made care bags to pass out. Guy bought waterproof Willy Pete bags from the army surplus store. They would fill two full carts at a time from the Dollar Mart with food, can openers, socks, underwear, wet wipes, toothbrushes, one-dollar King James Bibles, and anything else they thought people living on the street could use. They would drive around the Valley at night and pull over when they saw someone in need. There was a gathering spot around Sepulveda and Roscoe beside the freeway bridge. The Finnigans engaged in conversation—of course bringing in Jesus Christ. The recipients were so appreciative, as if they were given a bag of gold. Many opened a can of Chef Boyardee and began eating immediately, saying they hadn't eaten in days, as they cried. All were thankful.

The Finnigans weren't braggarts about it, though people could see gathered piles of items in the corner of their living room. Some people wanted to chip in. Guy and Marie had been at it since shortly after they had joined the Bush. Guy thought of the story of the poor beggar and Abraham, how it was God's desire for us to help the poor, the meek. The driving force for Guy was that he truly began to empathize with those who were broken. Some from drugs, some from poverty, some from mental problems or abuse as children. We bore responsibility for our actions, Guy felt, but he could have compassion for people's circumstances.

He couldn't imagine what it was like to sleep amid the stench of urine with roaches and rats running over you while you were exposed, hungry, scared and alone. When it got cold, Guy would pass out wool army blankets. Wool was the only material that kept you warm when it was wet. Guy wanted to show mercy to those the world wanted to forget. To let the homeless people know they were not forgotten, that God loved them.

As Guy and Marie brought God to the forefront of their minds and their days, they found opportunities. Things that they would have passed up before, things that they might not have even noticed. Like the long-haired man walking up the hill on the Five freeway. Guy had to get over from the fast lane quickly to pull onto the shoulder. It would have been easy to rationalize not getting over. Guy reversed down the incline slowly as the scraggly sandy-blond man ran up the hill toward Guy's car.

Peter was headed back to Alaska; that's where he was from. He had gone to Alabama for work, which lasted eight months. He was down to his backpack and hitchhiking. Guy was headed to church; it was Wednesday. It had been a long time since Peter had attended church. He would like to go, if his hair weren't so disheveled. Guy offered a haircut and a shave, which was eagerly pounced upon. Church attendance was of no obligation, however.

After a shave and a cut, Peter felt like a million bucks. He cried during service; that's why there were tissue boxes at the bottom of each row of chairs. Guy decided to buy Peter a bus ticket. They went to the Greyhound station; you could only buy a ticket to the northernmost station in the state of Washington. From there you had to purchase a separate ticket to Alaska. Guy told Peter to have the ticket counter employee call Guy's cell when Peter arrived in Washington. Peter thought there was no way Guy was going to answer. But he did. And Peter got to Alaska.

Once the Finnigans moved to the new neighborhood, they were quickly moved onto the church's leadership team. Guy would head the ushers; they spent time at Max's house with his wife and preteen daughter. They had regular leadership meetings and read John Maxwell together.

Guy felt honored when he was included on the list to attend the leadership training multiday seminar in Dallas at T. D. Jakes' church, The Potter's House. With entrance, airfare and hotel, it was a bit pricey, so Guy would go by himself, along with the Ebrahimis, and Ronnie—the guy who had first inspired Guy to tithe. Guy found the trip very enlightening.

Guy had never been to Dallas, but Dallas was not the point. T. D. Jakes was one of the most godly men in America. He had a massive following, and was respected by politicians and powerful men. The three-day leadership conference would help the Burning Bush get to the next level, to be more effective, to grow. With money, so many things were possible: missionaries, schools, more people, more staff. The Potters House was massive; the sanctuary must have seated ten thousand people. There were multiple seminars running throughout the day to choose from, some in the sanctuary, some in other rooms of the massive complex. Guy found the whole experience emotionally overwhelming. The energy when the sanctuary was filled with ten thousand people singing for Jesus was hard to express. Guy expected as much; he was emotionally sensitive in certain areas, and worshiping God always softened his heart. There were a few things, however, that truly changed his perspective.

Guy was well aware that such an organization took a lot of money to run, and that T. D. Jakes was certainly making money from books now. But what Guy found really staggering came after worship. At the beginning and end of each day, usher after usher would carry black cylindrical offering buckets—stacked so high over their heads that Guy was not sure how they accomplished the amazing feat. Guy wondered how much money people gave from their pockets each time the wall of buckets passed behind the curtain.

It's when people are squeezed that you get to see their true character. The same is often the case when they are relaxed. Max and Sue White, the Ebrahimis and Guy headed to Fogo de Chao for a fancy dinner out. Max picked the place; it was all-you-can-eat Brazilian barbecue. Servers came to the table with giant skewers of meat and cut pieces right onto your plate. There were over thirty different kinds. Any type of meat and cut you could think of: chicken, sausages, top sirloin, bottom sirloin. Everyone was given a circular cardboard chip. If the green side was up, the skewers just kept coming; if red was up, they would pass you by. The food and conversation were great. They spoke of conference highlights. George of course was his regular witty self.

As the night wore on, a friendly conversation began between George and Max concerning who could consume the most meat. As the evening progressed, George was himself, a little more wise, funny to a rare degree. As an athlete, Max was competitive; he was becoming indignant and serious over the matter of stomach size. As George feigned his own seriousness over the trivial matter, Guy and George became more and more amused at Max's increasing vehemence. George's wife, An, became more and more mortified. George found Guy's amusement, An's mortification, and Max's peculiar seriousness all the more reason to continue his role. He pressed down on the gas pedal forcefully. As if to prove a point, with green button raised, George yelled, "Hit me," and slapped the table as the cuts passed. George's unwavering stomach eventually caused Max to fold in irritated disgrace, as if he had missed the game-winning free throw in game seven of the finals.

The final day was closed out by T. D. Jakes himself in the large sanctuary. He was an electrifying speaker, charismatic. The crowd laughed, cried, jumped and sang down the list of emotions. Everyone was on fire; it seemed the house was filled with the Holy Spirit. T. D. Jakes got serious; he could feel in his spirit that some people here were under serious demonic oppression. That some people here were suffering with sin issues. That some people here were carrying burdens that they just couldn't let go. With his bellowing voice, T. D. Jakes declared, "The Lord says, if you come down to this altar with an offering of five hundred dollars, you will be freed from whatever it is that's oppressing you. Your offering is a sign of obedience and faith. The Lord says that, just as Pharaoh's chariots were washed beneath the seas, so too will you be freed from whatever it is that is oppressing you. It will not follow you back on the plane. It will stay right here. Do you desire to be free? Will you walk in faith or by sight!"

The tears began to stream down Guy's face. Fighting against pornography and masturbation was for him a brutal spiritual fight. One that left him on the floor in tears, crying out to God for victory. Not that it was regular or compulsive, but it existed. The conference was expensive, and Guy did not really have another five hundred dollars, but it was a cheap price to be freed from pornography and masturbation. He would walk out in faith.

God used Guy's faith. But, as is so often the case, it was not in the way Guy would have hoped for nor expected. When Guy returned from his trip, it was clear before long, that Guy was not freed. Not as if he had been freed and then the door had opened again, but simply that he was not freed. At first Guy was disappointed and sad. He wondered what was wrong with him, for the mountain of God had spoken. As Guy prayed, he saw things in an unexpected light. T. D. Jakes was not a man of God. T. D. Jakes was a liar. Jesus aside, when the Apostles spoke, spirits listened. Guy thought about Paul's travels to Ephesus in chapter nineteen of Acts. Men who were not of Christ tried to cast out demons in the name of Jesus. The demons responded that they had heard of Jesus and Paul, but not of these men. The demons leaped upon the men, overcoming and prevailing against them, until the men fled from the house in terror, naked.

Guy studied his textbooks to see what could be learned of false prophets. He found some interesting identifying characteristics; all false prophets speak lies against God, but not all men who speak lies against God are false prophets. There were certainly lots of other characteristics in common: large emotional gatherings, a charismatic leader, a striving to be recognized as great among men, a thirst for money. One stuck Guy hard, as it was particularly poignant and relevant. *Saying that God was going to do something, and it not happen.* T. D. Jakes was a false prophet. Though the situation was embarrassing, Guy would not keep it to himself.

Guy added this to the conversation he was having with anyone who would listen about the coming Tribulation, the time of great turmoil right before the Second Coming of Christ. Guy had known the word *tribulation* before, but not what it meant biblically. Sure, he heard one-third of the people and fish die, that there was a comet or meteor or something, but Guy had no idea of the specifics. It was not preached in church nor taught in Catholic school; finding out was his primary goal.

Guy was surprised people believed his testimony; it was part of the reason he felt connected at the Bush. They believed in the imminent return of Jesus Christ, as a real and imminent event. It was easy to see how debased the culture had become. That was part of the reason for the Burning Bush's nondenominational status—no big groups of representatives deciding among themselves—just a body of believers coming together for Jesus. Though they were not concerned about the end of the world. They believed in a pretribulation rapture, a dividing line that whisked away the believers to heaven before the start of any trouble. Since they weren't going to be around for the blood and fury of the Tribulation, they felt no need to study or prepare for it. As Guy studied, he confirmed what he already knew in his spirit.

Guy wondered why God would tell him to prepare if he was simply going to be whisked away. As he studied eschatology, the biblical proof was clearly against some sort of pretribulation rapture.

There were so many points, Guy tried to stick to some simple ones. He would read from Thessalonians, Corinthians, Matthew and Mark to show how Christ would return at the last trumpet blast, which occurs at the end of the Tribulation.

First Thessalonians Four:Fifteen–Seventeen (KJV)

For this we say unto you by the word of the Lord, that we which are alive and remain unto the coming of the Lord shall not prevent them which are asleep. For the Lord Himself shall descend from heaven with a shout, with the voice of the archangel, and with the trump of God: and the dead in Christ shall rise first: Then we which are alive and remain shall be caught up together with them in the clouds, to meet the Lord in the air: and so shall we ever be with the Lord.

First Corinthians Fifteen:Fifty One–Fifty Two (KJV)

Behold, I shew you a mystery; We shall not all sleep, but we shall all be changed, In a moment, in the twinkling of an eye, at the last trump: for the trumpet shall sound, and the dead shall be raised incorruptible, and we shall be changed.

Matthew Twenty Four:Twenty 9–Thirty One (KJV)

Immediately after the Tribulation of those days shall the sun be darkened, and the moon shall not give her light, and the stars shall fall from heaven, and the powers of the heavens shall be shaken: And then shall appear the sign of the Son of man in heaven: and then shall all the tribes of the earth mourn, and they shall see the Son of man coming in the clouds of heaven with power and great glory. And He shall send His angels with a great sound of a trumpet, and they shall gather together His elect from the four winds, from one end of heaven to the other.

Mark Thirteen:Twenty Four–Twenty Seven (KJV)

But in those days, after that Tribulation, the sun shall be darkened, and the moon shall not give her light, And the stars of heaven shall fall, and the powers that are in heaven shall be shaken. And then shall they see the Son of man coming in the clouds with great power and glory. And then shall He send His angels, and shall gather together His elect from the four winds, from the uttermost part of the earth to the uttermost part of heaven.

<u>Revelation Nineteen:One–Seven (KJV)</u>

And after these things I heard a great voice of much people in heaven, saying, Alleluia; Salvation, and glory, and honour, and power, unto the Lord our God: For true and righteous are His judgments: for He hath judged the great whore, which did corrupt the earth with her fornication, and hath avenged the blood of His servants at her hand. And again they said, Alleluia. And her smoke rose up for ever and ever. And the four and twenty elders and the four beasts fell down and worshipped God that sat on the throne, saying, Amen; Alleluia. And a voice came out of the throne, saying, Praise our God, all ye His servants, and ye that fear Him, both small and great. And I heard as it were the voice of a great multitude, and as the voice of many waters, and as the voice of mighty thunderings, saying, Alleluia: for the Lord God omnipotent reigneth. Let us be glad and rejoice, and give honour to Him: for the marriage of the Lamb is come, and His wife hath made herself ready.

It was pretty logical; the dead in Christ are raised, then we who remain are caught up in the air with Him. Revelation, chapter Seven, clearly showed that there were saints who are martyred during the Tribulation, after six seals are opened, not before the Tribulation starts. If the dead were raised at the beginning of the Tribulation, then what happens to all the saints who are martyred during the Tribulation? How are they resurrected? Was there a third coming?

<u>Revelation Seven:9–Fourteen (KJV)</u>

After this I beheld, and, lo, a great multitude, which no man could number, of all nations, and kindreds, and people, and tongues, stood before the throne, and before the Lamb, clothed with white robes, and palms in their hands; And cried with a loud voice, saying, Salvation to our God which sitteth upon the throne, and unto the Lamb. And all the angels stood round about the throne, and about the elders and the four beasts, and fell before the throne on their faces, and worshipped God, Saying, Amen: Blessing, and glory, and wisdom, and thanksgiving, and honour, and power, and might, be unto our God for ever and ever. Amen. And one of the elders answered, saying unto me, What are these which are arrayed in white robes? and whence came they? And I said unto him, Sir, thou knowest. And he said to me, These are they which came out of Great Tribulation, and have washed their robes, and made them white in the blood of the Lamb.

Some would tell Guy that the restrainer in Second Thessalonians was the Holy Spirit, but would God leave Christians without the Holy Spirit in their time of greatest need? The Holy Spirit had already revealed to Guy through reading and prayer that the restrainer referred to a powerful angel. Did anyone really believe it was God's character to wisk away His people from the face of adversity and judgment? Story after story from the Bible said otherwise, not to mention Matthew Twenty Four. God used the faith of Christians as an example during times of trial.

As Guy shared more information, he found people held on to their spurious beliefs tightly without having any factual knowledge. They didn't study to see what the Word said for themselves. There were some who were open to the information; most were completely closed, as if there were a concrete wall blocking them from hearing the truth.

After the conference, Max wanted to shake things up, get some growth. He invited K. C. Price down to preach at the Bush on a Wednesday night. It was a big deal; Price had a massive church in Los Angeles, and rubbed elbows with all of America's top Christian pastors and politicians. Max sent mailers out; it would raise visibility and could help add core membership. K. C. Price came to the Bush's expanded retail-located church driven in a Bentley and escorted by three large gangstas packing guns. Not *gangstas* because they were big, black and had guns, but because they were gangstas. Guy knew about gangstas. Reverend Price made Marisol, a young Mexican lady, cry when he yelled at her for not standing directly in line with the others up at the altar. Because she couldn't follow simple instructions, she would not receive God's blessing, he said.

Marie told Guy later that an old man she spoke with had driven fifty miles to come and see K. C. Price after watching him for so many years on TV. He was so overwhelmed that, when he went to say hello, he simply wept. The reverend asked the man if he was retarded or perhaps deaf or dumb. Marie told Reverend Price that the man had driven fifty miles, and he was crying because he was so happy to meet K.C.

When Guy spoke with Max about K.C., Max explained that Dr. Price was from a hard part of Los Angeles. *Surely a man who follows God deserves to be wealthy? Simply look at King David.* It just didn't sit well with

Guy, and, after Thanksgiving dinner, it was settled. The Finnigans had accepted a Thanksgiving dinner invite to eat at the Whites' house, along with the Ebrahimis, and Ronnie and Leda.

It was not what Guy and Marie had expected. There were waitstaff. They were served lobster bisque in gold bowls. Dinner, dessert, everything was incredible. Guy knew it must have cost a fortune. He would have preferred to just pick up a turkey. When they were home, Marie told him that she knew of several families in the church who were not celebrating Thanksgiving, because they had no one to celebrate with, or because they had no money. She hadn't said anything previously because they had already accepted Max and Sue's invitation. Guy was furious, not at Marie, but at the situation. He ranted until he wasn't mad anymore, then he prayed.

Guy was nervous as he pulled up to Pastor Max's house. Pastor Max had built the Burning Bush with his own two hands, along with Sue's devotion of course. Max had had a vision one night of a burning bush floating above him in bed. He had studied the Bible but wasn't formally educated, which Guy thought was great, seeing as the Apostles, aside from Paul, were unlearned men. The Gospel was for everyone. Guy was certain there were perspectives that Max hadn't considered. With some discussion and evidence, Guy was confident Pastor Max would thoughtfully reconsider some of his positions.

Guy had gone to speak with Max the week before in an effort to talk things through. He had some points he wanted to make, but he wanted to keep things light. Max knew that Guy was upset about the wealth of the megachurches. Max was charismatic; if any man should have great wealth, it should be a man of God. After thirty minutes Guy could see the allure of driving a Bentley and having 9 homes. Pastor Max told Guy to think about it, to come back if he wanted to talk more. As Guy reflected later that night, he truly felt deceived. As if he had been spiritually deceived when he had sat down with Max. A spirit of deception was actively at work keeping people from finding the truth about God, encouraging the acceptance of lies as truth.

As Guy prayed, he felt a lightheartedness about the situation. As if God found amusing the fact that Guy had gone off to do spiritual battle with no preparation. Amused like a parent by a young child who commits some unbeknownst wrong. Guy prayed and read. He sought counsel, then thought specifically about what he wanted to say and researched his points thoroughly. He set another meeting with Pastor Max, and decided he would pray and fast for three days beforehand so that he would not be deceived again. When he prayed, he asked God to make things very clear this time. Either soften Pastor Max's heart or make it stone. If it were to be stone, Guy prayed to make it very hard, so it would be abundantly clear that God wanted Guy and Marie to leave the Burning Bush. He asked George Ebrahimi to come in the spirit of Matthew Eighteen. George was the first elder in the church, and Pastor Max thought it was appropriate if Guy thought it necessary.

As Guy pressed the bell, the Whites' large front door opened. Pastor Max's big smile showed his nice straight white teeth. Pastor Max was always smiling. He must have just been to the barber as the sides of his head were buzzed close, the top was short and trim as usual. He was wearing his purple Burning Bush polo shirt; he was shorter than Guy and very muscular.

"Nice to see you, Guy. Come in. Come in."

"Thanks for making the time." Guy smiled and followed Max in through his entryway to the kitchen. George was already sitting at the large table that separated the kitchen from the TV room.

"Hey." George stood and waved from the table.

"Something to drink?" Max walked over to the large stainless steel double-door refrigerator.

"I'm good, thanks." Guy sat down at the table across from George.

Max sat down at the head of the table and placed his palms down. "So you had some more things you wanted to talk about?" He shook his head and said the words, as if he were making jest about being frustrated.

"Umm, yeah. We talked last week, and afterward I felt like I was still disagreeing with your perspective. So I prayed and read and found some things that I thought we could talk about specifically."

"OK, go ahead." Max turned up one of his palms, and George sat quietly with his Bible in front of him.

"At the end of every service, we hold up our offering and say into the Kingdom of God, I sow my seed, every penny shall produce for God and for me."

"Yes, yes. I know. I wrote it." Pastor Max looked intently at Guy, then chuckled a bit as he turned and looked toward George.

"Well, I looked in the Bible, and nowhere does it refer to *seed* as *money*. Aside from offspring, *seed* is usually used to describe *faith*. So it doesn't make sense to me why we hold up money and call it *seed*."

"It's an analogy. You can do lots of things with money, save souls," Max said excitedly.

"Well, God saves souls. We just preach the Gospel," George said, as he looked across the table at Guy.

"Of course, of course. I wasn't saying we save souls, just that money gives us more access. More opportunity for people to hear the Gospel." Max attempted to contain the grimace growing upon his face.

"Did you say that nowhere in the Bible is *seed* referred to as *money*?" George asked with an intent look on his face.

"Yep, I checked." Guy nodded affirmatively.

"How could you check?" George looked over, confused.

"With a concordance." Guy slid the concordance underneath his Bible across the table to George. "You can look up a word, and it tells you everywhere in the Bible where it appears."

"Really?" George ran his fingers through his thick black hair. "This is amazing. Oh, incredible." George flipped through the large Strong's Concordance.

"Keep it." Guy smiled.

"I couldn't." George tried to push the book back across the table, but instead he stood, holding it against the table with both hands, unable to push it forward as he continued to read from its pages.

"Please." Guy looked back over at Pastor Max. "So Creflo Dollar spoke when we were at the T. D. Jakes' conference."

"Mmm-hmm." Max nodded.

"I read this sermon of his, and I wanted to know what you thought." Guy passed a transcript of the sermon over to Max. "This is the whole thing, but basically Creflo says, that some men go before God like they are filthy rags, lying on the ground in shame. When Creflo goes to God, he stands upright. He says I am child of the Most High God. Creflo tells God the things that he wants because that is the right of a child to its Father."

"Mmm-hmm, true." Pastor Max looked up from the transcript. "I agree one hundred percent. You've got to speak it with your mouth." He pushed the paper across the table to Guy.

Guy opened up his Bible. "In chapter Sixty Four of Isaiah, verse Six, it reads, 'But we are all as an unclean thing, and all our righteousnesses are as filthy rags; and we all do fade as a leaf; and our iniquities, like the wind, have taken us away.'"

George let out a long, slow gasp that seemed awkward in the quietness of the room.

"Excuse me." George looked from Guy to Max. "What do you think, Max?" George extended his arm casually as he was still trying to catch his breath.

"Old Covenant." Max folded his arms.

Guy thought of Millie; she was a sweet elderly lady. Guy guessed she was in her late seventies or eighties. She had severe hip and knee problems; arthritis gnarled her hands.

"When you tell Milly that she'll be healed of her physical problems, if she accepts her healing in Jesus's name, it's hurtful. That's not the primary way I think of healing," Guy said as kindly as he could.

"We are healed by His stripes." Max waved his arm, as if swatting a fly.

"I agree, but the focus is being spiritually healed. Miracles happen, but what if God doesn't want Milly to be healed," Guy said calmly.

"Oh, He wants her to be healed, and she will be, if she has enough faith." Spittle came from Max's lips which seemed pale between his crimson cheeks. He startled himself as his palm came down upon the glass tabletop forcefully.

While Guy was researching, he had realized that some of Christendom called this version of Christianity "Health and Wealth," or "Name It and Claim It," as the Prosperity Gospel. He realized now that, rather than being surprised, Pastor Max was an adherent to beliefs that Guy had deep theological and moral problems with. Guy had come on a journey in search of truth. He was a man who hated lies, and he would have no part in half-truths concerning God. He had learned so much about God and His nature over the past three years. Guy was nervous again, but he was certain of one thing. God had not taken Guy this far to abandon him.

"I'm sorry, Pastor Max, but this isn't where God wants me to be anymore." Guy stood and began to take the key to the church's front door from his key ring. "I'll make sure the ushers are covered. I think Joe would do a good job running things." Guy placed the metal key down on the glass tabletop near Max.

"You're making a big mistake." He held up the key in his hand and looked over it toward Guy.

"I appreciate everything you've done. Thank you. Thank you, George." Guy looked over to George and extended his hand out to Max.

"All right."

Max and Guy shook hands. As Guy walked back to his car, he was thankful that God had made things clear. Marie would not be surprised, but he was sure she would be disappointed. Guy was curious to see what God had in store next.

BOOK THREE:
REVELATION

BOOK THREE: CHAPTER ONE

Guy leaned back in the armchair; it was comfortable. The room was quiet. The nurse had mentioned that this chair converted to a bed, and, though it was four in the morning, Guy wasn't in the least bit tired. He was exhilarated, serene. The labor had been taxing for Marie, and Guy felt an innate need to stand watch over his new precious babe and beautiful wife as they slept. Marie certainly did not feel beautiful; for the last few months, she had felt more like an overpacked suitcase, swollen and ready to burst at every seam. Her red hair was stuck to her forehead, dried with sweat; yet she looked peaceful as the IV replenished the fluids lost from her long labor.

Marie was adamant about giving birth naturally, no drugs, no epidural. Guy and Marie had gone to birthing classes together; Marie wanted to try the Braxton-Hicks method. They were diligent in practicing all the techniques, especially the breathing. Guy rubbed vitamin E oil on her ever-expanding belly, while he spoke to their little Peanut growing inside. Then he would read the Bible to their child in Marie's belly; this became their nightly routine. As the baby grew, they played a game where Guy would push his finger into Marie's belly and the baby would push back on the same spot with its foot. Guy would pick a different spot, and the baby would do the same. Marie found it cute but very, very peculiar.

Despite Guy's best efforts, Marie decided they would wait to find out the sex of the baby, hence the nickname Peanut. Green and yellow colors adorned the nursery. Guy had received strategic advice from everyone on his floor at work in attempts to convince Marie to find out the sex of the baby. They had all proved futile; Marie was steadfast. She would not be moved.

The labor languished. At around 11 p.m., no amount of showers, walking or breathing exercises could possibly dull the overwhelming pain. Guy was thankful Marie acquiesced at the last possible moment for an epidural. With as difficult and long as the pushing process became, she would not have had the strength otherwise. She was able to rest for an hour after the epidural, and then pushed in earnest for three hours. Guy didn't make up his mind until the last moment as to whether he would watch the baby's head come out. He did and was surprised by how much blood there was; it pooled onto the floor below.

His heart almost stopped when he saw the black hair and then heard the cry; it was a girl. Guy was surprised. For whatever reason, he thought they would have a boy, but his little girl melted his heart instantly. As she cried, he told her not to worry, that her daddy was here. She stopped crying instantly; the nurses were shocked and remarked that she clearly knew her daddy's voice. Well, Guy did speak to her more than most people in his life, as soon as she had developed ears in the womb, at around four months' gestation.

When Guy held her in his arms, she was so beautiful; she looked right into his eyes. At that moment, he loved her more than anything in the world; she was perfect. Before bringing her to her mother, Guy held her above his head and dedicated her as Faith Elizabeth Finnigan to the Lord God Almighty. As he prayed, he dedicated his firstborn child to the Lord, that she might be His, that He might direct her steps all the days of her life.

She bonded with her mother and ate hungrily from Marie's well-swollen bosom. Faith slept quietly in a small bassinet next to the bed, swaddled in a little hospital blanket with a pink cap upon her tiny head. Guy had never seen anything so beautiful; the simple sight of her brought tears of joy to his eyes, just as her arrival into the world had.

It was difficult for Guy and Marie after leaving the Bush. Guy was shunned by everyone. Pastor Max said Guy was a false prophet. Guy was not bothered by what came out of the mouth of liars; he prayed that God's truth would be revealed. About twenty people left when Guy departed, including the Ebrahimis. Not at Guy's request nor admonition. Simply because they had heard the truth and were convicted in their own hearts by the Holy Spirit. It wasn't long before the Bush shut its doors forever.

While Guy's thirst for God and truth remained unquenchable, he had no desire for church. When the Ebrahimis convinced him to come along to a new church they were attending, Guy acquiesced. The first message they heard preached was from Titus and concerned pastors whose mouths must be stopped because they subverted whole houses, teaching things which they ought not for filthy lucre's sake. The Finnigans and Ebrahimis looked at each other and chuckled; it seemed this was where God would have them for now.

Pennyhill, as it was called, seemed to be the church of seminary students associated with John MacArthur, a heavyweight in conservative Christendom. The pastor preached through the Bible one book at a time, verse by verse. Guy loved it; Sunday mornings were more like a college seminar. There was no building and no desire for a building, just a junior high school gym. Guy and Marie developed new friendships; many of their friends could read ancient Greek and Hebrew. They were voracious studiers of the Word.

There was a lack of emphasis on the Holy Spirit, however. It was most noticeable to Guy during worship, which was dull and quiet. There was no clapping, no raising of hands, no pouring your heart out to God. Guy didn't care; he still raised his hands and clapped. So did the Ebrahimis.

Guy made it to the major leagues at work. His boss, Bill Wilson, had made a switch over to J. D. Dordan Private Banking and, after a year, had convinced Guy to come along. It was a year later now, since Guy had made the move in Two Thousand Six after First City had shorted him on a promised raise by fourteen hundred dollars. It was the principle that made Guy leave as opposed to the money. He was their number-one producer several years and counting. The sixty three thousand dollars he was making was great, but that was still beside the point. Guy felt like he was shooting for the stars when he told J.D. that he wanted eighty thousand a year. They made him an offer on the spot, and Guy realized he had shot way too low. But, as was his practice, Guy simply wanted the opportunity to show them what he could accomplish. As usual he would let his numbers speak for themselves. He was confident everything else would fall into place. Marie agreed, and you couldn't shake a stick at eighty grand either. Not bad, but not quite the hundred K Guy had hoped to be making by the time he was thirty.

J. D. Dordan was quintessential private banking. Quintessentially good in that Guy was now commuting to downtown Los Angeles and working in one of the big high-rises that adorned the name of his new employer. There were guys in three-thousand-dollar suits wearing the equivalent of the price of a car on their wrists; most of them were stock brokers as opposed to bankers, like Guy. Quintessentially bad in that it was like working in a shark tank. Apparently, when there were lots of dollars on the table, people were willing to eat each other's faces in order to acquire them.

Guy was devastated with a coworker's reaction when she had wanted in on a prospect Guy was working. When Guy told her that he was working the opportunity with Bill, she started to cry hysterically. She sent Guy a "Dear John" email, relating how she had hoped they would be friends. She had hoped they would work on deals together. She wished him well in his future life and endeavors. Bill was Guy's mentor; Bill had showed Guy the new ropes. Still Guy felt horrible. That is until one of the guys in the office overheard her crying to a friend about how much she needed the revenue from the deposits expected to be brought

299

in from Guy's new relationship. Guy learned there was a lot he needed to learn.

His drumbeat that the world was about to come to an end began to seem ever more foolish to those around him; the country was never better. It was Two Thousand Seven, and people were making money hand over fist while the stock market continued to break new all-time highs. But, as Guy sought God's face, Guy would be brought back to Hebrews 11, where it was expounded that, by faith, Noah was warned by God of things not seen as of yet. Noah moved with fear and prepared; for in the days before the flood, they were eating and drinking, marrying and giving in marriage, until the day that Noah entered into the ark.

And so Guy tailored his conversations around such things. He found he had a much more receptive audience in some ways with the seminary students. They could clearly see the biblical truth against a pretribulation rapture. They too agreed the Bible showed that man would not be whisked away before the judgment. That they would need to stand. They could see the truth revealed by Matthew in chapter Twenty Five, when he spoke of Christ's return.

> They that were foolish took their lamps, and took no oil with them: But the wise took oil in their vessels with their lamps. While the bridegroom tarried, they all slumbered and slept. And at midnight there was a cry made, Behold, the bridegroom cometh; go ye out to meet him. Then all those virgins arose, and trimmed their lamps. And the foolish said unto the wise, Give us of your oil; for our lamps are gone out. But the wise answered, saying, Not so; lest there be not enough for us and you: but go ye rather to them that sell, and buy for yourselves.

And yet while they could see the truth, they still found no need to prepare in the physical world. Guy was nervous about getting Marie pregnant, because Matthew also warned in chapter Twenty Five of the danger to those with child and nursing babes during the time of the end. Guy prayed vehemently, however, and was on careful watch for signs. Once he felt it was right, he and Marie planned as they always did. They wanted to have a spring Two Thousand Seven baby, so their child would have an advantage in school. Marie even got a device that she peed on for a month that told her exactly when she was ovulating. She got pregnant the very first time they tried.

Marie started a home day care after she got pregnant so she could generate some income while she stayed home with the baby. When it became clear that Guy was going to be successful in his new job, Marie agreed to shut down the business. The stress of being eight months' pregnant and watching other children cry simply because they wanted their own mothers helped seal her decision. Guy and Marie were willing to make whatever sacrifices were necessary in order for Marie to stay home with their children. Thankfully God provided. They wouldn't have had children if it meant their children would be raised by someone else, while they both worked.

Making it out of Reseda was also necessary because of the schools and general environment. Reality showed them that most often homes where both parents worked involved choices. Guy came across many mothers in his office who needed to work in order to provide for their children. They all drove BMWs and carried Louis Vuitton purses. The same was true for those he knew in lower incomes; not having cable TV was simply too big a sacrifice to make. Some had no choice now, because they chose to have four or five children without the proper foundation to support them. There was no cable for Guy in the new house.

Guy looked over to the bassinet, and Faith opened her beautiful blue eyes without even a whimper. Guy would sacrifice everything to make sure she never walked upon the paths he had trod. He would protect her innocence like the most valuable treasure.

"Is she awake?" Marie turned onto her side, as if the opening of the babe's eyes had stirred her internal clock.

"She just opened her eyes. She's so beautiful. She was quiet the whole night. She never cried once. How are you feeling?"

"Better than I expected. She's hungry, I'm sure. Will you bring her to me please?" Marie smiled pleadingly. "Did you get any sleep?"

Faith was a little feather in Guy's arms. He couldn't believe the way she stared into his soul; she knew him. "Hungry baby, here's Mommy. I stayed up. I wanted to watch over you both." Guy smiled. He tucked little Faith into the crook of her mother's arm.

"She knows how to latch on. It's weird. I can feel my milk coming in. Well, I guess it's actually colostrum now. That's my sweet girl. You're a hungry girl." Marie stroked Faith's soft black hair.

Guy rubbed the back of her head with his finger as she ate from her mother's plump breast. "Look at all that black hair. Where did that come from?" Guy leaned down and kissed her little head. It was soft, and smelled new and fresh.

Marie giggled. "I know, right? You are too cute. You're OK that she's a girl?"

"More than I could have ever imagined. She's incredible. I could have never uttered the words to ask for something so wonderfully perfect." Guy's hand met Marie's, and they stroked her little head together as one. "Can I hold her when you're done?" Guy asked with longing eyes. "The nurse said she was going to give her a bath when you woke up."

"She's got a full little belly. She ate from both sides. She's already asleep, but she's still half sucking. There you go, sweetheart." Marie wrapped the blanket back around Faith's tiny body.

Guy sat down with her; he knew that he was going to love his child, but the joy was so overwhelming, something different than he had imagined. She looked so peaceful, Guy thought perhaps he would rest his eyes, but before the thought could roll over in his mind, the nurse opened the door.

"Is she ready for her first bath?" The stout morning nurse in rubber ducky scrubs strode across the room. Guy was surprised that Kaiser offered such nice accommodations. They had their own room for labor, almost like a little apartment. Guy looked down to his precious little bundle, and his heart stopped. "What's going on?"

Faith's skin had a pale blue hue; by the time the nurse ran across the room, Faith was as blue as a pair of denim jeans. "Oh, my God, what's happening?" As Guy stood, the nurse ripped the babe from his arms and ran out of the room. Guy was behind her as she exited the door and walked through the next, labeled Neonatal ICU.

"Oh, my God, what's happening? No, no, no, please!" The tears streamed down Guy's face, and in a moment there were ten doctors and nurses surrounding little Faith. They acted as if Guy were not even in the room. It confirmed what Guy knew in his heart: this was serious.

Guy dropped to his knees and extended his hands toward the heavens. "No, Lord. No, please, why! She's innocent, Lord. There's no fault in her. Did I not dedicate her to You, Lord? Please do not take her, Lord. Please, Jesus, in Your holy name, heal her, I beg of You. Please, Lord, restore her to health. Please, my God, let her be perfectly healed. She is in Your hands, is she not? Give these doctors wisdom, steady their hands. Let there be no consequence for my sweet Faith. Please, Father, in the name of Your Son, Jesus." The words groaned forth from his gut as the tears streamed down Guy's face mingled with snot, flowing over his mouth.

Guy felt a hand upon his shoulder as a doctor pressed and lifted him toward the double doors, all at once.

"She's having seizures. She stopped breathing. We've intubated her. She needs to be moved to the Woodland Hills facility right now. They have one of the top neonatal ICUs in the country. We're getting an ambulance ready to transport her."

It was a blur, a nightmare. It swirled around Guy as if he were pulled down a drain, gasping, and finding only water for breath—down, down,

down. Marie stood in the hall, pale, clammy, still attached to and hanging on to her IV.

Guy spit out the words through his sobs. "She's having seizures. She stopped breathing. They've intubated her. They're taking her to Woodland Hills in an ambulance. They don't know what's wrong. I have to go."

Marie burst into tears.

Guy pulled the phone from his pocket and dialed his father. "Oh, my God, Dad. There's something wrong with Faith. She stopped breathing, Dad. I need you to get here now. Please, Dad, hurry."

"It's OK. I'll be right there. Everything's going to be OK." Mack's voice was calm and collected on the other end of line.

"They're taking Faith to Woodland Hills. I need you to take care of Marie, Dad. I need you to get Marie over there, no matter what." The words came out like a roller coaster dipping through valleys, flooded with tears and heights of breathless pauses.

"I'm on my way. I'll handle everything. Go take care of Faith."

"I gotta go, Dad." Guy clicked the phone, as he and Marie fell against each other. "My dad's coming here to be with you. I have to go with Faith."

"Don't leave her. Go." Marie was in shock.

"I won't. I love you." The ambulance flew across the Valley with sirens blaring as Guy sat next to one of the technicians oblivious to anything, save his little treasure covered with tubes and tape. She was quiet and precious. Guy pleaded with his God.

Guy was reluctant to use Kaiser Permanente health insurance because he had always viewed them as the cheaper choice. But Marie had been with Kaiser since she was a child, and Guy never went to the doctor, so he never really cared. As they entered the Neonatal ICU, Guy could quickly see that it was a modern facility: new, clean and high-tech.

Any sense of time was wiped away; a minute was an hour and an hour a minute. The energy and resources of the facility were all clearly directed and focused toward his daughter.

"I'm Dr. Aggelos. She's intubated and medicated. It seems the seizures have stopped for now." The doctor, who appeared to be in his fifties, approached Guy with a presence of gravity.

"What's going on? What's wrong?" The words languished in Guy's mouth.

"We're not sure yet. We're running tests. This is a state-of-the-art facility. She's in great hands. I'm placing her under my personal care. I'm going to figure this out. Why don't you get some rest, and we'll let you know when there's more information." Dr. Aggelos placed his hand upon Guy's shoulder.

Guy, always a good reader of people, could tell that Dr. Aggelos, while remiss of tangible facts, was the right man. Not simply someone filling a spot, but a man of intelligence and a master of his craft. "I'm not leaving her side."

"There's nothing else you can do right now. Get some rest." Dr. Aggelos was calm, firm.

"Until she leaves, neither do I. I'm her father. I'm going to pray and read her the Bible quietly until she comes home. If that's a problem, you're going to have to call the police."

"OK, OK. I understand."

Guy's cell phone buzzed. It was Mack. "Dad."

"Is she OK? What's happening?"

"She's stable for now. They're still not sure what's wrong. They're running tests. She's on medication. She hasn't had any seizures for a couple hours. How's Marie? Why haven't they transferred her yet?"

"They don't have any available rooms. She's OK, but the doctors say she can't be discharged yet. I'm getting her a room there, no matter what. Don't worry about it. Take care of Faith." Mack's voice was stern, he was a man who knew how to get things accomplished, to overcome obstacles when he wanted to.

Marie was not OK; she had waited and planned for this day her whole life. It was supposed to be special and wonderful. Being separated from the daughter who had grown within Marie, unable to help, unable to even be by her daughter's side, was unbearable.

Guy read the Psalms aloud softly into his daughter's spirit; they brought him calmness as well. He spoke to her and to his God. She endured. Guy had seen the fire of her heart through her eyes when she was born.

His focused reverie was pierced by the touch of a pretty young nurse as Mack stood beside her.

"They're transferring Marie now. She wanted me to come over. They've got a room for you. You need to get some rest."

"I'm OK, thanks. How's Marie?" Guy asked calmly.

"She's a trooper. She'll be here soon." Mack knew there was no reason to tell his son of Marie's grief. It was to be expected, and there was no need for an additional burden on him. "I spoke with the doctors. They won't have any more information for a while. Marie told me that you stayed up last night. How long have you been awake now?"

Guy gazed down at this phone. "A little over forty hours, I guess, but I can't leave her, Dad."

"You need strength for the long haul. I'll sit with her."

"Come on. I'll show you." The pretty young nurse took Guy by the arm.

"OK, but don't leave her, Dad. Promise me. Not for one second." Guy floated along the floor, a balloon in the hands of a pretty young nurse.

"I promise." Mack set his heart upon it and his body upon the empty chair.

The nurse did find one room set aside for family emergencies that had just opened up. It was hygienic and felt like Guy's old room back at Camp Horno, with florescent lights, a mattress in the corner and a small bathroom. The weight of this crisis crushed Guy at once like the breaking of a dam. He stripped off his clothes and turned on the shower. The warm water washed over him as his spent tears and mucus flowed down the drain. There was no soap in the shower. Guy slid open the aluminum door frame and, with wet feet, stepped to the sink to fill his hand with liquid soap from the dispenser nearby. It was enough to make his body feel clean.

He turned the water off and once more stepped upon the linoleum floor, creating an ever-expanding pool of water. A quick glance around the bathroom revealed nothing to dry his dripping frame—no towels, not even toilet paper. He dripped into the bedroom, but the plastic mattress was not adorned with a blanket, not even sheets. The room was bare, save a drawer under the bed. Opening it revealed a gray sweatsuit. Guy pulled it out and over his soaked body. It was a woman's, too short to cover his calves or forearms. Still he zipped it up, flipped off the switch, and collapsed upon the pillowless bed into ineluctable sleep.

Guy's slumber on tax day of Two Thousand Seven, the day after the birth of his daughter, was pierced by the voice of Scott and John from Pennyhill. They were both students at The Master's College, fervent for Jesus. John was enlisted in the spiritual battle to snuff out masturbation and pornography, a battle that lingered for Guy but that he fought vehemently to eradicate. Scott was a scholar among scholars. Guy invited him over when the Jehovah's Witnesses wanted to stop by. The young guy who had initially stopped over brought back an elder ringer with him for the appointment. He was flummoxed by biblical truth and found a way to dismiss himself quickly when confronted with understanding.

The elderly man had actually left his aged wife in the car during the hot L.A. summer while speaking with Guy and Scott.

Scott also had a heart for the homeless. Guy was distributing his bags full of food and necessities primarily in the San Fernando Valley. There were lots of homeless folks, especially around the Four O Five and

Roscoe. But the first year Guy had worked downtown, he was extremely dismayed when Christmas rolled around. Just blocks away from the high-rises and the slick suits, he had found scores of merchants selling worthless garbage, trinkets. People walked out from the slummy little stores, bags packed to the hilt with junk, stepping over homeless people like cracks in the sidewalk. The dichotomy disturbed Guy to his bones.

When he spoke to Scott, Guy had discovered that this part of town was skid row, L.A.'s ground zero. Scott and his girlfriend, Katie, a fine young lady, went down at night to pass out tacos. Marie came along for their first visit. They had a hard time believing it was in fact America. There were hundreds if not thousands of people living in the gutter, shooting drugs, having sex on the street. It was like something from *Night of the Living Dead* crossed with Haiti and doused in urine.

When Scott and John arrived in Guy's room, they prayed and consoled, and then had a hearty laugh at Guy in his gray-and-red-striped woman's jumpsuit. Guy and Marie lived at the hospital for the next two weeks, surrounded by family and Pennyhill members, save Bear and Della. Bear was still in San Jose working on an engineering degree, and Della had scheduled two weeks of vacation with her friends in Texas starting the day Faith had come into the world. Mack exchanged Guy's jumpsuit for some clothes bought at the local Walmart.

The time at the hospital was anguishing. Guy and Marie stayed planted by their daughter's side the entire time. Faith was tested for everything under the sun, as were Marie and Guy. While Faith seemed to be on the mend, the doctors were still at a loss. They all had a smile when Mack's mother suggested to him that he be tested as well to make sure it wasn't a genetic abnormality. Mack gently reminded her that he and Guy did not share the same blood.

Faith's little head was wrapped in bandages, but the tubes up her nose and the ventilator were eventually removed, and she was able to bottle feed her mother's milk. The pain and fear of the unknown was eventually removed. The trauma was caused by a bleed on Faith's right temporal lobe, most likely from passing through the birth canal. The doctors could not say if there would be permanent damage; only time could tell. The Finnigans would have to wait and see if she hit milestones, like walking and talking, at the normal progression. She would have to take phenobarbital for six months to ensure she had no further seizures while the blood was absorbed back into her brain, plus regular visits with the neurologist until she was two.

When she came home after two weeks in the NICU, Faith sleeping in the nursery was out of the question. She slept in a cosleeper between Guy and Marie; it looked a bit like a shoe box with the bottom side cut out. Guy was fortunate that his new job afforded him five weeks of vacation. He had used four, two at the hospital and another two at home. In a time of need, his colleagues at old J. D. Dordan were extremely supportive. The instance seemed to help foster some camaraderie. Bill Wilson told Guy not to worry; he would take care of Guy's clients. Guy needed to focus on his family.

The first week of dinners at home were provided by Pennyhill congregants, which was nice because the Finnigans would have never asked for assistance. They received calls of support and cards from the likes of Mack's brother, Timmy, and his new family in St. Thomas, as well as from Della's sister Pricilla and Della's brother Carl, who, like half of New York, had migrated down to Florida. Pricilla had married Ray, a Long Island coke-dealer-turned-preacher. They ended up adopted a little Korean girl and her brother after the next door neighbor had called while in the midst of a domestic dispute. With cops surrounding the house, Pastor Ray had agreed to temporarily keep the man's children, before he then murdered his wife and took his own life.

Guy let Carl's message go to voice mail. Guy never really spoke with his uncle much since he was a child. Now he made a conscious point of avoiding it since he had learned his uncle was an incestuous pedophile. When Guy had gone back to New York to visit his biological father, after doing a line of coke, Roxie had casually shared how Carl had molested his sisters for years and years while hopped up on meth. She found it disgusting that the family pretended like nothing ever happened. Guy agreed.

Marie's mom, Aloha, proved to be a better grandmother than mother. It was hard to give individualized attention to a brood. Marie and her sisters had multiplied. Jackie's daughter Shyla was now seven and her sister, Shannon, was five. Their father, Lydel, was not bright or great with money, but he loved the girls and worked like a dog doing construction so that Jackie could stay home. They lived near Aloha in Sacramento so the girls got lots of Grandma–time.

Contessa Mara Amargado Trouble was the bohemian love child of Champagne and Facundo. While he was an illegal alien who spoke no English, Champagne found other ways to occupy their time as she spoke not a lick of Spanish. It unfortunately had relegated her to what seemed a permanent life of living in her father, Arnie's, house along with her wicked stepmother, Anastasia, who threw a fit if anyone called her Ana. Aloha stayed for two weeks once Guy went back to the office. She was beyond helpful: cooking, cleaning, doing laundry, all without being asked, and with a lightness of heart and a spirit of gratitude. She cried when she left.

Guy hoped that his mother's heart would be softened by her introduction to the Lord. She became slightly less caustic, and managed to work God and prayer into her conversations. While the time she spent visiting her granddaughter was infinitesimal when measured against her time spent feeding feral cats, she loved Faith dearly. She would rather buy Guy a shirt on double-double discount from Bloomingdale's, where she worked, than offer to babysit and drive the twenty miles from Hollywood. It was, after all, quite inconvenient. At least Guy was extraordinarily well dressed at the office.

His sister and Darnell stopped going to church altogether. They screamed at each other in the historical example of Della's motherly affection. Guy grew to disdain Darnell. He rarely held a job, had zero ambition for the future, and, besides the fact that he treated Pearl like dirt, he was also a mooch. In the several dozen times Guy had been out with him, he had never once paid for his own meal, let alone Pearl's.

While chivalry was dead for some, it was not for Guy, and he expressed his concerns to Pearl. She would simply reply that Guy didn't like her dating a black man. Guy only wished Darnell were a real man who happened to be black. Their relationship continued in a downward spiral of breakups that had turned the beautiful Pearl into a stalker who eventually threw a brick through the front window of Darnell's house. Darnell's mother's house, that is.

Herman moved from withdrawn to disturbing. He attended family functions as a perpetual black cloud donned in a black hoodie pumping Slipknot through his headphones. He was six foot four, blond and handsome, though chubby. He had a way with words that often left Pearl in tears. Guy told his brother that he loved him. Herman hated his father, even while living in Mack's house, completely on the dole, totally detached from the reality of his situation. He had had his college paid for but refused to get a job or even look for one.

Guy offered his help. He told Herman that he would feel better with some independence. Guy knew their family wasn't ideal, but Herman was his brother, and he loved him. Herman replied that, if Guy were dead, he wouldn't even notice; he wouldn't even care. Honest, he reiterated. If Guy hadn't worked hard on it, he would have knocked his brother's teeth down his throat, *honest*. John Brown said that was exactly what was needed.

John made great strides, for John. He found a girl with a job and a family that would give him a check. He became an exterminator for the family business and tied the knot quickly. That was good, as Bear and Guy thought there was a solid chance John would be lost to meth. There was no intervention possible until Carla came. John would lie to them about it until the cows came home. John often lied about little things, but it eventually became pathological.

It hit a deep nerve after he had begged Bea for a beautiful pit bull from her first litter, and it then disappeared. John swore up and down that he took the puppy, Jack, to live up on a farm for a better life. Bear and Guy suspected he gave the dog to some scum for drugs. John went on and on about the rolling hills. Carla was controlling, and it was good for John. She knew better than to let John out of her sight, and her family worked him like a dog. It was good for him; he stayed clean. He even started to attend church, it changed him. Guy was hopeful they would rekindle a meaningful relationship with John and Carla.

Guy even got Mack to sign up for extermination services; it was certainly necessary. In the years since the divorce, Mack had thrown himself into his work. He told himself it was to replenish the savings that was lost in the divorce, but Guy knew that working eighty hours a week was bullshit in the banking world unless you were making five million dollars a year. The guys making five million dollars were working thirty hours a week, if that. Only hedge fund guys making a hundred million a year worked that hard and not even most of them. Mack's calm, collected mind was maintained by his long hours at work, as his house became the dumping ground for his psyche, filled with three or four of anything that could be found on an infomercial, and, as John would find out, rats, lots and lots of rats. Mack had agreed that, with the arrival of baby Faith, the house needed to be rat-proofed. The house had a veritable infestation.

For twenty-six years now Jack had languished away in every filthy cell in New York. He called, through Della, to offer congratulations and a vote of support for the baby. When he got around to calling Guy, Guy offered to come out and visit with Faith the following year. He knew in his heart she would be healed by then. Jack declined; he didn't want his grandchild to see him like this. Guy thought it would be fine; Greenhaven was a nicer prison with a big meeting room. "No thanks" was all his father had replied.

While it all mattered, it mattered not. Guy had a real family now, a wife and child. He would always be there for his daughter, no matter what. To teach her, to instruct her. To protect her, to keep her heart guarded from a world that desired to steal the innocence of children. He would never let anyone hurt her, never let her feel alone or scared.

She wasn't scared. No one who wasn't already told had any idea of the trauma Faith's first two weeks had held. She was magnetic; she smiled and laughed hysterically. People thought babies couldn't laugh or even recognize faces that early. All who met Faith came to a different conclusion. She said *cat* when she was three months old, and, before six months, she was saying *Mom* and *Dad* clearly. The neurologist was stunned; she was off the medication at six months and walking the day she turned 9 months. One of Guy's Chinese clients told Guy that she was born in the year of the golden pig, something that only happened every sixty years. She was proof of an ancient proverb that all her trials were endured during her first weeks. The rest of life would be blessed.

Marie was the mother Guy always knew she would be: kind, loving, nurturing, instructive. She felt bad about the weight she had put on, but Guy didn't care in the least; he honestly didn't even notice. From their love, God had created this precious gift. Guy had wondered how he would fit a child into their lives, and now he knew he would never be whole without her. While the cyclone of life whirled through their families, Guy, Marie and Faith stood within the eye, calmly and firmly upon the rock.

BOOK THREE: CHAPTER TWO

"Frank, nice to meet you. Really appreciate you taking the time." Guy sat down in the armchair across the small table from where Frank Partnoy was already seated. It was the day before Thanksgiving Two Thousand Seven.

"My pleasure. I was glad you emailed me." Frank's refined nerdiness exuded through his glasses. He looked just like the picture Guy saw on the web. "I already grabbed my venti with nonfat. Starbuck's certainly has the secret sauce, don't they? Grab something. Must have been a long drive down from L.A. How long did it take you?" Frank took a long sip from the quintessential green logo'd white cup. He was dressed simply in khakis with a white-and-blue-striped polo shirt. His black hair was short and balding in the front. It added to his air of studious intelligence.

"I left early. It wasn't too bad. Took me about two hours and fifteen minutes from Santa Clarita. I think it was a bit lighter since tomorrow is Thanksgiving. Really nice of you to make the time. I had a cup on the way down. Thanks." Guy sat at the little table wearing a navy pinstripe Hugo Boss suit with a white Nordstrom shirt, a red Ferragamo tie and Ferragamo loafers, standard attire. No more shiny shirts with matching ties from his First City days. No more monochromatic combos along with his cream-colored patent leather shoes, which used to drive Bill crazy. But Guy's clients at the time had loved it. Private banking was different, much more traditional. Crisp white or blue shirts, very banker.

"So you're with private banking? How long have you been over at good ole J.D.? What sort of clients do you work with?" Frank asked inquisitively.

"At J.D. about a year and a half now. I've been really fortunate thankfully. I used to work at First City. My clients made the move with me. Business has really expanded. We have a minimum relationship of five million in liquidity to be held at the firm. I've got clients with five million, lots with net worths over a hundred, a few billionaires thrown in. We have a great platform. We help clients with everything from financing their five-hundred-thousand-dollar Maybachs, to paying bills and delivering food to elderly clients. We offer full-service investments, in-house and third-party managers. We work in teams. I specialize in debt, particularly commercial real estate finance. We use derivative swaps contracts to fix rates. I was unfamiliar with them coming from the retail banking world. I do my own research, a lot of reading."

"Good for you, but as they say, a fool's paradise is a wise man's hell." Frank shook his index finger in the air. "I should know. I worked at Morgan Stanley in their Derivatives Trading Group out of New York. I was a law clerk after graduating Yale and passing the bar. I guess I couldn't figure out what I wanted to do. I had a double major in mathematics and economics from Kansas. After working on Wall Street, I knew it wasn't that. But I found I have the best of both worlds as a professor here at UCSD." Frank nodded. "So you have some questions on derivatives? Let's see how far down the rabbit hole we get. Fire away." Frank let out a little chuckle, folding his arms across his chest as he leaned back into his seat.

Guy leaned forward. "So we use interest rate swaps to fix rates on loans for commercial real estate. When I first got into private banking, it was all new. What really struck me was how the bank made all this money on the trades, and it's wasn't disclosed to clients. With anything else, all the fees and costs are reflected." Guy's brow was furrowed, not out of anger, but with intense thought and reflection.

"Bingo." Frank pointed his finger, making a gun, toward Guy.

Guy chuckled. "You know, it actually makes me uncomfortable. But we're not allowed to say anything. It's like the big secret. Clients get a good rate, and it's how everybody hits big numbers. I've been doing what we call plain-vanilla swaps, just a fixed rate, no other variables. A lot of folks in the office do all these exotic swaps, where if this or that happens, you move back to floating rates, or maybe in the last year your exposure number triples. You can make insane revenue on the exotic swaps, but it seems way too risky to me."

"Derivatives hedging risk? Just ask Enron how that worked out." Frank smiled.

"That's why I'm here. I've been studying up myself, because, while everyone is selling derivatives like crazy, whenever I ask, it seems no one knows exactly what they are or how it all works together. We do a lot of schmoozing, fancy dinners, parties. We have suites at Staples for all the games—Lakers, Clippers, Kings—all the concerts, dugout seats at Dodger Stadium. So I go to all these parties and meet lots of guys who run their own hedge funds. Serious guys, worth hundreds of millions of dollars. I'll ask them to tell me a bit about derivatives. They all say, 'Oh, yeah, we use those. We buy them forward, sell them off at a profit. We make a killing.' But no one can tell me how it actually works together." Guy's Italian side was coming though with a double-handed chop as he got more animated. "So while I was researching, I came upon your sworn

testimony to Congress on Enron and the unregulated use of derivatives."
http://www.hsgac.senate.gov/download/?id=e61872aa-e5b1-4f41-a184-d4ebab8faa46.

"Then it looks like it's time to go down the rabbit hole. It's funny. More people have had their eyes opened by that piece. You're not the first person who's tracked me down." Frank looked pensive. "It's pretty amazing. No one really knows how all this stuff works together. Financial derivatives were cooked up by mathematical wizards, maybe at MIT. Complex functions that no one but hardcore math majors from top institutions can tackle. All completely unregulated."

"That's part of what seems so crazy to me. I've been in banking now for about a decade, and everything under the sun is regulated. From your testimony it seemed Enron was able to hide losses, hide debt, even count losses as profit. You mentioned it's all legal under Generally Accepted Accounting Principles. So I got to thinking. If this stuff is legal, there's no way Enron is the only one doing it. It has to be endemic. Then I started to think, wow. What if the banks are using this to skew their capital ratios?"

"Now you're onto to it." Frank slapped his knee; he was giddy as a schoolboy. "Be careful when you follow the white rabbit. You just might come out the other side of the looking glass." His grin widened. "Just like that"—he snapped his fingers—"*poof*, no more pensions, no more Four O One(k)s. Everything gone in the blink of the eye. Except what was raided by the brass of course. Even Warren Buffet called them time bombs in his Two Thousand Two annual report, not that it stops him. They are like moths to a flame." *http://www.fintools.com/docs/Warren%20Buffet%20on%20Derivatives.pdf.* "Do you have any idea how much derivative exposure there is?" Frank asked coyly.

"That's part of what I've been trying to find out. It seems to have led me here." Guy smirked.

"That's the thing. No one really knows. It's totally unregulated! From what I've been able to ascertain, it is somewhere in the neighborhood of a quadrillion dollars. Do you know how much a quadrillion dollars is?" Frank motioned with his left hand and took another sip of his coffee with his right.

"A thousand trillion," Guy replied.

"A thousand trillion, indeed, but let me put it a different way. A quadrillion is more than all the everything." Again Frank smiled.

"What do you mean, more than *all the everything*?" That was the question Guy knew Frank wanted asked. It was an appropriate one.

"*More than* all the everything. More than all the stock markets, all the stocks in the world. More than all the currencies. More than all the real

313

estate, all the houses, all the buildings, all the gold, all the oil. More than all the everything added up and put together."

Putting it that way, Guy's eyes began to fall out of his head. "We're in big trouble," Guy said flatly.

"Your thoughts about the banks"—Frank tapped his index finger against his temple repeatedly—"exactly." He held his finger straight up in the air. "Here, take a look at this. I brought a copy of J.D.'s annual report, the official Form Ten-K." He flipped through the stack and set it down on the round table between them. "See right here? Over thirty trillion dollars in derivatives." Frank pointed to the line items.

"What? How is that possible? That's tens of times our asset base. That's two hundred fifty percent of the country's GDP." Guy knew J.D. was in the business of derivatives, but the number was unbelievable.

"Leverage on leverage on leverage. Bets on bets on bets. That's all this stuff really is. A big casino, with no one watching the vault, until *poof.*" Frank touched his fingers to his thumb, and opened them quickly. "They'll say they all cancel each other out, but it's BS. The real problem is interconnectedness. Everyone is a counterparty to everyone else. It's like a big chain reaction, waiting for a catalyst. So what else have you been pondering?" Frank asked with prodding inquisitiveness.

"Well, honestly, I've been concerned the system is heading for collapse." Guy put his hands on the table.

"Not just a collapse like the dot com bubble in Two Thousand, or the real estate crash in the eighties. A really epic collapse. You know, during the Great Depression, everyone lost their shirts except the guys who saw it coming and bet on the opposite direction. They became robber barons." Frank pushed his spectacles up the bridge of his nose.

★★★

Guy could see the freight train barreling down the track; he was glad Jackie's husband, Lydel, was coming for Thanksgiving. In Los Angeles, you could have bet dollars to doughnuts that Lydel was a black man, but he was simply a Utah mormon. Everyone called him Dell. The Finnigans decided to have Thanksgiving dinner at their abode, since it would be Faith's first. Both Marie's and Guy's fractured but numerous family members were coming. Mostly numerous on Marie's side—her sisters were really something else when they all got together. On the phone it was hard to tell Marie and Jackie apart.

"So what do you think?" Guy asked Dell after Thanksgiving dinner while the family nursed their full bellies.

"Yeah, sure I can do it, if you're sure. I don't have to be back till Tuesday or Wednesday. This patio cover's still in good shape." Dell was extremely handy; he could tackle just about any job a house could toss at him. He was in construction, and he loved what he did. His passion for tools kept the family tighter on cash than they should have been. His hard work kept him trim. He was a few inches shorter than Guy and decent looking; he kept his brown hair buzzed short.

"Whatever you think's easiest. It just needs to be totally enclosed, no windows. How much do you think it'll run?" Guy stood out on the patio. The sun was just going down. There was a nice view of the mountains in the background; the air was still warm for November.

"Well, you'll have to get a dumpster for demo. That won't be hard. Materials, maybe five hundred bucks at most." Dell grabbed one of the beams which connected the patio to the roofline over the sliding glass door that exited from the kitchen/dining room area.

"That would be perfect. I was thinking I'd pay you a thousand for the work. Does that seem fair?"

"No way, bro. That's crazy. Just get me a couple twelve-packs of Mountain Dew and some pizza." Dell drank Mountain Dew like a well-hydrated marine drinks water.

"Of course I'll get you Mountain Dew and pizza. But I'm paying you a thousand bucks. No way you're gonna spend your holiday weekend helping me and not get paid." Guy knew Jackie and the kids would appreciate the cash. Plus they had a new baby.

Four girls between the sisters and now finally Maybel had a boy, JoJo. He was born a few months after Faith, a real tank. Marie's dad, Arnie, said her sister Maybel was the same way as a baby. Maybel looked like her sisters with red hair, lighter not as vibrant as Marie's. The family found out she had gotten married last year when the marriage certificate showed up at Arnie's house. Some tool who was kicked out of the Marine Corps got her hooked on speed. Guy had a few choice words with him; they were divorced in less than six months. Maybel seemed to be back on the right track.

Guy also had a stern talking to with Facundo. He showed up at Guy's house full of piss and vinegar demanding to see Champagne who was over visiting with Contessa. Guy met him out on the porch and closed the door behind him. Facundo had his long black hair pulled into a ponytail; he had learned enough English to have basic conversations. After he looked into Guy's eyes, not much more needed to be said. Guy informed Facundo, since clearly he hadn't heard, that Guy was not a man to be trifled with. If Facundo were to cause any more problems for Champagne or for any reason to ever, ever show up at Guy's house again, Facundo would find out personally how Guy had earned his reputation.

Facundo scared like a jackrabbit; Guy knew Facundo wouldn't be showing up again.

"Just letting us stay at the house instead of staying at Arnie's is worth a thousand bucks." Dell chuckled. "Can you believe last time we were down here, Anastasia called Shyla a little idiot? Arnie didn't say a word. I swear he's getting just as nasty as she is. I just about hit the roof, but I kept my damn mouth shut, because Jackie gets so upset. I swear Arnie has some sort of spell on those girls, everyone except Marie that is. He's so manipulative, and still the girls jump whenever he snaps his finger. I heard you had it out with him last year."

"Yeah, unreal. So you know they were getting the house redone. I advised them on how to get amazing financing, and, when they moved out, they asked Marie to watch the dog. Well, you know their dog Gily has epilepsy. She needs medication. She still has seizures, and Marie was pregnant. Well, after six months, it became way too much. Marie was still running the day care. It was nerve-racking to see the dog have seizures, plus she would defecate and urinate all over. Marie was so stressed over it. I told her six months was more than generous. So Arnie comes over to the house to get the dog and tells Marie, "Thanks for the help." He then says he is going to take Gily home and kill her, then bury her in the backyard."

"Are you kidding me?" Dell looked at Guy incredulously.

"Seriously, I was about to completely lose it, but I kept totally cool and just told him he needed to leave. Then I called him and asked him to come down to my office. I was already pissed because Arnie had already made Marie cry a few months before, by just being a dick. Well, he shows up with Ana, so I made her wait in the lobby. I told him flat-out, no one treats my wife like that. I suggested he do some soul searching, because if he didn't change his behavior, his time with my family was going to extremely limited. All he said was OK. Did Jackie tell you what he did next?"

"Of course not. She won't say a word against him. It's eighteen by twenty four. You got a little over four hundred square feet here." Dell was still listening as he draped the tape measure around the concrete floor of the patio.

"He mailed Marie a letter, saying he was never going to speak to her again. If it wasn't so hurtful to Marie, I would have just laughed. How pathetic. Who does that? Could you ever imagine doing something like that to your kids?" A look of disgust covered Guy's face.

"I'd die for my kids. Are you kidding me? What an asshole." Dell shook his head. "So you really don't want any windows in here? It's not a big deal to put them in."

"Nope, don't want anybody to see into the ark." Guy chuckled.

"So how much food are you getting?" Dell picked up a hammer and knocked at one of the corner beams.

"A Tribulation's worth, seven years." From what Guy was able to ascertain from the Bible, the Tribulation was a seven-year period. It seemed like you would need food when it hit the fan three and a half years into it, but he would rather be safe than sorry.

"You're crazy. How much food is that?" Dell looked over at Guy in disbelief.

"Well, seven years for the three of us—I used one of the mormon food calculators online. Found a great place, Emergency Essentials at beprepared.com. Still making a list, but it looks to be about ten tons or so." Guy followed Dell around the patio as he poked, prodded and measured.

"Bro, you're seriously crazy." Dell grabbed his head.

"That's what everyone keeps telling me." Guy smirked.

"How much is that going to cost you?

"Looks like about ten grand a person, but you could do it cheaper than that. Found fifteen-hundred-gallon water tanks. Going to get four and put them over on the side. I have that three-hundred-galloner, but no way that's enough." Guy had enough money to pay for the ark. He would have to find a way to get enough money for more food. "Especially when there's no rain, so no way to grow food, no way to buy anything without turning yourself over to the beast. How do you think the Israelites became slaves? During the famine they had to sell everything for food. Then when they had nothing left, they sold themselves. There's a big storm coming. Aren't the mormons supposed to store food? Why don't you guys have any?"

"Nobody stores food anymore, bro. It's hard enough to pay the bills."

"People waste money on all sorts of stuff. You could do it slow and for way cheaper than ten grand. You should read what the Bible says for yourself. Taking someone else's word for it is dangerous. You know I was catholic, with all the sacraments so far, confirmation, marriage. But when I saw them covering up for all those pedophiles—you know they couldn't even say they were sorry? They just made excuses—I did what God put in my heart and left. They made us sign something saying we promised to raise the kids catholic, whatever. I repented of it. You know when we went to church with you to see Shyla get baptized, and they had other men baptize your daughter, and made you sit there and watch because they said you were unworthy. That was cruel. It really bothered me." Guy put his hand on his brother-in-law's shoulder.

"I know. I know. I'm in good standing now." Dell's head hung down.

"That's not the point. You need to find out what the Bible says for yourself. Do you realize that mormons aren't considered part of Christendom?" Guy asked pointedly.

"What are you talking about? We believe in Jesus." Dell shook his head.

"You say you believe in Jesus, but you believe things about Him and God that are contrary to what the Bible says."

"Like what?"

"Well, just so you know, I had the same problem as a catholic. I mean catholics believe the pope's word is infallible, the same as God's. Are you kidding me? Have you seen all the evil things the popes have done throughout the years? Any heinous thing you can possibly think of. Hello, Dark Ages. And the words from those men's mouths were supposedly the same as God speaking? You have to be kidding me. Selling indulgences, seriously paying money to get out of limbo into heaven. Where is that in the Bible? How about praying to Mary ten times before you pray to God once on the rosary? Praying to saints? Hello, idolatry. The need to confess your sins to a man? We have an intercessor. His name is Jesus Christ. I went to catechism classes for years. In catholic school, you would think we studied the Bible. No, we studied rituals. But God is faithful to those who seek Him in truth."

"OK." Dell shrugged his shoulders.

"Look, the Bible warns that, during the last days, all sorts of men would come professing the name of Jesus, but many are liars and false prophets. Did you know that mormons believe, when you die, you become a god and can create your own world—that you would be god there? That means that our God was just some man, who had his own god. Really, Dell? I am going to shoot you an email with some stuff to read. _http://beatimundocorde.wordpress.com/2009/01/03/mormonisms-lie-of-eternal-progression-and-the-adam-god-doctrine/_. Take a look. It's in your own Journal of Discourses. Read some of the things that joseph smith or brigham young said."

"Hmm. I never heard that before." Dell looked puzzled.

"Despite the outrage, the mormons baptize people in the names of the dead Jews from the Holocaust. We have to make a decision for Christ before we're dead. All that 'sealing' is just nonsense. It's through Christ alone that we're saved. When Marie and I first got married, we went over to the house after Arnie got back from Temple with Maybel. She was being used to baptize as a proxy for dead people, and I could tell someone was baptized in my name too. That's crazy. You know they sent mormon missionaries to our house for years after we got married. They would come over and invite Marie to singles parties. She called the bishop and told him that she was a Christian and that mormonism was a lie, but Arnie still sent them over. I finally dropped the hammer and made her tell her dad to get her off the list or I was going down there personally."

"I've never done that," Dell said with some irritation.

"Listen, I'm not trying to bust your balls. I'm just saying you need to find out for yourself. Why would you be part of something that you have no idea what they really believe? Especially if it were things you didn't really believe in. That's what happened to me. I know you all spend time reading *the book of mormon*. Do you know what it says at the very end of the Bible, at the end of the book of Revelation?"

"What?" Dell asked drily.

"If any man shall add unto these things, God shall add unto him the plagues that are written in this book." Guy would leave it at that.

"Listen, I believe what I believe." Dell's mind was walled off, for in fact he had no idea what he actually believed.

Guy knew what he believed, and he began to feel as if the darkness was closing in. It didn't matter who he spoke to, family or friend, he found himself on an island. It was more worrisome than frustrating. It seemed logical that he was off base, because he knew many godly men and many men of means, yet neither group shared his concern with the end of the world or the collapse of the economy. As he sought God's face, Guy's spirit groaned with confirmation. Guy felt called to fast for assurance and enlisted Scott and John from Pennyhill as well. They knew of Guy's concerns and agreed to fast alongside him for an answer. After thirty days of nothing but fruit juice, they heard nothing. Guy decided he would break his fast at Christmas dinner, after thirty-four days of fasting. The din of the drums become a roar. Guy was more convinced than ever.

Guy had already moved the thirty grand in his Four O One(k) to cash when the Dow hit fourteen thousand in October. Business was phenomenal, and, as Two Thousand Eight opened, it seemed he was going to have his biggest year ever at work. If the year continued at this pace, he was going to be able to get everything on his ark list. Unfortunately a big bonus wouldn't come until February next year.

He took Frank's words to heart and found a way to bet against the economy. He would use derivatives, more precisely *option puts*. With option puts you could bet on a stock going down sometime in the future. It was like shorting a stock, but with a hundred to one leverage. Boom or bust, as you could lose all of your money. It wasn't like Guy was rolling in it, with a new baby and Marie at home. He wouldn't have it any other way though. He used the extra thousand dollars he had at the end of February to buy November expiration option puts against Merrill Lynch, Wachovia and Bank of America.

Faith was talking up a storm, Guy was thankful she started walking the day she turned 9 months. She never even crawled. A day earlier and Guy would have been able to tell people how she started walking at eight months. Guy never heard of a baby walking by eight months. The doctors were flummoxed. Not only were there no repercussions for her seizures but she was advanced beyond her age. The joy she gave to her father's heart was of an indescribable nature.

The merry-go-round of life continued. Guy received a call from a friend of his uncle Bobby's. Bobby was dead from HIV. He had contracted it from a prostitute he had let live in the house, which was now escheated to the state. Guy was hurt that he was only called after the fact, but it had been his uncle's wish. So said his only friend, Delilah. Guy didn't have an opportunity to say good-bye, which seemed cruel and yet appropriate for his family. What saddened his heart equally was that all of his family's history was gone. All of his grandfather's war medals, every picture, everything. He was glad he had taken his grandmother's pearls and his grandfather's cuff links when he had last left New York.

His biological father, Jack, was even more irritated. He had known Delilah for over two decades. He couldn't believe she didn't call. But, after all, she was a heroin addict. Bob of course relayed specific funeral instructions to her. He wanted to be at the same cemetery as her father. Of course she had no money to pay for it. Guy coordinated it so he could help his father get a guarded pass for a few hours to attend the service. It cost Guy almost ten grand, which he had to put on his credit card. The one day trip back and forth from New York and the hour spent with his father left his head spinning. It needed to be done. Another sad chapter completed.

After much beratement Della had convinced Guy to hire an attorney to see if there was anything to come from the estate. Surprisingly about eighty thousand dollars from the sale of the house was being held, along with some old stock certificates. Guy was named executor and, after paying attorney fees, was able to put sixty grand in the bank. Quite a windfall. The attorney suggested he wait several months to see if there were any claims by creditors.

Amazingly that summer his father was released from prison after twenty-seven years inside. It was the day Guy had dreamed of since he was a child. He would finally have his father back, and, with his daughter being so young, she would never remember anything else. Guy waited at the gate, just like he had always envisioned. He got an agreement from the parole officer to have a night with his father before he was to report to the Veterans Administration as part of his parole. They stayed in a nice hotel and had an amazing dinner. The next day he took his father shopping for clothes and food. They went to meet his parole officer and then got Jack checked into the VA.

It was wild for Jack, like stepping into a scene from *The Jetsons*. No computers, no Internet, no cell phones before Jack went into prison. He had never used an ATM machine or automatic doors. Guy paid the bill for a cell phone for Jack so they could stay in touch. Guy advanced Jack five thousand dollars, against the money from Guy's grandparents' estate, but his father adamantly refused. Jack wanted no part of the money, for his own reasons. His plan was to go to the monastery for a year, after six months at the VA.

It wasn't long after Guy returned home that he was informed that Delilah had produced a will naming her sole beneficiary of Guy's grandparents' estate. The will was drawn up the week of Bobby's death, while he lay in a hospice. The nurse on duty said Bobby had not been lucent for some time, but the will was notarized by an attorney. The attorney Guy hired said Delilah's attorney looked like a drug addict himself. That his clothes were filthy and disgusting. But he worked for the county, and Guy would likely lose and rack up some serious trial expenses. They wanted the full eighty grand, but settled for the sixty that was left over after attorney expenses. Between the funeral, his father and the attorney, Guy figured he lost close to twenty grand on the transaction. He still only wished he had one picture of his grandparents.

As the summer progressed the presidential race unfolded. It was no turkey shoot on the Republican side. No shining stars, no clear front-runners. Guy hadn't paid much attention to the Democrats, as their love of moral filth turned his stomach. The Clintons were so loved, it seemed Hilary was a shoo-in. Super Tuesday seemed to say the same. But then Guy began to hear that some no-name first-term senator seemed to be giving her a run for her money. barack hussein obama was a name that evoked thoughts of the Iraqi dictator, or even osama bin laden, making him a tough sell. He was black, which Guy imagined would garner him some favor in certain corridors, but the Clintons were political royalty.

When Guy began to hear talk around the water cooler that barack obama was going to secure the Democratic nomination over Hilary Clinton, Guy was shocked. While banks were generally conservative, there was no short supply of liberals in California, let alone Los Angeles. Many people Guy spoke to had a real passion for obama; they were energized. Hating Bush was generally sufficient enough, and Guy figured the Republicans were going to lose this election anyway, but the energy that Guy started to notice was palpable and different.

He decided to pull up an obama speech on YouTube to find out what all the fuss was about. As the clip began to run, Guy could see instantly how magnetic the man was, unusually and irregularly magnetic. As the clip rolled, Guy began to feel overcome by dread, as if his very spirit were being pierced. Then a woman in the crowd fainted, and Guy felt as if he would vomit. He clicked on the next link, *https://www.youtube.com/watch?v=yhzkltz3ipi*, and saw a spate of people fainting at rallies. Guy could not believe the size of the crowds that were turning out, and then finally obama saying his catchphrase, "Yes, we can," over and over as the crowd chanted it back. *https://www.youtube.com/watch?v=HoFqV3qVMGA*. Guy was't sure how or why, but he knew in his spirit that this was the man of sin. The one the Bible warned us to keep an eye out for, the one who would wage war against the saints during the Tribulation.

Guy was sure that people would say he was a racist, that he didn't want a black man to be president. What rubbish. Yet a very clever move, which Guy was sure the race-baiters would use to their significant advantage. If there was a black man running for president who shared Guy's morals and convictions, Guy wouldn't have thought twice. It didn't take much effort to see that obama was for partial-birth abortions, where a doctor grabs the leg of a fully formed baby, who could live if delivered. The doctor pulls the baby almost all the way out of the mother's vagina with forceps, leaving only the head inside, and then jams a pair of scissors into the back of the baby's head, into its brain. What a filthy disgusting pig.

The stock market was beginning to lose steam, and, when the Republicans decided to nominate the most left-wing person in the party to run against the most left-wing person in the Democratic party, Guy knew the Republicans were sunk. His friends and family all held out hope; they still felt confident that John McCain could win. Besides the fact that it was laughable, Guy knew it was fate.

The month before the election, the softness in the stock market would be another big plus for obama. Guy had a lunch he could not get out of on the tenth, so he decided he would have his annual commemorative fast on Thursday, the day before. On the 9th, the stock market had its second largest point drop in history: six hundred seventy eight point 9 one points. It was Yom Kippur, the Jewish Day of Atonement.

322

That night as Guy fasted, he meditated on the day quietly. As he sat, his mind was filled with a vision of skinny white cows with black spots eating, or more like swallowing, plump healthy cows. He knew it was the story of Joseph and the dream he had interpreted for Pharaoh. Guy opened his Bible and turned to Genesis, chapter Forty One, to reread the story. The Pharaoh of Egypt was having two troubling dreams. One with seven skinny cows who would appear and devour seven fat cows, one with seven withered ears of corn that would replace seven succulent ears.

Joseph told Pharaoh that it was a warning. There would be seven years of great abundance, followed by seven years of famine. The Pharaoh needed to save up grain in the good years, so that he would be able to endure the bad. Joseph was freed from prison and made second-in-command of all of Egypt to coordinate the efforts. The famine was so bad that the Israelites sold themselves for food, a tale of warning that Guy relayed regularly. Joseph was in a position to save his family when they came to Egypt in their time of need.

As he read, Guy was overcome by the Holy Spirit, once again feeling inconsolable despair and shedding many tears. It was seven years to the day tomorrow, since he had written his letter of warning.

BOOK THREE: CHAPTER THREE

As the sun rose, Guy was slow to rise with it.

"Good morning. We're going to run some errands." Marie was as bright-eyed and bushy-tailed as usual.

Faith, who she held in her right arm, was grinning from ear to ear. Faith was always so happy, they were consistently stopped in the markets by people looking to ogle at their beautiful daughter.

"Morning, lish. *Ooh*, I'm glad it's Friday. Any plans tonight?" *Lish* was short for *delicious*. Guy knew there were no plans. As if they were not already homebodies, Faith had certainly sealed the deal.

Guy and Marie never left Faith alone with anyone. These days pedophilia was a national pastime. And always someone everyone knew and yet no one expected. Guy certainly trusted Mack and, in theoretically controlled circumstances, Della, but neither Marie nor Guy felt any sense of urgency to be separated from their daughter. They made the decision never to let her spend unsupervised time with Arnie or Ana. Besides their cruelty, they knew Arnie would try to sow mormon hogwash into her heart.

Marie's uncle Saul, Arnie's brother, and his family were ardent Christians. His wife homeschooled their kids. They had had extreme difficulty over the years with Arnie pushing nonsense on the kids. When Saul would confront Arnie with the truth from the Bible, Arnie would shut down. He wanted no part of it.

Saul's son joined the army when he was eighteen, caught up in the nation's patriotic fervor. He wanted to be a light for Christ in the army. Guy warned him against it. He was an innocent kid and had no idea what it was like to do battle against real spiritual principalities. Guy warned Adam that, if his armor was not worn tightly, he would be overcome. While in Afghanistan, Adam was hit in the knee by a homemade hand grenade. While not physically disastrous, the experience was spiritually deadly. When he returned, he was not the same kid. He was empty, blank, withdrawn. He was never able to hold a job again. He drank. He had lost his faith in God.

He did bring back some interesting intel about one of the prisons he was guarding. There were lots of nonmilitary folks coming and going. One of the standard interrogation techniques proved particularly effective. A bearded man was strapped to a chair in a room by himself and pumped full of psychotropic drugs. They would leave him to watch the children's TV series *Barney & Friends* for days on end. The screams were blood-curdling. Guy found the story peculiarly disturbing.

"Snuggle time." Marie smiled. "So the doctor has been really harassing me about her shots." Marie rolled her eyes.

Her boobs really filled out her shirt this morning; they were swollen with milk. Guy tried not to be distracted as he smiled and sat on the edge of the bed. "You stood firm, I'm sure. Did you do any more research?"

"Like I'm going to let anyone tell me what to do with my own child? Don't you remember how crazy I drove them with my birth plan?"

Marie had won the Wolfson award when she had graduated with her degree in child development. Guy was proud. He stopped going to King's College after his experience with T. D. Jakes. Jack Hayford, the man who had founded King's, seemed like a godly man to Guy. But he regularly stood on stage with Jakes and called him a powerful man of God. Guy knew that if the apostle Paul were on stage, the Holy Spirit in him would call out the false prophet and liar, not exalt him. Guy knew the Lord had heard his prayers when Max's church, the Burning Bush, had failed.

"My baby." Guy squeezed his daughter's cute soft thigh. He looked forward to snuggling them both, though it hadn't been that long since they were both snuggled up to him in bed.

"Mine." Marie smiled. "So I found a place where you can order the MMRE vaccine. No mercury, all separate doses. Kaiser said they didn't offer it, but I told them that, if they didn't special order it, we would not be vaccinating, and I'm doing it on my own schedule, not till at least two, blah, blah, blah. They acquiesced." Marie jutted out her hip and put her left palm up in the air. "I also ordered a new water distiller." She smiled.

"Awesome!" They became much more diligent as to what went into their bodies when Marie had gotten pregnant. Reading labels became particularly disturbing, and the filtered water just didn't seem to cut it. After they bought the distiller they knew why. What was left over was like bile. Literally some sort of gross poison, totally disgusting. "All right, my lovely wife and my darling daughter dear, have a nice day." He kissed Faith's soft little head.

Her black hair had fallen out and grew in a light brown. Her eyes looked like they would be hazel, like her daddy's.

He touched his wife's hair; it was so full. He kissed her on the lips as Faith grabbed a handful of his hair. "Hey, you silly girl."

Faith laughed hysterically. What a riot.

326

As the garage door closed, Guy turned on the TV, so he could run his music through the speakers. Guy loved to worship his God, especially when it was just for Him. Guy put on his Time Life Worship Together collection. As the music played, Guy began to sing; he was overjoyed, overcome, and he cried out to the Lord in song. He worshipped Him. He danced before the Lord vigorously, until he danced out of his clothes and collapsed covered in sweat, naked before his God. Guy lay prostrate on the floor, his arms above his head, as if he were diving flat upon the ground.

"Lord, I come before You, naked, a broken man, who desires to be healed, a blind man who desires to see, a man who hates lies and desires truth. What is it that You desire from me, Lord? What is it that You would have from me? I am a man whose ears are plugged with cotton, Lord. Don't You know I am a fool who hears not? Lord I know Your Word is true. It says that, if I seek Your face, You will show it. Have I not sought, though everyone mocks me? Lord, please speak loudly, clearly. For You know I am just a fool who cannot hear Your words.

"Lord, I beg of You, please seal Marie, Faith and I. Protect us from this great wickedness that comes, for how else shall we stand? Do you desire our bones to be ground into the dirt, for my daughter's brains to be dashed upon the ground by wicked men? Let it never be so. She is innocent, Lord. Have I not spoken Your Word into her heart, made it my only goal to guard it? Please, Lord, protect us. I will do whatever You desire. Have I not built the ark? Will You not provide provision? I turn my will over to You, Lord. Let Your will be done in me, I beg of You." The words came out powerfully, forcefully, despairingly, as the tears pooled onto the wood floor, around Guy's face.

His tears were matched that day by the stock brokers' fears around the office, sorely and solely concerned with their pocketbooks. The days were emotionally draining, and, as Guy returned home, he was glad to feel his wife's embrace.

"Hi, honey. How was your day? I made pasta and meatballs, whole wheat." She smirked.

Marie took great pride in the transition of Guy's diet. She loved to remind him that he only ate Wonder bread when they first met. How the time passed. She thought it was cute. She packed his lunch every day and regularly sent homemade baked goods to the office for Guy to distribute around the floor. It was the first of December, only two months into the crisis and the bank had already downsized the floor from one hundred people down to around seventy.

"Going to be a rough week. The market closed down six hundred eighty points. People are really starting to lose it. I could seriously see some people would jump out the window like they did during the Great Depression, if this keeps going." Guy undid his tie and put his jacket over the railing. He always put his jacket on when he came in from the garage, so he would look nice for his wife.

"Oh, no. I've been praying for everyone." She gave her husband another big hug. "You should have seen your daughter today. She was running all over the house, chasing the cats around, *cat, cat.*" Marie pointed her finger upstairs. "Totally worn out. She's down for the count." Marie unbuttoned Guy's shirt. "I brought you down a change of clothes, so you wouldn't wake her."

"Thanks. Everyone at the office is thinking we might be nationalized." Guy sat down at the table and loaded up the pasta with parmesan cheese. "Looks delicious. Thanks, lish." Marie was a good and unique wife. A wife from the days of old who enjoyed being a mother and did the little things that wives used to.

"You really think so?" Marie's face looked concerned.

"Who knows? Not like it really matters. With all the money they've shelled out, they've transferred the debt to the government and effectively taken control anyway. My dad has a friend at Wells Fargo. Seems after the banks were told they were all going to accept bailout money, Hank Paulson had called a meeting with the heads of the major banks. Wells Fargo's CEO Dick Kovacevich said he didn't need the money and got up to walk out. When he stood up, good ole Hank told Dick that, if he didn't sit down, shut up and take the money, Hank would make sure Wells Fargo was finished." Guy twirled his pasta around the spoon.

"Shut up!" Marie gasped and covered her mouth.

"Not really a surprise. Paulson made Congress agree to a one-page document for the biggest expenditure in the history of the world. He told them, if they didn't sign, there would be martial law the next day." Marie's meatballs made him think of his grandmother.

"Are you serious?" Marie sat down at the wood table across from her husband. She wanted to know what was going on, but, then again, she really didn't.

"I've been warning people. No one cares. Well, they seem to care now, at least about their bank accounts," Guy said casually. He was staying ahead of the curve. He had moved all of his clients out of money market funds a month before the Prime Reserve broke the buck. People were surprised that their bank accounts were not actually cash but converted to invested shares overnight and then back to cash. All of the brokers had clients with money frozen in Auction Rate Preferred Securities. They sold them as cash equivalents, but, come to find out, they were actually long-term bonds spliced up and sold off. The brokerage houses were rigging the auctions, and, when they stopped buying, the clients were left holding the bag.

"Do you think we'll be able to get the rest of the food?" Marie had acquiesced on the ark; she had hung a curtain over the sliding glass door to keep it from her daily sight, but it now seemed prudent to her.

"Well, good news and bad news. Good news is I got paid on that deal, and between that and the ten grand we made on the options, we should have enough to get everything on the list."

"Oh, praise God!" Marie was relieved.

"Bad news is that the three hundred thousand dollar bonus that I was getting in February is gone." Guy had done more business than he had ever done in the first six months of the year and was due to get his first real payout. It was going to be a lifestyle changer. Well, not really a lifestyle changer, but he had plans for that bonus. After the hundred and fifty thousand dollars he would pay in taxes, he was going to be able to put at least a hundred and twenty five thousand toward his mortgage, after bills. Guy also found out that one of the executives from a failed institution which J.D. had gobbled up was receiving a 9 million-dollar bonus for staying on, six million in cash. After he drove his own bank into the ground. Disgusting.

"What do you mean, *gone*?" The tone in Marie's voice dropped.

"Well, they said that everyone's business was so good because the crisis caused everyone to flock to good ole J.D., so they feel they shouldn't have to pay." Guy's business came in early that year, before anyone even realized there was a crisis. His blood was boiling all day, but the steam was pummeled out of him when he realized he was going to have to take it on the chin like a chump.

"It's in your compensation plan. That's got to be illegal. What about an attorney?" That bonus was going to be their first real cushion. It provided Marie with a lot of mental comfort.

"It's like Bill Wilson always says, the bank's the mafia. They just said they have the right to retroactively change the comp plan. We could probably win in court, but then I would be fired like everyone else. We would be totally screwed and blacklisted. The industry is melting down. Everyone's fighting for their jobs. The bank knows they have everyone over a barrel. No raises or trips next year either." Guy was angry and dejected.

"You're right. Let's just be thankful you have a job." Marie was dismayed.

"I know you don't really like to talk about this stuff, but, just so you know, the definition of the melding of corporate and government interests is called Fascism. They're seizing control. We have to get everything on these lists now." Guy went over to his briefcase and pulled out the printed pages. "I'm going to need your help with some of this. Will you please make sure you buy Faith two sets of clothes and a set of shoes, for every year until she turns seven?"

"OK."

Guy flipped through the lists:

Emergency Essentials from beprepared.com

Superpail: Hard Red Wheat (two); Honey, sixty lbs. (two); Hard White Wheat (twenty-five); Lentils (twenty-five); Soft White Wheat (five); Regular Rolled Oats (five); Pinto Beans (five); Quick Rolled Oats (five); Small Red Beans (five); Pearl Barley (five); ABC Soup Mix (two); Small White Beans (five); Split Green Peas (three); Oat Grouts (five); Case [six cans] Blueberries (two); Broccoli (forty); Strawberries (forty); Scrambled Eggs (fourteen); Whole Eggs (forty); Real Cheese (forty); Tomato Powder (forty); Apple Slices (forty); Enriched White Flour (forty); Diced Carrots (forty); Chopped Onions (twenty); Yellow Cornmeal (ten); Bananas, Sliced (forty); Shortening Powder (fourteen); Instant Oatmeal (fourteen); Potato Slices (forty); Buttermilk Pancake (seven); Buttermilk Biscuit (seven); Chocolate Fudge Brownie (two); Sweet Cornbread (seven); Diced Potatoes (forty); Creamy Wheat (seven); Whole Wheat Flour (ten); Baking Powder (seven); Six-Grain Pancake Mix (seven); Vegetarian Broth (three); Potato Flakes (twenty); 9-Grain Cereal (fourteen); Baking Soda (seven); Muffin Mix (fourteen); Minced Garlic (three); Apple Cinnamon Muffin Mix (seven); Chicken Gravy (seven); Chocolate Chip Muffin (seven); Black Pepper (three); Cornstarch (ten); Italian Seasoning (three); Peach Slices (twenty); Corn (twenty).

Foodservicedirect.com

Purell Hand Sanitizer (one case); Blackstrap Molasses (four gallons); Aluminum Foil (two); Canned Apricots (twelve cans); Sugar (five hundred sixty pounds); Peanut Butter (eighty-four jars); Yeast (one pound); Canned Vegetables (twenty-four cans); White Vinegar (twelve gallons); Trail Mix (eighteen pounds); Chocolate Mousse (seven and a half pounds); Bleach (9 gallons); Blackberry Jelly (twelve jars); Fruit Cocktail (twenty cans); Pasta (one hundred pounds); Baby Wipes (forty-eight); Olive Oil (six gallons); Corn Syrup (four gallons); Shortening (thirty-six pounds); Instant Milk (three hundred fifty pounds); Canned Oranges (twelve cans).

Working list:

Bike pump and tubes; Extra magazines (9mm and .five five six); Wagons; Roof tar; Gas masks (seven); Cheesecloth and wax; Batteries; Bleach, four drops per quart / there are four quarts per gallon; *The Alaskan Bootleggers Bible* by Leon W. Kania; *Home Cheese Making* by Ricki Carroll; *Cheese Making Made Easy* by Ricki and Robert Carroll; *Cooking with the Sun* by Beth and Dan Halacy; Plywood, four x eight; Bolt cutters; Crowbar; Police scanner; Thermometer; Imodium; Solar concentrator; Grain mill; Pasta maker; Toilet paper; Wet wipes; Wood nails; Door secures; Maps; Compass; Ham radio; Propane, Charcoal; Sand bags; Games; Condoms; Cards; Clothes and shoes for baby; Rubbing alcohol; Gauze; Hydrogen peroxide; Booze; Cigarettes; Gold; Dog food; Bird food; Toilets and decomp; Sunscreen; Animal trap; People traps; Seeds; Sprouting kit; Soil; Pots; Fertilizer; Foam stuff; Bondo; Candles; Fire extinguishers; Books; Feminine pads; Formula; Diaper cream; Tissues; Bug spray; Colloidal silver; Vitamins.

Matches; Trash cans; Garbage bags; Drywall; Butter and cheese; Bear spray; Scope; Rifles; Bacon; Cast iron pot; Salt; Night-vision goggles?; Bible games; Walkie-talkies; Tent; Oxygen absorption packets; Plastic sheeting; Tools, saws, ratchets, etc.; Silicon tube; Radiation detector, Nukalert; Extra rubber plugs for water tanks; Log splitter + sledge; Drywall tape + mud; Canned bacon; Brownies + cookies; Rubber bands; Jeans; Fill the tanks; Mylar; Duct tape; More chicken wire; Rabbits??; Decontamination kits; Fruit trees; Soap; No-rinse body wash; Fire starters; Green-power science parabolic cooking mirrors; Solar oven; Ziplock bags; Drums, fifty-gallon (eight), to store one ton of rice, medications, antibiotics.

"I think the lists are pretty darn comprehensive. The Mylar is for when the forth angel pours out his bowl and the sun scorches the Earth. We also have to get enough plastic sheeting to be able to seal the house per the Department of Homeland Security. There will likely be a nuclear strike at some point and after a few days, the radiation intensity decreases significantly. When everything implodes, there won't be food on the shelves for more than a few days. Food is how they will be able to control the country. That's how they will get everyone to agree to go to the camps willingly, for food. What people don't realize is, that instead of simply selling their bodies for food, like the Israelites, this time they will be selling their souls. Once you are there, it will be too late. The only way out will be to lay down your life as a martyr. The booze, cigarettes and gold are in case we need to bribe any cops when they go around and pull everyone from their houses who refuses to comply." Guy looked back up from the lists and finished his last meatball.

"All right. I'll make sure we get lots of diapers too. And, honey, please don't be mad. I can't talk about all that. It's too much." Marie's face looked pained.

"I understand. It is too much. Let's just focus on the shopping. I'm sorry too, but let's be thankful that God has given us eyes to see."

It had been especially hard for Marie since they had left Pennyhill, but she was a strong woman. After Guy's fast in October, his spirit felt compelled to warn the pastor. Guy had dreaded it, as it was the last thing he wanted to do. He knew what the response would be, but God was so faithful, how could Guy turn his back? The pastor was only five years older than Guy. He was cool, drank beer, played poker, smoked cigars.

When Guy had warned the Pennyhill pastor that he was leading his flock into the Tribulation unprepared, he was furious. Then he laughed in Guy's face. He scoffed. "So you're saying I'm causing the Tribulation."

Guy repeated that wasn't what he had said at all, simply that the pastor was leaving the flock unprepared for the coming trouble. He told Guy to keep his mouth shut or leave the church. Guy knew he would be forced to leave before the conversation started. Guy had had enough of church. Churches had become cages for foul birds, their leaders. Not a one would even teach on Revelation, nor warn the body of Christ, for the church leaders had not eyes to see. How great the falling away would be when the sheep all realized they had been sold a lie and delivered right into the hands of the evil one.

Guy ordered all of the food online that week and set time aside that weekend to pray and give thanks to God for providing the food for the ark. He was thankful that, for whatever reason, God had chosen Guy's family along with others, out of all those in the history of the world to stand for its culminating event. He prayed for guidance and felt led to the book of Ezekiel. When he began reading the fourth chapter, his spirit was again compelled, much to his chagrin. It seemed that when you asked to be used by God, it ended up being something other than what you expected. Guy cracked a smile.

"OK."

God's ways were far above Guy's own. He grabbed the black Sharpie marker out his dresser and a ten-pound iron plate from his weight set. He was glad Marie was out for the morning as he walked out the front door and around to the side yard. He opened the white vinyl fence. It held up much nicer than the old wooden one he had replaced. The side yard would be filled with nearly seven thousand gallons of water tanks by next week. He grabbed one of the red bricks that had been pulled up when they had filled in with some extra grass around the perimeter. Guy knelt down on the dirt closest to the wall separating his yard from the neighbors.

As he did, he was flooded by the Holy Spirit. It was not despair, nor joy like worship. This time it was vehement fury. Guy took out the black Sharpie and wrote JERUSALEM upon the red brick, then lay it before him on the moist mud. He built mud into a little ramp against the side of the brick, then he grabbed some twigs and stuck them into the ground, encircling the brick. Guy broke a few more twigs and stuck them into the ground at an angle, so one tip of the sticks touched against the side of the brick. He did it around all four sides.

Guy lay in the dirt upon his belly and stared at the encircled brick. He grabbed the iron plate and put it before his face, between him and the brick. He stared at the brick through the hole where the barbell went through.

"JERUSALEM, THOU ARE BESIEGED!" Guy roared and slammed the iron plate into the brick, cracking it in two down the center. As Guy went back into the house, he felt drained of his energy, and, while it was still morning, he thought he might need to take a nap. He was looking forward to taking off a few days for Christmas. The mood was better around the office in December. The government was throwing everything including the kitchen sink at the crisis. The Dow was more than a thousand points higher than its November lows.

The crisis brought Guy a new boss as well. An experienced commercial real estate lender, extremely bright. Management thought they had stolen him away from the commercial mortgage originations group. The market for syndicated nonrecourse deals had evaporated. The pension funds were crushed as the AA-quality mortgages they had purchased for their portfolios had turned out to be garbage. Guy heard around the grapevine that his boss had been actually moved to the side after some of the recent mergers, for being erratic. Everyone in the office said it was just because he was a deal guy. Guy could tell it was because of cocaine. The guy sent emails at all hours of the night, blew his nose like crazy and would excuse himself to go to the bathroom multiple times during client meetings. It was obvious to Guy; he had spent enough time with his aunt and cousin, who were always high. The signs were so blatant he was surprised no one else noticed, but the times were distracting. No one noticed but Bill Wilson, that is; he was uniquely perceptive.

Guy took a couple days off for Christmas; he made it a big deal. They got a big tree, and he spoiled his tiny daughter. Guy and Marie hadn't done much about presents between themselves for a while. Everything came from the same pot, and, if they wanted something, they made the decision together. Faith was old enough to enjoy toys almost as much as tearing though the wrapping paper. Guy enjoyed the time with his family, unplugged from the cacophony. It wasn't until he went back to the office on Monday the twenty-ninth that he realized war had broken out between Israel and the Palestinians.

Guy called his mother on his BlackBerry. "Hey, ma. What's going on?"

"Oh, nothing. Just sitting out on the patio, drinking some coffee, enjoying my unemployment. Cinderlou's on my lap. She was out all night. Now she's being all lovey-dovey. Oh, I love it here in Hollywood. You guys have to move out here."

Guy got up and closed the door to his office. He had a nice view of the city, but his eyes were fixed on the breaking news flashing across Fox News on his muted television. "Mom, you've told me that like ten times. Hollywood is seedy. They have horrible schools. I would never move down there. How many times do I need to say it? Plus you keep saying you're moving away to Florida anyway."

While Della made it an excited part of every conversation, it drove Guy crazy. He was irritated by her lack of listening skills and that she wanted to move to the other side of the country to live with her sister and molester of a brother rather than spend time with her granddaughter.

"Oh, they have these beautiful houses right down the street. She could go to private school."

"Mom those houses are like five million dollars. My property taxes would be like five thousand two hundred dollars a month. I take home six grand." Guy tried not to sound exasperated.

"So I talked to Prissy. Kayla is pregnant. She's only sixteen. Can you believe it? Her and Ray are getting all sorts of fallout from the church. But she spoke to Roxie, who sounded really good, but she's depressed because Paulie got arrested, and Ted is shacked up with some hot, new thing. Their divorce is finalized now, but she's sure it started before that."

"Yeah, I know about Paul. I spoke to Jerry. He said it was for heroin. Paul's been living in some dope house. He said his mom's not doing good either, that she's been smoking crack. Jerry's doing good at least, a maniac as always, but he's making good money working as a carpenter in the same union as Ted." Other than the fact it was Prissy's adopted daughter, Guy didn't even know who Kayla was. They had never met; they had never even had a phone conversation. He knew Faith would never be able to build a real relationship with Della if she moved away to Florida.

"No way Roxie is smoking crack. That's crazy. I talked to her last week. She told me how she was praying. She sounded great. Paul on the other hand is going to end up dead in the gutter, just like his father, if he doesn't get his act together," Della said assuredly.

"Mom, you're being naive. Have you heard from Jack? He never picks up the phone when I call, and I have to leave like five messages before he calls me back. He told me the phone is a hassle to take around. I told him to just put it in his pocket." It seemed Guy spoke to his biological father less now that he was out of prison.

"I spoke to him last week. He decided not to go to the monastery. He's got a little stipend from the VA, and he's working a street jewelry stand for some lady he met out in the city. He said to say hello, asked about the baby. She was so cute. What a little ham opening up all those presents. Did she wear that dress I got her? It will go so nice with that little china skin."

"Yep, she looked adorable. I took a couple pictures. I'll email them to you. Did you see the news?"

"Oh, Israel, I know. What a mess. They cut into *American Idol*, but it was a rerun. Great season this year." Della's voice was animated; she never missed an episode.

"Mom, this is serious. I've been warning you. You made enough money on that last trade to buy some food. I'm telling you, you need to get it now."

"I'm just not feeling it, Guy. What did your dad say?" She had watched the news. They said the stock market was stabilized, and the worst of it was behind them.

Thankfully Guy didn't need to get into any of the spiritual reasons with his dad. Mack believed in God and Christ but had always hated churches. He said they were filled with charlatans trying to bilk people out of their money. Turned out he was right in some respects, but the matter was more spiritually dangerous. While he would make no prognostications, Mack agreed that the financial system was on thin ice, and a collapse was a real possibility.

Guy had emailed his father the list and had told him the amount Guy thought was necessary in order for Mack to weather whatever storm might come. Mack agreed without delving further and ordered enough for Pearl and Herman as well. While they were twenty-six and twenty-four, respectively, they were both still on the dole, living at home rentfree. Mack paid their expenses as well. "I spoke to Dad this morning. He's placing his order today."

"Really? Well, that's his choice. I'll make mine." Della was annoyed.

"Mom, I'm telling you, spiritually you need to do this now. When the trap shuts, it is going to be sudden. It'll be too late to make provisions then."

"Guy, you're taking this a little too seriously. Lighten up. I'm going to go have lunch with my friend Candy today. He's over at Nordstrom's now. Isn't that where you get your white shirts? Make sure you say hi next time you're there."

"I will. Tell him I said hello. I've got some stuff to do at the office. I'll call you later. I love you."

"Love you too. Give that baby a squeeze for me."

Guy hung up the phone and felt sorry for his mom.

As the New Year turned, Guy's food arrived. John Brown and Guy's brother, Herman, were nice enough to help Guy load it into the ark. The whole thing was packed, floor to ceiling, with some rows for access. It was the first time in forever Guy had been able to get either John or Herman to acquiesce to some face time.

Guy prayed diligently for Israel as the offensive raged on, and he was drawn back to the book of Ezekiel once again. As he reread the fourth chapter, his spirit groaned.

> Lie thou also upon thy left side, and lay the iniquity of the house of Israel upon it: according to the number of the days that thou shalt lie upon it, thou shalt bear their iniquity.

So Guy took a blank piece of paper and wrote upon it in large black marker The Iniquity of the House of Israel. He folded it in half and put it under the mattress on his side of the bed.

He was tired the next day and parked himself in Bill's office to kill some time and talk shop. Marie joked that Bill was his mistress, since they talked so often, but it was generally business, about the market, strategies. Bill was dressed conservatively as always; he liked gray suits and plain ties. He had a bigger office than Guy, but Guy had the better view.

"So how'd you golf last week?" Guy slumped back in the chair around Bill's conference table.

"Damn good for a kid from the Valley. Almost got a hole-in-one on 11." Bill chuckled. He was tan and played the public courses, which was unheard of in the office. All the inner-circle guys had country club memberships, Bel-Air or L.A. Country Club. Some guys played a hundred days a year. Being that Guy was extremely competitive, he didn't play. He joked that he preferred staying married to his wife. It was in part a joke, because there was no way Guy would spend enough time away from his family to become a scratch golfer.

Plus it was damn expensive; some of the clubs cost two hundred and fifty thousand dollars just to join and required you spend a few grand a month at the club. Guy was certain there were a few people hired by management just because they were ringers. Their skill set certainly didn't include generating revenue. That was one of the things Guy did appreciate about his job. It didn't matter if you had a degree from Harvard. At the end of the day, it was the numbers that spoke. Guy found the guys with the Harvard degrees were generally no competition at all.

"So I was talking to Avi. He thinks we've gotten a floor under the market." Bill turned away from his workstation toward Guy.

"Avi's a broker. Ask him when he's getting his clients' money back from the ARPS or that fly-fishing fund." Guy smiled.

"Yeah, right, seriously!"

"You know what I do love about Avi? He told me the truth." Guy smiled.

"Well, I wouldn't go that far." Bill laughed sarcastically. "About what?"

"So I've asked about a hundred brokers during the crisis, when is the right time to get your money out of the market? Every single one of them answered the same. 'We're not market timers. If you miss out on the twelve best days of the year, you've missed the whole market. In the long term the market always wins.' Blah, blah, blah," Guy droned sarcastically. "But I ask Avi, and he flat-out says, never. The right time to take your money out is never. Sure you can move it from this bucket to that bucket, but suggesting moving out of the market means nobody's getting paid. I was like, thank goodness, some honesty for a change." Guy laughed heartily.

"Avi is classic. But I don't know. I still think we could be nationalized. It doesn't feel like anything's been fixed." Bill grimaced.

"We've already effectively been nationalized. The government is certainly consolidating power. My dad heard from some guys over at BofA that Hank Paulson threatened Ken Lewis and forced him to buy Merrill Lynch, even though it's worthless. One of my dad's buddies told him that Lewis refused, but Paulson threatened to have him fired and make sure BofA was gutted afterward if Lewis didn't. Of course Lewis said OK."

"No way. He'd have to disclose that to the shareholders. Otherwise it's illegal. He could be put in jail." Bill pursed his lips and threw his hands up in the air dramatically.

"My dad knows some of the senior guys over there. He said they were credible. Hey, and it's not like he threatened Congress with martial law if they didn't sign the bailout for his buddies or threatened Dick Kovacevich, right?" Guy laughed heartily

"Those are just are rumors, like the telephone game." Bill shook his head.

"Are you serious? Have you seen the video of Brad Sherman? I'll shoot you the link, watch it. _https://www.youtube.com/watch?v=ArEf2kc1OLc_. Mack is friends with one of Dick's personal friends, and he was specific. He said Dick told him firsthand that, when he was there with the other banking heads and refused to take the funds because Wells Fargo didn't need them. Paulson looked over to Bernanke and said, 'Your primary regulator is sitting right here. If you refuse to accept these funds, he will declare you capital deficient Monday morning.' It's true. I'm telling you." Guy was firm, direct.

"Shit, looks like we're heading into socialism."

"Socialism isn't a political system. It's a bridge. It leads to Fascism or Communism, and this certainly smells of Fascism, with corporate and government interests melding."

"All right, you're killing me. Let's go get a shoe shine." Bill walked toward his door, and Guy followed.

★★★

Guy thanked God for His mercy, when Egypt brokered a peace deal between Israel and the Palestinians. As the first quarter of Two Thousand 9 came to a close, it appeared the country had weathered the worst economic storm since the Great Depression. The Dow was off its March 9 low of sixty five forty seven and trading back above eight thousand in April. The disaster was diverted, so it seemed to everyone, everyone except for Guy. He felt as if they were being led into a trap.

Guy prayed for guidance and direction; he asked the Lord for understanding. He prayed that he might be given discernment and eyes to see the plans of the wicked. Guy felt compelled to do some research. He took out his MacBook Pro and pulled up YouTube. He entered "government satan" in the search field and clicked Enter. Guy looked through the search results, and clicked on one that caught his eye: _http://www.youtube.com/watch?v=wtSVBTne-KY_. Some no-name in a suit, Alex Jones, began speaking. As Guy listened, it sounded like conspiracy nonsense. The clip was 9 minutes long, and generally Guy would have simply closed the video, but he felt compelled to keep watching. The man was talking about some New World Order. He claimed the world's elite were actually luciferians who worshipped satan, presidents on both sides of the aisle, past heads of the Federal Reserve. It sounded like nonsense. How could something like that possibly be kept a secret?

When the video was about two-thirds over, the footage changed. This man Alex Jones had snuck into someplace called the Bohemian Grove in northern California. As the video began, Guy started to sweat profusely. He felt cold, as if he were going to vomit. Demonic shrieking filled the background, and Guy immediately recognized the men in the video were reenacting an ancient amorite and canaanite ritual, one of the vilest, most despicable acts from the Bible.

The amorites lived just east of Israel in modern-day jordan. They worshipped the demon molech and would burn their babies alive in fires before his statue, as it was spoken of in First Kings, chapter 11, plus Leviticus and Jeremiah. It was the pattern of Israel to go whoring after the false gods of the pagans; nothing kindled God's wrath as greatly. He would punish the Israelites fiercely, having them slaughtered by enemy armies until they repented and turned back to Him. As they sought His face, He would bring them back to a place of glory and honor. When they came to believe they were great of their own accord, the cycle would begin anew.

It was public knowledge that the world's leaders and titans of industry had been attending the annual Bohemian Grove meeting for decades. Once Alex had shot his secret video, the industry powers could no longer deny what they were doing there. They simply kept their mouths shut. It was revealed into Guy's spirit that the things this man Alex Jones spoke of were true. The rulers of the world were taking counsel against the Lord and against His anointed, saying, *let us break their bands asunder.* Guy read that Alex Jones had snuck into the Bohemian Grove on July Fifteenth of Two Thousand, of his own accord. He was a man of fierce courage. Just a few months later God had spoken to Guy, warning him of what was to come. Clearly the Holy Spirit moved and guided Alex. God opened Guy's eyes, and, from that moment on, he was able to clearly see the physical world, as he had seen the spiritual.

Guy searched the Internet for "george bush New World Order." *http://www.youtube.com/watch?v=byxeOG_pZ1o*. He saw george bush sr., giving what would have previously seemed like an innocuous speech, calling for the ushering in of a New World Order before the united nations. But Guy could now see that it was a public pronouncement, a ringing of the bell, an ushering in of their dastardly plan. The bell was rung on September 11, Nineteen Ninety, the day of bush's speech. The bell was rung again loudly 11 years to the day later as at the planes crashed into the twin towers. Guy heard the fringe of society claiming 9/11 was an inside job. He thought it foolishness. He had never even researched the subject. He had simply dismissed it out of hand. Guy fell on his face, wept, repenting before his God. How he had called evil *good*. Guy realized he had been deceived, and his blood began to boil.

He had voted for george bush jr. twice and thought he was a good president, a good man, a Christian man who defended the country and kept it safe for eight years. Sure the left hated him, but it was because of their own ideology, not because he was actually a luciferian, a satan-worshipping piece of trash. Guy didn't need any proof. He knew in his spirit 9/11 was an inside job. He searched the Internet for "9/11 Truth" and watched a group of architects and engineers rip holes in the official story. *http://www.youtube.com/watch?v=YW6mJOqRDI4*. Guy heard there was controversy regarding building seven, but he had no knowledge why. He watched *http://www.youtube.com/watch?v=iEuJimaumW4* and *911: In Plane Site* on Netflix, which only further confirmed what he already knew. Unfortunately there was an abundance of such information, but no coverage. Guy could see the spiritual principle behind 9/11 now. Once a people agreed to believe a lie so large, it became nearly impossible for them to see truth. The attack on 9/11 was a veil, a screen that allowed lies to come through, perceived as truth.

The American people, like Guy, were played like a fiddle, choosing republican or democrat, as it appealed to them, believing that they had a choice. That if only their party's agenda were successful, all would be well in the world. But all would not be well in the world, because the filthy scum were simply liars, working in collusion to bring about the kingdom of their lord, the snake of old, lucifer, satan. These men and women were practiced and accomplished liars.

The democrats' wickedness was easy for Guy to see through, for they were the party of murdering babies and sexual immorality, constantly pushing the country into further moral debasement. But the republicans spoke to Guy's sense of morality, pretending to be a bulwark, all the while dancing the American public down the wrong road. Guy saw now that they were the party of patriotic death, murder in the name of comfort and freedom, all the while aligning the cards to further their nefarious agenda. Not all of them, just those who mattered. Guy wept bitterly as he thought of the babies, the women and children his country had blown to bits, while he had cheered the whole time. He was so disgusted and angry, so angry, but he thanked God for giving him the opportunity to repent.

God showed Guy many more things that night and over the coming weeks: how these luciferians operated, who they were. That, at the top, the democrats and republicans were both moving the country down the same path. As Guy's eyes opened, the news was filled with stories pointing the world's view to the man of sin. What Guy knew in his spirit, the Lord confirmed with mountains and mountains of evidence. Guy found that things sown into his spirit were often confirmed in the physical world by Alex Jones. Guy was relieved to find a man who spoke truth about the physical world. *Infowars.com*, it seemed, was the only place giving the real story. Guy bought a membership and watched all of his movies at *http://prisonplanet.tv*. While they were enlightening, *The Order of Death*, *https://www.youtube.com/watch?v=VhlRIH9iPD4*, was so compelling, he was certain it would wake everyone from their slumber. People would finally prepare for what was coming.

As summer unfolded, the country marveled at their men of unparalleled genius. Men who were wise enough to break the laws and economic principles that had bound empires since their dawn. The magicians conjured money from thin air. The fools of fallen empires had simply called it *money printing*. Our wise sages knew better and designated it *quantitative easing*. When that failed, a new name was set in its place, and all was well.

★★★

The evening was balmy. It was just after six p.m., and the temperature gauge in Guy's car read ninety-eight. The valleys of Los Angeles kept the heat trapped within their basins like a hot apple pie. His mother's and sister's cars were parked along the curb; he had forgotten that Marie had invited them over to dinner. Guy pushed the built-in garage door button and pulled into their two-car garage alongside his wife's Lexus RX. Guy was thankful the office allowed for business casual attire during the hot summer months, though one still tried to move from air-conditioning to air-conditioning.

Marie served spaghetti and meatballs, whole wheat pasta of course. One of his favorites, but his enjoyment was clearly surpassed by Faith who ate two whole meatballs and a full bowl of pasta. She could do it, "all by herself," which was evidenced by her sauce-covered face. She even had it on the back of her little head. The vigorous effort sent Faith into a food coma, and Marie took her up to their bed.

"That baby just lights up the room. Whenever you see her, you can't help but smile. I'm light for days after." Della beamed as she sat around the kitchen table.

"She's the best." Guy smiled; it was true. He wished his mother and sister spent more time with her; it would be profitable for their hearts. "You should have seen her last month when we went down to SeaWorld. We decided to take a tour of the hotel when we got there. She sees the pool and starts to get all excited, so I say to her, 'You want to go swimming?' She looks at me and says, 'Daddy, are you kidding me or what?' Marie and I almost died." Guy's expression softened as he thought of his darling daughter dear.

"No way!" Pearl smirked.

"Seriously. She had never been swimming before, but we brought her a bathing suit just in case. So I take her out to the pool, and Marie goes to work out in the little exercise room across the pool deck. Marie comes out to check on us, and Faith is standing on the edge of the pool. She jumped right in. Marie just about had a heart attack, but I yelled over that it was like her twentieth time in a row. She had made friends with this little girl, who was about seven or eight, and, as soon as the older girl had jumped off the side, Faith was like 'I can do that.' So cute! We did a special tour at SeaWorld. She got to feed the dolphins," Guy reflected, then the smile left his face.

"Aw." Pearl scrunched up her face.

"She's such a little ham." Della chuckled.

"All right, I know you guys think I'm crazy, but I want you to watch this." Guy pulled out his laptop and clicked on the video he had already queued up: _https://www.youtube.com/watch?v=VhlRIH9iPD4_, _The Order of Death_ by Alex Jones. It started off strong with the disturbing image of the world's filth performing the Cremation of Care ceremony at Bohemian Grove.

"Oh, come on. Are you serious?" Della rolled her eyes with gall.

"I'm dead serious," Guy said with the dead seriousness in his eyes.

"I don't want to watch this. Come on, enough already." Pearl huffed and crossed her arms.

"It's only forty minutes. You waste more than that on _American Idol_ every week. Just watch." Guy stepped back so as not to hover.

"Speaking of which, when are you guys going to get cable?" Della asked again for the tenth time.

"You guys don't have cable? That's why you're watching this nonsense. Are you kidding me?" Pearl looked perplexed.

"Like I said, we don't have cable. We're not getting cable. It allows us to control what and how much we watch. With cable you just watch hours and hours of nothing. It just pumps garbage into the house. We rent movies. We have a few shows that are appropriate for Faith. Using Apple TV totally allows us to control viewing."

"Time Warner is giving three months free plus free installation all summer," Della said casually and directly.

"Just watch the video." Aside from Mack, talking with his family was generally exasperating.

Alex exposed the New World Order, or the illuminati, as they liked to call themselves. They followed satan, lucifer, the one they considered to be the light giver, the illuminated one. Alex showed how the illuminati had infiltrated the highest levels of society, the seats of power. While the followers worked in the darkness, much of their symbolism was right out in the open. They operated through secret societies. Alex showed how their black spirituality came right from the ancient days of the egyptians and babylonians.

"Oh, come on. Do you really believe this nonsense?" Della was dismissive.

"What do you mean, do I believe it? Did you not see the video of them reenacting a child sacrifice to molech? Those are our presidents. Are you kidding me? Have you ever even heard of this?" Guy was befuddled, the evidence was incontrovertible.

"I'm sure it's not a real baby or anything. It's just some stupid men's club and rich guys getting drunk out in the woods, blowing off steam." Pearl was self-righteous and sure of her analysis.

"Wow, you have got to be kidding me. president bush and his father say they're both Christians."

"I think the president's a good man. He protected the country. We haven't had another attack in eight years." Della had been a democrat her whole life. She had voted for gore the first go-around. She regretted it when she became a Christian and voted for bush his second term.

"I know, Mom. I thought he was a good man too, but we were fooled. He's not. He's a liar. He and his whole damned family worship satan. You guys say you're Christians, but would you ever consider putting on black robes and pretending to burn a baby alive in front of a statue of molech? Doing the same damn things the ancient amorites and canaanites did that made God so angry He wanted Joshua to slaughter every last one of them? They were so evil, God even commanded their babies to be killed. Can you comprehend that?"

"That's just disgusting." Pearl sneered.

"The commandment of the Lord is pure. The judgments of the Lord are true and righteous altogether. bush and his illuminati buddies were the ones killing innocent babies on 9/11. All the while he sat there reading a children's book to little kids. That's disgusting." Guy was repulsed and more concerned than irritated at Della's and Pearl's refusal to open their eyes.

"All right, that's enough already. I've got to get on the road anyway, before it gets late." Della stood from the table.

"I'm warning you. These guys are laying a trap for us. Wake up." Guy was firm and direct without raising his voice.

"Give it a rest. Do you mind if I pick some roses? They look really great this year." Della loved to pick roses from Guy's bountiful garden; they always filled her house with the most delicious fragrance.

"Of course, go ahead. All right, drive carefully. I love you." Guy gave his mother a squeeze.

"I love you too. Give that baby a kiss for me. Tell Marie I said bye."

"I love you too." Pearl pursed her lips and gave her brother a peck on the cheek and a big hug.

After they left, Guy was disappointed. He took a moment to ask God to open their hearts and to thank Him for Alex Jones's courage. As he did, Guy could feel that something big was coming. The devil worshippers had installed their *Manchurian Candidate*, barak obama, the antichrist. Guy knew in his spirit that the devil worshippers were working full throttle to align the stage for their War of Armageddon. Guy felt it would certainly involve iran and Israel, as well as china and russia, then famine and death would follow.

There was only one man with a voice who even seemed to be concerned about their plans. Guy decided to send Alex an email warning him, letting him know that they were preparing a war with iran and Israel, that soon enough the second seal would be opened. Guy thought it best to use a dummy email address. And so he set up a Gmail account, thefoolwhohearsandspeaks, and sent off an email before bed.

The next morning's commute was deemed "summer-light traffic." It was pretty sad when an hour-long trek on the Five to downtown was considered *light*. Guy didn't mind the hour; he joked that it was the only time in his life he had to himself. He used the time to worship and to listen to Hardcore History or Infowars podcasts. He could deal with an hour; when traffic pushed his commute to an hour and fifteen or an hour and twenty, things seemed rough. That extra fifteen or twenty minutes each way made the ride unbearable, a crawl. If traffic hadn't been *light*, Guy might not have noticed the black Crown Victoria driving a few cars behind him shortly after he got on the Five at Valencia Boulevard.

There were a lot of cars taking the long commute down the Five, so it was nothing unusual. Except when Guy made multiple lane changes, the black Crown Vic did the same, all the while staying three of four cars behind. Guy began to find it troubling, and so he darted over quickly to the far right lane and slowed to nearly forty. The Crown Vic was caught off guard, but quickly changed lanes and slowed to the second lane from the right aside Guy's car. Guy looked out his window and into the eyes of a white man with brown hair and a bushy mustache, who was looking over directly at Guy. He was wearing a collared white shirt and tie. When Guy refused to break his stare, the other driver slowed further and dropped directly behind Guy. Guy felt his heart quicken. He finished the commute to work at the posted speed limit—the Crown Vic behind him the whole while.

When Guy exited downtown from the One Ten, the Crown Vic followed through multiple winding ramps, all offering multiple routes. The mustached man broke off and continued as Guy turned into his building. Clearly they were monitoring Alex Jones's emails. Guy was filled with apprehension and struck with the urgency of the hour. He knew talking with Bill would cool his nerves.

Guy went up the elevator and down the hall to his office. Bill, as usual, was in early and lollygagging in the hallway.

"Hey, come in here." Guy unlocked his office and sat down at his desk.

Bill followed in and sat comfortably on the couch.

"Somebody followed me to the office this morning," Guy said gravely.

"Well, you were probably driving like a *dick*." Bill extended his arms out along the back of the couch, making sure to emphasize the last word.

"I'm being serious. A black Crown Vic, all the way from Santa Clarita, until I turned into the office," Guy said again gravely.

"And?" Bill was nonchalant.

"And I was followed to work today." Guy was certain he was being clear, despite Bill's lack of concern.

"Really?" Bill was sarcastic. "Like you're not on the list, with everything that you look at, everything you're saying?" Bill continued with an acerbic tone.

Guy rolled his eyes and found the humor. "You're proving my point exactly."

"Well, if you don't want unmarked cars following you around, don't rock the boat." Bill was no-nonsense. He wasn't a Christian and didn't share Guy's perspective, but Bill also wasn't naive and understood the world wasn't all it appeared on the surface.

"Am I somebody who shuts up? Like I really care what people think at this point. Yeah, I'm really gonna to stop telling the truth because

345

some piece of refuse follows me to the office." It made Guy so hot he could feel his face get red.

"Well, there you go," Bill said matter-of-factly.

"Exactly." Guy was irritated, irritated at the whole damn thing.

"I'm just saying, don't be surprised." Bill lingered on his words, drawing them out.

"I think there's going to be enough surprises for everyone." Now Guy's voice captured a hint of sarcasm.

"Well, I'm sure they were just there to protect you." Bill's smirk grew.

"Just like the federal reserve is here to protect the monetary system right?" They both laughed heartily. "Did you know the federal reserve is actually privately owned?" Guy clicked on his computer. It was always great to have fifty new emails from the time you left in the evening until you arrived the next morning.

Guy had stopped using his BlackBerry altogether; it was cutting into his family time, and, as much as the bank would like to think so, they certainly didn't own him. He was due for a new model phone, and, due to policy changes with all the mergers, the bank had asked him to sign an agreement legally giving the bank ownership of his cell phone number. Seriously? The number he had had forever that his wife and family called him on? The bank had lost it's collective mind. Another ploy to take control of Guy and his clients. When he went into AT&T, to transfer his number to a different device, he was told that good ole J.D. owned the number. Guy went ballistic, and, after an hour of admonition on the phone, the bank acquiesced.

"What are you talking about? federal reserve? Federal—hello, McFly." Bill chuckled.

"*Hello McFly* exactly. The federal reserve is privately owned. Time to open your eyes, Bill," Guy said with a smirk. "Take a look for yourself." Guy shot off a link from his iPhone, *http://www.globalresearch.ca/the-federal-reserve-is-a-private-financial-institution/8518*. Per *Lewis v. United States*, the federal reserve banks are not federal instrumentalities for purposes of a Federal Tort Claims Act, but are independent, privately owned and locally controlled corporations. Go on. Take a read."

"Come on. Are you serious?" Bill's tone changed.

"Aren't I always?" This time Guy chuckled.

That was unfortunately or fortunately true, Bill thought. "I've been in banking for over twenty years. How have I never heard that?"

It seemed peculiar. Bill was having a hard time wrapping his mind around it.

"So who owns it?" Bill said incredulously, sitting forward on the edge of the couch now.

"Beats me. It's not like the owners even allow congress to see their books. They make agreements with foreign institutions, and yet congress isn't even allowed to see them. Ron Paul's been at it for thirty years. Nobody cares. See *http://www.ronpaul.com/misc/congress/legislation/111th-congress-200910/audit-the-federal-reserve-hr-1207/*. Ask around the office. We are at one of the world's elite banking institutions, and no one here even has a clue."

"Ah, that's kinda scary." Bill was being serious. "You know what, it probably has to do with is those thirteen families who run the world." Bill had long heard rumors around the fringes, all about how an elite group of families were pulling strings from behind the scenes.

"Hmm, haven't gotten that far yet, but I'll take a look. The number thirteen is certainly associated with the occult and satanism. We should be proud of our alma mater, maybe hang some banners."

"Why's that?" Bill was intrigued now.

"Who do you think created the federal reserve? Good ole j. p. morgan and his buddies? You should read *The Creature from Jekyll Island*. It's a good breakdown."

"Give me the Guy Finnigan CliffsNotes version." Bill could see this was important information, not just BS.

"So in Nineteen O Seven, j. p. morgan spread rumors about insolvent banks. It started a panic, a run on the banks." Guy ordered his thoughts. He wanted to be direct and clear.

"As a banker, why would he want to do that?" Bill thought it seemed strange.

"Bill, the same thing all these guys are about. Power and control, buying assets on the cheap. Just like the rothchilds did when they said the Duke of Wellington had lost at Waterloo to Napoleon. The financial market plummeted, and they bought everything up for pennies on the dollar."

"Ouch. They must be one of the thirteen families. You can count on that."

"I'm going to look in to it." As always Guy liked to do his own research.

"I have no doubt. *Hello, list.*"

That was the sort of humor that made Guy laugh these days. "So good ole j.p. and his buddies have a secret meeting on Jekyll Island in Nineteen Ten. They all went under aliases, including senator nelson aldrich, the chairman of the national monetary commission. The assistant secretary of the treasury was there too. Together, in secret, the heads of the banks and their cronies in the government created the federal reserve act, out of a panic that they freakin' caused." Guy spoke passionately. He enjoyed shining a light on the scum.

"Come on?" Now we were getting into the nonsense of conspiracies, Bill thought.

"Well, it's not like it's in Wikipedia or anything. Look at _http://en.wikipedia.org/wiki/Jekyll_Island_Club#Role_in_the_history_of_the_federal_reserve_. But of course they make it seem normal, not nefarious at all. The federal reserve, a private organization that controls our country's money supply, but isn't accountable to any representatives, was created by the banking heads and their purchased politicians in a secret meeting where they were so worried about anyone finding out that they used aliases, really?"

"Well, when you put it like that . . . Wow."

"So they pass the bill two days before christmas Nineteen Thirteen, when everyone is already gone for the holiday. Nice timing." Guy knew it seemed crazy, but he had done the research. It was all true.

"So where is all the fuss then?" If this were all true, Bill was sure someone would have made a stink.

Guy pulled out his phone. Bookmarks were great for these sorts of things. It amazed Guy how much power was packed into one of these little phones. Too bad most people just used it for drivel like porn and Facebook. People traded real connection and conversation for posting a few comments on a page. That was how people had friendships now; people felt proud of their thousands of so-called friends. Guy felt no connection to such things; they felt hollow to him. It was a pretty amazing change to life though—no more arguing over little details, like what year the Battle of Waterloo was, or is cheesecake a pie or a cake? Just pull out your phone and get the answer in five seconds.

"OK, well, here's what president wilson said after he signed the act into law." Guy read aloud, "'_I am a most unhappy man. I have unwittingly ruined my country. A great industrial nation is controlled by its system of credit. Our system of credit is concentrated. The growth of the nation, therefore, and all our activities are in the hands of a few men. We have come to be one of the worst ruled, one of the most completely controlled and dominated governments in the civilized world. No longer a government by free opinion, no longer a government by conviction and the vote of the majority, but a government by the opinion and duress of a small group of dominant men._'"

"OK, well, that's not good." Bill's outstretched fingers exuded concern.

"Well, just like mayer rothschild said, 'Give me control of a nation's money and I care not who makes its laws.' It seems like it didn't take long for us to forget the warnings of our Founding Fathers, men like Thomas Jefferson." Guy read again, "'*If the American people ever allow private banks to control the issue of their currency, first by inflation, then by deflation, the banks and corporations that will grow up around it will deprive the people of all property, until their children wake up homeless on the continent their fathers conquered. The issuing power should be taken from the banks and restored to the people, to whom it properly belongs.*' Going on he says, '*I sincerely believe that banking establishments are more dangerous than standing armies, and that the principle of spending money to be paid by posterity under the name of funding is but swindling futurity on a large scale.*'"

"I'd say that's about what we've done. *Ugh.*" Bill's groan was guttural and pleasing to Guy, because it was appropriate.

"Ever since then, they have been inflating away. First roosevelt seizes everyone's gold during the Great Depression and pays them twenty dollars sixty seven cents an ounce. Then once he has it all, he says it's worth thirty-five dollars an ounce. Well, since the dollar was backed by gold then, the government magically had more dollars, and so the printing began. With no restraint, we kept spending away, until we finally broke the buck in Vietnam. The French were certain we were printing the money we needed to fund the war. We promised we weren't. Well, they called our bluff and asked to redeem their dollars in gold. That's when Nixon said, screw off, we are officially off the gold standard. Since then we have been printing steadily. This last bout has been exponential."

"OK, I get it. We're screwed. So, what now?" Bill found the information not only intriguing but informative.

"Well, you know what got us out of the depression."

"A world war. Yeah, that seems about right." Conversations with Guy were less and less light, but the damn thing was, he wasn't wrong.

"World War —the war to end all wars. It doesn't take Einstein to know this is a game changer. That's what I'm saying. We've actually been in a depression since the fall of Two Thousand Eight. We've just been trying to print our way out of it. Yeah, solve a debt problem with more debt. As if that will work. Just like treasury secretary Henry Morgenthau said in Nineteen Thirty 9, '*We are spending more than we have ever spent before, and it does not work. . . . We have never made good on our promises. . . . I say after eight years of this administration, we have just as much unemployment as when we started. . . . And an enormous debt to boot.*' Sound familiar? Morgenthau was not just some shlep either. He was Roosevelt's closest advisor."

"OK, you're on the government's list for sure." While he said it again jokingly, this time Bill wasn't kidding.

"And just to make sure you are getting it, take a look at your paper money. *Annuit Coeptis Novus ordo seclorum*, which means to approve a new commencement, an undertaking, a new order for the ages. And that illuminated eye above is certainly the all-seeing eye of lucifer. While it is actually the reverse side of the seal of the United States, it was never used until it was put on the money by whom?" Guy asked.

"I'm sure you are going to tell me roosevelt," Bill said drearily. "OK, now I'm not going to be able to sleep. Thanks."

"What? You'd rather stay asleep and believe lies from these filthy pieces of trash?" Guy was not a man who enjoyed believing lies.

"You know most people like *The Matrix,* right Neo?" Bill smiled

BOOK THREE: CHAPTER FOUR

The fact that Bill had heard some of what Guy had said did smooth over Guy's concern about being followed to work. Talking with Bill provided some peace of mind. Sharing today's events with Guy's wife would only cause Marie to be frightened. Guy so despised these wicked men and women, and their plans for a New World Order. They were such practiced liars that the foul stench of their words polluted the minds of men. Their filthy deeds were done as by a master craftsman, creating a cage the world didn't even know existed. Until they pulled the trigger, until the eyes of the world were blasted open—but then it would be too late. The government's storm troopers, their militarized police force would do their job, placing the American people in their pens, where they would receive their mark or have their brains oozed from their heads. All the while posing as the saviors for the tragedy they had designed. Those who would give up essential liberty, to purchase a little temporary safety, deserve neither liberty nor safety. America was about to get what it deserved, for the citizens followed not the wise instruction of their forefathers. Resistance to tyranny is obedience to God.

As he got off the freeway, Guy saw a sign for the house of j p. morgan in the distance. He was overcome by wrath and pulled into a nearly empty parking lot. He found a space where he could clearly see the signage of the branch and spoke God's word.

"YOU THINK YOU SHALL STAND AGAINST THE LORD. YOU SHALL NOT STAND AGAINST THE LORD, FILTH. YOU WHO BUILD YOURSELF A HOUSE FOR THE AGES, YOUR HOUSE IS TORN DOWN! IT SHALL NOT STAND! THE HOUSE OF THE LORD GOD ALONE STANDS FOREVER!" Guy's voice was guttural; it seemed to overpower even himself. To another it would have sounded like boiling oil poured into the ear. Guy outstretched his hands toward their filthy sign. He felt drained afterward; he was glad it was a meatball-and-spaghetti night again.

Guy pulled into the garage and stepped out on the driveway to stop and smell the roses; they were in full bloom. The Bella'roma was covered with buds and fully open flowers—pink on the outside petals and tips, yellow on the inside. Guy could smell its fragrance from across the flower bed; it was more delightful than any expensive perfume; he inhaled deeply and looked up to the expansive blue sky. As he did, he could see what looked like little pinpricks of light, literally no bigger than the tip of a pin, in the uppermost regions of the sky. They were moving to and fro quickly. Guy squinted his eyes, concentrating on the little white pricks of light. Then he noticed little black dots, the same size, interspersed throughout and all swarming together. There seemed to be twice as many light dots as dark. A strange day, indeed, this was turning out to be.

Guy needed the snuggle time with his wife and babe before bed; it warmed his heart. As the family closed their eyes for sleep, Guy felt called to spend some time in prayer with his God. He went to the back bedroom where it was quiet. He lay in his boxers on the original white oak floor upon his belly, his hands outstretched in an act of obeisance.

"Lord Jesus, what is it that You desire of me? Can't You see that I am a fool, a man who asks to hear, but hears not? I beg of You, Lord, to speak loudly, to show me clearly, for I am a blind man who wanders in the darkness. A man, a man mired in the filth, who cries out to You. Do You not see how they follow me, how they hate You, how they make plans against You? Have I not laid myself bare before You, Lord, in all my shame? I've tried to do what You have asked of me, no matter how foolish in my eyes, Lord. They laugh at me for the things I say, but I care not, for it is You they laugh at, Lord. You who have become a fairy tale. THEY MURDER BABIES AND CALL IT GOOD. HOW LONG WILL YOU LET IT STAND, LORD? IS YOUR NAME NOT HOLY? IS YOUR WORD NOT TRUE? IS THEIR CUP NOT FULL? HOW LONG WILL YOU WAIT, LORD, WHILE THEY FEAST UPON THE BLOOD OF CHILDREN? IF THERE IS NO ONE WHO IS GOOD, LORD, WILL YOU NOT RIDE INTO BATTLE FOR YOUR OWN NAME'S SAKE? HOW LONG WILL YOU BE MOCKED? I'm sorry, Lord."

Guy began to sob. "Why, Lord? Why? Why have you shown me? Don't You see that they do not care? They love the antichrist. They hate You. Or is it me, Lord? Am I simply a crazy man, a man who knows nothing of You and Your nature? Is barak obama a man who You love? Do You love his works? Does Your face shine upon the bushes or the clintons, those vile pigs? I know it is not so, Lord. I know your anger burns as the sun toward these filth. Then why, Lord? Why show me these things? What is it that You desire of me?"

And the Lord spoke into Guy's spirit gently. *Why is it that you allow yourself to be baptized by pedophiles and false prophets?* Guy marveled how he was not able to see things that, once revealed, were so clear, so obvious. "You are a good and merciful Lord, a just Lord. Thank You for being so patient with me."

Guy stood and went to the restroom to grab his robe. He went down the stairs and out the front door. It was a dark, quiet night; there were no street lights. The warm night air was clear. Guy took off his robe and lay it on the weathered brick porch. Wearing only his boxers, he uncoiled the hose that was wound behind the Mr. Lincoln rose tree just to the left of the garage door. With the hose in his left hand, he held both hands toward the heavens and looked up to the firmament.

"My God, Father Yahweh, the God of Abraham, Isaac and Jacob. I renounce my old life. I dedicate myself to You and Your ways. Lead me where You may, do with my life as You would. I believe that Your Son, Jesus Christ, is the Messiah, that He died for my sins, that He was crucified, died and was buried, and that on the third day He rose again in fulfillment of the Scriptures. I put my trust in Jesus Christ alone, that through His sacrifice I might be forgiven and reconciled with You, Father." Guy turned the spigot on and let the cool water flow over his head, covering his body. "I baptize myself in the name of Jesus Christ, that my sins may be forgiven."

Guy put on his robe, wrapped the hose back into a coil and went in through the front door. He took off his wet boxers and draped them over the laundry machine. His robe was fluffy, and it absorbed the water from his soaking-wet body. Guy walked up the stairs, and, as he got to the landing, Marie opened the bedroom door.

"What's going on down there? Were you outside?"

"Yes, everything's fine." Guy was calm. To say Marie would think it peculiar for him to be baptizing himself in the middle of the night in the front yard was an understatement.

"Are you wet? What were you doing out there?" There was sleep in her eyes and irritation in her voice.

All right, he had hoped not to get into it, but he wasn't going to lie about it either. "I was baptizing myself. You don't have to say it, I know, but it was something I needed to do." Guy hoped his answer was satisfactory without drawing additional inquiry.

"Are you coming to bed or what? It's *late*." The emphasis on *late* was poignant. The sound of her irritation grew to one of anger.

"In a little bit, I'm praying." Guy's soul yearned for God tonight.

Marie went back to bed and closed the door behind her; she was clearly annoyed.

Guy walked from the landing, up the rest of the staircase and down the hall, back into Faith's never-slept-in bedroom. Guy loved feeling her little body squirm next to his in bed. She liked to touch him with her feet and rest them upon him like an ottoman while she slept.

Guy took off his robe and lay before God naked. "Thank You, Lord Jesus, for ordering my steps. For allowing me to see."

Guy felt the Lord speak into his spirit powerfully. *So you desire to see?*

"Yes, Lord, with all my heart. I am sick and tired of the lies. Please, Lord, show me Your truth."

The Lord turned Guy toward the book of Revelation. Guy sat upon the unused twin bed, the Bible upon his naked lap. Guy had read the book of Revelation numerous times; he had also read numerous books written about the book of Revelation. It was always intriguing. Revelation told of the specific woes that would befall mankind during the last days. This particular book of the Bible contained signs and information, but the things that were revealed clearly only took place when the Tribulation was already in full swing. Much too late to allow for any sort of preparation or advanced warning.

The rest of the book seemed to be locked away spiritually; it was indecipherable. Guy sat at the head of the bed, his back against the wall, his legs straight out in front of him. "God, if You desire me to see, then show me what You desire me to know from this book." Guy held his Bible in both hands above his head. "Send me Your Holy Spirit, so that I might have understanding, so that I might know Your truth. Guy was overcome by the Holy Spirit, and he began to read the book by the dim light of the room.

As he read Revelation Three:Sixteen, he felt nauseated, for Christendom had, indeed, become lukewarm. Guy could feel God's desire to vomit them out through His mouth. Guy could see clearly in chapter Six that, once the seal of war was opened, the seal of famine would come quickly and then the seal of death so fast that the three seals would seem to coalesce, as they spiraled together in a devilish dance. And as he read chapter Seven, Guy again fell upon his face. He believed in God's infinite might and mercy; Guy knew the Lord's judgments were discerning, for just as in the days of Noah, one would be taken and one would be left. It sure wasn't the godly folks who were taken during the flood.

"Lord, though I am a weak man, I have sought Your face. I have sown Your Word into my daughter's heart. Is she not innocent? Do you not see how she loves You? How pure her heart is? I beseech You, Lord, pass over my household as You did for the Israelites before the Exodus. Have mercy on my family, I beg of You. Please seal my wife, Marie Ruth Finnigan, my daughter, Faith Elizabeth Finnigan. If You would, Lord, place Your seal upon me, Guy Finnigan. For who can stand against these mighty men? These filth who have taken the whole world into their hand? Please, Lord, for Your own Name's sake, how much longer, my God?"

Guy sat back upon the bed and began to read farther. As he came to the 11th chapter, he wept bitterly, and, as he did, the truth behind 9/11 was revealed to him. As he read on, he was overcome by the Holy Spirit and began to have visions as parts of the book were unlocked. Not all things, simply the things that God desired Guy to know. The Lord showed Guy how the snake of old, satan, lucifer, the father of lies, the king of piss and shit, had created his unholy trinity, again trying to exalt himself above the throne of the Most High God. Trying to recreate in his fallen image the workings and miracles of God. God had revealed to Guy the dragon, the false prophet and confirmed the antichrist, that piece of garbage barak obama. The false trinity made a foul stench in the nose of the Lord. Their might, their black magic, was no more than parlor tricks before the Lord God Almighty, the Creator of Heaven and Earth.

Guy became aware of the nature of the one hundred and forty four thousand, and his mind was filled with a vision of the whore of babylon, and the mystery of babylon was no longer a mystery.

"THEN TEAR DOWN THIS ABOMINATION, LORD, FOR THEY ARE DEFILED!" As he stood, Guy outstretched his arms and looked up toward the heavens. He had a vision of a white horse in the distance galloping down from the heavens. Guy dared not look upon the face of the Lion of Judah, but only upon His thigh, and the Name written thereon. As he saw the name, the seven thunders began to sing a song that Guy already knew. He sang along through bitter tears.

Guy was able to see clearly the spiritual fight and how it manifested in the physical world, how intertwined they were. The spirit of deception had gone unchecked; it had grown powerful, overcoming the saints, both spiritually and physically. As they were beaten down and pushed into the mud like filthy whores, most did not even realize there was a battle raging, that the battle was so intense, that it raged toward its final climax. Guy lay down once more before the Lord and took comfort beneath the hem of His robe. Guy poured out his heart in prayer, and asked for guidance and direction as he prepared to stand. He stood and placed his robe back on.

"In the name of Jesus Christ, I cast you out, foul birds. Leave this dwelling. There is no place for you here. GO!" Guy was acutely aware now of the spiritual battle. Of demons that lurked in the shadows, influencing, spying. It was time for them to flee. Guy desired his house to be a place of respite, free from any dark pollution that would try to enter. Guy went around the house, from room to room doing the same. He knew that demons could take refuge in animals, as they had when they fled from the demoniac into the herd of swine, at the Lord's command as related in the Gospels. Guy went to the three cats and two dogs, one of them a toy poodle the same age as Faith. He commanded that any foul spirits in them must flee.

Guy went back to the bathroom and grabbed a small bottle of anointing oil from the medicine cabinet. He walked back out the front door as the blue of the night was beginning to meet the gold of the day. He walked down the driveway to the edge of his property line.

"AS FOR ME AND MY HOUSE, WE WILL SERVE THE LORD. ANYTHING THAT IS NOT OF HIM MUST BE GONE FOR THERE IS NO COMFORT FOR YOU HERE. GO NOW IN THE NAME OF JESUS CHRIST!" Guy walked his property line, the front, the sides, around the back. With his arms raised to the heavens, he said, "GO, IN THE NAME OF JESUS CHRIST! Lord, seal my yard that foul birds may not pass over it." He walked back through the front door, and, as he locked it behind him, he took the oil from his pocket and placed a dab over the entryway. "Lord, let no evil come through my door." Guy walked out to the garage, and placed his hand first upon his car and then upon his wife's. "Lord, let no foul birds enter these cars as we drive about."

Guy could see the sun coming up through the windows of the garage. He was tired—more than tired, drained. He was ready for sleep. As he walked back up the stairs, Marie caught him once again upon the landing.

"You're still awake?" Her voice was loud and filled with exasperation. "Have you been up all night?"

"I'm going to bed. I was praying." Guy was weary; he had no fight left in him. He and Marie had discussions but almost never argued.

"You have got to be kidding me. What's going on? You were up the whole night? That's not normal!" Marie was hot, which was all Guy could see, because her anger overwhelmed her deep sense of concern.

"I'm fine. I'm tired. I'm going to bed. I'm going to go lay down in the other room." Guy finished the climb to the top of the steps and kissed his wife upon her head. As he lay down upon the bed, he was asleep, it seemed, before his eyes even closed.

He was awoken by the touch of John Brown and greeted by his tattooed forearm. The front of John's forearm was covered by an innocent-looking child, yet the back of his forearm showed the back of the child holding a gun in his hands. John was crouched down beside the bed. His eyes looked out from beneath his shaved head. "Hey, are you awake?"

"What time is it?" Guy asked. He was still tired.

"Like 11 thirty. So what's going on? Everybody's real concerned about you." John's eyes did, indeed, hold a look of concern.

"Nothing's wrong, except everything I've been saying is true." Guy sat up on his elbow.

"Yo, you have to relax. I'm being serious. Marie is scared. You've got everyone freaking out."

"Everyone should be freaked out. They're walking around with their eyes closed. Everyone is in big trouble." Guy's tone was soft but serious.

"I'm telling you, you need to cut it out." Now John's tone was serious.

"John, you need to make a decision. Are you going to stand for God? The time is almost at hand."

"Of course I'll stand for God. Come on downstairs. Let's talk about it. Everybody's downstairs waiting for you."

"What are you talking about, *everybody's downstairs waiting for me?*" Guy was perplexed.

"I told you, Marie is all freaked out. She said you didn't even sleep last night. Everyone's downstairs. Mack, Marie and her uncle, your mom." John grabbed Guy around the bicep to pull him to his feet.

"Are you kidding me?" Guy was incredulous.

"I'm not kidding you. I told you that you needed to chill out."

"Whatever. Let me go get some boxers on. I'll be right down." As Guy walked down the hall, he could see the gaggle of folks, with chairs arranged in a half circle in his living room below. He slipped on a pair of boxers and walked down the steps, becoming more irritated with each one.

When he got to the bottom, Marie was standing there, her arms folded against her chest. He looked deeply into her eyes, and she began to sob.

"I can't do this anymore. There's something wrong with you. You need help."

"Marie, it's OK. I know what's going on. It's all true." Guy spoke kindly to her.

"It's not true, and it's not OK. You're not OK. Everyone knows it except you. They want to talk to you. Go sit down." Guy walked over to his family, who were sitting in the living room. "I can't do this. I have to go." Marie burst into sobs, and Guy could hear the front door close.

"So, Guy, what's going on? Marie says you've been praying a lot and reading the Bible. She said you didn't sleep at all last night." Mack's voice was calm.

Guy sat in the seat at the center of the circle. "I went to sleep. I just got up. Yes, I was up late praying last night. It's not like it's some regular occurrence. It's the first time I've been up this late since I was a teenager. How many times have you been at the bar until the sun came up, Dad? I was praying. Is that a crime or something?" Guy didn't want to turn last night into a big deal in front of his family. He could see now was not the time, they were not going to understand.

"OK, Guy, this has got to stop. Enough already, OK? Enough with the end-of-world stuff. Enough storing up all this crazy food. You need to drop it." Della was angry over the situation and let it show right off the bat. She had had enough with all this ridiculous talk.

"You better ask God to make it stop, not me. You're the one who's playing the fool, Mom. I warned you to go get food. And, when the time comes, it is going to be you who's unprepared." His mom was good at getting on his nerves.

"See, Mack? This is your damn fault too. Encouraging him with buying all that fucking food? You see what I've been saying now?" The look in Della's eyes was full of violence.

"Guy, we're all here to support you. This woman is a counselor. She's here to talk to you. We're all here because we want you to get help." Mack was firm; his words were even.

"Dad, I don't need to speak to a counselor, OK? I'm fine. It's you guys who should be worried all right." Guy wasn't about to speak to some damn counselor who walked around the world with her eyes closed tightly.

"Guy, it's not an option. You need to speak with her. She's a Christian. I talked to her. You're off base on all this shit." Della dug in her heels firmly.

"You guys are the ones who are off base. I've been warning all of you. We're on the edge of the Tribulation. God's judgment is nearly upon us. This country is going to be destroyed."

Marie's uncle, Arnie's brother, sat at the edge of the circle. He looked like Arnie, except taller, fatter and balder. He wore glasses as well. His family were ardent Christians; they homeschooled their three kids. He certainly was well versed in the Bible. He was dressed in full army fatigues, as he was in the National Guard Reserves. "Guy, I'm warning you. Who do you think you are, a prophet? You think you can speak for God? You better be real careful, son, because God has no forgiveness for people who speak lies using His Name."

Guy was on his feet in an instant. "YOU WHO SERVE IN SATAN'S ARMY, YOU THINK YOU KNOW THE TRUTH ABOUT THE MOST HIGH GOD? YOU ARE A BLIND MAN, A FOOL, SERVING THE POWER OF THE BEAST! IT IS YOU WHO BEST WATCH YOUR WORDS BEFORE YOU BRING

BURNING HOT COALS DOWN UPON YOUR HEAD! NOW BE GONE FROM MY HOUSE!" Guy's blood was at a boil. He would not be told the signs of the Lord's coming did not exist from a man who could not even see that he was serving in the army of the beast.

"Guy, settle down. Chill out, seriously." John stood up, like the third point of a triangle between Guy and Marie's uncle.

"Get out, now. You too." Guy looked down at the unnamed female counselor with short hair. Marie's uncle looked about the room for an answer.

"Get out of my house now, both of you." Guy looked directly at the counselor and lightly touched his uncle's shoulder, escorting them both to the front door. He opened it, and whisked them out, finding, to his dismay, that the front lawn was covered with cops. Not one or two, at least twenty. There were cop cars lining both sides of the street and an ambulance parked in the front. Guy walked back into the living room.

"Are you guys kidding me? Why are there police at my house?" This was getting absolutely ridiculous.

"I told you this wasn't optional, Guy," his mother said snidely.

He looked at her with burning eyes and then back over to John. "Really?" Guy said with mocking irritation.

"Yo, I was trying to tell you to chill out. Just talk to the counselor already." John tried to be nonchalant, though he was nervous.

"I'm not talking to some clueless counselor, all right?" They couldn't force Guy to do anything he didn't want to do. He hadn't done anything wrong.

"Is everything all right in there?" A burly voice echoed through the doorway. Guy walked over to the entryway.

"Everything's fine here, officer. Nobody is breaking any laws. No one is being violent. There's no need for you to be here." Guy spoke to him calmly, plainly.

"Everything's not OK from what I hear." His voice was sarcastic, sardonic. He stood on the porch and filled the space of the open doorway. He must have been six four, at least two fifty, his arms bulged from beneath his tight sleeves. "Why don't you come out here and talk to us for a moment?" He reached out his arm, coaxing Guy to come outside.

"I'm good right here, thanks. What is it that you wanted to talk about?" Guy was polite.

"Well, what I want to talk about is you coming outside first. It seems you've got everyone real upset here." It looked as if the police force for the whole small town must have been on Guy's front lawn.

"Well, I'm sorry if reading the Bible and praying has everyone upset, but I'm pretty sure it's not a crime yet. This is my house, and I'm asking you politely, Officer, to please leave." Guy's mind swirled; he could not believe this was actually happening. He was truly caught off guard.

"Look, we're not going anywhere until you come out here and talk to us first." The burly officer was insistent.

Guy was sure they were already informed that he owned three firearms and plenty of ammo to go with it. "We're talking now, aren't we? I haven't hurt anyone, Officer, and I'm not planning on hurting any one. You can see I'm calm and coherent. I'm certainly caught off guard having my whole family ambush me. But you can see I'm not being erratic."

"Who said anything about hurting someone? Have you been having thoughts about hurting someone?"

"I just said I have no plans to hurt anyone. I'm a Christian." Guy was beginning to tire of the conversation but was finding its unending nature worrisome.

"Being a Christian has nothing to do with you hurting someone one way or another. What do you have all that food and water stored up for, huh?" The officer was simply not going to give up.

"Officer, respectfully, open your eyes. This world is in big trouble. I'm a private banker, and I can assure you the economy has not been fixed. All this money that they've been spending, they're printing it out of thin air. It's going to have dangerous repercussions on the economy. If I were you, I'd be more concerned about your pension than the fact that I've stored up some food and water, or that I'm reading the Bible in my own house." Guy kept his voice calm, though he was irritated by the whole thing. The situation was starting to make him nervous.

"Sir, you need to come outside right now."

"No, thank you." Guy walked back to the living room, where Mack, Della and John were still standing. "Really, guys, thanks a lot." Guy grabbed one of the chairs from the living room and brought it over to the front entryway before the officer. Guy sat down in front of the open front door and began to read quietly from the Psalms.

One hour turned into two then three, and his front yard was like a hornet's nest of activity. Officers buzzing around, calling in on their radios. Multiple changes of guard duty across his wide-open front door, with each trying his hand, from friend to foe. Guy tried to let God's Word drown it out.

After three hours, it became clear the police force had no intention of leaving. Guy was quiet as a mouse, simply sitting and reading from his

Bible. He looked up to the officer at the door, and his heartbeat quickened.

This one had a similar look, but it was a different officer. His hair was buzzed high and tight as if he thought he was in the military.

"So are you going to come out and talk to us for a minute or what?" The officer was frank.

Guy stood calmly holding his Bible in his right hand. He asked the Lord for strength and protection. "Sure, I'll come talk. You can see I've been totally calm, right?"

"Come on out." The officer stepped to the closed side of Guy's double door. Guy could hear them all buzzing on their radios, "He's coming out."

Guy stepped out onto the brick front porch. There was an officer at the end, who seemed to be in command. The other rock of a man was standing behind Guy in the corner. It made him particularly uncomfortable.

"So what would you like to talk about, Officer?" Guy directed his remark to the slender man in charge.

"Sir, why don't you step over here on the grass, so we can talk." The officer motioned over to the front lawn on Guy's immediate right.

Here we go, Guy thought. This was not going to be good. He was starting to feel anxious, like he had made a big mistake coming outside. He asked the Lord quietly to protect him and walked over to the grass, still holding his Bible and wearing his robe.

Once he was on the grass, the big officer tackled him from behind, smashing Guy's face to the ground. It nearly knocked the wind out of him, but he tried to remain calm. If he resisted at all, he figured they would blow his head off. There were instantly eight or 9 officers on him, screaming and growling like rabid dogs.

"Don't fucking move, you hear me."

Guy had no intention of moving nor could he. The side of his face was pressed into the grass; someone had their knee pressed down upon his neck. Someone was sitting on his back, and there were multiple officers pinning his arms and legs.

"Do what you're told, and this is going to be easy. Don't move."

"Put your arms behind your back."

"I said don't fucking move."

Someone pressed their knee into Guy's ribs, and he felt as if he were going to suffocate. He would have cried from fear and anguish, not from the physical pain, but he had no air to sob.

"I got you, mutherfucker," someone's hot breath whispered into Guy's ear. One of his arms was wrenched behind his back so hard, he thought they would dislocate his shoulder. Someone else, with hands like a vise, twisted his left wrist behind his back. Guy had broken his wrist and elbow badly the year before, slipping on his wet concrete patio. He was in a cast from his hand to his shoulder for three months; it had been unbearable, but nothing like this. He felt the handcuffs close so tightly upon his wrists, he was sure there would be blood. The officers picked him into the air and placed him down onto a waiting gurney. The eight or 9 officers stayed on him and strapped him into the gurney tightly. The straps went from Guy's chest down to his feet which were bound multiple times with zip ties.

Guy was now thoroughly frightened and angry for being treated with such hostility, with such disdain. He looked to the heavens and pleaded for God's will to be done. For Guy knew, if it was God's will, this captain and his fifty could be consumed. Once he caught his breath, Guy cried out to the heavens. "If I be a man of God, then let fire come down from heaven. If I be a man of God, then let fire come down from heaven, and consume thee and thy fifty." And fire did not come down from heaven. God's will was done, and Guy was overcome by debilitating fear as he was loaded into the ambulance, and the doors shut, entombing him. "This won't hurt a bit" was the last thing Guy heard as his vision blurred, and he fell into unconsciousness.

When he opened his eyes, he was hazy, and so thirsty his tongue cleaved to the roof of his mouth. His left wrist was throbbing, still handcuffed tightly, but now to the side of a gurney or hospital bed. He was still strapped in tightly. He moved his neck to look about the room. It was some sort of hospital room but not a patient room. There was medication on the walls, and the room was not much wider than would allow for his bed and another. The clock on the wall read 9 p.m. Guy figured he must have been out for five hours or so. They must have shot him up with Haldol. He was pretty sure they didn't use Thorazine anymore. Whatever it was, it knocked him on his ass; he still felt foggy.

Despite the fog, he felt terror, abject fear, horror, as the possibilities swirled around his head. Where was he? Who had him? What were they going to do to him? Clearly whoever it was had full control, as Guy had done nothing illegal. He was polite, respectful to the police. Yet they had pulled him out of his home, had smashed his face into the dirt and had bruised his body as if he were a hardened criminal. He needed water desperately, but the fear of what was to come next kept him quiet until he could bear the thirst and the pain in his wrist no longer.

"Waa . . ." Guy's mouth was so dry, his lips and tongue could hardly form the words, and the air seemed to get lost in the barren wasteland of his throat. "Water," he choked out. "Water, please." There was no

362

answer. "Help, please. I need some water, anyone." It was as much noise as his body would allow for.

The door opened, and a black man with cornrows, who seemed to be about Guy's age, walked in wearing scrubs.

"Water, please." Guy had endured a lot more for a lot longer without water, but this was at the top of his list of dehydrations.

The man looked at him coyly. "You ain't going to cause no problems, are you?"

"No. Please, water." Guy begged with his eyes, like a puppy lying in the gutter after being hit with a car.

The man grabbed a disposable cup from off the counter to Guy's left and filled it with tap water from the small sink. Guy lifted his head from the bed, and the man placed the straw near Guy's mouth. Guy sucked down the whole cup quickly.

"Please, may I have one more cup? I won't cause any problems, I promise." The first cup allowed Guy to get out a sentence. One more cup would bring him halfway back to normalcy.

"All right, fine. But you behave yourself."

Guy sucked down the next cup just as quickly. "Where am I?"

"You're at a facility to help you get better. Don't worry," the man said casually.

The statement caused Guy no less worry, but, from the man's demeanor, Guy gathered he was not in the military, nor a man of power or influence. "Am I still in California?"

"Oh, yeah, man. You're in California. Don't worry about it. I'll get you some medicine in a bit. You can see the doctor tomorrow. He'll take care of you. It'll all be fine." The man had a real laid-back tone, and Guy knew it was time to play it cool. "Great. What about my wife, my daughter and my parents? Are they all right?" Guy inquired, making sure the tone of his voice had just a slight concerned NPR twang to it.

"Oh, yeah. They're fine. You'll see them in a day or two. You just be concerned about getting better." The man nodded his head.

"Thank you. I really appreciate it."

"No sweat, bro. You're gonna be OK."

"Hey, I broke my arm real bad last year." Guy lifted his left arm that was handcuffed to the bed. "This thing is on really tight. It's killing me. It's not like I've done anything. I've been calm and respectful the whole day, plus you got me restrained to the bed."

"That's not what I heard. I heard you're an ex-marine, martial arts expert. You got guns." The man put his hands on his hips.

363

"I haven't done anything to anyone. If you're really worried about it, put it on my other arm, please." Guy could tell the man was thinking about it. "Please, I promise."

"All right, but don't try anything funny, or you're gonna get it. I'm being serious."

"I promise."

"All right." The man grabbed his key chain and changed the handcuffs to Guy's right arm. It's not like he could move his left arm while it was strapped to the bed, but having the vise off his wrist made a world of difference.

"Thanks, I really appreciate it." Guy used the same words purposefully.

"You're welcome." The man smiled.

"So what's up? You guys gonna leave me tied to this bed all night? I promise I'll behave." Guy's body was starting to ache; he longed to be able to change position, to stretch. It made him feel horribly claustrophobic.

"Well, I'll come back and check on you in a couple hours. I'll bring you your meds, and, if you're still cool and take your meds without a fuss, I'll get you a bed." The man thought it sounded very reasonable, even kind.

"That sounds great. I really appreciate it. What's your name, if you don't mind me asking?"

"Shawn."

"Thanks, Shawn. I really appreciate it." Guy knew people liked to be called by their name.

"Oh, no problem, bro. You just chill out. I'll be back to check on you."

Guy seemed to be infected with a spirit of fear. It clung to him and would not let go. At least it seemed he was still on the grid. It must be some county facility, maybe some small private psychiatric hospital. Guy had a real disdain for medication; he wanted no part of it. But he could see clearly that he was not calling the shots here. He was a prisoner. He knew he would have to play along with whatever game they had in store, if he were ever to see the light of day again. He was scared and foggy, but he would have to be as wise as a serpent.

It was almost one in the morning when Shawn came back in, holding a little white paper cup that Guy knew contained his get-right medicine. Shawn filled up the disposable cup with water. "Open up."

Guy opened, and Shawn dumped what felt like two or maybe three pills into his mouth, followed once again by the straw. Guy sucked down the whole glass.

"Let's see, open up."

Guy opened his mouth and lifted his tongue. He had swallowed the pills. He was in no position to play parlor games. "Thanks. You know, I think I'm having some anxiety. What type of pills were those? Do you think it will help?"

"Oh, yeah. That was Ativan. It will kick anxiety right in the balls. Plus some Seroquel, to help you sleep."

"Thanks, Shawn. It'll be nice to get a good night's sleep. What do you think about that bed?" Guy asked casually.

"Well, you seem like you're calmed down, and you took your meds with no fuss. So, yeah, you can have a bed. But you go right to sleep. No problems." Shawn started to undo the restraints. On their release, Guy began to move his body. He sat up and rubbed his wrist. It hurt like hell and drowned out the tenderness in his left rib cage and in between his shoulder blades.

Guy, clad only in his boxers, walked beside Shawn through the lobby and down the hall to his room. Clearly a county or small private facility, nothing high-end. The room was small, but it had a bathroom and shower, very antiseptic.

"There's a gown for you over there. Bathroom, no showering until morning. Someone will come get you up. Walk you through the drill. You'll get to see the doctor. They'll explain everything to you. Get some sleep."

"Thanks again for all the help. Have a nice night, Shawn." Shawn closed the door behind him, and Guy drank heavily from the sink. As he lay in bed, he was tormented by images of wicked men, men of might who snarled and showed their teeth, the dragon in particular. Guy prayed that he would fall asleep quickly.

The next morning it was time for medication. Cafeteria-style breakfast was served upon a compartmentalized molded tray; he was told he would see the doctor shortly.

"Hello, Guy. My name is Dr. Greene. How are you feeling this morning?" Dr. Greene was an older man with a balding head ringed by gray hair. He wore thin spectacles and a white physician's coat over his well-fed frame.

"Good morning, Doctor. I'm feeling much better this morning. The medicine seems to be helping a lot." Guy sat in the chair opposite the doctor in an office that was not much bigger than a bathroom and cluttered with papers and books. Guy knew that if he were ever to be released from their clutches, he would need to say the things they wanted to hear.

"Very good. Medication can be very helpful, necessary. So tell me, what's going on? It seems you have everyone quite concerned."

"I know. I feel horrible. Well, I'm a private banker, and, as you know, it's been a stressful year, with the markets melting down. It's been really tough. They've laid off about forty percent of the people on my floor, people who had worked for the bank for twenty, thirty years, had poured their heart and soul into it." Guy made sure to look forlorn. While it was certainly a horrible year, for Guy it was simply a confirmation. He had positioned his clients well and was alone in beating the drum of caution well in advance. As the market collapsed, more people were interested in his thoughts on the matter.

"Oh, a private banker, interesting. Well, no surprise that you've been overwhelmed. I think the whole country has felt that way, but you're certainly at ground zero. So you've been telling people it's the end of the world." The doctor was frank.

"Well, you know, I do a lot of research, so I've been seeing this train coming for a while. I think when it finally hit, I was just so overwhelmed, that I developed this delusion so I could cope, kind of a way to make sense of things." The words were bitter in Guy's mouth.

"A delusion? Very perceptive. You're clearly an intelligent man, well spoken. You keep a good job, provide for your family. It would be a shame for all of that to be destroyed. So you really recognize this as a delusion now?" Dr. Greene looked down at Guy's chart and made some notes.

"Well, honestly, Doctor, what else could it be? The markets are way off their lows, the government has taken measures to get things back on track. I'm thankful I have supportive people around me to get me some help. I've been having a hard time sleeping. I think it was real helpful for me to get a break, have a good night's sleep." The doctor would eat this up.

"Having a support group is important. Letting people know when these feelings seep back in will be imperative for your recovery. I think this medication is going to be really important. You see what a good night's sleep can do? If you were released, would you agree to keep taking the medication, to see a doctor regularly?" The doctor looked at Guy over his thin black-framed spectacles.

"I think it will be really helpful in managing my anxiety." Guy disdained medication. His fear was debilitating last night, his anxiety overwhelming this morning at the thought of being locked away, but the medication had certainly taken the edge off. But it was false, clouding the mind instead of bringing clarity. That certain people benefited from medication seemed apparent, but Guy preferred to depend on the Lord despite circumstances. The burden did feel like more than he could carry, but Guy believed God's Word was true. That Guy would not be given a burden heavier than he could carry. He tried to place it at the Lord's feet, but it was difficult to put down.

"Very good. You said you spend a lot of time researching. Would you say that you've become obsessed with the news?"

"It's hard not to. I spend a lot of time studying the economy because of my job. I've been very interested in politics since 9/11," Guy answered truthfully.

"It's important to have a balance. Maybe just look at what you need to for the economy while you're at work. Don't go overboard. You need a break while you're not working. Spend it with your family. You should probably lay off the politics completely, stay unplugged while you're not working. What about alternative sites? Your family mentioned you've been listening to things like Alex Jones?" The doctor picked up his pen and looked back down at Guy's chart.

"Yes, but I can see how that hasn't been profitable. I think it's just added fuel to the fire." Guy again was honest. Alex Jones was one of the only men in the country telling the truth, certainly the man with the broadest reach. It wasn't just the loud voice, which some mistook for anger but which was clearly passion, frustration, and urgency. He was also a man who did his own research; he was sounding the alarm. Amazingly most of his research simply entailed shining the light on the things the New World Order were doing or writing about right out in the open. Things from their own manuals, books and articles. Laws and treaties that were never even mentioned by the media.

Guy had laughed in his heart at people like the soviets and the chinese with their glaringly controlled stream of information. Guy thought it was pathetic that their people seemed to be clueless about their own situation. america was in the same damn position. Though there was access to truth now, you had to go find it with discernment, as truth and lies were mingled together. While there was more information available than in the history of the world, it was extremely difficult to tell what was actually going on.

"I'm sure with your line of work, you have enough fuel for the fire." Dr. Greene chuckled. "Wouldn't you agree?"

"I think that's an understatement." Guy gave a bit of a laugh himself.

"Do you think you could agree to lay off completely from all the other wacky stuff that's out there? Keep it down the middle of the lane?"

"Oh, absolutely. This whole episode has been a real eye-opener. It's taught me a lot." It was true again. In these days men had become accustomed to lies. Truth was like a hot poker in their eye. Unfortunately it was the hot poker of truth that melted the scales from the eyes.

"Well, I feel like we've made real progress. You were admitted on a minimum seventy-two-hour hold. Let's see how the next couple days go, but I think you'll be ready to go home. Use this time wisely, decompress. I'll check in with the staff and talk with you in two days." The doctor stood to shake Guy's hand.

Guy shook it firmly, not too firmly and looked into the doctor's eyes. "I really appreciate all of your help, Dr. Greene. Thank you so much." Guy reached up and touched his left hand to the outside of the doctor's right as they shook.

BOOK THREE: CHAPTER FIVE

As Guy sat in a chair next to the delivery room, he was more nervous than for the birth of his daughter. This time it was Marie who wanted to find out the sex of the baby. Guy teased that he would forbid it, since he had languished for months on end with the desire to find out if their first peanut would be a boy or a girl. They were having a boy this time. They would name him John Stone Finnigan. More of a nod to Mack's middle name and John the Baptist, than to Guy's biological father, Jack. His grandfather John had been an honorable man, a man with character. Guy thought his grandfather would be proud of the life Guy had made for his family.

Guy was anxious about having a boy, because it meant he would need to teach his son how to become a man. While Mack was a man of character, he was also a man of few words. As Guy grew from a boy to a man, the dysfunction of his family had left Guy to grow alone into his manhood—no one to teach him how to shave. He found one of Mack's unused electric shavers below the sink to teach himself. Guy would teach his son how to shave, how to throw a ball. He would teach his son to be a man by example. He would compassionately teach him how to walk on the narrow path that leads to Christ. He was thankful for his daughter; she softened his heart so that he would not be too firm. He would kiss his son and tell him how much he loved him, how special he was. How he brought joy to his father's heart, just like he did with and said to Faith. He would call John *son*, something that Guy only received as a title in a letter from Jack.

The second pregnancy had been more nerve-racking than even the newness of the first. There was an additional worry since the family tests at Faith's birth had revealed Marie was a Factor V carrier, which meant she was prone to blood clots. After a thrombosis in her leg during the first trimester of this pregnancy, they had to give her an injection of Lovenox, a blood thinner. Guy gave Marie the injection in her belly every night, he never really got used to it. Marie also decided, upon advice of the doctor, to have a C-section in order to prevent any chance of a replay of the seizures caused from Faith's delivery. Marie was very nervous; she had no desire for surgery, but, of course, John came first.

Guy was dressed in a cloth hazmat suit, booties over his shoes, gloves on his hands, a hairnet over his head with a little doctor's mask over his nose and mouth. It was weird knowing exactly when the delivery would be. They were able to pick their son's birthdate. The doctors said the delivery would be June first, but Guy had refused and told them they would wait until the second. June first was Arnold's birthday, Marie's brother. Guy's son would have his own special day, and it certainly would not be shared with Marie's deceased brother, especially in light of his tragic end.

★★★

The last year had been a difficult one. Guy was initially furious upon his release from the mental hospital. He couldn't believe Marie had sold him out, that she was willing to have him locked away. He was a man who believed God's plan was perfect, however. He cried as he asked the Lord, why was he told these things only to be tied up and thrown away? The Lord had simply pointed Guy back to the Word, back to Ezekiel. Guy was right. Nobody cared; nobody would listen. And so the Lord had allowed them to carry Guy off in chains. God had cleaved Guy's tongue to the roof of his mouth, so that he would speak of these things no more.

Marie wanted to get pregnant shortly after Guy's release.

Referring to the events as a delusion made everyone quite comfortable, everyone except Guy. Continuing to take the Seroquel made everyone quite comfortable as well. Everyone except Guy, who felt as if he were run over by a Mack truck. Getting up in the morning was like rising from the dead. Guy was nervous about having another child, as the imminence of the end times still pervaded his being. He wanted to believe that he was wrong all along and, as much as he had tried to convince himself of the fact, the Lord would not allow it.

He had agreed with Marie's desire, but only if Marie would agree that he could go off his medication for a month before they tried to get pregnant. She was reluctant, but Guy would not allow his seed filled with poison to sprout in her womb. After he was detoxified, Marie was pregnant once again on their very first attempt.

The culmination of last year left Guy with a spirit of fear and a wonder that was more of a hope that he might in fact be crazy. Far better to be crazy than to be at the door of the world's end. He no longer desired to hear what the Lord had to say, but when Guy sought the Lord's face, the Lord told Guy that He had never said Guy was crazy, simply that it was time to keep his mouth shut. Although Guy no longer wanted to see, the Lord still had more to show him.

When Guy prayed, he became aware, in his spirit, that he was being listened to, spied on. Again the Lord told Guy to keep his mouth shut, that it was time to pray silently. Contrary to the belief of the filth, there were no plans other than the Lord's. The tinfoil hat that Guy figuratively wore was not lost on him. Still he got rid of the webcam, unplugged the cords on the computer and Internet when not in use, and put duct tape over the cameras on his laptop and cell phone. Everyone laughed heartily.

When Marie caught on, Guy said it was a small thing that gave him some comfort. Would she deny Guy the little comfort he could find? She reluctantly would not. Guy was acutely aware of how far the net of the New World Order was cast; it was pervasive. There were times at night when Guy's fear was so debilitating that he called Bear over to the house to hold his hand. To look outside and to make sure nobody was watching. To promise not to let anyone take Guy away again.

Despite it all, Guy's business was better than ever. He won the top producer's trip, and Guy, Marie and Faith were treated to a wonderful week at the Four Seasons by the beach, massages, parties and all. The bank changed the locks on Guy's cocaine-snorting boss, shipped him off with his personal items and replaced him with a darn good man. He was certainly a company man, but a man who loved his family, a man who shot straight. He wasn't full of BS, and he navigated the new environment of perpetual change like a true a captain.

Pennyhill closed its doors. Marie and Faith found a nice plain-vanilla church to attend some Sundays. Everyone understood when Guy refused, but he would never forbid his wife from finding some comfort in the fellowship it provided her.

★★★

Guy's excitement and nervousness grew as he sat peering at the door, awaiting the birth of his son. He wanted to look through its little glass window, but he was instructed to sit and to not get up.

"He's coming." The door cracked open to reveal a person similarly attired as Guy. Guy was through the door in an instant, to see his son lifted up through the tents surrounding Marie.

"Get this one on the scale. He's a big boy. You wouldn't have wanted to push this one out."

John let out a healthy cry, and so did Guy.

"9 pounds even. Do you want to cut the umbilical cord, Dad?" the doctor asked.

Guy was handed the scissors; the umbilical cord was tougher to cut through than he had anticipated. "He's so handsome, Marie. Beautiful. He has your hair." Guy picked up the beautiful babe in his arms. "I'm your daddy. I love you so much. I've been waiting for you, son. I'll always take care of you and protect you," Guy whispered. Then Guy held the babe wrapped in a little blue blanket to the heavens before his

God. "God, I dedicate my son, John Stone Finnigan, to You. May he follow You all the days of his life. Please sow Your Word into his heart and guide his steps that he might walk upon Your path always."

"I want to see. Bring him here." Marie spoke softly; her head peeked out from one side of the tent.

Guy walked beside her, holding their treasure. "Look at his hair. He's so big. He's just looking at me, smiling the whole time." Guy beamed.

"Oh, he's so beautiful. Look at that hair. Finally a redhead and a little boy. He's so precious. He's big. Look at that boy." Marie smiled; John was big, but not fat. His red hair was more strawberry blond, but definitely a redhead.

"Looks like he's going to have your fiery personality."

"Ha, ha." Marie laughed, it sounded as if little John laughed along with her. "It wasn't as bad as I had expected. But it was weird. I could feel everything. I could feel them moving around inside me, but it wasn't painful."

Guy placed John next to his mother's breast, and he ate vigorously. Mack was watching little Faith, who was so excited to meet her little brother. Guy knew she would be an amazing big sister. They spent the two days together in the hospital as a family. Guy took Faith home at night to sleep. Things went off without a hitch, and the Finnigan family was now four.

As time passed, Guy retreated into the comfort of his family. He had no desire for idle chitchat, nor the thoughtless conversations of fools. No desire to ride the merry-go-round of bad choices with friends and family. He tired of hearing the carnival music play, as they were all continually surprised by their own circumstances. Guy kept his mouth closed as tightly as the world's eyes.

Marie was convinced Two Thousand Twelve was going to be a year of healing and respite for the family. Guy hoped Marie was right. With the antichrist in office for nearly three and a half years, it seemed the clock was ticking. Guy prayed all would remain calm until November, that america be given a chance to repent and vote the man of sin out of office—though Guy knew in his spirit it was futile. While the economy was reinflated, people were still out of work, and things just didn't seem to feel right, even to the people on Main Street usa.

It was clear that obama's idea of change was radical, like him and his cohorts, radically different than the ideals the average american had believed for generations. america had grown in many ways along its journey, letting go of ignorant hatreds. The man of sin sought hard to redivide america, to break the individual and to replace it with the collective state. For big brother would clothe and feed you, tell you what

372

to think, how to live. All that was necessary was for you to bow your knee. And the country bowed.

Guy was seeing Milton Steiner with less frequent regularity. It cost him two hundred dollars an hour, eight hundred dollars a month. When he was first released, he had initially seen a doctor through his provider, Kaiser. Guy was a cheerleader for the HMO after the amazing care they had provided his family, but the psychologist didn't fit Guy's needs. Guy's mind was complicated, and the doctor's was not. He was mesmerized by Guy's knowledge of the economy and how much money Guy made that year. Guy had finally made his hoped-for salary of a hundred twenty five thousand dollars a year and got paid a bonus as well. The taxes cut it in half; it seemed things were expensive these days, and the money did not go far enough to afford the Finnigans any reasonable cushion.

"Good morning, Guy." Milton opened the door to the waiting room holding his cup of Peet's coffee, liquid rocket fuel.

"Good morning, Milt." Guy took his customary seat on the couch across from Milton's chair. The office was cozy, a small desk and computer in the corner. Two waist-high bookcases filled with all manner of books on psychology; a picture of Guy and his group mates from twenty years ago sat upon it. Milton's office was on the corner of Ventura and Sepulveda in Sherman Oaks, the center of the Four O Five and One O One interchanges. Which, depending on the year, was the worst interchange in america. Even meeting at seven a.m. meant taking the side streets.

"So what's been going on? How's the family? How have you been feeling?" Milton sat in his chair, crossed his legs and drank from his rocket fuel.

"Feeling pretty good. No more caffeine, so no more coffee. Even though the Seroquel makes the mornings tough, I found I just don't need the extra stimulation, especially at the office."

"How long has it been now?"

"About a year I guess. I really noticed it once I got on the medication. It wasn't easy at first, you know. I really enjoyed that cup of coffee with my hour drive in the morning. Started with half decaf, then moved to green tea, which only has a small amount of caffeine, but nothing for about a year. Quit sodas as soon as I was released. I found that sugar was making me feel anxious. For two years now, virtually no sugar. Trying to do what I can naturally to keep the anxiety in check."

"What about the medication?"

"I'm still taking it if that's what you're asking. It makes me feel like a zombie, but it makes everyone else happy. I've been working hard to find some comfort because there's no way I'm taking this stuff forever. I really don't care what people say."

"I don't think it's permanent. Just something to take the edge off." Milton looked nearly the same as he did twenty years ago, perhaps just a touch more gray.

"I feel like we're just surrounded by poisons. I've been cutting them out. No more gel in my hair, au naturel." Guy ran his fingers through his hair. He was getting more compliments on it. You could see the gray streak in the front more clearly. "Only distilled water. You know that fluoride is totally poisonous, and it's put in all our tap water. Really disgusting."

"Well, they say it's for your teeth."

"Well, I'm not too inclined to listen to whatever they say. Take a look at this." Guy fired off a link from his iPhone. *http://www.huffingtonpost.com/dr-mercola/fluoride_b_2479833.html*. "Harvard showed conclusively that fluoride in the drinking water creates neurotoxicity. In other words, it poisons the brain. They showed it significantly lowers intelligence and memory. The effects were much worse in kids. It makes them stupider."

"I never drink tap water. It tastes funny."

"Yeah, but that's not the point, Milton. The point is, if the government knows it's poison, what the hell are they doing putting it in our water? Same thing with the damn vaccines. We decided not to have John vaccinated anytime soon. It threw the doctors into a tizzy, as if we cared when it comes to protecting our son. Boys have a much thinner blood-brain barrier than girls. Why do you think boys have an autism rate four times higher than girls do? There are cases right out in plain sight where the government admits it, and even pays compensation. *http://www.infowars.com/breaking-courts-discreetly-confirm-mmr-vaccine-causes-autism/*."

"That seems pretty dangerous with all the deadly diseases out there." Milton uncrossed and crossed his legs.

"Really, Milton, all what diseases out where? Who do you know who has ever gotten measles, mumps or rubella? Anyone? Know anyone who knows anyone? Besides that, they are dangerous but rarely deadly. Bill, in my office, had the mumps. He said it was the pits. Oh, *the pits, darn.* Know anybody who has autism? Of course you do. Probably lots, and it crushes families. Now they are even pushing vaccines for STDs like HPV on little kids. You have got to be kidding me. First they sexualize the kids, then they give them poison to fix it. Disgusting." Guy shook his head. It really drove him crazy.

"Well, I have noticed that there seems to be significantly more cases of autism here in the united states than, say, the developing world. No one I knew ever had autism while I was growing up. You have to wonder about putting mercury in your body. It is highly poisonous. You're right on with the sexualization of children. Seeing the things my daughter's friends wore while growing up was, let's say, a challenge."

"I was in the mall the other day, and this girl who was not old enough to drive was wearing what looked like a tube top, except it was a skirt. You could completely see the bottom of her ass cheeks. Seriously what's the difference between that and what prostitutes wear? And I'm not saying *prostitutes* figuratively. I mean actual streetwalkers. It's the damn parents' fault. I would never let my daughter go out like that. Most of the moms want to dress like prostitutes themselves though, fake boobs, the whole 9 yards." It's not like Guy's eyes didn't appreciate it or that he had anything against prostitutes. In fact he had extreme empathy for them; he imagined it was hard to find one without an excruciating life story. The sexualization of america's children made him so sad and angry, but it seemed it's what the country wanted.

"Marie's been asking about fake boobs since hers were deflated from breast feeding. It certainly is alluring but putting a foreign object in your body? And what does it say to our daughter?" Marie had put on a lot of weight with Faith; it took her nearly till she was pregnant with John to get it off. She put on another sixty pounds with John, and the only place it seemed to be shed was from her boobs. They were, indeed, deflated. And, with all the weight she had put on, it had crushed Marie's self-confidence; she felt ugly. To Guy, she was still just as beautiful, just as sexy; he didn't care at all. He loved her so and, while he was aware of her body's changes, he didn't compare her now to back then. She remained Marie, his wife. He was supremely supportive both emotionally and financially of whatever new method Marie enlisted to get off the weight.

"Hard not to notice. One of the girls in my daughter's class got a set for her sixteenth birthday. Charming." Milton raised his coffee cup in a toast.

"Just wait till she gets to college. Now they have classes like Anal One O One and Rope Play." *http://mobile.wnd.com/2013/02/students-taught-oral-sex-tricks-and-more/*. "Or even better, being forced to masturbate or fail your class. Maybe write a paper about how you lost your virginity, how you masturbate, if you've ever been abused and what you enjoy sexually. All for some filthy professor to get his rocks off." *http://mobile.wnd.com/2013/02/students-taught-oral-sex-tricks-and-more/*. "That's college today. A system that brainwashes kids into degeneracy."

"Well, not my daughter. I still pay the bills and certainly check what classes she's taking." Milton shook his head, as if it seemed hard to believe.

"You know, Milton, the country has been debased. No one even cares. You have some filthy pig molesting little kids for decades, but no one cares because he's a football coach. *Oh, I didn't think anything of it, when I saw him taking a shower with a twelve-year-old boy in the locker room.* Child Protective Services? What an oxymoron. They even met Jaycee Lee Dugard and did nothing. How stupid do you have to be? Some sex offender has a young girl living with him, really? Pathetic. That's why I don't let my kids out of my sight for one second."

"Well, you'll have to sometime. How are the kids? How's Marie?"

"The kids and Marie are amazing. Everyone else is still riding the merry-go-round."

"John's a year now, isn't he? How do you like having a son?" Milton asked.

"He was a year in June. You know, I was nervous since I didn't have anyone to guide me into manhood. I was worried I would be harsh, but Faith changed all that. John is such a character—all boy, for sure. I tease Marie that he's so spunky because of her red hair. He loves to climb and jump and wrestle. He's a little comedian, always laughing and trying to make everyone else laugh. His smile is infectious. So I catch him using the iPad the other day. He knew how to open up the locked screen and was playing a game. I had never even showed him how. So I got him this Thomas the train game, where you can put together puzzle pieces. He was putting together these four-piece puzzles like a pro. I come home, and the puzzle is set to twenty pieces. I go into the settings on the game and change it back to four pieces. Well, he exits out of the game, goes into the settings and changes it back to twenty pieces. I was like, what? Then he put the whole puzzle together. He's not even two yet. Totally crazy!"

"Wow, it really is amazing how these kids are engrained with technology these days." Milton shook his head.

"It's hard to get away from it. We try to strike some type of balance. No cable, we use Apple TV, buy the shows we like and things that are child appropriate. That way we can control what they absorb. No commercials, so no marketing either, which is nice. Stream it to the TVs, you can put it on the iPad or iPhones. Our kids are very sensitive to any sort of conflict or people being cruel. We make sure the shows they watch are easy, kind. There's so much garbage being pumped into the home these days, you really have to be careful. The disgusting pigs in this country think it's funny to have a little five-year-old girl hold a giant pink penis cup and suck from the top. *http://www.breitbart.com/Big-Hollywood/2012/04/13/HBO-Children-Sex-Toys*. Really? So despicable. This country is going to burn, Milt, I'm telling you. We really think we can do whatever we want? Kill fifty million little babies and call it birth control? Women have made abortion a religious rite. They turn their wombs into sacrificial altars for satan." The war on the innocence of children made Guy sick and angry, so angry.

"All right, all right, cool it. Faith is going to be in kindergarten this year, isn't she?" Milton steered the direction of the conversation back to family, away from worldviews.

"Yep. You know we moved up to Santa Clarita because of the great schools, but we decided Faith is going to private school. I just can't stomach the propaganda, and I'm not going to let it be spoon-fed to my kids. You know, in California, they passed a law saying that kids have to learn about transgenders and homosexuals in first grade. Really? You know Faith can't even watch Disney movies without getting upset, and these scum think it is appropriate to talk to little kids about some guy getting his penis cut off. Absolutely disgusting.

"I've even heard rumblings that they are going to let boys use the girls' locker rooms and vice versa, depending on whether you feel like a boy or a girl. Maybe even let boys play on girls' sports teams. Can you believe that? Of course teenage boys want to see girls in the locker room, all in the name of fairness. Really, is it fair for boys to play on girls' teams? It would totally destroy sports, not that I care about sports in the first place or anything."

Guy sat back on the gray fabric couch. The cushions were soft; he was relaxed despite that content of his conversation. Guy actually despised sports, most actors and musicians as well. They made ridiculous sums of money, which Guy did not fault them for; it was a basic tenant of capitalism. But there was hardly a fingernail's worth of character in the whole lot. They were fools who spent their money frivolously, and, instead of being positive role models, they taught children that, if you had enough money, you could do anything you want. Act like a narcissistic piece of scum and be put on a pedestal for it.

"I think that would be a bridge too far, Guy. People wouldn't stand for it. So tell me about this school."

"You'd be surprised what people will stand for these days or even cheerlead for. The school's a classical Christian academy. They teach the way people learned until the fifties or so, the way the great men of history learned. Grammar, rhetoric and logic. They read the classics, learn Latin in third grade. What really sealed it for me was when I went to orientation. They had this 11th grade girl speak to the parents. As you know, I've been around the block a few times, and I can certainly tell an innocent girl. She looked pure, different from the girls you see walking around at the mall. Well, she starts talking about Milton's *Paradise Lost*, explaining the theological implications of demons being created beings. I looked around the room, and probably ninety percent of the parents had no idea what she was even talking about. I was like, this is where my kids are going, whatever sacrifices we have to make."

Guy was vehement about guarding his children's hearts, guiding them to the Lord without being oppressive or strict. He was rarely ever even stern. He laughed and giggled with his kids, and found that having conversations and answering their questions proved extremely profitable. It made him sick how wicked america had become. It was impossible to get away from the filthiness. You would have to burn your house down and move to the middle of nowhere with no technology. But then you would become isolated and weird. It was necessary to live in the world, but it had become increasingly difficult to walk through the mire.

"So I told Faith that we were sending her to a special school, where she would learn about God and be allowed to talk about Him." God could not in truth be separated from knowledge. He could not imagine little Faith being bashed down daily anytime she mentioned God in school. "She says to me, Conti can't talk about God in school? That's what she calls her cousin Contessa. I say, nope. In public school you're not allowed to talk about God. She says that makes God very, very mad. She's extremely wise spiritually."

"I'm glad you found something that makes you comfortable. My girls made it through public school, but it was a constant battle. What's going on with Della?"

"Tougher than usual. We don't really talk much anymore. She sends me a text every few months. We say hello at birthdays and when she comes to spend a couple hours with the kids a few times a year." His relationship with his mother had given him much sadness, but he had learned to let go of it. It was hard to understand why she didn't want to spend more time with his precious children. Especially when she had been out of work for over three years. She was collecting benefits, so enough to keep living, but she would rather spend her time drinking coffee with her friends.

"That's a shame. Did something happen or just the natural progression of the course?"

"I guess both, but the straw was John's first birthday. It was great, but Mack came with this gal he's been dating—first time in twenty years. She seems nice, has her own money, smart, certainly a little odd. Used to be the chief financial officer for a major bank. So the next day my mom calls

Marie, screaming on the phone. How dare Marie invite her to the party and not tell my mom first. On and on, totally crazy as usual. So of course I'm forced to go over to the house and to tell her that she's not allowed to talk to my wife like that. She's completely oblivious as usual, totally disconnected from reality.

"She was talking smack about Mack the whole while, how he just did it to throw it in her face. I was like, seriously, Mom? You slept with the pool man and how many other people over the years—in Mack's own house. It's been twenty years. Get over it. All Mack does is work. He deserves to have someone who treats him nice. All my brother and sister do is treat him like dirt, take advantage of him. My mom just wasn't hearing it. I left. You know he still invites her to every family event, pays for everything. Nobody appreciates it."

"Are the kids still at the house?" Milton referred to Pearl and Herman as *the kids*, like Guy did, which was appropriate because they had never grown up. One of Mack's big mistakes was indulging them because of the guilt of their destroyed family.

"Nope. They finally flew the coop. Pearl got a little place here in Sherman Oaks. Herman met a nice quirky girl, moved into a shoe box in North Hollywood, from what I hear."

"From what you hear?"

"Yep, haven't heard from him since before John was born. The kids moved out of Mack's house, but left their cats home for Mack to take care of. Pretty nice, huh? Mack never liked cats, but he still did it for them. Well, his new girlfriend, Ginge Ma, has been getting that house in order. She's not asian, just getting a divorce. I told her it's a metaphor for his mental health. It's been difficult, but she's getting it cleaned up, totally remodeled. Part of the impetus was Faith having an asthma attack. We ended up taking all the carpet out of the house, cleaning the vents, getting air filters. Well, it was the kick in the pants Mack needed to get his house in order. Actually, without Ginge forcing the issue, he would still be living in a rat infestation.

"So he had told the kids for weeks to come get their cats. Of course they had more important things on their agenda. He tells them the cats are going to start living in the garage on Saturday— still nothing. One of the workers left the side door from the garage open, and Herman's cat got out. Mack was out all morning looking for the cat, not that the cat didn't spend half his life outside anyway. But Herman went crazy, told my dad he's never going to talk to him again." Guy shook his head. He could hear the carnival music playing.

"So what does that have to do with you two not talking?" Milton furrowed his eyebrows, as if confused.

"Well, somehow Herman gets it in his head that it's Faith's fault because of her asthma. I guess I put Mack up to the whole thing or something. Totally untrue. I never even mentioned it. But I get a text saying—hold on. It's too good to paraphrase." Guy pulled out his iPhone. "'*It's been a good run, but I can no longer be a part of your family. Your words and actions have caused your father to throw my cats outside at night to fend for themselves and die. Please refrain from trying to contact me again.*'"

"Get out of town! Are you serious? Oh, how dramatic, very Shakespearean." Milton began to howl with laughter. "I'm sorry. I'm sorry. I know this is your family, but the irony, it really is sad. Did you respond?"

"Well, with some encouragement from my lovely wife, I did." Then Guy read from his phone. "'*Herman, in response to your text, Marie and I respect your decision and apologize if we have caused any pain. We only told Dad that we support him in any decisions he makes in an effort to move on in regard to his house, his life and his new relationship. We love you. Guy and Marie.*'" It saddened Guy to send it, but his wife's wording of the message did not surprise him. Marie was so nice to Herman. She always included him and treated him kindly, despite his cruelty. Guy even gave him his car, an Acura Integra, when he bought his new one. Guy had loved that car.

"*Ooh*, that's perfect. You took the high road. Kindness is like salt in the wound to arrogant little punks. I really am afraid to ask how Jack is." Milton grimaced.

"Funny you should ask. It dovetails nicely." Guy began to chuckle as well. "So not too long after I got out of the hospital, I come home, and Marie looks sullen. Everyone was already dancing on eggshells a bit with me. She looked so disheartened and said she wasn't sure how to tell me. As usual I just said, spit it out. She passed me this little brown box. I opened it up. In it were the cell phone I had bought for my dad and a little note saying, he was cutting off contact with the family, please don't try to contact him again."

"Oh, that's rich. After all those years in combat and prison, he sure turned out to be a pussy. What a man, huh?" Milton let his anger show, which was rare, but he knew how long Guy had waited and had hoped for a relationship with his father.

"Oh well. You know I paid the bill on that damn phone, but it was just such a hassle for him. I guess he just couldn't adjust to walking out into the future, like being in *The Jetsons*." It was hard for Guy, but it had pushed him toward God. He was forced to let go of the burden from his family, to let it go at his Lord's feet.

"I hate to say it, but it's probably better that your kids know nothing about him. They have people in their lives who truly love them." Milton swallowed the gall building up in his throat.

"Not surprisingly he still talks to my mom. She told Marie that he's still selling jewelry for some lady out of one of those little street vendor stalls in manhattan." He never did make it to the monastery for his year of reintegration. Guy suspected it wouldn't have made a difference, but Jack probably would have found more comfort in their prison without bars.

"Jerry Springer would be real proud. I'm sorry, Guy, I just . . ."

Guy cut him off. "It's OK, Milton. I know. Fortunately or unfortunately for Springer, he could do ten or twelve seasons on my family. I've let it go." Guy pursed his lips.

"I'm sorry, but, hey, you have a beautiful wife, two wonderful kids, plus Mack. Should I assume Pearl's the same?"

"The same, what a shame," Guy sang with a singsong cadence. "Seems she thought my mother was a good example. She only dates thugs who treat her like crap. Serious thugs. Felons who steal from her, never one with a job. They spend her money and, for whatever peculiar reason, they're all black. She's such a pretty girl, smart, funny. It's a real shame." Guy loved his sister; he felt bad for her. Everyone had their type. If his sister's was black, Guy just wished she would look to the content of their character. He spoke to her to no avail.

Took her out for her birthday to Mr. Chow, one of the most expensive places in Beverly Hills. She liked to dance, so he took her out dancing to a club one of his clients' owned. He wanted her to know what it was like to be treated special, to have the door opened for her, to have a meal paid for.

Della had convinced Mack to destroy her though, which he was happy to do. Pearl had run up thirty grand in credit card debt, and Della had manipulated Mack to give Pearl the money, with no strings attached. Guy proposed a plan with some oversight, which Della had been dead set against. Pearl spent all the money, since she was given it directly. She never paid off her bills. Things went downhill rapidly since then.

"Some people who feel like garbage like to get treated like garbage. You guys still speak?"

"At birthdays, not much point otherwise. All she does is lie. No one has a clue what she's really up to. Mack had a license plate sent to his house with her name and a business name written on it. When Mack and Ginge asked Pearl about it, she just lied for like an hour, saying it wasn't hers. Ginge did some research, pulled up all the corresponding documents she was able to find online. Well, Pearl finally said she had a business, and that it was nobody's business. Really? Start your own business and not ask the only two people you know with an ounce of business sense for any advice? So the license plate is for a trailer. I'm hoping she's growing pot, because the only other thing I can think of is prostitution. Still, to start a business growing pot and not ask her brother about it? Now that's funny," Guy said jokingly and with a laugh.

"I can see why you wanted off the merry-go-round."

"That's not even the best part. Mack told me that, after she left, Ginge's diamond ring was missing from the counter. A real rock, worth like seventy-five grand. Ginge said Pearl came over the week before and took all of her new cosmetics, which seemed weird. They searched the whole house for the ring. Mack called Pearl to ask if she had seen the ring while she was there, because they were going to have to call the police. Because of its value, there would be an investigation. It was a felony matter. Pearl says she's going to stop by and help look, since she has some laundry to do. She magically finds the ring right on the counter underneath a napkin."

"Same place that has been searched, I assume."

"Of course. I'm wondering if she has a drug problem. Not pot, but something like coke or meth. Whenever she comes over to my dad's, she just falls asleep. I asked her about it, but of course she's a liar so . . ." Guy threw up his hands to his shoulders.

"That would seem to fit the bill, but who knows? Nothing you can do until she hits bottom."

"I just hope everyone lets her, for her own sake."

"Well, onto better things. A busy year of traveling, right?"

"Wow, yeah, we went to new york in January for Mack's mom's ninetieth birthday. It snowed. The kids were in heaven. We had snowball fights. Faith was so cute. She wanted to sit next to her great-grandma the whole time. Every time she did, Faith would take Great-Grandma's hand in hers and stroke the back of it. We saw Roxie and Jerry while we were there too." Seeing his grandmother's old sun-spotted hand with big knuckles stroked by Faith's soft, pale little hands was peculiarly beautiful. Guy smiled.

"I'm afraid to ask about Roxie." Milton covered his face with his hand, leaving room for him to look between his fingers with one eye.

"Well, Roxie's in a wheelchair. She has Hep C and liver failure, from all the booze and drugs. They won't give her a new liver, because she won't stop drinking."

"So sad." Milton frowned.

"It's been hard for Jerry. He's had to go over to her house a few different times to throw scumbags out on their ass. He found a crack pipe and a slice of pizza in her pants last time. He told me his brother, Paul, shot her up with heroin, so she could know how hard it was for him. Very empathetic, right?"

"Wow." Milton, who was rarely at a loss for words, was.

"We went over to Jerry's house out on the island. He's really great with our kids. They totally loved him. Nice house, eighteen hundred square feet or so. He totally remodeled the whole thing with stuff from job sites. So there's this giant pile of trash in his neighbor's yard, like ten feet high, seriously half the size of a house. He tells me, when he remodeled the house, he just threw all the trash into his neighbor's yard." Guy chuckled.

"What? Didn't his neighbor say something?" Milton was shocked, but not really.

"Of course, and when he did, Jerry told him, why don't you keep your fucking mouth shut, retart. Jerry's a monster, six four, shredded. Everyone was like, wow. He looks so great. I asked him, 'So how long you been doing 'roids?' He says, 'I do 'em six months a year. How'd you know?' I was like, 'Come on, seriously?' So the neighbor finally gets cited by the city for having all this trash in his yard, and he comes over to have Jerry's wife sign an affidavit, saying that it's theirs. She looks at him and says, 'I never sign anything without my husband.'" Guy chuckled some more.

"Sounds like a great guy." Milton crossed and uncrossed his legs.

"For our family, he's top-notch, has a good job, treats the kids kindly. He works his ass off." Guy shrugged his shoulders.

"What about John and Bear? You still hang out with those guys?"

"John rarely. He's been the world's biggest flake lately, totally rude. Takes him forever to return phone calls or texts. Then he shows up like *no big deal*. When I talk to him about it, he acts conciliatory, then it's just the same old story. It makes me sad, I try not to be frustrated. He's getting divorced from that girl, but he's still married. He was out banging every girl in town. That is until he met some paralegal while spraying her building for bugs."

"Ah, a girl with money, classic John. He must have one hell of a pecker. Not sure what else he brings to the table." Milton laughed and slapped his knee.

"He's got a good heart. He's been wooing this girl for like a year. Not sleeping with her, being a gentleman. So he finally gets up to the plate and hits a grand slam. Gets her pregnant on the first try. I'm sure he was like, seriously? I've been waiting my whole life for this gal. I'm not going to mess it up now. *Bam!*" Guy makes an imaginary swing of the bat. "Retirement here I come."

"He got her pregnant. Oh, man." Milton scrunched up his face.

"She's going to go back to work, and John's going to stay home and play mom. They decided not to get married, alimony can cut both ways. She's a real sweetheart, totally accepts John for who he is. I think it's going to be really great for him. So, pretty crazy. John is married to someone else and gets his girlfriend pregnant, and Bear gets a married girl pregnant."

"What? Are you kidding me? Bear's having a baby with someone who is already married?"

"Crazy," Guy chimed in, in falsetto. "But this one is good, at least, because it's Champagne, Marie's sister."

"What? She's married?" Milton's head was spinning, and it showed. If he had kept longer notes, he would have written a whole book by now.

"News to everyone. Apparently she married that illegal alien so he wouldn't get deported and never told anyone."

"Oh, boy, Guy. When this is the good part of your family story, . . . wow. OK, go on."

"So it is good. Champagne and Conti have just been destroyed by living with her dad and stepmom. Has turned Conti into a spoiled little brat. She cries and throws temper tantrums over everything. We were having movie night on Fridays at our house, but that stopped because Conti would just throw a fit the whole time. Champagne never even got to watch one move. Well, except that new *Clash of the Titans* movie, and that was only because she let Conti watch. She's six. I was totally disturbed by it, but Champagne lets her daughter watch just about whatever she wants.

"Champagne feels guilty because she has to work, that plus her dad keeps her completely under his thumb since he babysits and lets her live at his house. Going to be a big wake-up call for Arnie, because Bear bought a beautiful house in Castaic. They're all going to move in. Conti will actually get to go to a school where they speak English. She's the only white girl at her school in the Valley. Half of the class is done in Spanish. It is going to be really great for them. Bear's really calm and logical. '*Little kids do homework when they get home from school,*' he tells Champagne. Of course Conti is going to throw a fit doing homework at eight o'clock at night.

"Classic, they're going to have their minds blown, but it is going to be great for everyone. Bear deserves to have a great gal, and Champagne deserves to have a guy who will treat her well. We've been trying to push them together. I'm totally stoked." It was going to be great to have

Bear as a real part of the family, a brother-in-law. Family gatherings were going to be a lot more enjoyable.

"After all of these years? What—is it almost twenty? Bear's going to be your brother-in-law. Well, after Champagne's divorce, I guess." Milton laughed heartily. "And what about you, Guy? How is Guy?"

"You know, Milt, it's been a tough road, but I keep on walking. I have a great, wife, beautiful children, a good job. I'm extremely fortunate." It had been hard, but Guy was fortunate. If your perspective was clear, Guy was one of the most fortunate men in the world. He wanted for nothing, except the righteousness of God and His justice.

"That's a healthy perspective."

"They don't call me Mr. Fabulous for nothing." It was harder to keep his chin up the last few years.

"And you're OK with not having the food?"

"Look, Milton, this country is cruising for a hard fall. I don't care what anyone says. Like I've been saying, it's the same pattern as the Great Depression. In Nineteen Twenty 9, the biggest crash in history to that date—no wait—in Two Thousand Eight, an even bigger crash. Well, what happened after Nineteen Twenty 9 was the biggest rise in history. No wait, *now* this is the biggest stock market rise in history. Well, what happened in Nineteen Thirty Two after the first leg down and the rebound, the biggest stock market crash in history, the market fell by ninety percent. So if the pattern holds true, the next leg down will be over ninety percent. Except this time around, with all the leverage and the dollar being the world's reserve currency, it will crash the entire system. Go take a look at the interactive historical charts. You can see the pattern clearly. No wait, they've all been removed from the Internet." Guy smiled broadly.

"What do you mean, *they've all been removed from the Internet?* Nothing gets removed from the Internet." Milton had a perplexed look mingled with disbelief, but he had learned by now that, when it came to research, Guy did his homework.

"I mean that every interactive chart on the entire Internet for the time period of the Great Depression has been mysteriously removed from the Internet. Yahoo *http://finance.yahoo.com/echarts?s=%5EDJI +Interactive#symbol=%5EDJI;range=1d,* only goes back to Nineteen Eighty FIve. Google only goes to Nineteen Seventy Four. *https://www.google.com/finance?q=INDEXDJX%3A.DJI&ei=GOwuVIjBI cariQLhtIDwBQ.* They both used to cover the Great Depression, but no more. When was the last time you saw the Internet get smaller? All gone from every public site? You can find static charts, but you can't manipulate the time period, so you can't see the correlation of the pattern. I checked our Bloomberg terminal. You can still see it there, but that's only for professionals, and they could care less. Interesting, huh?"

"I'd say disturbing, but it's never been your understanding of the economy that's been in question. Look, Guy, you have an amazing ability to take large quantities of information and see the bigger picture. All everyone has been saying is that your conclusion that this is the end of the world is wrong. Sure, certainly it seems we're moving to some sort of a new age, a time of change. Maybe we are even witnessing the fall of america, but that doesn't mean it's the end of the world."

"OK, Milton, fine. Look, I've done what everybody asked. I got rid of all the food, gave some of it away to Union Rescue Mission down on skid row, Mack took the rest to storage. He's still not convinced a collapse isn't coming. I tore down the ark and had a beautiful sunroom built for the family. All glass, even a glass ceiling, opens all the way around. Put our workout stuff in there, a couch, got a sixty-four-inch Samsung. Everyone loves it. You can see the mountains off in the distance. Added about four hundred fifty square feet to the house. They wanted seventy five thousand dollars to do it with permits. I got it for thirty five thousand. One of the benefits of the downturn I guess."

"Impressive negotiation as usual. So you're OK with all that, not having the food then."

"That day the cops told John to take my guns. I can technically have them back this summer, but I'm OK with it now. It's forced me to depend on God completely. If after all this, He wants me and my family to have our heads caved in on the concrete by these scum, then so be it. Because after the trigger is pulled and they tell people they need to leave their homes for their own safety and go to the camps, my household will not bend our knee. We will not go to the camps and not lose our soul to save our lives." The Lord commanded men to fight against the darkness, but instead men had embraced it, making it so strong that it filled every crack. This time the battle would be the Lord's. It was hard for Guy to lay down his sword as the enemy encamped round about him.

"That sounds a bit like the delusion creeping back in."

"Milton, I'll put it this way. I try to keep the so-called delusion in a box with the lid closed tightly. But, try as I might, the box will not stay shut. It's as if this world is the illusion, and the delusion is what's real. It's tiring. The fear and concern for what I feel is coming can be debilitating. But it has all pointed me closer to God. I try to relax, go to the sauna, sit in the ice pool. About the only thing that really brings me comfort is reading the book of Psalms. I was reading A *Tale of Two Cities*, and Dr. Manette develops this psychosis from being locked in solitary confinement for all of those years. He finds comfort in making shoes.

Eventually he's released and regains his health, but he keeps the little shoemaker's bench and falls back into a psychosis that he hardly makes it out of. His friend Jarvis tells him that he needs to let go and destroy the shoemaker's bench. I found it analogous to my food. So I let it go, but it still didn't seal the box."

"Well, you certainly seem less obsessed. It seems the anxiety has decreased significantly."

"I've learned to keep my mouth shut. Nobody cares anyway. I've taken a lot of steps to decrease my anxiety. I believe that God's plan is perfect, that He never gives someone more than they can endure." Guy was not a man who picked and chose truth from the Bible to suit himself. If you did, you could always rationalize your behavior and be righteous in your own eyes. "I swear, Milt, I do feel like I'm losing my mind sometimes. I even feel like they are passing information through the television and movies, like they're mocking us."

"The ever-present *they*?"

"The illuminati-scum *they*, who are trying to bring about their New World Order. There's this movie that came out called *Take Shelter*. The main character is married to a redhead and keeps saying there is this storm coming. Well, it consumes him, and he stores up all this food and starts acting crazy, pushing everyone away from him. He finally lets it all go and takes a vacation. When he does, this massive storm comes, a world-ending storm. He's there with his wife, trapped, away from his shelter. He's going to be killed. I felt like it was mocking me. I did some research. Maybe I have schizophrenia or something. At least that would make sense to everybody. I am worried about doing all this traveling this year." Guy was worried, but he put all of his eggs in God's basket.

"You don't have schizophrenia, Guy. That you can be sure of. I saw that movie. I thought your take on things was more broad-minded."

"If *broad-minded* is code for *disturbing*."

"I don't find any of this disturbing, Guy."

"That's because you're an atheist. For you the Bible is only a book of fairy tales."

"I never said I was an atheist, Guy. I'm a man of reason, a man who seeks knowledge's light."

Guy swallowed hard; a cold shiver ran down his spine. As he looked at the clock, his hour was up.

BOOK THREE: CHAPTER SIX

As Guy lay in his bed, he was pleased Marie was correct. She had told him that Two Thousand Twelve was going to be a great year for the family, a year of renewal. As Guy had placed more eggs in God's basket, Guy was able to come to terms with the impending doom more and more. Not that it was any less real, but he so enjoyed every moment with his wife and children. They provided him with overwhelming joy; they were his focus. The Lord spoke into Guy's heart: Guy could either learn to let the King of kings carry his burden or share it with his family, so that they trembled with fear. It was no choice at all. Guy kept his views to himself, and the loneliness of the burden only pointed him closer to God. It made him more reliant on God's mercy.

It was a great year so far. The Finnigans did more traveling this year than in nearly the twenty years Guy and Marie had been together. They had gone to new york, along with Pearl, Mack and Mack's girlfriend, Ginge, for Mack's mother's ninetieth birthday. It was a great time spent together.

The January timing for the new york trip couldn't have been better. Long Island was carpeted with snow. Faith and John had the time of their lives pelting Guy and Mack in the face with snowballs, and making little angels in the snow. Mack's grandma Lizzie grew soft in her old age. She was no longer harsh and cold as she was when Guy was a child. She was kind and adored Faith and John. She looked great for ninety; she was still living in her own apartment in an assisted-living facility. The image of Faith holding her great-grandmother's hand in hers was pleasurably seared into Guy's memory.

When her great-grandmother had asked Faith if santa claus had been good to her last month, Faith promptly replied that santa claus wasn't real. That it was a lie used to trick little children about Jesus's birthday. Guy smiled at the reaction upon his grandmother's face. When Faith was three, Guy started to take her out for daddy-daughter dates, so they could spend individualized time together. They would go for lunch and ice cream, play carnival games, go to museums, whatever Faith's little heart desired. Guy was looking forward to John being old enough so he could do daddy-son days too. Like most young children, he was still too attached to his mother. Guy found the switch changed from Mommy to Daddy around the age of three.

During a December outing when Faith was only three, she had asked Guy if santa claus was real. She had a knack for asking deep questions, like, "Where did satan come from?" Guy was always honest, and put things in terms she could understand but would not be overwhelmed with or scared by. He had told her how satan was an angel once. He had been created by God, but satan thought he was greater than God and led a war with one-third of the angels against God. satan was thrown out of heaven, and satan and his angels became the evil demons.

"*Pfff*, no one is stronger than God," she replied.

Guy knew it would likely bring up conversations with everyone else he knew, as santa was all the rage. But Guy was honest, and he told his daughter santa was not real. He didn't lie to her. If there was something that was not age appropriate, he simply told her so. He was glad he was honest, since the next question out of her little mouth, was "God's real, right, Dada?" *Of course He is, sweetheart.* "christmas is about Jesus, not santa. Why do parents trick their children about santa?" she asked. *Your daddy would never trick you, but that snake is very tricky. He's a liar*, Guy replied. "I don't like that snake one bit. I can't wait till Jesus locks him in prison for a thousand years," she said under her scrunched little nose.

Guy made the big bank trip again this year; this time it was in Miami. The bank treated the family like kings. Marie's mom, Aloha, came, so that Marie could attend all the events and dinners instead of watching the children. The water was warm and crystal clear; the family frolicked together in the ocean. The unending smiles upon his family's faces filled Guy with the utmost joy.

Who knew when they would ever get back to Florida again, so Guy decided to take everyone to Disney World. They stayed at Disney's Animal Kingdom Lodge. There were antelopes and giraffes right outside the balcony of the room, no more than fifteen feet away. There must be some sort of underground electrical fence, Guy thought. He wasn't sure who was more head over heels, the children or Aloha. She was a valuable addition to the trip. She loved taking care of the children; she would clean up the rooms and make sure everyone was taken care of, without even being asked.

Disney's attention to detail was staggering. Every time Guy's family walked to the lobby, someone would teach the children to play the bongos. When they went outside to look at the animals, people handed out sticks so the children could roast marshmallows. One morning the entire playground was filled with unlimited candy, so all the children in the entire hotel could collect a full bag without any skirmishes.

When they went to the Magic Kingdom, they were allowed to go in before the park opened—an extra benefit from staying at the hotel. They were greeted by a train coming down the tracks while Casey Jr. played a dance extravaganza with all of the Disney characters, followed by fireworks. As Guy, Marie and Aloha looked toward each other, there were tears in their eyes. Guy got to be a kid again with his children. When they went to the Animal Kingdom Park, everyone got their faces painted like different animals. Guy and John were both lions, with matching Pluto shirts. It seemed the family had a lifetime's worth of smiles and laughter.

When they returned, Guy and Marie left for what Guy envisioned would be a second honeymoon. They had never left their children for even a night before, but Guy had received tickets to a charity fund-raiser at the Cannes International Film Festival in france, a black-tie affair. He initially thought there was no chance they would actually attend. But the opportunity to take his wife to europe seemed unlikely to materialize again for at least another decade or two. Guy planned a first-class trip. They would initially stop at The Lanesborough in london, now operated by St. Regis. It had opened in Eighteen Forty Four and was within walking distance to buckingham palace.

Guy arranged for a private car, a Mercedes S Five Hundred, to pick them up from the airport. The driver waited for them at the departure exit, holding a placard with their name. When they arrived at the hotel, Guy was kicked out of the bar for not having a jacket. He thought it was great. They had a private butler, plus another driver in the same model Mercedes to take them to all the must-see spots around london. It made their time efficient. Their driver knew all the best spots, dropped them off at the front and waited until they were done. Then off to the next spot. While Marie tried to decline, Guy bought his wife a Louis Vuitton purse, so she would have something to remember the trip by. They saw the Tower of london, where many a good man was tortured by the crown. It was now filled with the empire's treasures. Guy had never seen a crown or scepter with so many giant gems, let alone hundreds and hundreds of them. God forbid there was ever a man without food in england.

Guy found the french characteristically rude, but their bread and cheese helped to smooth it over. Guy and Marie dressed to the 9s and enjoyed their time with each other at the festival, unassumingly amused by the self-importance of it all. At least their room had a beautiful view overlooking the Mediterranean waters.

rome was the Finnigans' favorite. They stayed at the St. Regis again, with a butler, a driver and all the rest. Their driver, Danilo, was a man of the city. He took them for the best pizza, the best coffee, the best gelato, and even organized a private tour of the vatican with an art history major. Guy was amazed at what the church had amassed over the last two thousand years. Guy and Marie held hands as they walked through the streets of europe, more in love than when they had first met.

Guy had his feelings bruised when he had asked his wife if she were proud of him for coming so close to the seat of wickedness. She belittled him for only a moment, and, as usual, Guy knew he should have kept his thoughts to himself. They let it go quickly and enjoyed the romance in the air.

They had a layover in munich. Guy arranged for a taxi to take them to dachau. Marie waited in the car, as she thought it was too heavy an emotion to bear. The site of the barracks, the ovens and the gas chambers made Guy weep bitterly. When he returned to the car, all he could say with hands over his mouth was "The horror." Marie sat quietly.

The children were watched for the first three days by Della and Champagne, and the last four by Mack and Ginge. There were strict house rules: no one other than those four, were allowed in the house, no matter the reason, especially Arnie. Twenty twelve was, indeed, shaping up to be quite the year.

★★★

Guy was still drowsy from the previous night as the night sky began to lighten. Faith's fifth birthday bash the day before was an all-out shindig. Faith had asked for two years if she could go to Disneyland for her fifth birthday. Guy had planned it out in advance; he had scheduled time for her to be made up like a princess at Bibbidi Bobbidi Boutique as soon as the park opened. Of course Mack and Ginge were there early. The look of delight on Mack's face was matched only by Faith's joy as she picked out her Belle dress with matching shoes and crown. Could she get a scepter too, Dad? Of course she could.

Bear, Champagne and Conti showed up half an hour late, which was early for Champagne and becoming normal for Bear, now that they were not only a couple but also having a baby of their own. Guy was thrilled. After twenty years, his best friend was actually becoming his brother-in-law. Finally a comrade at the dinner table. It was only when he pressed Bear about the marriage timetable that Bear let the cat out of the bag about Champagne being married to Facundo in order to prevent him from getting deported. No one knew, and they wanted to keep it that way.

Besides, Bear was adamant that Conti be treated the same as their new child. He didn't want to make a big deal about getting married before having the baby since Conti was born out of wedlock. Guy offered to sign on a loan for a ring, and Bear found a monster at a shop that one of

Guy's friends worked at. Bear was marrying a married woman who he had gotten pregnant, and John Brown, while married, got a gal pregnant who wouldn't marry him. How times had changed. Bear, John and Guy all had a good laugh.

Little Conti joined Faith in the princess transformation. They were so cute, tourists stopped them throughout the day and begged to take a picture—something Guy would have never allowed, but yesterday he acquiesced. Guy tried his best not to be irritated that his mother had scheduled a trip to new york, knowing it was during Faith's birthday, to meet her sister Prissy and spend time with Jack. She said her tickets were nonrefundable, but it wasn't like the day of Faith's birth had changed. Arnie of course had flaked as well. Guy had even purchased extra tickets for the giant laser and fireworks show, called *Fantasmic!* What a great way to end the night; they had their own special seats right up at the front, where they were served hot cocoa and cakes.

Pearl was a no-show as well. Guy gave away Arnie's and Pearl's *Fantasmic!* tickets to a family who seemed of modest means, sitting on the ground all the way in the back. The family was stunned. The fact that Arnie didn't even call Faith to wish her a happy birthday really grated on Guy's nerves. Almost as much as when Bear let it out that Arnie had called the day before, asking if he could take Conti back to Disneyland the day after Faith's birthday. What a piece of trash. The day was so special, Faith didn't even notice. A more magical experience than Guy's fifth birthday, that was for sure. Try as all the others might, the spiritual curse on his family seemed to be broken, for the Finnigan children loved the Lord; they were happy and safe.

"Daddy, Daddy." Faith tiptoed down the hall, followed in tow by her little brother.

"Dada." John tried to tiptoe as well but only managed to hunch his shoulders.

Guy had Faith sleeping in her own bed a year ago, but, not more than a week later, Marie moved Faith's mattress to the foot of their bed. John was still sleeping in bed with them, but, since they had arrived home so late, Guy took the opportunity to put them in their own rooms. He certainly enjoyed having the children sleep with him, but it seemed necessary for the health of the family that they stayed in their own rooms.

Marie had turned bedtime into quite an ordeal, lying down with the children every night for at least an hour while they fell asleep in their own rooms, and then moving them in the master bedroom when she and Guy were ready for bed. It significantly cut into the little evening time they had together during the weeknights.

"Too early, it's still nighttime, come on up." Guy rolled over on his side to check the clock. Not quite night, but certainly closer to five a.m. than six. The children had fallen asleep in the double stroller around 11p.m. on the way back to the tram. John had crashed with his little hiene up in the air.

"Did you have a fun time for your birthday, my darling daughter dear?" Guy scooped up his daughter onto the bed. She was solid; she was getting big now.

"That was the best birthday ever! You're the best daddy in the whole wide world. I love you so much, Daddy." Faith nuzzled her dad like a little kitten and kissed his check.

"What about you, my handsome son?" Guy could still scoop up his son with one arm.

"I shot those aliens. *Pechew*." John was already holding his little Buzz Lightyear ray gun.

"Buzz Lightyear, you sure did shoot all those aliens, my handsome son." Guy smiled.

John leaped to his feet, one foot astride Marie, like a heroic conqueror. "*Pechew, pechew*." He pointed his ray gun to the wall. "I got those aliens. They can't get me. I'm too fast. *Pechew*. Can we go back on Buzz Lightyear, please, Dada, please?" John's little face beamed.

"Your daddy took you six times yesterday, and you did so good. Daddy will take you back for your birthday, if you want." John did do well. He had scored better than his sister and nearly as well as Marie. Guy kept his score to himself, since it was more than Marie, Faith and John added up and tripled.

"Yeah, yeah." John giggled.

"Give your mommy a snuggle." Marie pulled Faith down on top of her and hugged her daughter tight. "And what was your favorite part, sweetheart?" Marie stroked her daughter's hair.

"Well, I liked being a princess with Conti, but I also liked driving the cars. Well, I also liked having lunch with Winnie the Pooh, and the hot chocolate with the fireworks, and that little boat thingy with the different people singing, 'It's a small world after all.'" Faith smiled wide, and moved her head back and forth trying to imitate the tone of the song.

"I drive fast!" John said, making a deep little voice and extending his hands out like he was holding a steering wheel.

"You drove so fast." Marie giggled. They had ridden on Autopia five times. John would laugh hysterically when he made the car jerk by intentionally steering the tire into the rail.

"I'm glad you both had fun. I had a great time for your fifth birthday, my darling daughter. And you children were so well behaved. Thank you so much. I really appreciate it."

"Thank you, Daddy." Faith gave her daddy a giant bear hug.

John leaped in as well. "Thank you, Dada."

"I love you, family." Guy's heart smiled even bigger than his mouth.

"My favorite part was Daddy dancing." Marie giggled.

"Daddy's still got moves." Guy shook his shoulders back and forth.

"Dada." John grabbed his father's face.

"Silly Daddy." Faith and John crinkled their noses.

There had been a giant XBox exhibit, and Guy had danced to Michael Jackson's "Beat It," along with Faith, John and Conti. It was pretty neat; you could see a very detailed infrared image of everyone dancing up on a big screen. Toward the end, Guy took turns picking up the children and pumping them in and out from his chest along to the music. It was great fun. Guy would have bought one for the house, had it not been for the degenerate filth who could use it to see through his walls and look at his family whenever they desired. Disgusting pigs.

"All right, who wants breakfast?" Guy rose to his feet. "How about a monkey tail sandwich?" Guy said jokingly.

"Daddy!" Faith looked incredulous, sitting upon her knees with her hands on her hips.

"One white and one brown." Guy pointed his finger from side to side.

"Dada, I want a sausage sandwich, Dada, and hot chocolate. Will you make it for me, please?" John pursed his lips together.

"OK, but first Daddy needs to eat some cookies. I am *sooo* hungry." Guy snatched a foot from each of his children and pretended to gobble up their little toes. "Mmm, delicious."

"Daddy, Dada," they rang out in unison.

"I want coffee, Dada. You babes are up *tooo* early." Marie pursed her lips as well and then let out a laugh.

Faith stood to her feet. "O God, my heart is fixed; I will sing and give praise, even with my glory. Awake, psaltery, and harp: I myself will awake early. I will praise thee, O Lord, among the people; and I will sing praises unto thee among the nations. For thy mercy is great above the heavens: and thy truth reaches unto the clouds." Faith reached her arms up to the heavens and extended them down to her sides in an arch.

"Wow, that was amazing and appropriate." Guy looked from his daughter to Marie, and their eyes smiled together.

"A psaltery is like a guitar. I learned it from Miss Bonhomie in preschool. I can't wait to go to kindergarten and my special new school.

I'm going to sleep in my own room, like a big girl, when I go to kindergarten." Faith beamed.

"I am so impressed. You are doing so well. You are such a smart little girl." She was getting so big, and she had no problem speaking her mind. Guy walked to the bathroom and grabbed his phone. It had gone dead around dinnertime from picture fatigue. He could see he had nineteen missed calls from his aunt Prissy. Guy rubbed the ridges above his eyes. While Prissy was kind, he was certain she didn't call nineteen times to wish Faith a happy birthday. He imagined it had something to do with the merry-go-round.

His mother and Prissy had decided to meet in new york to help Prissy snap out of her funk. Her pastor husband, who was making regular trips to the Philippines to do outreach work with the poor, found that he was most effective ministering with his pants off. He was moving one of his new congregants and their children to the states. They would be living with him, and Prissy's services were no longer required. She was humiliated and hardly able to get out of bed. Della found it to be the perfect reason to move down to Florida in order to rehabilitate Prissy. They could live in the little spare house that Prissy owned. It was a perfect location for Della's near dozen cats. Even the debilitated Prissy found it distasteful and shot down the idea out of hand.

It was surprising that Della was even up for the trip. She had just rehabilitated herself within the last few months, having contracted cat scratch fever from one of the feral cats she had trapped. The scratch had manifested as a softball-size lump in the lymph node near her left bicep. The doctor took out the lump of puss and left MRSA, the antibiotic-resistant bacteria, in its place. When Guy brought her over dinner after her surgery, he was surprised to find that the cat culprit was sleeping on his mother's pillow, next to her head. The small rented apartment in the divided house off of Sunset stank of cat urine, which appeared to cover most of the articles in the apartment. When she had recovered, she couldn't comprehend why Guy wouldn't allow the children to come over to the house for a visit.

Better to get it over in one fell swoop than piece together the chain of multiple voice mails, so Guy clicked his aunt's number, and she picked it up even before the first ring.

"Good morning, Aunt Prissy. What's up?"

"Guy, Guy." His aunt was hyperventilating on the other end of the line. "I tried to *huuuh, huuuh,* I tried to call, *huuuh, huuuh.*" Prissy sounded as if she were drowning, gasping for air.

"Prissy, calm down. We were at Disneyland for Faith's fifth birthday. My phone went dead from taking pictures all day. We got in late. What's going on?" Guy was calm and firm. He had closed the bathroom door and turned on the light.

"Oh, my God, Guy, oh, my God. He did it. He really did it," Prissy said hysterically.

"Slow down, Prissy. What's going on?" Guy lowered his voice.

"He did it." Prissy's voice was low, slow, gravelly, like a woman possessed.

"Who did what, Prissy?"

"She's dead," Prissy whispered into the phone, followed by a bout of hysterical sobs.

"Who's dead, Prissy? What are you talking about? What happened?" Guy asked, inherently knowing who *she* was.

"Della! Della, she's dead. He killed her," Prissy spit out feverishly.

"Who killed her?" Guy asked, already knowing who *he* was. Guy was still calm; he processed the information without yet internalizing it. When it all hit the fan, Guy was always focused.

"JACK!" Prissy screamed into the phone.

"It's OK, Prissy, calm down. Tell me what happened."

"He bashed her brains out, that's what happened. OH, MY GOD, OH, MY GOD, he bashed her brains right out of her head. They came right out of her forehead, and I was screaming, 'Stop, Jack, stop!' but he kept on hitting and hitting her, *huuuh, huuuh.*"

"Prissy, where are you?"

"He smashed her whole face gone."

Guy heard the phone drop to the floor. "Hello? Hello, Prissy, Prissy."

"Hey."

"Jerry, is that you? What the hell is going on?" Guy asked resolutely.

"Oh, my God, cuz. Holy shit, bro, holy shit. Oh, my God, I'm so sorry, bro."

"Yo, just tell me what's going on. What happened exactly? Start from the beginning."

"All right, all right. So Aunt Prissy was flying into JFK last night to meet up with your moms, right? I was going to pick her up from the airport, but I get a call in the afternoon from your moms, saying she and your pops are hanging out, and they're going to pick up Prissy when she gets in. I was like, that's not what I heard, and she says she already spoke to Prissy and got all the flight information, and it's all worked out, and I was like OK, whatever."

"All right, go on."

"So I get this call from the seven one eight that I don't recognize. I pick it up, and it's Prissy. She's screaming, all crazy. I can hardly understand a word she's saying. She's like, 'Jack's running all over the airport, and he's yelling that the c.i.a.'s coming.' And I'm like, 'Yo, I'm coming down there, just relax.' She starts screaming, 'No, no, there he is. He's got her.' She screams 'Jack,' and then just lets the phone go, nothing. All I could hear was some muffled noise. I yelled into the phone for like five minutes. Then I hung up and tried to call JFK—you know how that goes. Total monkeys on the line. They're talking to me like I'm a fuckin' moron."

"Oh, man, OK. So then what?" Guy ran his fingers though his wild morning hair and sat down on the toilet. The bathroom door cracked open, and Marie poked her face in. The shake of Guy's head and the look in his eyes let her know that it was something, not nothing, but something.

"It'll be OK," she mouthed and closed the door.

"So I'm going round and round with these t.s.a. idiots on the phone, when my other line starts buzzing. I click over, and it was some sergeant from nypd. He starts asking me who I am, and if I'm related to Prissy or Della, and can I please come down to security at JFK immediately. I'm like, yeah, but just tell me what's going on. He starts trying to play cop with me, and telling me, 'Sir, just come down to security, and I'll tell you all about it when you get here.' And I'm like, 'Listen here, you doughnut-eating mutherfucker, tell me what the fuck is going on, or we're going to have another fucking incident when I get down there.'"

"*Ooooh.*" Guy groaned. "I'd expect nothing less, Jerry, so then what?"

"So I'm like, 'Listen, you fat fuck, I've already been on the phone with the goon squad for like an hour while they're telling me not to worry and to calm down. Clearly someone should have been worried, huh? I'm coming from the island. You gonna make me go all nutso while I'm driving over there in traffic for an hour?' That's when he tells me that your moms is dead, and I keep pressing, and he tells me that your pops bludgeoned her in the head. So I get over there as fast as I can. I tried to call you." Jerry was apologetic in his tone.

"*Ugh.*" Guy groaned again. "I know. I know. It's all right. Not like it would have made a difference. We were at Disneyland for Faith's fifth birthday. My phone died from taking so many pictures. I just got up and saw all the messages."

"I'm so sorry, bro. It's sick. Our family is sick, just fucking crazy lunatics. Doctor says my moms is going to be joining her. Her liver's failing, and they won't get her a new one because she won't stop fucking drinking."

"I know. I'm sorry. That's why I keep my kids insulated from all this. My family's on a new path." Guy's head spun; it seemed the merry-go-round had caught up with him.

"Good for you, don't let this bring you down. I know it's hard. You guys are all about God, right? I guess now's when you really need that sort of shit."

"He's with us in good times and bad. We'll be all right." Guy was numb.

"All right, all right. So just the rest of the details. I get down there, and Prissy is totally in shock, blood all over her. We end up having to go down and ID your moms. Look, I know this is tough to hear, but I gotta say it anyway—you know me, I'm not gonna hide nothing."

"I appreciate it. Go ahead," Guy said uniformly.

"There was nothing to ID. Her face was gone, cuz. He just totally smashed it in. The cops had witnesses who saw the whole thing, said he was running around all crazy, dragging her by the wrist, yelling about the c.i.a. and shit. Then she started yelling for him to let go, and he just snapped. They said he punched her in the face, and she was out, but then he just started smashing her head against the floor. Everyone they interviewed said it happened so fast. They had her driver's license and everything, so they were sure it was her.

"When the cops got there, Jack was just sitting next to her, with his legs crossed, and his eyes closed, like he was fucking meditating or something. Fucking psycho, like something out of a movie. They have him in custody. Prissy is like retarted or something now. We got a doctor coming over to the house today."

"Wow" was about all Guy could muster. "All right, I appreciate everything you did. I got calls to make. I'll call you in a couple hours. I love you."

"I love you too, cuz. I'm sorry, bro."

Guy was tired, emotionally and mentally tired, but there were lots of people to inform. He had no desire to talk, but he would call his dad Mack first, after Guy spoke with his wife. Before he could even get a word out, Mack related that Pearl was in Northridge Hospital with a broken jaw, courtesy of the latest miscreant she was "dating" for the last five weeks. They were in love; he didn't mean to. She needed Mack's help to get the police to understand it was all just an accident, to make sure there were no charges filed. At least Faith had had a birthday she would never forget, completely and innocently unaware of the tumult in the background.

It was a day that Guy would never forget either. It left him with a feeling of incomplete completion. He was morose and wept privately over the next few days. The carnival music ceased. It was hard to find a sense of closure, but he told his mother how much he loved her, that he was sorry their relationship was not a closer one.

Guy spread her ashes in the ocean from the Santa Monica pier. Not because that was what she had desired—no one knew what she desired as the conversation had never came up. It was one of Guy's favorite places. The ashes of her empty body could finally be free to drift wherever the current wandered. He would think of her whenever the family stayed at the Loews Hotel, overlooking the pier and the ocean.

Faith wasn't sure why everyone was sad; Grandma was with Jesus in heaven. *Wasn't that great? Don't worry. We'll see her again*, Faith had said. *She'll have a brand-new body. She won't even have to dye her gray hair anymore.*

Pearl filed for bankruptcy, which, generally speaking, Guy was morally opposed to. But it was the right thing for her. Hopefully she would use the fresh slate as a clean start. Jerry called a month later. He got a call from Jack who had asked Jerry to let Guy know how much he had loved Della, that she was the love of his life. Even to Jerry it came off as twisted. Jack found out he had AIDS when he was reincarcerated. Of course Jerry pressed the subject. It wasn't from drugs, but twenty years of gay prison sex. He wasn't gay of course, but men had needs.

Guy focused on his wife and family, how beautiful they were and how much joy they brought to his life. Marie wanted to go back to school to become a nurse. Guy was a bit ambivalent because he didn't want her working simply to pay for someone else to raise their children. She wanted more interaction, something to do with herself when the children went to school full-time. Guy thought there were all sorts of activities she could get involved in, but he could tell this was important to her. She found classes she could take during the night as long as Guy could be home to watch the children. He was of course amenable to it.

Nurses had flexible hours, Marie said, they could work nights. It seemed likely to take up all of their free time together, but Guy knew they always found a way to make things work. They would cross that bridge together when they got to it. Having some extra money would be nice, though it wouldn't be as much as Marie expected. Because of his income, half of her anticipated salary would go to taxes. Having the children to himself some evenings was a true joy; they did whatever tickled their fancy.

Guy was no longer seeing Milton. His comment on not being an atheist gave Guy a strange feeling. Guy was able to get his anxiety down to near zero by turning ever closer to God, taking practical steps with his diet and getting a little exercise when he could fit it in. As the summer of Two Thousand Twelve closed, Guy could feel something big on the horizon, that it was time to clear his head. A time to listen carefully, to prepare for what God had to say next.

In order to hear clearly, Guy needed to have a clear head. He was back on the Seroquel since John had been conceived. It made everyone around him happy; no one cared that it made him feel like a zombie for half the day. He was on as low a dose as everyone felt comfortable with. Guy had asked lots of questions; the medication only helped with anxiety. The doctors confirmed it did not, could not and would not help with what was comfortably referred to by all as *the delusion*.

Guy knew it was time for him to stop taking the poison; he would wean himself off. Guy finally had Faith's bed in John's room so they could keep each other company at night, which was in reality a solution to provide Marie some comfort. John was fighting a cold, and Marie had spent the week sleeping with him, so she could attend to his needs. The timing was good, since Guy had had horrible night sweats and a nasty body rash while he was detoxing. He had timed it so he would be completely off the medication for 9/11. It seemed like an appropriate day to end a lie. Guy kept it to himself. He figured, after a few months, Marie would notice that he hadn't gotten his prescription filled. By then he thought her nerves would be soothed by knowing he was off the medication for months and months, without anyone even batting an eyelash.

As he detoxed, Guy noticed his appetite changing; he felt like a ravenous wild beast. He developed a hankering for midnight snacks, something he had never indulged in. He still went to bed around tenish as usual but would be woken up an hour or two later feeling as if he could eat a horse and unable to get back to sleep until he raided the refrigerator. He worried that he was becoming addicted, especially to Colonel Tsao sauce. He felt as if he could slather it upon everything he ate. The evening of September tenth, he ate with such fervor it felt like bloodlust. Guy was disgusted with himself.

When he was done, he lay upon the floor and prayed to God for relief from his growing gluttony. He asked God to give him strength, to free him from his gluttonous cravings. God simply asked if Guy enjoyed filling his bloated gut with babies? When he heard this, Guy was sick to his stomach. He hardly made it to the bathroom before he vomited. Guy's head spun. Eating babies? Guy wished he was losing his mind, but he knew well enough by now that, when God spoke loudly into Guy's heart, He spoke truth, no matter how nonsensical or unimaginable it seemed.

Guy booted up his laptop to see if he could find confirmation in the physical world. It didn't take him long to find out that, in fact, aborted fetuses were being used at research facilities for Pepsi–Cola and others. http://www.naturalnews.com/035276_Pepsi_fetal_cells_business_operations.html. Pepsi initially denied it completely, as they didn't see cells created using aborted fetuses as anything but lab research. http://www.washingtontimes.com/news/2012/mar/28/pepsico-denies-accusations-on-link-to-aborted-feta/?page=all. Guy knew everyone would laugh and scoff when he told them. Even if he showed them articles, they would simply say, *well, see? They say they don't actually put it in the soda.* But, as usual, it was a lie, like derivatives. It was endemic and secret. Things were labeled with peculiar names, refined, reprocessed, renamed, but the derivatives of aborted babies were being put into the food supply. Why? It was part of the luciferian illuminati's black magic, a way to debase the population. Simply another arrow from their quiver directed at humanity. With a little more digging, Guy found pictures of fetuses dipped in gold uncovered by police that were to be sold to rich clients for black magic rituals. http://www.dailymail.co.uk/news/article-2146396/British-man-arrested-Thailand-suitcase-dead-babies-used-religious-ritual.html.

Guy was sick and tired of being debased. He would switch his diet and eat only all-organic products. He long ago stopped putting chemicals on his body, whether hair products or the poison they called deodorant that went directly into the lymph nodes. Guy found, if he ate healthy, wore clean clothes and showered, he had no need of deodorant. He drank only distilled water. No more fluoride, a poison chemical so toxic that it's put below the foundation of buildings so any insects coming in contact with it die instantly. No, he decided, he would no longer put any chemicals inside his body either, no more preservatives, no processed food, only organic. It seemed the only way to ensure against being tricked into eating aborted children. He would find some organic soap too. One of the upsides of left-leaning los angeles was an abundance of all things organic.

On September 11, Two Thousand Twelve, Guy was poison free. He woke up feeling fresh and alive. He was thankful for God's mercy and curious as to what else the Lord wanted to show him. By lunch Guy's regularly read websites were ablaze with a new 9/11 attack on america's embassy in benghazi. Four americans were murdered, including an ambassador. The official story line was the attack was in retaliation for a YouTube video defaming islam—a video that no one had ever seen, made by some nobody which no one had ever heard of. Of course the muslims should be entitled to murder for any slight against their religion, even a mere cartoon would do. http://www.theobjectivestandard.com/2010/04/drawings-of-mohammed-in-defense-of-human-life/. While in america the government was happy to use tax money to pay artists to smear feces on the Virgin Mary or to have Christ on the cross placed in a jar of urine for all to admire.

Even the american public, so hungry for lies, couldn't swallow the government's story. There was no other reason given, just a closing of ranks, an atmosphere that said, don't ask questions, don't think for a minute that the president had any involvement in decision making. Of course not even the house or senate could have information pertaining to who was making what decisions when. The illuminati were using their New World Order power base, america, to rapidly destabilize the world as they sought to bring about World War , more aptly known as the War of Armageddon. It seemed their bombs of liberating love were not well received in libya.

It was, however, easy for anyone with eyes to see that the attackers in benghazi were simply weapons in the hands of a murderous american administration. It seemed likely the reason the ambassador was murdered involved using the consulate to run weapons to the syrian rebels. Perhaps the ambassador grew a conscious or maybe he just knew too much. Bits and pieces trickled out eventually, including that a portion of the facility was likely run by the c.i.a. *http://www.huffingtonpost.com/2013/08/02/benghazi-attack-cia_n_3695319.html*. Even more dastardly was the administration's demand to stand down, orders issued to two separate special operations teams, who were on their way to defend the consulate. Two us navy seals units near the complex were also told to offer no assistance three times; they disobeyed orders and lost their lives saving their comrades in the process. *http://www.forbes.com/sites/larrybell/2012/11/01/benghazi-stand-down-denials-dont-stand-up-to-reason/*.

john mccain met with the syrian rebels, declared them good and said america should supply them with weapons including antitank and antiaircraft missiles. *http://ronpaulinstitute.org/archives/neocon-watch/2013/may/27/mccain-spends-memorial-day-with-al-qaeda-allies.aspx*. The rebels in syria were al qaeda which was good, since america was now rooting for al qaeda after all. Guy wondered if mccain was able to eat a beating heart cut right out of an enemy chest, a favorite pastime of the rebel leader, his newfound friend. *https://www.youtube.com/watch?v=rpz8xKp9gS0*.

Things unraveled quickly as the luciferian illuminati used syria in an attempt to lure putin and russia into a war with america. The Gog of Magog, however, was not a man to be trifled with; he was a man of iron, and, on September Twelfth, he deployed russia's largest fleet since the days of the soviet union to the Mediterranean Sea. *http://www.theguardian.com/world/2013/sep/12/russia-sends-ships-mediterranean-syria*. The dividing lines were being drawn. What remained standing of the axis of evil, iran and north Korea, would assuredly side with their ally russia. china would eventually enter the fray as well, likely over some petty dispute concerning an island with an american ally or because of the intentional crash of the dollar.

After all, World War was simply to be a cover for the collapse of the dollar and a crash of the global financial system. china would not be happy about losing their trillions of dollars, but that was part of the point. For it was out of the ashes that the elite planned to bring their New World Order into the light.

It seemed the trigger could be pulled at any time. Guy wondered if the illuminati might use the nonsense of the mayan apocalypse date in December of Two Thousand Twelve to set things in motion, simply to increase the fear of the lemmings who believed in unending coincidences. Things would devolve quickly. While most would be happy going to a government camp for food, those who prepared in advance would be dragged out of their homes by the force of jackbooted police. Guy wondered if it would be prudent to flee with his family to the mountains for a time, once the devolution began, at least until his Valley was cleared out.

The weather was still warm, and a meeting that had ended earlier than anticipated afforded Guy the opportunity to scout a location he saw one day when driving through the canyons on his way to see Bear's brother, Diamond, in Lancaster. Guy pulled off the two-lane road onto the large dirt shoulder and changed out of his suit into a pair of shorts and sneakers. Guy grabbed a brown tarp from his trunk and set out toward the hill which appeared to be about a mile off in the distance. The road was lightly traveled, and the hill was far enough off to prevent a chance encounter. Guy walked through the dry bushes that would one day blow away becoming tumbleweeds. There was hardly a tree, but many of the bushes were large and grew together; they would provide excellent concealment if necessary. The hill was steep, and Guy broke a sweat as he arrived at the top. It looked like a perfect spot, a place where three hills came together into a small valley. Guy walked down the backside and found a relatively flat area to lay the tarp he was carrying.

Guy did his best to lay it flat and cover the edges with rocks. He would come back and bring a week or two's worth of provisions to hide underneath the tarp. It seemed a lot easier in his head before he made the hike. There was no way he could carry more than a box or two at a time. It would take multiple trips back and forth to the car, which was going to be a lot more arduous and time-consuming than expected. There was certainly no way to drive the RX to the base of the hill, due to a gulch.

As Guy finished securing the tarp with rocks, he heard a helicopter off in the distance. As it came into view, it hovered far enough off that Guy was sure he was not within their field of view. When a second helicopter hovered nearby and a third, Guy's heart began to quicken. Hiking certainly wasn't illegal, but it seemed past time for Guy to get back to his car. He climbed the back side of the hill quickly, and, when he got to the top, he could see that his car was boxed in by two police vehicles with multiple officers looking his way. Guy was overcome by fear, by panic, and he hit the dirt quickly. He laid down flat just below the crest and tucked as much of himself as possible beneath a bush.

It seemed unfathomable that the cops would trek out into the hills looking for him, as the area was vast. Guy prayed to the Lord for protection and was overcome by a vision of a babe left out in a field by wicked men. The baby's umbilical cord wasn't cut; the boy hadn't been washed in water, nor swaddled in any clothing. He was naked. The baby was thrown out into the field like garbage, without pity or compassion. The babe cried until it didn't. The Lord heard the cries of the babe and provided provision. Guy knew in his heart the baby was going to be OK.

As Guy peered again over the ridge; the officers were gone. Guy made his way back to his car as fast as his feet allowed. He noticed that somewhere along the route, he had lost his favorite pair of sunglasses. He had broken them once before and had purchased a new pair online, which had been a strange transaction. The company had sent him a reply email, saying it would take two months to receive the new pair. They were being specially fashioned in rome. Guy had found it a bit peculiar as the glasses were nice but pretty standard. They had only cost him two hundred dollars, which, while expensive, wasn't extravagant in the world of sunglasses.

Guy drove back toward the canyon. He was ready to be home. Shortly after he pulled onto the small winding two-lane canyon road, a police cruiser got on his bumper. Guy had traversed this canyon dozens of times, and there were never police on the road. Guy's body began to shiver; he asked the Lord to protect him, as he turned on his favorite CD, *Bible in Song*, eight Psalms set to music. In his personal time, the only music Guy listened to now was the Bible being sung. The canyon road was over twenty miles long, and the speed limit was never more than twenty five or thirty miles per hour. Guy kept right to the speed limit, and, with plenty of places to pass along the way, Guy was certain the officer would move on shortly. As the miles passed, the cruiser stayed right on Guy's bumper, and Guy could feel how wide the grasp of the New World Order actually was.

Guy could feel in his spirit they were monitoring everything now, through a nearly impermeable electronic grid. The Lord made it clear to Guy that there was no protection for what was coming, outside of full reliance upon the Lord. Evil had been allowed to grow so large, to become so powerful, that there was nowhere to run, nowhere to hide. Protection would come for those who received the seal of the Lord. Guy hoped that some were watching the times, that some had stored up their oil, that some would pray for the protection of God's seal. If they were wise when the time was at hand, they would pray for an earthquake so large it would cast the islands into the sea.

The officer stayed on Guy's bumper the entire forty-five-minute ride through the canyon.

The next morning, when the house was empty, Guy spent time worshipping the Lord in song and repenting of his weak and wicked heart while upon his belly. The Lord God, Who had all things beneath His feet, had taken Guy so far, shown him so many things, yet still Guy was overcome by fear yesterday. He cried out loud, "Lord, You are the Maker of Heaven and Earth. I am a man who trusts in You and Your perfect plan, yet this evil is so encompassing. Wicked men spy upon me continually. They listen to my prayers. Is there no solace, no privacy?"

The Lord spoke softly into Guy's heart. *I can hear you whether you speak aloud or not. It is you who brings their surveillance into your home.* Guy, as usual, felt like a fool next to the Almighty God. Praying in silence, unplugging his Wi-Fi and television when they weren't being used, was irritating but necessary. So was turning off his cell phone and leaving it in another room at night. All just more reasons for people to scoff at him, to laugh, but Guy didn't care. He knew in his spirit the filthy luciferians were listening.

"Lord, I have not looked away from the things that You have shown me, despite the consequences and ridicule heaped upon me. For who am I? Is it not You and Your name that they ridicule, Lord? I believe all things are within Your hand, yet I still tremble with fear at the might of the wicked. Help me, Lord. Why am I so fearful? Please deliver me." The Lord spoke more fiercely into Guy's heart. *Should not a man who calls out to God, yet surrounds himself with idols, be fearful? It is you who opens a door for the spirit of fear to come against you.*

Guy was humbled yet again as he looked upon his bedroom to the little personal trinkets he had collected. He decided he would keep no graven image of things in heaven or on Earth below. Guy began to see things in a new light: the little statue of caesar from rome, a monument to the destroyers of Jerusalem; an angel statue given to him by his mother. There wasn't much, but Guy gathered it up in a bag and took it down to throw away in the trash. As he walked down the staircase, he saw a giant upside down star hanging upon his wall, given to him by his mother. With new eyes he saw that it was a sign for satan, an uncircled pentagram, the sign of baphomet. _http://en.wikipedia.org/wiki/Sigil_of_Baphomet_.

When he did, it was as if a lightbulb went on. He ran up to his son's bedroom and pulled up his comforter. On the underside of John's Thomas the train comforter was a giant pentagram, an upside-down circled star. The tears ran down Guy's face as he realized that he was wrapping his son in a pentagram every night to sleep. He also thought of a pair of Faith's pajama's that were covered in nothing but upside-down stars. He put them both in the bag and repented to the Lord for his blindness. His children were innocent.

Faith had twenty pairs of pajamas; she wouldn't miss one, and John was now enthralled with Angry Birds. He would be excited about a new comforter, not disappointed. As Guy brought the blanket and pajamas down the stairs, he saw a pair of John's Spider-Man flip-flops, with Spider-Man giving the satanic salute. His son would no longer walk upon the satanic salute—in the trash the shoes went. It wasn't like John didn't have two other pairs.

Guy rid himself of any personal idols in the house, as well as the phallic sex toys he and his wife used for fun in the bedroom. Tomorrow he would throw away a beautiful chariot drawn by four horses he had at the office. He couldn't possibly ask his family to do the same, nor did he desire it. In today's world, getting rid of all their idols would require burning down the house and moving to the middle of nowhere. Being isolated was no way for a family to live; it was destructive, and groups who segregated themselves from the world usually became peculiarly disturbing. He would make sure that they were not buying things for the house or the children that were covered in satanic icons.

"Thank You for showing me, for I am a blind fool who does not understand unless You speak loudly so that what is hidden from me becomes clear. I worship You, Jesus, for Your name is above all others." And, as if he were hit by a bolt of lightning, a thunder roared within Guy's soul. WHO IS THIS JESUS YOU CALL UPON! If Guy could have melted into the floor, he would have, for he knew instantly, in his spirit, that his Savior's name was not jesus. It was so obvious, yet he had never even considered it, never even given it a thought. jesus was not the name of the Christ when He walked upon the earth, jesus was not the name that caused demons to flee from before the disciples; jesus was not the name that was above all others. Guy sobbed vehemently and cried to the Lord within his mind. Am I so debased, Lord, that I don't even know Your name, that I call upon you in a lie? As usual Guy knew people would think it was no big deal, but if your name was Steve and everyone just decided to call you Georgie, how would you feel? Did not our Savior deserve more reverence?

Guy could feel in his spirit and see with his eyes how rapidly things were beginning to move. He asked the Lord to reveal His true Name, to continue to show him the truth, for Guy would not look away. God spoke into Guy's heart that He would show Guy the truth, for He was so merciful that He had accepted the name of jesus for repentance. He knew our hearts, even while we used a lie when we called out to the Christ in truth. But the spiritual battle was about to spill over into the physical world, and, when it did, there would be no quarter for lovers of lies. God would no longer listen to the prayers of those who called upon the name of jesus, for it was the name of a demon.

The tears streamed down Guy's cheeks as he opened his laptop and began to research. He knew the Father YHWH was Yahweh, and he saw that Messianic Jews called the Christ *Yeshua*, but Guy continued to dig, until the Holy Spirit made it clear to him. As the Father was Yahweh, so the Son was of the Father, the Son whose name was Yahushua. Guy felt the power and freedom of his Savior's true Name. *https://www.eliyah.com/Yahushua.html*.

As the end of the year approached, Guy was excited for christmas. It was something to look forward to since america's fate had been sealed after the election. God was merciful and gave the country an opportunity to repent by voting the man of sin out of office. Guy knew america would not repent; it was now a country that loved filth, loved wickedness. america had decided which side of the battlefield it would stand on.

Marie always lobbied for a small tree, while Guy opted for giants. The smaller the tree the better it seemed to Guy this year. He wanted more focus on Christ and less focus on babylonian traditions. The joy Guy received from seeing the happiness and appreciation in his children's eyes was immeasurable.

Bear and Champagne's baby was due December Twenty Second. It was a girl; Champagne had decided to name her Aphrodite. Yet Aphrodite was quite comfortable where she was, and, like her sister, all indications pointed to a late arrival. While it was unlikely that the luciferian trash would pull the trigger on the mayan apocalypse, the twenty-second, Guy decided to consecrate himself at midnight. He showered singing praises to the Lord and washed his hair with organic soap. He dried himself with a clean towel and brushed his teeth with natural, nonfluoridated toothpaste. He shaved with a clean razor. He lay before the Lord and recounted the mighty deeds of His God, then confessed and repented of his sins. He prayed for the Lord's will to be done and anointed every inch of his body with organic argan oil.

On christmas eve, after the children had gone to bed, Guy and Marie went downstairs and piled presents underneath the tree. It made them smile with glee to see the dimmed lights of the tree flicker upon the wrapped treasures. Seeing the children run down the stairs was the only present they desired. Guy always waited till Marie fell asleep to get her present from the trunk of his car, hiding it underneath the tree as well. Marie was a fan of Disney movies. One year before the children were born, Guy found a lot of three hundred Disney movies on VHS for sale on eBay. The last time he went to Best Buy, they didn't even sell VCRs. Guy was pleased santa had no part in their christmas this year.

It must have been near four in the morning when Guy was awakened, feeling sick to his stomach. As he rushed to the restroom, he began to vomit violently. He felt as if his guts were being ripped out; he was sweating and cold all at once. The vomiting wouldn't stop, and, before long, Guy could not get up off the floor, nor even raise his head from the rim of the toilet. He was sicker than he had ever been in his life and literally felt as if he might die. Not only did he miss christmas morning but the entire day. He was so ill, he couldn't even lift his head to wish his children a merry christmas. If he wasn't so foolish, he would have gone to the hospital, but he couldn't even move. He lived on the bathroom floor and vomited for three days straight. His vomit became only bile, then dry heaves, then sips of water that he had been able to swallow.

On the fourth day Guy received a reprieve, but on the fifth he began to vomit again, and on the sixth day he promised the Lord he would forsake babylonian ceremonies—no tree in the house next year. He asked Marie to take him to the doctor and was prescribed medication that was given to chemo patients to prevent them from throwing up. It worked, and Guy stood to see what else God had in store.

BOOK THREE: CHAPTER SEVEN

As Two Thousand Thirteen took shape, the world slumbered. Guy was awakened by the voice of his daughter before dawn on March Twenty Second.

"Daddy, Daddy." The peep came quietly like a mouse from John's room.

"It's OK, sweetheart. Daddy's here. Daddy's coming." Guy threw on a pair of boxers and was beside his daughter before the words finished rolling off his tongue. "What is it, sweetheart?" Guy lay down upon his elbow next to his daughter.

John was sound asleep in his bed next to Faith's.

"Daddy, I saw God." Faith sat straight up in her bed; her eyes were as wide as silver dollars.

"What do you mean, sweetheart?" Guy stroked his beautiful daughter's golden-brown hair.

"God came to me in my dream right now, Daddy. He took me up into His throne room."

"He did? What is it like?"

"Well, God was sitting on His throne, and there was a river coming out from it, and it was like water, but it kind of wasn't. He had white hair, and there was a rainbow around Him, but it was only green. And when I saw Him, I knew to lie down on my belly, but then He told me to stand up, and He held out His hand to me, and He was holding Sally, my hamster, so that I wouldn't be scared, but I wouldn't be scared of the King, Daddy." Faith's face lit up with excitement and a look of courage, as she put her little hands upon her hips.

Guy had only asked as a comfort to his daughter, but he recognized some of the details came directly from the book of Revelation. Details from the Bible that had never been shared with Faith because she was simply too young. "Did God have anything to say?"

"Yes, He did, Daddy. But I was also wearing this beautiful white robe, and there were people sitting around the throne. They were wearing robes too, just like mine, but they had crowns, but they weren't kings, Daddy. God told me that I was special to Him and that He wanted to show me His face. That's why He was talking to me in my dream, because, if He did it for reals, He said I wouldn't want to come back home. But, Daddy, I really did want to stay." Faith wrapped her fingers around her father's forearm; her face was giddy.

"You are special to God. You have a heart just like His." His daughter exuded Christ's love; he was so fortunate to have such wonderful children. "Did He say anything else?"

"He wanted me to tell you something, Daddy."

"He did? What did He want to tell me?"

"Well, first He took my hand, and then I looked, and I saw the biggest wave in the whole wide world. It was so big, Daddy. It was bigger than the mountains. It even went all the way past martial arts. He asked me to tell you but don't be scared, Daddy. I can't wait to go back to heaven." Faith held her little hands to her face in glee, like a girl who was given her very own pony.

"Thank you for telling me, my darling daughter. I won't be scared. You are so special to me and to God. I love you *soo* much. Don't tell anyone about your dream, except for Daddy. We don't want anyone to be scared, OK?"

"I know, Daddy. God already told me that," Faith said matter-of-factly.

"You are so special to me. It's still nighttime, so get some more sleep. I love you, sweetheart." Guy gave his daughter a bear hug and kissed her little cheek.

"I love you too, Daddy."

Later that day, the Lord provided the whole world a sign. A sign that Guy was desperately waiting for. But the world never woke up that morning; the world never even noticed. Events began to speed up rapidly, but they only provided the world with a confused distraction. For the world loved not the truth, so God sent them a strong delusion that they might be believers of lies. That those who took pleasure in unrighteousness and loved not the truth might be damned.

As the days turned, the country prepared to celebrate its Independence Day, while Bear and Champagne prepared to make their love official.

"You look absolutely stunning." Though it seemed impossible, Guy loved his wife more and more with the passing years. Though the jeans with holes in the rear and the pert bosom were a distant memory, her beauty and his desire for her body left him satiated.

"Aw, thanks." Marie smiled, looking radiant. She was wearing a purple-hued gown she had bought at Neiman Marcus for their european vacation. She would have never chosen a purple dress, but, when she had tried it on at Guy's suggestion, it was a real head-turner. "I was worried it was a little too dressy, but when I asked Champagne, she said I should totally wear it."

"She was right." Guy smiled. Marie had put a little curl to her hair; she was wearing her diamond earrings. Guy pressed his body against hers and grabbed a handful of her butt, as he gently kissed her neck. "I hope this doesn't go too late, so I can take advantage of you later."

"Mmm, you better. Champagne said she's kicking everyone out by ten, part of the benefit of having it at their house."

"You are so beautiful. All these years later and I still can't get enough of you."

"You just love my booty." Marie giggled as she shook her tush.

"Daddy, look at me." Faith tore into the kitchen wearing a lovely red velvet dress, curtsying at her entrance to the kitchen.

"Wow, you look absolutely beautiful, my darling daughter dear. You are the most lovely girl in the entire world. Where did you learn how to curtsy like that?" Guy put his hands upon his hips, with an exaggeratedly puzzled look upon his face.

"I learned it at school. Royalty curtsies—well, boys bow—but I'm a daughter of the Most High King, and that's the best royalty of all." Faith beamed and shot her father an instructive glance over raised eyebrows.

"*Hiyah.*" John landed a solid punch to Guy's gut. "Yah, yah." He landed a second and a third.

"Look at you, my handsome son. You are getting so big." Guy whisked his son up above his head and buried his face into John's little belly, until his son howled with laughter. Faith had been training at Guy's old martial arts studio since she had turned four, over two years now. When she punched Guy in the belly, he needed to make sure he tightened his stomach. If she ever got into a fight with a boy at school, she would knock him right to the ground and leave him gasping for air.

John came home one day with a scratch on his nose. One of the older boys had pushed him to the ground. Apparently the boy had a habit of the unpleasant version of laying his hands on people. Guy told John, if the boy ever laid a hand on John again, to push the boy back as hard as John could. John said the teacher told him, no touching. Guy told his son that Daddy was the boss, that nobody touches his son, that John could tell the teacher his daddy told him to.

They practiced, and the look of pride on John's face was priceless two weeks later when he told his father how the boy had tried to push John, and John had pushed him hard right to the ground. John was so pleased with himself. When the teacher told him it wasn't allowed, he looked at her and said, "My daddy told me I could." Guy took him out for ice cream to celebrate. The boy never bothered anyone at the school again.

"All right, turkeys, time to get on the road. We don't want to be late to see Champagne and uncle Bear get married," Marie said.

"Daddy's being the turkey, Mommy." Faith squealed as she hung from her father's leg.

"You're the turkey, Dad!" John pushed against Guy's chest.

"I know. Daddy's the troublemaker. All right, let's go." Guy set John upon the floor and kissed the top of his soft head.

"Upstairs. Get your shoes on." Marie nudged John in the right direction. "So Champagne is going to get Aphrodite blessed next month, and I've been debating on whether to go or not. What do you think?"

"Do you really want to know what I think?" Guy asked, because he knew Marie did not like to have discussions on controversial topics, especially anything pertaining to religion, politics or the economy.

"I want to know what you think."

"If you want to know what I think, I'm going to be honest."

"That's why I asked. I want to know your opinion. I can't make up my mind."

"Well, the way I see it, our family is Christian. mormons are not Christians. They are outside of Christendom, just like muslims or atheists. Most are certainly moral people, but we both know morality doesn't get you into heaven."

"I know that, and I know that mormons aren't Christians. That's why I can't make up my mind." Marie was truly indecisive on the matter.

"Well, we are either of God or we are of satan. And mormons, though deceived, are of satan. So I would just ask, would you want to go see a baby dedicated to satan?" It was harsh, but it was true. For Guy it was as if poor Aphrodite had been birthed straight from her mother's womb directly into the waiting jaws of lucifer to be devoured. Guy had gone to a mormon temple years ago out of courtesy and was blown out of his loafers by the cultish deception. At the end of service, the congregants could stand and share their testimonies. Guy had always enjoyed hearing people's testimonies, about how they came to know God in a personal way, how He had transformed their lives. There must have been at least fifteen people who shared, and every person got up and said, "I believe joseph smith is a true prophet of God, and the mormon church is the true church." For many of them that was the entirety of their testimony. It was like something out of a horror flick.

"I was kind of thinking the same thing. It's so sad. I'm not going to go. Champagne said Bear's not going either."

"I don't blame him. Would you want to go and be told that you aren't worthy to dedicate your own child to God?"

Bear and Champagne's wedding ceremony was quick, no more than ten minutes performed by a mormon preacher. Bear set up chairs in the backyard and provided catered sushi from his favorite spot. They had strung lights and flowers around the fence and had ordered deli meat for the kids, which Guy found very thoughtful. It was perfect, and, after all these years, Guy's best and only friend became his brother-in-law.

"Yo, what up?" John Brown was decked out in leather chaps and a leather Harley vest.

"You made it. We were taking bets, but we couldn't find anyone to bet that you were actually going to come." Bear grinned.

"I made it, bitch, didn't I? Pay up! Congratulations, homey." John gave Bear a big hug.

"Of course he made it." Bear threw Guy a glance. "Well, congrats to you too. Baby's due soon, right?"

"Yep. Yep. You're looking at the new Mr. Mom. I'm going to get a reality TV show or something." John chuckled.

"Of course you are. Ha, ha. Congrats, bro. You ride the bike over? Bear's selling his, now that he's married. His snowboard too, if you want. And his 'vette only has two seats, so he's trading it for a minivan." Guy smirked. Bear had never run short on harassing Guy with marital comments over the years. Bear had never understood Guy's need to run things by Marie.

John chuckled.

"I'll take the 'vette," Diamond threw in, sporting a world-class lumberjack beard and flannel shirt.

"I ain't selling you shit." Bear looked at Diamond. "You can't even afford to pay me for your cell phone bill! Come, get some sushi." Bear nudged his brother in the shoulder.

"So is your son OK? He looks good. He had a problem with his bowel or something?" Diamond asked Guy with friendly concern.

"He's doing OK now. It was horrible. Marie was potty training him. He has the whole peeing thing down great, but, for whatever reason, he didn't want to go poop, and he started withholding. The day before Easter, Marie told me that John was sick, that he was having a hard time keeping down his food. Well, when he woke up on Easter, he was extremely lethargic. He was throwing up water. Clearly something was wrong. He was really sick. We took him to the doctor. He said John's bowel was completely impacted, and Kaiser said he needed to be rushed down to their new facility off Sunset for emergency surgery. It took all morning for them to make a determination, and, by the time we got over there, John was screaming in horrible pain, but they said they couldn't give him anything because it would slow down his bowels even further."

"Oh, man, that's horrible." Diamond grimaced.

"It was gut-wrenching. They made him wait till nearly two in the morning, and then they did a manual evacuation. I had to hold him down. Marie couldn't take it and left the room. Then they put a tube down his nose to drip the medicine and gave him an enema. It was horrible. He kept trying to rip the tube out of his nose. He had to keep it in for two days while we took turns keeping his hands from his face. A total nightmare."

"So he's OK now?"

"Well, the doctor said to lay off the potty training for at least six months, because his bowels just can't handle it. John has to take MiraLAX now, so his poop is pretty much liquefied. We have to watch him really close, and, if he doesn't have a bowel movement for a day, we have to let the doctor know. But he's back to being up at the crack of dawn, full of energy."

"Thank God. That's an easter you'll never forget, *ugh*."

"I'd like to forget it, believe me. We missed the whole day, no easter at all."

"So you're a picture bug. Did you get any good pics of Bear and Champagne?"

When Faith was three, Guy had felt like maybe he had missed out on some moments for the year, but, when he had looked at all the pics downloaded to his computer, he had taken over a thousand pictures—an average of three a day. He purchased an eight-terabyte Mac Pro with eight terabytes of backup after that. "Of course I did. Check it out. Here's a cute one of them kissing."

"Perfect timing. Why do you have duct tape on your phone?" Diamond looked puzzled.

"I put it on the front camera because I don't like being watched by scum all day." Guy smiled.

"What are you talking about? I could probably make you a tinfoil hat to help with that," Diamond joked, but not really.

"Time to wake up, Diamond. You don't realize it, but we're living in George Orwell's *1984* now. There was a time when people actually thought that book was disturbing, but now it's just life. The government has worked hard to make sure we don't realize or care, nothing a little poison can't help with. Poison fluoride in the water that lowers our IQ, *http://www.hsph.harvard.edu/news/features/fluoride-childrens-health-grandjean-choi/*, poison GMOs in the food supply, *http://www.naturalnews.com/037262_gmo_monsanto_debate.html* and *http://www.organicconsumers.org/ge/starlinkill.cfm*, poison in our vaccines, *http://www.infowars.com/the-ten-worst-ways-your-children-are-being-poisoned-right-now-vaccines-food-video-games-and-more-2/*, poison in our plastics, *http://www.webmd.com/children/environmental-exposure-head2toe/bpa*.

"I could go on and on about the sophisticated attacks that we're under. So I guess it's no biggie that the government records every phone call you make, every text, reads and stores every email, every website you've ever visited, every chat you've ever had, no matter how anonymous you thought it was. Nobody blinks an eye since they wear suits and ties instead of black uniforms and skulls. They can track your movements whenever they want from your phone because of the GPS. They can watch through your camera, listen through its microphone or through your TV. They can do it, even if you turn off your phone. That's the new america. No privacy for citizens, but everything the government does needs to be secret for the sake of our security. How pathetic." Guy found the whole situation disgusting.

"What are you talking about? You're crazy. If that were true, there would be an outroar. I've never heard of anything like that."

"Hate to tell you, but you're asleep at the switch, like the rest of zombie america. Will shoot you a link. *http://www.washingtonsblog.com/2013/06/the-single-most-important-step-to-protect-yourself-from-government-spying.html*. If the government wasn't full of quislings, someone would come out with proof and tell the people what's really going on, but the government would probably just kill them. Like they killed Aaron Swartz. Like that journalist they killed just last month, Michael Hastings. He was the guy who wrote that *Rolling Stone* article that got general mcchrystal fired. Hastings was working on some piece, apparently on obama, that he told friends was going to blow the lid off things.

"Well, it blew his lid off all right. He told his friends that he was being followed and that he needed to disappear for a while, go into hiding. He was paranoid that someone was tampering with his car, so he sent his friends an email. Then early the next morning, *boom*, his car blows up. They tried to make it look like he had crashed into a tree, but he had a brand-new Mercedes. The entire engine was blown over fifty meters out of the car." *http://www.wnd.com/2013/08/mystery-grows-in-journalists-death-prepping-obama-expose/*
http://en.wikipedia.org/wiki/Michael_Hastings_(journalist).

"Well, that sure as hell ain't gonna happen if a new Mercedes hits a tree. But come on, if you don't have anything to hide, who really cares? It's a different world now with the terrorists after 9/11."

"Oh, boy. Ever heard someone say, 'Those who give up essential liberty to purchase a little temporary safety deserve neither liberty nor safety'? Let me put it to you this way. Say a politician, judge, police officer, person of power, whoever, is sitting at a table. The person across from them says, 'We'd like your support in this matter, or we need you to take care of this.' The person of importance says, 'Absolutely not.' But the other guy says, 'Well, what would your wife or the public think of the pornographic websites you like to indulge in? How about these transcripts from your chats, these emails you've been sending, or these recorded phone calls? Have a change of heart?' Of course they have.

"The government has put a system in place that allows them to blackmail any person they desire. Not only that, but they know the innermost thoughts of your mind. Think about it. Everything that you have ever typed into the Internet, every search, every phone conversation? You have got to be kidding me. That's not freedom. Not even the soviets or the nazis had such a complete surveillance system over their people."

"Well, I can see your point there but doesn't that violate the Constitution or something?" Diamond was confused as to how it could be possible.

"Oh, you're still under the impression that we have a Constitution? The government already did away with that when obama signed the NDAA, the National Defense Authorization Act. You know, the bill that virtually every republican and democrat in both the house and senate as well as the president himself signed? The one that gives the government the right to throw american citizens in a deep, dark hole and never give them a trial or a lawyer? And when Bea comes asking what happened to Diamond, they can simply say, 'Diamond who?' They don't even have to say they arrested you. Diamond, that was called the Star Chamber back in england. It's a big reason why we fled to the New World in the first damn place." *http://www.forbes.com/sites/ erikkain/2011/12/05/the-national-defense-authorization-act-is-the-greatest- threat-to-civil-liberties-americans-face/*.

"Why isn't anyone talking about this? I've never even heard of this. I certainly never heard of anyone getting disappeared."

"I haven't heard of anyone *getting disappeared* yet either, Diamond. But that's not the point. Our constitutional protections have been removed. Why pass something so drastic if there is no intention of ever using it? Once the government pulls the trigger on war and collapses the economy, they will use it, believe that. Why else would the Department of Homeland Security have purchased over two and a half billion bullets for nonmilitary government agencies? That's enough for over thirty years of the iraq War."

"How is that possibly true, Guy?" Diamond was in disbelief.

"Take a look for yourself." *http://www.infowars.com/dhs-excuse-for-buying-billions-of-rounds-of-ammo-exposed-as-yet-another-blatant-lie/*.

"Oh, I've heard of Alex Jones. He's that crazy conspiracy nut." Diamond rolled his eyes.

"You should spend some time listening to him before you judge. He sounds crazy because he is so far ahead of the curve. He's been telling people the government has been monitoring us for years. Everyone said he was a nut. Well, now it's starting to come out. People said the same thing about all the bullets, until they saw the purchase orders. Most of this stuff the government hides in plain sight. It's just that the mainstream media doesn't do real journalism anymore."

"Well, if that's true, why doesn't the government just kill him? Maybe he works for the government."

"These days who knows for sure, but he has notoriety and such a platform that they would make him into a martyr and legitimize everything he's been saying. I'm sure, after they pull the trigger on WW, causing the world's economy to collapse, the government won't care anymore about what some people think. He's actually so dead-on, I had wondered if he might be part of the illuminati himself. Only because, with all he knows, I wondered how he could miss the top block in the pyramid. He was also using this microphone that was in the shape of a most important luciferian illuminati symbol. The symbol of thelema, created by aleister crowley, their most beloved and revered high priest. *http://en.wikipedia.org/wiki/Thelema*, *http://atwhistler.wordpress.com/2012/07/10/298/*.

"So, I was listening to Alex Jones one day and his young son, I think he's like ten, gets on the radio show for the first time. He interrupts his dad to correct him on the biblical story of Jacob and Esau. *https://www.youtube.com/watch?v=BnJIU6D7r_8*. The young boy recounted the story with such clarity and wisdom, it was clear he'd been taught the King James Version of the Bible at length in his house. He's homeschooled.

"I could understand, Alex has put everything he has into uncovering and showing the physical plans of these scum. He hasn't been able to invest the amount of time necessary to see their spiritual plans and the signs associated with them. His Bohemian Grove video is the best concrete proof we have that the world's leaders are in fact luciferians. If you want to have any idea of what's actually going on in the physical world, you need to listen to Alex Jones. Plus he changed his microphone, if it's God's will I hope his eyes are changed as well." Guy chuckled. *http://www.infowars.com/watch-alex-jones-show/*.

"Who does he think the top of the pyramid is?" Diamond was beginning to become intrigued.

"He thinks it's the central bankers, which is a good call, seeing as they are the weapon of our demise. Believe me, half my job has become dealing with government monitoring and compliance. If people had any idea, they would freak. Well, not really. americans will put up with anything these days as long as they have the entertainment of circus and bread. Nowadays we catalog people's dreams, desires, how they spend their money, how they plan to give it away, keep copies of their medical directives, wills, all in databases for the government. I get calls of clients being put on watch lists for no reason. Pillars of the community who I have to attest to the legitimacy of all their transactions on an ongoing and permanent basis.

"Of course you don't know why someone is put on the list. There's no appeal process. You can never get off, and the clients aren't allowed to know. All part of the new american freedom. But the central bankers are really just order takers. Throughout all time, behind kings and oligarchs are always the priests setting the agenda. Of course seeing how the top pieces in all the pyramids are actually run by luciferians, it's no surprise that they all answer to the luciferian high priests."

"It does seem the banks always have the advantage."

"They're good manipulators, and, as always, we were warned. Jefferson told us, if we ever let private banking institutions control our money supply, that our children would wake up homeless on the continent our fathers conquered, that banking institutions are more dangerous to our liberties than standing armies. The central banks are manipulators—manipulators of currency, of unemployment numbers, of debt loads. The system is ready to burst. It just needs a pinprick, and everyone believes the world is all fixed, because the stock market is higher than ever. What BS."

"If it were really fixed, then I'd have a job." Diamond hadn't been able to find a real job for years. If his house wasn't so far underwater, the bank certainly would have taken it by now. He hadn't made a mortgage payment in nearly four years.

"Does anybody really believe that the people running the show aren't abject criminals? I mean you can be a former marine like Brandon Raub and post song lyrics on your Facebook page and be raided by SWAT and forcibly committed, but, then on the other hand, Hank paulson can tell congress they need to sign the biggest bailout in the history of the world immediately or the whole system will collapse and the president will be declaring martial law the next day. _http://www.infowars.com/paulson-was-behind-bailout-martial-law-threat/_. Or maybe that ken lewis has to illegally buy Merrill Lynch without telling shareholders that it is insolvent or that hank paulson will have him fired. *http://online.wsj.com/articles/ SB124045610029046349*. The melding of corporate and government interests is called Fascism, Diamond."

"How can the government be doing things that are illegal without anyone getting in trouble?" None of this made any sense to Diamond.

"The Founding Fathers gave us clear guidance in many matters that we've just thrown in the garbage. John Adams was clear. Our Constitution was made only for a moral and religious people. It is wholly inadequate to the government of any other. Not only has our country become far from moral, america is anti–God. We have become a pathetic and despicable country. Women's freedom has come to mean the right to literally twist the head off your baby once it's born. *http://www.toomanyaborted.com/gosnell/*.

"Oh, they'll try to say gosnell was an anomaly, but even president obama is for late-term abortions. *http://wiki.answers.com/Q/ Did obama vote to legalize late term abortions in illinois and if the baby lived through the abortion then obama said the baby should be killed*. *https://www.lifesitenews.com/news/there-is-no-such-thing-as-a-humane-late- term-abortion*. I mean, a Texas senator wore a catheter so she could filibuster efforts to ban abortions after the fifth month of pregnancy. That's how impassioned we are for the right to murder our children. *http://www.breitbart.com/Big-Government/2013/06/28/State-Davis- catheter*. God forbid a politician would take such an extreme measure to ensure our real liberties.

"I do give the abortion supporters credit for at least being honest and chanting 'Hail, satan' around Christians who were singing "Amazing Grace."   *http://www.infowars.com/abortion-activists-caught-on-camera- possessed-by-spooky-hail-satan-chant-at-texas-state-capitol/*. *http://www.theblaze.com/stories/2013/07/02/watch-abortion-supporters- chant-hail-satan-while-pro-life-activists-sing-amazing-grace-outside-texas- capitol/*.

"At least we can use the murdered babies to create new flavors for our food, *http://www.lifesitenews.com/blog/confused-about-the-pepsi-fetal- cell-issue-here-are-the-facts*, or to burn them as the trash we think they are, using them to heat hospitals all for our own comfort. *http://www.telegraph.co.uk/health/healthnews/10717566/Aborted-babies- incinerated-to-heat-UK-hospitals.html*. People will say, *but that's the UK*, as if we aren't doing the same thing here. It seems about the only thing we love as much as murdering babies is molesting them. There's case after case of blatant serial pedophiles that everyone overlooked, simply because they   were   in   positions   of   importance.

http://www.foxnews.com/us/2012/06/12/teen-tells-court-sandusky-fondled-him-engaged-in-sex-act/. *http://21stcenturywire.com/2013/07/08/sex-pistols-star-johnny-rottens-warning-about-jimmy-savile-was-cut-by-bbc/*.

"The country feigns outrage and then turns on HBO, so they can laugh at how amusing it is to watch a little girl drink from a giant penis cup. *http://perezhilton.com/tag/angry_boys/*. I mean, all this country needs are people out in the streets dancing around a giant golden calf on satanic holidays. Oh, wait. america is so debased that when it happens, we don't even blink an eye, check out this video. *http://www.theblaze.com/stories/2013/05/05/is-that-occupy-portland-dancing-around-a-golden-calf-on-may-day/*."

"Yikes, OK, I'll give you that whole penis–cup thing is disturbing, but if people want to dance around a gold cow, I don't see the big deal. It's certainly their right."

"It's absolutely their right. We were given a choice in this country to follow God or follow satan. Dancing around a golden calf certainly seems like no big deal these days, but when Moses came down from the mountain after receiving the Ten Commandments, the people were dancing around a golden calf. It made God so angry that He was going to kill everyone. Moses pleaded for mercy so only three thousand men were killed, while the rest of the people were struck by a plague. That's how far we have fallen."

Guy had shown others the video, and what surprised him was that most had no knowledge of the biblical details linking the story. "Look, it's clear america no longer wants to be a nation united under God. In fact it has chosen to be against the things of God. The country was free to choose. But you can already see, our government is now run by liars and criminals who face no consequences for their actions. I mean, Sandy Berger can sneak out top secret documents from the National Archives in his underwear and get off by paying fifty grand and picking up some garbage. *http://www.wnd.com/2005/04/29721/*. That was classic.

"So now we have the government spying on journalists, *http://www.nytimes.com/2013/05/15/opinion/spying-on-the-associated-press.html?_r=0*, the government spying on american citizens, *http://www.theguardian.com/world/2013/jun/09/edward-snowden-nsa-whistleblower-surveillance*, the government using the i.r.s. to intimidate and shut down the free speech of its enemies. I mean they actually have the audacity to ask people for the content of their prayers." *http://www.theblaze.com/stories/2013/05/17/congressman-irs-demanded-to-know-content-of-pro-life-groups-prayers/*.

"But, no big deal. Hey, the head of the justice department, eric holder, runs guns for the mexican drug cartels that were used to kill countless innocents as well as american citizens. *http://www.theblaze.com/stories/2012/10/01/here-are-5-things-you-didnt-know-about-operation-fast-and-furious/*. Which really should come as no surprise since holder was the one who ran the cover-up for Oklahoma City. If you care, you should watch *A Noble Lie*. *http://www.anoblelie.com*. It's scandal after scandal, all to simply distract people from the real agenda. I mean, the marines are actually the ones guarding the opium fields in afghanistan now. Our military is guarding the heroin that floods our streets, kills our children and has our population thrown in jail. When I told Bear that, as usual, he just laughed, until I showed him this. *https://www.youtube.com/watch?v=AUATfLDiwVA*.

"Everyone thinks there's going to be giant blowback from all of these scandals, but nothing will come of it. It will be a shock if anyone even loses their job. There certainly won't be anyone held to real account. Lawlessness abounds with those in power. They think nothing of breaking your face now. This is one of my favorite examples—police breaking a defenseless woman's face. The despicable pigs should be put in a cage with a real man. *https://www.youtube.com/watch?v=SnjYrXd9ycA*. There's no short supply of people being shot with a Taser and beaten mercilessly by the cops. *https://www.youtube.com/watch?v=TPucQHtHZs*. Now we even have cops raping women. Putting the same gloved hand up the anus and then into the vagina of two different women—the same glove, all on the side of the road. Of course one of the women developed an infection. *https://www.youtube.com/watch?v=f6gOkDiUCA0*."

"OK, that's damn disturbing, but most of the cops are good. They're just doing their jobs."

"The police have been militarized, and unfortunately examples of brutality are happening with disturbing regularity, but, as usual, americans will put up with anything. We'll see if there are still any good men on the force when they're told to yank american citizens out of their homes, after the government tightens the noose that they have already placed around our necks. I'm sure the cops will fold like the cowardly thugs they are, seeing as the scenario has already been beta tested in New Orleans,*http://www.wnd.com/2013/02/see-police-confiscate-guns-from-americans/*, and Boston, where they forced civilians out of their homes at gunpoint. *http://beforeitsnews.com/politics/2013/04/shocking-footage-emerges-boston-under-martial-law-2511904.html*.

"Well, that was terrorism, and they did put the city under martial law." Diamond saw no problem with hunting down terrorists.

"Like most things these days, who knows what it really was? Though it is interesting that russia contacted the f.b.i. about the Tsarnaev brothers specifically, well in advance of the bombing. It's interesting that their pictures were still put out all over the media, asking the public if anyone knew who they were. *http://www.nytimes.com/2013/05/10/us/boston-police-werent-told-fbi-got-warning-on-tsarnaev.html*.

"How about the Craft mercenary agents, standing right next to the blast, who are seen carrying the same backpacks used in the explosion. *http://beforeitsnews.com/terrorism/2013/04/proof-that-craft-or-blackwater-agents-did-the-boston-marathon-bombing-2445882.html*. Of course they announced there was a terrorism drill running right before the bombing, so no one would be suspicious. I mean, they blew a hole in the top of the head of one of the bombers' friends while he was in custody. *http://www.theguardian.com/world/2013/aug/13/boston-bombing-suspect-friend-fbi-investigation*. And, as always, it is simply used to strip away our freedoms, to train us all for what's coming next."

"So what's coming next, and who's pulling the strings? I've heard people talk about the illuminati, but it seems like it's just some pop-culture thing, a way to be cool in hollywood or the music industry." A dumb fad, Diamond thought.

"Well, what's coming next is the end of the world as explained to us in the book of Revelation. The illuminati are certainly behind the coming New World Order, and while hollywood and the music industry are inconsequential to me, they are tools that the illuminati use to program and to prepare the minds of the populace." The entertaining fools were puppets on strings, dancing the public down the road.

"OK, I get that you're a Christian and all, but how do you know you're not wrong? Maybe the muslims are right? Or the catholics? Hey, the mormons even store up food."

"It ultimately comes down to faith. If you ask with an earnest heart, God will reveal the truth of His nature. For those with the Spirit of God, He is right now confirming His words from the Bible. As far as the others go, it's easy to see the delusion they are under and the lies they believe. I was a catholic, and, as I searched for God's face, He revealed His truth to me. It's not hard to see how wicked the catholic church is. They are the masters of intrigue and have been the force behind empires for millennia. Any simple read of history will show how vile and wicked the popes have been, some of the most wicked men in history. Not to mention the church is a den of pedophiles.

"But it is Scripture that shows us their true nature. The popes have taught heresies for money with the selling of indulgences. They kept God's Word, the Bible, a secret so they could manipulate it and hide it from the people. It wasn't until Martin Luther put his life on the line— less than five hundred years ago, translating the Bible from Latin into german—that people were able to stand against the wickedness of the church, that we were able to read God's Word for ourselves and uncover the lies of the catholic church.

"The pope equates his words as equal with God's word. Look at all the despicable popes. *http://theophanes.hubpages.com/hub/popes-Gone-Wild-What-the-catholic-church-Would-Rather-You-Forget*. Can you really believe that whatever they said was equivalent to the words of God? What a despicable and pathetic group of heretics. Those are simply the things done in the light. If people knew what they did in the darkness, how they fit into the illuminati pyramid, people would retch.

"mormons say they believe in the Bible, but the very end of the Bible warns that, to any man who adds to the things written, God will add to them the plagues of Revelation. The mormons added on a whole new bible addition with multiple books and heresies. *http://www.biblebelievers.com/jmelton/mormons.html*. They actually believe that they can become God, that they can go off and start new worlds, acting as the Most High God. Conversely they believe that God was simply a regular man, who attained godhood and started this world, meaning there are infinite worlds and infinite gods. *http://carm.org/mormonism*. The mormons can't even see how they cover their own temples with satanic pentagrams and the all-seeing eye of molech. How more blind could you possibly be? *http://vigilantcitizen.com/sinistersites/sinister-sites-temple-square-utah/*.

"It's the same with the muslims. They have been greatly deceived. It is pretty easy to see the fruit of their religion. The oppression of their women, who they treat worse than dogs, the utter violence they teach their children. How can you honestly believe that, if you murder people, you get a special place in heaven to sleep with seventy-two virgins? *http://www.theguardian.com/books/2002/jan/12/books.guardianreview5*. How uncharacteristic of God's nature. But if they gave even a moment to think about the ritualistic nature of their worship, the Most High God would open their eyes.

[Can two hundred and seventy words destroy the world? Only in the land of morons. And so it is with great regret that I have self censored myself and removed these words at the absolute last moment before this novel was to be sent for publication. For my dear readers, I apologize for the removal of the third wall. I was awoken last night, October Sixth two days before the second blood moon and four days before my annual fast. I can see clearly that the illuminati were going to use the words written here as a ruse, the pretext for their next false flag attack. As I have warned you, the next false flag *"terrorist"* attack will be devastating, dwarfing 9/11. It will be the beginning of WW, better known as the

War of Armageddon, things will move quickly after that. When the attack comes, and it still will, the illuminati were going to use these words as the reason for our destruction, much like they tried with the YouTube Video in Benghazi. However with the scale of this attack and the harsh truth of the words written here, as usual the world would dance to the tune of the piper. As you can see, I am concerned not with offending people, for these days truth is highly offensive. But for many, they would no longer be able to see the truth that is revealed in this book. And so it is with a heavy heart that I have censored the truth meant for the world's one billion muslims. To them, I say I am sorry.

To world's muslims, I know that you believe God is a God of truth, that in Him are no lies. You have been dealt a hard lot. As I have said my heart weeps for your woman and children. I beseech you, please do not engage with america, for the illuminati here have laid a trap for you and are looking for an opportunity to drown you in the blood of your poor babes. I am sorry I could not share the truth concerning the tools that have been used to deceive you. But God is a faithful God. In the privacy of your own mind please ask the Father in the name of His Son Yahushua to reveal His truth to you. Ask Him to reveal the truth behind the Kaaba to you. If you believe that Yahushua the Christ was no more than a man, what do you have to lose? If by chance you are wrong however, you have wagered your soul in a dangerous game. Now is a time for truth to be revealed. I beg of you, please before it is too late. To I, Pet Goat II, *https://www.youtube.com/watch?v=fP7lmTnqyxi* I say thank you. The darkness simply cannot hide it's desires.]

That's crazy weird, but what does any of that have to do with the illuminati? I'm curious as to how you think the entertainment industry is influenced."

"The sad thing is, Diamond, that the majority of catholics, mormons and muslims are moral people. But being moral doesn't get you into heaven. Their leaders have deceived them into believing lies. Because those religions are of man and are pyramids of their own that help form the structure of the illuminati. The top leadership certainly knows what their religions actually are—branches of luciferianism.

"The people at the top of the pyramid are in fact luciferian priests, who know the truth and practice satanism in secret, all the while intentionally leading their flocks astray. The Christian megachurches are the same, but even worse since their leaders hold themselves out as Christians and leave God's people spiritually unprepared for what's coming. There is going to be a special vengeance upon those pastors. It is impossible to grasp without the clarity of the Holy Spirit, as well as taking the time to research and study.

426

"The manipulation of the entertainment industry can be easier to see these days once your eyes are opened to it, because it has become so blatant, so out in the open, due to the lateness of the hour."

"What? Like Led Zeppelin music talking about satan when it's played backward?"

"Well, that was just an introduction. No need to keep things so secretive in our now debased society. I do like the fact that the Eagles' cover for their *Hotel California* album has satanic high priest anton lavey looking down on them from the window. There are all sorts of examples of rock stars from those days admitting they made pacts with satan in order to become famous. Of course it's still going on, but what seems to really get lucifer excited these days is turning supposed Christians, like Katy Perry, into luciferian whores. I always found Katy Perry to be inspirational. There's still that spark of a knowledge of God deep within her. She admits she sold her soul to the devil for fame. *https://www.youtube.com/watch?v=0ORgUzN-Qgs*.

"But what she forgot is that the devil is a liar, that God always offers forgiveness when we are truly repentant. I mean, how much money— how much adoration—does she really need? Doesn't she realize how she's been turned into a God–mocking puppet, dressed up in illuminati symbolism, glorifying those who enslaved God's people, those who He so hated He sent His plagues upon? Have you seen this? *http://www.vevo.com/watch/katy-perry/dark-horse-official/USUV71400083*."

"I think Katy Perry is damn hot." Diamond smiled

"Well, on that we can agree." Guy laughed. "I find hollywood more interesting these days. The illuminati scum are so brazen that they hide their plans in plain sight. It has to do with their luciferian black magic. They believe they receive power from showing us their plans in advance. They laugh at how stupid we are, that we can't see the truth even when it's shown to us. There have been some great examples lately. *The Dark Knight* movie shooting by James Holmes for example.

"He was clearly under mind control at the time of the shooting. He even told his cell mates as much when he was incarcerated. *http://www.prisonplanet.com/inmate-james-holmes-told-me-he-was-programmed-to-kill-by-evil-therapist.html*. Which of course sounds crazy, until you learn that this nobody and his father were both involved with d.a.r.p.a., the military research wing of the pentagon. Or that his psychiatrist, Dr. lynne fenton, had previously worked for the military."

"Well, that could all just be a coincidence. What does that have to do with hollywood and the illuminati anyway?"

"There's certainly no short supply of coincidences these days. I mean, just about every major event that's used to curtail our liberties has one peculiar coincidence after another peculiar coincidence. It was a pronouncement, a blood sacrifice to seal the truth that was hidden in plain sight within *The Dark Knight Rises*. For there is nothing the luciferian illuminati love more than killing innocent children. That is how these sick bastards believe they receive the most power.

"Someone on YouTube, Dahboo77, was the first to catch on. There's a scene in the movie, where Commissioner Gordon says, 'Figure out how to bring it down.' He puts his finger on a map of Gotham, except the town name that is originally in the comic is changed to Sandy Hook. *https://www.youtube.com/watch?v=whu4R6k4_Zs*, *https://www.youtube.com/watch?v=tOR67DOM-ZQ*. They even passed out Bane strike maps in connecticut, showing circled strike zones with Sandy Hook written on the map. Again something that's different from the original comic. *http://www.totalfilm.com/news/the-dark-knight-rises-viral-campaign-continues*.

"I mean, could they be any more blatant? Of course, meanwhile, Adam Lanza was doped up on psychotropic drugs, playing first-person shooter games all day long while worshipping satan, certainly under mind control."

"OK, that's supercreepy, I'll give you that." Pretty hard to argue with, Diamond thought.

"Most of it is more subtle, programing people to think or act a certain way. Like *World War Z* or *The Walking Dead* movies teaching people how it's necessary to act like complete animals in order to survive after the government collapses the economy. I enjoyed *Iron Man Three*. The bad guy—who was just an osama bin laden clone—was an actor controlled by the government and used as a tool to take away our freedoms. Maybe the new *Lincoln* movie—classic how everyone was calling obama the new Lincoln before he even did anything. He even announced his candidacy at the old state Capitol of Springfield, the same place Lincoln started his political career. *http://www.nytimes.com/2007/02/11/us/politics/11obama.html?pagewanted=all&_r=0*.

"When I saw the *Lincoln* movie, it all made sense. I was figuring it would be about the Civil War, but the movie was only about how necessary it was for Lincoln to break the Constitution in order to save the Union. What obama has planned for us, once they pull the trigger, will make Lincoln look like a rigid adherer to constitutional principles. The *Lincoln* movie was programming, so that once the government implodes everything and obama destroys the Constitution, we can all say that it's necessary for the Union, that Lincoln did the same thing to save the country."

Guy also felt drawn to see *Silent Hill: Revelation*, a horror flick. He hated horror movies but was amused to see them cutting people up to put in the fast food while the gluttonous population wolfed them down. While he was a big *Star Trek* fan, he knew in his spirit that *Star Trek into Darkness* was going to be interesting. He laughed heartily when they blew up his office building. They actually showed his office window before it was blown up—classic.

"Well, that just seems like them playing off of culture to me, except for that *Dark Knight* thing. That's really strange. But I still don't get it. I don't see how the illuminati is controlling things, or what they are really about."

"What they are about is controlling our perception of reality, so that we can't uncover the truth. So that we can't stop them from destroying our world and instituting their plan for a New World Order. A world where they rule over us as lords in some twisted dystopian cross between the Hunger Games and Elysium. In order to see clearly, there are some spiritual truths to understand. You have to take a closer look at some of the main culprits with eyes free from scales and ears free from cotton."

"Well, I do have to say, this is pretty wild. But if all this stuff is going on, why aren't Christians in an uproar?"

"Because in the last days, the bible says the deception has become so powerful as to deceive even the very elect. americans have chosen the comfort of lies and ritual. I don't think anyone believes that this country is actually a Christian nation any longer, but even those calling themselves by His name see no problem with reenacting the rituals of the ancient babylonian mystery religions. Sure, everyone knows Halloween is a pagan holiday. No one cares because it's fun. We are more concerned with fun than sanctification."

Although there were a growing number of Christians opting out of halloween. It wasn't something that they celebrated at Faith's school, and Guy was thankful for it. He would let the kids play dress up at home this year and bring ice cream, so they could have an ice cream party. Marie would have class that night.

"But the real tragedy is how we celebrate the birth and death of our Savior by reenacting ancient babylonian ceremonies. Why do we never stop to ask about what a christmas tree has to do with Christ? What we do is exactly what the ancient babylonians did—one of the most wicked nations to ever exist, a nation that brought God's people into captivity. They celebrated a big feast on the winter solstice, right around the Twenty Fifth of December. Of course they brought in a tree and

429

decorated it. It was symbolic to tell the story of their pagan gods. *http://www.christianmediaresearch.com/cmc-48.html*. Christians are even warned about it in the tenth chapter of the book of Jeremiah, verses Two-Four (KJV):

> Learn not the way of the heathen;
> And be not dismayed at the signs of heaven,
> For the heathen are dismayed at them.
> -
> For the customs of the peoples are vain;
> For one cutteth a tree out of the forest,
> The work of the hands of the workman, with the axe.
> -
> They deck it with silver and with gold;
> They fasten it with nails and with hammers,
> That it not move.

"But today's Christians could care less. It's the same thing for easter. The early Christians celebrated Passover. We don't even stop to think why we color eggs, why it involves a rabbit or why ham is traditional. It's all done because it was what the babylonians did in their worship of ishtar on the spring equinox. *http://mystery-babylon.org/easter.html*. The apostle Paul made it pretty clear to us too, in First Corinthians Five:Seven-Eight (KJV), but no one cares about truth anymore.

> Purge out the old leaven, that ye may be a new lump, even as ye are unleavened. For even Christ our passover is sacrificed for us: Therefore let us keep the feast, not with old leaven, neither with the leaven of malice and wickedness, but with the unleavened bread of sincerity and truth.

"We perform the same ceremonies on the same dates and then just wrap it in the veneer of Christ. If anyone thinks performing the religious ceremonies of a people most hated by God pleases Him, they are dead wrong. No one even realizes that we have the same customs and rituals, that we have become just as ancient babylon."

"Well, I think we've moved past the constraints of Christianity. I was never big on coloring eggs, but I do enjoy a good ham." Diamond smiled. "You know what bugs me about Christianity? The fact that they hate gays. I don't see how that's very Christian."

"There's a difference between hating sin and hating the sinner. A lot of people forget that. If you believe the Bible is true, then you have to believe homosexuality is a sin. It says so clearly many times. The danger of picking and choosing from the Bible is that we will always find a way to consider ourselves righteous in our own eyes. God's standards never change. As it states in Romans One:Twenty Six-Twenty Seven (KJV):

> For this cause God gave them up unto vile affections: for even their women did change the natural use into that which is against nature: And likewise also the men, leaving the natural use of the woman, burned in their lust one toward another; men with men working that which is unseemly, and receiving in themselves that recompense of their error which was meet.

"Homosexuality is a sin. So is adultery, but homosexuality is more dangerous these days, because it is glorified and called good. Sin is sin, and God offers forgiveness for those who repent, but there is no repentance from those who believe they have done nothing wrong."

"Well, I believe to each their own. I don't see why they should be treated any differently. I have some good friends who are gay."

"On that we agree, Diamond. I have some friends who are gay too, and the gay people I know are generally some of the nicest people in town. I don't agree that homosexuality is good for the family or good for the country, but if that is what the country wants, we should be able to come to a compromise. The gay community says that they want equal rights, but that's simply not true. They want equal morality. If a civil union came with all of the legal provisions afforded to married couples, then what's the problem?"

"Well, why should they have to have it called something different? That's not fair."

"Life is inherently unfair, Diamond. But if all of the legal provisions provided by the government were the same, it goes to show it has nothing to do with legality. They want to be viewed as morally the same, to have homosexuality taught to my children in school, to require priests to perform homosexual marriages. What they don't realize is that they are simply being used as a weapon by the fascists. Think it is immoral to bake a wedding cake for a gay marriage? Then your business is shut down. _http://www.christianpost.com/news/gay-activists-used-mafia-tactics-to-shut-down-bakery-says-christian-couple-103744/_. Think homosexuality is wrong?   Then   you   are   fired   from   your   job.

. The goal is to make the Bible hate speech, so that simply reading or believing it is a crime. That's the new america."

"Well, that does seem overboard to me."

"Overboard, Diamond? We're talking about considering the bible hate speech. Making words that forged the foundation of all Western culture illegal. That sounds a little more like china than america. But this country is going to get what it wants, what it deserves."

"Hey, the kids are getting wacky tired. We need to pack it up in a few." Marie was getting tired of standing in high heels.

"You know, your husband is really smart," Diamond said with wide eyes.

"Yeah, that's part of his problem." Marie grinned.

"Did you know that they had Sandy Hook on a map in that _Dark Knight Rises_ movie?"

"Are you kidding me? Are you back to this nonsense?" Marie's irritation was instant.

"Diamond, leave it alone," Guy asked.

"Hey, I'm the one who was asking," Diamond said to Marie. "I don't know that I agree with everything, but it's not like you were saying anything that isn't true."

As Marie shot eye daggers to Guy, Guy shot them back to Diamond, pleading with him to shut his mouth.

"OK, OK, we'll talk about it later," Diamond said to nobody in particular.

Guy looked up to the night sky. That was not the response Marie wanted to hear. Guy knew she hated hearing about anything pertaining to world events. He had made a conscious decision after she had called the authorities on him to not discuss anything related to the times or the hour, anything about the economy or politics. He didn't even discuss world events with her anymore, because she found them too disturbing. She had no idea what benghazi was, Operation Fast and Furious or Sandy Hook. She had never heard that north korea had threatened to blow up los angeles and austin with nuclear weapons. Guy had found that headline particularly amusing. He didn't blame her for it; the world was an especially disturbing place these days. It often required him to bite his tongue. He bit down hard.

The children didn't miss a beat on Halloween, and the Finnigans hosted Thanksgiving dinner at their home. A meal which had been normally prepared by Mack for the last decade. He was actually taking some time off at Ginge's prodding. They were back from their vacation in time to enjoy an organic turkey and organic rib roast. It had been a long time since Guy had cooked a turkey. He had never cooked a rib roast before; both were cooked to perfection.

As christmas approached, Guy was nervous when the bank decided to move his group up to the sixty-sixth floor. Working in one of the highest value buildings for a terrorist strike in downtown los angeles had never bothered him before. It was certainly unpleasant for a few years when the Occupy wall street folks were in full throttle. They would protest right outside Guy's office window, holding posters of his boss and chanting "Death to bankers." Guy actually didn't mind that at all; he found the whole thing quite amusing. Unfortunately they only had one side of the ledger correct. But going into his building flanked by militarized police really made Guy uncomfortable. Full black riot gear, shields and batons, shoulder to shoulder ringing the perimeter of his building. The counterterrorism drill right across the street certainly made him feel no safer. _https://www.youtube.com/watch?v=bK3LH_vVB_Q_.

Now as he looked down on helicopters, Guy realized just how vulnerable he was. From his new height, he had a great view of an illuminati temple they called a library, replete with pyramid top and the hand of lucifer holding the light of illumination. _http://vigilantcitizen.com/sinistersites/the-occult-symbolism-of-the-los-angeles-central-library/_. Guy had seen the footage of 9/11. After moving up to the sixty sixth floor of his building he realized that, in the case of an event at his office, there was simply no way out now. It had been so horrible for the people in the towers that some of them had jumped to their deaths rather than roasting alive.

★★★

Guy experienced his first bout of anxiety in some time. He was scared and asked Marie if she would stroke his hair while he put his head in her lap. She was too busy with homework. Guy knew she would consider it nonsense; he was right. She seemed a bit distant lately, and, when prodded, she admitted to being upset that her sister Maybel was sick— something to do with hormones but they weren't exactly sure.

Guy was given a mission by God, one that he had been preparing and working on for nearly two years now. He thought he should be done preparing by the New Year. The timing would be perfect. It was big, and Guy knew there would be consequences, but he would be obedient; he would put his trust in God. He wanted to be spiritually ready, so he began to fast in December, only organic food, no animal products whatsoever, a fast like Daniel.

As Guy walked into his office a week and a half before christmas, Bill took a seat in the chair across from Guy's desk. No more room for a couch; the offices were now corporatized. Guy eventually came to terms with the floor location of his new office space. As always he put his fate in God's hands. He did have an amazing view of the ocean. He teased the guys in the office that he had the best view for when the planes crashed into the building. How, if anyone saw him run, they shouldn't ask questions but just follow. He floated around the idea of getting a BASE jumping parachute. Of course you would need an ax to break out the thick windows. After jockeying the idea back and forth, some of the brokers thought it a very prudent idea, but Guy said, "Let God's will be done."

"So are you ready for christmas? Did you get a tree yet?" Bill was taking it easy through the end of the year. Most of his clients, as well as most of the office employees, were on vacation. Bill enjoyed wearing khakis and polo shirts—one of the benefits of los angeles: short sleeves in December.

"No tree this year. Wanted to try a year without a tammuz tree. Gave Faith the option of getting a tree or getting an iPad. She picked the iPad, said she didn't know what a tree had to do with jesus's birthday anyway. I gave my old iPad to the kids, but, with John, she's lucky to ever get her hands on it."

"tammuz tree of course." Bill laughed.

Guy always stuck to his guns.

"Those iPads are great—videos, games, the kids love them. Did you put up any decorations?"

"The whole house is decorated. We put up lights outside, lights inside. I have a great nativity set. The kids are gaga about the iPads. I already gave Faith hers, so she wouldn't feel bad about not having a tree. She didn't care in the least, and John is too little to even know about trees. We have to limit their time with the iPads though. We noticed a bit of a change in behavior. Nipped that in the bud real quick."

Marie had agreed it was wise to make the iPads a treat; then the kids' behavior was right back on track. Guy did love playing Angry Birds with his son, and now Angry Birds Go! John liked to race the cars. When he got stuck on a level, he always needed Daddy's help, because Marie could only pass the easy levels.

"So do you still have shopping to do? I didn't get my wife anything yet."

"The shopping's done. Did almost everything online this year as the kids had very specific requests for *Littlest Pet Shop* characters that you are just not going to find at Toys "R" Us. I think John is getting every Angry

Birds toy that has ever been made. Marie always harasses a bit, but what can I say? I love to see how excited the kids get. They're such good kids, so cheerfully obedient and kindhearted. I bought Marie a thousand dollars' worth of jewelry. Hopefully that will keep her distracted."

Receiving made Guy uncomfortable, but he received so much joy from giving. He looked forward to seeing their joy, especially since he and Marie had gotten in an argument a couple days ago about John being sick again. It had only lasted about two minutes, but they had both raised their voices. Guy never raised his voice. It always seemed inappropriate unless there was imminent danger. He was just glad the kids weren't in the room.

"Nice, that's because you're a good family man. christmas is such a different experience with kids. You still messing around on Twitter?"

"Nope."

"Why not?"

"You don't want to know." Unfortunately Bill was probably the only person who did want to know.

"Of course I want to know. What? Are they finally coming for you or what?" Bill was half joking.

"Funny you should say that." Though it was foolish, it gave Guy some anxiety.

"Oh, boy. Spill it already."

"So I'm sure you're not aware how crazy contentious Twitter is— lots of heated arguments. You know I'm not one to back down."

"Of course. Go on."

"Well, I've been doing it for a couple months now, and I had a few hundred people following me—mostly Christian-patriot sorts of folks, but a pretty wide gamut. Some of the people following me, who I'm having conversations with, keep getting muslim propaganda sent to them by this muslim gal. Well, who knows who it really is. So I get into it with this person, after asking them repeatedly to stop jumping into our conversation. I'm sure I should have just blocked them, but they said something defaming about Christ, so I told them to leave us alone or I was going to start defaming their prophet muhammad. Well they just kept going, so I started to send over cartoons I had found on the Net. The one of muhammad with a bomb for a turban that caused all that controversy and one of muhammad coming out of a pig's ass." Guy was going to show Bill the cartoon, but, when Guy had pulled up a Google search yesterday, it was, of course, gone.

"I would have expected nothing less. And?"

"Well, then a few days later somebody else I don't know jumps in my conversation. Well, actually gets brought into my conversation by this neo-nazi who I was tweeting with. It started by the nazi asking me about the Bible and spewing some hatred. Well, I start telling him that all men are created equally in God's image. He starts saying that he's done all these bad things, that there's no way God could forgive him. I ask him if he's murdered anyone to which he answers no. I tell him that one of the greatest men of God, Paul, who wrote most of the New Testament, went around murdering Christians. That David, who was a man greatly beloved by God, had his friend murdered so he could sleep with his wife. I actually thought it made an impact. I got him to take down his racist profile statement."

"You're too much. You are such a sucker for lowlifes running a snow job, just like that black lady who conned you into a frappuccino last week."

"Yeah, yeah. Well, you know my policy. I never give money, but I will always buy someone food. And not that I broadcast this, but I went down to skid row that night, and the same lady came up to me. She's homeless. She said buying her that frappuccino was the nicest thing anyone has ever done for her. She said I made her feel like a princess, and she started to cry." The thought that someone could say that being bought a six-dollar frozen coffee was the nicest thing someone had done for them made Guy sad.

"All right, you got me on that one. So what happened?" Bill found Guy generous to a fault; Bill thought it unwise to feed the bears, but it did make for some amusing interactions.

"So, back to Twitter. Some crazy liberal guy starts verbally attacking me, and I get into it with him all day. He's making jokes about abortion and stuff. He lays off for a week but then comes back with this other guy, who has no followers and is following no one except for me. The guy starts threatening me to shut my mouth, then tweets out my name and where I work downtown."

"What? Are you kidding me?"

"Not kidding you. Totally creeped me out."

"How the hell did he get that info?"

"Beats me, I was on there totally anonymously. Best I can think is that it was all some setup. I was emailing that nazi guy and this other lady. I accidentally sent her an email from my personal email that has my name. Well, the one guy says he's calling the cops on me, which is just nonsense, but I deleted my account anyway."

"I sure as hell hope you did. Were you threatening him?"

"Of course I didn't threaten him. I never threatened anyone—unless telling people they are going to burn in hell is a threat, but these people don't even believe in God let alone hell. And believe me, there are plenty threats of violence that goes on in Twitter. What did freak me out is I'm certain my phone and email were hacked. It seems crazy, but my email was being quirky. The profile picture of the girl pretending to be a friend, who might be involved, was popping up when I checked my emails for like a millisecond, so fast, you could hardly even notice it happened."

"Shit, are you being serious? I told you not to get involved in Twitter. What the hell where you talking about anyway? Stuff to get you on the list, I assume?"

Bill made jokes about a list, but the way things seemed to be going. "Well, that's why I was doing it anonymously. And what do you think I was talking about? The illuminati and the antichrist. It was a way for me to blow off some steam and inform people who actually wanted to hear. Well, I erased my phone and closed my email accounts too. No more Twitter, that's for sure.

"I did meet two really nice Christian families from Texas though. Real Christians. We pray together, separately, but at the same time once a week. One of them has three daughters. They're planning a Disneyland trip in the spring. I think we're going to join them." It had been a long time since Guy had been able to engage in corporate prayer; it was comforting for him to find some like-minded Christians who were aware of the New World Order. They weren't survivalists either—just regular folks with regular corporate jobs.

"Well, they can't arrest you for free speech yet, but when they do, make sure you don't give them my name." Bill, again, was only half kidding.

"You've already gotten too many emails and phone calls from me. Guilt by association, friend." Guy smirked.

"The biggest problem I have with all the stuff you talk about is that you're not wrong about the facts. Why aren't the churches talking about all this wild stuff that's going on in the country?"

"Because the churches and their leaders have all made a covenant with satan," Guy said matter-of-factly.

"How's that?" Bill asked, because he knew Guy well enough by now to know there would be specific information.

"Well, anyone with a moral compass can see how evil our government has become, a beast run not by bad or incompetent men but by wicked ones. The churches have all promised never to speak ill of the beast in exchange for money. They have signed a covenant, the Five O One(c)(Three)—nonprofit corporation, exempt from taxation— exchanging their righteousness for money. In doing so, they have become debased and blinded to the truth."

"Ouch. Well, it did always seem to me that a lot of the churches were all about money."

"Not some of them, any of them who signed the covenant. Of course they could repent. If they did, God would fill their coffers to overflowing. Then they could begin to speak the truth about the government. But the pastors are cowards and charlatans." Guy knew that the Bible warns pastors that they will be held to a higher standard and a fiercer judgment. How there will be a great falling away when God removes the veil and the flock can see how their leaders warned them not, how they were left unprepared to stand.

"Well, that makes sense to me. You know what doesn't make sense to me? Dinosaurs, aliens and evolution."

Bill was being serious; he didn't see how the Bible lined up with science. Well, aliens weren't necessarily science, but Bill believed they were out there. "Things certainly change as our knowledge of science increases. We once thought the Earth was flat, right? Things that we were sure about fifty years ago seem like nonsense now. So with radiocarbon dating and dinosaurs, who really knows how old they are? It becomes a sticking point because God created the Earth in six days, and then people try to add up all the generations to come up with the age of the Earth. A little hard for our minds to comprehend the process and timing of God creating everything. *Everything.* For one day with the Lord is as a thousand years, and a thousand years is as a day. Who knows what those six days really equate to?"

"That actually makes sense to me, but what about aliens? How do you explain that one, smart guy?" Bill's smile grew.

"I certainly don't believe in aliens. That much is for sure. But with all the weird stuff the government is doing in secret, who knows what they have concocted? I will say this though. The Bible speaks of Nephilim, who were the spawn of demons and women. They were extremely mighty. aleister crowley unlocked many of the ancient luciferian secrets. He was certainly into channeling demonic spirits for sex. He was an avid practitioner of sex magic. See *http://oz-mix.blogspot.com/2014/05/aleister-crowleys-sex-magick.html*."

"All right, you'll have to tell me who this aleister crowley is, but what about evolution? You skipped that fastball." Bill finally had Guy pinned down.

"Think about it a little bit, Bill. Evolution is deemed science now, and, if you disagree, you're some sort of religious zealot. But can you even think of one example of evolution? Science requires proof, doesn't it? Science isn't based on faith, is it? I'm sure you remember the story from school about the peppered moth that became dark with spots to evolve against growing pollution. There is even a Wikipedia page." Guy pulled up the website *http://en.wikipedia.org/wiki/ Peppered_moth_evolution*.

"Umm, I think you are proving my point, Guy."

"Unfortunately I'm proving mine, that we have become devoid of critical thinking. The moth getting spots, becoming darker, is an adaption, not evolution. Evolution is based on the theory that one species evolves into another, changing their DNA. So I'll ask you again. Can you think of even one case of evolution?" Guy was saddened by the systematic attacks that had left his countrymen debased and dumbed down.

"Whoa, I never even thought of that. I guess it is an adaptation. That's pretty crazy. All right, you've got me going now. Who is this aleister crowley?"

"That's where you really start getting into the rabbit hole. You know most people don't like the red pill of reality, Bill."

"I wouldn't have asked if I didn't want to know. What does this have to do with the illuminati and stuff?"

"And stuff, indeed." Guy smiled. The morning was clear, the view of the ocean was amazing.

"All right then, give me the whole enchilada."

"Are you sure?" Bill was the only one Guy knew personally who was not scared to talk about all of the crazy things going on these days. He was extremely knowledgeable and so perceptive. Guy had never seen him fooled.

"Look, I got my coffee and no breakfast. I'm hungry. Serve it up." Bill always learned something staggering after his conversations with Guy, whether it was economic, political, religious, or some fact he was sure couldn't be true until Guy documented it. Who knew Cleopatra wasn't egyptian? She was actually greek, and the royal court only spoke greek. Bill must have retold that story a dozen times; not one person had ever heard it before. Bill always wanted documentation; he just came to know on the front end that Guy did his research and would provide it.

"So, like I've been saying, the elites of this world are luciferians, top people in government, top people in corporations, top people in the military, top people in religious organizations. Alex Jones gave us visual proof when he filmed Bohemian Grove. Much of their vast attendee list has since become public. *http://en.wikipedia.org/wiki/List_of_Bohemian*

Club members. They have taken over the key points of control and have been actively working in secret to bring about their New World Order. aleister crowley, a thirty-third degree freemason, was their high priest and a cornerstone in bringing their plans to fruition. He was known as the most wicked man to ever live, which is certainly saying something. He was called *the beast*. *http://hermetic.com/crowley/confessions/fohi.gif*, *http://hermetic.com/crowley/equinox/i/iii/images/103_010.jpg*. He was a practitioner of luciferian black magic, and, through his wickedness, he was able to unlock the ancient babylonian and egyptian secret practices of demonology. *http://vigilantcitizen.com/hidden-knowledge/aleister-crowley-his-story-his-elite-ties-and-his-legacy/*. He's the one who wrote their book of the law, which is summed up as "Do as thou wilt." In his book, *magic in theory and practice*, he teaches luciferians the highest form of black magic, the sacrifice of an innocent male child of high intelligence within a pentagram, the sign of satan. *http://raumfahrer.wordpress.com/manson/crowley-on-sacrifice/*."

"I would ask if he actually wrote that, but, of course, he did. So, if this is true, how come someone doesn't blow the whistle?" If these sorts of horrible things were going on, Bill couldn't see how someone wouldn't talk about it.

"You think it was hard to break the mafia? Though it was common knowledge, no one could even prove they existed for decades. That's why the illuminati are based on a pyramid, so people take one step at a time. Everything is compartmentalized. You pass through one barrier by doing horrible things, before you get access to more information. At the highest levels, the luciferians murder little children and eat them as prescribed in their book of the law. They are, of course, child molesters as well. They believe they gain power from the screams of little children as they cry out for their mothers while they are tortured and have their blood spilled.

"Obviously they have each other on tape. How many people do you think are going to blow the whistle when there are tapes of them molesting, murdering and eating children? Even if they did, no one would believe it without seeing it with their own eyes. Besides the fact that these people are evil, this is their religion. They see and know who controls this world. There are certain families and bloodlines who have been at this for generations. They use mind control and torture on their own small children to program their minds."

"I've heard people talk about the thirteen bloodlines that control the world." Bill would have thought the whole thing was hogwash, but, with the way reality seemed to be shifting these days, he was finding certain things more plausible.

"If you really want to know how these filthy pieces of trash operate, read Fritz Springmeier's book, *The illuminati Formula Used to Create an Undetectable Total Mind-Controlled Slave*. *http://www.whale.to/b/ springmeier_formula.html*. It's a must-read if you want to understand how they are able to exert such control over people. They use the most horrible tortures you could never imagine to program people's minds, to break them and to make them forget anything has ever been done to them."

Guy had read the book after his experience out in the hills; it made his spirit shiver, but he felt the Holy Spirit calling him to press on. The illuminati did things like locking children in cages, making them kill other children, eat feces, plus sexual torture, and more degrading and despicable things than you could possibly envision. It was systematic and scientific, mixed with luciferian black magic, demonology. While Guy was reading the book, he had a vision of children stacked floor to ceiling in a warehouse, like some sort of disturbing puppy mill.

Guy saw a little boy in a white room with a table and a chair, a boy who had been tortured and abused. The child was dressed in a Superman outfit, and, when the man who was in charge of the torture came into the room, he pretended to be afraid of Superman. He let the boy chase him around the room, feigning fear, until the boy chased him out the door. The boy had a big smile on his face and made a Superman pose. They called it Superman training. It was all part of getting the children to put their faith in anything other than God for a savior.

"Sounds like twisted nazi stuff to me."

"Funny you should say that. What do you think happened to all those nazi scientists who were running experiments in the concentration camps?"

"I don't know. They were tried at the Hague, right?" Bill was pretty sure every one of those nazi bastards had been hunted down eventually.

"Wrong, they were brought to the united states to continue their work secretly in a program called Operation Paperclip, and that's not simply a conspiracy theory. It has since been declassified. *http://en.wikipedia.org/wiki/Operation_Paperclip*. They helped build the MKUltra Mind Control program alongside the c.i.a. *http://en.wikipedia.org/wiki/Project_MKUltra*. They said they had closed it down, but it really just morphed into the Monarch Project. That's the technique the illuminati uses now, though you won't find a Wikipedia page on it yet."

"We brought over nazi scientists. Are you kidding me? That's pretty despicable." Bill didn't care what the justification was; his grandfather had died fighting the nazis.

"It was an important part of how this country became infected with such darkness, such wickedness."

"Well, no surprise the c.i.a is engaged. I guess it doesn't bode well that bush sr. was the head of the c.i.a., huh?" Bill was disturbed.

"That's an understatement, but you're certainly on the right track now. Ever heard of lieutenant colonel michael aquino? He served in military intelligence and was involved in psychological warfare operations for the army. He was close friends with anton lavey, the author of the satanic bible. The colonel eventually founded the satanic temple of set. No surprise, he was a suspect in a massive pedophile ring. *http://www.bibliotecapleyades.net/vatican/esp_vatican16a.htm*."

"Let's just hope the republicans can get us out of this mess."

"Bill, you're not seeing the big picture here. The republicans are just another side of the same coin. For those with a moral compass, it's easy to see how morally repugnant the democrats are. They are overtly anti-God. It's harder with the republicans, because most of them hide under a veneer of Christianity. They are certainly pushers of war and the police state, but you can see, even when they are in power, they do nothing to stem the moral or economic slide of the country. You need to understand that the republicans are not our friends. Their leadership is wicked to the core and utterly compromised." Guy wished people would open their eyes and see that both parties were simply playing off each other, playing to their bases, all the while skipping hand in hand, leading the country to destruction.

"They certainly cave when it counts, but *evil* seems a bit harsh." Bill was a lifelong republican; Guy once was as well.

"Harsh, indeed. But see for yourself. These scum can't help but to broadcast. You know the upside-down star is the star of satan, known as baphomet. *http://en.wikipedia.org/wiki/Sigil_of_Baphomet*. So ask yourself this, Bill. Why did the republican party turn the stars upside down on their logo?" *https://www.youtube.com/watch?v=9kKEccwCkGg*. The country had grown so pathetically blind, Guy found it simply amazing.

"OK, that's weird. Why the heck would they do that?"

"They did it to show that they had seized control of the republican party, to show they were ready to move forward with their big plan, the opening salvo in bringing about a New World Order." Guy was stunned that no one even bothered to ask the republicans why they had turned their stars upside down. Sure, they would lie about it, but it was always good to put these scumbags in the hot seat.

"What plan is that?"

"Well, they turned the stars upside down in Two Thousand, when bush jr. took office. It was their sign to let the luciferians know that they were ready to move forward with 9/11."

"Come on. You really think the government was involved in 9/11?"

Not that Bill spent much time delving into the subject, but most of the 9/11 truther folks seemed a bit off their rocker. "Not at the time I certainly didn't. I was blowing the horn to go kill muslims just as loudly as the next patriot." The fact that Guy was deceived by a wolf in sheep's clothing and had cheered for bombs made him disgusted—angry and disgusted. "There are lots of videos out now that show all the inconsistencies and technical problems, the peculiar explosion of building Seven. Architects and engineers for 9/11 truth have some pretty good information on the subject." *http://www.youtube.com/watch?v =OQgVCj7q49o*. "The movie *911: In Plane Sight* is another great one on the Pentagon. You can watch it for free on Netflix."

"Yeah, there seems to be no consensus." To Bill it was one of those things people liked to squabble over, all the while claiming to be an expert.

"Like I said, Bill, these people love to show their cards. It's part of their luciferian black magic. Corrupting and feeding off the innocent, showing their plans in plain sight, making men become lovers of lies, they believe they gain power from these things. When a man believes a lie, it becomes harder for him to see the truth and brings him further away from Christ. It becomes easier for people to believe more lies, to become morally debased. What bigger lie than to rally the whole world around 9/11?

"They used it to wage war wherever they desired, to kill and torture. To take our freedoms and to set up a worldwide police state that we agreed too, all the while the plan was to use it all against us, the american people. For when america is destroyed, the light of liberty will have gone out, and the luciferians will be free to create their disgusting dystopian New World Order. So do you know what george bush was doing when the planes crashed into the buildings, Bill?"

"He was reading that pet goat book to those school kids."

"He was engaged in luciferian black magic when the plane hit the building, Bill. If this doesn't open your eyes, it's because you don't want them opened. president bush was in the classroom with young children. That's true. But the children were all chanting, *kite, hit, steel, plane, must,* in unison, over and over again, until the very moment the first plane hits the first building. Try and convince yourself once again that this is simply another coincidence."

"Get out of town." That couldn't possibly be true, Bill thought.

"Watch the video, Bill." *http://youtu.be/F-DTGdL6whY*.

"OK, what the hell is going on, Guy?" The video hit Bill hard. It wasn't fake, and the very moment the children stopped chanting, a man came and whispered in the president's ear that the first tower had been hit. Not while the president was reading a book. The look upon the president's face before he was told of the tragedy was peculiarly disturbed Bill thought. 9/11 had a big impact on Bill, he followed the news closely for months. He was absolutely certain, the president was reading a book when someone came and whispered in his ear about the attack. Certain, until he watched the video that is.

"What do you think I've been saying all this time, Bill? They've been planning this for a long time. Now if you research, you will see the written words are slightly different, *kite, kit, steal, playing, must*. But it is simply more luciferian charlatanism, it gives them plausible deniability. They use a homophone, two words that are pronounced the same way but differ in spelling. The teacher makes sure to tell the children to say the words, *"the fast way"*. I have listened to that chanting dozens of times, the teacher is clearly saying *hit* and *plane*, not *kit* and *playing*. Take a look at his piece-of-trash father, george bush sr., giving his big speech calling for a New World Order. *http://www.youtube.com/watch?v =byxeOG_pZ1o&list=PL0F22DEF818C2DE0B&index=52*. When do you think that was Bill?"

"I don't know. It looks old, I imagine while he was in office."

"He gave his New World Order speech on September 11, Nineteen Ninety, exactly 11 years to the day before the attack. Keep trying to convince yourself that all these things are simply coincidences. I mean george bush sr.'s father financed the nazis and had his assets seized in Nineteen Forty Two under the Trading with the Enemies Act. *http://www.theguardian.com/world/2004/sep/25/usa.secondworldwar*. These people have been wicked for a long, long time."

"Well, I have always heard rumors that certain bloodlines were involved in the illuminati."

"Most of the elite elites are actually related. Does anyone even realize that the wretched queen of england is german? The house of windsor changed its name during the first World War from the house of hanover because of war with germany. *http://en.wikipedia.org/wiki/ House_of_Windsor*. Look at how inbred these elite are. king george V of england and tsar nicholas II of russia are virtually identical twins. *http://en.wikipedia.org/wiki/George_V*.

"Wow, those guys are seriously identical. That's pretty creepy. Maybe that's why they're so crazy, all that inbreeding."

"They simply can't help themselves. Imagine how they just laugh at us. They show us what they're planning, and then say, 'Nope, look over here,' with some crazy concocted lie, and everyone just says, 'OK, you're the boss.' It is so over-the-top it just boggles me, like I'm living in *The Matrix*. Which of course is amusing, because in the movie, when Neo gets pulled in for questioning by the government, and they look at his passport, the expiration date is September 11, Two Thousand One. *https://www.youtube.com/watch?v=CxW79CwSK9M*.

"*The Matrix* came out in Nineteen Ninety 9 of course. Almost better was the pilot episode of *The Lone Gunmen*, a spin-off of *The X-Files* that came out in Two Thousand One, before 9/11. The premise is the government takes control of a commercial airliner and flies it into the twin towers. Well the pilot is stopped at the last second, but not before they show you the plane just about to crash into the tower and pull up at the last moment. *http://www.youtube.com/watch?v=9rsMG2hHsLo*.

"Check out what happens when you fold the newly redesigned currency from the five to the hundred in the shape of an airplane. It shows the twin towers falling. *http://www.youtube.com/watch?v=LpRLrga5mXQ*. Of course it was the first major redesign of the currency in sixty-seven years, and it was finished right on time in Two Thousand. The last major redesign was by fdr, when the illuminati pyramid and the all-seeing eye of satan were put on the currency, after they had seized control of the money supply with the creation of the federal reserve.

"I think I'm starting to get full." Bill feigned a chuckle and took a swing from his coffee, though his stomach was beginning to feel ill at ease.

"You asked for it! We're just getting warmed up." When shown the darkness, Bill was one of the few people who didn't flinch nor mock. When he was shown hard proof, he believed. He was wise, and, with as much discernment as he had, Guy prayed Bill would come to know the saving grace of Yahushua, the Christ.

"Of course we are. I didn't say *uncle*. Keep going."

"So, you've seen the bushes giving the satanic salute like it's going out of style. They use the fact that they are from Texas and say it's for the Texas Longhorns. bush sr. loves it so much, he even had to flash it while with the queen of england. But are all the world's elite Texas fans, or maybe just lovers of death metal, because they all seem to have an affinity for it. See *http://www.jesus-is-savior.com/False%20Religions/Wicca%20&%20Witchcraft/signs_of_satan.htm*."

"I go to lots of concerts," Bill said. "There are all sorts of people who give that sign." Bill was a big fan of concerts; he had friends who made that sign to be cool, not because they were satanists.

"That's a good point, Bill, and very true. Most of the folks today are unaware of the true meaning behind their actions. Again it's a systematic approach to debasing our culture. Unfortunately the elites in the illuminati are not people who are unaware. They are patient, calculating and powerful people of means. They have been working for generations to bring about their New World Order plan. The time has finally arrived with the enthronement of their king, the antichrist. You can see that 9/11 wasn't simply some random date. It was picked and planned long in advance. Just as president george bush jr. was the man they planned to have at the helm when the bell of 9/11 was rung. A man of great dark spiritual significance, whose destiny was planned well in advance as well."

"Why him?" Bill had voted for him and, at the time, had found bush to be very effective in fighting the war on terror.

"Why him, indeed. Because he is the grandson of their greatest spiritual leader, the one they call *the beast*, the one who is called the most wicked man to have ever lived, aleister crowley."

"Get out of town! Now you're just being crazy."

"These are crazy times we live in, where truth is a lie, and lies have become truth. There is no definitive proof, but when I researched it, the Holy Spirit revealed to me the truth of the matter. I know that's not in your wheelhouse, but take a look at this. *http://cannonfire.blogspot.com/2006/04/george-w-bush-barbara-bush-and.html*. george bush jr.'s mother is barbara bush. Her mother was pauline pierce robinson. In Nineteen Twenty Four, pauline traveled to europe to spend time with her friend nellie o'hara, which at the time caused a bit of a scandal because pauline was traveling alone without her husband, marvin. Her friend nellie was the unofficial wife of a man named frank harris. frank harris opened his home to aleister crowley, who was living with him at the time, after he had been kicked out of italy by mussolini for being too wicked. He was practicing his sex magic in italy when the public found out that someone had died or was killed in one of his ceremonies.

"During Nineteen Twenty Four, while living with frank in france, crowley was at the height of his sex-magic ceremonies. He obtained the highest magical achievement of his satanic order, the completion of a sex-magic ceremony known as the supreme ordeal. pauline pierce arrived back in the united states from her trip in October Nineteen Twenty Four, and barbara pierce, now barbara bush, was born on June Eighteenth, Nineteen Twenty Five. Viewed side by side the resemblance is striking." Guy pulled up the picture from *http://s889.photobucket.com/user/77forever/media/bowley_zps8b04034e.jpg.html*.

"They do look like two peas in a pod." The likeness of some of these folks was certainly peculiar, Bill thought. If it was one thing or another, it could be easily dismissed, but as Bill saw all the blocks being laid upon each other, it was harder and harder to deny the design. "It seems the bushes have some serious lineage, nazi supporters on dad's side and aleister crowley on mom's. A sad state when christmas dinner with the clintons looks more attractive."

"I wouldn't say that. They are certainly top-of-the-pyramid illuminati refuse. But you could help them decorate their tammuz tree with crack pipes, condoms, erect penises, marijuana, syringes, heroin spoons, animals having sex, some cock rings." Guy smiled.

"I don't think that would fly even with the clintons." Though Bill could understand the hyperbole.

"Bill, that's what was hung on hilary clinton's white house christmas tree per her official instructions. Of course, like everything else these scumbags do, we would have never even known about it. I mean, think about all the interns, all the people in the white house who saw it, and kept their damn mouths shut. Thankfully we know because Gary Aldrich from the fbi was assigned to the white house and had enough balls to open his mouth and put the information out in a book. *http://sweetness-light.com/archive/gary-aldrich-on-the-clintons-christmas-tree#.U3pJO15-8li*."

"The fact that I haven't heard about this stuff really stuns and disturbs me." Bill just couldn't understand how there wasn't national outrage over all of this.

"Looking at our real world's matrix from the outside in can be rather unsettling. Perhaps you shouldn't have opted for the red pill."

"It seems like some people are starting to wake up. I saw this article that had something to do with the last pope. Have you heard of that?"

"The book about it is called *Petrus Romanus*. I haven't read it but got the gist from reading articles. Glad some people are finally starting to get a clue. A nice piece of the puzzle but only a piece. It goes back to an ancient prophecy from a catholic archbishop from the twelfth century. The prophecies were first published in Fifteen Ninety Five, and a lot of people claim that's when it was actually written. But, suffice to say, it has a list of popes with a brief description of them, some rather accurate. The list ends with the pope who will be present at the end of days during the biblical Tribulation. The list ran out when pope francis took over from ratzinger."

The world believed that nazi piece of trash ratzinger was either a Texas Longhorns fan or a regular attendee of death metal concerts.

http://www.jesus-is-savior.com/False%20Religions/Wicca%20&%20 Witchcraft/signs/signs_of_satan3.htm. Even when he dressed like santa, you could see the evil exude from him. *http://www.godlikeproductions.com/ sm/custom/h/z/lrnqgqop.jpeg*.

"Yeah, that seemed pretty peculiar to me. I can't remember ever seeing a pope step down."

"That's because it almost never happens. I think about five times in two thousand years. The last time it happened was nearly six hundred years ago."

"Well, that seems like a bit of an ominous sign." The timing once again seemed awfully coincidental to Bill.

"I'd say the sign in the heavens came at ratzinger's resignation when the vatican was struck by lightning."

"Get out of town!" Bill threw his arms up in the air.

"Take a look yourself." *http://www.usatoday.com/story/weather/ 2013/02/12/lightning-bolt-strikes-vatican-pope-benedict- resignation/1913095/*.

"Where do you possibly find all this stuff?" Bill was stunned.

"Be careful if you ever ask God to show you the truth, to make you a hater of lies." Guy shrugged. It sounded like a smart request at the time. Though it had been a difficult journey, Guy would not change his request; he would not look away.

"So what does the catholic church and the pope have to do with all this? The pope just seems like a figurehead these days anyway."

"The pope has been the string-puller of empires' kings and queens for two millennia. The pope and the catholic leadership are wolves in sheep's clothing. But as always, people are content to keep their eyes shut tightly. They kept God's Word hidden from the people. As if it isn't enough that the popes have been some of the most wicked men in history, equating their words with God, the church is also a den and protector of pedophiles. At least now all that filth is right out in the open for everyone to see. Still people don't care. Of course they don't have eyes to see that rome is covered with Asherah poles, the wicked symbol of the ancient canaanites from the Bible. The popes have moved obelisks, their asherah pole, from some of the most wicked nations and rulers the world has ever known, to surround the vatican. They have the ancient obelisk of the egyptian sun god ra and the goddess isis—the most important gods of the egyptians who took God's people into captivity." *http://en.wikipedia.org/wiki/List_of_obelisks_in_rome.*

"I've never heard of either of them before, but it doesn't seem to make sense that people who say they follow jesus would surround themselves with things used for the worship of pagan gods." Bill found that rather peculiar. If you claimed to be part of the Christian faith, why would you surround yourself with evil artifacts?

"None of this makes sense until you come to the realization that it is not an accident, that it is all done by design. That these people are wicked, that they have been lying to us, that they are in reality luciferians. That they have been setting up a trap for us, preparing to destroy us. Now that they have everything in place, they are going to tighten the noose that we have allowed them to place around our necks. amun ra is the sun god, the most important god of the egyptian pantheon. Also known as amen ra. Want to know why Christians have no idea what's going on? Maybe when they pray to the Most High God, they should consider not ending every one of their prayers calling out to the sun god amen. *http://en.wikipedia.org/wiki/amun*.

"Christians have become so blind and ritualistic, they never even consider it. They're told maybe it means 'let it be done' and so they end every prayer with an oblation to the most high egyptian god. Pathetic. As if God needed some magical command at the end of a prayer. Some do study and see that it is also used by the Jews. But they stop there. The Jews started using it when they were taken into captivity. You certainly know isis also. I prefer to call her the whore of babylon."

"Somehow I don't think God would want his prayers ended with a salute to the egyptian sun god. What's with the whore of babylon?" Bill didn't know what it was, but it certainly sounded ominous.

"Well, the whore of babylon comes from chapter Seventeen of Revelation. She sits on many waters among a people of many nations and many tongues. Some might call it a melting pot. The entire world trades with her and becomes drunk because of her filthiness. She has a golden cup in her hand. Get it yet?"

Bill was silent.

"By your silence, I take it that you see that the whore of babylon is the statue of liberty."

Bill finished his last sip of coffee, and his mind swirled to come up with a cogent thought. "Didn't we get the statue of liberty from the french?"

"Yes, it was designed unsurprisingly by a french freemason to represent isis which is the greek name for the babylonian goddess ishtar. What do you suppose happens to the whore of babylon Bill?"

"I have a feeling I'd rather not know." Bill rubbed his temple.

"She gets destroyed with fire. If I were living in new york city, I would make my peace with God, because it's going to be destroyed." It was a bold statement, but Guy was tired of holding his tongue.

"Let's just hope it doesn't show up on the back of the twenty-dollar bill." Bill grimaced.

"Ha, ha." Guy chuckled. "Funny you should say so. The guy who found 9/11 on the currency just checked out the new bills with the gold-colored hundreds. It shows new york city being destroyed." *http://www.youtube.com/watch?v=E52mtSZN9D8*.

"Somehow I knew I should have just kept my mouth shut."

"That's what everyone keeps telling me."

"If you were as smart as I think you are, you would listen. I'm being serious now. You really should keep your mouth shut about all this stuff."

"I won't bend my knee to scum, Bill. You should know me better than that by now. I'm not going to shut up."

"You've got people hacking your email and tracking down where you work. Maybe you should take the hint," Bill said with deadpan eyes and as much sincerity as he could muster. "So, if this is all true, isn't there supposed to be like a bunch of dead fish and a third of the people getting killed and a rebuilding of the Temple in Jerusalem?" They were water-cooler slogans Bill had heard throughout the years, but he was pretty sure they had something to do with the Bible.

"Bill, the way this world operates in the shadows, most of what really happens is hidden from us. That's why people can't see the signs that have already been shown. Does anyone think we would know if these folks had made a covenant and then broke it? They'd do it all in secret. When the big signs come, like a flaming mountain into the sea that kills a third of the sea creatures or a third of the people, the Tribulation will be in full swing. It will be way too late by then to make any sort of arrangements. Not that it really matters, Bill, because the Bible says this world has become so wicked, that even when God brings back the same plagues that befell pharaoh and so much worse, even then, when there can be no denying it, the world will still refuse to repent.

"As far as the Temple goes, that is an interesting one. We can get into it later. Even the Christians who can see the truth behind 9/11—that it was orchestrated by the luciferian illuminati who have infected the places of power—still can't see the spiritual truth behind it."

"I'm following you now. It was their ringing of the bell for the bringing about of their New World Order."

"Yes, but it was more than that. I was pretty impressed with Jonathan Cahn's work on 9/11. He's a Messianic Jew and uncovered much of the spiritual significance behind 9/11, but he still didn't get to the core of the matter."

"I think I heard about him. He wrote a book called *The Harbinger*, right?"

"Yes, it's a must-read for an introduction into the deeper truths behind 9/11. He made important points and connections. How the Founding Fathers saw the united states as the new Israel. That they made a covenant. If our people followed God, we would reach new heights— but if we turned against Him, our blessings would turn to curses, just as with Israel. A central point of the book regards the words of the prophet Isaiah in chapter 9, verse ten, King James Version."

The bricks are fallen down, but we will build with hewn stones: the sycomores are cut down, but we will change them into cedars.

"OK, it sounds like a people standing strong, unified together." Bill could see how that was similar to 9/11. The country actually did come together.

"There was an initial attack before the Israelites were taken into captivity. After the attack the leaders uttered that statement. It sounds good on the surface, but what it showed was their reliance on their own strength to rebuild bigger and stronger, depending on their own devices instead of turning to God. It showed their lack of introspection, their lack of repentance, how far they had moved away from God. Since they didn't repent, God removed His hedge of protection and allowed them to be destroyed and carried into captivity. That verse is actually the Israelite's curse. It was God who was their strength, God who made them great, God who protected them."

"Well, I think you could make the case either way."

"The day after 9/11 the senate majority leader chose to read and proclaim the curse of Isaiah 9:Ten upon america. _http://www.wnd.com/2011/12/382289/_. On the third anniversary of 9/11, a senator proclaimed the curse yet again. obama summarized the verse in his first state of the union address and wrote a similar statement on a beam for the new freedom tower that replaced the twin towers." _http://www.wnd.com/2012/06/obama-fulfills-isaiah-910-prophecy-again/_.

"Well, that's probably not good." Bill didn't think it seemed particularly ominous either though.

"Certainly peculiar, but what was really fascinating was how we did the same things as Israel in deed also. We cut out hewn stone from the mountains above new york and had it placed in the hole at Ground Zero in a big religious ceremony. _http://abcnews.go.com/Archives/video/july-2004-ground-groundbreaking-10375296_. Even better, Cahn reveals how St. Paul's Chapel was saved from destruction by flying debris from a sycamore tree in front of the church. _http://www.thebanner.org/features/2011/01/new-york-city-s-tree-of-hope_. Well, the tree was destroyed, and, of course, in its place was planted a cedar or pine tree that was given by an anonymous donor. _http://www.wnd.com/2011/12/379829/_.

"Cahn makes some other important connections. How new york city was the original capital of the united states and that, when George Washington was sworn in, he led a procession to St. Paul's Chapel to dedicate the country in prayer, so the destruction of 9/11 happened at the place of our dedication as a country. He also shows how the biblical *shmitah*—a time when all debts are forgiven which happens every seven years on the twenty-ninth day of the Hebrew month of Elul—was the day of the largest stock market point drop, the day after the markets reopened following 9/11. The greatest point plunge ever was to happened seven years later to the day, when Lehman Brothers fell. Both on the twenty-ninth of Elul. *http://en.wikipedia.org/wiki/ List of largest daily changes in the Dow Jones Industrial Average*."

"Well, Cahn seems to be right up your alley. Is that the spiritual truth you are talking about?"

"It is only the beginning of the spiritual truth. Unfortunately he believes that our leaders uttered this curse upon us in ignorance, that the laying of the new *gazit* stone and the planting of the cedar tree were orchestrated by people who were unaware. Our leaders are aware though. They have done these things by design, for they are actively working toward our destruction. Yes, 9/11 was the sounding of the bell that our judgment is at hand. It was a coordinated effort. The spiritual truth is that 9/11 was not only done to sound the bell, but that it was a mocking of God planned long in advance. To laugh at Him, to say that the luciferians were in control, to pronounce judgment on God, to say that there was nothing God could do about it.

"9 is the biblical number of judgment, and the number 11 stands just like the twin towers that were destroyed. For at the time of the end, the Great Tribulation spoken of in the book of Revelation, God's judgments are released through his chosen vessels, his two witnesses, his twin towers. In the 11th chapter of Revelation, we see God's judgments called down upon the Earth by the two witnesses. On 9/11 the luciferians—whose magic is of charlatans—declared that they had destroyed the twin towers, that they would destroy the two witnesses. That they were now ready to finalize their plan for a New World Order with the installment of their king, the antichrist. They laughed and declared that there was nothing God could do."

"So it seems they have been working toward this end for some time."

"They have, indeed. Bringing in their king, the antichrist, has been the plan of their New World Order all along. They believe they will be able to redesign the world in their own grotesque image. For being so wise, these folks sure are stupid. Their father is the father of lies. Do they actually think that they are going to rule after this? It will not be so. Our

Lord will ride into battle for His own Name's sake. These scum are going to be caught in their own net. This could have very well been the design for the New World since our founding. At the very least our Founding Fathers made some sort of covenant to provide this New World with a godly form of government.

"Like Washington said, if we followed it, we would be blessed by God. If not, we would be turned over to lucifer for destruction. Washington certainly appears to have been a moral man. He was wise and gave us sound instruction. It also appears he was a thirty-third degree freemason, which is the rite of luciferianism. *http://33rddegreemason.com*. At Washington's inauguration, when he was sworn into office, he certainly did not reference God or Christ, simply the almighty being, which is certainly open to interpretation. *http://www.archives.gov/exhibits/american_originals/inaugtxt.html*.None of that really raises my eyebrows at all though."

"Mine either. It certainly doesn't seem as ominous as the rest."

"I agree. What I do find disturbing is the statue that was commissioned for his centennial where George Washington is represented as baphomet, the devil of old. *http://en.wikipedia.org/wiki/George_Washington_(Greenough)*.

http://en.wikipedia.org/wiki/baphomet. No shirt, the same peculiar hand gestures and all. At the time, they said it was a representation of zeus, the sun god, simply another representation of satan. The book of Revelation tells us that satan makes his seat on zeus's throne. Also Diane Reidy, a stenographer for the house of representatives, said she was repeatedly woken up by the Holy Spirit to give a message on the floor of the house of representatives. She did. She said that God would not be mocked, that this was not a nation under God. It never was. That the Constitution was written by freemasons, and they are against God." *http://wagpolitics.com/dianne-reidy-diane-reidy-house-stenographer-bizarre-rant/*.

"So to be honest I really don't know what to think, except that I know freemasonry is of the devil, and that whatever we were at our founding, we certainly are not a nation under God now. It would be some whopper of a lie to have a nation believe that they were good and dedicated to the God of Abraham, Isaac and Jacob if it were not so. Something interesting, but really inconsequential, with all the other proof and signs we have been given as to the hour and the day."

"Who knows these days? It all happened so long ago. I guess there's no way to really be sure one way or another. I did read something once about how washington, dc, is filled with masonic symbolism." Bill said.

"Well, that's definitely true. The whole city is like a masonic temple, obelisks and all. _http://www.jesus-is-savior.com/False%20Religions/ Illuminati/dc.htm_.My favorite is certainly the seat of our military might, the pentagram—uh, pentagon, I mean." Guy chuckled. "They even made sure it pointed the right way, with the devil horns pointing north."

"That seems appropriate. So shouldn't there be a false prophet, an antichrist or something?"

"Of course there is. As Christians we believe in the Trinity, one God—Father, Son and Holy Spirit. satan is a mocker and imitator of God. He has created his unholy trinity—the dragon, the false prophet and the antichrist. Anyone who has a clue should not be surprised to find out that the false prophet is the pope—pope francis to be precise. What better man to have the fools rally around when the world crumbles?

"Look how humbly he portrays himself, all the while being the luciferian's high priest. One of my favorite videos of that piece of trash is him sending a demon into a poor boy in a wheelchair. You can hear the poor boy grunt and groan as the pope lays hands on him. _http://www.youtube.com/watch?v=aBD-u8fJm-k_. Everyone was saying the pope performed an exorcism. But if it was an exorcism, wouldn't the boy be healed?

"The dragon is the black pope aldolfo nicolas. _http://en.wikipedia.org/ wiki/Superior General of the Society of jesus_.Very few people have ever heard of the term _black pope_. He is the head of the jesuits, which form the military wing of the catholic church. They have been thrown out of all sorts of countries over the centuries for their subversion and economic terrorism against empires. _http://en.wikipedia.org/wiki/ Suppression of the Society of jesus_. Now I'm sure that sounds crazy, and there is no proof for those conclusions. I can just say it was revealed to me by the Holy Spirit one crazy night while I was reading the book of Revelation.

"Now the antichrist, that is a favorite subject. Lots of proof against the most vile piece of garbage, barack obama, not that anyone cares or that anyone wants to hear."

"Hey, I'm in for the full ride. Shoot away." Bill could certainly agree that obama was a piece of garbage. He was stunned by how rapidly obama had changed the country, how quickly he was destroying it. He was certainly a bad guy, but the antichrist seemed far-fetched, science-fiction stuff.

"Well, I think we can agree that anything you research concerning barack obama, just doesn't seem to add up. It's easy to simply use pejoratives and call someone a _birther_, but if you have actually watched the press conference for the detective work done by Sheriff Joe Arpaio's cold-case team, obama's birth certificate is clearly a fake. *http://www.youtube.com/watch?v=XWmWO18GTc8*. There are so many inconsistencies with obama's birth certificate, starting with the fact that there is a typesetting that was done with a computer, but there were only typewriters at the time."

"No argument with me on that one. I watched the whole video, and there were multiple points that were incontrovertible. I made one of my cop buddies watch it. He said it certainly would be enough to have it ruled a forgery in court." The thought that life was imitating art and that obama was some sort of real-life version of *The Manchurian Candidate* had certainly crossed Bill's mind.

"What I think is even better are his school records. If he was some college wiz, why would his attorneys work so hard to make sure obama's school records weren't released? *http://www.wnd.com/2009/06/100613/*. It's easy to come up with some BS justification, but what is impossible to justify is that no one remembers ever seeing him at columbia university. Wayne Allen Root was a classmate at columbia during the same time period as obama, class of Nineteen Eighty Three, with the same majors, prelaw and political science. Not only did he never see obama at columbia, but at their thirty-year reunion, he asked every person in attendance. Not one person ever had a class with obama or even saw him on campus.

"Root called one of columbia's most famous professors after that, Professor Graff. Graff was a legend. Every student at columbia was required to take one of his classes. He's one of those men with an outstanding memory. He taught every significant american politician who had ever attended columbia and remembered them all distinctly. He unequivocally stated that he had never, ever taught barack obama and that no one at columbia ever knew him. *http://www.theblaze.com/contributions/ghost-of-columbia-part-ii-legendary-columbia-professor-never-heard-of-obama/*.

"Well, that's impossible."

"Not if his history is constructed, just a lie. Harry Lennix, an amazing actor who played the general in *Man of Steel*, told a talk show host named Mancow Muller that Lennix had trained obama for years on how to act presidential, like an educated southside African american. It was over ten years ago, and he said obama told Lennix that he was going to be president, which Lennix thought was ludicrous because obama was stupid. *http://en.wikipedia.org/wiki/Mancow_Muller*. Of course once the news went viral, Lennix backed off the story. *http://www.infowars.com/mancow-muller-obama-is-an-actor-trained-by-harry-lennix/*.

"They have certainly crafted him spiritually as well. The media literally made him the messiah on the cover of magazines. *http://christiannews.net/2013/01/21/newsweek-hails-obama-as-messianic-second-coming/*. And in the art world too. *http://hotair.com/archives/2009/04/27/outrage-du-jour-the-truth/*. When he went to egypt, they called him *pharaoh of the world*. *http://www.portlandmercury.com/BlogtownPDX/archives/2009/06/05/good-morning-news*. The one who really had it right was that guy in that miniseries, *The Bible*—the actor who plays satan looks exactly like obama. At least Hollywood is being honest for once." *http://www.theguardian.com/film/2014/feb/18/obama-son-of-god-satan-cut*. Guy smiled.

"The majority of this country sure has made him their savior. They wanted change, looks like we all got it. Unfortunately no one is paying my mortgage or filling up my car with gas. Although it did make for a great video. *http://www.youtube.com/watch?v=P36x8rTb3jI&feature=youtube_gdata_player*. You're not the only one who has videos." Bill laughed.

"Amazing, isn't it? Amazing how people actually think this man is a Christian, when he carries around magic talismans of pagan gods in his pocket with him at all times" *http://www.infowars.com/obamas-lucky-charms-a-hindu-god-in-his-pocket-a-masonic-emblem-and-a-ring-that-says-there-is-no-god-except-allah/*.

"I'm no Christian, but anyone who thinks obama is a Christian is just a moron, but we sure do have a country full of them these days." Bill found most folks knew more about reality television than politics or the economy.

"The obamas must enjoy hanging out with the bushes at Texas Longhorn games and ratzinger at death metal concerts because they love to throw up the horns too. barak does it regularly. *http://www.infiniteunknown.net/wp-content/uploads/2010/02/obama-hand-sign.jpg*. And michele is such a fan that she even threw it up on the cover of *Vogue* magazine. *http://www.vibevixen.com/2013/10/malaika-firth-and-15-other-black-celebrities-whove-covered-vogue/2/*. My favorite though is her standing in front of the veterans wearing a pentagram on her chest. *http://www.huffingtonpost.com/2011/10/20/michelle-obama-world-series_n_1021393.html*. Plus she was making some kind of luciferian hand signal. Who knows what the heck it means, but look at her hand. There is no way that's a natural gesture. Try to do it yourself. *http://www.whale.to/b/michelle_obama.html*. This photo used to be in a bunch of places, but it has pretty much been scrubbed from the Internet now."

"I can't stand to look at her man-shoulders." Bill cringed. "Maybe they met at a bath house. You know, there are rumors. *http://www.huffingtonpost.com/2012/09/12/obama-gay-rumors-chicago-jerome-corsi-_n_1877990.html*."

"I've read them. Who knows? There's much better evidence against this scumbag though."

"Well, let's hear it then. I agree that stuff all makes it clear this guy is not who he says he is, like he is some sort of puppet put in for a certain reason, but I don't see how that makes him the antichrist."

"That stuff has nothing to do with him being the antichrist. I'm just laying the foundation. It's clear this man is not who he says he is. He's not who he has been portrayed to be. *Puppet* is an apt description, but I would say more like an empty vessel. He has been poured out, so that evil can be poured in. As soon as I saw that man, my spirit jumped. I knew he was the antichrist, the man of sin. And I'm sure this sounds crazy to you, but, as with the rest of the stuff I've said, it works like this. God speaks something deep into my heart that seems crazy, then I go do research and find physical proof for the spiritual truth that was revealed to me.

"When I saw obama at rallies, I was stunned. I saw him saying his tagline, 'Yes, we can.' The masses of people would chant it back to him. 'Yes, we can.' 'Yes, we can,' back and forth to each other, as people are swooning around obama and falling to the ground unconscious. Not once or twice, but on all sorts of occasions. There was something about his catchphrase that really struck me. As I looked, I found out, when it's played backward, it says, 'Thank you, satan.' He was saying, 'Thank you, satan,' and people were repeating 'Thank you, satan' back to him and falling to the ground unconscious. *http://www.youtube.com/watch?v=C8g2nCxAVrk*."

"I saw that. I think it's just some YouTube hoax." It wouldn't be hard at all to fake something like that and put it up on the Net, Bill thought.

"Bear said the same thing when I showed him. He says, mockingly to me, 'I have an amp at the house. We can go try it right now.' He just about jumped out of his seat when we tried it, and 'Thank you, satan' came out of the amplifier, loud and clear."

"Get out of town! OK, that's definitely a creepy one."

"Something struck me about obama's name too. Besides the fact that is sounds so similar to osama, the name barack obama sounded so peculiar to me, I felt like there was something more to it. So I got a Strong's Concordance, which is a research tool for the Bible. You can look up words and see what the original Hebrew or greek word was, or look up Hebrew words and see what they mean and where they were used."

"Of course you did."

"So I looked up *barack obama*. Strong's number H1299 is the Hebrew word *bâraq* which means lightning, cast forth. *http://www.blueletterbible.org/lang/lexicon/lexicon.cfm?Strongs=H1299&t=KJV*. And Strong's number H1116 for *bâmâh* means from an elevated place, height, place of worship. *http://www.blueletterbible.org/lang/lexicon/Lexicon.cfm?strongs=H1116*. The O between them is the Hebrew *vav*, a conjunction that means bringing two things together *http://en.wikipedia.org/wiki/Vav_(letter)*. So in Hebrew, barak obama's name means lightning cast forth from the heights or place of worship. You can see the Hebrew word *bâraq* is clearly used as lightning in Psalm One Forty Four:Six.

"In the entire Bible there is only one place where satan is referred to by his name. It is in the King James Version, Isaiah Fourteen:Twelve:

> How are thou fallen from heaven, O lucifer, son of the morning! How art thou cut down to the ground, which didst weaken the nations!

"In the fourteenth verse, lucifer declares:

> I will ascend above the heights of the clouds; I will be like the most High.

"In Luke Ten:Eighteen, Christ is speaking and tells us what the consequence was for lucifer's arrogance:

> I beheld satan as lighting fall from heaven.

"So *lighting cast out from the heights of heaven* is the description of lucifer's fall and also the meaning of barak obama's name."

It doesn't matter how much proof people had, they still wouldn't believe, Guy thought.

"I don't think they are teaching that in Sunday school."

"Everyone is asleep at the switch. Once the veil is removed, people sitting in the pews are going to cower with fear. They are going to be caught in a trap and wonder why their leaders, their pastors, gave them no warning. They will be so crushed that their weak faith will be ground into dust. We will call that the Great Falling Away. So you will laugh at this one. Three days after the man of sin wins the election, the Holy Spirit speaks into my heart that his number is six hundred threescore and six. Everybody knows that one, as 666 comes from chapter Thirteen of

Revelation. And I swear, I'm like, huh? I'm going to check the winning lotto numbers for his district in illinois."

"There were *not*."

"The day after obama won the election, November Fifth, Two Thousand Eight, the winning lotto numbers for his home district in illinois were 6-6-6 and, for the pick four, 7-7-7-9, which represents perfect judgment. 7 is the biblical number for perfection. So three of them together, a perfect Trinity, while 9 is the biblical number for judgment."

"All right, that I don't believe." Bill thought that seemed too good to be true.

"Of course you don't. Take a look at the lotto website." *http://www.illinoislottery.com/en-us/Winning/Winning Number Search/ winning-number-search-game.html#loadingImg2*. Guy's bookmark list on his phone was longer than his arm.

"OK, why is it no one is talking about any of this?" There were certainly a lot of pieces to the puzzle, but Bill didn't understand how this stuff wasn't even being spoken of, let alone discussed.

"Because in these last days we love not the truth, so God has sent us a strong delusion that we would believe a lie. Certainly there should be more signs, right? Daniel tells us the antichrist will destroy through peace."

"Whoa. I did think it was pretty weird that they gave obama the Nobel Peace Prize. I mean, he just got into office. He didn't even do anything yet."

"But it was necessary for the man of sin to receive the world's prize of peace. The thing is though, these luciferian scum are imitators and mockers of the Most High God. For when Christ was born, there was a star in the sky, the star of Bethlehem announcing the birth of the King. So the luciferians must also have a sign in the sky for the announcing of their king. And so there was a sign in the sky the night before obama arrived in norway to accept his prize of peace. *http://www.youtube.com/watch?v=CBUW MZkQ30*. There was this crazy spiral of light in the night sky, unlike anything you have ever seen before. I'm sure it was man-made, since the luciferians are no better than carnies, but a sign nonetheless. *http://www.examiner.com/article/ mysterious-light-appears-over-norway-before-obama-peace-prize-speech*."

"That's crazy looking. Maybe they all got together and sang 'O Little Star of norway,'" Bill quipped, though he was having a hard time finding humor in any of this.

"There are plenty of other significant spiritual signs, like the fact that obama is the only president who was not sworn in with a Bible."

"That's not true. He used Lincoln's Bible. You know he's going to save the union in the next civil war. Hey, I pay attention."

"You do, indeed, Bill, but these days you have to pay close attention. chief justice roberts garbled the oath, after obama changed his response from 'I will execute the office of the president of the united states faithfully' to 'I will execute faithfully the office of the president of the united states.' http://voices.washingtonpost.com/44/2009/01/20/inauguration_flub_watch.html. A bit of a difference there, don't you think, Bill? obama changed the oath to say he would *execute*—or eliminate—the presidency. The next day it was done without a Bible in twenty-five seconds. http://www.nytimes.com/2009/01/22/us/politics/22oath.html?_r=1&. Of course they try to spin it, but, if the first oath was correct, then why did a second oath need to be taken? And where was the Bible, Bill? These folks are such two-bit cons. They play shell games, and no one even realizes there's no ball under the shell." Guy was no longer frustrated with the people's blindness. He would speak the truth regardless.

"I see your point there. Looks like he's executing the whole union. So what else have they been doing by sleight of hand?" Bill found the information Guy was sharing to be disturbingly poignant.

"So many to choose from, but here are a few of my favorites. The antichrist gave a speech in Gaston Hall at georgetown university. He chose to give the speech in front of a cross with a slogan, To the Greater Glory of God. Completely inappropriate for the man of sin, so they just had it turned into a black pyramid instead, one of their favorite symbols. http://www.nbcwashington.com/news/local/jesus-Missing-From-obamas-Georgetown-Speech.html.

"Seen the articles of obama being swarmed by flies? I find them amusing since a common Jewish reference to satan is beelzebub, which means lord of the flies. http://www.wnd.com/2013/01/is-obama-biblical-lord-of-the-flies/. How about the swine flu outbreak in mexico city that coincided with obama's visit and killed dozens of people? http://latimesblogs.latimes.com/washington/2009/04/white-house-says-obama-not-affected-by-swine-flu.html. A good one that just happened was when obama went to nelson mandella's funeral. Did you see the video of the man who was standing right next to obama? He was doing sign language for the audience, except it turned out he wasn't really doing sign language at all. He was just faking it."

"I saw that. What a nut job. People will do anything for money or a minute of fame."

"That's the truth. But after the event, the man was admitted to a psychiatric hospital. He said, while he was up on stage standing next to obama, he had a nervous breakdown, because he saw angels descend out of the sky and down into the stadium and onto the stage. *http://www.youtube.com/watch?v=7c33Omwka0A*. Unfortunately the man is spiritually blind, separated from God, so he didn't realize that what he saw were not angels but demons. Those are just some fun coincidences that follow that piece of human refuse around.

"I'm sure you don't remember, but, right after he took office, the luciferians gave a sign. There was an airliner flying real low, out of the normal flight paths over manhattan. People were freaking out, yelling and screaming, thinking it was another 9/11. *http://www.youtube.com/watch?v=lWARNUP07kQ*. It was the president's plane, air force one, doing a photo shoot, and the white house told the police not to inform the public. A photo shoot of what, you ask? All this to get a photo of the president's plane with the statue of liberty, the whore of babylon. Now that is an important photo and a signal to the rest of the illuminati that their king has seized control. *http://www.nbcnews.com/id/30435336/ns/us_news-security/t/obama-new-york-city-flyover-was-mistake/#.U35GYl5-9Fi*."

"Wow, that's out of control. What about those big signs I hear that everyone's waiting for? Isn't the antichrist supposed to get a head wound and rise from the dead? And what about that whole thing with the rebuilding of the Temple? Are you trying to avoid that one?" Bill gave a wide-eyed questioning look.

"Nope, again just laying the foundation first, Bill. So, for the head wound, again you have to realize that these luciferians are carnival hucksters. Sure, they have earthly power and communicate with demons, but their power is illusion, based on deception. So it's very interesting how osama and obama have identical markers used to recognize people, things that are difficult to fake even when changing someone's identity through surgery. Things like the distance between their eyes and the structure of their ears and the spatial relationship together. *http://www.youtube.com/watch?v=HuMShxAq7XQ*. The lines on their palms and the length of their fingers. *http://www.youtube.com/watch?v=SHXG-W0n1p8*.

"Now I'm not saying that there was no osama bin laden, just that, at some point, obama played the part of osama bin laden in videos. Nick Kristof heard obama recite the muslim call to prayer in arabic with a first-rate arabic accent. *http://www.weeklystandard.com/weblogs/TWSFP/2009/06/does_obama_speak_arabic_1.asp*. That was one of the few reasons I enjoyed *Iron Man Three* so much. They have a terrorist who looks almost exactly like osama bin laden putting out propaganda videos, while things are being blow up all over the place. It comes out at the end of the movie that the dangerous terrorist is just some government hack actor. That the government is using him as cover so they can blow up things themselves and use it all as a smoke screen so they can expand their power through war.

"Bill, does anyone actually believe the official story about the death of osama bin laden? What a joke! Especially that picture of the luciferian scum looking all concerned while they watched the raid on TV. Pathetic. _http://images.smh.com.au/2011/05/06/2346953/art_situation-room-420x0.jpg_.

"We have been hunting osama bin laden for over a decade. We're told that, because of him, it was necessary to have our rights stripped, our entire world turned upside down, that after 9/11 we lived in a New World with new rules. So with all of that, with the fundamental change thrust upon america, when we find the most wanted man in history, we offer the american people no proof that he was captured or killed? They have some BS ceremony at sea, that they pretend is to uphold osama's muslim dignity, that no one is privy to see. Meanwhile burial at sea is against islamic tradition. _http://www.theguardian.com/world/2011/may/02/sea-burial-osama-bin-laden_.

"Now, while these missions are secret, on this one we just happen to find out seal team six are the ones who captured osama, and then, within a few months of the capture, several members of seal team six are killed in a mysterious helicopter crash. _http://www.infowars.com/seal-team-6-families-force-congress-to-investigate-mysterious-chopper-crash/_. _http://www.teaparty.org/michael-savage-seal-team-six-executed-33118/_. Then there was another member of the team who was killed and another seriously injured in a training accident. _http://usnews.nbcnews.com/_news/2013/03/29/17520371-member-of-seal-team-6-killed-another-seal-injured-in-parachute-accident?lite_.

"And, with all that, the only proof the american people are given on the death of osama bin laden is a picture of him with a head wound, not _maybe_ a fake, a _confirmed_ fake. _http://www.cnn.com/2011/WORLD/asiapcf/05/03/bin.laden.fake.photo/_. _http://www.theguardian.com/world/2011/may/02/osama-bin-laden-photo-fake_. And so, with their carnival tricks, the antichrist, who has received a mortal head wound, still stands, and the luciferians laugh till their bellies ache, spiritually turning america's most hated enemy into our most revered leader."

"I never understood why osama, the man supposedly responsible for taking away our liberty and security, deserved so much reverence that we couldn't have any proof whatsoever that he was actually dead." Bill found the whole thing despicable. "They tell us they confirmed his DNA. Get real. They hung mussolini in the streets so he could get spit on, but we can't even get pictures or a video of osama dead. This just seems more and more like we've gone right through the looking glass. Really creepy."

"So the Temple—that was the sign I was really waiting for, but the Holy Spirit revealed the truth to me in advance through God's Word. Everyone keeps waiting for this rebuilt Temple. And I'd simply ask, where does the Bible say that? People will point to the the last portion of Second Thessalonians Four:Two, the King James Version:

> So that he as God sitteth in the temple of God, shewing himself that he is God.

"But the greek word used for *temple* is Strong's word G3485, which also means the place of divine manifestation. People will try to say it only refers to the Temple of Jerusalem, but Christ uses the exact same word to refer to Himself in the book of John. The same greek word is also used in Corinthians and Ephesians to refer to the body of the believer. But Christ Himself speaking of the antichrist gives us a very specific warning in Matthew Twenty Four:Fifteen.

> When ye therefore shall see the abomination of desolation, spoken of by Daniel the prophet, stand in the holy place, (Whoso readeth, let him understand:)

"So Christ does not say that the antichrist will be standing in the Temple of Jerusalem, but rather that he will be standing in the holy place. Now this is where it gets interesting, Bill. Christ made his triumphal entry into Jerusalem riding on the back of a donkey, the week before he was crucified. It is referred to as the Passion Week. He entered Jerusalem on the Tenth day of the Hebrew month Nisan at the same time the Paschal lambs were entering Jerusalem to be slaughtered for the Passover, pretty awesome symbolism. *http://www.fellowshipjasper.com/wp-content/upLoads/2010/03/Chronology-of-Passion-Week.pdf*.

"Well, obama, the man of sin, never made it to Israel during his first term. He did, however, make it when he started his second term. In fact he made his journey during the Passion Week. *http://www.christianpost.com/news/obama-visits-nativity-church-in-bethlehem-called-messenger-of-peace-92471/*. While he was there, he just so happened to visit the Church of the Nativity, the place of our Lord, the Christ's, birth. What day do you think he happened to show up standing in the place Christ was born?"

"No. Impossible." Bill didn't understand how all of this had remained hidden.

"Well, he made it there before sunset, so he arrived and stood in the place of Christ's birth on the tenth of Nisan. The man of sin made his triumphal entry and stood in the holy place, the place of Christ's birth, the same day that Christ had made His triumphal entry. And obama did it on the back of a donkey, the mascot for the democratic party. Now that's symbolism. It also happens to be the same day the Israelites entered the Promised Land, when the Lord parted the River Jordan. And just to make it a little more illuminati friendly, it was March Twenty Second here, with 322 a favorite illuminati number, the secret number of skull and bones. *http://www.secretsofthefed.com/wp-content/uploads/2014/04/maxresdefault-13.jpg*. And so I say, 'He that hath an ear, let him hear what the Spirit saith unto the churches.'" Guy was sick and tired of the lies and deception.

"OK, I think I'm ready to go hide in a cave now." Bill could feel himself sweating through his shirt; his face was feeling clammy.

"But wait, there's still more," Guy said, smiling, speaking in his best game-show voice. "Now this one has got to be my favorite. It's just so brazen, and the same thing happened. Nobody even blinked. In the book of Revelation, chapter Two, verse Thirteen, Christ speaks directly to pergamos or pergamon and says He knows it is where satan's seat is, satan's throne, which is Strong's Number G2362. Pergamon is an ancient city in Asia Minor outside of constantinople, the capital of the eastern roman empire after the fall of rome. The famous pergamon altar was built in the second century BC and was the center of pagan worship. *http://www.cbn.com/700club/features/ChurchHistory/pergamon/EZ28_seat_of_satan_part_2.aspx*.

"The pergamon altar was also called the temple of zeus, king of the gods, another representation of satan. It was lost to antiquity, likely sometime in the Fourteen Hundreds after the fall of constantinople. *http://en.wikipedia.org/wiki/pergamon_altar*. But it was rediscovered in the Eighteen Sixties by a german archeologist, who excavated the altar and moved it brick by brick to Berlin. The reconstruction was completed in Nineteen Thirty just in time for hitler's rise to power. In fact the podium at Zeppelin Field was designed based on the pergamon altar. It's where hitler gave some of his most dastardly speeches including the nuremberg laws and the final solution." Guy paused and took a sip from his water. He always made sure to keep distilled water in his office.

"And?" Bill asked reluctantly.

"And obama gave a big speech in berlin before he became president, near the pergamon altar under the victory column that hitler had erected. Atop the column stands the goddess victoria, also called nike, who is said to be zeus's charioteer. *http://www.theoi.com/daimon/nike.html*. The name of his speech was, The World that Stands as One, much too tricky for people to make the leap to 'One World.' When he was done, a german radio announcer declared that we had just heard the next president of the united states and the future president of the world. There are rumors that obama went to go see the pergamon altar while he was there."

"So?"

"So hold on. We're just getting to the good part. He was there in July, and, when he comes back, he accepts the democratic nomination in August of Two Thousand Eight at Mile High Stadium, Invesco Field, now known as Sports Authority Field, in Denver. obama has a replica of the pergamon altar built at Mile High Stadium. So when obama accepts the nomination for president of the united states, and the whole world knows he's going to become president of america, he does it from a re-creation of satan's throne, with the white horse of Revelation, the white horse of the Denver Broncos, directly above his head while he spoke. *http://www.utexas.edu/courses/fallofgreece/great_altar_reconstruction.jpg*. *http://gospel-of-christ.weebly.com/uploads/2/0/4/2/ 20422437/7088924.jpg?650*. *http://www.isawthelightministries.com/obamahorse.jpg*."

"OK, I'm officially speechless. I think I'm going to go throw up." Bill struggled to implement his joking tone, in an attempt to diffuse his own apprehension. He found the information was nothing to laugh at— nothing funny at all, not in the least bit humorous.

"Well, with that, I think I've said enough. If that doesn't open someone's eyes, it is because they have willfully chosen to keep them shut. They have said in their own heart that they would rather be a lover of lies."

"I think you've said more than enough. But I'm going to say it again. You need to keep your mouth shut about all of this. I know you realize who you're messing with here, so don't poke the beehive. You're going to end up getting stung." Bill was not joking, not joking at all.

"Bill, I'm not sure how I can be more clear. I'm not going to keep my mouth shut. I'm not going to bend my knee to scum. I'm not going to submit to filthy satan-loving pieces of trash." Guy realized there would likely be consequences for shining the light on the darkness, but he had a plan. It was almost finished, and he was going to carry it through to the end, no matter what.

"Don't say I didn't warn you."

"You and everybody else, Bill."

"So it looks like these people really have us cornered. What do we do?"

465

"What we should have done was vote every single incumbent out of office, some sort of slogan like "not one"—not one incumbent left in office who voted for the NDAA and not one voted in thereafter, unless they promised to repeal the NDAA, as a start to restoring our liberty. Then we should have taken back the privatized federal reserve and abolished it. The evil ones are smart though. They've already packed the system with dynamite. Taking back control of the money supply now would explode the entire system, because the only thing keeping it together is printed money and manipulation.

"Unfortunately we have moved past the point of no return now. God gave us one last opportunity to repent, when obama was up for reelection, but instead we said, 'Lord, we're sure we want the antichrist to be our king.' What we need to do now is repent, pray and resist this filth at every level. Resist the poisons, resist the lies, resist the police state, its surveillance. Resist the prison planet they have created on every front. No more *bending of the knee*, period. These luciferian illuminati are all-in now, Bill. They're going to start World War as a cover, so they can collapse the dollar and the world economy, then take total control, because we have become reliant on them for our food.

"There will certainly be resistance, and it will be a bloodbath, especially when we all find out what we already know in our hearts, that the majority of the police and military will have no problem following orders as blindly as the nazis did. They certainly have no problem actively participating in training for war against the american people. http://www.infowars.com/dod-training-manual-suggests-extremist-founding-fathers-would-not-be-welcome-in-todays-military/. Or shooting up targets of pregnant women. http://www.infowars.com/dhs-supplier-provides-shooting-targets-of-american-gun-owners/. The illuminati are dug in so deeply that they will have no problem with nuking american cities, if the resistance is too fierce. We have let the evil grow too large, too strong.

"Unless God moves for the sake of His own Holy name, the evil is going to grind us into dirt and remake the world in their own despicable, pathetic image. But our God will not allow it. Our God will move. It is the evil ones who are about to be caught in the net that they have laid. Repent, store up your oil, refuse to bend your knee to scum, pray that God moves, pray that seal of God be placed upon your very forehead. If you are wise, pray for an earthquake to rock the very islands from their foundation." That was Guy's advice. He had nothing more to say.

★★★

For Guy, there was nothing sweeter than the joy that emanated from his children as the holidays brought the year to a close. With the first week of the New Year Two Thousand Fourteen, Guy pressed feverishly to finish crafting the sword he would use to strike at the very heart of the luciferian's power. On the morning of the fifth, a Sunday, Guy finished all of his research, all of his preparation. The sword he had crafted was finely sharpened, like a razor. It was time to break his fast, a celebration of what was completed and what was to be done.

Guy took Marie, Faith and John bowling. Marie's father, Arnie, came along with his wife. It was nice to have Bear, Guy's new brother-in-law, along with Bear's wife, Champagne, and their children, Contessa and little Aphrodite. The kids bumper bowled. It was Faith's and John's first time. Guy couldn't wipe the smile from his face. Faith wanted to do it all by herself; she won all three games on the kids' lane and even scored higher than her aunt Champagne on the last game. Though by Faith's modesty, you wouldn't have guessed. Guy got a kick helping John roll the ball from between his legs, as they watched it bounce back and forth between the bumpers. Guy came from behind and beat Arnie and Bear, who were up for most of the day. He was modest also, though it was more difficult for him, and he knew his heart was dimmed by the purity of his daughter's.

Breaking a fast with bread was never necessary after the iron gut the marine corps had helped Guy forge. He treated his family and Bear's to their favorite barbecue joint. They enjoyed some delicious ribs along with an ice cold beer. You couldn't possibly pass up on the wings, so he split an order with Bear. The day's events had left the children dazed and ready to collapse into the sweet slumber of childhood.

With his family's heads safely upon their pillows, Guy basked in the love he felt for his precious family. He stared out into the black of the night. He put the darkness on notice. The sword he had crafted for the dark evil forces was ready. He was ready to wield it and strike them a fierce blow. He had resisted them long enough. It was time to gain ground. It was time for battle. It was time to go BANG!

EPILOGUE

EPILOGUE

As Guy drove home from the office on Monday, January Sixth, Two Thousand Fourteen, he was relieved the heavy lifting was over. He was filled with anticipated nervousness at what was to come next. At least it would all be over soon. As he neared home from his daily drive, he received a call from the father of a girl in his daughter's class. She was a real angel of a girl. Guy could see her lovely spirit and heart for God instantly. He had fostered the girl's friendship, and the two families had shared some meals together, while the wives had become friends.

The girl's mother, Jane, was an executive at the local community college and was able to get Marie into a class last semester that she was having a hard time enrolling in. This semester there was a biology class which was nearly impossible to get into. Jane had secured Marie a spot, and Marie needed to pay online by the end of the day or she would lose her place. Jane had been trying to reach Marie unsuccessfully all day. Guy said he would take care of it when he got home. He gave Marie a quick ring, but she didn't pick up, which was unfortunately rather standard. It was one of those irritating habits of Marie's that Guy had just learned to let go of.

As Guy pulled into the driveway and opened the garage, there was a chair pulled into his parking spot. He could see a note duct taped to the back of it. His heart sank instantly. *Guy* was written across the top in large black marker.

The children and I will not be going on the camel joy ride to the bunker with you and your Twitter friends. I am afraid of you, and what you will do to me and the kids. I fear for my life as you have threatened me and have become increasingly irrational. I fear for the safety and emotional well-being of Faith and John too.

I am getting help, and I pray you get psychological help. I know there is no going back from this path, but I have no choice. You scare me, and I know you will kill me for defying you.

Marie

Guy was instantly in a panic. What was Marie talking about: a bunker, hurting her? As he ran into the house, he was left with the remnants of a hurricane. The dogs' area was covered in dirt and hair, because their cages had been moved. The bird's cage was empty, and, as Guy called out, there was no answer. There was a table set up in the kitchen, with nearly a hundred picture frames thrown about, the glass and backings were strewn everywhere. As Guy ran to the stairs, every picture in the entire house was gone. Every picture except his wedding photos and two pictures of the children, which were only left because those pictures included Guy. The tears streamed down Guy's face, and he sobbed, hysterically, violently, as a man dying from a mortal wound.

As he ran to the children's room, they were empty, except for the furniture. Every toy gone; every shred of clothing gone; every book gone. Marie's clothes gone; her jewelry gone. His eight-terabyte computer gone; his backup server gone. The two cats gone; the two guinea pigs gone; the two dogs gone; the bird gone. Guy ran back to the garage; his laptop was gone, along with all of his handwritten notes. All of the work, all of his research, all of his plans gone, though it concerned him not. Guy knew something was dreadfully, dreadfully wrong.

As he looked throughout the house, he saw that his only set of house keys were gone: his spare car keys, the keys to the shed, the keys to sprinkler box. He checked the safe. His passport was gone along with Marie's and Faith's. The children's birth certificates and all of their medical records gone. All their wedding china, in the china hutch, was gone. A large bookcase Marie's grandfather had made was gone. And in an instant, Guy realized he was destroyed.

He called Bear, who was almost home. Bear was sure Marie would be at his house, but Guy knew his family would not be there. The letter Marie wrote made no sense. He realized she must have been secretly reading his emails. *Camel Joy Ride* was the email he had set up to correspond with the two families he met in Texas after his email account was hacked three weeks ago. While he didn't speak to Marie about it, it certainly wasn't a secret. It was all on his laptop, which he had left next to his bed every day; no passwords needed. He had nothing to hide from her. He had never threatened Marie, not once; he loved his wife. The tone and language seemed uncharacteristically Marie, as if she were coached on what to say, though the letter was certainly in her handwriting.

Bear's callback revealed that Marie had stopped by their house at ten thirty that morning with the children, that she had told Champagne that Marie was going to disappear. Faith was in her school uniform, but Marie told Champagne it was a pupil-free day. Guy was stunned, instantly shattered. Bear would call Guy's sister Pearl, and they would come to the house. When Guy called Mack, he passed the phone to Ginge, who was hysterical. She said Marie showed up at Mack's house around two thirty with a stack of emails and tweets for Ginge to leaf through. Ginge said

Marie was going to divorce Guy, and he deserved it. She had read the tweets. How could Guy say that people were eating babies?

"How disgusting, Guy. What's wrong with you?" she said.

Guy tried to tell her about the Pepsi testing, but she just said he was out of his mind and continued with her hysterical ranting. When Guy asked, she said Faith wasn't there, that she was in school, and that Marie had left quickly to pick her up.

Guy confirmed that, in fact, there was no school that day and found the information terrifying. Who was Faith with when Marie was at Mack's? Guy and Marie trusted no one with their daughter alone, not even Marie's father. It was clear to Guy that there were other people involved. Marie could never have moved in her small SUV all the stuff that was taken, even with multiple trips. Her grandfather's bookcase would never fit. Who was watching Faith?

Everyone was quick to assure Guy that no one really disappears, that he would be served with divorce papers any moment and to stop being so hysterical. They were concerned Guy would kill himself. Guy stayed home from work, as the tears and sobs never ceased. He cried continuously, endlessly, for days on end. Hurt his wife or his children? Unthinkable! He would let himself be ripped apart by wild dogs before he would let any harm come to his wife or his children, ever.

On Wednesday night he called Mack to see if Ginge would bring him over to something to put him to sleep. He hadn't slept in three days, and he was choking on the glut of his tears. Ginge was the queen of medication; she took nearly thirty pills a day, which she mixed and matched personally, purchasing many from the Internet and multiple doctors to help with her numerous physical and mental illnesses. They were ecstatic when Guy asked for medication.

He was sure Marie would use the information in his laptop against him, to say he was crazy because of the thoughts of his mind, his personal religious beliefs. He was sure it would work in the new america, as it had in the old soviet union where *thought* crimes were much more dangerous than *actual* crimes. Crimes of the mind were not to tolerated as the New World Order was birthed. Though he had done nothing wrong, and had never offered his wife and children anything but love and provision, it was a time when the country found the thoughts of a man's mind more dangerous than his actions.

Guy could see she was going to try to keep the children from him, even though he had kept his thoughts in his own mind for the last years, never verbalizing them to his immediate family. He was innately aware that they all knew what Guy believed, that they thought his mind was more dangerous than Marie's actions.

He decided he would go back to see Milton, for Guy knew, if he didn't, everyone would side against him—even though everyone knew what an amazing dad Guy was, that his children were the most kindhearted, loving and obedient children any of them had ever run across. They were never sad; they were never scared. Still people would gladly say Guy should be banned from seeing his children, if he didn't recant of his own mind. He figured seeing Milton would help stave off the calls for his necessitated medication.

On Thursday, Guy received a call from Bear. Bear's wife Champagne had called Bear to say that Guy's little poodle, Rupert, and Guy's two cats were left in a cage on Bear's front door step. Guy was stunned; it seemed very peculiar. He thought it seemed likely their large dog, Duke, might have been left at Marie's father's house or perhaps Mack's. Duke was only two, a Doberman-poodle mix, and often of questionable behavior. If Marie were going to leave a dog behind, it would be him. Rupert was always well behaved and easy to take care of. When Guy arrived at Arnie's, Duke was not there.

Nothing waiting for Guy at Mack's either, which Guy found very odd. What he found even more peculiar was that Ginge was not home. She was always home, as she didn't drive, except perhaps once in a blue moon for an emergency. But as a matter of fact and practice, it hadn't happened since Guy had known her. When he gave her a ring, she was hysterical. On a whim, she had decided to drive down to Mack's storage unit. It was empty. The twenty thousand pounds of food that Guy had given to his father to keep harmony and to further Guy's dependence on God was gone. His assault rifle, shotgun and handgun that he gave to his father were also gone. Guy wanted to go see for himself. Ginge said she would be home shortly, that they could go together.

When she arrived, she was in a panic, as Guy stood at his father's front door at the top of his long pathway. Ginge froze at the bottom and started screaming hysterically that Guy was scaring her. He hadn't said a word, then asked her what she was talking about. The whole thing seemed to be getting more peculiar by the moment. Why was she down at the storage unit, when she never drives, coincidentally the same day the dog showed up at Bear's house. She just felt like checking. The lock wasn't broken, so how did Marie get a key? Ginge gave it to her around Thanksgiving, because Marie wanted to move the guns from Mack's safe into storage. Hmm. Marie gave it back on christmas. Interesting, indeed, Guy thought.

After that Guy hired a high-powered Beverly Hills attorney who was a friend and required a sizable retainer. Guy thought perhaps he should hire a private investigator, but he was a thousand dollars short and not due to receive his bonus until April. He asked Mack to lend him the paltry sum. He had borrowed money from Mack in the past, when a bonus was late or there was an emergency. Guy had always paid him back quickly, every last dime, unlike his sister. Mack repeatedly had said it was a pleasure to help. But now he said he didn't have the money and told Guy to stop making such a big deal of things. His response was immediate and canned. It sounded of something whispered in his ear by Ginge.

The attorney agreed with the family—people just don't disappear these days. Especially with two children and a flock of animals. He had experience in these matters and said Marie just needed to blow off steam. She was clearly scared and pursuing her would only confirm her fears. While the attorney advised against it, Guy sent Marie a text letting her know he understood she was scared, though there was no reason for it. He told her that he was nervous himself after Faith's tidal wave dream. He was sorry. He loved her dearly, and she could take as much time as she needed. He could have the attorney send her and the children some money confidentially, no strings attached, no ruses.

He told her that, despite what she believed, the only reason there was no coming back from this path was because she desired it, not because it was so. He imagined she was staying in some sort of shelter, since she was trying to return the little dog and two cats. There was probably a limit on the amount of animals, and, if she was staying in a strange environment, Duke would have made her feel safe. He was a guard dog after all. That was the reason Guy had lobbied for him.

He told her that he had stopped talking with his friends in Texas. Though they were godly folks, they were certainly a bit Midwestern–peculiar by los angeles standards. While Guy would pray for a hedge of protection, they would pray for a holy cheese dome. When Guy would pray that the words of evil men would not be able to come against them, they would pray that the Lord would seal their mouth with Holy duct tape. Guy sent the Texas family presents for christmas, money for the girls, a T-shirt for the husband and a coffee mug for the mother. They had sent Guy a Bible, Marie some custom wine glasses, jewelry for Faith and trucks for John.

Guy was waiting for the presents to arrive so he could introduce them to Marie. He knew she would find the fact that he had made online friends intolerable, but he thought the presents would break the ice. Then he would propose that they all meet at Disneyland for spring break. Except Guy never got the box, and, when he spoke to his friends after the matter, they were devastated. Marie must have found the box. They had put a roll of gold-colored duct tape in the box as a gag gift, along with all the other presents in the box. Guy was mortified. While it made no sense for Marie to be scared, she was clearly not in her right state of mind, and he could see how it would have affected her.

Over the last several years, Guy was often fearful over events, until God had removed Guy's fear. People had told him that his fears were irrational, but the fear was real nonetheless. He knew Marie's fear was irrational. There must have been twenty rolls of duct tape around the house after Marie had left. Marie had stuck the note to the chair with duct tape. If Guy was planning something nefarious, to tie up his wife with duct tape and murder her, would he really have someone send duct tape to the house? It was irrational nonsense, but Guy felt compassion.

When he ran it by Bear, it seemed Champagne happened to remember more details that she had kept to herself. Yes, Marie was scared. She said Guy was going to kidnap the kids and take them to Texas, then have an affair with this woman. Marie had even showed Champagne a picture on the woman on the Internet. They thought she was very pretty. Guy's head spun. His wife was secretly reading his tweets and emails. Not that Guy kept them secret. He had spoken to his wife about his Twitter account, how he had actually found some nice people to speak with, to let off some steam.

There were over seven thousand tweets and tons of emails going back and forth with the family. Guy never mentioned taking the children to Texas or having an affair. Marie was petrified of any talk concerning worldly events, let alone the illuminati and their plans for a New World Order. He could understand how she could have worked herself into a frenzy, though he wondered why she wouldn't have said anything to him. He left everything right out in the open. If he was making these crazy plans, why would he make no effort to keep them secret?

He was sad and dismayed. He could understand how Marie could have taken some things out of context, if she were only reading sporadically. He said he believed his family would be taken by God as first fruits when the great earthquake happened, as Guy knew his daughter's dream about a tidal wave coming over the mountains was prophetic. The Internet picture of the gal in Texas which Marie had looked up was from twenty years ago. The woman was fifty, and Guy corresponded with the entire family. Did anybody really believe he was going to have an affair with a married fifty-year-old woman from Texas?

Guy spoke to the whole family on the phone together and sent them all christmas presents. In the finance world half the guys he knew were having sex with nineteen-year-olds, whether the guys were married or not, whether the girls were professionals or not. Guy found the whole thing to be preposterous that he would stand accused of such; still he was not angry with Marie. There was a picture of the girls in the family all wearing fur coats. The mother's was made of beaver. Guy had made a joke and said "Nice beaver." It was inappropriate. But it was a comment flooded by the deluge of comments that spoke of the love he had for his wife and children.

The wife was a real prayer warrior; she prayed fervently for Guy when he was concerned about his building being blown up. She told him not to worry, that God would protect him; he found great comfort in it. He mentioned that He thought God had a sense of humor finally providing him with spiritual friends that included a blonde cheerleader. Guy had always found blondes attractive. He had been sure to include how God was honored by faithful families and fidelity. There were hundreds of emails on prayer and God's Word.

Still he could see how it would have hurt Marie's feelings, making her angry and jealous. He had been spiritually lonely for so long, he was simply overjoyed to have some spiritual friends that he could speak honestly with. People who didn't mock him, who didn't laugh at him, a family who was willing to pray alongside him. Yet he was ashamed that he was not perfect in his communication.

There was no one he ever desired like the beautiful Marie, no one he ever desired to share his life with, to share life's memories with, to spend all of eternity with. It was something he had voiced to Marie regularly, and everyone who knew him heard the same ad nauseam, especially his new friends from Texas.

Guy loved Marie deeply. He was devastated that his love wasn't clear to her. Though he didn't understand how, obviously he hadn't made it clear. If she was unhappy, why had she never said so? Guy would do anything for her. He had thrown out his T-shirts that she might have found offensive, sporting lines like End the fed or There is Poison in the Water. If she had wanted a christmas tree so bad, why didn't she just say so? If it was a big deal to her, Guy would have said fine. He would agree to see a psychiatrist permanently if that made her feel comfortable.

He let her do whatever she wanted when it came to religion and church, for her and the kids. If she wanted him to go to church also, he would acquiesce. There was nothing he wouldn't do for his wife. He gave her anything she had ever asked for. He let her stay home with the children, paid for her martial arts classes, paid for her to return to school, to go to book studies, Bible studies, weight loss clinics, watched the children so she could go out with friends whenever she desired. Anything she had ever asked for. He cherished her; he would do anything for her.

When she had severe postpartum, he had paid for counseling and for a sitter to come over three times a week. After John was born, she had wanted to keep the sitter, so she could have more time to herself. Though it was a lot of money, he of course said yes. He just hoped that after everything they had been through over the past twenty years that she would at least agree to marriage counseling. To see there was no need to rush, to at least be willing to talk. He would do it on her terms—however she was comfortable. She and the kids could live in the house; he would stay with a friend—or vice versa, for however long, whatever she wanted. Marie and the children were his everything. His heart was broken, and he thought he would drown upon the tears that never stopped flowing.

As the days turned to a week and then to another, everyone was sure Marie would reach out at thirty days. Though they were surprised Guy hadn't been served with papers yet, this time would give her enough distance to cool down.

Though Marie was very close to her mother and sisters, none of them had heard from her. Guy took some solace looking at his Find iPhone application. Though Marie had turned off the location services, her phone was still on. It was stupid, but it provided Guy some comfort. On day twelve when he checked, he saw his laptop was turned on. It was near a McDonald's or a coffee shop, near the Four O Five and Ten freeways about thirty-five miles south of Guy. The laptop must have connected to a free Wi-Fi and had updated its location.

His heart leaped with joy, and he called his attorney, who happened to be right around the block. He would stop by and see if Marie and the kids were there. Guy was reluctant; he thought maybe it would scare her, but the attorney said he would be tactful. The laptop was only on for two minutes. When he had arrived, there was no trace of Marie or the kids, no trace of her car. That evening the green light on Marie's phone went off. The little lifeline that Guy had previously had was now extinguished. He was crushed, ground into the dirt.

He looked at their phone bill and saw that, while Marie's phone was on and he thought she was using the Internet, a closer look showed it was only an automatic update the phone was doing at the exact same time in the middle of the night. Guy realized she was not using her phone at all, that it must have been stashed somewhere. When he did some further reading on the subject, he saw that an iPhone could stay on for twelve days if it wasn't used at all. Marie wasn't even checking her messages; he doubted she had even seen his text. Guy looked through her telephone records for December and saw there were all sorts of women that she was in contact with who Guy had never heard of before. Women that none of her friends had ever heard of.

There was also a call to an abortion clinic and planned parenthood, followed by a call to her gynecologist. Guy was floored. Marie was ignorant concerning the workings of the world, but how could she possibly call planned parenthood? They were one of the most wicked organizations in the world, slaughtering children by the millions. Guy was confused and devastated.

Marie had had a miscarriage in April. She probably wouldn't have even noticed, as she was only ten days' pregnant. But ten days earlier, while they were having sex, the condom had come off, and Guy knew immediately that he had gotten her pregnant. She couldn't believe it and wanted to try a douche, which Guy said was nonsense. Three home pregnancy tests had confirmed it quickly, and then what would have just been seen as a heavy and slightly late period had passed the little babe. Perhaps it took a greater toll on Marie that he had thought.

The buzz of activity of calls to unknown women came the day that Guy was outed on Twitter, the day he was threatened. Guy thought perhaps a group of people had contacted his wife to scare her, which would not have been hard. Clearly Marie had received organized help. There were also some calls to a family from Pennyhill, the Ports, as well as the pastor who had moved out of town. Guy wondered if they were involved. The Ports' son had cystic fibrosis; Guy had thrown a charity poker tournament and had raised Fifteen Thousand Dollars for the family, so they would not have to worry about medical expenses for a couple of years.

As thirty days approached more slowly than molasses, more arduous than a plow ox in a muddy field, more painful than torture, Guy realized that Mack had never called him once during the entire ordeal, not once. When he finally called, Guy suggested they go to lunch. As Guy expressed his hurt, Mack said callously that he didn't see what the big deal was. Everyone gets divorced after all. After Della had left, he got a call one day from an attorney telling Mack that he needed to be out of the house. Did Guy think Mack liked that?

Guy expressed his concern for the children. What reason could they have been given for not being allowed to go to school anymore, for not being allowed to see their friends or their family, that they couldn't see or speak to their father? Guy was not just a good dad, he was a great dad. A dad who used every vacation day, so he never missed a school event. He went on every field trip. There had been six or eight for Faith alone, along with countless school events. He was almost always the only dad in attendance. He made sure the children always felt safe; he protected their innocence. How hard he had worked to make sure their lives were on a different path, a godly path. Marie had stolen their innocence.

Mack scoffed and said that Guy did scare the children. That when Faith was over, she told John not to use a red straw because God would be mad. Guy was flabbergasted and said what an ass Mack was for making assumptions. Any fool could see it was because they used a color-coding system at Faith's new school, and different colors meant you were being bad or good. She never said anything like that in front of Guy, as always Guy would have lovingly corrected her mistake.

Mack said Guy threw out all of the children's clothes and toys. Guy's blood began to boil. Guy had thrown out a blanket and a pair of pajamas with a pentagram. The children had so many toys, they took over nearly every room in the house. They had more toys than just about any kid in america.

Well, Mack continued, Guy had forcefully baptized his wife and the kids, held them underwater. Guy was infuriated. You mean two years ago, when he asked Marie if she wanted to be rebaptized because she was baptized by a charlatan? She said yes and was baptized in the tub. The whole thing took about fifteen seconds. Marie held her own nose and put her own head underwater for one second, like you do to rinse your hair.

Faith was baptized over three years ago, when they were on vacation. He was in the hot tub with her as they were talking about Christ. Faith had knowledge beyond her age and was giddy when Guy had asked her if she wanted to ask Christ into her heart. Of course she did, silly. He told her baptism was the sign of acceptance, to go all the way under the water. She did, just like she had twenty times before in the last fifteen minutes.

John was baptized in the tub about a year ago, while taking a bath with Faith after she had told him that he could ask God into his heart. See, this is how you get baptized, just like washing your hair. She dunked herself underwater. Always wanting to copy his sister, John did the same.

Guy was furious. He could see the web of lies and cruelly twisted truths they had been weaving against him. When he mentioned that Mack hadn't called him the entire time, his father said sorry with as much vehemence as he could muster. A friend of Marie's was the emergency coordinator at Faith's school. For some peculiar reason she had called Ginge after three days of Faith not showing up at school. Why didn't Mack ever mention that?

Guy found out why when he called the woman. She was certain Guy must be beating his wife for her to take such drastic action. She advised Guy to get help. Guy had never laid a hand on his wife in twenty years; he had never even grabbed her wrist or shoulder. Not because he controlled himself, but because he found any sort of physical aggression toward women to be vile and repulsive. Physical violence toward a woman was always inappropriate in Guy's mind, but as usual his thinking was simply outdated. According to many, there was a time and place to smack a woman around, just ask whoopi goldberg or tim mcgraw.

Mack said the information wasn't important. Guy was disgusted. The principal called on the fourth day. Guy explained the situation. Although it was a Christian school that Guy paid handsomely for and was thoroughly involved with, they never called again.

Guy called his attorney as thirty days passed. The attorney recommended they wait ninety days before filing paperwork. He was certain the situation would resolve itself before then. Though Guy received much contrary advice, he felt in his heart this was the best action. Marie hadn't yet reached out to anyone, and, because Guy had remained calm and reserved, though crushed, there were no consequences yet for Marie's abduction of the children.

Once Guy got law enforcement involved, he was concerned about the consequences for his wife and children. The children would be interrogated by police and likely the wicked child protective services. Depending on the vile things Marie hurled at Guy, his attorney would demand he defend himself. Marie's actions were so outrageous, along with plenty of other dirt from over the years that the attorney would want to use against her, Guy then realized the children could actually end up in the hands of the state. Nothing could be worse. Children in the hands of the state often had unspeakable things done to them. He felt like the mother who was asked if she wanted her baby cut in half by King Solomon

Once charges were filed, the DA, if engaged, would pick up the case independently. Guy could not drop charges later. Marie could face a felony and up to three years in prison. He was certain now that someone had coached her to write the letter, because it was almost taken word for word from the district attorney's website. You could take children if you were concerned for their physical or emotional safety. There was a big *but*, however, the district attorney must be notified within ten days. Guy thought Marie could believe she really needed to disappear if there were serious consequences for her actions.

He thought perhaps Marie was waiting till the Passover, till Faith's birthday, which fell on the blood moon. The blood moons were something Guy spent time ranting about on Twitter. There were four, falling on the four Jewish holy days for the next two years—in the middle was a solar eclipse. These rare occurrences birthed significant spiritual events, the founding of the New World, the founding of Israel, the Six-Day War. It was the sign of Joel:

> The sun shall be turned into darkness and the moon into blood,
> before the great and terrible day of the Lord come.

The sign of Acts:

> The sun shall be turned into darkness, and the moon into blood,
> before the great and notable day of the Lord come.

Since Guy was talking about the Passover blood moon on Twitter, perhaps Marie had decided she needed to stay away until it passed. The family agreed that, in light of the circumstances, it made sense. No one wanted Marie to be in trouble.

Guy had called George Ebrahimi, who was a congressman now. He revealed his daughter had babysat a handful of times in October. Marie had said she was going to AA meetings, that Guy was drinking. Guy didn't understand why his wife was crafting this web of lies. Guy had grown to acquire an affinity for martinis when he had first been introduced to private bank functions, which all revolved around alcohol. It had waned quickly, and he had learned a valuable lesson after his DUI, especially at AA. He had learned all about alcoholism and could see how it had ruined generations of his family. That was five years ago. Since then he had an occasional beer, and usually not for months and months. Marie on the other hand was a wine enthusiast and had switched to drinking Sailor Jerry rum. To say she drank ten times as often and frequently as Guy was an understatement. He didn't see it as a problem. It was always after the kids were asleep, and the worst thing it did was make Marie frisky, which he rather enjoyed.

Guy expressed how he thought Marie must be in a shelter because of the dog and cats she returned. Also, since she was out of contact with all of her family and friends, he thought it seemed likely they had a no-policy contact with the outside for thirty days. But George had contacts at the shelters; they told him that they never have women cut off contact with their family and friends. That if a woman comes in for help from a spouse, that a police report and restraining orders are filed immediately. Guy's heart sunk.

When he next spoke to Bear, Champagne suddenly regained her memory once again. Oh, yeah, Marie had asked if she could stay with them when this was all resolved. She was scared. Did Guy tell her that he would bury her in the backyard if they ever got divorced, italian style? Guy had also threatened her when they had the fight about John. It was more nonsense. Guy did joke he would bury her in the backyard, italian style, if they ever got divorced—twenty years ago when they used sit around smoking pot with their friends. They were so in love, it made

482

everyone sick. Everyone including Marie laughed handily, because it was a joke, and, at that time and place in life, it was funny. The thought of Marie and Guy ever being apart was ludicrous; they couldn't even stop staring into each other's eyes for hours on end.

When Guy came home from work in mid-December, they did have a fight about John. Marie had told Guy that John wasn't able to keep down any food, that he was throwing up, that he hadn't gone to the bathroom in days. Guy was stunned. Why did she wait till it was at a crisis level? The doctor had said he needed to be made aware immediately, if John didn't have a daily bowel movement, so John could get extra medication. She had said, "Whatever," and had rolled her eyes at him. Guy had asked her if his gentleness toward her over the years had made her forget that he was a man who wouldn't tolerate being treated with such disrespect, such disdain.

Guy's blood had boiled, and the conversation got heated. Guy closed the glass doors to the kitchen so that the children wouldn't hear. Marie and Guy had both raised their voices, but it had lasted less than two minutes. It was the only the second time Guy had ever raised his voice to his wife. The first was eighteen years ago, when he had found out that she was smoking behind his back and that all his friends knew. He had told her that he wouldn't marry her if she was smoking, that he didn't want to watch her die of lung cancer one day.

He had thought the argument about John had resolved itself reasonably well. Marie had turned the conversation to money, and Guy asked her where her faith and gratitude were. God was so generous with them; she was afforded the luxury of staying home. They wanted for nothing. In fact God even fulfilled their desires. Marie was able to engage in any activity she ever wanted, fly down to visit her mother anytime, give money to her sisters when their finances were tight. Guy and Marie's children went to one of the best classical Christian academies in the country. Guy and Marie went to europe with private drivers and a butler. The family went to Disney World. They lived richly; they never wanted for anything; they were never even forced to cut the fat. Marie needed to change her perspective. Maybe she should come back down to skid row or take a look around the world to see how others lived, crushed under the weight of poverty.

Things were a bit frigid after that, but it had been twenty years now that they had been together. They had weathered all sorts of ups and downs. That argument didn't even register on Guy's radar. In fact, the night before she had kidnapped the children, Guy had said he felt like the gap between them was still growing, that he didn't like it. He loved her; he didn't like when they argued; he didn't want the gap to grow any larger, did she? She said she didn't.

The week before she had abducted the children, Guy had gotten a babysitter so he could take his wife out on a date. He took her out for her favorite wine, Chateau Montelena, and a movie. They made out in the movie, hot and heavy like they were teenagers. Marie actually put a sweater on her lap and let Guy take her pants halfway off. They were so worked up, they hardly made it through the movie. They tore each other's clothes off when they got home.

Guy was flummoxed now.

Bear told Guy to look on the bright side. He had a great job, a sexy car; he could go out and bang hot nineteen-year-olds all night long.

Guy loved his wife. If he wanted to bang nineteen-year-olds, he would have already been doing it. He told Bear that he didn't believe in divorce. That if Marie filed, he would not sign. A judge would have to order it without his concurrence. He would not fight Marie, because, while she didn't realize it, there were larger forces at work. Guy would not step into a trap that would allow any harm to come to his wife or children, no matter the harm or consequences he might face.

Bear thought Guy was crazy. If someone did something like this to Bear, he would divorce her in a second and make sure she was the one who was destroyed. He wondered how much longer Guy would wear his wedding ring. Bear never knew someone personally who was treated so cruelly.

Still Guy loved his wife.

★★★

He thought of the hell his life, his children's life would become. The thought of never being able to kiss Marie again, never being able to touch her skin, to stroke her hair. Never being able to embrace her, to hold her. His tears would never cease. The thought of his wife being touched, having sex with other men broke his heart. All the while he would have to pay her, pay her to have sex with other men. The children's futures, their innocence would be destroyed. There was no way Guy could afford to pay for two households and send his children to private school.

They would have to go to public school, to be taught how to be sluts and pigs. To be taught the common core curriculum statements like: government officials must be obeyed by all. _http://www.tpnn.com/ 2013/11/04/common-core-indoctrination-the-people-must-obey-government-commands/_. They'd be forced to read books about pedophilia sex instead of the classics that drove the great minds. _http://www.theblaze.com/ stories/2013/08/22/pedophilia-incest-and-graphic-sex-excerpts-from-a-_

common-core-reading-list-book-for-11th-graders-that-will-make-you-blush/.
Guy was mortified; he didn't understand how his wife could be so selfish. How could she treat the family, treat Guy, so cruelly? He had never treated anyone that cruelly, let alone Marie.

The credit check run by the attorney showed nothing. The women no one recognized from Marie's phone calls were from Marie's martial arts class. Guy decided to have the private investigator run Marie's license plate number through the system. The investigator said it would let them know if she went through any cameras at intersections. It would at least let them know if she was in town and could provide Guy with some comfort. Guy was doing his best to hang on, to try to hold on to some ray of fading hope. What came back broke him completely. It took the air from his lungs, the light from his eyes; the darkness enveloped him completely. The day after she left, Marie had sold her car. She was never coming back. When he mentioned it to Bear, he was already aware. Marie had told Champagne that she was going to sell her car, so she couldn't be tracked.

As six weeks had nearly passed, Guy's desperation and desolation squeezed out his very life. The week after Marie left, he had decided to military detail the house. It would keep him occupied. Champagne mentioned Marie was overwhelmed by the house. Guy had tried for years to get her to accept a housekeeper, but she had always refused. Guy spent every night and all weekend cleaning the house. He took everything out of every shelf, the fridge, the oven, the pantry, cleaned underneath and around everything. While he had never realized it before, the house was filthy. Yet it was spot cleaned so he had never noticed.

He wanted to make sure everything was immaculate, like brand-new, so Marie would have something nice to come back to. It took Guy six weeks to clean the bottom floor. He thought he would feel a sense of accomplishment. But it only increased his despair. The house was sanitized, but empty; his family was not coming back. He hired a cleaning crew to deep clean the upstairs; he couldn't bear to do the children's rooms. He asked them to be straightened, since everything had been thrown all over when Marie and her helpers had loaded up the house. They left boxes of plastic bags everywhere. Guy hired the cleaners to come back once a week. He couldn't even bear to look at his children's faces upon the two pictures that were left. It was simply too painful.

At six weeks there was a supposed sighting of Marie at the Dollar Tree right on the corner, a mile from Guy's house. Peculiarly the information came once again from Ginge. She had received a call from one of Marie's friends, whose mother saw her there. No they did not see what type of car she was driving, nor the children, but Marie looked great, happy. It was clear to everyone, except Mack, that Ginge was a lying piece of trash. The friend asked that no one contact her, that she knew nothing except what she told Ginge. The friend had called Guy no less than a half dozen times to get information about the situation, but Guy didn't know her well enough to feel comfortable sharing. Ginge was so happy; she was sure we would be seeing Marie in a week or two.

It was also clear Ginge had lied about the storage unit. She had said she got the key back on christmas, but Guy found out that the food was moved after christmas, while he was spending the day with Marie. The removal took two days, and Guy was with Marie for both. The only way to view the storage facility's security tape was to get the police involved. Guy was sure it would show some nondescript rental truck with unknown figures. As every private investigator put it, Marie had been criminally cautious. None of them had ever seen anything like this before, many with over thirty years of prior police experience.

It was also clear that Ginge had coached Marie to her mental breaking point. Ginge was a hysterical woman; she had counseled Marie, helping her to attain the same grade of insanity. When Guy checked Marie's phone records, the two women were speaking twenty times a day for months. Marie was always extremely close with her mother and sisters, but she spent exponentially more time on the phone with Ginge. While Ginge made it out like she was shell-shocked about the whole situation, with no prior knowledge, she again simply showed what a lying piece of garbage she was.

She called and said she forgot, but Marie did mention that she was having someone look at Guy's tax returns. Clearly Marie was trying to see how much money she could get out of Guy. When Guy spoke with Pearl next, she mentioned Ginge told her that Ginge saw Guy trying to place a tracking device on Ginge's car, outside their father's house. What a filthy disgusting pig, Guy thought. What type of person could make up something like that, especially in light of the current circumstances?

When Mack's birthday rolled around, Ginge sent a text saying that they would be celebrating it with her family two hundred miles away just in case Guy and Pearl wanted to join. How pathetic and despicable Mack had become. In Guy's desperate hour, when he was enduring one of the cruelest things a person could ever endure, Mack had showed what sort of father he was—no father at all. He showed what sort of man he was, a man now devoid of character. He would rather spend his birthday out of town with people he hardly even knew, than to be here for his son.

Guy renounced Mack as his father. Ginge was leading him around by the nose. Guy saw clearly now that it was purposeful. She had destroyed Mack's relationship with Herman, then Pearl. Then either facilitated the abduction or helped to create the mind-set that caused Marie to see no other choice than kidnapping. How despicable. Mack showed he was a man who loved lies and filth; it was his own choice. He would pay a harsh spiritual price for it.

Guy realized that Ginge wasn't simply a bad person or a wicked person, she was evil and calculating. She had lots of money and had used it to help Mack remodel his house, so he owed her that too. She took complete control of his life, isolating him by destroying his family, and he loved it. If anyone tried to call her out on it, she simply broke down in tears like a hysterical teenager playing the victim. Mack ate it up and asked for seconds.

Pearl relayed the story of being accused of stealing a seventy-thousand-dollar ring from Ginge. Guy had heard the story earlier from Ginge and Mack; at the time he had believed it. Ginge and Mack were convincing, and Pearl was having money trouble as usual. Guy didn't have a good relationship with his sister, because she lied and never shared what was really going on with her.

Pearl related the story of a little black pig from her preschool class. She waited all year to play with it, but the other children were very aggressive. She never got to play with it until the last day of school. She put it in her pocket and took it home. She didn't understand what stealing was, but she hid it in her room, and her guilt prevented her from being able to enjoy playing with it or even just looking at it. When she was six, she told Mack, through streaming tears, what she had done. He sat her upon his lap and told her that stealing was wrong, but that she was remorseful, that she was sorry, and so God forgave her. He said the tiny pig no bigger than her pinkie was probably long ago forgotten by the teacher but suggested they take it back to the school anyway.

Pearl never forgot that lesson. Mack apparently had. Guy knew Pearl hadn't stolen the ring then. Ginge had told her story about how it was right on the counter, but then it was gone. After they all searched for hours, and then threatened Pearl with calling the police, the ring showed right back up on the counter. It was clear now that Ginge had concocted the whole scene. Just like she had accidentally let Herman's cats out of the house, and had no idea about anything relating to the kidnapping of Faith and John, except that she had been lying about it all along.

The situation repaired Guy's relationship with his sister and moreover created something special that had never even existed between them. She called every day and stopped by his house often. She even told him what

487

the trailer was for without him asking. It was a business to grow pot. It failed; pot was actually hard to grow. Guy laughed—a pot-growing business without asking her brother. He knew a couple of people from his past who were legends in the growing industry. It made them even closer. It also repaired his relationship with his brother, Herman. He wasn't much of a talker, but they spent time together and exchanged a few texts. Herman had a lovely girlfriend; Guy was happy for his brother. It also gave Guy an opportunity to speak with Jack and forgive him in Guy's heart. Jack called for two weeks, until he stopped. The last interaction was a letter that suggested Guy get a brain scan. It was typical. He was thankful for the brief reconciliation with his biological father.

The days turned to weeks, and the weeks to months, and as his anniversary and Faith's birthday approached, the light went out from Guy's eyes, from his heart. He stopped taking phone calls, and, though it was just over three months, he still cried continuously, all day, every day, all night, every night. He sat in his office and cried; they suggested he take leave. While no one knew what was going on except for Bill, they knew it was something serious. They were compassionate; Guy was reluctant to take the time off, but it seemed necessary. Hearing clients and colleagues continually ask how his wife and children were was like a sword twisted in his stomach.

Guy decided that he would simply lay down and die. Not kill himself, because he didn't want to burn in hell, but die nonetheless. He would stop paying his bills though he had the money. But, as smart as he was, he couldn't figure out a way to die without it being considered suicide in the eyes of the Lord. He thought of engaging in reckless behavior or not eating. But, if ultimately his goal was to die, it was suicide nonetheless; he couldn't find a way around it. Guy simply laid upon his floor in the fetal position and cried and cried.

He thought he would just walk away himself. Become homeless, and live under a bridge or with the rats in skid row. But he was thoroughly disgusted by rats and had a hard time coming to terms with eating garbage. He would stop eating, but then someone would just throw him in a hospital and force-feed him. There seemed to be no way out. Marie had gotten what she wanted: Guy was destroyed. It seemed she wanted more than that; she wanted him to kill himself. For she knew he couldn't possibly live without his beloved children. To be the man who forever introduced himself as the man whose children were kidnapped. The man whose children would forget his face; Faith didn't even know his cell phone number. Soon his son would forget he ever had a father.

Milton tried an intervention, calling Pearl and Bear to a therapy session. Guy couldn't even get off the ground. His sister was compassionate; so was Bear. Though he found Bear disingenuous. Through the years there was no end to Bear's busting on Guy for having to run things by Marie. Still Guy always made time for Bear. Now Bear made no time for Guy. Bear insisted he was making the time to Milton, that Guy needed to understand Bear had a family. But in reality he made no time for Guy.

Champagne went to mormon temple on Sunday mornings and told Bear that was his designated time. If Guy wanted to spend time with Bear, it was only Sunday mornings. Which was OK, except that it showed Bear wasn't willing to make any time for Guy at all. Guy was just thankful Bear was compassionate and emotionally there for him, however, when Guy went to Bear's house to see him. It was harder to see Champagne. She had known his kids were going to be kidnapped and had said nothing. Along with Ginge, they said they were concerned Guy was going to hurt himself.

Yet they were both so unconcerned that, when they knew Guy was going to come home to an emptied-out house, with everyone gone, that they made sure no one would be there waiting for Guy. There would be no emotional support for him. If Guy had killed himself then or gotten sick or in a horrible car accident, his children wouldn't even know. There would be no visits to the hospital, no family at the funeral.

When Guy did take a leave of absence from his job, he truly had nothing left, nothing left of his heart. He told his sister, he never cared if he saw his children again. It was a lie, and she knew it, but Guy could not bear to see what they would become after Marie had stolen their innocence and had turned them over to the public school system so they could play perverted Dr. Seuss games. Boys using the girls' bathrooms; girls using the boys' bathrooms. Boys playing on the girls' teams; girls playing on the boys' teams. How could Marie ever be so cruel, and yet Guy still loved her. He sent her a text letting her know as much on their anniversary, and one letting his darling daughter dear know how much he loved her, that he would never forget her. Telling her to let her brother know that he was loved and not forgotten. He sent a link to Fievel of american Tail singing "Somewhere Out There." *https://www.youtube.com/watch?v=dan6g5a3Dgg*.

For Guy's wedding anniversary, Diamond suggested they go to the lowest place in the Western Hemisphere—Death Valley. It seemed appropriate. Diamond drove; Guy wept. He had spent his birthday alone, because that seemed appropriate as well. Though he hadn't heard from anyone in Marie's family, Jackie and Maybel had sent a card after the months of silence. Marie's mother, Aloha, left a message. It was the first one since Guy had called her a few weeks into the ordeal. She had cried on the phone then; she didn't understand how Marie could have done this. She was angry now; she didn't understand how Guy wasn't hateful.

After months of silence, Mack called and left a message saying, "Let's grab dinner," like it was no big deal. Guy didn't call him back; it was pointless to speak with a blind and deaf man. Guy had no father save his Father in heaven. Champagne said she would make an effort, a few months back in a text. She had at least texted him on his birthday; he declined the dinner invitation.

The pit of Guy's despair seemed to have no lower limit. He wished he could just be held in Marie's arms and cry forever. He tried to find someone online, that maybe he could pay to hold him while he cried. But when he looked, it seemed they all just wanted sex. He decided to go to a high-end strip club. He got a booth way in the back and was immediately accosted; he turned down company, until a young lady who exuded compassion sat down. She called herself Jadzia, clearly a Stark Trek fan. He said he knew this was crazy, but could he pay her to hold him while he cried? The tears came out almost before she could answer. Guy laid his head on her shoulder and wept the tears of gods. He cried and cried for five hours straight, as snot and tears rolled down the girl's neck, assuredly on her beautiful and covered bosom. She wiped his tears and and nose regularly, and Guy paid her thousands of dollars to do it. They ate dinner together in the club, and then Guy cried for another five hours on her shoulder. He was thankful for it.

When Faith's birthday on the Passover came and went, as well as the ninety days suggested by the attorney, Guy was a walking dead man, except that he walked not; he simply lay down to die. John Brown showed the sort of man he had become. When Guy stopped taking phone calls, he simply showed up at Guy's front door on a Friday night. He said he wasn't leaving until Guy let him in. He would be back every Friday whether Guy picked up his phone or not. To help another when they can no longer help themselves, that is the nature of true friendship. John proved he was Guy's true friend.

Pearl could take it no longer; she went to the police herself. Guy received a call from a detective, and, through his sobs, he heard the detective say she was sending a sheriff to the house to take missing persons' reports.

The sheriff was like an order-taker at a fast-food restaurant, checking off boxes on a form, with no ability to ask questions of her own. Guy called the National Center for Missing and Exploited Children. Guy had previously looked at their website, and they wouldn't help unless there was a police report. Guy sent over the file numbers along with pictures of his family. They said they would be in contact.

A week later, while in the car on his way to see Milton, Guy got a call from another local detective, heading the investigation. The detective said he would call back the next day to ask questions. The detective never called. They never called Guy to ask questions, never called a single family member, never asked for a piece of information; they simply did not care.

Guy found it interesting that Marie's car was sold to a police captain who lived right up the block, Evin Ebert, who ran the local prison facility. However, when Pearl went to the station and mentioned it, they said it was purchased by someone else. When Guy reran the car fax report, the police officer's name was gone. As the weeks passed no one called him from the National Center for Missing and Exploited Children either. The shatters of the man who Guy once was were ground into dirt, and the dirt cast into the bottom of the sea.

The police showed how pathetic they were; they never called, never asked a single question. They never called other family members. Guy asked the family to call the detective. The police never did a damn thing to warrant their taxpayer-provided salaries. When Guy went down to the station to meet the lead detective, detective soup, it was clear Guy was right in his perception. The man was a real piece of trash. He refused to share any information; he saw no need to interview the person who had purchased Marie's car. He didn't think it was helpful to know how they met, who was with Marie or how she was paid for the car. Guy explained that, unless she was paid in cash, there would be a record of the bank account that Marie had deposited the check into, and it certainly wasn't Guy's. detective soup saw no point, he saw no need to interview the people related to Marie's sighting.

When they spoke on the phone, Guy asked about putting up missing poster flyers. The detective asked him not to. Perhaps it could affect his investigation, Guy thought. Guy mentioned it at their next meeting, and the detective denied the conversation entirely. He was also a liar, unsurprising. When Guy asked if they had followed up when Marie's cell phone was turned on in April, he simply said no, that it was too late to check now; the records were gone.

After a couple of months, Guy finally got a call from someone at the National Center for Missing and Exploited Children. The woman was nice, compassionate; her children had also been kidnapped. They had been restored to her. When they called back after Guy's children were gone for four months, he inquired why their pictures still weren't in the online database. They decided police reports weren't enough and that Guy would have to get an emergency custody order, that he needed felony charges filed against his wife. He was disgusted.

Marie had kidnapped the children, had sold her car the next day, had stopped using her credit cards, had stopped using the bank, had stopped accessing her email, had turned her phone off, had cut off all contact with family and friends, had pulled his children out of school. But if Guy made her a felon, they actually thought that would make her come back? It was preposterous and stupid. No one cared about Faith and John. That they had no father, no friends, no relatives, no school. Everyone simply said, *too bad*.

Guy cried out to the Lord in his anguish, was Job not restored? The Lord spoke into Guy's heart. *Did not you say you would follow Me at all costs? Did I not tell you this would be a hard road? Did you not say that you would wield the sword that I had given you?* But Guy said his strength was gone. He promised to wield the sword if God would restore his strength. God said there were no plans except for His.

On Resurrection Sunday, Guy's strength was restored. He was able to kneel and then to stand. To praise his God, Who was just and merciful. To thank Him for His wisdom, for His perfect plan. To thank his God for never abandoning him. Guy prayed for the safety of Marie, Faith and John. For the content of a man's character is measured not when the sun shines brightly upon his face but when the storm leaves him gasping for his last breath.

And so, while Guy's computer, server, backup server and all his handwritten notes had been stolen the day after they had been completed, he had rightfully been paranoid when he had hidden a USB drive with the information. It wasn't everything, only about eighty percent. But the form of his sword, the words, the book he was commanded to write, they were still there. The last two chapters were missing, everything about the Lluciferian illuminati and their New World Order plan for instilling the antichrist, the man of sin. The information was seared upon Guy's mind, however. It was difficult and painful, for he had to recount in part about his family, about the life he once had. He set to the task, to rewrite what was stolen. And as he worked through the pain and through the tears, God made him in a way stronger than before.

As he did, america continued on its path, working hard to draw the Gog of Magog into war with america via the Ukraine, turning more citizens into thought criminals, like the CEO of Mozilla, or the HGTV stars who were simply not allowed to work in the new america, because they believed the Bible was true. *http://www.theguardian.com/commentisfree/2014/apr/07/brendan-eich-has-the-right-to-fight-gay-rights-but-not-to-be-mozillas-ceo, http://www.rawstory.com/rs/2014/05/13/fired-hgtv-hosts-satan-using-his-gay-demonic-agenda-to-silence-us/*.

Six months turned to seven, then eight and on, and on. Guy and Diamond decided it was time for another road trip. They saw the wondrous sequoias and hiked the Grand Canyon. They were going to camp at the bottom, but there were no campsites left. They wanted to hike all the way to the Colorado River, but they showed up late in the afternoon, nearly two thirty. While everyone said it was too late to start the trek, it felt like an opportunity they couldn't pass up. They hiked all the way to the Colorado, and back up twenty miles straight. It took them till five thirty in the morning. On the way Diamond had convinced Guy to buy him a headlamp, which Guy thought a waste, but he had purchased it anyway.

Trying to make the climb back up the canyon, in the shadow of Diamond's footsteps was brutal. Diamond had bought a dollar lighter from the liquor store that had a little LCD light on the bottom; Guy used the light to scale the Grand Canyon. It hardly illuminated the giant black scorpions that shared the path in the dark of night. They were aggressive and charged at your feet if you stepped anywhere near them. After twelve hours climbing the mile-high elevation, Guy was so exhausted that he thought he might take a moment to lie down with them. It was the hardest physical feat Guy had tackled since the corps. It was a great bonding time for him and Diamond; they felt a sense of accomplishment.

★★★

When he returned, he could see Mufasa, his orange tabby, was not long for the world. The last few months had showed his age; the vet said his liver was failing. She would do her best to make sure he was comfortable. Guy made sure Mufasa got to go outside every day, that he knew he was well loved. When the day finally arrived, Guy took him out on the front porch step. Guy pet his cat's head and read aloud from the book of Psalms. As they watched the sunset, Mufasa passed peacefully, bathed not in the love of a family but only in the tears of a man. A man who decided it was time to stand.

> For the seven thunders sing:
>
> Holy, Holy, Holy, Lord God of power and might. Heaven and Earth are full of Your glory. Hosanna, Hosanna in the highest. Blessed is he who comes in the Name of the Lord, Hosanna, Hosanna in the highest.
>
> And the Lord of Lords, Yahushua Ha Moshiach, prepared to ride upon His white horse. For out of His mouth goeth a sharp sword, that with it He should smite the nations: and He shall rule them with a rod of iron: and He treadeth the winepress of

the fierceness and wrath of the Almighty God, for on His thigh, He has this Name written: YHWH.

Misguidedly yours,

J

★★★

There once was a poor boy who lay in the mud,
A spirit beaten and battered with a mighty loud thud.
As he grew and he grew, in the mud he did stay.
Should he have gone, he knew not the way,
Until the Lord God extended His hand.
He opened his eyes, and God taught him to stand,
And stand the man did and shouted out loud.
But satan grew angry, for lucifer's proud.
The devil destroyed the man's life; he ripped it a shred,
Until the man thought he'd be better off dead.
But God forsook not Job, nor the poor boy.
It was the devil, in fact, who God would destroy.